DIMENSIONER'S REVENGE

ALSO BY S.K. RANDOLPH

VARTERELS' UNIVERSE™

(as paperbacks)

Part I - UnFolding

1. DiMensioner's Revenge

5. ConDra's Fire

8. MasTer's Reach

10. Jaradee's Legacy

Agothany 1 (Companion Shorts 2, 3, 4, 6, 7, and 9)

Part II - CoaleScence

11. Incirrata Secret

13. Corps Stones

16. Mocendi's Gambit

19. Queen's Quest

Agothany 2 (Companion Shorts 12, 14, 15, 17, 18, and 20)

Part III - Quickening

(a work in process)

Told with words and art,

contained in novels and companion shorts,

available in print and eBooks.

DIMENSIONER'S REVENGE

ILLUSTRATED BY THE AUTHOR

VARTERELS' UNIVERSE™
BOOK ONE

S.K. RANDOLPH

Cover & Illustrations by
S.K. RANDOLPH

CheeTrann Creations LLC

DiMensioner's Revenge: Illustrated by the Author (VarTerels' Universe™ Book 1)

Previous published as "The DiMensioner's Revenge"

ISBNs
color eBook 978-1-962777-24-7
B&W Paperback 978-1-962777-23-0

Self Published by S.K. Randolph
CheeTrann Creations LLC
Suite 316-160
1410 Valley View Drive
Delta, CO 81416 USA

Web Site: www.skrandolph.com
Substack: skrandolph.substack.com
Facebook: http://facebook.com/S.K.Randolph11

Revised 2026

VU-125-J VU01-DR 260704-0129 IS-PB-BW | V231129 PlbtA VUPt-1.vellum | 6X9-642

*For Tom, Sean, Courtney and Jared
who love me no matter what.*

VarTereIs' Universe ™
SCIENCE FANTASY

DIMENSIONER'S REVENGE

FOOTHILLS
GRASSLANDS

DOJANACK MOUNTAINS
meredith
SEKAN RIVER
TERCES WOOD
Brie As Tar

Arrival
Prologue

From her balcony, Almiralyn Nadrugia gazed over the grounds of the Temple of Mahyinaeh on the planet of KcernFensia. "I am about to leave behind the only home I've ever known." Her whispered words stirred the butterflies fluttering in her stomach into a frenzy. She pulled her long, silver-blonde braid over her shoulder, stroked its silky weave, and gazed at the tranquil beauty of the deep aqua sea sparkling in the distance.

The sapphire blue of her eyes deepened and her butterflies calmed as dignity enveloped her. *I, Almiralyn Nadrugia, have completed the training for my role as the Guardian of Myrrh. Today, I assume the responsibility for protecting the last remaining piece of Old Earth. Today, I will step into the dimensional portal that will carry me to my new home.*

The bell at her chamber door chimed. With a lingering glance at the familiar surroundings, she stepped into the cool interior of her suite of rooms. "Please enter."

The Galactic Guardian, who oversaw her training, ducked through the open door and straightened, his blond hair almost brushing the ceiling. "Hello, Almiralyn."

"Good turning, Chealim." She smiled up at him.

Lowering his tall, muscular frame onto a sofa, he waited for her to take the seat opposite him. Ancient wisdom glowed in his cool blue eyes. "KcernFensian's solar cycle 33-63-33 begins this turning, Almiralyn. It is time for you to travel to Myrrh."

The warm resonance of his voice vibrated through her. "I'm excited to see Myrrh, to explore, and to meet those who live there." Her gaze grew distant before returning to his face. "It seems as though I've been waiting for this turning all my life."

The Guardian's expression grew somber. "I've received some disturbing news, Almiralyn."

Her brows arched. "News?"

A frown thinned his generous mouth. "An evil presence has made itself known in the Inner Universe. Thus far, it has eluded our attempts to discover its origin. The Galactic Council believes it will usher in The Unfolding sooner than expected." The mouth pursed. "Not good or bad—simply the way destiny works. Perhaps more important...the Mocendi League searches for you, the Prima Crystal Evolsefil, and the other treasures we are placing in your protective care."

Chealim's words inspired a chill-induced shiver. Almiralyn hugged herself and focused on her mentor. "Has the Counsel discovered who the Mocendi leader is?"

Chealim shook his head. "It is a mystery—one we are working to solve. Not your concern, my dear. You will have plenty to keep you busy as you establish yourself on Myrrh." He regarded her with slightly narrowed eyes.

"It is good Karrew and Allynae accompany you. The Five Fathers of Idronatti have proved to be less than honest about their actions. You hold the keys to The Unfolding and to the maturing of the Inner Universe. Remain vigilant. The Fathers are greedy."

"I will do my best not to disappoint the Galactic Counsel, Chealim."

He inclined his head. "We are certain, Almiralyn, that you will make us proud."

The entrance bell chiming produced a knowing smile. "That will be Relevart." The Guardian rose as the VarTerel of the Inner Universe strode into the room. "Your timing is impeccable, Relevart." Chealim's large, cool hands sandwiched hers. "I must depart. If you have need of me, Almiralyn, consult Elcaro's Eye." Light flared. The Guardian vanished.

Almiralyn smiled at the VarTerel. "I'm so happy you could be here today. Without you, Relevart, this new beginning wouldn't have felt right."

He offered a hand, clasped hers, and tapped his rowan wood staff against the floor. The stars and night sky of Mittkeer, the Land of All Time and No Time, embraced them.

Almiralyn's stomach grumbled. Her vision blurred. Relevart's light touch on her forehead dispersed the disconcerting symptoms of their arrival. She swallowed and stared at the endless expanse of universal beauty flowing in all directions around them.

Relevart studied her. "Do you remember your first visit to Mittkeer?"

"I do." She felt a wave of nostalgia. "It was after my initiation from child to young adulthood."

His appreciative gaze warmed her. "This turning, you are beginning the journey you have trained for all your life." The face grew serious. "Chealim warned you about the Mocendi League. I had hoped you would have more time to enjoy your new land."

Amber eyes looking deep into hers reflected the arc of a shooting star flashing across the endless night sky. "Heed Chealim's warning and take care." The crystal topping his VarTerel's staff glinted as he spoke. "It is time for you to go. Enjoy your first turning on Myrrh, my dear Almiralyn."

He and Mittkeer vanished, leaving her alone in her chambers. Her thoughts racing, she entered her sleeping room, gathered up a blue velvet pouch, and looped its matching ribbon over her head. Clasping the pouch in her hand, she pressed it to her heart. *Your gift, Maman. I am so glad to have a small piece of you with me.*

Her reflection in the mirror made her pause. She touched the arc of her cheekbone and studied the slope of her nose. *I love seeing the resemblance to you in my face, Maman.* She traced the curve of her full-lipped mouth. Its tendency to curve up in a smile made her think of her father. *I miss you, Papa.* Sadness clouded her eyes. *I wish I knew where you were, if you're alright, if I will ever see you again.*

Urgency nudged. One last appraising look in the mirror produced a slight smile. *Dark green slacks, a long-sleeved white shirt, and sturdy hiking boots are a far cry from the flowing garments and sandals that marked my years of training at the temple.*

Inhaling a calming breath, she verbally reviewed her preparation for the role of Myrrh's Guardian. "I have studied Earth's history and its geological importance to the Inner Universe; the analysis of Myrrh's host planet, Thera, and its symbiotic connection to the last piece of Old Earth; the politics of the Fourth Galaxy and the Clenaba Rolas Solar System which includes Thera, KcernFensia, and six other planets." Confidence voided any lingering self-doubt. "I *am* well prepared."

Readiness cloaking her, she walked into the main room of her suite, gazed around it for one last time and announced, "Almiralyn Nadrugia, Guardian of Myrrh, your new home awaits."

A large raven glided through the open window and landed on her offered arm. It cawed, then spoke in human language. "You had your final meeting with Chealim?"

"I did, Karrew. Relevart stopped by as well. They both had news." She shared what she had learned.

Her friend and protector flew to the back of a chair and pranced an agitated jig. "The Mocendi League." He stopped. A single ebony eye focused on her face. "We knew complications could arise, Mira." He flew to her shoulder. "It's time to go."

Grateful that Karrew and her brother, Allynae, joined her in her new adventure, she opened the door. Crossing the spacious hallway to a veranda bordering the top of a wide stone stairway, she took a moment to absorb the beauty of the temple grounds one last time.

Allynae glanced up and waved. Excitement bristled around him as he and the High Priestess conversed.

Karrew cawed next to her ear, "Time passes, dear one. We must be off."

She nestled her head against his blue-black feathers and sighed. "Do you think we'll ever return to KcernFensia?"

"Time and your destiny will reveal the future." He launched into flight, circled, and came to rest on a flowering tree near the translucent spin of the dimensional portal to Myrrh.

Almiralyn descended the steps and traversed the garden. At the foot of a shimmering crystal spire, long-time friends said their goodbyes. Eager to be on her way, she faced the spinning vortex. At her command, Karrew flew into the portal and disappeared.

Karrew exited Demrach Gateway into early morning in the Terces Woods on Myrrh. Landing amidst silvery leaves on the low branch of a gnarled and ancient Tirips Tree, he anxiously awaited his mistress.

The shimmering portal, shadowed by tall trees and the dim light of predawn, began to spin. A hush settled over the forest. Almiralyn arrived in the clearing and stood tall and regal and still as stone. A delicate shaft of sunlight shot through the forest canopy, washing her upturned face with warmth and bleaching her white-blonde braid to silver. Like deep mountain pools, her sapphire eyes absorbed the first rays of the rising sun as she absorbed the beauty of her new home. More magnificent than the dawn, she turned to greet her brother, who strode from the portal, his rugged features alive with curiosity.

"Alli, listen." She tipped her head. "Life is stirring, and we are part of it."

He moved to her side. Karrew flew to her shoulder.

"We're finally here." Her whispered words quivered. "I've waited so long." She looked at her brother. Eyes a lighter blue than her own, mirrored her radiant smile.

He gave her braid a playful tug. "I imagine you and Karrew want to explore. I'll follow the path to the cottage."

"You could shape shift and join us, Alli." Hope filled her pronouncement.

A crooked smile twitched his mustache, a new acquisition of which he was most proud. "You know I hate shifting. Never liked it, never will. A walk in the woods will bring me closer to the land. Besides, I can't wait to see the cottage. I'm told your design is quite wonderful. Off you go." He strolled toward the path, his lanky body and long legs easy, his gait relaxed. Speckles of light leaking through the trees shimmered on his dark hair. He glanced back and waved.

Karrew flew to a Tirips Tree and cocked his head, one obsidian black eye focused on his motionless mistress.

Almiralyn absorbed the sounds of the forest. At its center, the pulsing of magic as ancient as Old Earth informed her CheeTrann, the Sentinel in the Tower of Nemttachenn, sensed her presence. Beneath her feet, the heart of the land beat to the rhythm of her own. *Home. I am here!* She inhaled the smells of cedar and pine, of oak and maple, of moss and spores and forest creatures. Exhaling, she grinned at Karrew. "I'm ready to fly."

He ducked his head in a mimicked bow. "I await your lead, my lady."

Delight gurgled up from her belly in a full-bodied laugh. "We are here!" She raised her arms. An iridescent oval flared around her as she shifted. Her bird form, smaller than Karrew's and white as the first snow of winter, soared upward. Gold-tipped wings carried her through the loosely woven canopy and into the dome of the morning sky. Delicate swathes of pink and lavender drifted above her. Below, the emerald depths of the Terces Wood flowed unbroken to the eastern horizon. To the west, the forest bordered the Grasslands, which rolled into the foothills snuggled against the mighty Dojanack Mountains. A thrill coursed through her as she skimmed the treetops. *This is my land!*

At the edge of the Terces Wood, the terrain transitioned from forest to prairie. A desire to stand in the tall grass—to experience the air weaving through it—made her land and change form. Summer breezes whispered their secrets in her ears and sent wispy, silver curls to caress her cheeks and forehead. She shaded her eyes with a slender hand and let her hungry gaze devour the landscape.

Around her, the grasses swayed like the ebb and flow of ocean waves on the beach. She loved the feel of it—the scents of flowers and rich, dark earth. Her long legs stretched in an easy stride as she walked westward. The sound of water made her pick up her pace. Soon, she discovered a meandering river gleaming like a snake in the grass. Shading her eyes, she scanned its length in both directions. *I can't wait to catch my first fish.*

Her training came to the fore. She shut her eyes and allowed her senses to show her the villages, farms, and hamlets dotting the landscape along the outer edges of the prairie. *Soon, I'll travel to meet the people of Myrrh, but not today. Today, it is vital that I create the oneness that will allow me to understand and protect this last piece of Old Earth.*

Karrew's deep caw called her to join him. She embraced her bird form and, sailing on warm currents of air, soared over the Sekan River and into the foothills. The Dojanack Mountains rose to unimaginable heights, creating a skyline of crystal, obsidian, granite, and rose quartz peaks that caught the sunlight and tossed a medley of colors into the morning sky.

Landing in human form, she pressed a hand to her heart and soaked in the spectacular beauty of Myrrh.

Karrew came to rest on her outstretched arm, one gleaming eye fixed on her profile. He ruffled his feathers and croaked his appreciation. "The Dojanacks underwent some spectacular changes because of the upheaval on Earth. They are even more amazing than I imagined."

Almiralyn inhaled the fresh mountain air and let it sit in her lungs until they forced her to exhale. A laugh of sheer joy burst up from her heart. Karrew flapped his wings and cawed.

When their chorused response faded into the sounds of Myrrh, she gazed back the way they had come. "We must find the cottage, Karrew. The sun is already past its zenith. Alli has been alone long enough, and I'm starving."

She shifted once more and soared upward until the sheer splendor of the world below sent a rush of intense love and the desire to protect it at all costs surging through her. From a distance, she watched a family of wolves sprawled on a rock, enjoying the afternoon sun. At the bottom of a steep ravine, a large mountain lion glanced up from its fresh kill. Over the grasslands, she observed mice, butterflies, bees, and rabbits going about the business of living. The trees of the Terces Wood whispered her name. Birds chirped a welcoming song. Squirrels sat, bushy tails flicking and noses twitching to pick up her scent. Chipmunks scurried among the dried leaves, spreading the word that the Guardian of Myrrh had arrived.

With her heart overflowing, she soared over the big, red barn at the edge of her acreage and alighted in human form. The barn, already full of livestock—horses, chickens, a dog, and a cat with a litter of kittens—made her smile. A half turn brought her around to face the cottage. She sensed its magic and knew it would shift to serve her needs.

Circuiting the end of a beautiful pond, she crossed the garden to a tall maple tree where Karrew perched on top of a tree house. "Isn't it wonderful?" With a pleased smile, she sat on a wooden swing and set it in motion.

The back door opened. Allynae leaned against the doorframe. "I thought I heard you. Are you happy?" He laughed. "What a silly question. I can see it in your face. You love this land, and we've only just arrived."

She jumped from the swing and strode toward the cottage. "Wait until you have explored more, Alli. The forest, the grasslands, the foothills...and the mountains! I can't wait for you to see the Dojanacks." At the foot of the back steps, she stopped and grinned at him. "I'm starving. What have you discovered in the pantry?"

He led the way into a bright, homey kitchen, where pale peach walls glowed in the afternoon sun, and a fire in the wood-burning stove heated a kettle of water for tea. On a rectangular table at the room's center, freshly churned butter, honey the color of amber, and creamy goat cheese in small wooden bowls surrounded a large plate of ripe peaches and a round loaf of warm, fragrant bread.

Her stomach responding with a deep, hungry growl made Almiralyn grin. She arched a delicate blonde brow. "You've been busy."

"I can't take credit. It was all here and ready. All but the bread, that is. A small man who introduced himself as a Wood Tiff delivered it."

Almiralyn smiled. "Wood Tiffs are the guardians of the trees of the Terces Wood. I'm sorry I missed him."

Karrew swooped in through the open window and landed on his perch. "Home at last," he croaked, eyeing the feast.

Allynae set a bowl of fresh berries and nuts near his perch. "Whoever arranged this meal didn't forget you, Karrew Castilym."

Karrew dipped his head up and down and cawed. "I repeat...home at last."

Gratitude welled up from somewhere deep inside her as Almiralyn took her place at the table. Opposite her, Allynae spread fresh bread with butter and honey. He caught her eye and beamed. "What's first on the agenda?"

"Since the sun will set soon, I suggest we ride over to your cabin to ensure it meets with your approval. Will you stay there tonight or return here?"

"You have Karrew to protect you. I'll stay at my place. I could use time to myself." He swallowed the last of his bread and brushed the crumbs from his hands. A yawn spread into a full-bodied stretch. "It's been a long turning."

Almiralyn enjoyed the last bite of a ripe peach. "It has been wonderful."

When the kitchen was tidy, they strolled across the back garden and stood, arms linked, absorbing the beauty of sun's light splashing across the pond as it began its slow descent below the western horizon.

Allynae grinned. "Race ya to the barn." He shot ahead of her.

Myrrh's Guardian sprinted after him. They arrived at the paddock behind the barn, gasping for breath and laughing like a couple of children.

Four horses and a pony whinnied a welcome. A rooster strutted over to greet them, and a big, shaggy dog bounded in from the field, tail wagging and eyes bright with delight.

Allynae scratched his ears. "Buster, my friend, good to see you."

Almiralyn bent to scrub her hands up and down his sides. A wet, pink tongue soaked her cheek. "Good dog!" Straightening, she opened the gate. "Alli, your cabin is midway between the cottage and Demrach Gateway—a substantial walk. Which horse would you like?"

He patted a large stallion the color of ebony. "They bred Gemlucky for you." A low whistle summoned a roan mare. "I rather like Saylo." He scratched the roan's ear and led her into the barn.

Almiralyn rested her forehead on Gemlucky's forelock, stepped back, and looked into the dark eyes observing her. "I'm glad to see you, my friend." He snorted a response, tossed his head, and ambled after her. Once saddled and ready to go, she led the stallion from the barn. With the ease of an experienced rider, she mounted and guided him to the woodland trail.

The forest, a unique environment when the light followed the sun lower in the sky, greeted them with silky shadows and the coolness of the coming night. Ahead of her, Allynae scanned the trail, glanced back at her, and frowned. He reined Saylo to a stop and waited for her. "Something's strange. Can you sense it?"

Closing her eyes, Almiralyn concentrated on the subtle silence hanging like a filmy curtain in the woods. The trees seemed to hold themselves at attention. Wildlife paused in the twilight, alert and searching. Birds grew silent.

Gemlucky's skittish prancing forced her to refocus. She patted his neck. With a soft snort, he dropped his head and nibbled the grass at the trail's edge. A bird chirped. A small critter scurried through dried leaves. Whatever had disturbed the peace had passed.

Allynae shrugged. "Guess I was imagining things."

Almiralyn frowned. "No, something was here. Now it's gone. Let's get you home, so I can return to the cottage before night sets in."

Nudging Saylo into a slow trot, Allynae followed the trail to a large clearing where his cabin sat close to the trees at the far side. Karrew landed on a wooden rocking chair next to the front door. Allynae dismounted and led Saylo into an outbuilding on the opposite side of the clearing. Almiralyn tossed Gemlucky's reins over a bush, patted his neck, and joined Karrew.

"Did you sense something odd just before we arrived?"

His neck feathers ruffled and settled. "I did, but could find nothing. I'll keep watch while we wait for Alli."

With a sigh, she relaxed in the rocker, closed her eyes, and lost herself in the peaceful sounds of dusk.

"He comes." Karrew's soft caw snatched her from the verge of sleep.

Beneath half-closed lids, she observed her brother. *I'm so grateful life on Myrrh appealed to your easygoing nature, Allynae Nadrugia.*

The porch step creaked, and he smiled down at her. "Come on, sleepyhead, let's explore." Without waiting, he pushed the door open and stepped into his new home.

Almiralyn luxuriated in a full-bodied stretch, allowing him time alone in the dimness. His soft laughter brought her to the doorway. He grinned, walked to a small table, and removed the glass chimney from an oil lamp. Although he could have lit it with the snap of his fingers, he struck a match and touched the wick. The flame flared. A slight adjustment softened it to a warm glow that pushed away the shadows of turning's end. He raised it to eye level and surveyed the cabin's interior.

The front room was functional. On the west wall, a fire laid in the fieldstone fireplace was ready to be lit. An array of comfortable furniture in rich autumn tones formed a semi-circle around it. Bookcases filled with a variety of his favorite books lined the walls on either side of the fireplace. A nook of a kitchen provided what he would need to cook. Against the wall were several boxes and a large trunk waiting for Allynae's attention. Up a steep stairway, a sleeping loft nestled beneath the eaves.

Almiralyn watched him explore. Karrew flew through the doorway and perched on her shoulder, his glowing eyes taking in every detail.

Grinning from ear to ear, Allynae descended the loft stairs. "It's perfect, Mira. I have everything I need." He set the lamp down, smiled at her, and opened the door. "Go. You have things to do before bed."

She walked onto the porch and gazed at the fading streaks of orange and salmon arcing above the edge of the clearing. Allynae's arm around her shoulders made her smile. She glanced up. "Thank you for coming with me. It means more than you know."

He gave her a quick hug. "Couldn't stand to be left behind. Now, off you go, so I can unpack." He scanned the clearing and gave her another hug. "Keep your eyes open, Mira."

"I'll stay alert, and so will Karrew." She jogged down the steps and mounted Gemlucky. When her protector had settled on her shoulder, she waved. "Until later, Alli."

Knowing Gemlucky would carry her home safely and Karrew would warn her of danger, she allowed herself to become immersed in her surroundings.

Above the canopy, the sun dropped below the horizon, and velvet black night prowled through the forest like a predator, devouring the color and leaving the greens and browns of the turning's light muted to shades of gray. Gemlucky sniffed the air, flicked his tail, and continued his ambling pace toward the cottage. In the distance, the sounds of night filled her hearing— the deep croak of a frog, the hoot of an owl, a cricket's song. On her shoulder, Karrew remained silent. She knew that, like his mistress, he listened and absorbed.

The barn, a dark shadow against the vanishing light, loomed ahead. Almiralyn dismounted and led Gemlucky to the tack room. After removing his saddle, blanket, and bridle, she rubbed him down and released him in the paddock.

As she strolled through the garden, Karrew landed on her shoulder. "Does help arrives tomorrow?"

"Yes. Allynae has arranged for a couple from a nearby village to assist with chores. They will live in the cabin across the pond." Almiralyn climbed the porch steps, crossed to the back door, and paused to stroke his breast feathers. Excitement tingling, she pushed the door open and stepped into the kitchen. Delighted laughter chimed. "Look, Karrew, the walls have changed color, just like I wanted them to."

Karrew landed on his perch and cocked his head. "They were pale peach earlier, and now they're a soft, cozy yellow. You look happy."

"I am. I can't wait to explore the cottage and spend time in my sanctuary. Are you coming?"

His blue-black feathers ruffled and resettled. "You need some time alone. I'll keep watch here."

She slid a gentle hand down his back. "Thank you, Karrew."

An oil lamp in hand, she stepped into the hall. With the quiet dimness of the cottage embracing her, she explored the first floor: a study/library, a formal dining room, a comfortable living room, a guest bedroom and personal needs space, and an empty room that would become whatever she required.

Before climbing to the second floor, she tested the fourth step. A squeak brought a nod. *Just as I requested.* On the upper level, she discovered an elusive number of bedrooms, designed to shift and change depending on need. She paused in a doorway, a hand on her heart. *My sanctuary!*

As though on cue, shafts of soft light from the full moon shot through the window on the eastern wall, washing the room in cool, white luminosity. Brightness bathed the opposite wall in shimmering iridescence and highlighted the map of Myrrh engraved there.

She placed her lamp on a side table and sank into the cushioned softness of the only chair in the room. "I'm finally here."

A flash of golden light next to the window faded and left a battered trunk in its place.

She crossed to it, knelt, and placed a hand on the ancient brown leather. "Chealim told me you would arrive during my first visit to the sanctuary." Unbuckling the leather straps, she opened the lid. "Tonight, I have things to do."

Moonlight casting its magic glow over the trunk's contents inspired a wave of emotion. *These, and my mother's gift, are the treasures of my office— the things that will help me keep Old Earth safe.* She lifted a leather scabbard, held it up, and withdrew a knife. Amethysts in the gold handle sent beams of purple darting throughout the room. Emerald mist rose from etched symbols on the silver blade. Efillaeh, forged in the heart of the Evolsefil

Crystal, began to glow. It trembled and grew warm in her hand. Beams and mist joined in a cocoon of shimmering color around it.

Almiralyn's voice, raised in song, filled the room.

"Efillaeh, the healing blade,
Bless this cottage, wood, and glade.
Heal all those who enter here.
Open hearts and melt their fear.

When The Unfolding begins to rise,
Keep my heart and mind apprised
Of who must next receive your gift
In time to mend the coming rift."

The glowing cocoon evaporated, leaving Efillaeh cool and motionless in her hand. She returned it to the scabbard and replaced it in the trunk.

Her hand strayed to the blue velvet pouch hidden beneath her shirt. Removing the ribbon from around her neck, she cupped the pouch in her hands and closed her eyes. An image of her mother's lovely face teased a faint, sad smile to her lips. *I wish you could see Myrrh, Maman.* Loneliness mingling with sadness, she tipped a piece of Zullia the size of a quail's egg onto her palm. Cobalt blue and veined with gold, Zullia, mined on Tao Spirian, was rarely allowed off the tiny planet. Known as The Stone of Remembering, it stimulated memory, magnified courage, and soothed away sadness and fear.

Almiralyn smiled as its satiny surface glowed, enlivening its rich colors. Happy memories washed over her. *Grandmama received this piece from the hands of a Tao Spirian mystic and presented it to Maman at her temple initiation. Now, I am its steward.* Again, her mother's face filled her sight and faded. The stone's inner light muted. She smiled, returned it to the velvet pouch, and placed it next to the knife.

Chealim's trunk contained three more precious items. Moonlight highlighted the circular face of the Compass of Ostradio. Hefting its solid weight, Almiralyn closed her fingers around its sleek smoothness. She admired the red lettering on the pale gold face and smiled at the slender, gold needle jiggling when her hand moved. Turning it over, she examined the deep blue metal and the sprinkled glints of white representing the stars in the night sky. A tiny asteroid, nestled at the center of the compass in a nest of spun quartz crystal, enabled it to absorb the geography of any planet or place. A warm tingling spreading over her palm prompted her to hold the compass up in the light of the full moon and whisper the words taught her by Chealim.

"Patterns of Myrrh's landscape rare...
Forests, grasslands, mountains fair...
Absorb these secrets into thee
And all else that we should see."

The needle spun in a golden blur. Letters blazed the fiery crimson of the Great Central Suns. Glints of white on the cobalt back rearranged themselves into the constellations and galaxies of the Myrrhinian sky. The needle stopped. Crimson letters returned to a dulled red. Almiralyn pressed the compass to her heart before returning it to its place in the battered leather trunk.

Awed by the trust placed in her, she focused on the most important item of all, the oracle fountain, Elcaro's Eye. Miniaturized for travel and carved from the rarest alabaster in The Universe, it sat on her palm and drank in the moon's luminosity like an elixir. Reverence embracing her, she knelt and placed it on the hardwood floor at the center of the sanctuary. With the faint scents of wood and stone tickling her nostrils, she rose, and, stepping back, chanted the words that would bring the fountain into place and time.

> *"Elcaro, the All-Seeing-Eye,*
> *Grow to size that I may spy,*
> *Within your depths, the heart of things,*
> *And all that The Unfolding brings.*
>
> *Expand your width and height to be*
> *The center of my sanct-u-ary.*
> *I clap my hands to call you forth.*
> *Spring to size from your true north."*

Three claps rang out. The sculptured stone quivered. Azure mist swirled around it. A flash of blazing white light preceded the resounding crash of thunder. The cottage rocked on its foundation. Darkness enveloped the room. Sudden silence left Almiralyn holding her breath.

A radiant shaft of moonlight shot through the window and pooled around the full-sized alabaster fountain, enlivening the crystal, Vesen, within the sculpted pedestal. The carved likeness of Myrrh's new Guardian knelt on the circular rim, her cupped hands above the waiting emptiness. Water trickling from the upraised palms filled the sanctuary with the sound of its rippling arrival in the fountain's round bowl.

Almiralyn stared in awe. "Elcaro's Eye, you are so beautiful! The greedy covet your sentient awareness and potential for prediction. I promised the Galactic Guardians I will protect you with my life."

Almiralyn knelt and slid her arms around the cool smoothness of white alabaster and pressed her cheek against the fountain's rim. "This is the gift of gifts." Trembling fingers caressed the carved weave of the braid circling halfway around the bowl. "Elcaro's Eye, please help me steer a true course through the upcoming Unfolding and to protect Myrrh and the Clenaba Rolas Solar System."

After a moment of reverent quiet, she rose and gazed down at the last item placed in her care, an alabaster ladle with a sapphire cabochon in the handle. *Sipping water from this ladle will enhance my perceptive power.* She dipped it, drank the refreshing contents, and replaced it in the trunk.

Moving to Elcaro's Eye, she touched its rippling surface. *I wonder what Allynae is doing?* The spilling water ceased to flow, and the surface calmed. A whirlpool formed at the fountain's center, spun into a frothing swirl, and sucked the foam into its vortex. Stillness brought Allynae's face to the mirror-like surface.

"Good evening, Mira. I gather all is well?"

A laugh of genuine delight bubbled up. "Oh, Alli, everything is wonderful. The cottage is exactly as I imagined. I love my sanctuary. The trunk is here, and its contents are intact. The full moon blessed each gift. I am happy and content. Are you still pleased with your cabin?"

"It's exactly as I wished. I, too, am content—and exhausted. Portal travel always wears me out. Unless you need me, I'm off to bed. I'll be there in the morning to meet the caretaker, Katerrace, and help him settle in. Does he bring his companion to help you in the cottage?"

"I believe she will join him. Tomorrow will tell all." Feeling the depth of her fatigue for the first time, she yawned.

Allynae grinned. "Sleep well." He gave her a mock salute.

Water spilled from the statue's hands, scattering his image and reclaiming the fountain.

A wave of contentment flowed through her. She rested a hand on the fountain's rim. "Thank you, Elcaro."

She pivoted, absorbing the simplicity of the sanctuary, the map of Myrrh, and the graceful lines of the fountain. The rhythmic sound of water spilling into the bowl accompanied her to the window. She gazed at the moonlit back garden—the shadowed shape of the barn, the sparkles of starlight on the pond. The curtain fluttered. A breeze caressed her cheek as she bent to close the trunk and secure its buckles.

The flame in the oil lamp tossed strange shadows around the room. The sounds of water died, leaving tension in the air.

Hastening to the fountain, Almiralyn observed a furtive figure flitting through a blistered landscape. A man's hand flashed across the surface. The image vanished. Chealim's face focused.

"Beware, Almiralyn. Evil is loose within the Inner Universe. Let Myrrh be your primary concern. The Galactic Guardians will keep your presence hidden as long as possible." A smile replaced his stern expression. "Your first turning in Myrrh draws to a close. Rest well."

Water tumbling into the bowl scattered the image and erased the anxiety of Chealim's unexpected visit.

Fatigue nudged Almiralyn across the hall to her room. After preparing for bed, she slid between crisp, cool sheets, and let her sleepy gaze absorb her surroundings. White walls with pale green accents, a window seat with a view of the front garden and its border of sunflowers, and a cozy chair and footstool produced a heartfelt sigh.

She plumped her pillow and extinguished the flame in her lamp. A yawn squeezed her eyes shut. The smell of summer flowers and the rustling of curtains in the gentle evening breeze were the last things she remembered before sleep wrapped her in its peaceful embrace.

Birds chirping their welcome to the sun enticed her from dreams of the Dojanack Mountains to the muted light of early morning. Waking for the first time in her new home, she lay motionless, listening. The unfamiliar sounds of Myrrh's awakening sent a newfound joy thrumming through her. A luxurious stretch brought with it a deep inhale of morning-fresh air.

Swinging her legs over the side of the bed, she padded to the double glass doors and stepped out onto a small veranda. A view of the Terces Wood, wrapping around the northern edge of her acreage, greeted her. Tall trees stretched their leaf-laden branches toward the cottage, shading the furthest bank of the pond. *This is my home now.* The realization left her breathless.

After her morning cleanse, she dressed and stood in the doorway to the sanctuary, braiding her long hair, her gaze resting on Elcaro's Eye. Its exquisite beauty and the knowledge that the Vesen crystal in its pedestal possessed awareness more acute than her own awed her. Foreknowledge of coming events and the intelligence to predict outcomes made the fountain a prize worth fighting for.

She frowned and gazed at the rippling water. "Who was the figure in the fountain last night? Chealim would not have taken control if he had not been concerned." She flipped her braid behind her shoulder. "He told me the Guardians would handle it, and I trust him. Patience is key. Elcaro will share at the appropriate time."

With her thoughts refocused, she headed for the kitchen. *Wonder what color it is today?*

"Good morning, Mira." Karrew's cawed greeting ended with a deep gurgle.

"Good morning to you." She stopped, hands on hips, and surveyed the room. "It's the pale blue of a bird's egg. What fun!" Crossing to Karrew's perch, she ran a finger over his glossy feathers. "It's so peaceful here. I slept better than I have in ages. How about you?"

His neck feathers fluffed into a collar of black. "Why do I feel the peace will be short-lived?"

Almiralyn told him about Chealim's appearance in Elcaro's Eye.

He sidestepped along his perch. "Guess we'd better enjoy the tranquility while we've got it. Breakfast?"

After preparing his food, she rummaged in her well-stocked pantry and found the leftovers from last night's snack. Spreading butter and honey on a crust of bread, she wandered onto the back porch. The rising sun, soaking the sky in a pastel wash, arced above the garden.

With hope filling her heart, she inhaled a long breath of fresh Myrrhinian air. *Today, my new life begins.* Back in the kitchen, she set breakfast goodies on the table.

The back door closing heralded Allynae's appearance in the kitchen. "Good morning. The turning's awake and wonderful." He helped himself to bread and goat cheese, popped some berries in his mouth, and plunked down on a chair. "I passed Katerrace and his wife. They'll be here soon. I checked their cabin. It's ready. So...what's next, Mira?"

"Let's take a quick peek at Elcaro's Eye and see what's happening in Idronatti. Chealim hinted that the Five Fathers might be a problem."

Allynae scratched his chin. "I hear Elcaro can be pretty cantankerous. Will it show you what you need to know?"

"We shall see." She offered Karrew her arm, and he hopped on. Taking the lead, she climbed the stairs to the second floor and entered the sanctuary.

Karrew fluttered to her shoulder while she and Allynae took their places by the fountain. Almiralyn glanced from the raven to her brother. "I'm so glad you are both here."

She snapped her fingers. The water spilling from the statue's open palms ceased its cascading song. Elcaro's cognizant awareness steadied the reflective surface. An image took shape.

Five uniformed men sat around a table, arguing about a document spread out in front of them.

A squat man with dark hair jumped to his feet and pounded a fist on the tabletop. "We must stop the proposed tours to Myrrh and erase all memories of it from the minds of our people."

"How do you propose to do that, Soru?" The older man next to him glowered.

"We use memory adjustment. The tests are showing it works on anyone over thirteen sun cycles."

A third man spoke up." And we destroy the portal to Myrrh."

Soru slouched into his chair and scowled at the man across from him. "Don't be ridiculous. If we destroy it, we won't be able to monitor what's happening there."

A calm, calculating voice entered the discussion. The speaker sat with his back to the observers in Myrrh. "Please, gentlemen. PPP patrollers guard the portal—" He held up a hand, stopping a rebuttal from the second man. "The PPP monitor it, Jarel. We will adjust the memories of all Idronattians over thirteen. They won't remember Myrrh exists."

The speaker shifted in his chair and stared over his shoulder. Sharp, narrow features accented the harshness of his expression. Beady eyes blinked and stared again. He turned back to his comrades. "Idronatti's citizens will not travel into or out of Myrrh. The PPP will arrest anyone who tries and send them to the Five Towers." He shot another glance over his shoulder.

The fountain's water swirled, erasing the room, the men, and the anger.

Karrew flew to the windowsill, flapped his wings, and pranced from one foot to the other. "A lust for power is never attractive. What is it about Humans that they thrive on making other Humans subservient?"

Allynae fumed. "Fear, Karrew. Fear drives a lust for power." He shook his head. "What kind of life will people have in that city?"

Almiralyn's mind juggled thoughts like a circus clown juggling balls. The papers on the table, entitled The Plan, laid out rules and regulations to control and censor the lives of Idronatti's citizens. Scheduled from morning to night, they would be monitored by the Peoples Progress Protectors, the PPP. The right to choose their own paths through life would cease to exist. She feared what would happen to those who rebelled. And she hated that The City's children would never know the joy of making their own choices.

Allynae's voice intruded into her thoughts. "You're pretty quiet, Mira."

"We have to help Idronatti's children. We can't let them live their lives not knowing about freedom and play and the delight of escaping into a good book." An idea took hold. "I know what we'll do."

Karrew flew to her shoulder. "What have you come up with?"

"We will create a secret gateway to Myrrh only the children will know about." Happy laughter bubble up. "This will be fun. It's time to eat and make plans."

From his perch in the kitchen, Karrew watched a flush tint Almiralyn's cheeks pink and her eyes sparkle with pleasure. She loved a challenge, and the Five Fathers had definitely presented her with one.

Across from her, Allynae slathered cheese on bread and listened while she presented one idea after another for discussion.

A knock interrupted the rapid flow of ideas. "Excuse me? Hello?" The voice was low and weathered like an ancient tree.

Allynae, nearest to the porch door, went to welcome the caretaker and his companion. "Come in. We've been expecting you." He showed the couple into the kitchen.

Almiralyn came around the table. "Welcome. I'm Almiralyn."

The man, well past middle age but bristling with energy, held out his hand. "Katerrace is the name, but friends call me Race."

She smiled and shook his callused hand. He was tall and lean with a huge smile and bright, intelligent eyes the color of roasted chestnuts. His thinning gray hair was cropped short. He was tidy as a pin in his overalls and green plaid shirt.

A petite woman peeked from behind him. He drew her to his side and put a protective arm around her. "This is Feela, my companion. She's a great little cook and cleans plenty good."

Almiralyn offered her hand. "I am so pleased to know you and so grateful for your help."

Feela dropped her gaze and bobbed a curtsy. Fawn-colored eyes with flecks of green lifted to meet Almiralyn's before the woman's shyness settled around her like a cloak.

Almiralyn smiled and returned her attention to Race. "Allynae will show you to your cabin. Please take the rest of today to settle in. Let me know if you need anything. Tomorrow, we can discuss responsibilities and what works best for all of us."

Race nodded. "Thanks, my lady."

"Please, call me Mira."

He nodded again and flashed his smile.

Allynae led the couple across the garden. Almiralyn watched Feela's short roundness disappear after the men. *She's interesting.*

"Shy little thing." Karrew sidestepped along his perch. "I imagine you'll bring her out of it, though."

"She just needs time." Almiralyn pursed her lips. An enlightened smile smoothed them into an elfish grin. "Karrew, I have a plan to provide a playground for the children of Idronatti."

He cocked his head and listened as she paced and explained the details.

When she finished, she made her favorite tea in a flowered teapot, poured it into a matching mug, and sat down at the table. "Unless you noticed something I've missed, we'll run it by Allynae and see what he thinks."

"I believe you have thought of everything." Karrew pecked at his belly feathers. *It's a good plan...if nothing interferes.*

When Allynae returned, they resumed their meal, and Almiralyn sketched out her proposal. "The first thing I'll do is close the gateway in the Five Towers."

"The Fathers won't like that." An affirmative nod and eyes gleaming with a gleeful twinkle accompanied Allynae's reply.

She sipped her tea, savoring its sweetness and her own sense of right.

"The Fathers do not control the gateways of Myrrh." Her eyes narrowed. "It will not hurt them to feel the power wielded by the Guardians."

"So, if you close the gateway, how will the children find us?"

"I'll create three new portals to insure their safe passage to and from Idronatti. The first one will be located in The Borderlands, the buffer zone between Idronatti and Myrrh. It will move from place to place and bring the children from there to our sunflower field here on Myrrh. Next, I'll create the portal the children will use to travel from the city to The Borderlands and a different one they will use to return to Idronatti."

Allynae tugged his mustache. "That should keep the PPP guessing." He selected a handful of berries and popped one in his mouth. "Won't we need a portal custodian for the one that travels around The Borderland?"

She nodded. "We will. I have an idea, but first, let's set up the portals."

He swallowed another berry and asked his next question. "How will the children discover them?" His brows bridged. "And how will they find the traveling portal to Myrrh when they arrive in The Borderlands?"

"We'll plant the secret of the three portals' whereabouts in the mind of one special child who will spread the word." She looked toward the back door, where a smoky gray cat sat cleaning her ears. "And we'll provide a guide for Myrrh's portal in the buffer zone."

The cat strutted into the kitchen and jumped into her lap. Round amethyst eyes stared up at her. Almiralyn stroked her silky fur. "This is Majeska." She scratched her ears and ran a hand down her back. "You'll be our guide and go between, won't you?"

The cat's purr filled the kitchen as she jumped to the floor and crouched beneath Karrew's perch. One easy leap landed her on the windowsill beside him. He lengthened his neck to touch her pink nose with the tip of his beak, then bobbed his head up and down and pranced along his perch. "Hi, Jeska."

She blinked her purple eyes, opened her mouth in a wide yawn, and stretched out in the sun.

Allynae leaned back in his chair. "One more question... What will contain and support the traveling portal?"

Eagerness made Almiralyn grin. "Have you read anything by the Old Earth author Lewis Carroll?"

"You mean *Through the Looking Glass*?" Sadness flickered, but only for a moment. "Maman used to take me to the Galactic Library at the temple when I was young. Lewis Carroll fascinated her." Merriment lit his eyes. "A mirror, right?"

She smiled a knowing smile.

"Perfect! Maman would approve." He leaned his elbows on the table and rested his chin on his knuckles. "You've thought of everything, Mira. When do we close the Idronatti Gateway at the Five Towers and open the new ones?"

She took a breath. "Tonight, we'll wait until the moon begins to rise, so our illusions will achieve their full strength when it reaches its zenith. The process will take most of the night."

After clearing away the remains of their meal, she turned to her brother. "How about a walk in the garden? I haven't had time to explore."

Arm in arm, they strolled past the maple with the tree house and the swing. By the pond, they watched ducks paddle. They looked in the chicken house, where Almiralyn cupped an egg's warm roundness in her hands before returning it to the nest. In the barn, they discovered Race feeding the horses and Feela with a lap full of kittens. A trip to the paddock brought a tan and cream pony to the gate.

Race and his companion joined them. Feela rubbed the pony's nose and smiled shyly. "This is Tamboreen. She likes to be called Tam."

Almiralyn rubbed the pony's nose. "She told you her name, didn't she?"

Feela nodded. "How did you know?"

"Because you have special gifts. I felt them when we met. I'm so glad you're here."

The woman blushed but kept her eyes on Almiralyn's face. "So am I."

A further exchange about what time to meet the following morning ended with Almiralyn bidding them good turning. With a smiled farewell, she guided Allynae around the cottage to the front yard, where flowers grew in abundance. Vines intermingling with pink roses crawled up trellises and tumbled over the white fence. Just beyond the gate, she stepped away from her brother. The air made her skin tingle. Squinting, she peered into a field of tall, golden sunflowers.

"What's up?" Allynae's quiet question intruded into her silence.

"Tropal Portal, the dimensional gateway leading to the Five Towers in Idronatti, is hidden amongst the sunflowers." Her brow wrinkled. "I believe someone has attempted to mask it. Tonight, we will close the portal's destination point at the Five Towers and reroute it, so Tropal becomes the gateway from here to The Borderlands. The gateway back to Idronatti will be beneath a street lamp at the fringes of the buffer zone. Its destination and anchor points in The City will be determined by Elcaro's Eye and the Compass of Ostradio."

Allynae pursed his lips. "Have you decided where to anchor the portal from Idronatti to The Borderlands?"

She tapped her chin. "I believe the SunSpire, the City's tallest building will be the perfect place." A yawn brought tears to her eyes. "A nap is calling."

"You never nap." Her brother's laugh deteriorated into a cough as she shot him a quizzical look and pushed open the front door.

I n the quiet of her room, she stretched out on the bed. When asked what type of home she wanted on Myrrh, she had spent hours in the temple's library, poring over old books until she could picture it exactly. She smiled to herself. *It's more wonderful than I imagined.* Sadness tinged her smile. *I wish you could see it, Maman.*

Fatigue left her yawning. Even as she wondered if her parents had returned to KcernFensia, her eyelids closed and she slept.

The weight of Karrew landing beside her woke her. Outside her bedroom window, the sun slid along its western arc. Dusk would arrive soon.

Pushing herself to sitting, she leaned against the headboard. "When the architects were designing the cottage, I asked for an attic full of forgotten treasures, but I haven't explored it yet. Do you suppose we might find a mirror up there?"

Karrew hopped to the end of the bed. "We won't know—"

"Unless we look." She followed him from the room.

He flew the length of the hall and landed by a recessed door. An age-darkened brass key hung on a hook beside it. Almiralyn inserted the key in the lock. A quiet click sounded, and the door swung open. Inside, a narrow staircase angled up between two walls. Feeling a quiver of excitement, she ducked through the doorway and climbed the wooden steps.

Her anticipation increased as her head arrived above the level of the floor. *The attic holds an abundance of treasures!* Six more steps brought her into a spacious area with beamed ceilings and dormers with shuttered windows. Scattered throughout were odd shapes hidden beneath gray covers, piles of books, and baskets filled with surprises.

Karrew flew up the stairwell, circled the room, and landed on a gray mound.

Allynae's head appeared at floor level. "Anybody home?"

"Alli, help us search for a mirror!"

He surveyed the space. "We'll need more light." Moving from one dormer to the next, he opened the shutters, inviting late afternoon's golden light into the attic. His eyes held a smile when he turned to her. "Let's get started."

One by one, treasures emerged...a rocking horse, handmade with a black horsehair tail and mane; a box of leather-bound books that made Allynae coo with pleasure; and an antique desk and matching chair. Almiralyn opened and closed the center drawer. "Oh, Alli, won't this look great in the study?"

"Mira!" Allynae's voice held a note of suppressed excitement.

She looked up to find her full-length reflection in a large oval mirror with an intricate gilded frame. "Alli, it's perfect. Help me teleport it to the sanctuary."

Allynae stepped to her side and groaned. "You know how much I hate practicing DiMensionery. Can't we just carry it down together?"

She shrugged. "We can, but the stairs are pretty steep."

He glanced at the stairwell. "You're right. I'll help, but just this once."

She raised an eyebrow at his reflection in the mirror.

"I'll be helping tonight. I know." He clasped her hand and shut his eyes.

His energy flowed in concert with hers. Focusing her intention, she formed a detailed image of the sanctuary in her mind and pictured the mirror in the corner by the window.

Karrew gave a gurgled caw. "The mirror is gone."

Allynae opened his eyes and stared. "You never cease to amaze me, Mira."

"Thanks for your help, Alli. I will need all the strength I can muster for tonight's work. Shall we check and see if it's where it's supposed to be?"

Karrew swooped ahead of them down the stairwell. When she entered the sanctuary, he was perched on the rim of the fountain, one eye observing her. The mirror rested against the wall in the corner.

Allynae lounged in the doorway. "Did you think it wouldn't be where you pictured it?"

Her eyes searched his face. "Do you even begin to know how powerful you are?"

"Leave it, Mira. I need to eat before our work begins." He disappeared down the hallway with Karrew flying in his wake.

For a moment, she allowed the quiet of her special place to fill her. She knew the Five Fathers would fight her for power over the Idronatti portal. Without Allynae's help, she might fail. Inhaling the fresh summer air, she headed for the kitchen.

· · ·

Almiralyn relaxed on the window seat in her room. A cool glow heralded the moon's appearance in the eastern sky. At dinner, Allynae had accepted her need for help and ceased his denial of his gifts and his power. They separated to rest and prepare for the night's work with smiles of anticipation. Gratitude filled her. *How lucky I am you came with me, Alli.*

The curved edge of the moon crested the trees. *I'm glad the moon is full for three turnings here.* She crossed the hall to the sanctuary and gazed into the rippling depths of Elcaro's Eye. The whisper of raven wings announced Karrew's arrival. The fourth step creaked. Allynae was on his way.

After opening the trunk to make the treasures accessible, she placed twelve white candles in a circle around the outer circumference of the room. Incense filled the sanctuary with her favorite scent. One by one, she lit the candles, waiting for the last two until Allynae had entered the circle.

She picked up the alabaster ladle from the trunk, dipped it into the fountain's bowl, and offered it. "Drink this water with clear intent for the success of tonight's work, Alli. It will support your talent and give you strength."

He drank deeply and handed it back.

She focused, followed suit, and then offered it to Karrew, who bobbed his head and dipped his beak. When he had finished, she hung it from the fountain's rim and smiled at Allynae. "Ready?"

He placed his hands on Elcaro's bowl. She took her place opposite him and curled her fingers over the carved weave of the statue's braid where it circled the rim. The water spilling from the alabaster hands ceased. Sentient awareness smoothed the ripples away, leaving moonlight from the open windows glistening on the water's satin stillness.

Almiralyn glanced up. Allynae remained motionless in the candlelight. His eyes were closed, his breathing even and quiet. She leaned forward and blew. An image emerged from the depth of the bowl.

Like menacing ghosts, Idronatti's Five Towers loomed on the surface. Spotlights on each building shot beams of light down empty streets. The image zoomed closer and steadied. Two PPP patrolmen stood at attention on either side of a vault entrance. Another zoom pulled the picture into focus beyond it, where a vortex swirled in the subdued light.

Almiralyn centered her thoughts and created a contracting boundary line around the portal. Her clear, commanding voice chanted,

> *"The time has come to close the gate,*
> *To save it from the Fathers' hate.*
> *I draw the string up tight and bind*
> *This gateway 'til the end of time."*

A soft caw from Karrew warned of trouble. The vault door flew open and light exploded into the space. Almiralyn snapped her fingers. The boundary surrounding the vortex contracted. Bit by bit, the portal grew smaller until only a minuscule opening remained.

A furious face filled the fountain. Dark eyes searched. A mouth, twisted with hatred, opened in an ear-slitting scream. "Who dares to defy me? Who dares to destroy what belongs to the Five Fathers of Idronatti?"

Almiralyn projected her holographic image into the vault. "I, the Guardian of Myrrh, close what you have defiled. Give the people of Idronatti their freedom, and I will return the portal."

The man's face contorted with loathing. "We will not give up what we have created. *The Plan* will save the people. The People will obey *The Plan*. Idronattians will *never* visit Myrrh again."

"So be it." Almiralyn snapped her fingers. The opening vanished as the man's comrades flooded the vault.

Anger infused their features. Hatred hurtled toward her hologram.

A wave of her hand deflected their emotional charge. Dignity and power radiating around her, she addressed the gathered men. "Fathers of Idronatti, the Guardians granted you the privilege of building The City and the responsibility for protecting it, its citizens, and Myrrh. You have chosen instead to use your authority to control and constrain those placed in your care. Until The Unfolding is complete, this gateway will remain closed."

A man started toward her. The hologram faded. Garbled voices shouting profanities were cut short by the water boiling up in the fountain, sloshing over the rim and down the smooth bowl onto the ivy-sculpted pedestal. A whispered word brought the water to a standstill. Silence settled over the sanctuary.

Allynae released his hold on the fountain and stretched. "You've made powerful enemies. They will not soon forget tonight's work."

Brushing tendrils of hair back from her face, Almiralyn shrugged. "They made their choice. I made mine." She picked up the compass and held it out to him. "Take this, please." She strapped Efilleah's belted scabbard around her waist and slipped the ribbon of the Stone of Remembering pouch around her neck.

Her brother fingered the compass. "What's first, the mirror and the traveling gateway or the portal into Idronatti?"

Karrew cawed. "Clearing the anchor point at this end will be important, as well."

Almiralyn tossed her braid over her shoulder. "That's our next goal." She smiled at Allynae. "Remember, the cottage portal is called Tropal. Are you ready?"

He slipped the compass in his pocket, placed his hands on Elcaro's rim, and nodded.

She removed Efillaeh from its scabbard and leaned over the fountain. "Tropal Gateway." Clouds rolled up and obscured the water's surface. Moonlight drenching the fountain turned its alabaster opaqueness translucent. From the bowl's depths, a shaft of Vesen's cool, crystal light dispersed the mist and highlighted Tropal's faint vortex emerging in the water. Almiralyn pointed the sacred knife at the portal's center. The etchings on the silver blade began to glow. Drops of emerald light dripped from its tip and dispersed into the swirling vortex. Blackened debris flew from the gateway. Purple light from Efillaeh's handle absorbed it, transmuted it, and beamed it back into the center of the bowl.

Tropal ceased its spinning and Elcaro's Eye returned to its original opaque alabaster whiteness. Efillaeh's blade and handle grew cool in the moon's light. Almiralyn exhaled. Beside her, Allynae's gaze lifted from the fountain's surface to her face.

"I knew the knife was powerful, but..." He shook his head, pulled a handkerchief from his back pocket, and mopped the beaded sweat from his brow.

Almiralyn offered him a ladle full of water. When he had drunk his fill, she quenched her thirst. Refocused on Elcaro's Eye, she absorbed its omnipotent magic, the candlelight in the sanctuary, and her brother's power. A deep breath cleared her mind. "Tropal's old anchor point is gone. The next step is a destination point for the new portal. Please hold the compass above the fountain, Alli."

Withdrawing it, he held it face down over the water. Almiralyn cupped her left hand over his and recited,

> *"Elcaro's Eye and compass fine,*
> *Join forces to give us a sign,*
> *Where destination points can stand*
> *In Myrrh's buffer, The Borderlands."*

In rapid succession, a series of pictures shot to the water's surface...a house; a flower shoppe; an old, deserted chapel. Faster and faster the images appeared, blurred, and vanished—then ceased.

The Compass of Ostradio glowed. Almiralyn removed her hand. Allynae turned the compass over. The spinning needle's blurred impression obscured the face. Three sharp claps brought it to a standstill. Identical pictures of a shoppe front materialized on the compass face and on the water's surface. The weathered sign on the dark blue door read, "Antiques by Q." A cross-fade erased the door and brought a decrepit two-story building into focus.

Karrew landed on Allynae's shoulder and peered at the image. "The mirror can move within the shoppe, and the shoppe can travel throughout The Borderlands."

Almiralyn nodded. "It will do." She tipped the Stone of Remembering from its blue pouch, whispered a few quiet words, then touched it to the compass face before placing it in the kneeling statue's open palms. "That will secure the memory to both. Now, it's time for the mirror, Alli. Keep the compass close."

After slipping it in his pocket, he clasped her offered hand. Together, they teleported the mirror inside the circle of candles. She released Allynae's hand and placed hers on the fountain's rim. "Hold the compass in your right hand, facing the mirror. I'll tell you when to switch it to your left."

She gazed at her kneeling likeness and took a breath. "I'll create the portal within Elcaro's Eye. Karrew will transport it through the mirror and into The Borderlands. Timing is critical."

Alli placed the compass as directed. She summoned her protector to her shoulder. With his presence reassuring her, she let her mind grow empty. A picture of the new gateway formed as she recited:

"A new portal must come to be.
In the fountain, let us see
It arise from its beginning;
Swirling, whirling, vortex spinning.

Make a keyhole at its center,
Hidden until one would enter.
Index finger makes the sign
To open up this portal line."

Elcaro's Eye shimmered translucent. Golden light soaked the base of the pedestal and radiated upward, coalescing into a pearl-sized seed at the fountain's center. Beneath it, the water churned, opening a funnel from the surface to the tip of the oracle crystal, Vesen, where it gleamed at the bottom of the bowl. Luminous light shot upward, exploded into a rain of diamond sparks that pelted down into the All-Seeing-Eye, and merged with the seed into a spinning phosphorescent vortex at the fountain's center.

Almiralyn clapped her hands. "Eero Tye Como!" The vortex swirled out to fill the bowl. "Oree Eyt Omoc!" It shrunk to the size of a coin. Karrew swooped, snatched it in his beak, and landed on Allynae's shoulder.

The Compass of Ostradio's golden needle began to spin. Almiralyn's voice rang out.

"Whirling vortex, compass points,
Join to mirror like bones to joints.
Spin within the captive space;
Remain forever in this place.

Transport to The Borderlands,
Hidden secret from brigands.
To the shoppe, Antiques by Q
Anchor there this portal new."

Pale blue mist filled the mirror. A large keyhole appeared at its center. Karrew shot through the keyhole and vanished.

"Other hand, Alli. Now!"

Allynae fumbled, caught the compass midway to the floor, and switched it to his left hand.

Karrew's deep caw preceded his reappearance from the haze as thunder clapped and the mirror flashed from sight. He landed on the rim. "That was close."

Allynae ran shaking fingers through his hair and flashed Karrew a strained smile. "I almost dropped it. Sorry, old friend. Good thing you're quick."

Almiralyn stroked her raven's back and offered him a dipper full of water. "Good work, Karrew."

He gave a low gurgle and dipped his beak. Lifting it, he ruffled his feathers and croaked. "Thank you, Mira. What's next?"

She returned the ladle to its hook on the rim, straightened to her full height, and squared her shoulders. "Now we must create the portal from The Borderlands to Idronatti. This time, Elcaro will place the anchor and destination points, but we have to decide where they should be."

After the compass and the fountain had discovered the correct placement—one at the far edge of The Borderlands beneath a street lamp and two in downtown Idronatti—Almiralyn spoke the charm to create the new portals, substituting appropriate instructions in the second stanza.

When all was complete, once again she offered Allynae water. "We have one more thing to do; then we can rest."

After a long drink, Allynae's tired expression shifted to a smile. "Who will be the first child to visit Myrrh?"

She nodded, reached for the Stone of Remembering, and held it next to her heart. "Right, Alli, let's begin." With her free hand on the fountain's rim, she whispered,

> *"Elcaro's Eye, help us to find*
> *A child with curiosity of mind,*
> *Who will spread the word around,*
> *Where Myrrh's new portal can be found."*

The water remained motionless. No image emerged. Total silence gripped the sanctuary and the cottage. Then a breeze rustled the curtains; a moonbeam skittered across the water; and on the surface, a picture formed.

Curled up in bed, his black hair tangled on his pillow, was a boy of about ten cycles. As they watched, he sprawled onto his back and mumbled in his sleep. Almiralyn held the Stone of Remembering above the fountain. A ray of light shot from its glowing center, piercing the water's surface, highlighting the boy's dark skin in a blue aura. Eyes filled with wonder opened. A sleepy smile ended in a yawn. The boy rolled onto his side and slept. The stone lay dull blue and lightless on her palm.

Karrew cawed. Allynae exhaled, a breath long held.

Almiralyn smiled. "Our first young guest..."

Tired but satisfied by the night's work, Almiralyn sat on her bed, absorbing the quiet. Allynae remained at the cottage and slept down the hall. Karrew stood guard in the kitchen with Majeska. A yawn nudged her into bed, where the lullaby-like whisperings of the pre-dawn breeze sang her to sleep.

The sun rising above the trees and the aroma of fresh baked muffins coaxed her from her bed. Dressed and excited for a new turning, she arrived in the kitchen to find Feela setting the breakfast table. Allynae and Race sat chatting about Myrrh and making plans for the turning.

"I seem to be the lazy one." She smiled and sat down at the table. "Everything looks and smells amazing. Thank you, Feela."

The woman returned her smile, still with a touch of shyness. "Eat while things are warm."

After a comfortable breakfast, Race and Allynae headed for the barn. Feela hummed as she cleared the table, and Almiralyn slipped away to her sanctuary.

From the doorway, she surveyed the room, then crossed to the fountain. "Good morning, Elcaro. What have you to share?"

The oracle's mirror-like surface shimmered. Almiralyn's reflection steadied, but her body throbbed. Gripping the alabaster rim, she closed her eyes and slowed her breathing. Cool energy tiptoeing up her spine, prompted her to blink and to focus. The fine-lined face of Mira, the persona she had created for entertaining Idronatti's children, smiled up at her. Gray hair, tied back in a bun, seemed intent on escaping. Blue eyes twinkled. All of four feet, ten inches tall, Mira was round in a comfortable, grandmotherly kind of way. "This will do." She tucked a renegade lock back into place.

A knock at the front door prompted her to hurry downstairs. Feela whispered from the kitchen doorway. "Exactly how I pictured you..."

Mira nodded, then straightened her apron, patted her flyaway hair into place, and opened the door. A boy in a blue uniform stood on the steps with Majeska sitting primly at his feet.

Surprised confusion lit his face. "Where am I?"

"You are in Myrrh. I'm Mira. What's your name?"

He gave her a nervous stare. "I'm Wilith Whalend, and I dreamt about you.

She opened the door wider. "Come in, Wilith. Fresh-baked cookies await you in the kitchen and a back garden is ready to be explored."

From the kitchen window, Mira watched the boy from Idronatti overcome his fear of anything new. Allynae coaxed him onto the swing and taught him to pump it higher. They visited the tree house, where Wilith used a hammer for the first time to fix a loose step on the ladder. When Buster ran barking from the barn, fear flared in the boy's dark eyes.

Alli called the big dog to heel and gripped his collar. "I promise he won't hurt you, Wilith."

The Idonattian boy rubbed a hand over his black hair. "I have never seen a dog up close. What do I do?"

A short time later, his laughter drifted over the garden as he chased Buster and together they rolled around in the grass.

When it was time to go, he exploded into the kitchen, an imp of a smile erasing his earlier nervousness. "Please, can I come again?"

Mira kept her face neutral. "Yes, you may. But your visits must be our secret, and you may only come when it's safe."

Wilith gave her a studied look. "I will be careful and only tell friends I trust about Myrrh." Apprehension flickered. "How do I find my way home?"

She smiled and escorted him down the hall. "Majeska will show you."

Delight highlighting his features, he dashed after the gray cat. At the portal, he turned and waved. "Thank you, Mira." He jumped into the swirl of light and was gone.

Karrew landed on her shoulder. Allynae joined them and slipped his hand into hers. "What do you think, Guardian of Myrrh?"

She let her gaze come to rest on the new Tropal Gateway. "I think our life in Myrrh has begun."

Upstairs in the sanctuary, the water spilling into Elcaro's Eye ceased. Stillness polished the surface silver. An image formed. Four young people, a tan pony, and a dog ambled in a dispersed group along a forest trail. A silhouetted shape swooped from the top of a tall granite tower, gave a great horned owl's shrill screech, and soared out of sight.

Water trickled from the statue's alabaster palms. The image vanished, leaving only the memory of what was to come.

1

Prophecies tell of those who will lead
The battle to thwart rising darkness and greed.
Their arrival will herald the Time of Unfolding,
A cycle of growth and Universal remolding.

Ancient prophecies quaked to life on the last remaining piece of Old Earth. Raging winds stirred in deep mountain passes, charged across the grasslands, and whipped the treetops of the Terces Wood into a wild frenzy. Where the forest bordered the land surrounding the Guardian of Myrrh's cottage, the tempest calmed to a gentle breeze.

Curtains rustled at the window of an upstairs room. Inside, the carved statue of a woman knelt on the rim of an alabaster fountain, her gaze fixed on the turbulence in the water-filled bowl.

The breeze dissipated. The water stilled. A blurred image floated to the surface and focused. Uneasiness filled the room.

Almiralyn Nadrugia, her eyes narrowed in thought, gazed out her kitchen window. With a contented sigh, she murmured to herself. "Time has flown by since we arrived in Myrrh." Her gaze roamed from the pond to the swing in the maple tree, to the tree house perched high up in its leafy branches. Since we established a pattern of visits from the children of Idronatti, my turnings are filled with the joy of watching them discover who they truly are. I've paid visits to the farms and hamlets boarding the grasslands." She tapped her lips and nodded. "Most importantly, I have forged relationships with the inhabitants of the Terces Wood and the Dojanack Caverns deep beneath the mountains. I am also know and respected by those in The Borderlands.

A gust of wind lifted the curtain. Her contented smile tugged into a frown. Over the past few turnings, subtle changes had occurred in Myrrh—changes that inspired a deepening sense of unease.

The desire to know more sent her from the kitchen up the steps to the second floor of her cottage, where the all-knowing fountain, Elcaro's Eye, waited. A glow of heightened expectancy shimmered on the water's mirror-like surface, then floated upward to fill the room, leaving her sapphire-blue eyes filled with questions gazing up at her. A long braid hinting of sunlight and moonbeams caught the light and gleamed.

She stared at her reflection and almost smiled. "I see you've been expecting me, Elcaro."

In response, water spilled from the upturned palms of her sculpted likeness and sent ripples in concentric circles toward the bowl's curved sides. Its rhythmic drip, drop, drip erased the image, but failed to dispel Almiralyn's growing apprehension.

Crossing to the window, she stared out at the back garden. "Where are you, Karrew? Have you found anything that might help us unravel our mystery?" She scanned the garden once more. "I wish you were here. Elcaro is about to share information." With a disappointed sigh, she returned to the fountain and fixed her attention on the image-free water.

Curtain's fluttering and a soft caw alerted her to her protector's return. A large raven glided through the open window, landed on Elcaro's alabaster rim, and cocked his head. One dark obsidian eye studied her.

She smiled her relief and ran a hand over his glossy feathers. "I'm so glad you're back, Karrew. What did you discover?"

A deep-throated gurgle preceded his verbal response. "Tension, as tangible as the wind in the trees, is spreading throughout the land, but I couldn't find the reason." His neck feathers spiked and resettled. "Do you think the fountain will show us what we need to know?"

Almiralyn focused her intent on the undulating surface. "Let's find out. Elcaro, the All-Seeing Eye, show us the source of the uneasiness creeping over the Land of Myrrh."

The water ceased its rhythmic splashing and rippled into stillness. A blur of colors swirled and quieted into an image from an earlier time. She glanced at Karrew. "The fountain's showing my first visit to this sanctuary on the turning we arrived in Myrrh. I wonder how that impacts what's happening now?"

Her raven gave a throaty gurgle and returned his attention to the fountain.

Intrigued by the memory from the past, Almiralyn opened to what Elcaro's Eye was choosing to share and fixed her gaze on the image on the water's surface.

Kneeling in front of a battered leather trunk, Almiralyn reverently examined each item placed in her protective care by the Galactic Guardians of the Fourth Galaxy. Efillaeh, the healing blade, the Compass of Ostradio, the Stone of Remembering all left her humbled and in awe.

Giddy from the power emanating from the trunk, she picked up a miniature fountain sculpted from the rarest white alabaster in the Inner Universe. Cupping it in trembling hands, she carried it to the room's center and held it up. "I have great things to accomplish, Elcaro's Eye, and you are the key."

Placing it in a pool of moonlight at the room's center, she stepped away and pressed her hands to her heart. The moon's radiance enhancing the beauty of the carved alabaster magnified the emotions threatening to overwhelm her.

After a steadying breath, she recited the ancient words taught her by the Guardians. Three sharp claps rang out. The tiny Elcaro's Eye quivered. An azure mist swirled around it. Blazing white light flashed and faded, leaving the full-size fountain glowing with the radiance of alabaster and moonlight.

The past faded. Almiralyn shifted her gaze from the water to the sanctuary window and then to her protector. "I brought the All-Seeing Eye to size many sun cycles ago, Karrew. Why is Elcaro showing it to us now?"

The raven's feathers ruffled. "It must relate to the growing tension in Myrrh. Does the fountain have more to share?"

Almiralyn touched the water and stared at her glistening fingertip. The immensity of her role and the responsibility she carried made her square her shoulders. *So many seek this land and the secrets it holds.*

Karrew's soft caw brought her attention back to Elcaro's Eye.

On its reflective surface, the bowl's alabaster rim framed Old Earth in its hidden dimension parallel to the planet of Thera in the Clenaba Rolas Solar System. Two silhouetted figures soared high above it, their shadows darkening the land below. The image wavered, then scattered into tiny pieces that sank into oblivion.

Water, overflowing from the statue's upturned palms, sent ripples dancing over the fountain's surface.

Fingering her long, silver-blonde braid, Myrrh's Guardian frowned. "Uninvited visitors are flying this way, Karrew. I know you have just returned but—"

"It won't hurt to take another look around." The raven cawed and unfurled his wings.

Mira crossed to the window and held a curtain aside. "Be careful. Don't let whoever's out there know you're abroad."

Karrew alighted on the windowsill and touched her hand gently with his beak. "Stay alert, Mira. I'll be back as soon as I can." He launched into flight and streaked toward the Terces Woods.

With her instincts thrumming an urgent warning, she watched her friend and protector disappear in the clouds rolling over the forest bordering her land. His absence further amplified her sense of foreboding. She shivered. *I always feel less vulnerable with you nearby, Karrew.*

Worry nudged her back to the fountain. She studied the gently undulating water and reviewed her options. "Until you return, patience is the key." Her spoken words hung in the air.

Frustrated but knowing Elcaro would share more when the time was right, she left the sanctuary and descended the stairs to the first floor. In the pale blue kitchen, she poured herself a cup of her favorite Dojanberry tea.

As her footsteps faded, an opaque fog billowed upward from Elcaro's basin, obscured the carved likeness of Myrrh's Guardian, and cascaded over the alabaster rim onto the floor.

The song of swirling water stilled. Mist hovered above the fountain and floated out the window, leaving the image of a large oval mirror in a gilded frame gleaming on the water's surface. Silence hung like thick velvet curtains around Elcaro's Eye.

A small, boot-clad foot kicked the shining glass, unleashing the full force of childish rage. Panted breaths accompanied the web of cracks that sent shimmering shards flying. A long fissure careened upward.

Triumphant laughter echoed through the sanctuary and down the stairs to the kitchen.

Almiralyn paused, her mug of tea midway to her mouth. A second laugh brought her to standing, her eyes glued to the ceiling. *What's happening in the sanctuary?*

Racing up the stairs, she went straight to the fountain. Her alabaster likeness sent sparkles of light into the air. The water's surface glinted. She leaned closer. "Elcaro, show me the recent past."

At the bottom of the bowl, the tip of Vesen, the quartz crystal encased in the fountain's pedestal, glowed red. The cottage staircase flashed into being. Her image sprinting up the stairs quivered and dissipated.

Ripples filling the bowl informed her the occasionally contrary fountain had nothing more to share. Worry narrowed her eyes. The responsibility for the hidden remains of the once great planet Earth pulsed through her veins. She hurried to the window. Her gaze darted over the landscape. Nothing triggered an alarm. Still, growing apprehension raised the hair on the back of her neck.

2

Almiralyn's throat tightened. *Where are you, Karrew Castilym?* A cool afternoon breeze tossed the curtains inward. A squawk of warning announced the return of her protector. Relieved and anxious for news, she moved aside.

Karrew skimmed the sill, landed on the back of an overstuffed chair, and cocked his head. "Better shut it, Almiralyn. Storm's on the way."

She pulled the window closed. For a moment, she stared at the raindrops splattering against the rectangular panes, then faced her friend. "Did you discover anything new?"

Zigzags of lightning flashed. Thunder rumbled. The raven ruffled his feathers. When they had settled along the curves of his body, he hopped onto her offered arm. Happy to have him home and safe, she smiled and arched her brows in a question.

"I visited the folk of the woods and mountains. Everyone I spoke with shared a similar message—something's amiss on Myrrh. They described two silhouetted figures flying repeated patterns over the Dojanack Mountains, the Grasslands, and the Terces Wood. Even the DeoNytes, who rarely leave the caverns deep in the mountains, are sensing danger they do not understand." He fluttered to the padded arm of the chair.

Almiralyn sank down beside him. "Did you discover anything about what or who might be out there?"

"Nothing." Blue-black wings fanned the air. "Has Elcaro's Eye shared anything useful?" The raven bobbed his head. "I don't suppose Chealim has been in touch?"

Before she could answer, blinding pale-blue light filled the room, leaving the subject of Karrew's inquiry towering over her. The Galactic Guardian's radiant gaze held hers, then Karrew's.

"Almiralyn Nadrugia, Guardian of Myrrh." His deep voice, softened to accommodate human ears, warmed her. He bowed his head and touched his heart. "Karrew Castilym of Roahymn."

One long stride carried Chealim to the window. He stooped to peer out, then straightened to his formidable height and faced them. "Darkness the Galactic Council has yet to define gathers in the Clenaba Rolas Solar System. We believe whoever controls it is searching for you, Almiralyn, and the hidden secrets on this last piece of Old Earth."

The Galactic Guardian stood even taller, his head brushing the high ceiling. A long, silent moment passed. The seriousness in his expression when he returned his attention to her sent a chill skittering up her backbone.

His brows drew together. "The evil Mocendi League is expanding its reach. Its DiMensioner-trained assassins are spreading their malignant destruction throughout our galaxy without regard for life forms or solar systems. Unlike the Order of Esprow's DiMensioners, whose aim is to accomplish good, the Mocendi are intent on upending everything positive in the Inner Universe. Their greed keeps them from progressing higher than the lowest level of DiMensionery, yet they wield their power with remarkable skill. Beware, Almiralyn. Do *not* underestimate them."

Almiralyn rose, her gaze fixed on his. "I promise I will neither underestimate them nor disappoint you."

Chealim almost smiled. "The Council knows you will continue to be vigilant and to do what you know must be done."

A smoky-gray cat sprinted into the sanctuary, howled in distress, and darted beneath the chair.

Chealim's eyes became mere slits. "Your unwanted visitors are drawing closer to your acreage. I suggest you shield the cottage and grounds from view." Blinding light flashed, leaving the spot where he had stood empty.

Majeska darted from the sanctuary. A clipped meow filled the stairwell.

Karrew cocked his head. "Even Majeska is feeling the strangeness."

Almiralyn motioned for him to precede her and followed him down the stairs, through the kitchen, and into the back garden. Grateful the summer squall had passed, she scanned the paddock, gardens, ponds, and fields comprising her home.

Karrew perched on the peaked roof of the nearby tree house. Majeska paused on the back step, her tail twitching and nose sniffing. Almiralyn stooped to look the smokey gray cat in the eye. "Go, Jeska, warn the Wood Tiffs and the Nyti. Have them tell all forest creatures to stay hidden until I send word."

As the cat darted across the garden into the Terces Wood, Almiralyn sang out,

> *"Shields, my cottage and gardens surround.*
> *Hide them so well they cannot be found.*
> *Send any strangers wandering away;*
> *Lost and confused, lead them astray."*

The shields shooting upward into place left her tingling. She rubbed her arms and projected her senses outward. Satisfied her intruders would see only forest and meadows, she fixed her attention on Karrew. "We must discover who our enemies are and inform Allynae and the residents of Myrrh to be on the alert. I will join you in flight."

She stepped away from the tree and prepared to shift shape. An iridescent oval flared around her. Her bird form, somewhat smaller than Karrew, flashed into being. White as the first snow of winter, she unfurled gold-tipped wings, fanned the air, and soared upward. Scanning the horizon, she replayed Chealim's warning in her mind. *We must find the intruders before the intruders find us.*

Side by side, she and her protector flew a crisscrossed path high above the immense field of sunflowers bordering the cottage on one side. As they swooped over the Terces Wood, Almiralyn sent Karrew ahead to confer with the Wood Tiffs and then soared higher. Far below, the mountains, prairies, and forests formed a patchwork of varied hues, shapes, and textures beneath her. When nothing sparked an alarm, she swooped into the forest. The transition carried her into silky shadows smelling of damp earth and the coolness of the coming night.

Landing in the leafy protection of a tall Tirips Tree, she merged into the silvery leaves and cocked her head one way and then the other. *Something feels strange.*

A mental search ruffled her white neck feathers into a bristly collar. Silence enshrouded the woods. Trees held themselves at attention. Wildlife paused in the twilight, alert and watchful.

In the cottage sanctuary, the turbulence in Elcaro's Eye stilled. The crystal Vesen's sentient essence welcomed the fiery rays of the setting sun that shot through the cottage window and glistened on the water's calm surface. A small hand holding up a shard of broken glass emerged from the fountain's depths. Silver light darted along the sharp edges.

Ripples scattered the image into small pieces that sank like bits of sparkling sand to the bottom of the bowl.

In the Terces Wood, a bird's chirp broke the silence. Small critters chattered. Almiralyn's bristling feathers smoothed. *Whatever disturbed the peace has passed.* She fluttered to the ground and materialized in human form.

Karrew alighted across the way. "Tibin says he and the Wood Tiffs have seen nothing since late yesterday, nor have the tiny, winged ones, the Nyti."

Almiralyn gave a tendril of silver-blonde hair a tug. "We need to share what has occurred with Allynae."

Her protector cawed his agreement and launched into flight. She shifted and shot after him. Within a short time, they arrived at the large clearing where Allynae's cabin sat in the shadow of the trees. Karrew flew to the back of a rocker on the porch.

Almiralyn shaped Human, sat next to him, and scanned the clearing. "Alli's feeding Saylo. He'll be here shortly."

Karrew fanned his wings. "He sure loves that horse."

She smiled inwardly as her tall, lanky brother stepped from the outbuilding and strolled across the clearing. Their parents had disappeared not long after his tenth Sun Cycle Celebration. She had been fifteen when she had taken him on as her responsibility. Since their arrival on Myrrh, a subtle change had occurred. Allynae had become her equal.

The porch step creaked under his tread. "You look serious, Almiralyn Nadrugia."

She took his offered hand and stood. "I just hope you won't regret coming with me to Myrrh when you hear what I have to tell you, Alli."

"I wouldn't worry if I were you." He pushed the door open.

She glanced around the clearing. "Karrew, please keep watch."

The large raven flew to an evergreen and alighted in the shadows.

Allynae studied him for a long moment before motioning her into the cozy interior. While she settled in a comfortable chair, he fetched water, handed her a filled glass, and sat down. "You and Karrew are worried about something. What's happened?"

With the glass cupped in her hands, she focused on a droplet sliding from the lip into the water. A long sip later, she described all that had occurred. Her brother listened with total attention. His eyes, a lighter shade of blue than her own, narrowed in thought. She finished with a slight frown. "I hope I can live up to the Council's expectations."

Allynae stood, pulled her to her feet, and gazed down at her, his eyes gleaming with pride. Strong arms enveloped her in a bear hug. "You have already established Myrrh as a haven for the children of Idronatti; you've neutralized the City Leaders' control of the portal from the Five Towers into The Borderlands; and you've established yourself as a power to be reckoned with throughout the solar system. I think you're living up to expectations." He pointed at his fieldstone fireplace. "Chealim paid me a visit, as well."

Leaving the comfort of his arms, she crossed to the mantel to study a quartz crystal the size of an ostrich egg. "It's beautiful, Alli. Does it have a name?"

"Yes. Novissi. Once it's connected to Elcaro's Eye, I'll be able to help monitor what's happening on Myrrh." He edged her toward the door. "Karrew's getting impatient. Go, Almiralyn. He wants you safe at the cottage before moonrise. So do I. When shall we connect Novissi to the fountain?"

"I'll contact you later tonight." She walked onto the porch and gazed at the fading streaks of salmon and gold arcing above the clearing. Her brother's comforting arm around her shoulders made her smile. "Thank you for your support, Alli. It means more than you know."

He gave her a quick hug. "Keep your eyes open, Mira."

"You, too. I'll stay alert. So will Karrew." She kissed his cheek, shaped the white bird, and flew after her protector.

3

Quiet filled the Guardian's sanctuary. As though painted by an artist's brush, the portal mirror, appeared in Elcaro's Eye. A circular web of cracks glinted near its bottom edge. Pieces of shattered glass dotted the basement floor. Reflected on the marred surface, the silhouette of a young boy holding a silvery shard lifted his hand and sliced his right cheek. Droplets of blood oozed from the wound. The boy dropped the shard. The mirror vanished. A single drop of scarlet floated on the fountain's calm surface.

Above the forest canopy, the sun descended below the horizon. Velvet, black darkness slipped through the forest like a prowling panther, devouring the color and leaving the turning's greens and browns muted to grays. Nothing ominous distracted from the sounds of night.

Almiralyn arrived at the border between her lands and the forest ahead of her friend and protector. An unexpected sensation of peril propelled her toward the barn, through the hayloft's open doors, and into human form. A quick check of the shields affirmed they held strong. She frowned.

Karrew's arrival on her shoulder steadied her. Neither moved nor made a sound. Raven claws gripped harder. His telepathic message filled her mind. *"I'll discover what I can at the cottage."*

"I'll do a mental search from here." Almiralyn's quiet exhale ruffled the single white feather on Karrew's breast.

Powerful wings carried him from the loft. Moments later, he swept in and alighted once more on her shoulder. *"Something is strange in the sanctuary. I suggest we teleport."*

Almiralyn pictured the upstairs room. A breath later, they stood beside the fountain. Her eyes widened. At the calm center of the All-Seeing Eye floated a single, luminous drop of blood. Karrew's talons dug into her shoulder. A shudder shook the bowl. The drop dissipated into a crimson sheen. Water overflowing the statue's upturned palms, sent undulating ripples to disperse it.

Determination firmed her chin. "Elcaro, show what caused the blood?"

The water spilling into the bowl ceased. Light swirled up from Vesen's crystal tip. Sunlight danced over the gilded frame of an oval mirror standing beside the fountain. The unmarred surface gleamed; a book rested on a table nearby. The fountain zoomed in on the book's cover. The title read *Through the Looking Glass*, authored by Lewis Carrol. Sunlight changed to moonlight on the mirror's surface. A raven cawed. The picture zoomed out to show Allynae, herself, and Karrew gathered around Elcaro's Eye. To one side, the battered leather trunk sat open, exposing its treasures.

Karrew cocked his head. "A flashback?"

She nodded. "I'm uncertain why, but perhaps it will help us determine what's happening now."

On the fountain's calm surface, the flashback played on like an old-fashioned movie, pulling Almiralyn and Karrew into the past.

In quick succession, images of the night the new portals came into being flashed like cards flipping. The creation of Tropal gateway's, destination point, the sunflower field on Myrrh, focused and vanished. The portal mirror formed beside the fountain. With the help of the compass of Ostradio, Almiralyn created the new anchor point at the center of the fountain. Her voice filled the room.

> *"A new portal must come to be.*
> *In the fountain, let us see*
> *It emerge from its beginning,*
> *Swirling, whirling, vortex spinning.*
>
> *Make a keyhole at its center*
> *Hidden until one would enter.*
> *Index finger makes the sign*
> *To open up this portal line."*

The mirror and the anchor point vanished, leaving behind a large keyhole that undulated into nothing as water cascaded from the statue's alabaster palms.

Almiralyn frowned as the water stilled. "I asked what caused the blood." Her brow furrowed. "The fountain can be abstruse, but I believe it just gave us an answer."

Karrew's wings quivered. "The mirror portal..." He glided to the windowsill. "Allynae may have a thought or two. Why don't you contact him? I'll do a quick patrol and then stand guard." The wha wha of raven wings faded over the garden.

Almiralyn gazed into the water and directed the fountain's magic.

> *"Elcaro's Eye, please thread the web*
> *Before the full moon's power ebbs.*
> *Connect Novissi to your heart,*
> *So Allynae may do his part."*

A whirlpool formed at the fountain's center, spun into a frothing swirl, and sucked the foam into its vortex.

Stillness brought Allynae's face to the mirror-like surface.

"Good evening, Almiralyn. Novissi is glowing. I gather it is now connected to Elcaro's Eye?"

"Yes, Alli, and through it to the Prima Crystal, Evolsefil, which will allow it to keep you informed regarding Myrrh, Thera, and beyond." She bit her lip.

"You look worried. Better fill me in."

She described the blood in the fountain. "I asked Elcaro where it came from. Do you remember the night we created the mirror portal in The Borderlands?"

"How could I forget? I almost ended Karrew's life. Why?"

"Karrew and I just watched a flashback in the fountain. I'm certain the mirror portal has something to do with the strangeness on Myrrh."

His rugged features, so like their father's, grew thoughtful. "Why isn't the fountain showing what you need to know?"

"What it shows us may seem arbitrary, but I've never known it to play games. It responded to my question." She yawned. "I'm simply too tired to see the answer."

Allynae studied her. "You're fighting exhaustion. Get some sleep. I'll ride over in the morning. We can figure out Elcaro's message when we're fresh." He gave her a clipped salute. "Goodnight, Guardian of Myrrh."

She stifled another yawn and grinned. "Goodnight, my favorite brother."

He chuckled. "I'm your *only* brother."

Spilling water from the statue's hands erased his image and reclaimed the fountain. The soft, rhythmic sound soothed her frayed nerves. Moonlight beckoned her to the window. She sighed and soaked in the beauty of her land—the shadowed shape of the barn, the sparkles of starlight on the pond. A full-bodied yawn brought tears to her eyes. "Our mystery can wait. I need a good night's sleep. I'm more tired than I have been since I first arrived in Myrrh."

In her bedroom, she stripped off her clothes, pulled on her nightdress, and slid between the crisp, cool sheets. The night's quiet and the knowledge her protector would return soon lulled her into a deep sleep.

Perched on the thatched roof, the raven Karrew kept watch. His eyes, gleaming like polished obsidian, scanned the night sky. *For the moment, you are safe, Almiralyn.* His neck feathers spiked. *I intend to keep you that way.*

4

Almiralyn woke as dawn's warm light penetrated the sheer curtains covering her bedroom windows. Rolling onto her back, she stared up at the ceiling, her sapphire blue eyes narrowed in thought.

Allynae will be here soon. Today, we must discover who terrorizes the Land of Myrrh. Her lips pursed. *Why do they bring hatred and fear into the land? Is this the beginning of the prophesied Unfolding?*

She slid from beneath the covers, gathered her clothes, and crossed to her personal needs space. A fine mist of water warming her skin refocused her thoughts. With a sigh, she gave herself permission to relax.

In the sanctuary, morning light illuminated the fountain's glistening white alabaster. The statue's sapphire eyes gleamed. Water droplets slowed, then ceased. A hint of red glistened as scattered shards of glass formed on the water's surface. Elcaro's Eye zoomed out to show the portal mirror with a web of breaks and a long, vertical crack bisecting the surface all the way to the center. A boy's silhouetted hand touched a shadowed cheek, then held a blood-soaked finger up in the dim light. His voice rang out. "You will be sorry, Mira. Someday, I will find my way back to Myrrh." A quick, calculated movement smeared sticky scarlet down the length of the crack. Angry footsteps retreated, echoing through the cottage before diminishing into silence.

Almiralyn finished dressing, pulled on her boots, and glanced at herself in the mirror. The faint sounds of a youthful voice and retreating footsteps informed her the fountain was awake and sharing. She hastened to the sanctuary, where the image of the mirror portal in The Borderlands gleamed on Elcaro's calm water, its diagonal crack filled with blood.

Swirling water erased the mirror and stilled. Images of Allynae, his skittish roan mare, and two silhouetted figures high overhead, flashed in a rapid sequence and vanished.

The sound of cascading water filled the sanctuary. The whisper of a light breeze lifted the curtains at the window, kissed the cheek of the alabaster statue, and grew still.

A rush of foreboding left Almiralyn breathless. She slowed her racing thoughts and formulated a question. "Elcaro, please contact my brother, Allynae."

Murky darkness cycloned upward from the depths of the basin. Distorted images flickered and faded. Water's rippling song informed her Elcaro had shared all it was willing to reveal.

Hurrying downstairs, she arrived in the kitchen as her protector glided through the open window and alighted on his perch. "Karrew!" She hurried forward. "Have you made your morning patrol?"

The large raven made a clicking sound, opened his black beak wide, and snapped it shut. A deep gurgle preceded his croaked response. "The protective wards shielding our acreage hold steady; all is as it should be at Allynae's cabin, but I saw no sign of him or his horse. You look worried. Is everything alright?"

She shared what she had seen in the fountain. "I know Alli is in trouble. When I ask the fountain to contact him for me, a series of images flashed, but nothing concrete." She frowned. "Maybe I didn't ask the right question."

Karrew ruffled his neck feathers. "Perhaps we should allow the fountain to share in its own way."

Almiralyn tilted her head and tugged at her long silver-blonde braid. "Come with me."

From the sanctuary doorway, she watched her protector land on the fountain's rim. Then, fixing her attention on the continuous flow of droplets, she joined him. "All-Seeing Eye, please show us what you know of Allynae's whereabouts."

The drops ceased their gentle cascade. Smooth water glistened, forming an image of the mirror portal leading from the Borderlands to Myrrh. The diagonal crack glinted in the dim light before the picture dissolved into nothing.

Water overflowing from upraised palms created a quiet, rhythmic song. Elcaro's tranquil presence filled the sanctuary.

Karrew cocked his head. "I believe we have a lead."

Almiralyn blew out a relieved breath. "Let's go see what we can discover."

With hope ignited, she shifted shape. Her white bird, gold-tipped wings gleaming, shot through the open window, and soared over the garden to the sunflower field bordering her land. A soft whinny brought her to the ground near Saylo, Allynae's mare.

The horse greeted her materialization to Human with a nervous toss of her head. Almiralyn approached, her movements slow and non-threatening. The mare's nostrils flared; her ears flattened. Almiralyn laid a gentle hand on the white blaze on her forehead.

Karrew landed nearby on a large sunflower. "What frightened her?"

Careful not to startle the horse further, Almiralyn made a cautious mental probe. Memories of ominous shadows passing overhead flickered and faded. Saylo took a restless step sideways and nickered.

Almiralyn's brows bridged in thought. "I just saw the sinister shadows Elcaro shared in Saylo's mind. Has anyone mentioned seeing them to you, Karrew?"

He fluffed his feathers. "Several villagers reported the shadow of doom flying over their fields."

She nodded. "More about our strange visitors after we find Alli."

Her protector fluttered to her shoulder. "He's not anywhere near here. I think we should explore the portal."

"I agree." Almiralyn patted the horse's flank. "Stay here, girl. We'll be back."

After moving away from the skittish mare, she whispered the Key for the Tropal Portal. A spinning circle began as a twinkle of golden light and grew to the height of a tall Human. "You take the lead, Karrew."

A low croak of acknowledgement, and the raven swooped into the swirling gold vortex.

Almiralyn ran toward the gateway to The Borderlands and leapt into its center. Suspended aloft in the tunnel between dimensions, she watched her protector floating in the distance. Streaks of shimmering color flashed by. Intense silence pressed against her eardrums. Karrew vanished through the portal exit. Accelerating time propelled her after him. She landed on hands and knees in a darkened basement smelling of dampness, dust, and the mustiness of old, abandoned things. She forced her body and mind to be still and listened for her raven.

The soft wha wha of his wings alerted her to his presence. "All clear, Mira."

She rose and held out an upraised palm. A ball of blue light glowed. Squinting to see through the darkness, she rotated slowly. The crack in the mirror's surface glinted a dull silver. Her light illuminating the floor revealed a foot. She lifted her hand higher. Allynae lay sprawled on his side, unmoving.

Dropping to her knees beside him, she touched his brow. "Alli?" His lack of response made her throat tighten.

A soft moan and fingers grasping her wrist sent a wave of relief rushing through her.

Karrew landed next to them.

Allynae's eyes blinked open. With a gulped breath, he struggled to sit up. "Mira?" His confused gaze darted from her face to the mirror. "What—where—Ouch!" He groaned, touched a large lump on the back of his head, and stared at his blood-sticky hand.

Footsteps in the shoppe overhead acted like a shot of adrenaline.

Karrew pranced from one foot to the other. "We need to leave. Can you stand, Alli?"

"I th-think so."

Almiralyn helped him to his feet. With a deft flick of her wrist, she drew a keyhole on the mirror's surface. A roiling mist tumbled onto the floor as the portal entrance expanded.

The door at the top of the stairs creaked.

Raven wings unfurled. Karrew shot into the gateway. Allynae stumbled after him. Almiralyn followed. Streaks of color rushed by. The keyhole-shaped outlet formed in the distance. Time sped up. Energy caught them and tossed them head over heels into the sunflower field. Behind them, the vortex spun faster in preparation for another exit.

Jumping to her feet, Almiralyn grabbed Allynae's arm. "I'm teleporting Alli to the cottage, Karrew. Make sure no one follows."

She pictured the kitchen. They arrived in an instant. Allynae gripped the firmness of the table's smooth, rounded edge and lowered himself onto a chair.

Almiralyn touched his shoulder. "I'll check the shields, then take care of your wound." As he lowered his forehead onto folded arms resting on the table, she hastened from the kitchen and up the stairs to her sanctuary.

A quick mental survey of the protective wards satisfied her the cottage and land remained invisible. She retrieved the healing knife, Efillaeh, from the trunk and returned to the kitchen.

After examining the gash on Allynae's head, she withdrew the blade and held it up in the light. She had only used it on two occasions since her arrival in Myrrh and knew its simple beauty belied its power.

"Are you ready, Alli?"

"Yes." Pain saturated the whispered reply.

Almiralyn touched the tip of the silvery blade to the gash. The amethysts in the hilt glowed and sent a lavender mist to surround her brother's upper body. From the etchings on the blade, tendrils of emerald-green, writhing like tiny snakes, encircled the wound. Allynae shivered and grew still. The ragged, bloody edges of the deep laceration stretched upward, met over the gaping cut, and reknit, leaving only a faint white scar. Amethyst and emerald light withdrew and faded. Efillaeh, which had grown warm in her hand, cooled.

Allynae's pain-filled breathing quieted. He sat up, touched the back of his head, and stared at his clean hand. Cloudy-blue eyes gazed up at her. "I knew the knife was special, but I did not understand its power until now. Thanks, Mira." He reached out. "May I hold it?"

Her smile broadened as she handed it over.

Reverence filling his expression, Allynae removed it from the leather scabbard and ran a finger down the blade. "Thank you, Efillaeh." He let out a long sigh, returned it to the scabbard, and smiled. "Even my headache is better."

Almiralyn took the knife and planted a sisterly kiss on his cheek. "You relax while I take this upstairs; then we'll talk." Eager to learn more of his misadventure, she replaced the sacred blade in the trunk. After a glance assured her the fountain had nothing to share, she hurried back to the kitchen, fetched a pitcher of water and glasses, and sat down.

"How did you get to the basement of *Antiques by Q*, Alli? Do you know who hit you?"

His brow wrinkled. "When I rode this way earlier, two shadowy figures flew circles over the sunflower field near the portal. By the time I reached it, they were gone. My research into The Unfolding hinted that the mirror portal from The Borderlands to Myrrh is important, so it seemed prudent to make certain everything was as it should be at *Antique's by Q*."

He took a long sip of water, set his glass on the table, and stared into the distance, his brows bridged in thought. "I recall exiting the portal in the shoppe's basement. Moments later, I heard a sound behind me." His brow smoothed and a wry smile tugged. "The next thing I remember was you kneeling beside me."

"Alli, I'm sorry…"

He patted her hand. "Don't look so worried, Mira. I'm fine, just annoyed at myself for letting my guard down." He leaned back in his chair. "What made you check the portal?"

"I asked Elcaro where you were. After a pause in the water's flow, it showed the mirror surrounded by darkness. I put two and two together."

She ducked into the pantry and returned with snacks. "Let's eat while we talk." She bit into a rosy red poma, savored its sweetness, and swallowed. "I'm sure our visitors are connected to The Unfolding prophecy."

Karrew glided through the open window to his perch. "Nothing exited the portal; no one followed us. Saylo is safe in the paddock." He sidestepped along the smooth, round wood and cocked his head. "You're looking much better, Alli. Any theories on what's happening in Myrrh?"

Allynae leaned his elbows on the table. "When I was a boy at the Temple on KcernFensia, where Mira trained to be Myrrh's Guardian, I studied The Unfolding." He steepled his long fingers. "The age-old battle between good and evil is about to create havoc throughout the Inner Universe. The prophecy predicted it will begin with a menacing threat here on all that remains of Old Earth. Four young people, destined to lead the fight to save the Land of Myrrh; its host planet, Thera; and our solar system, will follow. I believe our mysterious shadows are the prophesied danger."

A contemptuous snarl rumbled in the room above them.

Goose bumps racing brought Almiralyn to standing. Karrew gave a shrill squawk.

Allynae's startled gaze shot to the ceiling. He stood and clutched the table. "I'm still feeling dizzy. I'll join you in the sanctuary when my head stops spinning." He inhaled a calming breath.

Almiralyn's cautionary gaze rested on his face before she sprinted from the kitchen up the stairs and straight to the fountain. Raven wings fanned her hair. Karrew's talons gripped her shoulder. Glad for his presence, she watched the last fading edges of a silhouetted form melt away and a new image take shape.

The mirror portal, covered with an old tapestry, emerged on Elcaro's surface. Three youthful figures gathered in front of it. One pulled the aged fabric aside; another drew a keyhole at the mirror's center. It shimmered and expanded to allow the trio to enter the gateway into Myrrh.

As trickling water erased the image, a predatory shriek echoed through the land. Unexpected darkness enshrouded the sanctuary. Karrew cawed and flew to the windowsill. Almiralyn hurried after him, her gaze riveted to the silhouette of a massive bird of prey, talons extended, hovering overhead. Another ear-piercing screech shook the cottage. Immense wings carried the raptor above the trees.

A second sinister shadow took its place. Coldness unlike anything Almiralyn could remember left her gasping for breath. Fear fought for control. Ignoring it, she watched the cloud of glacial darkness soar higher, then swoop into the Terces Wood. At the forest's center, Nemttachenn Tower quaked. Shockwaves of terror rolled over the Land of Myrrh.

A shiver shimmied over her entire body. Unsure whether fear or cold provoked it, she hastened back to the frost-coated fountain, her mind buzzing with questions. Frozen water filling the bowl remained solid and opaque.

Two long strides brought Allynae from the doorway to her side. "I believe we just experienced what the inhabitants of Myrrh have been feeling." He shuddered. "The fear of death almost strangled me."

Almiralyn whispered a single word and snapped her fingers. An aura of pale-yellow light encompassed Elcaro's Eye. Warmth permeated the sanctuary, vaporizing the frost and ice into a fast-fading haze.

Karrew alighted on the rim. Almiralyn clasped her brother's hand and gazed at their reflected likenesses forming on the glassy surface. Droplets from the statue's palms dispersed them, one face at a time.

Tropal Portal spun into focus. A slender boy shot clear of the vortex beneath a large sunflower. His bald head gleamed in the sun as he peered up at the sky. The shadow of an enormous bird of prey circling lower and lower transitioned into a funnel-shaped opening at the center of the bowl.

A kaleidoscope of butterflies with scarlet-veined black wings spiraled upward. Once free of the fountain, they flew in unison from one side of the room to the other, then gathered in a fluttering cloud over the alabaster basin.

Almiralyn held her breath. Allynae clutched her hand. Karrew landed on her shoulder.

Nineteen butterflies quivered. Scarlet droplets rained down on the water. Stark black butterflies formed a line above Elcaro's Eye and morphed into letters:

The Unfolding Begins!

As the words faded, a verse appeared on the surface. Almiralyn studied it, then recited it aloud.

"The children of many bring truth to light,
Their courage challenges the DiMensioner's might,
The Unfolding sets the stage to reveal
Their futures and then their destinies seal."

Elcaro's Eye glistened as a breeze lifted the sanctuary curtains and sent a series of wavelets chasing across the water. The words scattered and dissolved. The fountain grew still, and the statue's cupped palms filled and overflowed.

5

Almiralyn felt her brother sag. She squeezed his hand and peered at his tired face. "I'm taking you home, Alli, so you can rest. Karrew, please go ahead with Saylo, and make certain the cabin is safe."

The raven gave a deep caw and flew out the window.

Allynae touched the statue's alabaster cheek. "The prophecy's prediction is coming true, Mira." He sighed. "I don't want to leave you, but I'm too exhausted to be of much help. What will you do first?"

Her brow wrinkled, then smoothed as she gazed at the map of Myrrh on the opposite wall. "I believe the young people shown to us by Elcaro are the ones predicted by the prophecies. Based on what the fountain showed us, they may already be on their way. While you rest, I'll track their journeys to Myrrh."

She touched his arm and teleported them both to his cabin. Fatigue bleached the color from his face as he sank into an armchair.

Crossing to the mantel where the large, egg-shaped crystal, Novissi, glistened in the late-turning sun, she observed her brother's reflection gleaming on the glossy surface. She turned to gaze down at him. "We can stay in touch via the fountain and your crystal. Please rest. I want you with me as soon as you're able."

Karrew flew to the arm of Allynae's chair. "The Terces Wood is quiet for the moment." He cocked his head, one eye on Allynae. "I'll remain here for a time."

Almiralyn hugged her brother, nodded at her protector, and teleported to the kitchen at the cottage. After refreshing herself with a mug of cool water, she hurried upstairs.

A frown tugged as she reviewed recent events. *I'm certain our interlopers are the spark igniting The Unfolding. Our young guests will speed up the process. I must discover what connects the children to our mysterious visitors.*

She opened the battered leather trunk under the window and allowed herself a moment of pleasure. *It seems like the Galactic Guardians presented these to me so long ago.*

After acknowledging the power of the sacred blade, Efillaeh; the magic compass, Ostradio; and the velvet pouch containing the Stone of Remembering, she picked up a ladle carved from the same white alabaster as the fountain. The sapphire cabochon in the handle sent a star of blue light to hover over Elcaro's round bowl.

Droplets falling from the statue's palms slowed, then ceased. The star floated lower and sank beneath the water's shimmering stillness. Almiralyn dipped the ladle in the fountain, drank deeply, and returned it to the trunk.

Resting her hands on the carved braid circling the bowl, she focused her intention.

"Elcaro's Eye, show our champions of The Unfolding."

A city bathed in morning light rose to the water's surface. The fountain zoomed in. Almiralyn held her breath as her eyes widened with surprise and understanding.

Sleep-tangled copper-red curls framed the sparsely freckled face of an adolescent girl peering from a bedroom window. Her gaze traveled the landscape of identical buildings across the way. Each one duplicated the next —the same twenty-five stories; the same gray with a slight blue tint; the windows positioned in the exact same place. Far below, the pristine streets were empty but for an occasional PPP RiaCruiser.

Her aimless thoughts collided. *Ari and I will soon be fourteen sun cycles. The Peoples Plan Protectors will wipe our memories clean of anything they don't want us to remember.* She frowned. *Then they'll assign our professions. What then? I don't want to forget Myrrh and Mira and Buster. I want to remember all the good times we've had and all the people and animals we love.*

She turned back to the room. Her chestnut-brown eyes came to rest on her identical twin sister, sleeping with such a peaceful expression it gave her hope. *Something will save us, Arienh AsTar. I'm sure of it.*

Smothering a yawn, she slipped across the hall to her mother's art studio. A freshly painted canvas sat on the easel. Menacing shadows soared over mountains of salmon-colored granite, black obsidian, and shimmering quartz crystal. The haunting beauty of the painting terrified her. She gasped, hugged herself, and exhaled a shaky breath.

Her mother walked into the room and stopped beside her. "What do you think, Brielle?"

"Where are those mountains?" Brie gave her mother a quick sideways glance before returning her attention to the painting. "They're so beautiful."

"I believe they're on Myrrh, although I don't remember seeing those particular ones when my family lived there."

Brie faced her mother. "And..." Brie swallowed. "...the shadows?"

SparrowLyn AsTar smoothed a strand of brown hair behind her ear. "I'm not sure. They just appeared as I worked." Her sleepy expression changed to serious. "Are you and Ari still planning to go to Myrrh today?"

"Mornin', you two." Brie's twin sauntered into the room, gave Sparrow a quick hug, and shot her sister a quizzical look. "You're awake early." Her eyes widening, she stared at the painting. "Mother, those mountains are amazing. But the shadows—" A slight shiver turned into a full-blown shudder.

"Mother thinks the mountains are on Myrrh, Ari. Wouldn't it be fun to go see them?"

"Not if those shadows are there." Ari tugged a tangled coppery curl. "Hey, today's Torgin's Sun Cycle Celebration. Remember, we're taking him to meet Mira, so we'd better get ready."

Sparrow's worried gaze flicked from one identical face to the other. "Would you consider taking Torgin another time?"

"Mother, it's his *fourteenth* Sun Cycle." Ari's deep voice held a hint of exasperation. "Today will be his last opportunity to visit Myrrh."

"In two moon cycles, the City Fathers will assign his profession and erase all memories that might promote a spirit of independence." Brie shook her head. "Afterward, he won't know Myrrh even exists."

Sparrow sighed. "I didn't intend to spoil your plans." She glanced at the painting and back at her daughters. "It's just that—" She bit her lip. "Please be careful. If something happened to you, I—"

"Nothing's going to happen," the girls chorused.

Ari shot her a crooked smile. "Just think, Mother, if you were like the other adults in Idronatti, you wouldn't know anything about Myrrh."

"And," the twin's announced in unison, "you wouldn't worry!"

"You're incorrigible—both of you." She studied her daughters. "I am grateful that because I didn't grow up in Myrrh, the PPP were unable to force me to have my childhood memories erased." Sparrow glanced at the miniature chronometer near her easel. "You'd better hurry if you plan to make it to Torgin's before Early-Morning Walk is over. I'll fix you a quick breakfast."

After they'd eaten, Brie sat on the bed and pulled on her uniform. "I had the strangest dream last night, Arienh." She stood. "That's why I woke up so early. And guess what?"

Ari raised her auburn brows.

"The shadows in Mother's painting were in my dream."

"You're kidding, right?"

"No." Brie frowned. "I wish I was."

"You can't tell her, or she won't let us go today."

"I won't, but—" Brie flinched and rubbed the back of her neck.

Hands on her hips, her sister voiced her disgust. "Brielle AsTar, nothing's going to happen to us on Myrrh. Mira will see to that." She buttoned the last button on her uniform and sat down to put on her shoes.

Brie sighed and studied herself in the mirror—spotless cobalt blue coveralls, a matching bandana tied just so, shoes polished to a glossy black shine. She tucked a shiny curl out of sight. "How can we avoid being noticed when everyone can see our hair is red?"

A pillow whizzed through the air and smacked her on the shoulder. In one smooth movement, she picked it up and hurled it back at her attacker. Ari caught it and chortled.

"Ready to go?" Brie grinned.

Ari plopped the pillow on the bed. "You bet I'm ready!"

"No, Arienh, you're not." Their mother stood in the doorway. "If you intend to walk down the streets of Idronatti unnoticed by the Peoples Plan Protectors, you'd better be presentable." She picked up a hairbrush. With a quick flick of her wrist, she tamed her daughter's long red curls into a braid. Deft fingers twisted a blue band around the end and pinned the braid up in a low bun. She tied her daughter's blue kerchief in place and turned her to face the mirror. "Much better, don't you agree?"

Brie laughed at her sister's scowling reflection.

Sparrow stepped between her daughters, her dark head topping their coppery ones. "Goodness, when did you two grow so tall?" Identical faces grinned back at her. "And how on Thera do people know who is Brielle Ralyn AsTar and who is Arienh Lynae AsTar?"

Ari grimaced. "I don't understand why people can't tell us apart. We sure don't act alike."

The sharp sound of a warning whistle blaring outside sent the girls into a frenzy. Brie tucked another wayward curl beneath her bandana while Ari did a last-minute check in the mirror.

Sparrow put her hands on her hips. "Let me see you both." Her worried gaze traveled from the top of their heads to their feet. "You look good.

Never forget we're on the Watch List, don't call attention to yourselves, and don't leave for The Borderlands until Late-Morning Exercise."

Ari kissed her cheek. "Gotta go if we're gonna make it to Torgin's before the next whistle blows."

Sparrow gave Ari a hug. Her eyes twinkled. "Take care of your younger sister, Arienh."

Brie scowled and scurried after her twin. "She's only four clicks of the chronometer older than I am."

When the girls rushed out, the door across the hall opened a crack. One magnified violet eye peered after them.

"Good morning, Henrietta." Sparrow smiled.

The eye disappeared. The door shut without a sound.

Returning to her studio, Sparrow crossed to the open window. Twenty-two stories below, blue-uniformed figures walked in unison down both sides of the immaculate street. She sighed. *We are all scheduled to the moment. Blue clad, brown clad, green clad, gray—all taking our regimented walks or eating our meals or sleeping or working or studying—all at the same time in different parts of the city.* She turned her back to the window and heaved another frustrated sigh.

After placing a clean canvas on the easel, she perched on the edge of her stool, picked up her palette and brush, and began to paint. Unbidden thoughts disrupted her usual ability to escape into her art. *What kind of future will my girls have in Idronatti? Their fourteenth Sun Cycle is only a moon cycle away. How will I keep the PPP from erasing their memories of Myrrh?* She added a second color to her wash and lowered her brush. *It's only the PPP's suspicion about their father's identity that keeps us from being sent to the Five Towers.* Another color joined the first two. *They're hoping he'll seek us out, and then—* Aggressive brush strokes flashed over the canvas.

The shrill sound of a whistle made her jump. Pulled from her artist's trance, she studied the painting. *Mira's cottage and—* She shivered and stared at the shadow of an enormous bird of prey hovering above it. "I wish the girls weren't going there today."

6

The scene on the water's surface swirled into a rainbow of colors. Mira drummed the rim with restless fingers. "Well, my dear Sparrow, they are on their way. Soon their friend will join them."

Elcaro's surface quieted to a mirror-like gloss. The details of a new image materialized.

Torgin Wilith Whalend, tall and lanky with warm brown skin and eyes as green as the first leaves of spring, stood opposite a large, arched window in his parent's luxury apartment, muttering to himself. "Why, in the name of the Five Fathers, did I allow the twins to talk me into visiting Myrrh? I have never broken a PPP rule in my fourteen sun cycles." He groaned and shuddered. "I am about to break one of the biggest."

The last Early-Morning whistle shrilled. Uniformed people on the avenue below made a rapid but orderly entry into their buildings. Torgin checked the street in both directions. "Where are you, Ari and Brie? Why do you always cut it so close?"

Two officers of the Peoples Plan Protectors emerged from a side street to walk their inspection route down the deserted Avenue of Trees. Torgin glanced at the Theran chronometer on the mantel and back at the avenue.

A bandana-covered head appeared from behind a building across the street. A twin looked up and waved. He shook his head. *That has to be Ari. She is the only person I know who is that brazen.*

Ari watched the officers march down the avenue and turn the corner. Gripping Brie's hand, she pulled her across the street and into the pass-through next to Torgin's building. Crouched low, they watched the patrollers in a PPP RiaCruiser glide by on a cushion of air, inspecting every entryway they passed.

"Should be clear in a moment." Ari peeked down the avenue as the cruiser disappeared around the corner. "Now!"

The twins dodged into the building's portico, where a uniformed doorman held the door ajar.

"One of these times, you are going to get caught." The tall man scolded with a slight twinkle in his eye.

"Thank you so much, Dalan." Brie whispered. "We didn't mean to be late."

"You never do. Hurry upstairs before there's trouble."

"Thanks, Dal." Ari clicked her heels together, gave him a smart salute, and followed her sister to the drop car.

Torgin yanked the apartment door open, his eyes blazing. "By the Fathers, you gave me a fright. The PPP almost caught you."

Ari snickered. "We're safe, Torg. No one saw us except Dalan, and he'll never tell."

Brie grinned. "Happy Sun Cycle, Torgin. Are you excited?"

"Shhh! Nanny is down the hall."

Ari put fists on her hips. "You aren't going to chicken out, are you?"

Torgin frowned. "No, but—is this a good idea?"

Brie tilted her head to look up at him. "It's your last chance to see Myrrh. Two moon cycles from now, the PPP will adjust your mind and assign your profession. Besides, it's what you said you wanted, isn't it?"

"Yes. No. I don't know." Torgin fiddled with a button on his uniform. "Why do we get our minds adjusted when we turn fourteen?"

Ari glanced at Brie and bit her lip. "You know what they teach us in school, right? Fourteen is the Time of Induction—the end of childhood. That's why they assign professions then."

His brow wrinkled. "It is more than that, correct?"

"Listen, Torgin, the truth isn't what we're taught, and you may be better off not knowing it."

"Why do you always treat me as though I am younger than you, Arienh? Tell me the truth or—"

"Okay, Torg." She sank onto a dark blue leather couch. "What do you know about the PPP?"

"The Peoples Plan Protectors take care of us—they make certain we are happy and safe."

"Not exactly." Brie joined her sister. "Their actual job is to make sure we obey all the strict guidelines laid down by the Five Fathers."

"It is not. You know the Fathers set everything up for our own good." His tone dared her to disagree.

Brie shrugged and jumped up. "Torgin, please play one of your compositions for us while we wait for the next whistle."

"Oh yes, Torgin." Ari linked an arm through her sister's. "We love your music."

"I do have a new piece I would like you to hear." He led the way to the music room, paused by a shiny, black keyboard, and patted a smallish silver case. "Anopi or the flute?"

"Anopi." The twins plopped down on a padded window seat.

Torgin settled himself at the air keyboard, closed his eyes, and inhaled. On the exhale, he began to play. The first passage, moody and dark, depicted feelings of repression and sadness, then transitioned to a section so quick, light, and free it resembled laughter. A rising arpeggio repeated over and over and culminated in a final crashing chord. He held his breath. The feelings he could only express through his music resonated in a complexity of dissonant harmonies and faded into silence. When he looked up, the wide-eyed twins smiled their awe.

Nanny stomped into the room, her big bosom heaving. "Can't a person take a nap around here?" She shot the twins a hard stare. "Hello, girls. What are *you* up to?"

"We're scheduled to work with Torgin on our home study project, so we came early to do Late-Morning Exercise before we start." Ari flashed her an innocent smile.

"That'd better be all you're here for!" Straightening her brown uniform skirt over her ample girth, she made an accusatory sound and marched from the room.

Ari imitated her waddled-gait, then grinned. "Loved your music, Torg."

Brie chimed in. "You're so talented. Do you think the City Fathers will assign the Musical Arts for your profession?"

He scowled. "Father expects it will be mathematics because I am so good with numbers. He does not think my music is worth much."

"Your father doesn't realize how gifted you are." Ari handed him his blue uniform hat. "It's time to go. Let's get moving."

Torgin opened his mouth to speak, but Brie piped up first. "We'll take good care of you, Torgin. I guarantee you'll love Myrrh and Mira."

Ari adjusted her bandana, tucked a persistent red curl out of sight, and opened the apartment door as the whistle sounded and the Theran chronometer chimed the time.

Torgin straightened his hat, ignored his growing sense of guilt, and followed the twins to the drop car.

Once outside, Torgin hung back and watched the twins melt into the burgeoning crowd of blue-uniformed citizens marching along the Avenue of Trees. *I am breaking the rules.* He swallowed and wiped the sweat beading on his brow. *Calm down, Torgin.* Scanning the avenue, he gulped. *Where are the twins?* A flash of copper caught his eye. He pulled his cap lower and stepped into line beside Ari.

"Can you believe these?" She made a subtle gesture toward the trees planted equidistant apart as far as the eye could see. "Why do they clip them to look identical?"

"Excuse me?" His voice, too loud in the oppressive atmosphere, made him glance up. An older woman glared over her shoulder, her finger on pursed lips. She faced forward and continued her measured walk. He lowered his voice. "The symmetry is perfect, balanced, exactly as it should be."

Ari made a face. "Bor-r-r-r-ring."

"You two'd better keep it down, or somebody'll turn us in." Brie adjusted her step to match her twin's.

Torgin lowered his eyes and immersed himself in the crisp swish-swish of uniformed legs, setting the cadence for the ritualistic march. He smiled and hummed the complementary melody taking shape in his mind. Absorbed in his passion, he failed to notice a nudge in the ribs. When he glanced up, he panicked. *Now, where are the twins?* He stepped from the crowd. *I almost wish I had stayed home.* Again, sunlight on coppery hair alerted him to the girls about to enter the RiaTrain station. Relief sent him scurrying after them down the spotless steps, his PPP ID in hand.

"Put that away," Ari hissed as he fell in step beside her.

"How will I get on the train?"

She herded him away from the well-ordered crowd. "If you use your card, the PPP will track you. And guess what? We're scheduled for home study today." Ari's hissed tone blistered his ears. "We reviewed this with you already. Have you forgotten?"

He glowered. "My memory is exceptional."

Brie stepped between them. "Enough." She directed them away from an overly interested bystander. "The train's almost here."

"I know what to do." Torgin clamped his mouth shut.

Brie squeezed his arm. "Good. I'll signal you when to get off."

The long, sleek RiaTrain whooshed to a stop.

"Come on." Ari nudged them back into line, pressed as close as possible to a sturdy middle-aged lady, and slipped undetected through the P-Scan.

Brie ducked through, unnoticed.

A large woman stepped up to the scanner, blocking the twins from view. The "GO" flashed. The woman moved her ample figure forward. Like a shadow, Torgin followed, dodged beyond the scanner, stepped onto the waiting RiaTrain, and wedged himself between expressionless adults.

The train pulled away from the station into a dim tunnel. Air hummed as it rounded a turn. Torgin fought the ingrained instinct to grab one of the clear transmitter poles at the center of the car. *I do not want my fingerprints sent to the PPP's Central Data Depository.* He stared at the floor. *Another rule broken.* His gaze flitted around the car. *What if they catch me?*

At the next stop, several passengers disembarked. He sank onto a bench beside the twins, hands folded and eyes down, the perfect demeanor for an Idronatti youth.

Brie leaned closer. "We get off at the next stop. Remember to watch for surveillance lenses."

A soft whoosh brought the car to a halt. Torgin's stomach tightened. *Idronatti Central. What if the PPP are waiting to arrest us?*

With his gaze fastened on Brie, he exited through the doors and crossed the platform. A quick sidestep carried him out of the mainstream and behind a support beam. A calming breath later, he climbed the stairs and took a tentative step onto the street. His head jerked right, then left. *Now what?* A hand on his arm hauled him into the space between buildings.

He pushed Ari's hand away. "Stop yanking me around."

"Then stop being such a Drotti." Her eyes snapped.

"He's not being a Drotti." Brie's calm tone soothed his bruised ego. "Remember our first time down here?"

"We can't stand around gawking." Ari glared at him over her shoulder. "A PPP patrol is due here any chron-click. Late-Morning Exercise is over, or hadn't you noticed?"

Brie urged them forward. "There's no turning back now."

Ari led them between towering buildings, onto an empty street, and into a shadowed doorway.

Torgin studied his surroundings. At the end of the street within a circular compound, five identical steel-gray buildings seemed to lean inward like co-conspirators sharing an ominous secret. Narrow slits served as windows. He didn't see any doors.

"What are those?" A shudder quaked through him.

Brie and Ari exchanged glances. Brie answered. "The Five Towers."

His eyes widened. "You mean..."

"The headquarters of the Peoples Plan Protectors." Ari's tight-lipped expression made his heart race.

"Is that where they take you when you do not follow The Plan?" His voice cracked.

Both girls nodded. Neither smiled.

He suppressed a desire to run all the way back to his parents' apartment and lock himself inside. "Oh."

Her eyes brimming with understanding, Brie took his hand. "It's alright, Torg. We're almost there."

Ari looked up and down the street. "I'll go first." Before he could object, she stepped into the open.

"Hey, you! Stop!" A pistol-sharp shout exploded from somewhere behind them.

Ari sprinted across the street.

Torgin froze.

"Come on!" Brie pulled him with her and raced after her sister.

Not daring to look back, he followed, his heart pounding louder than any of the percussion sounds on his anopi. Running faster than he had ever run in his life, he dodged between buildings, down a side street, and burst into the open.

His fear melted into amazement. The Sun Spire, Idronatti's tallest building, stretched upward in front of him, gleaming ruby red in the brilliant light of the sun. Trees and flowers overflowed its extraordinary gardens. The wide moat surrounding it—where building and sky lay captive on the water's surface—took his breath away.

Ari, pointing, snapped him back to the moment. "Run!"

He glanced back.

Three patrolmen exploded into the open street. "Stay where you are!"

Panic catapulted him over a small drawbridge and across the garden. Two pairs of hands hauled him into the glass drop car on the exterior wall of the Sun Spire. The door slid into place. Ari touched a button; the car sailed upward. Gasping for breath, Torgin watched their pursuers grow smaller and smaller.

"That was close." Ari slapped him on the back.

"Too close." Torgin wiped sweat from his face with the back of his hand. "I have never been so scared in my life."

"Neither have I." Brie's brown eyes looked even larger than usual. "We almost got caught."

"But we didn't." Ari's powerful voice reverberated in the closed space. "What fun!"

Torgin shook his head. "You are the strangest girl, Arienh."

"Maybe." She shrugged and pushed three numbers on the touch screen. One hundred twenty popped up on the readout.

The drop car jerked to a stop. The doors slid open. A long, white corridor loomed in front of them. Roiling mist obscured the far end of the hall.

A khaki-clad officer stepped into view. "Do not leave that car."

Torgin and Brie gasped.

Ari stepped in front of them.

"Where do you think you're going? Myrrh?" His cynical laugh punctuated his sarcastic tone.

Ari slammed her foot down on his well-polished boot, gave him a quick shove, and dashed past him.

Brie shot after her.

Fueled by terror and desperation—and the stories about those who ended up in the Five Towers—Torgin raced down the hall until they reached the mist.

"Now w-w-what?"

The twins each seized an arm. "Jump!"

Torgin lurched forward. With nothing but mist above him and the water of the moat rising to meet him, he squeezed his eyes shut.

Elcaro's Eye gurgled as water spilled from the statue's palms. Mira stretched and paced to the window. Moving the cotton curtain aside, she took a moment to appreciate the beauty of her back garden before returning to the fountain.

Gazing into the water, she leaned closer. "Show me Esán Efre."

In a private room in Idronatti's Center for Advanced Healing, a slender boy studied his reflection in the mirror on the closet door. "I have so little time."

The round smoothness of his bald head, the purple crescents beneath large, stormy-blue eyes, the paleness of his skin all made his thin shoulders droop. "Life's just not fair."

He held up pale, thin hands, curled them into fists and challenged his mirror image. "What do you think?" For a moment, he appeared to listen. His brows arched. "Miracles happen all the time, you say. Why not for me?" Rubbing a hand over his shiny head, he gave a rueful grin. "Why not for me, indeed? Tomorrow, I'll be fifteen, and I'm going to Myrrh—no matter what."

A woman's reflection smiled at him from the doorway. Esán turned and hurried to meet her. "Aunt Merrilea, is there any news?" She embraced him. He rested his head against her strong shoulder, absorbing her strength and her calm. Stepping back, he examined her face—her tired eyes—her sad smile. "Well?"

"They haven't found a donor, Esán."

"I know *that*. Did you contact the Guardian of Myrrh? Will she let me come for one last visit? Did you tell her it would be for my fifteenth Sun Cycle Celebration?"

His aunt's weary expression melted into a smile. "Mira would be delighted to have you visit Myrrh tomorrow. There will be three other young people as well."

"She'll let us explore the Terces Wood?"

"I think she'll let you do whatever you wish, Esán. What's the safest way to get you there?"

He squared his thin shoulders. "I'm going up in the Sun Spire through the portal like everyone else. Majeska will lead me the rest of the way."

She placed her hands on his shoulders. "The Holistic Healer told me yesterday he felt certain you were fading. This morning you took a remarkable step forward." Her healer's eyes studied him. "Do you know what caused the change?"

Esán rubbed his head. "I dreamt an elderly lady came to visit. She told me I must go to Myrrh as soon as possible. When I woke up, I felt better than I have in turnings."

"I see." She held his gaze. "A patient at home in SumnerTyme needs me. How would you feel if I left for a couple of turnings?"

"Is it Deora?"

She nodded.

He hugged her. "I'll be fine."

"Let's tuck you in, so you can rest up for tomorrow's adventure."

Esán sat on the edge of the bed. "Thanks, Aunt Merrilea, for everything. Don't worry about a donor. One will show up. I'm sure of it. And don't worry about me while you're gone."

She smiled. "I won't leave until after I've taken you to The Borderlands. Sleep well." Dimming the lights, she slipped into the hallway.

He slid under the covers. Outside the window, the Sun Spire glowed red against the night sky. "Tomorrow," he murmured, "tomorrow, I'm going to Myrrh." Yawning, he curled onto his side and drifted into sleep.

His sleeping image blurred and reformed. The sun, framed by the window, tinted the city in warm morning colors. Esán tossed and turned and finally pushed himself to sitting, his eyes wide and startled. "Those shadows were scary!" He shivered. "Just a dream, a terrible dream."

Throwing back the covers, he swung his too-thin legs over the side of the bed and grinned at the SunSpire. "I am going to Myrrh today!"

7

Mira touched the oracle's swirling water. Shades of blue settled into another scene. She smiled as she watched her guests arrive in Myrrh.

Torgin's feet hit the ground with less impact than a normal running step. His eyes flew open to find a grinning twin on either side of him. He looked from one to the other. "What just happened?"

Ari folded her arms and rocked back on her heels. "We jumped dimensions."

"What?"

"We jumped to another dimension." Brie's reassuring tone helped. "I know it was scary. If we'd told you we had to leap from one hundred and twenty stories up, would you have come with us?"

"No-o-o!" His eyes grew even bigger. "Will the PPP patroller follow us?"

"Don't be silly." Ari yanked off her bandana, stuffed it in her pocket, and released her long curls from their braid. "Turn around, Torg."

Brie gave him an encouraging smile.

A slow pivot left him gaping. Brilliant colors exploded from flower boxes to beautiful silk scarves dancing in the sunshine to brightly painted trim on pastel cottages to the people crowding the cobblestone streets. The unexpected beauty and bustle took his breath away.

He glanced down at his blue coveralls and then at the twins, his eyes filled with questions.

"We look pretty drab, don't we?" Brie's eyes sparkled. "We'll get some different clothes before we go to Myrrh."

"This isn't Myrrh?"

"No, Drotti." Ari smirked. "This is The Borderlands."

Torgin's anger flared. "I am not a—"

"Stop it, Arienh." Brie shot her sister an exasperated look and turned back to him. "It's between Idronatti and Myrrh, Torgin. When the guardians of this solar system decided they must hide the last remaining piece of Old Earth to protect it, they concealed it in another dimension and created The Borderlands as a distraction or buffer zone."

"Anyone seeking it must find their way through The Borderlands first." Ari linked her arm through his. "I say we go buy some different clothes. Then we can find Majeska."

"Majeska?"

"You never listened to other children talk about how to find Myrrh?"

"Not really. I was not that curious."

"Or you were afraid." Ari chuckled and punched him on the arm.

Torgin crinkled his face into a scowl. "I just prefer what I know. Life should be predictable. Isn't that what the Fathers teach us?"

For once, Ari stepped into the breach she'd created. "I'm sorry, Torgin. My mouth gets away from me sometimes. You're right. That is what we're taught. Let's not argue. This is your turning to discover all kinds of fun."

That is a first—Ari admitting she is wrong. His scowl melted into a tiny smile. "This is rather exciting. Tell me about Majeska."

"You'll see." The twinkle in Brie's eyes hinted at mysteries to come. "We'll show you Worldness Way first."

Torgin trailed after the twins, his gaze darting from one quaint shoppe to the next. Window displays of delicious-looking candy, colorful clothing, strange furnishings, and unusual plants left him shaking his head in wonder.

Voices and laughter drew him around a corner. The Borderlands' Outdoor Market opened up in front of him with vivid banners flying and smiling vendors competing to sell to the highest bidder. Townsfolk meandered from one booth to the next, laughing and chatting and stopping to buy. The noisy, chaotic, mind-boggling blend of color and sound left him dazed. Unable to process it all, he held back, shoved his hands in his pockets, and stared at the multitude of shoppers.

"Torgin, where are you?" Brie's voice floated over the cheerful buzz of the crowd.

"Here I am. Over here." He frowned. *I sound so forlorn.*

She stepped from behind a bulky man with shaggy hair and a full beard. "It's a lot to take in, isn't it?"

He tore his gaze from the bustling market. "I did not know people lived like this. How do I—" He shrugged.

Ari ambled out of the crowd. "I found Nans' tent so we can buy new clothes." She dodged away between the booths, red hair gleaming in the sun. Brie chased after her. Afraid to get separated, he followed. Ari disappeared and re-emerged by a booth with a green awning. She stopped and waved. "Hey, I'm thirsty. How about a glass of red berry juice?"

Torgin grinned. "I could use a drink."

Ari waltzed up to the counter. "Three red berry drinks, please."

"You from Idronatti?" A man with straggly salt-and-pepper hair peered down at her. Torgin tried not to stare at his glass eye.

"We are." Ari met his gaze.

"How do ya expect to pay?" Doubt filled the man's voice.

She pulled a small pouch from her pocket. Fascinated, Torgin watched her bounce it on her palm where it made a strange clinking sound. She smiled sweetly at the man. "Of course, we could go somewhere else if—"

"Now, missy, there's no need to be hasty. Give me four repocs each, and it'll get ya three tall glasses of juice. What do ya say?"

Torgin licked his lips in anticipation. Ari turned to Brie. "What do you think, sister dear?"

A broad smile spread across Brie's face. "Four if you can tell which of us is the oldest, and three if you cannot.

He folded his arms. "How do I know ya won't lie?"

Stepping up to the counter, she pulled her braid aside. Nestled at the edge of her hairline was a tiny red star. "The Star of Truth." She smiled. "I can't lie."

"You got the Star of Truth, do ya, girl? Who are ya, anyway?"

She shrugged and let her braid fall back into place. "So who's the oldest?"

The man examined each girl. He walked around them, stared first from his real eye, and then turned the glassy one that did not blink toward them.

Grinning, he pointed at Brie. "You be the eldest."

Ari swept him a mock bow. "Nope, I am...by four chron-clicks." She stacked three repocs for each of them on the counter.

Muttering under his breath, the vendor filled the tall glasses. Ari flipped an extra repoc up in the air and caught it.

"Thank you." She dropped it in his hand. After she finished her juice, she set her glass on the counter. "I'm ready for new clothes."

"Me, too." Brie put her empty glass next to her sister's.

Torgin downed his last swallow and scurried after the twins. "Where did you get repocs? I have never seen them except in books."

"Mother always makes sure we have Myrrhinian money before we leave for Myrrh." Ari pulled out the pouch and handed him a coin. "Keep that in case you need it."

"Thanks." He examined the engraving on both sides. "You are so lucky your mother knows about Myrrh. I wish mine did."

"Someday, she might remember." Ari tucked the pouch away. "Some adults do, you know."

"Once they assign my profession, I will not remember either, so I guess it does not matter." An unexpected rush of sadness tightened his throat. He swallowed and slipped the repoc into his pocket. "You did not tell me why the PPP adjusts our minds when we turn fourteen. I need to know."

Brie clasped his hand. "Are you sure, Torgin? It won't be what you've learned."

"If they are going to erase my memories of Myrrh, I want to know why. Please, Brielle."

Brie took a deep breath as Ari joined them. "A long time ago, after the gravitational pull of Thera attracted all that remained of Old Earth, the

Galactic Guardians of this solar system hid it in a parallel dimension, named it Myrrh, and appointed the Five Fathers to build Idronatti."

Ari's deep voice picked up the story. "Pretty soon, the Fathers started to realize Myrrh had become a deterrent to their vision of the perfect society."

"Why?"

"Myrrh's residents are encouraged to be individuals." Brie's expression was serious. "The Five Fathers want everyone to be the same."

"So, what did they do?" Torgin listened intently.

"They created the PPP to keep Idronattians under control while their scientists developed a way to extract Myrrh's memories from their minds."

"Why did they not adjust their memories when they were younger? Then they would not have known about Myrrh."

The twins moved closer to each other. Ari's solemn gaze held his. "They discovered their mind-wipe destroyed the brains of children younger than fourteen sun cycles."

"Oh…" He felt sick to his stomach. "I guess I would rather not know any more."

They had stopped in front of a red and white striped tent. "We get our new clothes here." Brie smiled at the woman leaning on the counter.

She smiled back. "Hello, twins. Are you headed for Myrrh?"

"Yes. This is our friend, Torgin. Today's his Sun Cycle. We're taking him to meet Mira."

"Happy Celebration, Torgin. I'm Nans." She beamed at a tall man and two youngsters who had joined her. "This is Saaul, my mate, and these are our children, Tima and Tansy."

Tansy smiled at Torgin. "You have pretty eyes."

"Thank you." *Meeting these people feels good. I am surprised.*

Saaul nodded at the twins. "We've been hearing strange stories from Myrrhinians who've visited The Borderlands in the past couple of turnings. Make sure you stay alert."

Torgin's feel-good response plunged into wariness. "What stories?"

Saaul frowned. "They're saying that—"

"We'll be fine." Ari brushed his concern aside.

Torgin refused to be sidetracked. "Do we have time to visit Myrrh today?"

"Time's different here, Torg. We have all we need. Let's get new clothes." She guided him through the racks in Nans' tent.

Brie held up a yellow T-shirt. "I love all the colors!" She disappeared into a changing cubicle and re-emerged wearing it and a pair of blue jeans with brightly embroidered patterns on the back pockets. "All I need are shoes."

Torgin pointed at her black leather uniform shoes. "Why not wear those?"

"I want something more fun. And here they are!" She slipped on a pair of orange rubber-soled sneakers that matched the trim on her shirt and pants.

Torgin ran a finger along a rack of shirts. "I have never picked out my own clothes."

"In that case, you're about to have a novel experience." Ari held up a bright green shirt.

"I cannot wear that."

Ari's eyebrows shot up. "Why not? It matches your eyes."

"It is not...me."

She sighed and prowled through the racks with Brie, making suggestion after suggestion. Finally, he agreed on jeans, a navy-and-white striped T-shirt, and dark blue trainers. Mumbling under his breath, he headed to the dressing cubicle.

When he came out in his new clothes, Ari posed in front of a mirror, admiring her jeans, purple shirt, and trainers.

"We look great!" She gave her reflection a grin of extreme satisfaction.

Saaul stuck his head in the tent. "Fadin says PPP patrollers just made the jump into The Borderlands. They're lookin' for twins and a brown-skinned boy. You'd better hustle. We'll create a diversion." He disappeared.

Nans hid their uniforms in the bottom of a trash can, accepted the repocs Brie offered, and ushered them out the back of the tent. "Majeska is waiting on Chance Lane. Keep your eyes open. Hurry!"

The sound of water spilling into the bowl and mingling with the wha wha of raven wings alerted Almiralyn to Karrew's arrival. A short glide brought him to a landing on Elcaro's rim.

"Alli sent me to tell you he is doing much better and should be fine by tomorrow." He fanned his wings, then folded them close to his body.

Relief made Almiralyn smile. "I'm glad he's on the mend. We could use his help. Our young people are almost here." She moved to the window. "Did you see any sign of our intruders?"

Karrew clicked his beak. "None. The woods are quiet, although CheeTrann continues to be concerned."

"We'll make certain our young guests know to stay away from Nemttachenn Tower." She approached the fountain and shifted to Mira, the grandmotherly persona she adopted when entertaining Idronatti's children. Fly away gray hair pulled back in a bun accented the twinkle in her eyes and the fine smile lines around her mouth. She touched the water with a finger and watched the ripples chase over the surface.

"I suggest we continue to monitor the young people until they enter the portal. Then I will go down to greet them."

8

The water in Elcaro's Eye grew still. An image floated upward and settled on the surface. Mira glanced at her protector, then fixed her attention on the action taking place in the fountain.

Panic chased Torgin through the crowd to the far side of the Outdoor Market. Darting from shadow to shadow, he followed the twins between stables and outbuildings to the dark, narrow lane called Chance, where vibrant village colors evaporated into peeling paint and grime-covered walls. Irregular shaped buildings leaning at odd angles created a jumble of eerie shadows. Trash littering the lane made him wrinkle his nose in disgust.

"Do you know where you are going?" He cupped a hand over his nose and mouth and groaned.

"We do." The girls replied in unison and jogged deeper into the closely packed streets.

His sour expression twisting into a scowl, he ran after them. "I dislike this smelly place. I want to go home."

Ari stopped and eyed him with disgust. "And how do you expect to get there? Ask the PPP to take you?"

Brie, who had jogged further along the narrow lane, halted and turned, her tense expression changed to relief. "Majeska." She pointed.

Up ahead, a smoky-gray cat reclined with leisurely grace on a dirty white stoop, her bright amethyst eyes glowing in the single patch of sunlight which permeated the dismal surroundings. She yawned and stretched, her tail waving above her head like a cobra rising from a snake charmer's basket.

Torgin glowered. "You didn't tell me Majeska was a cat."

A distant volley of shouts sent a wave of fear careening up his spine. The cat's ears twitched. She flickered her tail and trotted down the dingy lane.

Ari dashed to Brie's side, grabbed her hand, and glanced over her shoulder. "Majeska's leaving. Come on, Torg."

The girls scurried down a side street that curved and disappeared into the murky depths of The Borderlands.

Brie looked back and paused. "It's okay, Torgin."

Ari pranced from one foot to the other. "Let's go, you two. We don't want to lose Majeska. And I'd prefer not to get caught."

Another series of shouts, closer and more distinct, set all of them in motion. With their four-legged pied piper in the lead, they sprinted down one street after the other until she stopped in front of a small shoppe with large, filthy windows. Faded gold lettering on the dark blue door read *Antiques by Q.*

Brie knocked. An old man with bristly gray whiskers opened the door and squinted at them over wire-rimmed spectacles. Majeska rubbed her sleek body against his legs and meowed.

"So ya got trouble on your tail, do ya?" He tickled her under her chin. "Well, take 'em to the mirror." He nodded toward the children. "Don't stand there. Get going." He shuffled into the dark interior of the shoppe.

Brie stared after him. "I don't trust him."

"You always say that. He's just old." Ari shrugged. "Where the mirror goes, he goes." She hurried after Majeska.

Brie preceded Torgin down a dusky hallway.

The cat rounded a corner and stopped in front of an unobtrusive wooden door.

Ari scratched her ears. "Thanks, Jeska."

A purr rumbled in the quiet. With an air of nonchalance, their feline guide meandered away into the gloom.

Torgin stopped and folded his arms, resistance radiating from his entire being.

Ari flashed him a taunting grin and pulled the door open. "You first, Torg?"

He shot her a dirty look and took a step back.

Crowding together, the twins stared down a steep wooden staircase.

Torgin peeked over their heads. "Where is the light?"

Muttering under her breath, Ari started down the rickety stairs. "Your eyes'll adjust, Torg. Come on."

Brie followed her sister into the dimness.

"Do you know what is down there?" Their disappearing backs left him in a quandary. He glanced down the hall. Majeska sprinted past him and bolted after Brie. The muted tinkling of a bell propelled him down the steps in her wake. "I heard a bell ring up there. Now what?"

"We're looking for a large oval mirror." Brie glanced around and moved further into the space.

"A mirror? Whatever for? You could not see your reflection in this light."

"The mirror's the portal into Myrrh. It's never hidden in the same place twice. That's why we followed Majeska. She always..."

Ari gasped and pointed. "Over there!"

The gray cat clawed at a faded tapestry, stopped, and clawed again.

The twins each grabbed a corner and flipped the tapestry, revealing a mirror in an ornate gilded frame. A single crack ran diagonally from the upper left to merge with a series of spider-web breaks near the bottom edge.

Torgin stood in front of it. "I cannot see my reflection. Is the mirror magic?"

"Yes." Brie cast a harried look up the staircase and pressed her palm against the dust-covered glass above the jagged crack. When she lowered her hand, an impression remained.

Torgin gasped. The handprint formed a fist with the index finger extended and sketched the shape of a large keyhole at the mirror's center.

"Let's go!" Brie reached for his hand.

He hid it behind his back. "Where?" Apprehension left him breathless.

"To Myrrh, of course."

His gaze flitted from the twins to the mirror. Dust tickled his nose. He threw back his head to sneeze. The last thing he saw—Ari disappearing into the keyhole.

A jerk propelled him through space. He opened his eyes and gasped. The basement and the mirror had vanished. He stood next to the twins in a field of sunflowers.

The Guardian of Myrrh's gentle face focused on the fountain's surface. Mira smiled at her fading reflection and smoothed her gray hair. "Our guests have arrived. It is time to meet them." With a final glance at Elcaro's Eye, she strode from the room.

Torgin could only see yellow sunflowers and a cloudless, blue sky. He pushed aside a large leaf and stared at a thatched-roofed cottage in the middle of a garden. Beautiful flowers tumbled over a white picket fence, hummingbirds played chase, and bees buzzed a merry song as they flitted from one blossom to the next. In front of the bright red door, an older woman with fly-away gray hair pinned up in a bun waited, one hand shading her eyes. She welcomed the twins with a hug.

"We almost got caught today." Ari grinned at Torgin over her shoulder.

"I know you did, Arienh. You were very lucky. I understand the folk in The Borderlands created a diversion. The patrollers returned to Idronatti, but the PPP now knows the portal's location. Please be more careful. It would be unfortunate if they caught you and took you to The Five Towers."

Ari blushed. "I'll be more careful in the future."

"Torgin." Brie waved him forward. "Come and meet Mira, the Guardian of Myrrh."

Mira's welcoming smile melted away his reluctance. "Hello, Torgin. It appears you've had quite an adventure today. I hope it won't negatively affect your time on Myrrh."

Torgin couldn't take his eyes off her. "My father thinks you are just a story."

Mira nodded, her expression solemn.

"Mother said you are a fantasy."

"Your mother used to love fantasy." Her deep blue eyes twinkled with a hint of mystery.

"You know my mother?"

"When she was a little girl, I knew her well. Come in so we can get acquainted. It's not often that I have guests whose parents were some of my favorite visitors when they were children."

He followed the girls into Mira's cottage. The aroma of cinnamon and baking apples made his mouth water and tempted him down the hall to a large, comfortable kitchen. At the center, a table laden with goodies unavailable in Idronatti took his breath away.

"Before we eat..." Ari grabbed his hand and led him to the back porch. "We have something to show you."

Brie grinned and followed. "The PPP may not allow pets in Idronatti, but here in Myrrh..." She introduced him to Millie and her four kittens and a large, shaggy, brown dog named Buster, who soon sat with his head in Torgin's lap at the table.

"I understand today is your fourteenth Sun Cycle Celebration." Mira put a thick piece of chocolate cake in front of him.

Torgin laughed. "My favorite! Thank you." He took a huge bite and savored every last crumb.

While her young guests enjoyed the Celebration cake she had provided, Mira sat back to study them one at a time. The Galaxy's Guardians hinted that these three young people, along with Esán, would lead the fight against the evil erupting in the Inner Universe. The twins were not new to her, and she watched them with interest, wondering how much longer she could keep the secret of their true identities. Torgin was an unknown, although her knowledge of his parents suggested high intelligence and yet undiscovered talents.

Her attention drifted to Brie, whose demeanor suggested a growing disquiet unusual in the younger twin.

9

Only half listening to her friends' animated conversation, Brie savored the sweet aroma of Dojanberries and mint. *Why do I feel so anxious? The PPP has gone back to Idronatti, right?* She sipped her tea. *Maybe Saaul's warning about Myrrh triggered it, or perhaps it was Mother's painting coupled with my dream.* She set her cup on the table and watched the kitchen walls change from blue to pale green. Whatever its source, the sense of foreboding persisted.

A soft knock at the front door startled her back to the present. Dread raised its snake-like head.

The Guardian caught her eye. "Brie, will you please answer that?"

The solitary walk through the cottage did little to relieve the knots in Brie's stomach. She shook herself. *Everything's fine. You're being silly, Brielle Ralyn.* The Star of Truth's affirming warmth calmed her agitation. Shaking her red curls back from her face, she opened the door.

A boy about her age leaned on the doorframe, his weary blue eyes seeking hers. His face, ravaged by illness, struck such a deeply empathetic chord she found it hard to gather her thoughts.

"Is Mira at home?" His soft voice, though steady, sounded strained.

Brie stepped aside. "She's in the kitchen."

The boy took a tentative step across the threshold, paused, and struggled to catch his breath.

"Are you alright?"

"I'm fine." He attempted a weak smile. "Just not as strong as I thought I was." He seemed to gather his remaining strength to precede her down the hall.

His bald head, his pallor, and his fragile frame spoke volumes. A wave of sympathy washed over her. *How did you ever make the trek through Idronatti, to the Sun Spire, and all the way through The Borderlands to Myrrh?*

At the kitchen doorway, he hesitated. Mira welcomed him with a smile. "Esán, come in!"

Brie stepped up beside him and guided him into the room.

Torgin glared at the newcomer. "Who are you? And...*what* are you doing here?"

The unfriendly tone propelled Esán a step backward. Faint pink splotches tinted his pale cheeks.

Mira patted the chair beside her. "Esán is my guest, Torgin. Like you, his Sun Cycle Celebration is today."

The thin, bald boy slid into the seat next to her and glanced around the table.

Ignoring Torgin's stiff grin, Brie moved to Ari's side and together they chimed, "Happy Sun Cycle."

A beautiful smile softened the pain on Esán's face. "Thank you."

Mira placed a cup of tea in front of him. "Cake?"

"I'm not hungry, Mira, but thank you for the tea." Pale hands trembling, he raised the steaming drink to his lips.

Brie's sadness deepened. She moved closer to her twin.

Mira touched Esán's arm. "May I tell them?"

Esán set his cup on the table. "Yes, of course."

Her gaze, as she looked from one young person to the next, proclaimed the importance of what she was about to share. "Esán's long illness has made it impossible for him to visit Myrrh, which makes today extra special."

Esán's hand glided over the smooth, roundness of his bald head and came to rest on the table. His weary, blue eyes sought Torgin's. "It's even more special now, Torgin, because you and I are sharing a Celebration."

The annoyance drained from Torgin's expression; he almost managed a smile. "Uh, thanks."

"How about a celebratory picnic?" Mira's gaze darted to the window, then back. "But first, I have something important to share. Rumors about strange shadows flying above Myrrh are spreading throughout the land. Please stay within sight of the cottage." She smiled. "There are plenty of places to picnic nearby. In the woods behind the barn are several small clearings. Or lunch by the pond is always an option." Her eyes narrowed. "What you must *not* do is go anywhere near Nemttachenn Tower."

With dread quaking in her belly, Brie noted Esán's excited smile and stifled a negative reaction. "Do you have the strength to walk in the woods, Esán?"

Myrrh's Guardian smiled. "Don't worry, Brie. Tam will carry him, and you can make sure he doesn't overdo it."

Esán beamed. "We would love to go exploring, Mira. I'll be fine."

Brie hid her unease and smiled at his obvious delight. "We promise to take good care of you."

Torgin pushed his chair back, stood up, and folded his arms across his chest. "Should he not stay here and rest? He looks too weak to do anything."

"What's wrong with you, Torgin Whalend?" Disgust lathered Ari's voice. "Esán is sitting right here, and you're talking like he's invisible."

Esán shifted uncomfortably in his chair. "Perhaps I should stay here."

"If you stay, Esán, so will we." Brie's expression and tone challenged anyone to argue.

Mira moved around the table. "Esán has a gift for each of you. When you come back, you can share what it is." She fetched a pair of packed saddle bags from the pantry and smiled at Torgin. "Why don't we fetch the pony, Tam, from the paddock, Torgin?"

Blank-faced, he nodded and followed Mira from the kitchen into the back garden.

The twins escorted Esán after them. As they neared the barn, they paused to let him rest.

Brie cleared her throat. "We're sorry Torgin was so rude. He isn't usually like that."

Esán sighed. "He probably thinks I'll ruin his turning."

Torgin walked up, leading a tan and cream pony. "You will not ruin it, Esán. I am sorry I was so mean."

"Well said, Torgin." The Guardian smiled at him and then grew serious. "Have fun and please remember to stay within sight of my acreage. Tam and Buster will warn of danger. If anything disturbs you, come back immediately."

Brie's sense of misgiving returned. The star on her neck twinged as Torgin and Ari helped Esán onto Tam's back and settled the saddle bags in front of him.

Ari grinned at Torgin. "Race you to the barn."

Not even their mad dash across the garden or their shared laughter lightened Brie's mood. All she could think of were the shadows. She frowned and touched the back of her neck.

Esán stretched his arms skyward. "Let's go have an adventure!"

Brie gathered the pony's reins, and, forcing one hesitant foot ahead of the other, led Tam and her rider around the barn.

When they were no longer within sight of the cottage, Ari grabbed Torgin by the arm and dodged deeper into the Terces Wood.

He yanked free and skidded to a halt. "Mira said to stay in the woods behind the barn."

She threw her head back and laughed. "It's a beautiful turning. There's nothing in the woods to hurt us, you silly Drotti."

A scowl twisted Torgin's full-lipped mouth. "I'm not a Drotti. Unlike you, I do what I'm told."

"You, Torgin Whalend, are a scaredy—"

Buster dashed past, gave a sharp bark, and disappeared around a bend.

Ari's hair formed a cloud of red as she whipped around. "Buster's not afraid, so neither am I." With a final glance in his direction, she sprinted after the big furry dog.

Secure on Tam's back, Esán began to relax. Inhaling the scents of earth and evergreen, he smiled at Brie. "Tell me about Idronatti. I've only visited the healing center. It must be strange to grow up in a big city. I can't imagine living stacked one on top of the other or not having trees."

Torgin strode toward them. "We have lots of trees." He sounded defensive.

"Only three streets in the entire city have trees of any kind." Brie stroked Tam's sleek neck. "Of course, the Fathers' City Park has lots of trees." She smiled at Esán. "Idronatti has twelve city districts. The Benisuss District is Downtown."

Torgin jumped back in. "That's where my father works. He's the Advisor to the Premier of Idronatti. My mother is a research chemist. We live in Domlenah Uptown Blue."

Brie glanced behind him. "Where's Ari?"

He scowled. "She called me a Drotti, because I do what I'm told, and then she took off after Buster."

Ari strolled from the trees. "You're just afraid of anything new, Torg." She rolled her eyes and looked at Esán. "For the record, Uptown Blue means rich."

"It does not. Idronattians are all treated equally." Torgin frowned. "I am not afraid of new things. I just like life to be predictable." His eyes dared Ari to disagree.

Ari's eyebrows shot up. She looked at Esán. "That's because the PPP makes certain we do nothing the Fathers haven't scheduled." She kicked a pebble down the trail. "Idronatti isn't perfect, you know, Torgin. We're just taught that it is."

Esán wrinkled his brow. "I guess that tells me all I want to know about Idronatti." He looked from one to the other. "Isn't it wonderful in the woods where we can do whatever we wish?"

Shaking her hair back from her face, Ari grinned. "Buster and I found a great place to picnic."

Buster barked in agreement and bounded down the trail. Torgin and Ari, their differences forgotten, raced after him.

Esán watched them go. "Life is too short to waste it on disagreement."

"You are so right." Brie ambled along beside the pony.

Esán patted Tam's neck and allowed himself to be lulled by the beauty of the surroundings and Brie's easy companionship.

Brie tried to enjoy the sunlight slipping between the summer-green leaves and playing in filmy patches on the forest floor. Her gaze leapfrogged from one splash of light to the next until it came to rest on Torgin and Ari, whose animated conversation showed their friendship, at least for the moment, unimpeded by bickering. Buster dashed back and forth, sniffing at trees and bushes with his ever-curious nose. *He doesn't seem concerned.* Even so, her anxiety nagged. She glanced over her shoulder and frowned.

Esán followed her gaze. "Is something wrong?"

"Yes—no. I don't know." She shrugged. "I've had the strangest—"

"Hey, you two, come here!" Torgin hollered from further up the path. "And hurry!"

"Hold on tight." Brie grabbed Tam's reins and dashed down the trail toward her friend's voice.

At the cottage, Mira mounted the stairs to her sanctuary. Brie's anxiety underscored her own uneasiness. *Are the young people safe? Should I have kept them with me?*

Shedding her Mira persona, she tossed her long braid over her shoulder and moved to the fountain, where an image taking shape on the water's surface quivered and steadied.

Perched on top of an ancient evergreen, a great horned owl the size of a man swiveled its head and gazed with rapacious intent at four young people, a pony, and a dog who approached the tall stone tower at the center of the forest. Like an actor preparing for an entrance, it preened sleek black and silver feathers until they glistened in the mid-turning sun. Hazel eyes blinked and stared. A deep "Whoo! Whoo!" shattered the woodland silence.

With outstretched wings casting a menacing shadow, the owl's massive body launched into the air and climbed skyward.

Almiralyn Nadrugia raised troubled eyes from the scene playing out on the surface of Elcaro's Eye. Crossing to the window, she leaned out and listened intently. Deep at the center of the forest surrounding her land, the magic within Nemttachenn Tower sent its urgent message throughout Myrrh. *The Unfolding has passed the point of no return.*

Brow furrowed, she returned to the fountain and studied the reflected image of the four young people racing toward Nemttachenn.

Ari and Brie, why did you ignore me? I warned you to stay close and not to go to the tower. Water cascading from the statue's open palms sent the shattered image into Elcaro's depths.

Her carved likeness kneeling on the fountain's rim reminded her of the weight of responsibility she carried. *The twins do not know how important they are to The Unfolding. Should they fall into the wrong hands...* Her sapphire blue eyes narrowed. *Who is shaping the great horned owl?*

Staring into the fountain's depths, she willed herself to be patient. The rhythmic song of trickling water grew silent; the surface calmed. From the bottom of the bowl, an image floated upward. Black and silver wings lifted the owl high above the forest. Then, swooping lower, it dropped from sight. The image dissolved.

Almiralyn gripped the rim and leaned forward. *Where have you gone?* She focused on her quarry and projected a mental probe into every corner of the land.

A picture of the Dojanack Mountains emerged in the fountain and steadied. The shadow of the owl, a stark silhouette against their shimmering beauty, materialized, dodged skyward, and vanished. Malevolent laughter echoing through the room churned the water into a frothing whirlpool. A bolt of lightning exploded from its center, hovered, and flashed into nothingness, leaving behind the heavy aroma of ions. The mountains faded. Water rippled into stillness.

Frowning, she straightened. Premonition prickled. *You are a rogue DiMensioner of the Order of Esprow.*

Eyes squeezed shut, she pinched the bridge of her nose. Conviction pulsed through her as she descended to the first floor and into the the kitchen.

10

In the cottage kitchen, the raven Karrew drew the feathers of his blue-black wings through his beak one at a time and savored the resettling of each in its place, cleaned and shiny. Footsteps in the hall alerted him to his mistress' arrival. He tilted his head and watched her pause in the doorway.

"I'm so glad you're back, Karrew. One of our intruders is a renegade DiMensioner." She crossed the room and ran a finger along his back. "He seems to have taken up residence in the Dojanack Mountains. I'm still unclear who or what his companion is or where he is."

The depth of her concern ran straight into his heart. "You're worrying about the twins and their friends?" He bobbed his head and peered at her from one glistening eye.

She left his side to look out the window. "I warned them to stay away from the tower." Mixed emotions flickered across her face and lingered in the silence between her words. "They're at Nemttachenn, Karrew."

Opening the window wider, she moved aside. "I believe the DiMensioner led them there. Go quickly, my friend. See what you can discover."

The urgency in her voice heightened his own. Clinging to his perch, he fanned his wings to prepare for flight. "Stay alert, Almiralyn. I'll be back when I can." His deep caw reverberated off the kitchen walls as he soared out the window and over the Terces Wood.

The sun hung just above the forest canopy, a lazy orb in Myrrh's cloudless blue sky. His wings pressed against the air and sent him higher and faster toward its warmth. The Terces Wood—honey oaks, maple nut, other deciduous trees, and willowy, long-needled evergreens—slid by beneath him. He loved Myrrh, but he missed his home planet of Roahymn. Sometimes the longing became so great, he fought the urge to fly through the forest portal and go home.

Nemttachenn Tower breached the canopy, caught the sunlight, and tossed it skyward. A threat, like a billowing cloud, hung in the air. Concern for Almiralyn's young charges drove his homesickness away. Banking left, he began his descent.

Mira watched Karrew's graceful flight with a sense of foreboding. As he vanished over the Terces Wood, the need to contact her brother sent her from the kitchen up the stairs to her sanctuary. When she reached Elcaro's side, she quieted her churning thoughts. A whispered word calmed the water's rippling surface. Her own worry-clouded eyes stared up at her. She forced a small smile and waved a hand above the fountain.

Her mood lightened as Allynae's lean countenance floated up from the bottom. Next to Karrew, her brother was her best friend. His reflected face steadied. A slightly crooked nose seemed almost too big for his face. Dark hair touched with flecks of silver stuck out like straight pins in a pincushion. Laugh lines around cloudy, blue eyes crinkled at the sight of her.

"How are you feeling, Alli?" She tried to muster a bigger smile.

"I'm fine. Just woke from a nap. You look serious. What's up?"

"One of our intruders is a renegade DiMensioner, and he appears curious about the four young people visiting today."

Allynae frowned. "Is this related to The Unfolding?"

She pursed her lips and nodded. "I believe our young guests are a catalyst for the quickening of this process. The DiMensioner is the spark that has ignited its beginning. I'm uncertain what or who his companion—"

A cough behind Allynae interrupted her. The reflection pulled out like the zoom on an old-fashioned camera. A tower of a man leaned against the door frame, a slow grin spreading across his black face.

"Hello, Paisley." Allynae cocked his head. "I don't suppose it occurred to you to knock?"

"I did. Ya didn't answer."

"That might've meant I wasn't home."

The man's round, full mouth stretched into an even bigger grin. The mustache tucked under his nose jiggled. "But ya are, aren't ya?"

Allynae chuckled. "I guess I am."

"You talkin' to Mira?" He pointed to the large crystal Allynae cupped in his hands.

"Yep."

"Hey, Mira."

"Good to see you, Paisley." She smiled at the man who had befriended them soon after their arrival on Myrrh.

As a child, his formidable size and gentleness had made him the brunt of bullying and taught him to keep his fists ready. Allynae had been on the receiving end of those fists only one time. When Paisley James—hand bruised and bleeding and eye blackened—picked himself up off the ground, he acknowledged Allynae to be a worthy adversary. Their friendship had sprouted from there and matured over the sun cycles.

"I came to tell ya there's an enormous owl flyin' around Myrrh. The Wood Tiffs are worried enough to gather in their homes way before the sun sets. The Nyti are hiding, too."

"Thank you, Paisley." Her brow knitted. "Stay close to your cabin, Alli, and keep Paisley with you. I need to check on some things. I'll be in touch." She lingered a moment.

Paisley rubbed his grizzled chin. "What's for lunch? I think I missed breakfast."

"You never miss breakfast." Allynae stifled a grin. "And who said you're invited to lunch?"

"Mira said to keep me with ya, didn't she? So I guess she invited me."

Allynae laughed. "It appears she did."

Fragmented images scattered against the side of the bowl, leaving Almiralyn to ponder her next move. She made a decision and gripped the fountain's rim. "Elcaro's Eye, show me more about Esán's illness."

A new image came into focus.

At Idronatti's Center for Advanced Healing, a Holistic Healer studied a blue screen covered with medical symbols. Esán's Aunt Merrilea sat beside him, her face mirroring his frown.

"Esán's heritage is causing us problems." HH Zarron tapped the screen. "We still haven't found a suitable donor for the cell infusion to reprogram his immune system. The synthetics we've developed that work so well for most patients won't help those with his genetic background. I was hopeful you would be the right cell type, but you're not. Any suggestions on where to look next?"

Merrilea looked thoughtful. "His father is living, but all my efforts to locate him have failed. How much time does Esán have?"

"It's hard to say. Several turnings ago, he made an unexpected improvement, so he's stable for the moment. However, in his weakened condition, any infection could end his life."

Merrilea's breath caught in her throat. "I understand." She remained quiet for a moment. "I need to return to SumnerTyme. One of my patients there has taken a turn for the worse."

The HH nodded. "I'll take care of Esán. If there's a change, I shall contact you."

The imaged blurred into the calm surface of the water.

Mira's eyes narrowed. "Show me who else will play a role in The UnFolding."

In Elcaro's eye, the water swirled and steadied. A high mountain tundra filled the surface. In the distance, smoke wafted from the chimney of a rustic cabin. A man strode around the corner, paused, and pulled a battered hat lower on his forehead.

The water rippled into a third image. Mira leaned closer.

SparrowLyn AsTar sat at her easel. Her hand hovered midway to the canvas. Frowning, she turned her head and looked in Mira's direction.

The Guardian stepped back. Had Sparrow sensed her presence? *Impossible. And yet...* She watched the twins' mother return to her work, dab her brush on her palette, and add a bold swathe of silver to her painting. *I want to glimpse more, but dare not take the risk.*

The scene faded, and the motion in Elcaro's Eye ceased.

Three more players and secrets to be discovered. Her eyes came to rest on the kneeling statue. Its serene expression soothed her frayed nerves.

Water droplets sent a gentle chorus of sounds into the room, suggesting that more information would not be forthcoming. With a sigh, she hurried downstairs, opened the window in the front room, and invited the afternoon's warmth into the cottage. Then, she headed for the kitchen, where the walls changed color in response to weather or mood, children or song. Their warm yellow brightened the room and eased her mind. A kettle bubbled on her wood-burning stove, and the aroma of fresh-cut flowers filled the air.

With a DiMensioner on the loose, she dared not do a mental probe or teleport to the tower. Until Karrew returned, she must remain at the cottage and vigilant. She poured a cup of her favorite tea and sat down at the table. A calm, quiet moment would rest her mind before she tackled the perils she knew were on the way.

Torgin's arrival and his mention of his parents brought with it a flood of memories. Idronatti's children had been coming to Myrrh since her arrival many sun cycles ago. The secret of its whereabouts and her miracles—passed down from one generation to the next in soft, excited whispers—never failed to bring a new influx of visitors. The younger ones spent happy times in her protected back garden, where a majestic maple occupied them with its swing and tree house tucked into its low-hanging branches. They fed ducks, gathered eggs in the chicken coop, and played with Millie the cat, Buster the dog, and Tam the pony. Older children roamed further afield, experiencing a rare afternoon free of regimentation. And when, after their fourteenth Sun Cycle Celebration, they returned no more; she felt a substantial loss; for she knew the PPP had ripped their memories of Myrrh from their minds, replaced them with a programmed existence without fear as long as they obeyed the rules. But it offered no joy.

She swallowed the last of her tea, cleaned her mug, and put it away. Myrrh offered many adventures. The Unfolding, however, would be unparalleled in the land's history. Changes were afoot. They didn't come without danger.

Where are the children now? Where are you, Karrew? What have you discovered at the Tower of Nemttachenn?

11

Brie halted on the trail and listened. Since Torgin's urgent call, an ominous silence had settled over the forest. The Star of Truth tingled, then burned a warning. Esán straightened on Tam's back, his narrowed eyes squinting into the distance, his expression intense.

A sharp, excited bark shattered the quiet for a second time. Brie tightened her grip on Tam's reins. "Hold on Esán."

A short time later, they burst into a clearing dominated by a tall, majestic stone tower. Buster charged back and forth at its base, the shrillness of his bark increasing with each pass. Torgin and Ari stared upward. Perched high above them, its luminous eyes glowing, was the biggest owl Brie had ever seen.

Black and silver and the size of an adult man, it lifted into flight, soared in a wide arc, and spiraled downward. Wind from its huge wings caught Brie's braid and tossed it into the air. Her startled scream echoed through the woods. The owl's silhouetted shadow cloaked Esán in darkness as it flew low over his head. With a shriek it streaked upward and circled.

A second swoop left Brie ducking, with her hands covering her face. Ari dropped to her knees. Buster leapt at the descending raptor—his teeth bared, his bark a percussive threat. Tam snorted in terror, reared, and sent Torgin tumbling backward.

Esán wrapped his thin arms around the skittish pony's neck and fought to keep from being thrown. Tipping his head, he stared up at the mighty owl hovering over his head, its piercing eyes riveted to his wide-eyed gaze. Huge wings pressing against the air lifted it higher and higher until it soared up and disappeared over the trees.

Torgin scrambled to seize the pony's reins. "It is good, Tam. It is gone." He spoke softly until she stopped her agitated prancing.

Ari stroked the pony's neck, then helped a stunned Esán down from her back. "Are you alright?"

"Yes." His eyes tracked the path the black and silver owl had taken. "I dreamed about that owl last night and—"

"We must to go back to Mira's." Torgin's trembling voice cut him off. "This place is not safe."

Esán gulped a breath and leaned against Tam's side. "I don't want to go back. The owl's gone. We're all fine. Please let's enjoy our afternoon together."

Ignoring Torgin, Brie brushed red curls from her unraveled braid away from her face and examined Esán's pale features. "Did you see how it stared at you, Esán?"

"Listen to me!" Torgin's voice grew more insistent. "We have to go back."

"That owl sure seemed interested in you, Esán." Ari regarded him with curiosity gleaming in her chestnut eyes.

Grumbling and shuffling his feet, Torgin glared. "Where are we anyway? I don't believe in Myrrh. It is not on any map I have ever seen."

Brie and Ari turned exasperated faces to their friend. "If you didn't believe in it," began Ari.

"You wouldn't be here," finished Brie, gathering her hair back into a braid.

Torgin kicked a twig. "I just hate not knowing where I am."

"Get over it, Torg." Ari's brusque statement elicited a hard, frustrated glare.

"Wait! I have something that might help." Brie pulled a folded piece of paper from her pocket and handed it to him. "I made this for your Celebration, Torgin, and forgot to give it to you."

Still sulky, he took it. "Uh, thanks."

His companions gathered around him. Blowing out a breath, he unfolded his gift. After flipping it this way and that, he finally held it up so they could see.

Ari moved closer. "Not bad, Sis."

"What is it?" Torgin stared at the paper.

"It's a map of Myrrh." Esán studied it over his shoulder. "Good work, Brie. There's Mira's cottage and the Terces Wood."

Brie pointed at the mountain range. "The Dojanacks. I wonder if they're as beautiful as Mother's painting of them. I sure would love to go there."

"It even has the tower." Torgin's voice held a sudden note of interest. "What is it called?"

"Nemttachenn Tower." Ari snapped her mouth shut and glanced at her twin.

Torgin's eyes rounded. "Nemttachenn! Mira said to stay away from—"

"By the Fathers, Torgin, are you afraid of *everything*?" Ari shook her head. "It's a tower—it's granite. We're over here; it's over there."

Brie hugged him. "We promise to keep you safe, Torg. Esán needs to rest—"

"And I'm starving." Ari shot him a pleading smile. "What do you think Mira made for our picnic?"

Esán smiled. "Even I could eat something."

Torgin bit his lip and folded the map. "At least we're not lost." He slipped it into his pocket. "Thank you, Brielle."

Ari punched him on the arm. "We'd never let you get lost, Torg."

The twins unpacked the saddlebags. Brie pulled out a red blanket and glanced at Torgin, who stood lost in thought, his gaze fixed on the tower.

"Hey, Torg, are you hungry or not?" Ari shook out the blanket.

"Yes." He sounded surprised. "I am hungry." He grabbed a corner of the blanket and helped to spread it on the forest floor.

Esán sank onto it with a contented sigh.

Ari handed around thick sandwiches and flasks of chilled lemonade. A comfortable silence settled over the group.

Torgin finished his last bite. "Wow! That was great."

"Wow?" Ari's guffaw turned into a snort. "You'd better be careful. You're beginning to sound like us."

Torgin looked surprised, then laughed. "That is scary, Ari." He cocked his head and grinned. "But maybe I am at that."

Esán licked his lips. "I ate a whole sandwich. Haven't eaten that much in —" He laughed. "I love it here! Take a deep breath. No antiseptics or other Healing Center smells—just plain, fresh air." His thin arms stretched above his head, he tipped his face toward the sun.

Brie glanced at her twin. *We're so lucky.*

"Where are you from, Esán?" Ari made herself more comfortable on the blanket.

"I grew up in a beautiful, little village in the Central Mountains called SumnerTyme. Have you always lived in the city?"

"All three of us were born there." Ari picked up a small twig and twirled it between her fingers. "Tell us about your family."

Esán's thin shoulders sagged. His happy expression grew sad. "My mother left right after I was born. My father disappeared not long afterward. Aunt Merrilea raised me." His face brightened. "I love her so much. She's my mother's sister and a nurse-midwife. Like your mother, Ari, she's from Myrrh, but she's been with me in SumnerTyme since I was born." Esán's smile dimmed. "She doesn't say much about either of my parents."

Brie squeezed his hand. "Your parents didn't know you, Esán. Don't let thoughts of them make you sad."

He gave his bald head a quick rub and smiled. "How can I be sad when I feel good for the first time in many moon cycles, *and* I have three great new friends?"

Torgin got up and wandered across the clearing. *I have both parents.* He glanced back at his companions. It had never occurred to him the twins might feel sad about not knowing their father. Now Esán had neither father nor mother. *How would I feel if my parents disappeared?* Stopping by Tam, he absorbed her calmness. *I am so lucky to have them both!* Tam nibbled his hand. He gently stroked her nose and switched his attention to his friends. The twins' curls glowed a rich burnished copper. Their faces, animated and bright as they talked, made him smile. And Esán seemed less pale—more alive.

He left Tam's side to lean against the tower wall and study the thick growth of trees and wildflowers scattered around the edge of the woods. An alarm went off in his astute, young brain. *Now, what? I refuse to let fear take over again.* Walking the clearing's perimeter, he worked to contain his emotions. The alarm sounded again. He hurried to his friends. "The path has disappeared."

"Don't be silly, Torg." Brie and Ari said together.

"I am *not* being silly. Look for yourselves."

Brie's dread washed over her again as she and Ari circled the clearing. "There's no visible way out." She slipped her hand into Ari's.

"Mira said Tam and Buster always know the way home." Torgin patted the pony's neck. "Show us the way, Tam."

The pony pranced the clearing's circumference with Buster sniffing at her heels. She shook her head and nickered.

Esán scrambled to his feet. "We haven't come that far. I bet if we climb to the top of the tower, we'll be able to see Mira's garden."

Ari joined him. "Good idea, Esán, but you need to rest. Brie will stay with you. Torgin and I will do the climbing."

Brie started to protest, but one look at Esán's face made her nod her head in agreement.

Torgin and Ari headed for the tower. The tall, arched entrance faced away from the setting sun. No light welcomed them, and none found its way into the dark interior.

Torgin took a step back. "I am not sure I want to go in there."

Ari grabbed his hand and pulled him after her into the blackness.

Brie's heart shuddered in her chest.

12

The pulsating darkness inside the tower snatched Torgin's breath away. "Don't let go of me."

Ari squeezed his hand.

"Maybe there is no way up." His fear-filled words floated into the gloom.

"There has to be a stairway." Pulling him after her, Ari crept forward.

A sudden icy chill pervading the tower's interior made Torgin gasp. A slap of glacial cold stung his cheek. Icicle tendrils slithered over his body and turned his breath into an icy white cloud.

"By the Fathers!" He staggered backward. Ari's hand jerked free. Terrified, he went rigid. "Ari? Arienh, where are you?"

Cold pressed closer, bound him, trapped him, froze him one limb at a time. Frost coated his tongue. Words refused to form. Panic screamed through his horror-struck mind. *Arienh, help me!*

Alone in silence that grew colder by the moment, Ari fought her growing panic. "Torgin, where are you? Answer me! Torgin?" She strained to pinpoint his position in the darkness, but failed. *By the Fathers, Torg, did you leave the tower?*

Sidestepping along the interior wall, she searched for the entrance. Her toe striking a hard surface sent her to her knees. Blinded by the pitch blackness, she stretched out a hand. Tentative fingers found the jagged edge of a rough stone step. *If you're in the clearing, I'll see you from the top of the tower.* Pressing close to the rough wall, she began a tentative climb up stone stairs she could not see.

Brie, her imagination working overtime, paced the clearing. Stopping at Tam's side, she stroked the pony's mane. "Why did I agree to stay out here? I should never have let Ari and Torgin go into the tower without me." The Star of Truth's throbbing became more urgent. Hastening to the arched entrance, she peered inside. Impenetrable darkness blinded her. Fear pulsing through her entire body, she hurried to where Esán rested.

He sat up and patted the red blanket. "Don't worry, Brie. They haven't been gone that long."

She cast a troubled glance over her shoulder, stifled her fear, and plopped down beside him. Although his blue eyes, bottomless pools in the paleness of his face, mirrored her concern, he remained calm. An inhaled breath kept her from pressing the issue. Instead, she gazed at the blue veins etching map-like patterns beneath his translucent skin. "How sick are you, Esán?"

He stared at his thin hands, rubbed the palms together, and met her gaze. "Unless they can find a donor for a cell infusion, I probably won't recover."

Sadness falling like tears from each word made her heart ache. "What's it like to know you might die?"

He inhaled and seemed to savor the fresh air in his lungs. "At first, it scared me, then I got really angry." He wrapped his arms around his knees. "It's strange to think of not being here. But I guess I'm getting used to the idea because I don't think about it much anymore. It seems silly to finish my life afraid and unhappy, so I try to make the best of every moment."

Brie swallowed the lump in her throat. "I'm really glad I met you."

His radiant smile erased the melancholy from his face. "Me, too!"

She touched his arm. "You need to rest. I'll keep watch with Buster and Tam. Torgin and Ari should be back soon."

Esán tipped his face up as though afraid to miss even one ray of sunshine, stretched out on the red blanket, and slept.

She gazed at his pale, relaxed face, felt a wave of sympathy, and sighed. *You have more courage than anyone I know, Esán Efre.* Wiping a tear from her cheek, she shaded her eyes with a hand and watched the fluttering leaves catch the glow of the late afternoon sun.

A dark shape spiraling downward over the clearing produced a rumble of fear in her stomach. Her first thought was the owl had returned. When a large raven landed on the branch of a dead tree near the tower, she climbed to her feet and took a step closer. "Karrew?"

The raven lifted its head. In the fading light, a single white feather contrasted with the sleek blue-black of his chest feathers.

Giddy with relief, she ran to the tree. "Karrew, it is you."

He blinked. A deep croak rattled up from his throat. "Where are they?"

The unexpected sound startled her. "In the tower. You talk?"

His ebony eyes gleamed. "Obviously. Stay here." He gurgled deep in his throat. "Under no circumstances enter Nemttachenn." With a parting caw, he flew through the entrance and blended into the darkness.

In the instant before the opening vanished behind him, Karrew glimpsed Torgin, imprisoned within an undulating body of dense, vapor and ice. Frozen in mid-stride, mouth wide and arms thrown out before him, the boy from Idronatti neither moved nor spoke.

Karrew flew the circumference of the tower, his thoughts in turmoil. *A death shadow. How did a death shadow find its way to Myrrh?*

The creature's icy gaze tracked him. A silent threat radiated from the glacial mist cloaking it.

Karrew croaked, then spoke. "Who holds the guest of Almiralyn captive?"

Angry words thundered from the frigid mist. "Who dares to confront Wodash od DerTah?"

"I am the Raven Karrew, protector of the children of Idronatti. Release the boy."

"This boy invaded the domain of my body." A snarl shook the tower. "I claim him for my master."

Karrew circled again. "Who is your master?"

"What makes you think I would tell you?"

Karrew's deep caw echoed. "If you are afraid to speak your master's name, he must be mighty indeed."

A wicked laugh sent an avalanche of small stones tumbling from the ancient tower walls.

"You fear him!" Karrew soared upward.

"I fear *nothing*. Fear *me*, Raven! For I carry death in my breath." He sneered. "If I choose, you will drop like a stone, dead before you hit the ground."

Karrew swooped lower. "Since I cannot escape death at your hand, I would go to my ending with the knowledge of who sent me from this world. Who do you serve?"

"It is not Seyes Nomed who sends you to sleep in the heart of SeDah, Karrew, Raven of Almiralyn. Beware! It is I, Wodash od DerTah, who will freeze your heart."

With a blast of frigid air pursuing him, Karrew shot up the winding staircase into the warmth of the summer evening.

Ari leaned over the stone parapet. Far below, Brie knelt on the red blanket beside Esán, talking and pointing at the tower. A further search of the clearing produced a worried utterance. "Torgin, where are you?"

Ari's gazed flitted over the trees. The height of the tower's pinnacle allowed her a full view of the Terces Wood. *I wonder if I can find the path leading from the clearing?"*

A large black bird swooped from the tower's dark interior. With a percussive caw, caw, it alighted on the parapet's ledge and tilted its head. A flash of white caught her eye.

"Karrew?" She peered closer. "What are you doing here?"

"I came to discover why the paths of the Terces Wood are—"

"Wait!" Ari sputtered. "I didn't know you talked?"

Karrew cocked his head. "I only speak in times of need."

Ari stared. "Why..." She licked her lips and frowned.

"Almiralyn sent me to make certain you did not enter this tower." One coal black eye fastened on her face. "It appears I am too late."

She shook herself, glanced down at the clearing, and back at him. "Did you see Torgin in the tower?"

Karrew's neck feathers spiked. "A death shadow has trapped him within its frigid cold."

"A death shadow?" She wrinkled her brow. "Can we rescue Torgin?"

"Pay attention, Arienh AsTar!" She flinched under Karrew's sharp stare. "Do not go back into Nemttachenn. Above all else, *do not* show fear. The death shadow cannot harm you unless you are afraid."

His blue-black wings unfurled. "I must inform my mistress. I'll return as quickly as I can." With a final caw, Almiralyn's raven streaked away over the trees.

Arie stared after him for a long moment, then shook her head. Turning her gaze, she watched the blazing sun begin its slow descent below the horizon. *Soon, night will arrive in the Terces Wood.* Her jaw tensed. *I refuse to remain captive above the treetops.* She moved to the stairs, peered into the dark, and shivered. "If I don't go back into the tower, I can't help." Another shiver shook her. "Karrew's gone. It's up to me to save Torgin."

She sucked in a breath and stepped onto the first granite step. A penetrating chill slipped icy fingers around her bones. She exhaled a wintery cloud and focused on slowing her pounding heart. *I will not show fear. I wish Brie were here. I must not show fear.*

Wodash tracked the progression of Torgin's terror. Coherent thought was now gone. The hands, thrown out before him, tingled as they gradually froze. His feet, dangling like dead weights above the tower's floor, prevented the boy from recovering equilibrium in the unlikely event he gained control over his fear. Wodash delighted in his power. A hideous laugh rolled into the confined space.

Fixing his full attention on his victim, the death shadow reveled at the boy's youthful vitality. *Your fear made you easy prey.* Thoughts of drinking the boy's life energy to feed his own made his mouth water. A blue-gray tongue slipped over his white lips. A scowl distorted his hideous, icy-white face. *You are lucky, boy. I know better than to disobey my master.*

He glanced up the stairway. *The girl slipped around me, unafraid. She will return. And she, too, will be mine.*

His thoughts churned the coldness surrounding him. Seyes Nomed, a DiMensioner of tremendous power, was not to be trifled with, and he, Wodash od DerTah, owed him. Nomed had found him wandering battered and alone in the desert on the planet of DerTah, nursed him back to health, and brought him to Myrrh. Wodash now did the DiMensioner's bidding, which today had been to capture these children. What did Nomed want with them? He knew better than to ask.

"Ah, ha! The girl reenters the tower." He sent another dose of cold into his prisoner. "My master will be pleased."

13

rie stared at the tower. Beside her, Esán slept, his face half hidden by its massive shadow. She hugged bent legs close to her chest and rested her forehead on her knees. *I don't know what to do.* Lifting her head, she squinted up at the distant parapet. A black bird soared over the clearing. She scrambled to her feet and sprinted after it. At the edge of the trees, she stopped and waved her arms. "Wait, Karrew! Come back. Why didn't you bring—" The Star of Truth's throbbing became more insistent. *Ari's in trouble.* She ran back to the red blanket and knelt beside Esán.

He stretched and sat up. Stormy blue eyes gazed at her. "What's wrong? You look like you saw that enormous owl again."

"I'm going into the tower after Ari and Torgin."

"I'm coming with you." He clambered to his feet.

"We don't know what's in there, Esán. Maybe you should wait here."

His thin hand grasped hers. "I'll be fine."

Side by side, they waded into the pitch-black darkness of Nemttachenn.

Ari sagged against the tower wall. Short, quiet sobs formed a frosty cloud around her. Chills ricocheted up her neck and over her scalp. She whispered, "If the death shadow comes, don't show you're afraid." A quivering inhale produced a shudder. *How can I not show it? Fear is all around me.* Her thoughts jumped to Torgin. *How will I find you, Torg?* "Brielle, I need you." Her call for help floated down the stairs.

An answer penetrated the icy darkness. "Ari! Ari, where are you?"

She struggled to speak. Only a cloud of white formed.

"Ari, answer me!"

Oh no! Brie's in the tower! Concern for herself melted. Fear for her sister propelled Ari down the crumbling stone steps. "I'm up here! Stay there." Pebbles bounced ahead, announcing her rapid descent.

"Esán, did you hear that?" Brie squinted, straining to see. "I think she's coming down steps."

"Get out of the tower!" Ari's frantic yell unnerved her. "Quick, before it gets you, too!"

"We're not leaving without you!" Brie's shout echoed off the granite walls.

Esán stiffened beside her. "Brie, look over there."

His urgent whisper amplified her fear. She peered into the darkness. "I can't see anything."

"To the right of us. Something has Torgin."

She tightened her grip on Esán's hand. "Don't let go." A firm squeeze reassured her.

Ari reached the last stair and took a cautious step onto the tower floor. "Brie, where are you?"

"Ari. Here."

Moving toward the familiar voice, Ari gave a hiccuped sob. Something brushed her cheek. She stumbled. Brie caught her and held her so close they felt like one person.

When the twins tumbled into each other's arms beside a thin, bald boy, Wodash licked his lips and hissed in delight. *Three together!* He chortled. *So much easier than catching them one by one.*

His prisoner struggled to call out. Wodash hissed again. *Be still, boy.* Tightening his icy grip, he sent him somersaulting into forgetfulness and returned his attention to the three young people on the other side of the tower. His wraithlike body floated forward, encircling them with frosty tendrils of fear.

The girls froze in each other's arms, their cheeks touching. The boy remained unaffected.

Curious. Wodash narrowed his eyes. *The boy is not frightened. Very curious indeed.*

Esán realized the twins could not see the undulating creature and kept his hand firmly on Brie's shoulder. Beneath his grip, she turned cold and still.

The shadow controls the twins, but it doesn't control me. If it wants me, it'll follow me. He took a step backward, another and another. A breeze tickled his bald head. In one quick movement, he dodged out the entrance into the night. Above him, the bright curve of the full moon cresting the trees illuminated the clearing. He faced his pursuer.

The ghost-like creature hovered, the rise and fall of its body mass repulsing the moon's rays. White, haunted eyes studied him.

Esán felt only curiosity. "Who are you?"

"Who are you?" The creature's snarl reverberated around the clearing.

"I asked you first." Esán kept his gaze locked on the mottled white face. Beneath heavy, white eyelids, oblong irises—the color of blood opened and closed. Strange images flooded Esán's mind. His brows arched. *The creature's thoughts are pouring straight into my brain. Telepathy. I wonder...* He took a slow, measured breath.

Blood-red irises snapped closed. "I will kill your friends."

Esán sent his reply directly into the death shadow's mind. *"If you kill my friends, I will not go with you. And, Wodash od DerTah, you cannot kill me. Your master would be furious if you harmed any of us. Free my friends, and I will go willingly."*

"Why are you not afraid? I could kill you with a single breath."

"Death and I have walked over half my life together. It bides its time. And, Wodash od DerTah, I am not afraid." Esán almost smiled at the creature's rage. "You fear being disembodied."

Anger twisted the already grotesque face. The death shadow lunged. The howl of a disappointed hunter filled the night.

Esán stood on the far side of the clearing, his thoughts racing. *What just happened? How did I get over here?* Excitement charged his weak body like a battery. *I teleported!* He quieted his churning thoughts. "Wodash od DerTah, take me to your master."

With the creature's departure, the cold drained from Brie's body. "Ari?" Her sister moved against her. "Are you alright?"

"C-c-cold." The staccato clicks of her chattering teeth echoed off the stone walls. "T-t-torgin?"

Brie looked over her twin's shoulder. A shaft of moonlight from the tower's entrance formed a rectangular shape on the floor. Torgin knelt at its center, rocking back and forth and rubbing his hands up and down his arms. "Behind you, Ari."

They hurried to his side.

"I-I've ne-ne-never b-b-been so cold or s-so scared in all-all my l-life." Covering his face with his hands, he began to sob.

Ari helped him to his feet and put an arm around him. "It's alright, Torgin. We're right here."

"We won't let anything else happen to you." Brie hugged him. "Not on your Sun Cycle Celebration."

"S-some Ce-Celebration. I didn't think I was going to live to ever see another one."

"The death shadow's gone, Torg. You don't have to be afraid." Ari moved toward the entrance. "Let's find Esán."

"W-where is h-he?"

"He led the death thing away from the tower." Brie chafed his icy hands. "Can you walk?"

He nodded, wiping away his tears.

"Come on, let's go."

Ari stopped them at the entrance and pointed.

Brie gasped and gripped Torgin's hand tighter.

"Whoo! Whoo!" The black and silver owl, its gigantic wings glistening in the light of the moon, descended into the clearing. "Whoo! Whoo!"

A mix of anticipation and excitement sped up Esán's spine as the owl's talons touched the ground and the huge raptor disappeared.

In its place stood a man, his gleaming hazel eyes as cold as the icy shadow that lingered nearby. The silver-lined black cape, draping his lithe body, added to the aura of predatory power surrounding him. His face, with its high cheekbones and elegant patrician nose, would have been handsome but for the jagged scar that pulled the corner of his mouth into a sneer.

Wodash shrank into the darkness.

Curiosity danced a jig through Esán's thoughts.

"So you barter your life for that of your friends?" The man's deep voice resonated in the night quiet. "What makes you think you are of more interest to me than they are?"

Esán remained still and watchful. Their minds touched.

The man flinched. One dark eyebrow hiked his forehead. "Don't play games with me."

"I didn't mean to do that."

The hazel eyes seemed to dissect him. He knew they saw much more than his fragile exterior. Masking his thoughts, he remained quiet.

With the silver-lined cape swirling around him, the man turned to Wodash. "Go. Prepare a place for our guest."

The death shadow frowned. "What about the others?"

"Leave them for now. Go."

His expression blank, Wodash od DerTah lifted into the air.

The man faced Esán. "I have your word you will come with me?"

"You have my word."

"Would you like to ride on the back of an owl?"

"Yes!"

The man laughed. "Well, come then."

"Before we go, what is your name?"

After giving him a long, searching look, the man said, "I am Seyes Nomed."

"Thank you, sir. I'm Esán Efre."

A crooked smile played across the man's face. Like a whispered word, he vanished, and the owl materialized in his place. Esán mounted, slid his arms around its strong neck, and pressed his knees into its muscled sides. In one swift movement, the enormous bird took flight. Energized by the adventure and a feeling he didn't quite understand, Esán watched Nemttachenn grow smaller beneath him.

Brie dashed from the tower with Torgin and Ari close behind. Far above them, the dark silhouette of owl and rider melted into moonlight.

"Wow! Did you see that?" Ari's delighted laugh rolled across the clearing. "I'd just love to ride on that owl!"

Torgin's expression turned Brie's concern into giggles. "No one will make you fly on an owl, Torg. I think it might be quite wonderful, though."

The relief in Torgin's face sent the twins into more peals of laughter.

"Stop laughing at me or I will—" His voice cracked.

"You'll what?" Ari threw a fake punch.

His face hardened. His spine stiffened and his fists came up. Buster bounding into the clearing saved the moment. Anger forgotten, Torgin scratched the shaggy dog's ears. "I'm glad you had enough sense to hide. Where is Tam?"

Buster barked. An answering whinny came from the woods. Tam trotted toward them. Brie slipped her arms around the pony's neck. "I'm so glad you're safe!"

Ari dodged the exuberant dog. "Wasn't Esán clever? He made sure we had the man's name. Seyes Nomed. I bet he's a DiMensioner or something."

"Do you think Mira knows who he is?" Torgin combed Tam's forelock with his fingers.

Brie's nod sent copper curls tumbling around her face. "Mira knows everything. Let's eat something and get some rest."

Torgin frowned. "And then?"

Brie knew he wouldn't like her answer. "We need to find Esán, of course."

"I was afraid you would say that."

Ari set Tam's saddlebags on the blanket. "First things first. I'm starving."

Torgin gave Brie a grim look. "I remember reading, a quote from turnings long past."

"And what's that?" She flipped open the bag and pulled out a flask.

"The condemned ate a hearty meal..."

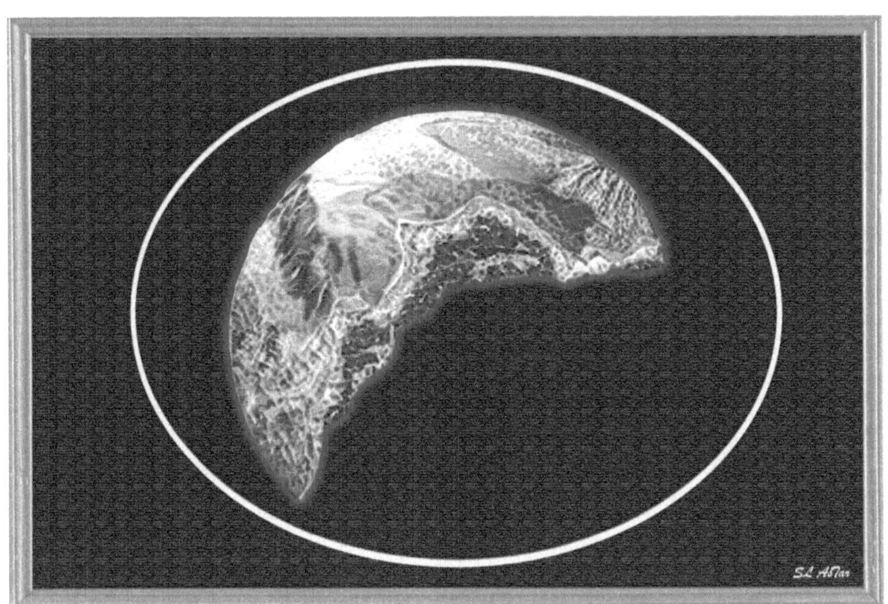

14

Karrew swooped over the back garden, glided through the open kitchen window, and landed on his perch. Ruffling his plumage until he looked twice his normal size, he pranced like a step dancer from one foot to the other.

Almiralyn observed him from the doorway and might have laughed outright had she not been so concerned. "What did you discover?"

The raven paused one foot lifted and tilted his head. "The young people were already in Nemttachenn. At least Ari and Torgin were." Both taloned-feet gripped the perch. "A death shadow had frozen Torgin just inside the entrance. Ari escaped and climbed to the top of the tower."

"A death shadow— That's the companion of our intruder. Did you learn who controls him?" She sat down at the table.

"The shadow calls himself Wodash od DerTah. He let slip he does the bidding of Seyes Nomed."

"Seyes Nomed." The power in the name washed over her. "Why is he disrupting the peace in my land?"

The feathers at the back of Karrew's neck puffed up and flattened. "Only time will tell."

"Have you alerted Allynae?"

"On the way here."

"Rest, Karrew. I'll need you later."

While her protector tucked his head beneath his wing, she pondered Seyes Nomed's intrusion into her land. *His presence on Myrrh is no accident, nor is his timing. Until I understand his intentions, no one else must enter or leave Myrrh without my permission.*

Determination escorted her from the kitchen and up the stairs. *This was not the adventure I envisioned for Esán, nor the way I imagined The Unfolding would develop.*

She stood before the engraved map in the sanctuary, brows bridged in thought. With a piece of invisible chalk, she drew a circle around her domain, connecting its beginning and end so no break occurred. In the tradition of her lineage, she chanted an ancient verse.

> *"None may come and none may enter,*
> *None may leave or go;*
> *Only when events are centered*
> *Will the gateways flow."*

Never, since her arrival on Myrrh, had she shut the magic gateways. Vital to the land's survival, they stabilized the half-sphere that had once been a vibrant part of the planet Earth. Closing them could create problems, but only if closed for too long.

She crossed to Elcaro's Eye. A snap of her fingers brought the flow of water to a standstill.

Allynae's serious face came into focus on the calm surface. "What's up?"

"I've sealed the gateways, Alli. Now we must join in the DiMensioner's game."

"He has Esán." Allynae's expression was grim.

"I thought as much. Where has he taken him?"

"Into the Dojanacks. Paisley and I were about to embark on a rescue mission. Will you go to the others?"

"Yes. The young people are the key. Take care, Alli. The hatred of Seyes Nomed fills the land. And, Allynae, the DiMensioner's companion is a death shadow. Tell Paisley to show no fear."

"We'll be careful." He waved. The image faded.

Water slipped again through carved fingers. A fluid song—in sharp contrast to the growing tension all around her—flowed through the sanctuary.

Without a backward glance, she hurried down the stairs and through the kitchen. "Karrew, it's time! Let's fly."

Walking briskly into her garden, she lifted her arms to the star-studded heavens. Her tall, lithe body, evaporating into a luminescent ball of light, filled her with joy. She shifted instantly into her white bird form. Gold-tipped wings lifted her into the air, a sparkling diamond against the clear night sky. Sapphire eyes scanned the forest's canopy. With Karrew at her side, she streaked toward the tower in the Terces Wood.

Torgin lay on his sleeping mat under the red blanket, huddled between Brie and Ari. Even with Buster curled up at his feet and Tam munching nearby, he could not shake the haunting memories of the death shadow. Like aftershocks, the creature's devastating chill quaked through his body. Snuggling closer to the twins, he rubbed his throbbing head and cleared his throat. "I wonder what it is like, flying on the owl's back."

"If the owl isn't Seyes Nomed, it would be great. Seyes Nomed was scary." Brie's musical voice always soothed him, even when her words didn't.

Ari cracked open an eye. "Would you two *please* be quiet? I need to get some rest. So do you."

"I can't sleep." Torgin pushed himself to sitting. "Every time I close my eyes, I see and feel that horrid, icy darkness. My heart is still freezing cold."

"I know. I couldn't think or move." Ari propped herself up on an elbow, a riot of coppery curls framing her face. "It had you under its power much longer than it did either of us. I can't even imagine how you feel."

He hugged his knees to his chest to keep the memories at bay.

Brie scooted next to him and put her arm around his shoulders. "We're sorry we didn't get to you sooner."

Ari sat up. "When I lost your hand, I thought you'd gone back to the clearing. If I'd known about the death shadow, Torg, I would've tried to help."

"You did the right thing. It would have captured you, too. How did you learn about the death shadow?"

"Karrew, Mira's raven, told me. He came flying from the tower and nearly scared me to death."

"Come on, Ari." Skepticism soaked his voice. "Ravens don't talk."

"Of course, he talks. I mean, really talks like us. He gave me a bunch of orders like 'don't go back into the tower' and 'don't show fear.' Fear's what gives the death shadow control."

Torgin hugged himself and shuddered. "I believe that. It caught me before I could even think."

"I know what you mean." She shivered. "Were you afraid, Brie?"

Her twin hesitated. "As long as Esán held my hand, I wasn't afraid. But when I let go to hug you, it froze me on the spot."

Ari looked thoughtful. "How about Esán? Was he afraid?"

"He didn't show any fear." Brie twisted a strand of hair around her finger and pulled on it. "That's what made the death shadow follow him into the clearing."

Torgin frowned. "What *is* a death shadow?"

"I'm not sure." Ari shrugged. "Karrew just called it that."

"It seemed afraid of Esán." A ringlet slipped from Brie's finger. "I wonder—" Sadness overwhelmed her.

Torgin touched her hand. "What's making you so sad?"

"Esán told me he may die." Her voice broke. "He seems pretty calm about it. Maybe that's why the death shadow didn't frighten him." She brushed a tear from her cheek.

"I didn't realize he was *that* sick." Ari hugged her sister.

Buster's ears twitched. He lifted his head, sniffed the air, and growled.

Brie put a finger to her lips and motioned them deeper into the tower's long shadow.

Scurrying feet and muffled whispers moved toward them through the woods. Torgin gripped Buster's collar. Tam remained statue-still, her creamy mane and tail gleaming in the moonlight.

Three little men scampered into the clearing—their noses sniffing like mice after nut butter. Half as tall as the twins, they wore shades of brown, yellow, and green. Leafy hats bounced on heads that seemed too big for their round bodies. Tweed jackets buttoned over jiggling bellies topped brown knickers. Their feet, encased in uncomfortable looking bark boots, made Torgin grateful for his blue trainers.

"Woof! Woof!" Buster yanked him into the moonlight. The big dog's deep bark and the sudden appearance of a stranger sent the trio backing toward the trees.

"Buster, sit!" Ari pointed at the ground. "Sit!"

The big dog dropped to his haunches.

Brie stepped into the moonlight. "Please wait." The soft lilt of her voice seemed to ease their apprehension. They paused, staring at her from large, almond-shaped eyes.

"We won't hurt you."

Three noses twitched.

"Who are you? Where did you come from?" Her gentle questions elicited no response.

"I bet they don't understand us." Torgin snickered. "They certainly look silly."

The tallest of the three bristled. "Don't be rude. We are not silly. This is our home." Ignoring Torgin, he addressed Brie. "Why does the smell of death fill the clearing?"

Tam gave a welcoming nicker. A tall, slender woman clothed in silver—a raven perched on her shoulder—emerged from the trees. Warm and beautiful, she glided toward them, long, silver-blonde hair floating around her in the cool breeze.

"Good evening." Her voice, brimming with the magic of Myrrh, held them captive.

No one moved or spoke until Brie's soft voice broke the spell. "Is that Karrew?"

"It is." Her smile encompassed all of them.

The three small men pulled their hats off their heads and knelt. Again, the tallest one took the lead. "Sweet Lady Almiralyn, you honor us with your presence." With a broad sweep of his hat, he acknowledged the children. "These are strangers to us. We hope they do not offend you."

"Have you been frightening my young friends, Tibin?"

"Lady, had we known they were *your* friends, we would have welcomed them into your woods. Will you forgive us? Can we make amends?" The three heads bowed low.

"Please stand." Her smile warmed them as they rose. "What brings you out at night, my friends? This is not your custom."

Tibin's nose sniffed the air. "We smelled death on the wind and came to investigate."

She nodded. "I see. Tibin, please introduce your friends."

The second little man bowed. "Tuper at your service."

"I'm Fen." The smallest of the trio twisted his hat in his hands and ducked behind Tibin.

Serious but smiling, Almiralyn addressed them. "I forgive you for scaring my young guests. Now, I need your help."

Tibin, Tuper, and Fen listened, heads bobbing.

"Your first duty is to carry a message to the little people of the Terces Wood. A DiMensioner and a death shadow have come to Myrrh. Tell them not to panic, but to prepare to assist me if I require their services. When you have completed this task, wait in your TreeOms until I summon you."

Ari poked Torgin in the ribs and whispered. "I told you he was a DiMensioner."

"A DiMensioner *and* a death shadow." Tibin and his companions scuttled closer together. "Thank you for your trust, my lady." He addressed the children. "We're so sorry we startled you. Please forgive us."

The three little men bowed in unison and scurried away through the trees.

Brie studied the beautiful woman. "I know you're Almiralyn, but you're Mira, too, aren't you?"

Almiralyn nodded. "I am seen in many forms, Brie, but this one expresses most fully my role on Myrrh."

Shyness holding him silent, Torgin glanced at the twins, and realized they, too, seemed a bit intimidated—even Ari.

"You must have questions." Myrrh's beautiful Guardian sank onto a sleeping mat. "Please sit with me, and I'll try to answer them."

They all began talking at once.

"The DiMensioner kidnapped Esán." Ari plopped down near her.

"Who are those little men?" Torgin sat cross-legged opposite her.

Brie sank down next to her sister and pulled the red blanket around her shoulders. "I'm so glad you came to find us!"

Almiralyn laughed. "One at a time, but first... Karrew, please fly to the top of the tower and keep watch while the children and I catch up."

Torgin stared after the raven. *Why does he need to keep watch? Surely, Almiralyn has the power to protect us without the help of a talking bird.*

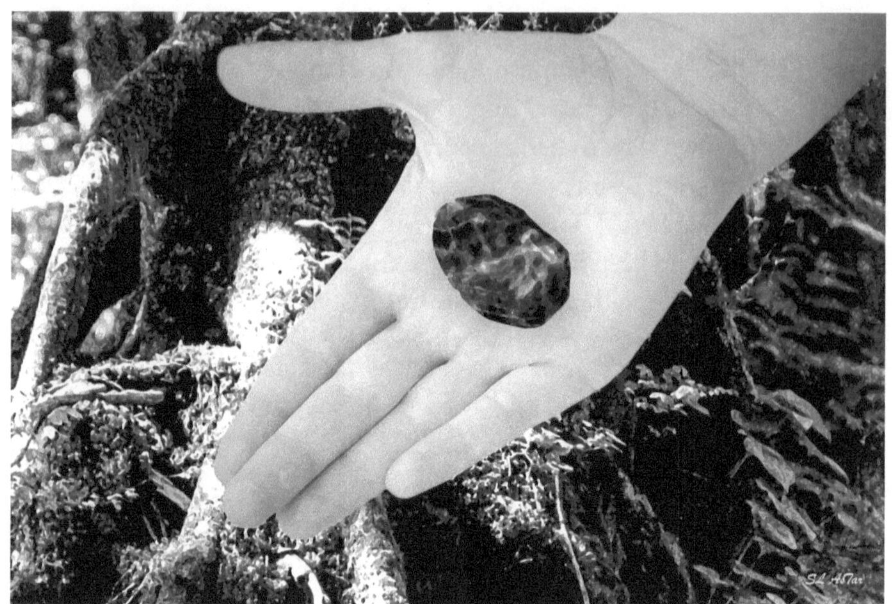

15

The thrill of flight and the world slipping by beneath him invigorated Esán. To the West, the beauty of the sun's final glow highlighting the horizon left him breathless. Spectacular mountains to the East grew bigger and more magnificent with each wing stroke. *Everything is so beautiful from up here.* He grinned. *I can't believe I'm riding on the back of a great horned owl.*

Even though the owl's undulating muscles carried him away from all that he knew, he didn't fear what lay ahead. Illness forced him to focus on the gifts of the moment.

Pressing against the feathered body, he watched the land below change from forest to grassland. Wind whipped his thin jacket and danced around his bare head. Rhythmic power generated by the owl's wings intoxicated his senses. *I wonder what it's like to become an owl.*

Dizziness squeezed his eyes shut. His heartbeat altered. Owl's eyes blinked open. Blurred vision sharpened. In the grasslands below, he picked out each blade of green or yellow; watched a small brown mouse scurry from one rock to the next and a rabbit disappear down its hole. His hunger blazed.

As quickly as the owl's senses had embraced him, he found himself back with his arms clasped around its feathered neck. He laughed out loud. "Thank you!" The wind snatched his words almost before they left his mouth.

An immediate response formed in his mind. *"You are welcome. We will be in the mountains soon. You can rest. I won't let you fall."*

Too energized to sleep, Esán allowed himself to relax. No sound came from the owl's powerful wings. Only the air whistling by and the mountain range cresting higher on the horizon alluded to their forward motion. A strange sensation—one he almost didn't recognize—washed over him. Happiness left him grinning.

S eyes Nomed flew onward. *I am fascinated by you, Esán. You are the reason I shape shifted and flew back to the tower.* Owl wings pressed harder. Training you is a priority.

Why he felt so drawn to this boy puzzled him. Early in life, he learned to keep others at a distance, especially those who professed to love him. The lesson had alienated him from his family and everything he had known. When a portal appeared and took him away from Thera, he celebrated.

I'm back, and I will have my revenge. With Wodash to do my bidding and now Esán... Why am I cold and dry inside? Efforts to silence his invasive thoughts failed. *Perhaps when I attain this goal, life will be more bearable. Enough!*

His strength waned. Shape shifting taxed his endurance and flying with someone on his back added to the drain. He pressed his great wings faster. *Wodash must not know of my weakened state. He will take advantage of any vulnerability.*

Mountain peaks looming on either side helped him to refocus his thoughts and energy on increasing his speed. Soon the Cliffs of ReVod, bathed in the light of the full moon, rose to meet him. Talons reaching for a firm foothold, he landed on a high, rugged trail.

Esán slid down from the owl's broad back. The exhilaration of flying sent vitality pulsing through his veins. He hugged himself. *I feel better than I can ever remember.* With an inner smile, he watched Nomed shift from owl to man.

Sweat covered the DiMensioner's brow. He balanced himself against the cliff face and appeared to struggle with the lethargy clinging to him like a dense fog. When he finally straightened, he removed his cape and draped it over Esán's shoulders.

"Thank you, sir." Grateful for its warmth, he pulled its folds tighter around his too-thin body.

"Come." Nomed strode up the rough-hewn path and reached into a high crevice. A rock rolled aside, revealing a gaping entrance. Motioning him forward, Nomed waited until he was well inside before following.

The rock slid back into place. Esán faced the DiMensioner in the total darkness of a mountain passage.

In the Terces Wood, Torgin stared at the elegant Guardian of Myrrh. Only a hint of the comfortable older woman he had met earlier appeared in the lovely lines of her face. The tall, lithe body and long, flowing hair bore only a slight resemblance to Mira's short roundness and fly-away gray locks.

Brie interrupted his musings. "Those little men... Who are they?"

Almiralyn smiled. "Wood Tiffs—guardians of the trees of the Terces Wood who live in sweet little bungalows high in their branches. To you, they may seem silly, but they are quite perceptive and clever."

"I apologize for calling them silly." Torgin's cheeks burned.

"Unknown things often appear odd to us, Torgin. Awareness is the key to not embarrassing oneself or others." She grew serious. "They wouldn't have ventured out at night unless something disturbed them. Wood Tiffs are creatures of the turning's light and prefer to be snug in their warm homes before the sun sets."

Ari leaned forward. "Were we the reason they came out?"

"I bet it was the death shadow and Seyes Nomed." Torgin jumped in, hoping to regain the Guardian's favor.

Almiralyn looked surprised. "You know his name?"

"Y-yes. Esán made sure we heard it before the man shifted back into the owl."

"Why did Esán go with the DiMensioner?"

"To save us." Brie's voice grew thoughtful. "Esán wasn't afraid of the death shadow. He led it away from us. Once it left the tower, we broke free from its hold." She shivered.

Ari took up the story. "We peeked from the entrance as a huge black owl landed and turned into Seyes Nomed."

"It was so creepy." Torgin shuddered.

Brie scooted closer to her twin. "His voice was hypnotic, but Esán didn't seem affected by it. He just stood there, watching and listening."

"Do you know who Seyes Nomed is, Almiralyn?" Ari slid an arm around her sister.

The Guardian wrinkled her brow. "Not where he's from or why he's here, but he's a DiMensioner, which is worrisome."

Torgin cocked his head. "What *is* a DiMensioner?"

Almiralyn's expression grew thoughtful. "It's the lowest ranking for an initiate into the Order of Esprow. If rooted in honesty and the quest for truth, an initiate may achieve the most exalted rank of VarTerel. Seyes Nomed, however, does not use his training for the good of Humankind."

Time seemed to hesitate. Then, with the sound of Almiralyn's voice, it picked up speed. "I need to open a gateway so you can go home."

Brie sat up straighter. "We're *not* leaving without Esán."

Ari nodded her agreement.

Home. A rush of relief made Torgin giddy. He glanced at his best friends. "Are you sure we should not go? The death shadow is not something I wish to run into again."

Almiralyn regarded each of them. "If you decide to stay on Myrrh, you must remain until the danger passes. And I will need your help to rescue Esán."

The twins caught each other's eye. "We're staying." Their voices rang out as one.

Torgin's voice shook. "I do not think I—"

"Please stay, Torgin." Brie touched his hand. "We began this adventure together. Let's finish it together."

"Do you realize how much I need to go home?" He forced the words around the lump in his throat.

Ari draped her arm over his shoulder. "I know how awful it was in the tower. If you want to go, we'll try to understand. But we'll miss you."

Brie massaged his icy fingers between her warm palms. "You're our best friend, Torgin. No matter what you decide, that won't change."

His heart and his head fought—one for home, his parents, his nanny—the other for his best friends. The battle brought him to standing. He crossed the clearing to where Tam grazed, wrapped his arms around the pony's neck, and snuggled his face against her mane. Her calming warmth eased his fear of the unknown. He squared his shoulders and faced his friends. "I w-will stay."

Almiralyn's expression remained serious. "Remember, there is no turning back, Torgin. I cannot open the gateway once you and your friends are closer to the Dojanacks."

The Guardian's solemn words tempted him to change his mind. He looked down at the twins. Their eyes held his. "I understand." His voice shook a little less.

Brie and Ari pulled him down on the ground between them. Brie squeezed his hand. "We're so glad you're staying."

He inhaled a long, steadying breath. "Please tell me what a death shadow is, Almiralyn. Maybe if you explain, I won't be so afraid."

"Death shadows are the fear of death we carry within ourselves. The fear becomes externalized in places where death is ever present, such as execution chambers, battlefields, abodes for aged ones. I imagine this one was cast out into his own darkness, and Seyes Nomed rescued him and kept him from destroying himself. Now, the death shadow must obey the DiMensioner until he's released from servitude. His name is Wodash od DerTah."

"Can he hurt us? I mean, more than wrapping us in freezing cold." Torgin thought he knew the answer.

"Only if your fear becomes too great. Fear makes you vulnerable. The death shadow manipulates it. If you give in to it and give up, the death shadow will freeze your heart and feed on your vitality to increase his power."

Ari frowned. "Can he kill us?"

"He can leave you apathetic, depressed, and lost in the dreariest parts of your mind. In time, you would give up on life."

"If someone gives up, is there a way back?" Brie held her breath.

"There is, but it takes courage and a great deal of love." Almiralyn peered up at the forest canopy and frowned. "Soon, I must leave, and I may not be back by morning. Even if I am not here, you must start your journey to the Dojanacks."

Torgin withdrew Brie's map and studied it. "The Dojanacks are these mountains, right?"

"Yes, they are a mountain range of unsurpassed beauty." The Guardian smiled. "Before I leave, Torgin, I want to share some of Myrrh's history with you. Perhaps it will help you not to be so afraid."

He sat up straighter and fixed his full attention on her. "I'd like that."

Her beautiful, sapphire-blue eyes gleamed. "Long, long ago, the second Millennium of the New Age dawned bright and clear throughout the Inner Universe. Ancient stars died and new ones exploded into life, gathered in clusters, and came together to form new Galaxies. And so, the universal journey continued.

"In the Milky Way Galaxy's outer spiral arm, the planet Earth traveled an uninterrupted orbit around the sun, until, from the depths of space, an asteroid of unprecedented size rocketed toward it, intersected its orbit, and collided with the Southern Hemisphere. Massive explosions beneath the planet's surface flung chunks of debris far and wide, creating havoc throughout the solar system."

Ari spoke up. "It was a terrible time for Old Earth, Torgin. Blistering winds roared from North America to the coldest reaches of Siberia, scattering cities and woodlands like pickup sticks. Their horrific power crushed all living things and flung them like so much litter over the quaking terrain."

Despite his fascination, Torgin shuddered. "How did it get so close to Thera?"

Brie glanced at Almiralyn, received a nod, and picked up the narrative. "The Galactic Guardians of the Fourth Galaxy were monitoring the situation and observed the large portion of the Northern Hemisphere hurtling beyond the Milky Way. To preserve the imprint of Earth's diversity and its history, they guided its remains to a parallel universe and into the gravitational pull of Thera, a small, Earth-like planet in the Clenaba Rolas Solar System."

Torgin's brow wrinkled. "How do you know so much, Brielle?"

"Standin, our mother's father, grew up on Myrrh and learned its history in school. He shared what he knew with Mother, and she shared it with us." Brie smiled. "You look confused."

"I am. Why are we not taught about this in our educational studies? It is an important part of Thera's history."

Ari shook her head. "Seriously, Torgin? We aren't taught anything that might inspire questions the Five Fathers can't or don't want to answer. Rather than risk Idronattians becoming independent thinkers, they keep us ignorant."

He shot her a dirty look and turned to Almiralyn. "How did the piece of Old Earth develop into Myrrh?"

Almiralyn's serious gaze traveled over the faces of her audience. "Through extensive research and scientific experimentation, the Guardians developed a new and innovated process to insure the safety of Thera, the Terran remains, and the solar system. Crucial to their plan was the Prima Crystal Evolsefil, a quartz crystal of extraordinary power, hidden in deep caverns beneath what had once been the Cascade Mountains."

Torgin held up Brie's gift and pointed. "The Cascades are the Dojanacks, right?"

Almiralyn's eyes twinkled. "You are correct."

He grinned, folded the map, and tucked it away. "What happened next?"

"In order to stabilize their gravitational attraction, the Guardians' scientists connected the cores of the two astral masses and created portals to help establish a shared ecological system.

"Over time, life began to reappear. By the end of one hundred solar cycles, the Galactic Guardians established a human colony and chose Almiralyn to train for the position of the Guardian of Old Earth's secrets. They then selected five fathers to design and build the city of Idronatti. What had once been Earth became known as Myrrh."

"Think about it, Drotti." A hint of scorn laced Ari's voice. "The City

Fathers have misled you all your life. They may never allow you to develop your potential because your intelligence and talent make you a threat."

"That's not true! And I'm not a Drotti."

"Let's not argue." The Guardian glanced up at the forest canopy. "This may be Torgin's only opportunity to visit Myrrh and learn something of the world beyond the regimented streets of Idronatti. We also have Esán to rescue." Almiralyn rose. "Toward that end, I have a gift for each of you. Please stand."

The trio scrambled to their feet. Anticipation and excitement sparked around them.

The Guardian of Myrrh reached into a pouch at her waist and withdrew a round compass on a leather thong. "Torgin, you are the navigator." She placed it on his palm. "Speak the name of your destination, and it will point the way. It is called Ostradio and holds the secrets of Myrrh's geography, so you must keep it safe."

Pride overcame his uneasiness. "I will take *excellent* care of it." He returned her smile.

Almiralyn placed a small blue pouch on a matching ribbon around Brie's neck. "This holds the Stone of Remembering. My mother gave it to me when I was very young, before they took me to the Temple of Mahyinaeh to train as Myrrh's Guardian. If you are afraid or lost or confused, hold it next to your heart. It will assist and protect you. But use it only when all else has failed. Its power dissipates with each use and takes time to rebuild."

Brie wrapped trembling fingers around the gift at her throat. "Thank you, Almiralyn."

Ari took an eager step forward. The guardian's expression grew serious. In her hand, she held a small, silver dagger with amethysts gleaming in the hilt. "You must be my warrior, Arienh." She slipped the knife in a scabbard made of plain brown leather and strapped it around Ari's waist. "This blade carries the promise of life and healing. When used with honest intent, miracles may happen. Wielded by the wrong person, it can kill in an instant. Awareness is essential, Ari. If the bearer forgets to walk in truth, the knife can leave of its own accord. Its name is Efillaeh."

Ari stood even straighter. Her hand rested on her gift.

Almiralyn scanned the night sky.

Above them, in the moon's light, Karrew soared in a wide circle. A wave of the Guardian's hand brought him swooping in her direction. While he flew to join her, she instructed the children. "You must sleep now. In the morning, Torgin will lead you to the Dojanacks. Tam and Buster will accompany you. Trust your hearts and may the love of the Goddess Mahyinaeh surround you."

One last smile and Almiralyn disappeared into the forest with the raven Karrew on her forearm.

Torgin touched the compass and tried to ignore his ever present apprehension as Myrrh's Guardian faded into the night shadows.

With the Remembering Stone clutched in her hand, Brie watched Almiralyn vanish into the Terces Wood. Once again, they were alone, the enchanted tower's shadow merging into the night. Buster's ears drooped. Tam tossed her head and nickered. Ari and Torgin, their expressions grim, stared into the darkness.

Brie opened the blue velvet pouch. The Star of Truth tingled as she tipped the midnight blue stone onto her hand. "Almiralyn gave us such lovely gifts." When they continued to stare into the woods, she poked Ari in the ribs. "Snap out of it. The Guardian has given us an opportunity to save Esán. I can't wait until morning!"

Ari shook her red curls back from her face and touched the lapis-blue stone. "It's so beautiful."

Torgin peered over her shoulder. "I wonder if it truly helps people to remember things? Do you think it might help Idronattians recall the past after the PPP erases their memories?"

Brie replaced it in the velvet pouch. "I guess we will discover its power as we go."

Ari pointed at the sky. "Look." Above the clearing, two birds soared into the radiant path of the moon. "I wonder if Almiralyn ever takes the shape of a bird?"

"I bet she does." Torgin looked up at the sky, then held out his gift. "I've never seen a compass except in books."

The twins peered closer at the shimmering blue Ostradio. About the size of his palm and edged in gold, it had red numbers on the face that glowed in the dark. A small, golden arrow danced about whenever he moved his hand. He slipped the leather thong over his head and tucked the compass beneath his shirt. His face brightened with confidence and pride. "Tomorrow, this will help us find the Dojanacks."

Ari withdrew the knife from its scabbard. The blade spanned the length of her hand from her wrist to the tip of her middle finger. Its silver surface glinted with a satiny sheen. Two purple stones, set one above the other, adorned a gold hilt. She held it out. "There's a pattern etched on the blade."

Brie leaned closer and gasped. "When I look at it, I see ancient legends coming to life." She glanced up. Reality snapped back into focus. She ran her finger over the flat, cool surface. "It's exquisite, Arienh."

"It makes me feel stronger and braver." Ari seemed to grow taller. "I am a protector of Myrrh."

Torgin stared at the knife. "My fear is fading away. It is melting just like snow on a spring morning." He yawned behind his hand. "We had better get some sleep. Tomorrow is going to be busy."

Brie winked at her twin. Torgin appeared to be taking his role of navigator to heart. Using the red blanket as a cover, the three snuggled close together and gazed at the stars.

The sounds of the forest, Ari's soft breathing, and Torgin's intermittent snores comforted Brie like a cup of Mira's special tea. A shooting star trailed across the sky. Trees, the sentinels of the night, cast long shadows over the clearing. *What a turning.* She looked at her sleeping sister. *I wonder what tomorrow will bring. And I wonder if the mountains in Mother's painting are the Dojanacks. What if those shadows...*

Snuggling closer to Ari, she allowed herself to drift into dreaming.

16

The young DeoNyte Crystal Keeper, Zugo, crept down the labyrinth of tunnels winding through the bowels of the Dojanack Mountains. As he often did, he stopped to imagine the spectacular beauty of peaks he knew rose to great heights beneath the open sky. *Someday I will see them—no matter what my father says.*

Wary of false passages and dead ends, he slipped into a narrow tunnel near the Lake of Rorret. Scattered bones bore testimony to the many explorers who lost their way and died in the intricate maze beneath the mountains. He didn't intend for his bones to be among them.

Arriving at his destination, Zugo assured himself all was as it should be. Large, pale blue eyes that missed very little, especially in the cavern's darkness, focused on his target for the second time that turning. An effortless leap landed him on a ledge above the entrance from the Cliffs of ReVod. Crouching low, he peered at the massive rock shielding the tunnel from the outside world. *My father and our people will not understand my curiosity or my quest for knowledge. But change is coming to Myrrh. I can feel it. As the future leader of my people and the protector of the Prima Crystal, Evolsefil, I seek to understand the source.*

A Human male with a scarred cheek and a creature emitting intense cold camping in the upper caverns had left him curious and fearful. He thought back to the events that brought him back to the ledge.

Footsteps approaching the ledge from the cavern drove him—heart pounding—into a fissure. The scarred one and his frigid companion passed below him. Chill bumps chased one another beneath his white fur. A brief shaft of sunlight sliced through the darkness. His eyes snapped shut. The memory of blinding light lingered long after the entrance stone rolled into place.

Once assured the two interlopers had disappeared beyond the stone, he jumped from the ledge, his bare feet soundless against the cold stone of the passageway. Shaking his fur-covered body to remove the chill still lingering along the surface of his black skin, he took a moment to recapture his curiosity and slow his heart rate. For the briefest instant, he wished he could be like the rest of his people.

He made no sound as he sprinted upright down the tunnel. With excitement beating like a small drum in his chest, he stepped into the cavern. The fire near the center cast strange shadows up the walls. To his right, a subterranean lake formed a natural boundary. Near the edge of the lake, furthest from the entrance, a passageway disappeared into the depths of the mountains. Opposite the fire, he peeked behind a dark curtain covering the alcove where the scarred one slept. Further around the perimeter, he discovered another tunnel that wound into the mountain's innards. The last mouth-like opening led into a small, barren cave.

Cold clutching at his body spun him around. Fear sent him scurrying up to a ledge on the cavern wall. The shadowed one entered and crossed to the small cave. Zugo, adrenaline pumping, jumped to the floor and sprinted down the passageway.

His insatiable eagerness to know and understand what was happening in his world had nudged him to return to the ledge. Tempted but afraid, he balked at venturing into the land beyond the caverns when the brightness of the sun's fireball traveled across the sky.

Now the cool darkness of night beckoned. His face pressed to a narrow crack, he inhaled the mysterious fragrance of the outer world. Cool air rustled his silky, white fur, creating a strange and wondrous feeling unlike any he had ever experienced.

Muffled footsteps on the ledge outside announced the scarred one's return. Zugo shot back into the fissure as the large stone moved to reveal the narrow opening. A cloaked figure preceded the scarred one into the passageway. The stone rolled back into place. When a hairless head emerged from the folds of the black cloak, Zugo pressed his hand against his mouth to keep from gasping. *A Human child!*

"Come, boy." The scarred one strode down the passageway toward the main cavern.

Boy? A male child like me! Zugo wanted to jump up and down with excitement. Instead, he leapt to another ledge and crept after them.

The boy entered the subterranean grotto and stared in awe as the gemstone walls, reflecting the glow of the fire, sent colorful ballerinas of light leaping across the space.

"It's so beautiful!" He removed the cloak from around his thin shoulders and handed it to the scarred one.

"So it is." The man turned as the shadowy figure of his minion materialized from the darkness. "Is all made ready?"

"The small cave is prepared, just as you ordered, Master."

Zugo shuddered at the hollowness of the dark creature's voice and crouched lower on the narrow outcropping.

The scarred one returned his attention to the boy and pointed at the small cave. "Your quarters. You need rest. We'll talk further in the morning." He handed him a small packet of biscuits and a flask of water.

"Thank you, Seyes Nomed." With no detectable fear, the boy walked across the cavern.

Zugo slipped along the ledge and sidled along a narrow fissure until he squatted behind a large rock with a view of the small cave. The boy entered and surveyed his surroundings. Dark circles beneath his eyes seemed even darker in the light of the oil lamp glowing by a pallet on the floor. He sagged onto the makeshift bed and sat nibbling a biscuit. When he finished, he sipped water from the flask and lay down. Sleep came instantly.

Although Zugo's curiosity flicked like sparks in the council fire, he made himself stay hidden. The temptation to climb down and touch the smoothness of the boy's skin nagged. *Patience.* He smiled. *I sound like my father.* In time the Human boy's slow, even breathing showed he slept the deep sleep of one whose exhaustion demanded relief.

Without a sound, Zugo descended and crept closer until he sat on his haunches next to the boy's elbow. Ever so slowly, he extended his hand. One slender black finger hovered, then traced the cool curve of the Human's face and arm. Leaning closer, he looked at the smooth white cheeks, the roundness of the bald head, the ears that were so different from his own hearing hollows.

The sleeping boy stirred. Zugo jumped back, knocking over the closed water flask. A rattling sound echoed throughout the cave. Hidden in the shadows, he held his breath as the hairless one's eyes flew open.

Esán, his gaze darting around the cave, pushed up to a sitting position. In the soft light of the lamp, a white creature stood out against the dark wall. The creature blinked its light blue eyes and stared back. It crouched, and with surprising agility, leapt to a ledge and vanished.

Esán retrieved his water flask and drank deeply. No further sound broke the silence. He moved the curtain aside just enough to peek into the main cavern. The only visible light came from the fire close to Seyes Nomed's personal space.

He turned to examine his sleeping cave. High on the wall, he could make out the narrow ledge. His memory flashed to the dark triangular face, huge pale eyes, and white, furry body. The creature had appeared to be about his height. He had sensed no fear or predatory intent, only curiosity in his visitor.

I sure hope it comes back. He yawned, curled up on the pallet, and succumbed to his need for sleep.

Dreams of adventures with the white creature took him down secret passages that opened before them as they journeyed deep under the mountains. He rolled onto his side. His dream changed, and he soared through the air in pursuit of the great black and silver owl. Below him, total darkness prevailed. Around him, ancient voices whispered. He turned again, bumped the small lamp by his pallet, and woke up. His eyes flitted around the space. "Just a dream."

He rose from the pallet and tiptoed to the curtained entrance. *Dare I take a closer look?* Chilling cold penetrated the curtain. Not wanting to alert Seyes Nomed's servant, he tiptoed back to bed.

From the ledge, Zugo watched the boy toss and turn in his sleep. *I want to know more about this Human. Why does the scar-faced man keep him here? Will he harm him?* Fear for the boy's safety kept him from leaving the ledge.

His father, Yookotay, would not approve of his interest in Humans. Zugo shrugged, his fingers caressing the sapphire that hung on a gold chain around his neck. *Yookotay is old-fashioned and afraid. Humans do not remember the DeoNytes exist. Over twelve cycles have passed since one has wandered deep enough to get close to the underground city and mines. Besides, I must know why the scarred one is here. Does he seek Evolsefil?*

He glanced down. The boy looked up. Their eyes met and held for the briefest moment—before the curtain to the sleeping cave was pulled aside.

Esán dropped his gaze.

"Good morning." Seyes Nomed held the curtain open. "Come. It is time to begin the turning."

After a quick peek at the ledge, Esán followed the man out to enjoy the fire.

Under lowered lids, he observed the stranger opposite him. *Who are you? Where are you from? And why do you seem so familiar?*

Seyes Nomed handed him a battered metal mug. Esán sipped and smiled. The taste of honey and spices left his mouth tingling. "What is this?"

The words bounced against the cavern walls and chased themselves back to him. Startled, he looked around.

The response filled his mind. *"Echoes are interesting, are they not? One hears one's words repeated over and over until they fade into eternity."* Nomed looked around the space. *"Because of the structure of this grotto, named Oche Cavern, echoes sound in what appears to be a random fashion. We may speak through thought, which is easier than words and less noisy."*

Esán studied the scarred face, the crooked smile, and the flickering light in the hazel eyes. *"What do you want with me?"*

A curious expression crossed Seyes Nomed's face. *"When did you first notice you could communicate telepathically?"*

"In the clearing with the death shadow, I realized I puzzled him. Then I was in his mind." Esán glanced around the dark cavern. *"Where is he this morning?"*

"Wodash has gone on an errand for me. He will return soon." Seyes Nomed observed him with a critical eye. *"When you were in his thoughts, what did you discover?"*

Esán stared into the fire. Memories buzzed around his mind. *"I saw fast changing images of his fear. Desert sands painted blood-red shifted into pain-wracked bodies. Tears fell in torrents and evaporated into ghosts that moaned in anguish for their lost lives. Shadows watched, cringing when light touched their undulating masses and sent them shrinking into nothingness."*

Nomed's eyebrow arched. *"You went that deep? Are you positive you've never experienced telepathy before?"*

Esán warmed his hands over the fire, his eyes fixed on the flickering red and gold flames. *"I have no memories of it, but I understood what was happening as though I'd done it all my life."*

"And I suppose you have never experienced teleportation before, either?"

Esán shook his head. *"Not until yesterday."*

Nomed stood. *"I have things I must do. Here is your task."* He pointed at a large dark rock that glittered with emerald flecks of light. *"Use telekinesis to move that boulder to the other side of the cavern. If it is too big, then begin by moving smaller ones and graduate upward until you can manage it. Questions?"*

"I feel your anger. Why are you here on Myrrh?"

A swirl of silver and black settled around Nomed's shoulders. Long, elegant fingers fastened the cape. *"You will know soon enough."* He exited the ring of light cast by the flames. *"And, Esán, try nothing foolish while I'm away."*

Grateful for its light and its warmth, Esán stared into the fire, then studied the large stone. *Does he honestly think I can move that?* He walked over to inspect it. *Do I think I can move it? I wonder...*

17

High above the Terces Wood, Karrew savored the opportunity to fly with his mistress. In tune with her every move, he matched his speed and trajectory to hers.

Around them, morning's welcoming light returned color to the landscape below. Flying high in the first moments of the turning made his heart throb with joy. Even the urgency of this flight could not detract from the thrill he felt as the sun crested above the horizon.

Ahead of him, his mistress dropped without warning into the trees below. He banked sharply and followed her down through the silky dimness of the forest.

Paisley sat by the small campfire, fascinated by the play of flickering light changing Allynae's face from light to shadow. Instinct sent a tingle over his skin. He sensed Almiralyn's quiet approach before he saw her. Karrew perched on her arm made him nervous. He'd never come to terms with the bird's ability to talk.

Allynae looked up. His eyes held a fire-lit gleam. "Welcome. Hey, Karrew, it's good to see you."

The raven cocked his head and cawed.

"Cat got your tongue?" Allynae laughed. "Or is it Paisley?"

"Behave yourself, Alli." Almiralyn's pale, blonde hair glistened as she turned. "Hello, Paisley. Thank you for joining us."

Paisley nodded but said nothing. Almiralyn made him ill at ease. He liked her Mira form better.

Karrew flew to a low branch and perched, grooming his feathers. He chose not to speak in front of Myrrhinians. Tonight, he would join in if asked. Until Almiralyn gave him the sign, however, he would remain silent and attentive.

Allynae waited until his sister joined him on a large log by the fire. "How are the children? Did you get them home?"

"They refused to leave without Esán and will remain in Myrrh until he's safe. These are most unusual children, Alli. I believe this is their story, even more than ours."

Almiralyn grew silent. Paisley seemed entranced by her beauty. A sigh made his mustache quiver.

"You okay?" Allynae's eyes twinkled. "Or are you mooning over some pretty girl?"

Paisley coughed.

"Don't let Alli's teasing bother you." Almiralyn smiled and then addressed her brother. "We have some decisions to make. I need someone to go to Idronatti to find Esán's Aunt Merrilea and also SparrowLyn AsTar. Both women may help us. Also, we must discover what Seyes Nomed is after, why he's in Myrrh, and what he's planning. I feel sure he is seeking revenge for something. We need to know what it is. Do you have any suggestions, Alli?"

The raven tipped his head. One glowing eye regarded Allynae, who sat in silence, his face a picture of changing emotions.

The mention of Sparrow's name left Allynae fighting for breath. Picking up a small stone, he pressed it between his palms. The idea of Idronatti made him sick to his stomach. *Why does Mira want me to bring Sparrow to Myrrh? The last time I visited the city, the PPP almost caught me; the Five Towers loomed bigger than life.* He swallowed his escalating dread and glanced up.

Almiralyn's eyes overflowed with questions. Paisley sat wrapped in silence, his eyes never leaving the fire.

Allynae tossed the pebble and caught it. "You must remain in Myrrh, Almiralyn. Seyes Nomed will expose his hand soon, and you need to be here. That leaves me to make the journey to Idronatti. What about Paisley?"

Almiralyn looked at the black man whose dark eyes reflected the color of fire. "I have an important task for you if you're willing to help."

Paisley squirmed. "I've never been outside Myrrh. I'd be afraid to go to Idronatti, even with your brother. Is it somethin' I can do here?"

"Don't worry, you need not accompany Alli. Your job is close to home. Many sun cycles ago, a gentle, sad man came to Myrrh. He called himself One Man. I granted him permission to remain, and he did so. For a time, he worked at the cottage. Eventually, he left. Although I have not seen him since, I know he lives deep in the Dojanacks near Timreh Pass. Would you be willing to find him and bring him to me?"

Paisley looked relieved. "That's a job I can do well, my lady. I've hiked those mountains all my life. When would you like me to start?"

"You can leave first thing this morning. Alli, when do you want to depart for the city? I'll give you the key to the gateway so you can come and go as needed. Choose your times with care. No one must know a portal has been breached. And no one must know you have ventured into Idronatti."

"I'll go as soon as I reach the cottage." He grimaced. "You know how much I hate leaving Myrrh, Almiralyn. I understand the need. I just dread the journey."

Almiralyn put her hand on his. "Thank you, brother. Take care of yourself. Do you want Karrew to accompany you?"

"No, keep him with you." He stood up and slipped on his backpack. After embracing his sister, he tapped Paisley's shoulder. "Watch your back, Pais. That DiMensioner may not play fair. Besides, who would I tease if you didn't come back?"

A chuckle rumbled in Paisley's throat. "Take care. See ya soon."

Head high and spine rigid, Allynae strode into the trees.

Karrew watched him go, then eyed the two by the fire. For a time, Almiralyn and Paisley sat, gazing at the dying embers while birds welcomed the rising sun. Squirrels scurried about, gathering nuts and seeds. Somewhere a crow called, and another answered. The turning had begun.

Paisley stood up, stretched, and reached for his pack. "Guess I'd better be goin'. How do ya s'pose I'm gonna find this One Man?"

"There's a small cabin near Timreh Pass by the Ylenol Spring. Try there first. Keep your eyes open for the Enots. They might know where he is."

"I haven't seen an Enots in many a sun cycle." He pulled at his mustache. "They're shy things, ya know. I've climbed all around those avalanche areas where they build their homes and have never seen a single one even peek from a crevice. Some guardians of the Dojanacks they are!"

"You know they come out only when they sense danger. Perhaps they don't consider you dangerous."

Karrew watched her suppress a smile.

"I can do without the danger," Paisley groused, "but their help would be nice."

Almiralyn raised an eyebrow. "If you need them, they will know."

He slung his backpack onto his broad shoulders. "Anything else ya need before I go?"

"No, I'm about ready to leave myself. Take care, Paisley James. When you find One Man, bring him to the Tower of Nemttachenn. The Wood Tiffs will let me know when you arrive."

"And if I don't find him?"

"Go there anyway. I'll decide then what to do next."

Paisley bowed and disappeared into the woods.

At the center of the small clearing, Almiralyn continued to sit by the fire, her expression stern.

Karrew respected her silence and waited.

At the clearing by Nemttachenn Tower, the sun's return sent streaks of lavender and peach pink across the Myrrhinian sky. Torgin yawned and stretched his long legs.

"Hey, you two, time to wake up." He nudged a girl on either side of him and got to his feet. "We have a big turning ahead of us."

The twins stretched and sat up.

"What woke you so early?" Ari opened one eye and yawned.

"Torg knows what we need to do, and he's ready to do it." Brie grinned, but neither eye opened.

Tam nibbled dew-soaked grass, her tail switching from side to side. Torgin stroked her neck. His heart grew heavy with dread that would not quite go away. Tam moved against him until her beautiful brown eyes came in line with his. Her trust-filled gaze melted his fear. "Are you magic, Tamboreen?"

Tam tossed her head up and down and stamped her hoof.

Torgin laughed. "You are wonderful."

He looked at the twins' sleep-smudged faces.

Ari pushed the blanket aside and stood up. Stretching to one side and then the other, she gave him a lazy grin. "Mornin'." Her grumbling tone had disappeared. "How'd you sleep?"

"Better than I expected. How about you?"

"I'm stiff but good." She bent forward and put her hands flat on the ground.

Torgin winced. "By the Fathers, Ari, does that not hurt?"

"Nope." She rolled up through her back and grinned. "It feels great."

"It looks painful to me." He turned his attention to Brie, who sat in a puddle of red blanket, absently fingering its soft-edge. "What are you thinking about?"

"I had the strangest dream—dark shadows and bats and a creature I've never seen before—" She shivered and pulled the blanket tighter around her.

"What kind of creature?" Ari stopped stretching and plopped down next to her.

Brie closed her eyes. "It was about the size of Esán and covered with soft, white fur. It had pale blue eyes in a dark face and hid behind a pile of rocks. Ari, the dream was so real."

"Do you think the creature wanted to hurt him?"

"No, it just watched and waited."

Torgin dropped Tam's saddlebags beside them and sat down. "How about some breakfast?" He pulled out a small, nutty loaf and a piece of fruit and handed them to Brie. "Eat. A full stomach will help to chase away bad dreams."

She bit into the loaf. "Yummy."

"Apples and cinnamon." Ari mumbled with her mouth full.

When they finished, Brie brushed the crumbs from her hands and grinned. "Much better."

Torgin nodded. "See, the world is already brighter." He began to repack the leftovers. "I hope we never lose these saddlebags. We would get pretty hungry without them."

Brie gave Buster his ration of biscuits while he and Ari gathered the sleeping mats, folded the red blanket, and packed them away.

Ari flung the saddlebags over Tam's back. "Get out your compass, Torg, and find out which way we're heading."

Withdrawing Almiralyn's beautiful gift from beneath his shirt, he squared his shoulders and held it out so the twins could see. "The Dojanack Mountains."

The golden needle spun in a blur above the compass face and stopped, pointing due West. He looped the thong back around his neck. "West it is. I hope we discover a trail once we move beyond Nemttachenn."

"We will." The twins chorused response made him smile.

"Let's take turns riding Tam." Ari looked at her sister. "Why don't you go first?"

"Sounds good. I'm still unnerved by my dream."

Torgin helped Brie settle on Tam's back. With a glance around the clearing, he led the way into the forest. Buster loped ahead, sniffing out the best way through the trees.

Their journey had begun.

18

Nomed strode down the passageway, plans spinning through his mind. *Soon, I will destroy this last vestige of Old Earth and gain the recognition I deserve.* He laughed with greedy delight. "I'll travel the Universe like royalty." The scar on his cheek pulled the corner of his mouth up at an odd angle. He touched it, then smiled. *No matter. My face still has charm.*

During his careful research into Myrrh's history, he discovered its five gateways were its weak points. He paused and stared ahead. Confidence filled his verbal pronouncement. "As soon as the Prima Crystal, Evolsefil, is mine, I will destroy all the portals and thus guarantee Myrrh's demise."

He strode forward. Thoughts of Esán prompted a satisfied smile. *The boy came into my life at a perfect time. Somehow, he will play a part, and his role will be a crucial one.* The connection he felt to this bald child stirred up memories he preferred not to revisit. He shook his head. *I am softening the control I have imposed on myself since leaving Thera. It makes little sense, but it's happening.*

Reaching into the crevice, he pulled the hidden lever and stepped onto the mountain ledge. The large rock slid back into place behind him. Early morning sun blurred his vision; then the landscape came into focus.

The exquisite beauty of Myrrh—unsurpassed anywhere in the solar system—made his heart ache. But the hatred he'd carried for so long crushed his love and left him empty. *Nothing must impede punishing Mira and destroying all she holds precious.* Loathing welled up in his throat until he tasted its bitterness.

Memories of his childhood flared. His father's enraged face nose to nose with his, the agony of the man's fists hammering his small body, the yelling... Nomed's fists clenched and unclenched. The memories refused to be stifled. He was eleven again.

The mirror bore witness to his beating. Davin glared at the bruise spreading across his cheek. "I hate you, Father," he growled, staring into his own over-bright eyes. "Today, I'm going to Myrrh."

He eased the bathroom door open a crack and peered down the hall. The yelling ceased as his father stormed from the house. After making certain he was not coming back, Davin tiptoed to the room he shared with his younger brother. In the closet, he discovered Somay sitting on the floor, tears streaming down his cheeks.

"Come on." Davin held out a hand. "We're going to Myrrh."

With his brother in tow, they fled through the streets of Idronatti, took the drop car up in the SunSpire, and jumped through the mist into The Borderlands. Majeska guided them to the mirror. They stepped through the keyhole into the Land of Myrrh, the only safe place he had ever known.

All he wanted was time to forget, but anger overtook him as he watched Somay cuddling Mira's kitten. In a fit of raging frustration, he grabbed it and flung it against the wall across the room.

Panting, he touched his swollen eye and stared at the small, still body. "That's what I will do to you, Father. Just wait until I'm bigger."

"Davin." The sadness in Mira's soft voice interrupted his ranting and put him on the defensive.

He flew at her, fists flying. "It's not my fault the stupid cat died."

Her silence brought him up short. He dropped his hands and glared.

Nomed stared at his clenched fists. Hatred still gripped his heart. Sure, he had lost his temper; sure, he had killed a kitten. So what? That was no reason to ban him from Myrrh and return him to his father's anger. The scar on his cheek burned where he had cut it with a shard of glass from the portal mirror.

More memories assaulted him.

Two months after his fourteenth Sun Cycle Celebration, the PPP announced his Time of Induction, the turning they would assign his profession and adjust his memories. Grabbing his pack, he crept from his building, through alleys and back streets to the Onom Lira station and stowed away on a train to the Central Mountains. No one was going to erase his memories of Myrrh. Nothing would keep him from getting his revenge.

He found an uninhabited cave high in the mountains. Ten sun cycles of living hand to mouth strengthened his body and toughened his mind. Little by little, he began to change. Talents, including his ability to protect his memories from being accessed and expunged, emerged. It was time to venture out of hiding and find his brother.

The moon cycles he lived with Somay and his wife, Tianna, were some of the best and the worst of his life. Love for Tianna had hit him with the force of a flash flood. When he declared his feelings, her rejection, though gentle, sent him into a rage that took him back to Idronatti and eventually to Tower Five. His imprisonment was short-lived. Using the cunning he had gained from his unsettled life and with the help of a fellow prisoner, he'd soon escaped. Demrach Portal in the Central Mountains took him away from the planet of Thera.

His goal of destroying Mira and Myrrh, foremost in his mind, he arrived on the planet of DerTah. There, Wolloh Espyro, a High DiMensioner, whose anger and genius exceeded his own, helped him hone his talent for the mystical arts into DiMensionery and directed his anger into military prowess.

With the maturing of his skills and temper, Wolloh arranged for his initiation into the DerTahan Order of Esprow. Unbeknownst to his mentor, the leaders of the planet christened him Seyes Nomed and set a proposal before him.

"Now here I am—in the land that has fueled my determination to survive, the land I will destroy." He squared his shoulders. "How dare you ban me from Myrrh, Almiralyn Nadrugia?"

With his shout echoing off the mountains, he leapt from the cliff and shaped the owl midair. Its powerful wings carried him deeper into the Dojanack range to the portal he had used to return to Myrrh. Certain Mira would close all the gateways, he had placed a spell on this one, ensuring its availability.

Landing in Human form between the cathedral-like walls of an obsidian gorge, he surged forward. "Great Pentharian, come forth!" The words echoed like crashing thunder. An answering roar issuing from the portal sent Nomed's cape flying out behind him. Five exotic creatures leapt through the vortex and landed in the narrow ravine. Blacker than the obsidian surrounding them, the Pentharian shape shifters each assumed a unique form. Snake, hyena, panther, wild boar, and vulture swarmed around him, their golden eyes gleaming. The odor of death filled his nostrils. He knew their breath could burn the heart from a living body. Their skills combined with his own assured the gateways to Myrrh would be destroyed forever.

Undaunted by their ancient and deadly power, or the lies he had told to gain their allegiance, he faced them. The scar on his cheek tingled in the sunlight. His fearless eyes met theirs. "The time has come. Follow me."

He sprinted down the ravine. His cape flared into owl wings that lifted him into the summer-blue sky. Behind him, Pentharian vultures formed an ominous trail of black.

K arrew waited, his feathers gleaming with the freshness of morning as Paisley disappeared into the Terces Wood. Almiralyn, his mistress since their childhood, stood in silence at the center of the small clearing. Head tipped to one side, he absorbed her beauty. Long hair caught the light and spun it around her slender tallness in a halo of shimmering, silvery gold.

Her sapphire eyes glowed with determination. Soon she would decide, and their journey would begin.

She paced toward him. "I'm distracted this morning, Karrew." Her fingers twisted a strand of hair. "Do we join the twins and Torgin or head for the Dojanacks?"

"Do you think Nomed will try to capture the children?"

"I think he will gather them into his net."

"The fountain could help us find him. Do we have time to consult it?"

"If we hurry..." Almiralyn strode to the center of the clearing. "Let us fly east and then return to the children." A brilliant ball of light flashed, sending her white bird form soaring up through the trees.

Once again, he allowed himself to revel in the joy of flying beside her. His devotion intensified as they matched speed and wing stroke. Cresting the forest canopy, they emerged into the light. Feathers prickling on the back of his neck propelled him in a wide circle.

Above the western horizon, menacing shadows ascended from the canyons of the Dojanacks into the late morning light. Karrew shot toward his mistress, adrenaline pumping. Age and experience informed him that Seyes Nomed led great evil over the Land of Myrrh and was closing the gap between them.

"Hide!" His cawed warning ripped through the morning silence.

The white bird shot toward the treetops and disappeared into the shadowy darkness of the Terces Wood.

Karrew streaked after, his heart tight with foreboding.

Allynae emerged from the dust-covered mirror dressed in brown coveralls. His combed hair lay flat against his head; his beautiful mustache no longer adorned his face. He touched his top lip and sighed. In Idronatti, no one under the age of sixty sun cycles boasted facial hair of any sort. He could not afford to attract attention.

Rubbing his right arm, he grimaced. The crack in the mirror had gotten longer since he had last used it to enter The Borderlands. Children did not seem affected by the change, but adults found it painful. He remembered the turning thirteen sun cycles ago when he had escaped the PPP. The crack had only reached the center of the mirror. Attempts by his pursuers to follow him had caused the crack to continue its diagonal journey across the surface. Mira's skill had held the mirror together and saved his life.

The idea of the Peoples Plan Protectors, appointed zealots whose purpose was to seek those Idronattians who did not adhere to *The Plan*, made him shudder.

They had created five levels of correction for those pinpointed as offenders. Each level had its own building. Lawbreakers sent to Tower Five were never seen again. He had barely escaped incarceration in Tower Four. Now he was once again making his way to the city that had almost deprived him of his freedom.

The importance of his task forced him to abandon his fears as he headed up the rickety staircase in *Antiques by Q*. In the dusty hallway, he stopped to get his bearings. A deep rumbling purr alerted him to Majeska darting toward him. Smiling, he picked her up.

"So, you're still hanging out here, are ya?" He rubbed the underside of her chin as he walked toward the front of the store. A noise down the hallway made her wiggle and jump from his arms. On silent paws, she faded into the darkness.

The old man who kept track of the mirror limped into the hall, smoothing a green vest over his round belly. "Who's there?" He squinted over his wire-rimmed spectacles.

"Nice vest, Dom." Allynae moved from the shadows.

Dom looked surprised. "What's brought you out of Myrrh? You know the PPP still has you on the Watch List."

"I know. I wouldn't be here if it weren't urgent."

Dom pointed toward the small hidden door. "I thought the gateways to Myrrh had been closed. I got a message from Mira via Majeska. What's up? Are the young people involved?"

"They are. And the less you know, the safer you'll be." They moved toward the front of the shoppe. "If a quick exit is necessary, will the mirror be here?"

"As long as the gateway remains locked, the mirror will stay where it is. If the portal opens, the mirror may move, and Majeska will be your guide."

After searching through several drawers in his office desk, the older man handed Allynae a PPP ID Card.

Allynae read the bold print out loud. "Jonn Menalow 275770, Type B." After committing the information to memory, he shoved the card in his uniform pocket.

Dom removed his specs, rubbed a lens clean on his vest, and returned them to his nose. "Don't forget to use the ID to enter and exit every place you visit. Where are you headed first?"

Allynae paused, his hand on the front doorknob. "What do you know about SparrowLyn AsTar?"

The old man peered at him over the top of his spectacles. "She's one of Idronatti's most prominent artists. *And* she's on the PPP Watch List. Do you know why?"

Allynae ignored the question. "How do I find her?"

Dom hesitated so long that Allynae began to wonder whether he would get an answer. "I believe she lives on the Avenue of Trees around One Eighty-Seventh Street."

"Is the portal between The Borderlands and Idronatti still operational?"

"As far as I know, yes."

"I'm off then. Thanks, Dom. Take care and stay out of sight." Sidestepping out the door of *Antiques by Q,* he slipped away into the dim morning light.

"I'm not the one who needs to take care." Dom stared after him, his eyes narrowed. "It's not me who's got a price on his head."

In his office, he found Majeska curled up on a pile of papers. Absently, he traced the arc of her back and tipped her small chin up. "Allynae's headed for trouble, my friend. You'd better go with him."

Majeska stretched out to her full length and sent papers flying in all directions. With effortless grace, she jumped to the floor and padded soundlessly to the front door. He opened it a crack. She meowed and disappeared, like smoke in the wind, after the man from Myrrh.

19

Brie, astride Tam for the second time, gripped the pony's mane and fixed her attention on their descent down a steep incline.

A fallen tree had forced them up the side of a hill. Now, rocks and small twigs scattered beneath their feet and cascaded ahead of them as they slipped and skidded their way back to the path.

Once more on the level ground, she heaved a sigh and allowed the warmth of the sun and the rhythm of Tam's gait to lull her into a dreamlike state. A series of images formed and melted away—Ari, Torgin, Buster, and Tam gathering around her on a narrow trail; strange creatures with golden eyes chasing them into the dark trees; rocks and hanging branches blocking their way—

"Brie?" The voice sounded distant. Someone shook her.

The rising tide of her dreams fought her desire to surface. Another shake. Her eyes blinked open. Ari and Torgin stood beside Tam, their worried gazes fixed on her.

"Are you alright?" Ari's question held a trace of alarm. "We've been trying to get your attention."

"Tam stopped and refused to move, Brie." Torgin rested a shaking hand on the pony's neck, his expression uneasy.

Still disoriented, she brushed a hand across her forehead. "I must've fallen asleep. I dreamt something followed us and forced us to leave the trail. Dark creatures with yellow eyes—" Creeping cold made her skin crawl. "It was awful." She slid down from Tam's back. "Why am I having such strange visions?"

Ari hugged her and held her at arm's length. "It was just a dream, Brie. You're fine, and so are we."

Brie made herself focus on her surroundings. The trees, less dense near this part of the path, allowed patches of blue sky and the light of the summer sun to come through. Delight in the afternoon heat soaking into her cold bones changed to a thrill of fear. The Star of Truth burned a warning. She rotated, exploring the terrain, then shaded her eyes with a hand and searched the sky.

A dark cloud moving their direction blotted out the sun and chilled the land below.

Buster growled. Tam pranced a skittish dance beside them.

Torgin's hands clawed at his throat. His face paled. "It's like the death sh —" The words garbled into gulped breaths.

Brie slipped her hand into Ari's. "Quick, into the trees. And be quiet!"

Torgin gripped Tam's mane, took the lead, and clambered up the hillside. On the ridge above, a grove of evergreen trees beckoned. Cold nipping at his heels drove him toward it. His teeth chattered a distinct counterpoint to his heartbeat. Legs aching and throat dry, he scrabbled into the shaded protection of the trees. The others crowded in after him.

He looked back at the path and froze. Wodash od DerTah, his dank, vapor-filled darkness spilling around him, moved back and forth, sniffing like a hound stalking its prey.

Frustration fueled the death shadow's search along both sides of the trail. He had been positive the children were right below him. Now that he was on the ground, nothing suggested they had ever been there. On one side of the trail, fallen trees formed matchstick patterns down the hillside. No one had passed that way. On the other side, he sensed a faint resonance of a recent presence, but saw nothing to suggest the passage of three children, a pony, and a dog.

Huddled together in the hemlock grove, Brie, Torgin, and Ari released long-held breaths when he disappeared around a bend.

"That was way too close." Torgin's whispered words made them all shiver.

"I wonder why he didn't follow us?" Ari edged closer to Torgin, her voice tense and low. "It was like we hadn't been there. I know we must've left some sort of trail."

Brie, distracted by the beauty of the grove, wandered further into the trees. A deep inhale filled her nostrils with the scents of hemlock and moss and moist earth. The trees stretched skyward. Sunlight filtering through their branches sent shafts of shimmering light to warm her face and splash golden patterns on the mulchy ground.

Drawn forward by something she could not see, she pushed a branch aside and stepped into a small clearing. A gnarled and twisted tree dominating the center bore the aura of antiquity. *It must be older than Myrrh, perhaps even older than time.*

Approaching it, she pressed her hands on the rough bark. The Star of Truth grew warm. Energy pulsed through her palms, filling her body from head to foot. Light cycloned around her until she thought she would spin into it forever. A deep voice whispered her name.

"Brielle. Brielle! Welcome to the Grove of Mehloc, Bearer of the Star of Truth. Stay within these sacred trees, and evil cannot harm you. When it is time to step beyond our branches, take a small twig of hemlock with you. It will protect you on your journey. WeHem holds you in its memory."

The light faded, and the voice softened into silence. Brie backed away from the tree. Wonder, like an unexpected summer shower, washed over her.

"Brielle AsTar, where are you?" The alarm in her sister's voice snatched her back to the present.

"Ari, I'm over here."

A low hemlock branch quivered and moved aside, escorting Ari into the small clearing with Torgin at her heels.

"By the Fathers, Brie, you scared me to—are you alright?"

"I'm not sure." She sank down on the needle-covered ground. "It spoke to me."

"It?" Ari gave her a quizzical look.

"The tree."

"You are kidding." Torgin gaped in disbelief.

"It knew about the Star of Truth, Torg, and said the death shadow couldn't see us because we were in this grove of trees. It's called the Grove of Mehloc, and it's very sacred. We're each to take a sprig of hemlock with us for protection." She reached for Ari's hand and drew her down next to her. "What's happening to me? I feel the earth beneath me breathe, hear trees talk, and dream strange dreams. I'm scared." She gulped a breath. "Really, truly scared."

Her sister's firm hand squeezed hers. "Brie, we're in a magic land. Each of us carries a magic gift, and we're all involved in a magical venture. You're just responding to the magic, that's all."

"So, why aren't you having dreams?"

Ari shrugged. "You've always been more sensitive to things than I am. Are you hurt?"

"No."

"Are any of us hurt?"

Brie shook her head.

"See, there's nothing to be afraid of."

Brie touched the blue pouch at her throat and smiled. Her fear evaporated, and the wonder of the experience returned. She stood up and pulled her twin into an embrace. "Thanks, Arienh."

Her sister returned her hug. "You're welcome."

Brie caught Torgin's eye. Stark fear flashed back at her.

He pivoted and walked away from the clearing, tension in every step he took.

Ari jerked a thumb in his direction. "I bet he wants to go home again."

"You alright, Torgin?" Brie kept her voice calm.

He whipped around. Over-bright green eyes raked their faces. "If it were not for Esán, we would be home and safe. And Wodash would not be hunting us. Why did Esán go with the DiMensioner, anyway?"

Brie walked over to him. "Torgin, you *know* why Esán went with Seyes Nomed."

Torgin's shoulders drooped.

"It's okay to be afraid. Wodash frightens all of us, but we each made our choice to stay in Myrrh." She slipped her arm through his. "What's our next move, Mr. Navigator?"

Her words seemed to nudge his anger into confidence. He scanned the area. "Since Wodash appears to have gone, we had better be going, too. I think we need to stay off the trail, though."

Ari cleared her throat. "I agree. Can your compass lead us another way?" Her respectful tone made Torgin smile.

"We can ask." He withdrew the compass and held it so they could see. "Show us the way to the Dojanacks without using the trail." When the needle stopped spinning, its gold arrow pointed to the far side of the Grove of Mehloc. He let out an audible sigh. "It looks like we can stay within the hemlocks for a while."

With Tam beside them and Buster in the lead, they wandered between the ancient trees, the sound of their footsteps absorbed in the deep layer of hemlock needles carpeting the ground. Too soon, they reached the far side of the grove.

Torgin hesitated. "I hate to leave here."

Buster licked Ari's hand. She scratched his ears and glanced back the way they had come. "It feels so safe, doesn't it?"

"Don't forget to take a sprig of hemlock, and be sure to say thank you." Brie broke a small twig from a gnarled old tree, attached it to Buster's collar, and fastened another to Tam's halter. After she tucked a piece in her pocket, she gave the tree a gentle pat. "Thank you."

Ari and Torgin each broke off a small piece and expressed their gratitude.

Buster loped ahead. Tam whinnied softly. Brie slipped one hand into Ari's and one into Torgin's, and they stepped free of the grove into the afternoon sun.

Esán sat contemplating the fire for some time after Nomed's footsteps faded. *Can I move something with my thoughts?* He looked up and surveyed the subterranean cavern. Wood piled to his right, along with candles and a large container of water, offered possibilities.

He took a breath, focused on a single candle, and attempted to move it. At first, the occasional sound of water dripping or the fire crackling pulled his attention away from his task. Gradually, however, he became more and more engrossed in the candle's molecular makeup. In the instant he understood it, it rolled in his direction. Surprise shattered his concentration. The candle stopped just short of the fire.

He picked it up and held it out to the flames. The wick sprang to life. Astonishment made his hands tremble. *For a moment, I became the candle I hold in my hand.* Awe left him breathless.

A deep, steady inhale calmed his excitement. He turned his attention to the big, emerald-flecked rock Nomed had instructed him to move. With the candle held high, he walked over to inspect it. *It's as tall as I am. Doubt I could even wrap my arms around it. If Nomed thinks I can move this, he must be crazy.* He took a step back and grinned. "But it'll be fun to try."

Eyes squeezed shut, he wrinkled his brow in concentration. His first attempt to teleport the rock failed. He wiped the sweat from his forehead and tried again. It remained undisturbed. A frown of discontent accompanied him back to the campfire. He set the candle down, drank from the water jug, and returned to stand facing the rock.

Grinning, he murmured to himself. "I do love a challenge." He planted both feet on the cavern floor, placed his hands on his hips, and studied the rock with even greater intensity than before. "And I love to succeed." Closing his eyes, he calmed his thoughts and projected his full attention into the stone. Its molecular pattern, fuzzy at first, sharpened. When it felt familiar, he *thought* it across the space.

A gasp bounced from wall to wall. Esán's eyes flew open and flashed from the empty spot where the rock had been to the intriguing white creature who stood revealed by its disappearance.

With his excitement held in check, Esán remained still. After several intense moments, the creature stepped into the fire's warm glow, its pale blue eyes calm and curious.

Esán moved his hand, pointed at himself, and spoke aloud. "Esán." He waited while the echo repeated his name.

The creature touched its white chest. The word *Zugo* flashed across Esán's mind.

He forced a calm he did not feel and responded telepathically. *"Is that your name? Do you understand me?"*

The furry head nodded. *"Your words are like my language, so I understand you."*

"I am a Human, Zugo. I'd like to be friends."

"Me, too. I am a DeoNyte." He shot a nervous glance toward the passage entrance.

"You fear something?"

Light eyes refocused on his face. *"Your companions frighten me. But you do not seem to fear them. Why?"*

"They can do nothing more than kill me. I've already come to terms with dying, and I don't fear it."

"You are very ill, yes?" The creature's telepathic voice filled with compassion.

Esán nodded.

"I am sorry."

Rubbing his bald head, Esán shrugged. *"Let me tell you about my captors. The dark creature is called Wodash. He is a death shadow who thrives on fear. I refuse to feed his lust. Seyes Nomed is more complicated. I know he has some diabolical plan to destroy Myrrh. He wants to involve me, but I won't help him, Zugo. I won't."*

The DeoNyte regarded him for a long moment. *"Will you tell me about the land outside the mountain caverns?"*

"Of course. Will you tell me what lies inside the depths of the Dojanacks and about your people?"

Zugo nodded. A questioning grin spread across his face. *"How did you move that stone?"*

Esán eyed the emerald-flecked rock and looked at his new friend. *"I simply became the stone and thought it across the space."*

"Could you do it again?"

"*I hope so. I don't want Seyes Nomed to know I moved it.*"

Zugo seemed to study him. "*Do you want to stay with the DiMensioner?*"

"*No, but I do not know how to get back to Mira's or how to find my friends.*"

"*Who's Mira?*"

"*The woman who guards the portals of Myrrh and protects the inhabitants of the land.*"

Zugo's eyes widened. "*You mean Almiralyn? She's the Goddess of my people. I've only heard stories of her beauty and her power. You're so privileged to have met her!*"

"*She promised me an adventure, but I never expected this.*" He grew serious. "*Can you help me find a way out of the caverns?*"

"*Yes! But if you're ill, can you travel?*"

"*Since I've been in Myrrh, I've grown much stronger. I think I can manage. If I need to rest, I'll tell you.*"

Esán walked over to the large rock and focused his intention on it. Again, he examined each molecule and each space in between until he knew every minute particle. Then he pictured the spot near Nomed's sleeping alcove where he wanted it to be. When he opened his eyes, it had moved. He faced Zugo. The young DeoNyte stared at him, admiration shining in his enormous pale eyes.

Esán smiled a lopsided smile. "*I couldn't do that until today.*"

Zugo shook his white head. "*Do you need anything before we go?*"

Esán filled his water bottle, fetched the rest of the dried biscuits from the night before, and rejoined his friend. "*Which way?*"

Zugo pointed at the passage leading to the cavern entrance. Esán took one last look at the emerald-flecked stone, then followed him out of the firelight into the blackness.

20

The trees beyond the grove of Mehloc grew close, tall, and forbidding. Torgin urged Tam toward them. She tossed her head and balked. He rested a hand on her back. "Well, Tam, if you refuse to go in there, so do I."

Brie joined him. "Check the compass again."

"Good idea. Maybe I need to change what I am asking for." He pulled it out, squinted, and nodded to himself. "Compass of Ostradio, keeping us off known paths, please show us a safe way to the Dojanacks."

The compass needle spun clockwise for two circles and stopped. Its face dissolved into a picture of a faint trail winding beneath the brush and close-knit trees.

"Don't move, Torg." Ari clasped Brie's hand. "We'll try to find the trail."

With a tingle of misgiving, he watched the twins scurry down a small hill. Ari took the lead. Brie searched the underbrush at the edge of the forest.

She paused, pushed aside several large ferns, and swept away the dried leaves with her foot.

"Over here! I think I found it."

At Brie's call, the picture on the compass faded. Torgin slipped it beneath his shirt, grabbed Tam's reins, and whistled for Buster. "Come on, you two, let's see what they have discovered."

Ari walked up as he arrived beside Brie. "Where's the compass, Torg?"

"The picture disappeared." He patted the hidden gift. "I hope that means Brie found the right spot."

Brie slipped into the gloominess of the forest. When she reemerged, she gave them a relieved smile. "It looks passable. Let's see if Tam will go in now." She gathered the pony's reins and led her down the trail.

Tam showed no fear. Buster dodged ahead, sniffing the mysteries on the forest floor.

Torgin checked the compass one more time. "This is definitely the right trail. If we plan to be free of the woods before dark, we need to go."

Brie sensed her twin's eyes on her back as she ambled along the trail, Tam's reins wrapped around her hand. *Arienh, you are the dearest person in my life along with Mother. I love that as alike as we appear on the outside, we are as different as Myrrh and Idronatti on the inside.* She peered ahead and smiled.

People thought she was timid, but they knew nothing of the quiet courage that often surprised even her. Ari was outgoing, brave, impatient, and given to snap judgments. *We balance each other's weaknesses and strengths.* She glanced back at her impetuous twin. *And I love the fact you trust no one more than you do your "little" sister.*

Absorbing the quiet of the woods, she pondered recent events. *This turning has been full of miracles: dreams, visions, talking trees. Something is changing inside me, something I don't understand. But I know it will alter my life forever.*

More curious than scared, she gave herself permission to become a part of everything around her. She sensed the ground's patient acceptance of their every step and understood the trees' whispered message about three Humans, a pony, and a dog.

Light in the forest dimmed. She examined the canopy and then the scattered patches of fading light on both sides of the path. *The sun can't have set yet.* She pulled Tam to a stop and listened. No birds sang. Not one squirrel or chipmunk stirred. *How strange.*

Torgin joined her and slipped a hand into hers. "I hope we don't have to spend the night in here. There's nowhere to set up camp." He bit his bottom lip. "I bet it gets really dark."

A sharp bark made them both jump. Tam twitched her tail and tossed her head. Torgin's grip tightened. Ari rushed to her side. Brie's fingers closed around the Stone of Remembering as the Star of Truth sent a sharp pain up her neck. Teeth bared, Buster continued a low warning growl.

"Do you feel that?" Brie kept her voice hushed.

"What?" Torgin still clung to her hand.

Ari's gaze darted along the trail and back to her face. "What is it, Brie?"

"Something has changed in Myrrh. I don't know what, but it's in the ground and in the air we're breathing. Even the trees have grown silent. They seem to be listening for something just as we are."

Ari grabbed Tam's reins and handed them to Torgin. "We'd better keep moving. The faster we reach the opposite side of the woods, the better."

"For once, Ari, we agree." Torgin matched his stride to hers and pulled Tam after them along the trail. Buster ran ahead, his nose sniffing the air, the narrow trail, and the roots of the trees.

Brie remained stationary. She peered behind her and then turned back to stare ahead. *Nothing seems amiss. But nothing seems right either. What is happening in Myrrh?*

S eyes Nomed flew west with the Pentharian. They soared over the gleaming crystal Mountain of Niar through the Esor Trazuq Canyon and across Timreh Pass. Focused on dual goals—finding Mira and destroying her domain—he ignored the breathtaking beauty below. With uninterrupted rhythm and unbroken silence, they raced toward the Terces Wood.

Far ahead, his owl-sharp eyes spotted two birds, one black and one white, flying above the forest canopy. Light shimmered around them, then dissipated into a trail of fading brightness. *Have I found my prey?* As he drew nearer to the tall trees, Wodash od DerTah rose to meet him.

"The children were under me one moment and gone the next." He flew beside his master.

"Where were they?" Nomed's owl eyes gleamed.

"Between here and Nemttachenn."

Seyes Nomed glanced ahead. Side by side, the two birds descended into the forest, heading toward the tower. Realization ripped through him. *"Show me where you last felt the presence of the children."*

Wodash raced above the trees. Their darkness soaking everything below them, Seyes Nomed and the Pentharian streaked after him. *What a coup to be waiting with the children already in my power when Mira and her raven arrive.* The potential triumph of the moment thrummed in his veins. If he could have rubbed his hands together in glee, he would have done so.

"Faster, Wodash! Faster!"

The death shadow increased his speed and then swooped over a path. *"This is where I saw them."*

Seyes Nomed signaled his followers to land. Snarling and snuffling the air, the Pentharian touched down. A shudder-like quake rumbled through the ground beneath them and rolled across Myrrh.

Nomed placed an image of the children in their minds. "Spread out. When you find them, summon me at once. Do them no harm. They will be our bait!"

Panther and hyena moved to the right, snake and wild boar to the left, and a vulture rose in the air, circling high above the hemlock grove.

Almiralyn and Karrew swooped down through the canopy of the Terces Wood. Deep in the forest, they came to a three-crotched birch standing at the center of a large swamp and took refuge high in its branches.

"What was that in the sky?" Karrew ruffled his blue-black feathers. *"I've experienced nothing like it!"*

Almiralyn cocked her white head to one side, her sapphire eyes alert and gleaming. *"Seyes Nomed has breached the gates and brought aliens into Myrrh."*

Karrew heard the foreboding in her words. *"What is it?"*

"Pentharian hunters. They are part Human and part Reptilian in their truest form, but they shape shift into whatever serves their needs. We must find the children. This has become a serious game."

Almiralyn took flight. Karrew shot after her, his mind racing. Pentharian hunters were known for their cunning and their ability to catch their prey. They were always successful, always deadly. *What are they doing in Myrrh?* A chill ran through his body. It had been a long time since he had accompanied his mistress into battle. He was about to do so again.

Karrew knew she cast her senses like a fisherman's net throughout the Terces Wood in search of the children. To the Northeast, he detected a ripple in the calm of her land. Myrrh cringed beneath them.

"The Pentharian landed!" Almiralyn's urgent telepathic message stunned him.

Closing the gap between them, he felt her search increase in intensity. Her focus sharpened as she located her objective and shot deeper into the forest. Sensing her relief at finding the children, he felt her anger dissipate and her attention refocus on her primary goal: protect the children at all costs.

21

As Myrrh shuddered with the coming of evil, Elcaro's Eye boiled up in the center and spewed frothy geysers into the air. Cascading back into the alabaster bowl, the water beat against the curved sides like waves in a hurricane. For a few moments, as in a storm's eye, the water stilled. In rapid succession, images flickered across the surface—a dark cloud passing over the land, small animals scurrying to safety, birds landing, silent and watchful.

More images flared and disappeared—Myrrhinians wringing their hands in despair; farmers scanning the sky to see what blocked the sun; children crying out in terror, their faces hidden in the skirts of their mothers; Wood Tiffs clinging to each other in their TreeOms in the Terces Wood. The fountain roiled with the fear in their hearts.

The figure of Allynae bubbled to the surface and focused. He ceased his long strides through the city of Idronatti, his hand on his aching heart. Majeska growled low in her throat and moved closer to the man from

Myrrh. In the Central Mountains, Esán's Aunt Merrilea froze with a cup of tea midway to her mouth.

And in The Borderlands, Dom opened the hidden door in Antiques by Q and descended the stairs to the basement. He recited the sacred words Almiralyn had given him for emergencies, stepped up to the mirror, and disappeared. The water settled into an uneasy calm.

Nomed could hardly contain his impatience as five dark Pentharian forms melted into the trees in search of the children. *Success is almost within my grasp.* He flashed Wodash a crooked smile. The scar pulled taut, a constant reminder of his reason for revenge. "It's time to find the Guardian of Myrrh."

"As you wish, Master." The death shadow bowed his ugly head and lifted his bulk into the air.

Nomed embraced his owl form and, streaking skyward, flew in ever-widening circles above the Terces Wood. His highly developed senses picked out the Pentharian and, in the distance, the children. But he could find no trace of Almiralyn or the raven, Karrew.

A rabid desire to achieve his goal urged him to fly faster. Only sun cycles of disciplined training enabled him to maintain his concentration. He flew lower and lower until he discovered lingering traces of the raven's recent presence. With a sense of purpose rather than urgency, he allowed Karrew's trail to pull him down through the forest canopy. Landing on the branch of the big birch tree where Almiralyn and Karrew had rested, he swiveled his owl's head to one side and then the other. Hazel eyes gleaming, he materialized in Human form on the ground next to his henchman.

"Wodash, fly back to the Dojanacks and bring Esán to me at once. I want him to see my power, yours, and that of the Pentharian."

The death shadow disappeared into the approaching night.

Paisley paused at the edge of the grasslands, narrowed eyes scanning its width and breadth. His peaceful journey through the forest ended with the shudder that announced more evil had found its way into Myrrh.

A shrug loosed his pack from his shoulders. He sank to the ground, his back against a tree, and watched the sun's fiery descent splash color across the western sky. The mountains soaked up the last of the turning's light like colorful sponges; red, salmon, rose, and glowing crystal stood majestic and tall, draped in the sunset's glory.

He sighed. *Is Allynae safe? Has Almiralyn found the children?* He could only hope for the best.

An ominous shadow flying toward the mountains sent a shiver of foreboding down his spine. *What is that?* He stood up, brushing stray grass and leaves from his pants. *At least it's flying away from me.*

He grabbed his pack and withdrew a mottled green cape. Once his backpack was in place, he draped its folds around his shoulders and stepped into the grasslands. He planned to travel at least halfway across before stopping for the night. Dusk and his cape hid him from sight as he stretched long legs in an easy stride, carrying him closer to the mountains and, he hoped, to the hermit.

An intimate knowledge of the terrain allowed his thoughts to drift through the events of the past two turnings and to explore his options for finding the man at Timreh Pass. His stomach growled. Refusing to yield to its demand for food, he tightened his belt and continued his journey.

Torgin couldn't remember when he had been more tired. He felt his control slipping as light leaked from between trees, one ray at a time. Further up the trail, night wrapped its gloominess around the twins, leaching the copper luster from their curls. They moved closer together. Tam's bouncy trot slowed to a walk, and Buster ceased his sniffing to stay close beside Ari. Torgin's toe hit an exposed root. Muttering under his breath, he caught Ari's eye. "What should we do? We don't want to wander off the trail in the dark."

"Hold on. I'll try to find a light." Ari rummaged around in the saddlebag closest to her. "Ah ha. These saddlebags are amazing." She withdrew a glowing, slender stick about length of her hand, wrist to fingertip, and gave it to Brie. "What do you make of this?"

"I've never seen anything like it. Have you, Torg?"

Savoring the light's positive effects on his fear, he peered over her shoulder. "I don't know what it is, but I'm sure glad Ari found it. Is there another one?"

Ari moved around Tam and searched the other saddlebag. "Here's one more. So what will it be? Do we stay here or keep going?"

"I vote for here and rest." Torgin surveyed the area. "It is flat and—"

The forest floor quaked. Around them, the trees trembled and grew as still as death.

Brie's gaze darted from one tree to the next. "What was that?"

Ari frowned. "I don't know, but I don't think we want to attract whatever caused it." Ari shook her light. "Do these lights turn off?"

Brie held hers up in front of her. It went out and came back on.

"What did you do?" Torgin's curious gaze darted from her to the slender light.

"I thought it off, then on. Here. Try it, Torgin."

He took it and concentrated. The lite-stick grew dark and then sprang back to life. A sigh of relief escaped his lips. "I wasn't sure I could do it."

Brie drew him into a huddle with Ari. "Something is wrong in the forest. The trees are spreading the word strange creatures have entered the Terces Wood—creatures that are sending evil to the very roots of Myrrh. We have to hide."

"Where?" Torgin looked around frantically.

Brie's hand on his arm calmed his fear. "Torgin, Almiralyn told you the compass holds the secrets of Myrrh. Use it to find a hiding place."

Handing her the lite-stick, he fumbled with the thong around his neck, withdrew the compass, and with trembling hands held it out. "Show us a safe place to hide."

The compass needle spun until the picture of a staircase leading beneath the forest floor appeared.

"How do we find *the* staircase?" Anxiety clipped his words short.

Brie shielded the lite-stick inside her jacket and nodded her approval when Ari did the same. "Come on. We can't stay on the trail."

With instinct as her guide, she stepped over big roots, pushed aside low-hanging branches, and led the way through the thick underbrush. Torgin grunted and lurched into her. She stumbled and glanced back. Her heart leapt into her throat. Behind Buster and Tam, a pair of molten-gold eyes moved toward them through the darkness. Her eyes flashed to her twin's face. As one, they extinguished the lite-sticks and shoved them in their pockets.

Ari grabbed Torgin's hand. "Go, Brie!"

"What's the—"

"There's something stalking us, Torg." Brie projected a sharp whisper over her shoulder. "Quiet!"

Behind a tall Tirips tree, she discovered a large hollow space at the base of its trunk. It was deep enough for all three of them and Buster to huddle inside.

"I can't go in there." Torgin folded his arms.

"Sure you can." Ari pushed him ahead of her.

Brie shoved Buster in after Ari. Before she followed, she saw Tam disappear into the night, a decoy she hoped would fool whatever was on their trail. She squeezed in beside a quiet Buster. Not one growl or bark disturbed the silence gripping the Terces Wood.

Almiralyn sensed the children's presence nearby. The Pentharian were closing in fast. Somewhere above her, Seyes Nomed narrowed the distance between them. *If only, I could consult Elcaro's Eye.* She frowned. *There's no time.*

Since she realized she dared not confront the Pentharian or the DiMensioner before getting the children to safety, she left Karrew concealed high above her and perched on a low branch close to the children's hiding place. The silent approach of two Pentharian sent her to the ground in Human form at the foot of the children's tree. To her surprise, she found it filled with protective magic. With no time to discover its source or to move her charges, she placed them under a spell of silence.

Pressed against the trunk, she transformed her body into tree bark, camouflaging the hollow center and hiding the children. Moments later, a Pentharian panther and a hyena rounded the Tirips tree.

Karrew watched the two Pentharian shift to their Human-Reptilian shape—one blue, one green—and shivered. Two vultures dropped through the trees near his hiding place and landed in their true form, adding the glow of red and orange to the grouping below.

Silent as the moonlight glistening on the jewel-colored scales of their lizard-like tails and legs, Karrew flew to a lower branch. Another shiver ruffled his feathers as their lidless golden eyes scrutinized the area. They would miss nothing.

From his new vantage point, he did his own scrutinizing—human-like faces tattooed with their birth clans' symbol, thin-lipped red mouths each boasting at least one gold ring, and narrow aquiline noses pierced with carved stone loops made him shiver. On either side of their Humanesque skulls, pointed ears covered with gold and silver rings that ran from their tips down to their gem-encrusted lobes twitched.

The blue Pentharian emerged from the shadows and made a slow turn. Multiple braids the color of his sapphire scales cascaded over broad shoulders and onto his tanned, muscular chest, where more tattoos depicted his bloodline and heritage. Miniature scales slithered down his spine like tiny drops of iridescent light and widened onto his low back and long tail. A grinding, guttural sound brought his comrades to his side.

Karrew withdrew further into the foliage, his evolved sense of smell recoiling at the stench of swamp water emanating from the creatures below him. He marveled at their beautiful colors and their aura of predatory ease. Although Pentharian rarely killed in their natural form, he remained motionless. *How had such alien beings come to Myrrh?*

A whinny echoed in the distance. The Pentharian shifted. Four panthers sprinted toward the sound.

As soon as they were out of sight, Almiralyn shucked her tree bark shell. Karrew flew to her outstretched arm.

"I will see to the children, Karrew, and alert Tibin to aid and protect them. Can you shield Tam from the Pentharian?"

"Of course."

"Then go. She will be terrified and for good reason!"

On swift wings, he followed the smell of the swamps of ReTaw au Qa, home planet of Myrrh's invaders

The children looked mystified when Almiralyn appeared at the hollow tree's opening. Buster sniffed and exited, his tail wagging. The wide-eyed twins followed, arms wrapped around each other's waist. Torgin peeked out, his face a portrait of disbelief.

Ari opened her mouth to comment.

Almiralyn shook her head and gathered them close. "I must go, or Seyes Nomed and Wodash will find us all. Tibin, the Wood Tiff, will be here soon to lead you to safety. Until then, stay hidden and quiet. Do you understand?"

The children nodded.

"Take care of each other." Like mist in the wind, she vanished.

Tibin, the Wood Tiff, hurried along the hall to answer the insistent knock at his door. He pulled it ajar and stifled a gasp of surprise. Almiralyn waited outside his TreeOm. Bowing, he opened the door wider and stepped aside. "My, my. Ahhh, welcome to my home."

The Guardian ducked her head to enter, then straightened. "I wish this were a social call, Tibin, but I'm here on a matter of the greatest urgency. We have a most serious problem in Myrrh."

"Does it have to do with the quake that ran through the Terces Wood a short time ago?" He struggled to control his concern.

"You are aware of the Pentharian?"

"Pentharian? In Myrrh?" His head bobbed like a cork in a river. "I've heard tales of their notorious hunt—oh dear. Are they here with the DiMensioner?"

Almiralyn's beautiful eyes narrowed. "Seyes Nomed has summoned them to destroy the peace in Myrrh. And my young guests are in grave danger."

"The children I met in the clearing?"

"Yes."

The seriousness in that simple word almost undid him. He hesitated, then gulped. "Does this mean the Terces Wood and the grasslands are in danger?"

"It may mean Myrrh and Thera could cease to exist. I need you to warn the Wood Tiffs and other tiny folk of the forest. But first I need you to hide the children."

A hand went to his throat. He swallowed and nodded. "It will be safe to have them stay here, at least for the night. Where are they?"

"The twins and Torgin are in the hollowed Tirips tree. Will you bring them back through the Intersect?" She ducked out into the night.

"It's the quickest way. I'll leave now. What about..." He frowned. "The bald boy?" He grabbed his hat and prepared to follow.

"Esán is already the DiMensioner's prisoner. We will deal with his rescue. Thank you, Tibin. I knew I could count on you." She ducked out into the night and departed with soft flutter of her white wings.

Honored to serve but quaking with fright, he slipped down through the branches of his TreeOm and scurried off through the woods, the three children's safety his primary goal.

I n vulture form Yaro, the Pentharian, wrapped sharp talons around the branch of a dead oak near the hollow Tirips tree. Piercing raptor eyes searched the small clearing at its base. Although he saw nothing in the deepening night, he *knew* the children were there—he knew, and he waited.

22

In her apartment on the Avenue of Trees, SparrowLyn's chair crashed to the floor behind her. The painting on her easel depicted three children, a pony, and a dog, huddled together in a dark forest. Two lite-sticks illuminated their faces and highlighted the menacing creatures creeping toward them.

The brush in her limp hand dripped black blobs onto the polished studio floor. Tearing her eyes away from the painting, she gasped as the puddles shifted to form a panther and a hyena, a snake, a boar, and a vulture. Her world flipped upside down. *My daughters are in grave danger and need my help.* Her hand clasped a small gold locket hidden beneath her blue uniform. *I must go to Myrrh at once and find—*

A ringing bell startled her from frantic thoughts. It rang a second time and an insistent third. She hurried down the hallway. *How on Thera did someone slip past the doorman?* She pressed the switch on the V-Viewer and, in two quick movements, opened the door and pulled her visitor inside.

The tall man, a tentative smile on his clean-shaven face, closed the door and waited.

"Allynae!" She rushed into his outstretched arms, her tears soaking his uniform where her head rested on his shoulder. "How did you know I needed you?"

He stroked her hair. "I didn't until a short time ago when my heart turned cold. Mira sent me to bring you to Myrrh. Four children are in danger, and she thinks you can help."

Sparrow examined his face. Almost fourteen sun cycles had passed, yet her love for him was as strong as ever. She took his hand and led him to her studio.

"Look." She pointed at her latest creation.

He studied the large painting, then scanned the room as though searching for something and stopped, riveted to the silhouettes on the floor. In one deft motion, he grabbed a cloth hanging on the easel and erased the Pentharian images. Their malevolent power dissipated. Her tension eased.

He drew her back into his arms. "How did you know?"

"I see things. All morning these images have been coming to me. At first, they didn't concern me, but when those creatures leaked from my brush onto the floor, I realized this painting was about destroying Myrrh. And our daughters are there, right in the middle of everything." Sparrow's hand flew to her mouth.

Allynae held her at arm's length. The cloudy blue eyes she loved so much bored into hers. "What did you say?"

"Oh, Alli, I wanted to tell you, but I was afraid you would come back to Idronatti. I couldn't take the chance." Her hands clasped over her heart, she tried to explain. "The PPP would have found you, and I would never have forgiven myself." Her voice shook. "Alli, please don't be angry. I never meant to hurt you, only to keep you and our daughters safe."

He took her hands in his. "How could I have not known?" The pain of loss soaked his craggy features. "I'm not angry, just sad not to have been a part of your lives."

He kissed her. The lost time melted away. She felt young and alive and in love again. Her heart skipped a beat. *Not again—still.*

"Does Mira know?" He gazed down at her with tear misted eyes.

"I'm not sure." A tear slipped down her cheek.

He cupped her face in his callused hand. "Will you come back with me? It'll be dangerous for both of us."

"Of course. When do we leave?"

"We have to find Esán's aunt before we return to Myrrh. She lives in SumnerTyme in the Central Mountains."

"Who's Esán?"

He pointed at a painting, where a bald boy rode on the back of a black and silver owl.

Her breath caught in her throat. "You mean he's real?"

Allynae leaned forward, pointing to a man in a silver-lined black cape. "And so is he. I'm almost certain this is the DiMensioner called Seyes Nomed." His finger touched the scar she'd painted on his right cheek.

He gathered her into his arms again. The love she had yearned for flowed from him to fill her heart.

"I've missed you every turning of my life." The breath in his words ruffled her hair.

She touched his cheek and traced the line of his jaw with a forefinger. Shaking her chestnut curls back from her face, she moved from his embrace. "You must get back to Myrrh, Alli. Mira needs you, and so do Brie and Ari. I'll go to SumnerTyme and find Esán's aunt."

"I can't let you—"

Sparrow placed a finger on his lips. "I'll be safer if I go alone. What's Merrilea's family name?"

"I don't know, but she's the town's midwife and nurse."

"I'll find her. Go back to Myrrh and save our daughters." She edged him toward the hall.

He lingered for a moment. His arms encircled her again. "I love you, SparrowLyn."

She tensed and looked back across the studio.

"What's wrong?"

"Several times today, I've sensed someone watching me. It's the strangest feeling."

Allynae's eyes narrowed. "It's probably your imagination." His lack of conviction mimicked hers.

Sparrow held him a moment longer. With reluctance, she slipped from the warm protection of his arms. "Be careful. I don't want to lose you again."

He brushed her lips with his. Like a sigh, he was gone; the door closing softly behind him.

At Mira's cottage, Dom entered her private sanctuary and crossed the room to the alabaster fountain. On the water's smooth surface, he observed Sparrow's hand fly to her mouth and noted the surprise on Allynae's face when he realized he was a father. He eavesdropped on the plans for Sparrow's trip to SumnerTyme and Allynae's return to Myrrh.

Curiosity made him lean forward to get a better look at Sparrow's painting. The twins' mother turned and stared straight into his eyes. He jumped back. Not moving a muscle, he waited as Allynae kissed her and slipped out through the door.

Dom smiled to himself. *Hmmm. So that's the lay of the land.*

Downstairs in the blue and white kitchen, he rummaged around in Mira's cupboards until he found a small pack. When he had filled it with food and a canteen of water, he limped his way to the barn, where he found several horses. He led a coal black stallion to the tack room and threw a saddle on his back. After a final glance around, he mounted and rode toward the Terces Wood.

In Mira's sanctuary, the alabaster woman locked her gaze onto Dom's image, capturing it in the cool, clear memory of her waters.

Allynae's measured gait carried him down the hall in Sparrow's apartment building. Apprehension and concern for his daughters pressed him to hurry. He slipped through the service door and jogged down the stairs. On the second-floor landing, a stranger blocked his way.

"Your identification." He held out a hand, his gaze riveted to Allynae's face.

Allynae plastered on a pleasant smile to cover his dismay, pulled out the ID card Dom had provided, and handed it over.

"Jonn Menalow? What is your ID number?" The crisp command held a hint of suspicion.

"Number 275770, Type B."

"Where are you from?"

"I live in Domlenah Brown in the Redart Apartments."

"What are you doing here?" The third degree continued.

"Checking a duct on the tenth floor. Were you the person who sent the request order?"

The man frowned. "Follow me." He turned and led Allynae down to the first floor.

Fight or flight responses surged through Allynae's body. He wanted to run. *Steady, boy. An opportunity will present itself. Just stay calm.*

At an office marked "Overseer," the man paused and knocked. A muffled voice bid him enter. He motioned Allynae toward a chair next to the door. "Have a seat, while I speak to the boss."

Forcing a relaxed appearance, Allynae sat down. The door snapped shut, leaving him alone in the hall. *What made the man suspect me?* The thing that came to mind was his fake ID.

A quick glance at the office door and he dodged out of the apartment building and down the Avenue of Trees. With his harried gaze focused straight ahead, he put as much distance as possible between the apartment building and himself. When he dodged into an alley or pass through, he sprinted. On the major streets, he adopted the unhurried walk of a citizen of the city. At a RiaTrain station several blocks from Sparrow's, he followed a sedate Idronattian down the polished steps.

Since he no longer had an ID, he waited for an opportunity to slip unobserved through the People Scan. *I'll have time on the train to decide the best way back to Myrrh.* He shoved his growing impatience away and surveyed the area.

A group of blue-clad children marched in proper Idronatti fashion down the stairs and stopped beside him just as the train arrived. Enclosed within their ranks, he passed through the scan. One calculated sidestep placed him on the platform with a group of workmen in brown overalls, his heart pulsing in his throat.

The doors slid open. Surrounded by a crowd of uniformed workers, he boarded the train. *I'm trapped.* Panic burned in his belly. His survival instincts urged him to keep moving. Logic and reason held him still.

Careful not to touch the clear poles monitoring the passengers, he sank down onto a hard bench and forced himself to look straight ahead with vacant, staring eyes. At the third stop, he exited the train and crossed to the opposite side of the pristine platform. *They won't expect me to go back uptown.*

Two PPP patrollers scanned the crowd. Without missing a step, he turned and walked in measured Idronatti cadence back the way he had come. Not far ahead, a cat the color of smoke caught his attention. *Majeska?* Amethyst eyes blinked.

Without waiting, she darted into a dark space between two walls. He moseyed after her. Pitch-black nothingness smelling of rotting trash and raw sewage assailed him. He smothered a choked cough. *So much for the immaculate cleanliness of Idronatti.*

As his eyes adjusted to the dim light, he picked out Mira's cat silhouetted against the dingy white wall. She flickered her tail and, with feline grace, led him down one tunnel after the other. Time ceased to exist. Majeska never faltered. Whatever served as her guide, he trusted it implicitly.

23

SparrowLyn closed the door behind the man she loved. *Did the PPP see you enter my apartment, Alli?*

Urgency propelled her down the hall to her bedroom, where she packed a People's carry bag with a change of clothing. In the kitchen, she tossed a ripe quwee and a container of water on top of her things. *What if they catch him?* She hurried back to the studio and added paints, brushes, and a sketchbook to her bag. After she cleaned up the remains of the black paint on the floor, she faced her paintings to the wall. *I can't be too careful. The PPP will be watching. What if...* She shoved aside her fears. They would only cloud her thinking.

With practiced efficiency, she tucked her hair under her uniform cap and stepped in front of the mirror. A quick pinch brought some color to her pale cheeks. Her light-filtering glasses hid the strain at the back of her eyes. The mirror assured her she looked less frazzled.

One last check of her carry bag and she opened the apartment door. A fist poised to knock brought her up short. "Henrietta, what are you—"

Her elusive neighbor shook her head and pointed at her door across the hall.

Sparrow frowned. "I don't..." Stopped again by a warning in Henrietta's expression, she mouthed the word "what?"

The older woman toddled to her apartment and pushed the door wider.

Torn between her need to leave and an overwhelming feeling the woman might have something important to share, Sparrow followed.

Henrietta closed the door, led her into a small, cool room, and sank onto a pale blue chaise. Brows raised, she patted a place beside her.

Sparrow's mind screamed, "Go!" Her heart said, "Sit down."

Henrietta leaned close and spoke in a whisper. "The PPP stopped your visitor, the tall man, and took him to the Overseer's office."

Every muscle in Sparrow's body tensed.

"It's alright, deary. He got away, at least for now. A gray cat followed him." She tilted her head. "Do you know that cat?" Not waiting for an answer, she hurried on. "We'll need her help."

Sparrow removed her glasses and examined her elderly neighbor. "Who *are* you? How do you know all of this?"

Satisfaction flittered across Henrietta's face. "Ah yes. Majeska is her name. She's our guide to Myrrh." Her brow creased in thought. "Although, I believe all the gateways may be closed. Did the tall man tell you the Key to open them?"

Sparrow shook her head. "Who—"

"Let me see." Henrietta tapped her chin. "I used to know the Key." She shrugged. "Oh well, I'll remember it. Now, deary, we must go."

Sparrow put her hand on Henrietta's. "Please, tell me who you are and how you know about Myrrh."

Henrietta's violet eyes blinked. "I came from there, deary."

"You came—"

"I came to Idronatti when you moved here to your apartment. Almiralyn asked me to watch over you and the twins."

"Almiralyn asked you—"

"Sparrow, we have little time." Henrietta spoke as though she were talking to a child. "I'll be happy to answer your questions later."

"What do you mean, *we*? I'm going to the Central Mountains." She gave her reclusive neighbor a long, hard look. "You can't travel all that way."

Henrietta raised her eyebrows. "You'd be surprised what I can do, deary. Now listen. The Overseer suspects the tall man came to see you. You and I will leave together. You have been with me all morning. Did you clean up your studio? Do you have your special artist's pass?"

Sparrow gave a nervous laugh. "Okay. I give up. Yes, I cleaned the studio. And I have my pass in my carry bag."

Henrietta teetered across the room and paused by the door, her gaze fixed on her guest's face. "What else did you pack?"

Sparrow gave her a list of her bag's contents.

"Good girl, you did what I would have done myself. Wait here. I'll hurry."

Sparrow sat, trying to make sense of the conversation. *Almiralyn knew about the twins from the beginning. All these sun cycles she's been watching over the three of us.*

Henrietta returned with a carry bag over one arm. On her head rested a straw hat decorated with bright purple flowers that deepened the violet of her eyes. *The Plan* allowed women to wear hats after sixty.

"Henrietta, what a pretty hat. Now, tell me where we're going."

"On a trip to the Central Mountains. Never lie, Sparrow, when you can tell the truth. Since we know we're under surveillance, let's be as honest as possible."

The women walked down the hallway to the Drop Car. Neither spoke while they waited. When the car arrived, they got in. Whoosh! They arrived on the first floor and the doors slid open.

Sparrow's heart jumped into her throat.

"Come with me." A stern young PPP patrolman prepared to lead them to the Overseer's office.

"We have an Onom Lira to catch, young man, so please make this quick." Henrietta's purple flowers bounced as she accompanied him across the foyer to where the building overseer waited.

Sparrow followed, her mind overflowing with questions,

The Overseer ushered them into the office and took a seat behind his desk. "Sit." He pointed to the straight-backed chairs opposite him. "Where are you going?"

Henrietta folded her hands in her lap. "SparrowLyn is accompanying me on a trip to the Central Mountains. My best friend is ill, and I will spend as much time with her as possible. While we visit Sparrow plans to do some painting. She's a famous artist, you know."

Both men listened to Henrietta, but their eyes bored into Sparrow. She did her best to remain relaxed and smiling.

The patrolman leaned in, his nose almost touching hers. "You had a visitor earlier today. What was his name?"

Sparrow forced a puzzled expression. "I've been with Henrietta all morning. If anyone stopped by, they missed me."

"Are you positive you were with her *all* morning?" The patroller's hot breath tickled her cheeks.

Henrietta made a strangled sound. "Do you think she's daft? Of course, she was with me. Look." She pulled a small canvas from her bag. "This is the painting she helped me do for my friend. Isn't it lovely?" Henrietta held up a picture of two yellow flowers in a blue vase. "Now, are you finished? We do *not* want to miss our Onom Lira."

The patrolman straightened. "Well, ah..."

The Overseer reached across the desk. "Your travel papers, Miss AsTar."

She withdrew her pass from her carry bag. "I have a special pass."

He snatched it from her hand and shifted his attention to Henrietta. "And you?"

Feigning confusion, the elderly woman rummaged in her bag. "Ah, yes." She pulled out an official-looking envelope and held it a moment before handing it over.

Sparrow glanced at it and smiled. The paperwork bore today's date.

The Overseer's eyes glinted with anger as he stood up. "Where are your daughters?"

"They're with a friend."

"Who is this friend?" His anger sparked in glaring dark eyes.

Henrietta rose, her gaze fixed on his face. "Enough is enough, Overseer Tilt. I don't know what you suspect, but you have the wrong people." She shifted her attention to the patrolman. "If you don't let us go now, I'll place a call to Major Jordett. He'll straighten this out."

The patrolman blanched and returned their papers. "That won't be necessary." He cut in front of the Overseer and escorted the ladies to the door. "We apologize for the inconvenience."

Purple flowers bobbing, Henrietta led Sparrow from the office and through the double doors to the street. A shiny white Ria Transport floated at the curb. An older man in a brown uniform assisted Henrietta into the back seat. Sparrow slid in next to her.

Henrietta sighed when the driver closed the door. "That was fatiguing."

Sparrow let herself relax. "You were wonderful! Where did you get the painting, and what made you bring it? Who is Major Jordett? And how did you get travel papers stamped with today's date?"

Henrietta patted her carry bag. "I painted it some time ago. I brought it because I knew we would need a reason you spent the morning with me. Major Jordett is my friend's co-worker and the superior of the young patrolmen. The Major, I've heard, is *not* a patient man and is intolerant of errors among his underlings. And the paperwork..." She shrugged.

Sparrow leaned over and kissed her soft, wrinkled cheek. "I can't thank you enough. Do you think they'll follow us?"

"All the way to the Central Mountains, my dear. All the way to the Central Mountains."

They rode in silence while the Ria Transport skimmed above the ground, humming the song of matter cutting through air. Its monotone lulled Sparrow into a dreamy state, and soon she drifted into the memories of Allynae's face, his wonderful warmth as he held her close for the first time in what seemed like an eternity.

Memories of their glorious yet heartbreaking summer together overwhelmed her. The present fell away. Her mind went back, back, back.

Home from the Art Institute for the summer, she helped her mother prepare the mid-turning meal. Uninhibited laughter filled the big, cozy kitchen. It felt so good to be home.

A knock at the back door interrupted their fun.

Gerolyn paused. "Please get that, Sparrow. I can't leave this for even an instant."

Sparrow crossed to their screened porch. A tall, lanky man waited on the back steps. "Is Gerolyn here?"

His voice, deep and pleasant, made a blush rush to her cheeks. "May I tell her who's calling?" Her voice sounded breathless.

"Allynae." His smile lit up eyes that were blue as the summer sky.

"Sparrow, who is it?" Her mother appeared in the doorway behind her. "Allynae! How are you? And how is Mira? Don't just stand there. Come in." She gave him a hug and led him into the kitchen.

Sparrow took a breath and tried to calm her pounding heart. Her mind repeated his name... Allynae. *What is Almiralyn's brother doing here? And why am I acting like a love-sick schoolgirl? I've only just met the man.*

"Sparrow, join us." Her mother's voice, often tinged with sadness, rang with joy.

Setting aside her confusion, Sparrow sat with them at the kitchen table.

"Mira asked me to check on you." His eyes rested for a moment on her face before returning to her mother. "I'm afraid the PPP are looking for me, though, so I need to leave soon."

"The PPP never journeys as far as Singtil. Why don't you stay for a while?" Gerolyn smiled at her life-mate who had appeared in the doorway. "Standin will alert the villagers. They'll warn us if any strangers or patrolmen show up."

"It is good to see you, Allynae." Her father's voice held an eagerness she didn't recognize. "What brings you out of Myrrh?"

"I'm on an errand for Mira."

The conversation faded into background noise. Sparrow realized she was staring at the man's face and lowered her eyes. *It seems so familiar—the nose that looks a bit too large, his eyes and the lines that crinkled around them when he laughs.* She peeked under her lashes. *His dark, unruly hair made her fingers itch to touch it. He laughed again. Even his laugh is...* He caught her eye and smiled. Her heart gave a happy skip.

"Well, that settles it." Her mother nodded and smiled.

Sparrow forced her mind back to the conversation. "Settles what?"

Standin gave her a knowing look. "Where have you been, girl? Allynae agreed to stay for a while."

She gazed out the window of the Ria Transport at the city flying by. That turning long ago, her life had changed forever. She and Allynae talked, walked, and shared life stories. Half a moon cycle later, sitting under a crag that shaded them from the afternoon sun, he brushed the back of her hand with his fingertips, then he jumped to his feet, and pulled her up after him. They ran laughing like children through the blue and yellow flowers dotting the mountain meadow.

Even then, she now believed, they knew they were in love. And so did everyone else. Sparrow's mother, a citizen of Myrrh, had cautioned her. "A relationship with Allynae can only end in sorrow."

Sparrow had refused to listen.

She let herself slide again into the past.

The sun hung in the western sky, ready to begin its downward glide to the horizon, when Allynae pulled her down beside him under an ancient and gnarled Spirit Tree. He leaned over and brushed a soft kiss across her lips.

"I need to tell you something." His voice and face, usually filled with laughter, were solemn.

"You sound so serious." She tried to move into the crook of his arm. Instead, he turned to face her.

"You know I am Almiralyn's brother. What you don't know is that I am from a dimension where longevity isn't measured in sun cycles."

Her heart grew quiet. "How old are you?"

"My age doesn't matter. I've loved you, SparrowLyn, since the turning I arrived. I don't want to lose you, but life with me would not be easy."

She put a finger on his lips. "Sh-h-h." She reached up and kissed the place where her finger had been. "Alli, you are my heart. Nothing will keep me from wanting to be with you."

His arms encircled her. She felt his heart, a chorus in his chest. Hers sang in response. Their kiss sealed their love.

His eyes smiled into hers. "We must be Joined. If you will have me, I will pledge my love to you forever."

"Of course, I'll be Joined to you. But I haven't reached the age of decision. I can't do so without my parents' consent. Mother will never agree, and my father..." Tears spilled down her cheeks.

With the back of his forefinger, he wiped them away. "I met an official a short distance from here who will perform the rite without reporting us." He held her hand and pressed a kiss into its palm. "The man's a romantic. He won't question your age."

She traced a heart on the window. The official had followed the prescribed protocol, wished them well, and then disappeared—to Myrrh, she now supposed. He generated a V-Chip they could file when a favorable opportunity presented itself. The opportunity had never materialized. Her hand moved to the small locket nestling close to her heart on its gold chain, the chip still secreted inside.

Divinely happy with each other, their love grew richer with each sun's turning and each moon cycle. Then, six moon cycles after Allynae had arrived, a friend came to the house. "The PPP are in Singtil. They're looking for Allynae."

She would never forget the last time he held her or the words he spoke for her alone to hear. "I will love you until I no longer have memory or breath. My heart stays with you always." He left without looking back.

Soon after she returned to Idronatti and her training at the Theran Institute of Art, she realized she carried Allynae's child. She told her parents late in the pregnancy. Her palm pressing against the locket trembled.

Henrietta placed a small, wrinkled hand on hers. "Are you alright, deary?"

"I was just caught in a memory." She sighed again.

Henrietta smiled, a knowing twinkle in her eye. "I understand, especially since he just walked into your living room."

"Why did Mira ask you to guard me?"

Henrietta adjusted the angle of her hat. A pensive expression settled over her face. Sparrow wondered whether she might have some sad memories of her own. "Your mother got word to Mira about your pregnancy." The purple flowers caught the light and glowed in the afternoon sun.

So, Mother knows Allynae is the father, and kept his identity a secret. Gratitude filled her heart. Both Almiralyn and the twin's maternal grandmother had protected them.

Henrietta continued. "After painful consideration, Mira chose not to tell Allynae. She realized he would do anything to return to you and his child. After the twins were born and PPP gave you permission to live on the Avenue of Trees, she knew you were being used as bait. They suspected Allynae was the father. Mira wanted you and your girls safe, so she brought me to Thera from KcernFensia to serve as your protector. Living here has been interesting."

Sparrow looked confused. "From where? I thought you were from Myrrh."

"I am from the planet and dimension where Almiralyn trained to be the Guardian of Myrrh."

"What will you do once we get to Myrrh?"

"Whatever Almiralyn needs. Ah, here is the Onom Lira station. Look relieved and happy and stay close to me."

Sparrow assisted her companion onto the platform, slid her ID into the passage slot, and followed Henrietta through the P-Scan. A quick glance over her shoulder revealed a man in gray trailing after them. Once through the scanner, he moved up the platform, close to where they stood. His official color added significant credibility to Henrietta's statement that the PPP would follow them.

Henrietta slipped her hand around Sparrow's elbow and leaned close to her ear. "All the way to the Central Mountains."

A whistle of air announced the long, sleek train that sent a wind-tide through the waiting crowd.

24

Yaro, the Pentharian, stretched his long vulture neck for a closer look at the tall Tirips tree. A woman's form had emerged from its rough bark and gathered an invisible presence to her. He stifled the temptation to follow her into the night. His hunter's instinct told him his quarry was nearby, so he focused his unwavering attention on the small clearing. When the children appeared, he would be waiting.

A stealthful crunch in the underbrush alerted him to company. Had he been in natural form, he would have smiled at the three small men who appeared from the thicket of the trees. More from curiosity than any predatory instinct, he studied their round bodies, funny hats, and bright-colored vests and scarves.

One of them leaned into the tree's hollowed center and then backed up next to his comrades. They stood still and appeared to be waiting for something. Then, in the cool light of the rising moon, the dim outline of three huddled forms, and a dog took shape. Yaro pulled his neck back into his shoulders and, head aslant, stared.

Suddenly, a male child became visible.

Tibin fought a wave of impatience when Torgin dropped to his knees and began searching the ground with his hands.

"I've lost my piece of hemlock." The whispered explanation held a touch of panic.

Striving to control his own fear, Tibin touched the boy's shoulder. "We must go. Evil hunts in these woods tonight and is much closer than we think. Come. I'll lead. Tuper and Fen will bring up the rear."

"What about my hemlock?"

"Torgin, I'll share mine. We need to hide." The urgency in Brie's voice brought him to standing.

Tibin ducked into the hollow tree and ran a hand along the back wall. His fingers closed over a metal ring hidden in the rough wood. "Thanks be!" Giving it a twist, he whispered the Key. "Teek, Toope, Treddle." A panel in the ground slid aside, revealing a gaping hole. "Follow me." He gripped the handrails on either side of a steep staircase and descended into the root system beneath the floor of the Terces Wood.

Behind him, the children moved in single file, first Ari with Buster, then Brie with Torgin at her heels. Tuper and Fen slid the panel back into place and hurried down the stairs after them.

Midway down, Fen swiped at the side of his face. "What was that?"

"What was *what*?" Tuper looked around, his head bobbing with a nervous tic. "I don't see anything."

"Something flew past me just before the panel closed. A moth, I think."

"You know you're not supposed to let anything beyond the panel."

Fen flounced down the stairs. "It didn't ask permission."

"Adolescent Wood Tiffs." Tibin shook his head and returning his attention to his charges. They stood on the platform, wide-eyed with astonishment. On tiptoe, he peered over the railing at the extraordinary view.

The trees of Myrrh sent their roots down into a vast night sky. Stars sparkled in bright jewel colors, and a creamy moon hung radiant below them. In silhouette against this breathtaking backdrop, the roots intertwined in intricate woven patterns. Sprinkled throughout, where root crossed over root, swirls of iridescent turquoise light shimmered.

"It's so beautiful." Brie's tone held a touch of reverence.

Ari leaned over the balustrade. "What are the swirls of color?"

"We call them Intersects." Tuper bobbed his head. "Each of them takes us to a different place in the forest."

Torgin joined Ari. "How can there be a sky under the ground?"

Tibin beamed up at him. "That's a good question, Torgin. When we have more time, we'll explain. Right now, we need to get moving." He glanced around the assembled group. "Tuper, you take Torgin with you. Fen can take Ari and Buster, and I'll follow with Brie."

Tuper slipped his small hand into Torgin's and studied his fearful expression. "Don't be frightened—just hold tight. When I squeeze your hand, say with me 'ZeeAck od Thrice.' Ready?"

Torgin nodded and closed his eyes. Tuper squeezed and together they recited the unfamiliar words.

The air, cool against Torgin's face, smelled of rain and sunshine and like nothing he had ever known. When he opened his eyes, he stood on another platform with Tuper smiling beside him.

"That wasn't so bad, was it?"

Torgin grinned. "It was quite wonderful."

Ari watched Torgin and Tuper flash across the night sky and vanish. Fen took her hand. Gripping Buster's collar with the other, she whispered the magic phrase. The next instant, she stood beside Torgin. "By the Fathers, that was quick!" Her delight bubbled into a full-bodied laugh.

Hand in hand, Brie and Tibin waited for their turn. The Wood Tiff nodded. "ZeeAck od Thrice." The words had barely left their mouths when Brie arrived on the platform beside her twin.

Ari laughed and hugged her. "Wasn't it wonderful?"

Brie ducked and brushed her cheek. "What was *that*?"

"Something small and black." Ari frowned. "I saw it fly toward you, but I didn't see where it came from."

Brie's gaze darted from one direction to the other. "Something's wrong. Can anyone else feel it?"

"I felt nothing." Ari's matter-of-fact tone didn't ease the tension.

"Me neither." Torgin sidled closer to Brie.

Fen snatched something from Tibin's hat. "Ouch!" He flung it away and peered at his hand. "It bit me!"

Ari pulled a lite-stick from her pocket and thought it on. Light flared just in time to illuminate a black and gold snake slithering into the root system surrounding them. The Wood Tiffs exchanged concerned glances. Tibin grabbed her hand and pulled her after him up a steep stairway. In total silence, the others followed.

Relieved the Wood Tiffs watched over the children, Almiralyn shifted to her bird form and flew in search of Tam and Karrew. She discovered the raven sitting in the leaf-covered branches of an old oak. In the clearing below, four Pentharian, one in its true form and three as panthers, circled an agitated black horse and its rider.

A wave of foreboding washed over her. *"That's Dom on Gemlucky. What is he doing here?"*

Karrew kept his attention on the clearing. *"I think you will find his conversation most interesting."*

Dom peered at the Pentharian through smudged spectacles. "I'm telling you, I know Seyes Nomed and have important news for him."

"Where are the children?" The rasping question from the sapphire blue Pentharian sent a chill down his spine.

"I haven't seen them since they came through my shoppe two Myrrhinian turnings ago. Take me to Nomed. He will be furious if I don't get this information to him."

A panther shifted into a large vulture and lifted into the air. Gemlucky shrieked and reared. Dom lost his grip on the reins and hit the ground with a thud. The terrified horse bolted into the trees, his hoofbeats like a hammer striking an anvil in the oppressive silence of the Terces Wood.

Vulture and panthers flashed from sight, leaving three more Pentharian in their places. The last glow of dusk illuminated their strange bodies and tattooed faces. Deep sapphire blue, emerald green, ruby red, and carnelian orange scales gleamed in the fading light as their tapered tails twitched. Never had Dom seen creatures like these.

Elongated fingers on tattooed hands reached down to pull him to standing. He rubbed his bruised backside and listened to the Pentharian converse in a rasping, guttural language. Their unexpected shift into vulture shape left him cowering. Three lifted into the air and headed back the way they had come. The fourth rose above Dom's head and, grasping him by the shoulders, flew off to the West.

Almiralyn and Karrew remained silent for a short time after the clearing had emptied of its strange visitors. Karrew's neck feathers spiked and resettled. "They are almost beautiful in a deadly sort of way."

Almiralyn fluttered to the ground and resumed her Human form. "Where's Tam? How did they miss her? She must have been closer than Dom."

"I hid her in an outcropping of rock after they passed right by her."

"Show me where she is, and then we'll decide how to proceed. Maybe Nomed hasn't picked up our trail." The white bird lifted into flight.

Staying within the shadow of the trees, Karrew led the way. Not far ahead, he banked to the left and came to a rock-covered hill, where Tam stood hidden behind a tall bush, her soft eyes flecked with fear.

Almiralyn materialized and ran a hand over the pony's taut body.

Reaching up to scratch her ear, it surprised her to find a sprig of hemlock tucked in her halter. "No wonder they missed you. The question is, what's best for you? Home will be the safest."

Tam shook her head and snorted.

"I know you want to return to the children, but they've gone where you cannot go. When it's safe, you can rejoin them. Now, Tamboreen, run swiftly and with utmost care. Karrew and I will follow soon."

Almiralyn planted a kiss on Tam's soft nose and sent her trotting toward the barn, the cottage, and the swing in the old maple tree.

Paisley's long stride ate up the distance across the grasslands. Nothing would keep him from fulfilling his mission. Few people realized the true character of the man named Paisley James Tobinette. Life had dealt him cards from an interesting deck. Because of his size and the unmerciful teasing of the boys in his village, he had learned to play the fool to cover up his shyness and sensitivity.

"I'm sure grateful for Alli's friendship." He stretched, resettled his pack, and resumed his trek. Allynae's trust and that of Almiralyn, whom he adored, brought great joy to his heart. He squared his shoulders. *I will not break their trust or fail in my mission.*

The sky's last glowing memory of the turning disappeared below silhouetted mountains as a large, dark bird flew from the East, its captured prey thrashing in the grip of its talons. Malevolence washed over the grasslands. Paisley doubled over, dropped to his knees, and fought to catch his breath. *What on Myrrh...*

As silent as an animal being stalked, he tracked the bird of prey until it was no longer visible, then shook fear aside and climbed to his feet. *Soon, I can rest.*

After taking a deep drink from his water flask, he slipped like a mottled green ghost through the grasslands.

After Wodash departed to fetch Esán, Nomed flew through the forest, his owl eyes scanning the landscape for any trace of Almiralyn or Karrew. Struck by the silence and the absence of life, he landed. His owl head swiveled. *This is not the vibrant Terces Wood I remember from my childhood.* Had he been in Human form, a satisfied smile would have tugged at his scar and brought joy to his vengeful heart. *My long-awaited destruction of Myrrh has begun.* Arrogant anticipation launched him again into flight.

His owl senses alert, he flew a zigzagged path through the forest, picked up Karrew's trail, and followed it to a Tirips tree with a hollow center. The faint aromas of swamp water and evergreen and the even fainter scents of Human and dog gave him a moment of triumph. In a clearing further along the trail, the raven's scent disappeared amongst that of Pentharian, horse, and man. He found no evidence of the children's presence. *So who was the man? And what were the Pentharian doing here?*

Circling, he followed their distinctive odors. One had flown toward the mountains with the man. Three headed back through the forest. *This is not in the plan. What's going on? And where is the fifth one? The Pentharian will do my bidding, or they will get a taste of my wrath.*

He landed on the branch of a deciduous tree and pondered the behavior of his hired mercenaries. *How did they miss the children? I sensed them near the hollowed tree.*

Owl's eyes blinked. Pentharian hunters never lost their prey. Magic was the only thing that impeded their success. They understood nothing magical. *I'm betting Almiralyn interfered.*

A rabbit hopped through undergrowth at the edge the clearing. Hunger growled. He swooped, snatched the small mammal in his talons, and alighted. Tearing at his victim with his powerful beak, he began to feed, blood streaming in rivulets down his black-feathered chest.

Rarely had he succumbed to the appetite of his shifted form. Tonight, frustration and hunger combined to drive him deeper into the wild instincts of the owl. He knew he would regret it, but he savored the moment and the subsiding emptiness in his belly.

After finishing the last morsel, he cleansed his feathers of all signs of his feast and spiraled upward through the trees until he emerged into the moonlit sky. The time to send the Pentharian to their posts at the gateways drew near. Their presence would begin the deterioration of these magic portals. The children would finish the job.

Below in the forest, Almiralyn and Karrew found the remains of Nomed's meal. He would be easy to follow with the smell of fresh blood on his feathers. Of the Pentharian, there was no sign.

Almiralyn flew to the top of a tree. *"Stay here, Karrew!"* Leaving him hidden, she flew into the moonlight, her white wings shimmering, their gold tips on fire.

Nomed circled and swooped to meet her. The weight in his belly nagged him to rest, but he rose with her. Together, they spun in an intertwining helix. Diving, banking, and free-falling, he engaged her in a winged *pas de deux*. A mental probe for information found her love for the land, her people, and the young guests who visited her home. He did *not* discover the whereabouts of the children.

The tingle of her mind probe sent him soaring upward while striving to veil his consciousness. Gluttony slowed his mental acuity. She scanned his memories—his brother, his parents, and even the magic mirror—all before he could react. His plans for the destroying her land and his affinity for Esán flowed past. He fought to stop them, then felt them go.

His too-full stomach had weakened his defenses. Anger at himself pushed him to attack as the white bird swirled with grace and power around him. Aiming for her soft underbelly, he swooped in for the kill.

Out of the night sky, a missile of black slammed into his side and pitched him wing tip over wing tip. Just as the trees of the forest reached up to tangle him in their branches, he regained control and glided into the night shadows of the Terces Wood.

I will find you, Guardian of Myrrh. And when I do...

Almiralyn and Karrew circled until he disappeared into the trees and then streaked homeward.

25

At the top of the stairs, Buster scrambled through the door after Torgin and Ari. While Brie and Fen waited their turn, Brie scanned the Intersect for the black and gold snake.

Fen groaned and grabbed her arm. "I-I feel f-funny—" He collapsed on the stairs in a heap. His hat, knocked from his head, bounced to a stop on the platform below. A ragged breath shook his small body.

Brie dropped to her knees. "Help me! Something's wrong with Fen."

Tuper appeared at the top of the stairs and descended to kneel on the step above the younger Tiff. "What happened?"

"He groaned and collapsed. Do you think it's the snake's bite?"

Buster's low growl rattled through the opening. Tuper's head bobbed. "Better hurry."

Brie darted down the steps, grabbed Fen's hat, and bolted back. She and Tuper lifted the limp Tiffin and carried him to the entryway. Torgin and

Tibin pulled him through. As soon as she and Tuper had crawled clear, Tuper closed the panel.

Brie gazed at the unmoving Wood Tiff. "Do you think we locked it down there?"

Tuper straightened his lopsided hat. "I hope so. Nothing followed me through."

Everyone gathered around Fen's pale form. Brie knelt and touched his forehead. "He's icy cold." The Star of Truth burned. Her heart grew as cold as Fen. A tear slid down her cheek. Clutching the stone in the velvet pouch, she made herself focus. "The snake poisoned him. We have to act quickly, Tibin, or he'll die."

Ari gripped Efillaeh's handle. *Almiralyn said it could heal. But how?* Withdrawing it from the scabbard, she knelt opposite her twin.

Brie nodded in relief. "Place it over his heart."

The moment the knife touched Fen's chest, the etched design on the blade glowed emerald green, and the jewels in the handle sent purple light spinning around his small, rigid body. Black venom trickled from two small holes in his palm and pooled on the ground.

When the light faded, Ari picked up the knife, touched the tip to the wounds, and held her breath. The dark viscous fluid changed. Clean blood erased all traces of the venom. Her exhaled breath accompanied the closing of the small punctures. Not even a scar marred the Wood Tiff's palm. She rocked back on her heels and touched the pool of poison with the knife. The residue sizzled and flashed from existence in a puff of greenish smoke.

Her vision blurred. The world tipped and spun. For an instant, she thought she might faint. Brie's hand on her shoulder steadied her. The spinning ceased. Her gaze found Fen. He lay breathing softly, his flushed cheek warm beneath her cool fingers.

Brie helped her up and drew her aside to give Tibin and Tuper room to kneel by the young Tiffin.

"Fen? Can you hear us, little brother?" Tuper's voice trembled.

Fen's eyes fluttered open. His small brow furrowed. "What happened?"

With Tuper's help, he struggled upright. His once-injured hand held close to his heart, he repeated the question. "What happened?"

Everyone looked at Ari.

Tibin spoke. "Where did you get *that* knife?"

"Almiralyn gave it to me, but I didn't know how to use it. Brie told me what to do."

Her twin hugged her. "I only told you how to begin. You completed the process. You are amazing, Arienh AsTar."

"May I hold it?" Fen's small hand trembled when she placed the silver knife on his palm. He stared in awe. "It's Efillaeh, isn't it? I've only heard of it in tales." With a soft sigh, he handed it back. "You have my loyalty for the rest of my life, Ari. You need only call, and I'll be at your side."

Unable to speak around the lump in her throat, she replaced the knife in its simple sheath.

"That is some knife!" Torgin draped an arm around her shoulder.

Brie's bright smile warmed her. "You did great."

Tibin and Tuper helped Fen to his feet. Tuper slid an arm around his waist. "Can you walk?"

The Tiffin nodded and rubbed his curly head. "My hat? I left my hat in the Intersect."

"No, you didn't." Brie handed it to him and received a shaky smile as he patted it in place.

Tibin looked at the gathered companions. "I need to get you to safety. Follow me." He proceeded them down a low corridor to a small wooden door and opened it a crack. After surveying what lay beyond, he pulled it wide and beckoned them. Soon they gathered beneath a large tree. Tibin yanked a hidden cord. The sound of rustling leaves accompanied the arrival of a small seat attached to a stout rope.

"We're sending you up to stay with a friend for tonight. Her name is Sibine, and she'll take good care of you."

"What about Buster?" Ari knelt with her arms around the big dog's neck.

"We'll keep him safe. Up you go. Who's first?"

"Wait." Torgin raised his hand. "What about Tam? We can't leave her alone in the woods. She must be frightened."

Tuper's head bobbed. "Don't worry, Torgin. We'll send a message to all the forest folk to watch for her. When she's found, we'll bring her to you."

"Thank you." Fatigue and relief rang in the simple words.

Brie stepped up. "I'll go first, Tibin."

The Wood Tiff helped her to settle on the small seat and pulled the cord again. The seat ascended, taking Brie higher and higher until she was no longer visible. When the seat reappeared, Torgin jumped on and vanished into the lush greenery. Ari climbed on last, grabbed the stout rope, and hugged it to her chest. She twisted to look down at the Wood Tiffs and then leaned back to gaze up through the leaf-covered branches. Laughing from sheer delight, she rode to the top of the tree, where a small house sat hidden from view.

*B*eneath the Terces Wood, the black and gold snake glided onto the stairway. Yaro materialized and regarded the closed panel. *I missed the opportunity to slip through. Unless I can open it, I'm trapped.* He trod up the stairs, searched for a lever, and found nothing. When he grabbed ahold of the small handle and pulled, it wouldn't budge.

Now what? He surveyed the vastness of the night sky below him. *I, Yaro, Pentharian of ReTaw au Qa, am a prisoner in the root system of Myrrh.*

*D*arkness closed around Esán as he followed Zugo from Nomed's cavern toward the outer entrance at the Cliffs of ReVod. *I need to get as far from the DiMensioner as possible.* He stared ahead, trying to pick his companion out of the blackness.

"Don't get too far ahead of me, Zugo. I don't want to lose you."

"I'm right here." Zugo's fur brushed his bare arm. *"Your eyes will adjust. Come, we're getting close."*

Esán formed a picture of the DeoNyte in his mind and followed. A soft phosphorescent light began to glow around his new friend's white, furry body.

A whispered clunk brought them to a halt. Mountain air tinged with a foreboding iciness turned them back toward the cavern. Zugo slowed and pointed higher up. The space where he'd been standing emptied. At a loss, Esán threw a frantic glance over his shoulder. Zugo's hand brushed his cheek. Esán grasped it and scrambled onto a narrow ledge beside him.

Masking their thoughts, they sidestepped their way to a half-hidden opening where they slipped through into pitch black darkness. Esán forced his heart to slow its wild beating and pressed his back against the tunnel wall. Icy fingers of cold crackled through the tunnel. A hand grabbed his wrist and guided him into a wide fissure. Chilled to the bone, he huddled next to Zugo until the death shadow's wintery presence faded. Esán's mind snapped open. *"We have to hide. Wodash will find us if we stay here."*

Still holding his wrist, Zugo guided him around a tall, flat boulder, sat down on the ground, and scooted forward. *"Hurry. Sit and put your arms around my waist."*

Esán sat down, maneuvered until his upper body pressed next to Zugo's back, and wrapped his arms around his chest.

Zugo spoke over his shoulder. "Match your body's movement to mine. *Hold on!"* Leaning back, he pushed hard with his hands and shot forward.

Esán smothered an astonished squeak of surprise as they slid down the slippery surface of a small tunnel just high enough for their heads to clear. Slowly at first, and then gathering speed, they shot deeper and deeper into the bowels of the mountains.

Wow! This is... Wow! Esán's body tilted to the side as they rounded a sharp curve and shot upright when they hit the next straight stretch. Zugo's fur tickling his face and the delight of the ride made him laugh out loud.

A gradual change to the surface of the tunnel slowed their descent. They came to a stop on cool sand. Zugo jumped up and offered his hand.

Esán took it and climbed to his feet. *"That was great. Now what?"*

"This way." Zugo strode over the sand onto a hard surface.

Esán matched his stride. *"Where are we?"*

"Rorret Cavern." Zugo came to a halt at the edge of an underground lake. "Keep quiet. The lake can be dangerous."

"Do we cross it?"

"Yes. Stay close to me."

They followed the perimeter of the lake until they reached a pile of rocks near the arc of the cavern wall. Zugo reached into a gap and began to pull. *"Go around to the other side."*

Esán dodged around him and gripped a rough, rounded edge. *"What is it?"*

"An aqua glider. Keep pulling. Just a little more…"

One last heave brought it to the lake's edge and into the water. *"Be careful. The lake has no shallows. It drops straight down."*

Zugo held the glider steady and helped Esán step aboard. Once he settled at the bow, Zugo stepped in and sat down. Grabbing the one paddle, he pushed off and guided the boat across the blue-black expanse.

Cold fury washed over Wodash when he discovered Esán's absence. *I knew the boy would be trouble. Why did Nomed leave him to wander free?* A fruitless search of the cavern left him even more angry. *How dare that boy leave! Now I must search for him.*

Since he had just passed along the passage from the Cliffs of ReVod, he chose one leading deeper into the caverns of the Dojanacks. Anger propelled him into the labyrinth riddling the mountains, the maze that had become the final resting place of many men. He relished death's presence, totally at home among the skeletal remains.

Wildness pulsed through Nomed's owl form. Talons reaching for purchase closed over a moss-covered log beneath the trees of the Terces Wood. His head swiveled left, then right. Huge owl eyes blinked. Human thought fought for control. The effort to shift quaked through the feathered body. A rush of blood filled Nomed's Human mind with the roar of a pounding surf. Change wracked his body. Feet—talons, face—beak, skin—feathers battled to hold him until, exhausted, he fell to the ground, his Human body wracked with sobs.

Digging his hands into the rich black dirt, he smelled the pungent odor of sweat and felt the coolness of the summer night's breeze skitter through his sweat-soaked hair. The beat of his heart slowed. He forced himself to a sitting position, his dulled mind struggling to come to life.

What craziness drove me to feast on that rabbit? What arrogance drew me into battle with Almiralyn? I spilled my plans like water from a bucket. He crawled to a nearby tree, leveraged his shaking body to standing, and gulped air into his lungs. *I acted stupidly, but I am not a fool. The game has just become more interesting.* He frowned. *My next move will be crucial. As in the ancient game of chess, I need a strategy.*

Gradually, his breathing calmed, and the strength in his legs returned. *I have to find the Pentharian, and I dare not shape shift to do it.* He sagged against the tree trunk and groaned. *How am I going to travel at the speed I require?*

The sound of pounding hooves disrupted the stillness. Black and shiny as polished ebony, a stallion exploded through the trees, terror blazing in its eyes. A mental probe of the frightened animal's mind netted Nomed the memory of Pentharian. With the gentleness of a caress, he erased it. *"Whoa, Gemlucky. Whoa."*

The stallion came to a halt. His sides heaved. Sweat coated his muscled body. He stared at Nomed, shook his head, nickered, and dropped his nose to nibble a patch of grass. When he raised it, his eyes were soft.

Nomed removed his cape and stripped off his damp shirt. Gemlucky tossed his head but allowed him to grab the reins. Whispering soft, calming words, the DiMensioner wiped away the sweat. Another gentle mind touch produced a soft whinny for the stallion. His nostrils flared. He dipped his beautiful head.

Nomed smiled and stroked his black forehead. "I christen you in the language of DerTah, TroeEen, the Mighty One."

He tossed the sweat-soaked shirt on the ground, donned his cape, and mounted TroeEen. Guided by the swamp water smell of the Pentharian, they traveled southward. Scattered thoughts organized into goals. *I must gather my resources and begin the attack on the gateways of Myrrh. The children must be captured and hidden in the Dojanack Caverns. Last but not least, I will claim the Prima Crystal Evolsefil for my own and end time on this last stronghold of Old Earth.*

Like the call of the battle drum, his triumphant laugh mingling with the stallion's hoofbeats echoed through the Land of Myrrh.

. . .

Nomed found Voer, Stee, and Yuin in their Pentharian form outside the hollow Tirips Tree, conferring in guttural, throaty voices. For a moment, he remained hidden, considering their divergence from his meticulous plans. After dismounting, he tied the skittish TroeEen's reins to the low branch of a tree and strolled into their midst.

Alien eyes scanned his bare chest. Sensitive noses sniffed the scents of sweat and blood. Unabashed, he met their gaze.

Stee shook emerald braids back from his face. His Reptilian eyes narrowed. A sneer of contempt contorted Yuin's facial tattoos.

"We speak of the disappearance of Yaro and of the children. It is good you come." Voer, the Pentharian leader, bowed his head.

Nomed allowed his cold hazel eyes to travel from one Pentharian to the next, ending with the sneering Yuin. "Remember who I am and what misfortune I can bring to you. If you forget, you'll regret it for the rest of your shortened life. Why is it you have deviated from my plans?"

Yuin's expression didn't change—his disgust palpated the surrounding air. "We deviated from nothing. Circumstances sometimes require a change in tactics."

Ignoring Yuin, Nomed swirled his cape around his bare torso and addressed the others. "We will return to the mountains. The children will come to us. Trust me—they're planning to rescue their friend. We will intercept them in the grasslands. As for Yaro, he's strong and smart. He'll join us when he can." He watched Voer and Stee evaluate his words. They knew how he had earned his name. None of them, including Yuin, would test his patience. "We'll travel together." He mounted TroeEen and galloped away through the trees.

The moon hung high over the plains when they reached the edge of the grasslands. Nomed slid to the ground, held TroeEen's head between his hands, and blew into his nostrils. "You are mine. When I call, you will come. Until then, you are free to run." He pulled off the stallion's saddle and bridle and hid them in the trees. With a slap on the rump, he sent the beautiful animal to graze in tall grass and moonlight and turned to the Pentharian. "I will need a ride to the mountains."

Voer bowed his head. "Ride upon my back." He shifted to panther, a sleek silhouette against the grass of the plains.

"Thank you, Voer. I will not forget this gift."

Like the wind across a stormy sea, three panthers sprinted across the open prairie. A bare-chested man rode on the leader, his cape sailing out behind him. Tall grass bent before them. Night animals scattered. The moon's shimmering light vanished as the huge cats leapt into the air and changed, mid-leap, into vultures. Their massive wings cast absolute darkness over the grasslands below.

Paisley sat up, sweat glistening on his forehead. *Was that a dream? It seemed so real.* He rubbed his eyes and searched the sable sky, where impending doom had drowned the moon and the stars.

A black velvet curtain of foreboding enshrouded him. He rested his head on his bent knees and hugged his legs close to his chest.

When at last the moon reappeared above silhouetted mountaintops, he settled his backpack in place and strode toward the rolling foothills that would take him closer to mountains and to the malevolent shadows of the night. He dared not even guess what awaited him there.

26

Majeska led Allynae through the tunnels under the city of Idronatti. His safe return to Myrrh was her aim. The magic mirror would remain in its present location as long as the gateways were closed. *It* was their destination.

She preferred not to expose him to more danger, but they had to re-enter the RiaTrain station. Since the PPP allowed no cats in the city, she, too, was a liability. Her ears twitched. The sounds of the Idronatti Central underground station alerted her she had achieved her first goal. She stopped.

Allynae scooped her up. "Well, Jeska, where are we?"

She looked up and blinked. She liked this Human. He had always been kind to her. Besides, he belonged to Almiralyn.

Jumping down, she walked sedately to a break in the wall. As middle-night neared, only a few workers waited, Idronatti-fashion, for the train. Most citizens were inside their apartments as required by *The Plan*. She skulked from the opening across the platform and into the shadows. A glance in Allynae's direction made her pause. He appeared uncertain.

Allynae hated to abandon his hiding place. After a quick look in both directions, he forced himself to step onto the platform. Majeska trotted to the exit and merged once more into obscurity. Mimicking the prescribed gait for city workers, he followed, dodged unobserved through the People Scan, and took the floating stairs.

He emerged onto a deserted street, where the unnatural lighting cast an eerie glow over the cityscape. *Nothing but buildings, buildings, buildings.* He craned his neck to see upwards. *How do people live here?*

Majeska observed him from the opposite side of the empty street. Humans were an odd lot. Trapped in mental monologues about things they couldn't change, they had to be among the most indecisive of creatures.

With the calm indifference of her species, she waited until his eyes picked her out of the night before trotting between tall buildings. When she reached the street on the opposite side of the block, she halted. It, too, was empty of people and of PPP officers.

She stepped onto the walkway. Allynae, a shadowy figure behind her, stared at five steel-gray buildings at the end of the block. Searchlights midway up the façade of each structure shot moving beams of light down the darkened streets. Allynae squatted beside her, his fear scenting the air. Amethyst eyes gleaming, she dodged a circle of white light, sprinted across the street, and turned to observe him.

Allynae broke into a cold sweat. *The Five Towers.* He forced himself to breathe. "Concentrate on the timing of the lights instead of the terror in your gut." *One, two, three, four...* Majeska's eyes glinted in the wash of light skirting her hiding place. *Five, six, seven, eight...*

The beam swept back and forth, an eight-count each way. He glanced up. The light shot above his head and pooled a block or two further down the street. A quick calculation later, he tensed and exploded into motion. The sound of his pounding footsteps compelled him to double his speed. He hit the walkway and dodged into the darkness between buildings with no time to spare. Majeska, already halfway to the next block, gave him no time to fret.

He jogged to a stop behind her and stared at the Sun Spire, Idronatti's most magnificent building. Though he'd heard about it, he never expected to be gazing at it. Lights at its base and on its uppermost story washed one hundred and thirty floors with soft rainbow colors. The surrounding gardens stood in silhouette against the warmth of the submerged lighting in the shimmering blue water of the moat.

Allynae groaned, glanced down at the cat sitting unperturbed beside him, and looked back at the glass drop car on the building's façade. Frustration, anger, and fear flew like frightened bats through his mind. *How on Thera am I going to reach that building without alerting an entire regiment of PPP patrollers?*

Majeska meowed. With complete disregard for danger, she sauntered across the street, walked over the bridge, and sat beside the drop car.

Allynae studied her while she licked one gray paw and groomed her ears. *She would never lead me into danger.* Still, his fear imprisoned him in the dark alley.

Majeska's tail flipped back and forth. Her ears twitched to catch some sound he could not hear. She widened her amethyst eyes to look at him. He swallowed. *My time's up.* Dashing into the open, he arrived, panting with exertion and a touch of panic, at the drop car and pushed the "up" arrow. The glass wall melted away. He bolted inside. Majeska flashed past him, her meow clipped and urgent. The doors whooshed shut. The car shot upward. Below, PPP patrollers flooded the gardens and formed a semicircle around the front of the building. Searchlights popped on from every direction. Majeska stared at him and then at the glowing touch screen. *"By the Fathers, I almost forgot."* He tapped three numbers. The car shuddered to a standstill. The doors slid open, revealing a long, white corridor ending in a roiling mist.

Majeska trotted toward the swirling haze. Allynae hesitated. The drop car jerked. A lunge through the closing doors sent him stumbling after the cat into the mist. He jumped and landed on the ground in a glowing pool of light beneath a streetlamp on the outskirts of Old Earth. *The Borderlands! Thank Emit!*

Majeska let out a hiss and crouched. A smothered cough behind him brought Allynae around—fists ready.

In shadowy edges of darkness beyond the light, two grim-faced PPP patrollers waited. One lunged through the air, tackled him around the waist, and knocked him to the ground.

From the corner of his eye, Allynae saw the second patrolman throw his hands up as a hissing cat missiled toward his face. Her bared claws left a bloodied pattern on the man's cheek. Letting out a howl of pain, he tripped backward.

Allynae sent his attacker flying, scrambled to his feet, and bolted after Majeska down Worldness Way with the two PPP patrollers at his heels. A path cleared as people on the street dodged into doorways or ducked between buildings. A sprint across the town square took him into an alley. Halfway down, a man lurking in a darkened entryway motioned him inside. The door closed behind them. Allynae found himself in total darkness with a man's big hand on his shoulder.

"Shh." The low voice stilled.

Footsteps hammered by, faded, and grew louder again. They stopped just outside the door.

"They have to be around here someplace." One patrolman growled and kicked a trash can over.

"They can't have evaporated into thin air." The other's reply carried an edge of anger. "No matter what the old earth adage said, cats do *not* have nine lives; and I plan to see that one gray feline learns it the hard way."

"You take care of the cat. I'll get the man. I'm pretty sure he's the one Jordett's after."

A shout in the distance made Allynae tense.

"Hear that?" The patrolman barked the question.

"Yep. Let's go!"

Footsteps thundered down the alley and faded.

Allynae fought to calm his pounding heart and slow his breathing. The man beside him opened a door into a dim room. "In here." The subdued voice was rough, but pleasant. "Ya can wait here 'til we get word that it's safe for ya to leave."

Allynae and his host sat down at a rickety table. The man across from him pushed straggly dark hair back from his face and watched him from an unblinking glass eye.

Allynae extended his hand. "Allynae."

The man met his steady gaze. "Not *Almiralyn's* Allynae?"

Smiling, he nodded. "No other."

The big man took his hand and shook it. "Fadin." He jerked a thumb toward the alley. "They've been prowlin' here a couple of turnings. First, they were after three kids, twins and a mix-blood boy. A bit ago, they got all excited and set a trap by the entry point. You know them kids?"

"They're in Myrrh. Can you tell me how many PPP patrollers I'm up against?"

"Five, maybe six. We got men posted to keep 'em busy. Ya going to *Antiques by Q*?"

Allynae nodded.

"They be watchin' it, but we can help get ya inside. PPP patrolmen used to be rare here in The Borderlands. The few times they come, it were by accident. They be pretty dumb, ya know. Couldn't figure how they got here or where they was. These officers come on purpose. Word of their presence spread through the outer reaches like a prairie fire. Ya see, we don't take kindly to manhunts or them that's conductin' 'em. We gotta network of folks ready to lend a helpin' hand to whoever the PPP's after."

A soft knock brought Fadin to his feet. He opened the door a crack, listened, whispered a reply, and beckoned to Allynae. "This be Saaul. He'll show ya the way to the antique shoppe. Don't worry, we be glad to help."

"Thanks, Fadin. I won't forget your kindness."

"It be good." The man pulled the door wider. Allynae slipped through.

Saaul cracked open the outer door and listened before drawing Allynae into the night. One alley after the other, they traveled without seeing another soul. At the sound of a soft meow, Allynae glanced down, relieved to see Majeska keeping pace, her cat ears twitching to pick up any strange sound. Saaul stopped in the shadow of a derelict building and placed a steady hand on Allynae's arm. He pointed to Chance, the street that led to the antique shoppe. Not far away stood the two patrolmen.

"Now what?" Allynae whispered.

"Patience."

A man dashed into the street and dodged down an adjacent alley. The patrolmen took the bait, ran after the decoy, and disappeared around the corner. Saaul and Allynae traversed the narrow street and ducked down Chance with Majeska, a flash of gray streaking ahead of them. Following the dingy, twisting lane past several even less inviting ones, they stopped in a doorway, where Almiralyn's cat sat, washing her face.

"Do you know where you are?" Saaul murmured the question in his ear.

"Yes."

"Remember, the shoppe's guarded. Majeska'll lead you around back. If a distraction's needed, we'll provide it. Safe journey, and take good care of those twins."

"You can be sure of it." He smiled. "They're my daughters."

The two men shook hands, and Saaul melted into the night.

Allynae followed Majeska to a doorway several stores down from the antique shoppe. Everything looked quiet. A gap between two dilapidated buildings provided a path to the back of Dom's shoppe. An open window on the first floor waited like an empty eye socket. *Handy*. A drop of sweat slid down his neck. *Perhaps too handy.*

With practiced skill, Majeska leapt to the windowsill and vanished into the gloomy interior. Allynae knew to stay put until Majeska reappeared, but everything in him wanted to get under cover.

Loud voices sounded at the front of the building. "I'm telling you, Jordett said the guy would come here."

"Where is he then?"

"How should I know?"

"Have you checked around back?"

"No, just inside, and it's empty as a dead man's cell."

"Nice description. I'll take a look."

"There's nothing back there."

"Humor me."

"Whatever suits the Fathers."

The crunch of gravel warned of the patrolman's approach. Allynae climbed in the window, eased it shut, and locked it. Pressed against the wall, he listened to the man checking windows and jiggling the doorknob on the back door. A yell sounded from the front of the building. The patrolman sprinted toward it.

Allynae heaved a sigh of relief and bent to scratch Majeska's ears. Silent as ghosts, they moved down the hallway to the hidden door. It opened without a sound and ushered them into the murky basement below *Antiques by Q*. Allynae pulled the tapestry aside and placed his palm on the cloudy glass.

"Stand right where you are and take your hand off that mirror." The voice came from behind him.

Allynae froze for only an instant before whispering the Key Almiralyn provided. "Eero Tye Como."

As he felt himself being pulled through the keyhole into Myrrh, a hand gripped his shoulder. With Majeska and the hand's owner on his heels, he flashed through dimensional space.

In the distance behind him, the two voices from outside Fadin's door in the alleyway chased them. "Did you see that?" The astonished question ended with a choke.

"Where did they go?" A touch of fear leaked into the second voice. "I don't like this at all. In fact, I think we should get out of here."

27

Sparrow would have enjoyed her trip to SumnerTyme, but for the man in gray. Afraid to bring up the questions she most wanted to ask, she exchanged casual pleasantries with Henrietta, napped, and watched the city slip into the distance and green, rolling hills transition into the Central Mountains. Absorbing the beauty of the scenery, she wondered what, besides the PPP, had kept her in the city.

The village of SumnerTyme sat near the top of SunRise Mountain. Since it was about the size of Singtil, Sparrow felt confident finding Merrilea would be easy.

Henrietta mumbled in her sleep. Her gray head dropped forward, tipping her purple flowered hat at a precarious angle. Sparrow sighed. *I wish you had made yourself known long ago, Henrietta. The richness of your friendship would have warmed the many turnings I've spent alone over the last fourteen sun cycles.*

The elderly woman stirred and blinked. A yawn morphed into a warm smile as she sat up and straightened her hat. "We're almost there. Let's go to my friend's then take a walk in the countryside. It's so lovely this time here."

She really has a friend here. Sparrow tried to cover her surprise. "That would be fun. SumnerTymn is new to me."

"I know that, dear." Henrietta patted her hand. Her eyes held an impish sparkle.

Sparrow gathered her belongings and prepared to disembark as the Onom Lira pulled into the enchanting country station. They stepped onto the platform amidst happy, rosy children who waited to climb on board with their mothers. Tanned fathers in farmers' coveralls stood ready to assist their wives. Sparrow couldn't help making a comparison between the boisterous spontaneity happening all around her and the hushed conversations and regimented movements of residents in Idronatti.

Henrietta led the way through the crowd and onto the main street of SumnerTyme. "Deora's cottage is this way." She moseyed down a colorful side street, where striped awnings and flower boxes in full bloom lined the cobbled street. Its quaint charm reminded Sparrow more than ever of her home village of Singtil.

Rounding a corner onto a lane leading toward a long, high hedgerow, Henrietta toddled along, humming to herself. She pushed open a white gate in the hedge and walked along a path to a fieldstone cottage back by tall, willowy trees. Eyes twinkling, she climbed the porch steps, grasped the hummingbird knocker, and rapped three times.

When the door opened, a woman about Sparrow's age regarded them from fatigue-filled eyes. "May I help you?"

"I'm Henrietta, a friend of Deora's from Idronatti, and this is Sparrow AsTar. Is Deora here?"

Henrietta's tone made Sparrow glance from her to the woman in the doorway. The fatigue faded as she watched, and a smile brightened the gray-blue of her eyes.

"Please, come in. Deora is sleeping, but she should awaken soon."

She motioned Henrietta and Sparrow into the cottage and escorted them to a comfortable sitting room. "Did you arrive on the Onom Lira? Can I get you some tea?" Looking somewhat bemused, she ran a hand over her blonde hair. "Oh, I'm so sorry. I'm Deora's nurse, Merrilea."

Sparrow's hand flew to her heart. "Merrilea!"

The woman's eyes widened. "Is something wrong?"

"No." Sparrow smiled as she noted the twinkle in her companion's eyes. "Everything is perfect. Henrietta and I came from Idronatti to find *you*."

"To find *me*? Whatever for?"

Henrietta moved to the window, peeked between the curtains, and gave a tiny nod.

"You have a nephew named Esán, correct?" Sparrow noted the woman's worried expression.

"Yes, is he alright?"

"Esán is in trouble." She drew Merrilea down on the sofa beside her. "He needs your help."

"If he's worse, he must return to the hospital at once."

"To my knowledge, he isn't ill, or at least not more ill; but he *is* in danger. Almiralyn sent word she needs both of us in Myrrh right away. Will you come?"

Merrilea sat in silence, her emotions in obvious turmoil.

Sparrow frowned. "Do you know about Myrrh?"

Eyes overflowing with memories, Esán's aunt smiled. "Myrrh was my home before Esán's birth. When he was tiny, we moved here." She rubbed the center of her forehead. "I hated to leave him in the city when he's ill, but Deora took a turn for the worse. She needs constant care. No matter how much I want to help Esán, I can't leave her."

Henrietta joined them. "Well, it's a good thing I came along then, isn't it? I'll stay with Deora, and you can go to Myrrh."

Sparrow laid a hand on her arm. "But, Henrietta, I thought you wanted to go home."

"I do, but the situation has changed. Deora, my friend since I arrived in Idronatti, taught me to live in that horrid city. I encouraged her to follow her dreams. That's why she moved here." She patted Sparrow's hand. "The least I can do is stay with her now."

Merrilea looked doubtful. "You're sure?"

"If Almiralyn needs you in Myrrh, you must go. She rarely asks for help, so this must be a serious matter. I'll take care of things here."

Merrilea gave the older woman a hug. "I can't thank you enough. Come. I'll show you where she's resting." The two women left the room, speaking in soft tones about their patient's needs.

Sparrow paced to the window and back. *How will I find Myrrh without Henrietta? And what about the twins?* A series of strange images flashing through her mind brought her to a standstill. *Oh dear, what kind of danger are they in?*

She hurried to the sofa and pulled her sketchbook and stylus from her pack. Quick, smooth strokes generated three figures—a panther, a vulture, and a man in a cape leaping high into the moonless sky. Powerless to stop the flow of images, she sketched a small triangular face, dark against silky white fur. Behind him stood a bald boy, his rounded eyes mirroring a grotesque skeletal face.

A soft noise made her glance up from her work to Merrilea standing at her elbow. She pointed at the dark face. "That's a DeoNyte." Her finger moved. "And that is Esán. What is he looking at?"

Sparrow shook her head. "I don't know. We need to leave for Myrrh soon. I wish the portal to The Borderlands wasn't in Idronatti."

"A trip back to the city isn't necessary."

"I don't understand, Merrilea. How will we get to Myrrh?"

"I know another way, but I'm sure Almiralyn has closed the portals. We'll need the Key to open the gateway. Do you know what it is?"

"No, but I think Henrietta knows if she can remember."

"Your Henrietta is quite a lady. Deora is already looking better."

"I am pretty amazing, aren't I?" The elderly woman chuckled from the doorway.

Sparrow's worried expression relaxed, and she and Merrilea laughed at the comical look on Henrietta's face.

Merrilea grew serious. "Henri, we need—"

"I know, deary, you need the Key. I've been wracking my brain, trying to remember the darn thing." She rummaged around in her carry bag and pulled out a pair of spectacles. The large round lenses made her violet eyes look twice their normal size. "I only wear them for thinking." She wrinkled her brow in thought. "Eet... No. Ea rose. Ah, Eero. Eero is the first word. Dye. Rye. Try. Oh, got it. Tye, that's it. Now the third word—"

A sharp knock on the front door froze the women in place. Henrietta put a finger to her lips and nodded at Esán's aunt.

Straightening her apron and smoothing her honey blonde hair, Merrilea walked down the hall and opened the front door.

A gray clad PPP official glared down at her. "Is Deora Lane at home?"

"Yes, but she's ill and napping. May I help?"

"Does she have a friend from Idronatti coming to see her?"

"You mean Henri, of course. She arrived on the last train." Merrilea kept her expression serene.

The man flashed an impatient scowl. "Get her."

"Just a moment, please." She turned and stepped aside as Henrietta tottered with elderly elegance down the hall and peered up at their visitor.

Her expressive face, a picture of confused interest, she pressed a hand to her cheek and smiled. "I'm Henrietta. May I help you?"

He stared at his notes. "Your full name is Henrietta Avetlire, correct?"

"Yes, it is."

"You plan to be in SumnerTyme for a Theran turning or two?"

"That's correct."

"And SparrowLyn AsTar traveled with you." He projected his voice down the hall." *Where* is she?"

Henrietta ignored the question and studied the official from behind her large spectacles. "Do I know you? You look so familiar." A quizzical expression added to her air of elderly innocence. "Oh my dear, I know who you are."

His brows bridged over a snub nose and a mouth fighting a scowl.

Sparrow walked into the hall, her attention absorbed by the sketchbook in her hand. She nibbled on the tip of her stylus, then glanced at Merrilea. "Did you need me?"

Henrietta gave a merry laugh. "Sparrow, it's the man from the train."

A dark flush crept up his neck as his hard gaze raked Sparrow from head to foot. "Where are your papers, Miss AsTar?"

"Oh." Sparrow, distracted by her work, bit her lip. "I'll get them." Attention glued to her sketchbook, she ambled back to the sitting room. With her artist's pass and paperwork in hand, she rejoined the group by the door.

The PPP official, his annoyance obvious, compared the face on the pass to hers and returned the papers.

Henrietta smiled up at him, her magnified eyes guileless. "It's all right, dear officer. Your secret is safe with me. I won't tell anyone we spotted you." With an expression of child-like sweetness, she turned to Merrilea. "This man came all the way from Idronatti to make certain we arrived safely." Her innocent smile beamed with gratitude. "Thank you for checking on our safe arrival. How thoughtful of you." Confusion flitted across her face. His presence seemingly forgotten, she patted her stomach. "I'm starving."

Merrilea fought the urge to giggle. "You'll excuse us, won't you? My guest appears to need her supper. She's had such a long afternoon, and she's exhausted. Thank you again for checking on my friends." Without giving him a chance to respond, she shut the door and left him standing on the doorstep.

Henrietta tottered to the sitting room. "Thank the Fathers *that's* over."

Sparrow peeked out the window. "He's gone."

Girlish giggles filled the room.

"Oh dear, Henrietta." Sparrow hugged her and chuckled. "You sounded so Idronattian."

"You were wonderful!" Esán's aunt wiped a tear from her cheek. "I doubt he knows yet what hit him."

Henrietta paused midway to a chair. "Co. Cos. Col." She removed her spectacles and tapped them on her palm. "Con. Com. Como. That's it! Eero Tye Como is the Key."

Merrilea and Sparrow grinned at each other over her white head.

The amethyst-rimmed spectacles disappeared into the carry bag. "Now, I *am* starving."

Henrietta's pained expression triggered another round of giggles and sent them all scurrying to the kitchen, where preparations for dinner were soon underway.

"Merrilea, you mentioned going to Idronatti to get to Myrrh is unnecessary." Sparrow tossed greens in a bowl for salad. "Is there another gateway near here?"

"There's one in the Central Mountains. We can take the train to RemMus Lake and hike into Demrach Canyon." Merrilea sliced a loaf of freshly baked bread and set it on the table. "I think—"

A tiny bell ringing interrupted the conversation. Henrietta picked up the tray Merrilea had prepared. "Girls, I'll just take this and sit with Deora while I eat. You have plans to make."

"Thank you, Henri. She'll be happy to have your company." Merrilea watched her toddle from the kitchen and turned back to Sparrow. "We should leave pretty early in the morning."

"Do you think our PPP official will attempt to follow us?"

"Based on who you are, I would be surprised if he didn't. So you and I will slip away before sunrise."

"What if he follows us?"

"That's something we'll try to avoid. The authorities know nothing of Demrach Gateway where we're going. We don't want its location discovered." Sparrow put down her eating utensil. "And if it is?"

"The consequences could be disastrous." Merrilea's expression was as serious as her tone.

28

B rie rode the seat up through green leaves to where a smiling female Wood Tiff waited.

"I'm a Tiffet, and my name is Sibine." The diminutive creature smiled shyly and helped her onto the platform. "Welcome to our TreeOm."

"I'm Brie. Thank you for letting us stay with you." She peered in amazement at the charming little cottage.

From its sloping, leaf-covered roof to walls fashioned from branches bound with clay and flowering vines, it reminded her of a cottage from one of her mother's paintings. On either side of a floral-painted door, where roses, daisies, and daffy-down-dillies all nodded their brightly colored heads; red shutters bordered windows gleaming with a welcoming light

"The door looks alive."

"It is, Brie. Everything in this TreeOm has a spirit. If you are sensitive enough, you can feel it." Sibine tipped her head back and smiled up as Torgin arrived on the platform.

Brie beamed. "This is Torgin, my best friend, and—" Ari arrived, grinning. "This is my sister, Ari."

The Tiffet bobbed her head. "I am Sibine, and I welcome you all to our TreeOm. You honor us with your presence."

She led the children through a cozy sitting room into the kitchen. "I thought you might need a snack before bed." Sibine invited them to gather around a table made from an old tree stump. Toast slathered with jelly stacked on pretty pink plates and warm acorn milk, steaming, frothy, and white, in tall mugs enticed the children to sit and enjoy.

Sibine perched on a stool, observing her guests. Curly, light brown hair tied up with wildflower garlands framed her large, brown eyes and rosy cheeks. Her hands rested on a round little belly that she patted as she talked. "Our wee one is due at the end of this moon cycle." Her eyes filled with wonder. "This is our first babe, and I'm very excited."

Brie sipped her tea. "Do you know if it's a boy or a girl?"

Sibine shook her head. "No. I'll love whomever chooses to come."

"What do you mean *chooses to come*?" Torgin popped another bite of toast in his mouth.

"Babes pick their families. Parenting is an important responsibility and an honor. When this babe is born, the entire community will celebrate. Everyone will help to raise the child to be a good Wood Tiff."

"Do you have any names picked out?" Ari licked jelly from her lips.

"We'll know the name on the turning of the birthing. Our wise woman will come to bless this house and give the babe its name."

Brie smiled. "I like that. I'd love to meet your wise woman."

"Perhaps you will someday." She slid off the stool. "Now it's time for you to sleep. I understand you've been most busy."

Ari nudged her sister. "Look, Brie, Torg is almost asleep at the table."

Torgin shot up straight and glared at the twins. "I am not sleeping." He smothered a yawn.

Grinning, the twins, with Torgin trailing behind, followed Sibine up a spiral staircase. The loft had three mattresses arranged side by side on the floor. Each had a handmade leaf quilt, a soft lichen pillow, and a colorful nightshirt.

"Oh, my." Brie pressed her palms together. "This is beautiful, Sibine."

Ari chimed in. "Thank you so much for taking such good care of us."

"Yes, thank you." Torgin smothered another yawn. "I am more tired than I imagined."

After they had washed and prepared for bed, Brie watched her sister and friend doze off almost before their heads touched their pillows. She tried to stay awake and think about all that had occurred since coming to Myrrh, but slipped into a deep, dreamless sleep.

Sibine peeked in the doorway. She had seen few Human children—especially those from Idronatti—and these made her curious. Tuper had told her Almiralyn was their protector. But he had shared only a bit of their story.

She blinked back a tear. Her heart knew the shudder rippling through the land earlier in the turning was a harbinger of change. She hoped, for the sake of her babe, life on Myrrh would not change too much. Sighing, she returned to her little kitchen. After placing the kettle on the bright red stove, she cleared the table and then sat thinking, her small, protective hand resting on her belly.

Tibin was her Tiffin, and she was uncomfortable with his being out after dusk. Wood Tiffs belonged indoors as soon as the sun sank beyond sight. He brought the children across Terces Wood through the Intersect. Few Wood Tiffs knew about the secret world under the forest. She hoped Tuper, Tibin, and Fen were safe.

To help ease her concern, she crooned a lullaby to the unborn babe she already loved. Steam from the blue-flowered tea kettle began ringing the tiny bells on its spout. She poured water into a mug of gering nut tea and inhaled the wonderful aroma. Her thoughts wandered. *Tomorrow, the sun will rise, bringing with it the song of the birds. Tibin will return, and the children will continue their journey. Somehow, they will affect our lives in ways I don't even know now. But I know this will happen.* She pressed a hand to her belly. "*I love you, dear babe. But I'm so afraid for you...*"

As Yaro, the Pentharian, explored the area below the roots of Sibine's tree, he felt the magic of the land filling his heart. Determined to escape from the root system of Myrrh, he shaped a small blackbird and soared into the night sky.

This land inspired thoughts of his family and clan, the swamp where he was born, and the beauty of his freshwater home. Gliding upward, he came to rest on a large root and feasted his eyes on the expansive panorama stretching below him. *How I ache to go home.* He blinked. *Soon, my mission here will be complete.*

The DiMensioner and the Dreelum of DerTah had hired the Pentharian to steal the Prima Crystal. It wasn't until after they arrived in Myrrh that Nomed divulged his personal plan to destroy the land. Yaro's manufactured enthusiasm for his leader's goal waned, dissipating into the vastness and beauty of the Intersect. Sadness invaded his thoughts. He pushed it away. *It is my job. It must be done.*

"Well, Jordett, how do you like Myrrh?" Allynae observed the stunned PPP officer gaping in disbelief.

"Where in the name of the Five Fathers am I?"

"You're in Myrrh, Major. Pay attention. Or have you forgotten you spent time here as a child?"

Major Jordett tore his gaze away from the charming white cottage, the gardens, and the Terces Wood to look at the man standing beside him. "Myrrh? I spent time here as a child? I learned about it during officers' training but never believed it was real." He frowned. "The Borderlands... that's another story. Magic mirrors leading into yet another dimension?" He shook his head.

"Oh, it's *very* real. And you'll be staying until Mira decides what to do with you. Let's see if she's around anywhere."

Allynae pushed the cottage door open. Majeska strutted down the hall, the tip of her tail teasing the two men to follow. Just as she arrived in the kitchen, Almiralyn, in bird form, and Karrew flew in through the open window.

The raven cawed and landed on his perch. "Hey, Jeska, welcome home."

The white bird landed. Myrrh's Guardian materialized as Major Jordett stepped into view.

"Alli, what is *he* doing here?" She gave her brother a stern stare.

"Come in and sit down, Major." He then described his adventures in The Borderlands and how Jordett had arrived in Myrrh. When he finished, Almiralyn studied the Major where he sat, absently petting Majeska's silky head.

She smiled. "It appears you've made a friend, Jordy. I find it most interesting that she seems fond of you."

"I like cats." He ran his hand over her back. "How do you know my name?"

"Although you don't remember, you and I share a history."

Jordett looked puzzled.

Almiralyn gazed at Majeska. "How do you know you like cats since the PPP does not allow cats in Idronatti?"

"I just know, that's all. What happens now? Allynae said I can't go back through the mirror."

"No, you cannot. In fact, until events here are resolved, you can't go back, period."

"Now wait just a chron-click." The blustering major shot an indignant glare from one to other. "I have things to do. My team will miss me."

"They won't miss you for a while." Almiralyn looked thoughtful. "*My* question is, what do we do with you? I'll need to ponder that. Meanwhile, make yourself at home. Alli and I need to catch up. Please help yourself to a snack." With a sympathetic nod, she glided across her yellow gingham kitchen and into the hallway.

Allynae followed her upstairs to her sanctuary and faced her. "I almost didn't make it back. We need to fix that mirror. Why didn't you tell me about my twins?"

"I'm so glad you're here, Alli. We'll do something about the mirror, I promise. And I *couldn't* tell you about the twins. You were young and hotheaded, and I would have lost you to the Five Towers."

He sank into Mira's big, overstuffed chair and put his head in his hands. "Sparrow and I are Joined, you know."

"I know."

"All those missed sun cycles. And now my daughters, whom I've never even met, are in danger. What were you thinking, Mira?"

Almiralyn sat down on a footstool opposite him and took his hands in hers. "Your daughters have a destiny they must fulfill, Alli. Neither you nor I can interfere with that. I protected them while they were in Idronatti, and I will continue to protect them while they're here. I know you're angry and hurt. Try to understand I did what I did because I love you. When we've resolved the issues we're facing, I promise you time with Sparrow and your girls. But now, Myrrh is in trouble."

Allynae pulled his hands from hers and ran a finger over his bare upper lip. "Give me some time, Mira. They are almost *fourteen*. I've missed so much of their lives." He stood up and walked to the window. Anger at his sister warred with his love for her. Sadness left him shaking. He inhaled and faced her. "I understand you were protecting me and my family. It doesn't make it easier but..." A sigh filled with loss floated out the sanctuary window.

The sympathy in Almiralyn's eyes almost undid him. A glance out the window helped him gain control. "Tell me what occurred while I was gone." Still fighting his emotions, he forced himself to pay attention. When she finished, he told her about his reunion with Sparrow and his harrowing race through the city.

"Where is Sparrow now?"

"She sent me back to help you save our daughters and went to find Merrilea."

"I expect Merrilea will bring her to Myrrh through the gateway in the Central Mountains. She has used it to visit back and forth. Alli, someone set you up. Any idea who?"

"It had to be Dom. No one else knew I was in Idronatti. When I came back through the shoppe, he had disappeared."

"Let's check Elcaro's Eye and see what we can discover."

"Too bad it won't give us everything we need." Allynae heaved himself from the chair.

"It gives us what we *need*, just not what we think we *want*." Almiralyn turned to the fountain.

"Rather like life." Allynae muttered a profanity or two and joined her. Captured on the water's calm surface was Dom's face. "Well, I'll be..."

"Interesting. Let's see if it will give us a bit more information." With a wave of her hand, Almiralyn asked her first question. "Please show Dom... Recent past." The picture shifted to show Dom standing in front of the fountain, watching Sparrow and Allynae.

"Ah, he knows you're the father of the twins. Karrew and I discovered him in the middle of a pack of Pentharian, demanding to be taken to Seyes Nomed."

"That little turncoat."

"There's nothing we can do about Dom. We need information, so let's get down to business." Her hand moved over the water, erasing Dom's picture. "Show us Seyes Nomed." A dark cavern became visible. Six shadowy shapes sat around a small fire—Nomed, Dom, and four Pentharian.

Allynae leaned closer. "Weren't there five mercenaries?"

"There were. Elcaro, show us the fifth Pentharian." The picture continued to show Nomed and his minions.

Allynae scowled. "See what I mean? Do ya think it'll show us Esán?" The picture shifted. Esán and Zugo climbed down a rope ladder hanging over the side of a steep cliff.

"Well, well... A new player." Almiralyn sounded pleased. "I couldn't have chosen better myself."

"What about Paisley?"

Almiralyn touched the water's surface. "Paisley Tobinette." A new image came into focus. Paisley strode across the grasslands toward the Dojanacks.

Allynae leaned over the water and studied the image. "He's made good time."

"He's a good man." She squeezed the bridge of her nose. "It's late and I'm exhausted."

They returned to the kitchen and their unexpected guest. The major sat glaring at Karrew. "Come on. I heard you talking to Majeska when I came in. Say hello, Jordy. How about...goodbye. Say *something*."

Allynae laughed. "He's as stubborn as you are, Jordett. Prove you're a friend, and he might surprise you one of these turnings."

"Humph!" The major's snort elicited a caw and the flapping of Karrew's black wings.

Almiralyn put warm bread, sweet cheeses, and fresh fruit on the table. After they'd eaten their fill, she left.

The men headed to the barn. When they had settled in for the night, Jordett rolled onto his side. "What makes you think I won't take off after you fall asleep?"

"Where would you go?" Allynae yawned

"Anywhere. This is a big place."

"True. But, Major, Myrrh's under siege. Do you know anything about Seyes Nomed and the Pentharian?"

Jordett gave him a long, hard look. "No, I don't."

"They're here, and they're deadly. And no one in Myrrh or on Thera is safe until they're neutralized."

"And just what makes you think I believe you?"

Allynae shrugged. "I'm going to sleep, Jordett. Either you'll be here in the morning or you won't. The choice is yours."

29

In the depths of the Dojanack Caverns, Zugo's paddle pulled through the water, each stroke propelling the glider further over the smooth surface. At the bow, Esán sat in silent contemplation. The unusual energy radiating from him fascinated Zugo. His new friend seemed a curious mix of Human and magic. Despite the ancient taboo, he was taking him to Meos to meet his father. Yookotay was a formidable adversary, but he'd also earned the reputation of being fair and understanding.

The uneventful journey across the water gave Esán time for reflection. He marveled at his newfound talents and embraced the unfamiliar stirrings within him. Everything had its reason, and he knew he was in Myrrh for a purpose. Even meeting Zugo was important. The young

DeoNyte's role in the unfolding events would be as essential as his own; of that, he was certain.

When they reached the other side of the subterranean lake, Esán clambered ashore, helped Zugo to hide the aqua glider behind a granite outcropping, and squinted into the darkness. "Which way?"

Zugo guided him to a narrow cleft in the wall and took the lead. Esán sucked in his breath and crept along like a crab in a crack, keeping his focus on the vague outline of his friend's white, fur-covered body. The outline stopped. Esán sidestepped into the open and exhaled.

Zugo led him to a rocky cliff, where he could just make out a knotted rope stretching into the pitch-black emptiness below.

"We have to go down another level." Zugo knelt near the rim. *"I'll go first. When I tell you to start, you begin. I knotted the rope so we can climb down."* He grabbed the rope and swung over the edge. *"Are you ready?"*

The darkness wrapped around Esán like the wings of a bat. A deep breath helped him to focus his thoughts on the climb. *"I'm ready."*

Zugo started his descent. *"Come on."*

Esán knelt, and clutching a large knot, lowered himself over the edge. Zugo's weight below him provided tension on the rope and a sense of safety. Before he knew it, he stood on solid ground. *"That was quite something."*

Zugo laughed softly. *"You do well for an ill Human."*

"I am feeling a lot stronger. How much farther?"

"Not too much." The DeoNyte's hand on his elbow guided him into a tunnel.

Down they walked, side by side. Down. Down. Down...

The death shadow's rage teetered near the freezing point. He had searched the two tunnels exiting from Oche Cavern. Finding nothing in either to suggest Esán had passed that way, he returned to explore the passageway leading to the cavern's outer entrance. Esán's fading essence hung in the air. And he was not alone. Sniffing like a bloodhound, Wodash followed the trail to the edge of a subterranean lake. Acute night vision informed him his quarry was nowhere to be seen. He lifted into the air and skimmed over the water.

Below him, the lake shimmered, then smoothed. A creature rose to the surface, its grotesque face twisted into an angry scowl. Sunken white eyes with pulsating, crimson pupils trapped his gaze in a vise-like grip and sent him somersaulting back in time.

Memories rushed around a racetrack in Wodash's mind—his beautiful wife and daughter lying in a pool of blood—the rage that drove him to avenge their deaths; how the need to kill took over his life.

His last turning rose like the spectre in the water below. He stood on the edge of a seaside cliff, the ocean pounding on the rocks, the father of his latest victim sobbing at the side of his dead son. Anguish for the man and for himself sent him plunging into the sea—the cold, the liquid filling his lungs, the heaviness—the realization that his choice to kill had made him a deathless thing, destined to wander forever, feasting on the life energy of others.

A panicked spasm flung him from his memories into stalactite-filled space. Boney hands reached for his throat. Down he plummeted. Cold water snatched at his body and hauled him below the surface. Struggling to break free, he thrust his water-weighted bulkiness upward and launched into frantic flight. Terror propelled him to the far side of the lake, where, coughing and sputtering, he collapsed. Cursing with each rasping breath, he shook his waterlogged form like a soggy dog. Heavy droplets rained around him in a wide, wet orbit.

Gathering his courage, he stepped to the water's edge and scanned the surface. The ugly white face glared up at him. He jumped back. The face vanished. He leaned forward. It reappeared, gruesome and leering. Wodash stretched a boney, white finger in its direction. Its finger reached toward him. Their tips touched. The face rippled, scattering—a torn photograph on the currents of time.

Wodash gaped. *A reflection!* He took a jerky step away from the edge, his gaze digging into the darkness. *What is this place? By the burning sands of DerTah, I'm glad Nomed wasn't here to see me battle with my reflected image... my own memories.*

He sank to the cavern floor, wrapped his fearsome cold in a tight cloak around him, and shoved the last remnants of memory into an unfathomable place in his mind. His anger returned. "Where in SeDah is Esán? He will pay when I find him." Nostrils quivering, he followed the fast-fading scent to the rope hanging over the cliff.

Behind him, the smoothness of the lake's surface once again projected the image of his horror-stricken face. The Lake of Rorret had savored every moment of the death shadow's terror. It had tasted it, relished it, and would remember it forever.

The water swirled, eradicating the gruesome image. For one moment, the hairless boy appeared—eyes filled with knowing—face pale and expectant. And then, like a memory wiped clean, the lake lay blank and calm in the lightless cavern. The Time of Change had come.

Birds bursting into song teased Brie to wakefulness. At first, the pale green room and sunlight warming her face confused her. She blinked and sat up. A smile of recognition tugged at the corners of her mouth. "We're in the TreeOm." She rolled onto her side and nudged her twin.

Ari peeked from one eye. "Good morning. I sure slept well. How about you?"

"Great." Brie yawned and stretched. "It's so good to feel safe."

Ari laughed. "Look. Torgin sleeps with his mouth open."

Torgin groaned and yawned. "I do not."

Brie grinned and pulled Ari up beside her. "I smell something yummy. You'd better hurry, Torgin, before we eat it all."

She preceded Ari down the spiral staircase. In the kitchen, Sibine stood by the stove, a pan of muffins hot in her hand. A centerpiece of fresh flowers sat at the table's center with a banquet of delectable breakfast treats surrounding it.

"Good Morning, Sibine." Brie linked elbows with her sister. "The table looks so pretty. I love the flowers."

Ari clapped her hands in delight. "It looks like a party."

Sibine studied their faces. "You are identical." She laughed. "How do people tell you apart?"

"Listen to their voices." Torgin joined them, still yawning. "Brie's is softer and sounds like a melody. Ari's voice is deep and more resonant. That is how I tell them apart."

Sibine's dark eyes twinkled. "Say something."

Brie grinned. "I'm Brie, and I love your TreeOm."

"I'm Ari, and your breakfast table looks beautiful."

Sibine smiled. "I see what you mean, Torgin. Thank you, girls. Now, before we eat, you can freshen up down the hall. You'll find your clothes clean and folded on the bureau behind the spiral staircase."

"Thank you, Sibine." Brie gave Ari a playful shove and followed her down the hall.

Ari returned to the kitchen and took her place at the table. "It feels so good to be clean."

"It sure does." Brie plopped down beside her.

Torgin ambled into the room. "I think *I'm* awake now."

Sibine motioned him to join them at the table. "Now let us give thanks for the gifts given by so many." She remained standing, her head bowed.

> *"To the Plants, to the Tree, to the Flowers and Vine,*
> *For the food on our table, these presents divine,*
> *We thank all who've given of body and soul*
> *To keep our lives healthy, abundant, and whole."*

Sibine slid into her chair. "Now, we'd better eat before Tibin arrives, or there will be nothing left."

Happy chatter accompanied the meal. Ari swallowed the last bite of her third muffin. Her deep laugh of delight made Brie grin.

Torgin ate nonstop without looking up. At last, he leaned back in his chair. "That was wonderful!" "What were those muffins?"

"Birchberry and pansy flower. They're my favorites." Sibine smiled.

Ari smacked her lips. "I loved the redberry jelly."

Brie drank her last drop of acorn milk and set the cup on the table. "Thank you so much for making us such a lovely breakfast. Can we help clean up?"

"You may, but are you sure you've eaten enough?"

"I couldn't take another bite." Brie pushed her chair back.

Ari began to clear the table. "I can't remember the last time I was this full."

Bells in the hall rang, sending a wind-chimed song throughout the TreeOm. "That will be Tibin." Sibine scurried from the kitchen.

"I suppose that means we have to go soon, doesn't it?" Torgin frowned. "I know we must find Esán, but it is nice not to be afraid."

Ari nodded. "It has been good to feel safe. We'll just have to stay out of harm's way, that's all. Come on, Torg. Smile. It isn't so bad."

"We have each other, and that's what matters." Brie hugged him.

Tibin walked into the kitchen. "Good Morning. Sibine tells me you ate all my breakfast."

"We did not." Torgin pointed at the table. "See, we saved you a whole plateful. I loved the muffins."

"He ate at least five." Ari chortled. "But there are still some for you."

Torgin grinned and punched Ari in the arm. "And how many did *you* eat?"

Ari considered Tibin's sad expression as he watched their playfulness. *Does he know something we don't?* She shrugged her apprehension away. "How's Fen?"

"Better than ever. He and his mother send you their regards. I need to eat, then we'll leave. We must arrive at the grasslands before the sun reaches its zenith. You should try to make it at least halfway across today if you can." He savored a couple of bites. "You will find a grove of trees with a spring on this side of the river where you can spend the night. Torgin's compass will guide you."

"How did *you* know about the compass?" Torgin wasn't smiling.

"Almiralyn told me. She must trust you, Torgin, or she would never have given it to you."

Torgin blushed. "I did not mean to sound so testy."

Tibin smiled. "It's okay. You have every right to be wary. A lot has happened to you in the past couple of turnings." He finished his last bite. "It's time to go."

Sibine greeted them in the front room with an anxious smile. Three backpacks sat on the floor beside her.

"Since you've lost your saddlebags, we thought you should have these." Tibin handed them around. "Each one has a blanket for the cooler nights in the mountains, dried food, a lite-stick, and water. You can refill your water bottles in the streams and springs. I included a rope in each pack and flint for making a fire."

After profuse expressions of gratitude, the children slipped on their packs and hugged Sibine one last time. Brie's eyes glistened with tears when she stepped back from the Tiffet. "Your babe *spoke* to me."

Curiosity and surprise filled Sibine's face. She cupped Brie's hands in hers. "What did it say?"

"It's a Tiffin, and his name will be Adin. He'll be born by the light of the new moon." She blushed, her eyes still damp with tears. "Should I have told you? I'm not a wise woman."

The Wood Tiffs exchanged glances. Sibine put her arms around her. "You are a wise woman in the making, Brie. I sensed it when we first met. Tibin and I are honored you have blessed our TreeOm with your knowing. Travel with the blessing of the WeHem and the love of the Wood Tiffs. Remember your beds and your nightshirts will be here for you when you pass this way again. You are always welcome."

Brie hugged her, settled on the seat, and vanished through the deep green foliage. Torgin followed.

Ari watched them go with a fresh wave of anxiety.

When her turn came, Sibine hugged her. "Stay safe, Ari."

Ari nodded and climbed onto the seat. Apprehension, clinging to her like a spider's web, eclipsed her delight in the ride. *I wonder if this is how Brie feels.* The chair stopped. She slid off, her eyes searching for her twin.

Sibine remained on the porch after the children left. She knew they faced dangers she couldn't even imagine. With a sigh, she patted her belly. "I hope they return to us, Adin. I'd like you to meet the young woman who named you—the wise woman who doesn't yet know her destiny."

30

With the death shadow sniffing at their heels, Esán and Zugo fled deeper into the Dojanack caverns. As they rounded a bend, Esán reached for his friend's arm. Emptiness sent a wave of panic through him. His heart pounding, he started back up the tunnel. "Zugo? Where are—"

"I'm here." The shaky voice produced a small, hazy cloud. "I-I'm so cold, I can hardly move."

"Steady." Esán laid a hand on his friend's icy arm. "The creature following us feeds on our fear. If you aren't afraid, he can't harm you."

"I've seen him in the upper cavern and not felt like this. Why now?"

"He knows someone's with me, and he's concentrating on you. Where are we going?"

"To my father in the City of Meos."

"We can't lead the death shadow to your people." Esán rubbed his bald head and narrowed his eyes. "Hide, Zugo. We can't let him find you, either."

The DeoNyte hugged his furry body and shivered. "I won't leave you."

"Zugo, he's faster and stronger than either of us. I'll try to teleport behind him and lead him back the other way. If he catches me, you can rescue me later. It's vital *you* remain a secret. Seyes Nomed will use you. Just like he's planning to use me. Please hide."

"We'll do it your way, Esán, but I will be close by." Zugo shivered and melted into the darkness.

A numbing cold rushing down the tunnel left Esán hugging himself to keep warm. *Sure hope I can repeat what happened in the clearing at Nemttachenn.*

"I know you're here, bald boy." The frigid voice was grim. "I know someone's with you. Stay where you are, and I won't harm you."

Esán gauged the slant of the passageway, pivoted to face uphill, and shut his eyes. Relief washed over him as the paralyzing cold of the death shadow hit him from behind. With growing confidence and the need to protect his friend, he envisioned himself at the base of the cliff near the Lake of Rorret. The knotted rope brushing his arm made him giddy with excitement. *I did it!*

Alert for the approach of his adversary, he edged along the rough wall until he found the tunnel opening. A blast of cold slamming into his chest knocked the breath from his lungs and sent him staggering backward.

The death shadow loomed over him. "You think you can trick Wodash od DerTah? You're a naïve little fool." White eyes narrowed to mere slits. "Who led you into this part of the cavern?"

Esán gulped a breath, and rubbing his chest, masked all memories of Zugo. "My guide fled, frightened by you and your frigid cold."

An icy hand shot out and gripped his chin. A probe ripped his mind in two. "Tell me who he is."

Esán pushed the hand away, but kept his gaze fastened on the death shadow. "A man stumbled into Oche Cavern and told me he could lead me out. Instead, he got me lost."

Wodash scowled in disbelief. "Enough lies. Seyes Nomed sent me to bring you to him. By now he will have guessed something's amiss." Boney fingers tightened around his arm. "Come."

Esán jerked free. "And if I choose not to go with you?"

Wodash glared, pressed him against the wall, and fastened a thin white collar around his neck. "Try to get away, and you'll discover just how tight that cord can get." His attempt at a smile contorted his face into a hideous mask. "Let me show you how it works."

Esán gasped and clawed at the tightening cord. Wheezing attempts to breathe forced frozen clouds of air between his lips. Ice formed on the surface of his tongue. A gurgling spasm shuddering through his body dropped him to his knees.

Wodash yanked him to standing. "Will you do as you're told?"

"Ye-e-s." The strangling pressure released. Warm air sliced through his lungs. Esán flinched and brushed a tear from his cheek.

"How wise you are for one so young. Follow me to the top of the cliff." Wodash shot upward.

Esán massaged his throat with shaking hands and relished a moment alone.

Above him, a disembodied voice growled. "What are you waiting for, boy? Get up here."

His mind racing, Esán grabbed the rope. *Climbing will give me time to think.* One knot after the other brought him closer to the enemy, but not to a solution for his predicament. *My only choice is to follow the death shadow's instructions.* He gritted his teeth. *But I will escape. I have to.*

Wodash hauled him up beside him on the cliff's edge. "Why didn't you teleport?" Annoyance made his harsh voice more abrasive.

Feigning fatigue, Esán relished the touch of triumph his minor rebellion provided. "I thought I should save my strength."

"Don't play me for a fool." The death shadow dragged him along until they stood a short distance from the Lake of Rorret.

Sensing trepidation in his enemy's mind, Esán glanced up. Fear registered on the ugly face and then vanished behind a mask of hesitant control.

"You go first." Wodash shoved him to the lake's edge. "And don't do anything silly. Wait for me on the far side."

Esán glanced down at the lake. His eyes widened as snakelike tendrils of dark, shimmering water slithered over the rocky edge and encircled his ankles. The next thing he knew, water gurgled and splashed around him. Arms flailing and feet kicking, he fought an unbeatable battle to stay afloat. Powerful currents sucked him under, pulled him into fluid obscurity beneath the lake's surface. A low, languid voice penetrated the intense silence—a voice that mesmerized, hypnotized, and enthralled him. *"You are safe. Relax. Do not fight."*

Propelled by the unseen, he drifted deeper and deeper, until, when he thought his lungs would burst, he broke the surface in a space filled with radiant light.

"Nooo!" A scream of anguished rage exploded from the death shadow. Gawking at the lake and unable to believe Esán had disappeared beneath its surface, he wrestled with his personal fear of Rorret. Dread left him shaking. *The lake terrifies me more than the wrath of my master.*

Unrelenting fear forced his wraith-like body into flight. A nagging desire to look down sent him racing to the far shore. The walls of the crystal tunnel closed around him. Too soon, he arrived in the passage leading to Oche Cavern. He shuddered. *Now I must face the anger of the man with the demon's eyes.*

As the death shadow disappeared, Zugo crept from the narrow crevice near the knotted rope to the edge of the blue-black lake. He had watched the watery tendrils drag Esán into the water and his friend struggling until he disappeared into its murky depths. Uncertain about what he should do next, he stared at the unruffled surface. *Father told me you were dangerous, Rorret. Now I believe him.*

He trotted back the way he had come, grabbed the rope, and began his descent. *Only one person can tell me what has happened to my friend—only one can help.*

Seyes Nomed preceded three Pentharian through the entrance at the Cliffs of ReVod and charged down the passage and into Oche Cavern. He came to an abrupt halt with his black and silver cape swirling around his bare torso like a lightning-streaked thunder cloud. Wodash and Esán were nowhere to be seen. Dom, a disheveled, crumpled heap, sat alone beside the campfire. On his long nose, gold-rimmed spectacles reflected the dancing flames and stressed the wrinkled pallor of his aging face. Jeet, his Pentharian escort, stood a good distance away, gazing at Remmihs Lake. He turned as his three comrades joined him.

Nomed's harsh glower twisted the scar at the corner of his mouth. "Where's Wodash and the bald boy?" His piercing hazel eyes narrowed. "And what coaxed you from your safe little antique shoppe?"

"We haven't seen the death shadow or the boy." The old man grimaced.

Cursing under his breath, Nomed strode toward his alcove.

"Wait, Seyes. I have something important to share."

Nomed paused at the curtained entrance and turned. "What could be so important you would travel all this way?"

"I saw—"

"Give me a moment, Dom." He ducked into his sleeping space, tossed his cape onto the pallet, and crossed to a makeshift washstand to splash water on his face and neck. After patting himself dry, he drained his water flask, pulled a clean shirt from his pack, and slipped it on. Much refreshed, he rejoined his companions.

"So, what's your news, Dom?" He sat on a rock opposite the old man. "And how did you enjoy your journey here? I understand Jeet most graciously transported you."

Dom scowled and rubbed his shoulder. "He carried me like vermin."

The four Pentharian joined them by the fire. Jeet shrugged. "He squirmed like vermin. He should be grateful I didn't drop him over the grasslands."

Dom threw the carnelian alien a dark look and then peered over his spectacles at Nomed. "I thought you would want to know some news I've discovered about the twins."

Nomed realized the old man paused for dramatic effect. "Continue." The word, clipped and laced with disinterest, had no effect on the older man.

"Guess who their father is."

Nomed picked up a small piece of wood and tossed it on the fire. "I do not know. Is there some reason I should care?"

Dom's wrinkled mouth puckered into a tight circle. "It's Allynae Nadrugia."

"Almiralyn's brother?" The wood burst into flame, and so did his interest.

"The one and only." Dom's dour expression turned triumphant.

"How very interesting. It would appear even more important for them to come under my influence, wouldn't it? But then, we seem to have lost them. In fact, we can't seem to keep our hands on any of these young people." He glanced around the cavern. "Where, on DerTah, is Wodash? And what has become of Esán?"

From the passageway, Wodash heard the last part of the DiMensioner's angry question with a wry expression. *A little bravado won't hurt.* As though in response to a theatrical cue, he entered.

Nomed came to standing and glared. "Where have *you* been?"

He performed a deep bow. "Chasing the bald boy. When I arrived back here to fetch him, he'd vanished."

"It appears..." Nomed stared beyond him into the tunnel. "...that he continues to be absent. Am I correct?"

The sarcasm in the DiMensioner's voice made him bristle. "I found him. We were almost here when he tumbled into the lake and disappeared."

"You mean he drowned?" The knife-sharp question ricocheted off the stone walls until only silence remained in Oche Cavern.

Wodash pressed thin, blue lips together.

"Answer me, Wodash." Nomed's eyes flashed. "Did Esán drown?"

"He fell into the lake and did not resurface. I assume he drowned."

In two strides, Nomed reached the tunnel entrance. "Take me to that lake."

Fear rose like a sour lump in Wodash's throat.

The scar on Nomed's cheek pulsed with rage. "Are you going to hover there like the SeDahan coward you are? Show me now."

Wodash swallowed. "Yes, Master."

"Does anyone care to join us?" Nomed's query sparked an immediate response.

Voer conferred with his comrades, then moved to Nomed's side. "I come. Yuin and Stee will remain here."

Jeet's gaze rested on Wodash. "I wish to see this lake that so terrifies a death shadow."

With a glare of loathing, Wodash turned his back on the orange Pentharian and floated down the passageway. When they reached the narrow crevice, Nomed pushed him aside and peered into the tunnel.

"We need to fly." Changing to the owl, he swooped between the crystal walls.

Voer and Jeet assumed bat form and flew after him.

Dread hammering through him, Wodash followed.

From its fathomless depths, Rorret witnessed their approach, read their fear, and understood their quest before their shifted forms touched down at its shore. Savoring the death shadow's apprehension, it prepared to listen.

"Where's the boy's body?" The DiMensioner snarled at Wodash.

A long, boney finger pointed to the far side of the lake. "He fell in over there."

Rorret tracked the course of the owl to its opposite shore. As Nomed shifted and knelt to peer into its depths, it captured his human visage on its surface.

"Nothing." Nomed's scarred face twisted with frustration as he stood.

Voer sat on the lake's edge and motioned for Jeet to join him. "We'll find the boy."

After sliding into water, they shaped two rainbow-striped fish and, with a flip of their tails, shot below the surface.

Rorret explored their alien strangeness and tasted the bitterness of their dislike for the DiMensioner. *To kill or not to kill?* Deeper still, it discovered innate goodness buried beneath the instincts of the hunter. *Live, they must survive.*

The unexpected benevolence filling their hearts with desire for home, family, and the swamps of ReTaw Au Qa confirmed his decision. It caught them in its current and pushed them to the surface. They clambered empty-handed onto the rocky edge, their golden eyes drenched with longing.

Nomed strode beside the water's edge and stopped in front of them. "What is this lake?"

The Pentharian shook their braided hair back from glistening tattooed faces and lowered their eyes.

The DiMensioner swung around and glowered at the water's fluid darkness. "I know you keep a boy who is mine, and I will have him back." Shifting the great horned owl, he streaked across the cavern and up the crystal tunnel.

Rorret watched Wodash follow in his wake, fear chasing him as surely as he chased his master. The two Pentharian hesitated. It understood their water-hunger and waited.

They moved to the edge of the lake, stared into its restlessness, then shifted and flew after the DiMensioner.

In rapid succession, the Lake of Rorret sent images flashing across its dark surface. Delighted laughter flooded the cavern. *A good turning's work! Very good indeed.*

More than satisfied, it shifted its attention and focused on the bald-headed boy and the crystal heart of Myrrh.

In Oche Cavern, Dom sat opposite Yuin and Stee. They made him uncomfortable. But then, so did Seyes Nomed. *Whatever possessed me to chase the DiMensioner across Myrrh?* Loyalty, he supposed. They had spent time in the Five Towers together. Seyes had helped him escape. *Now I'm caught in this so-called adventure with no foreseeable way out.* Antiques by Q and its comfortable quiet sounded better than ever.

Avoiding the Pentharian's alien gaze, he cleaned his spectacles and stared at the fire, contemplating his next move. When two bats, an owl, and the death shadow flew into the cavern, he replaced the specs on his nose and trembled as all but Wodash shape shifted. *I'm certainly keeping strange company.*

Nomed paced to the tunnel entrance and back before he faced those around the fire. "Tonight we must rest. Tomorrow, Voer, you and your comrades will find the twins and bring them here. Wodash and I will discover the truth about Esán. Please make yourselves comfortable. If you're hungry, you'll find food in the containers behind the woodpile. Good night." He stepped into his sleeping alcove. The curtain swished shut behind him.

Wodash turned to Dom and pointed at Esán's cave. "You rest there." He looked at the Pentharian. "And you do whatever it is you do at night, as will I."

Dom remained by the fire for some time after his odd companions dispersed. It crossed his mind that this might be the time to escape. *And how would you find your way home, old man?* Muttering under his breath, he shuffled to the small cave.

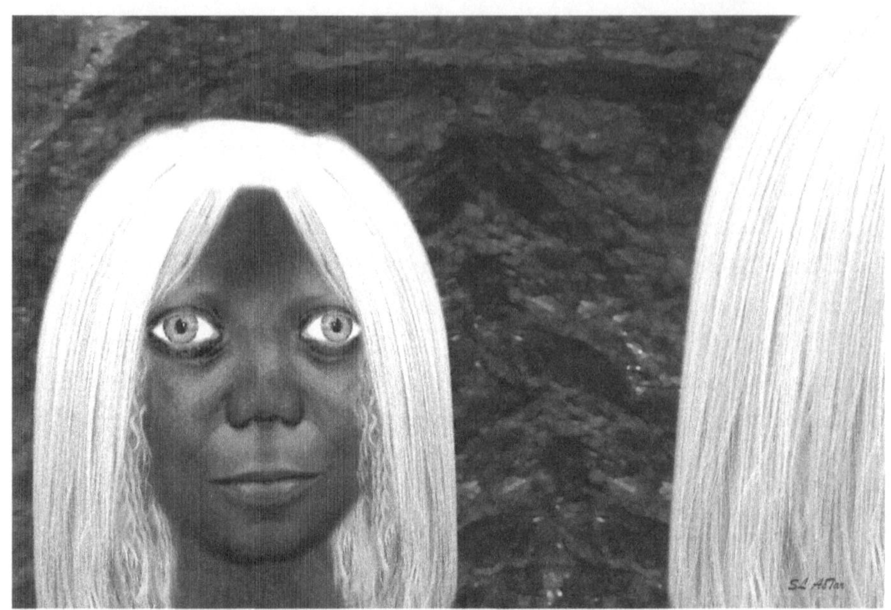

31

Zugo gripped the Sapphire of Descendence and squared his shoulders. "I have one more thing to share, Father." He swallowed. "I met a new friend. His name is Esán."

His father's penetrating gaze drilled into him. "Esán? What kind of name is that, my son?"

"It is a Human name. Esán is Human."

For one long, agonizing moment, his father said nothing. His gaze did not waver. When he spoke, a stern expression belied the soft cadence of his words. "You know about the ban on Humans, do you not? You know, we do not associate with any humanoid species. How is it you are now involved with this..." He pursed his lips. "...Esán?"

"He is not at all like the Humans my tutors warned me about. In fact, he drew the death shadow away from me and allowed it to capture him so it wouldn't find our people. He has special gifts, Father."

"How are you aware of these gifts, Zugo?"

"I've seen him use some of them. And I can perceive others."

Another long silence made Zugo squirm.

"Where is this Esán now?" His father's face looked grave, but not angry.

"The lake took him."

"I don't understand, my son."

"The Lake of Rorret wrapped tendrils of water around his ankles and pulled him down so far I couldn't see him anymore. Do you think it took him to the Cave of Canedari?"

"There are many stories about the lake." The ReDael's stern tone matched his expression. "Some survivors tell stories of it and the cave. You know it is not safe to anger Rorret, Zugo."

"I've crossed the lake many times, Father. It has always behaved calmly. But it was not calm when it grabbed Esán away from the death shadow."

"Why did the lake do that, son?"

"I don't know."

"You realize your curiosity about the world outside our boundaries has gotten you into serious trouble. Now you must appear before the council."

"Yes, Father." Zugo's trembling fingers tightened around his pendant.

Yookotay listened to what Zugo shared verbally and deciphered what he left in the silence between words. His son had broken many taboos. He had also proven his courage and honesty by sharing the truth with his father and leader.

Yookotay drew Zugo down beside him on a carved granite bench and studied his face in the dim lamplight.

"Zugo, my son, what you have done has placed our people in danger. Now you and I must decide how to approach the council to get their support and their help for your young friend."

"I'm sorry to bring danger here, but I'm not sorry to have met Esán, Father." Zugo's tone carried a touch of defiance.

"He is, from what you've said, a very special Human." Yookotay's tone reflected his respect for his son. "It is good your young friend knew not to bring the death shadow close to Meos. He also protected you, and for that, I'm grateful."

"Father, tell me about the Cave of Canedari. You've been there. Can we find it and save Esán?"

Yookotay crossed to the large round table at the center of the chamber. He did not let Zugo's impatience hurry him as he paced around its diameter, pausing at each of twelve evenly spaced gemstone markers. When he finished his circuit, he held out the Sapphire of ReDaelum, which hung on a thick gold chain around his neck. A shaft of radiant blue light shot from it to the inset sapphire marking his place at the council table. Both jewels glowed with an inner fire that faded.

He regarded his young son. "We can find your Esán, but we must speak with the council first. It is imperative that all hearts perceive the truth and that all minds join in one accord."

A knock on the door interrupted them.

Yookotay turned. "Come in."

A young female DeoNyte entered and bowed her head. "They await your summons."

"Send them to us."

With a nod, she left the chamber.

A solemn procession, composed of eleven DeoNytes, five male and six female, entered and took their places around the table. Yookotay bowed his head in respect before aligning his Pendant of ReDaelship with his sapphire place marker. As the council members followed his example, rays of light connecting their pendants to their markers formed a circular rainbow of jewel colors. The last connection created a fountain of light that rose from the table's center and sent a shower of diffused radiance to tint the whiteness of their fur. In unison, they repeated,

> *"As in times gone by, as in days of old, in a galaxy far away*
> *Let us gather here, around the round, to discuss our coming day.*
> *As in days of old, bring your heart and mind to the table of the one*
> *In this moment you and I are joined, the Unfolding has begun."*

In the silence that followed, Yookotay released his pendant. The light vanished, and the members took their seats. Gathering his thoughts, he addressed his fellow Crystal Keepers.

"My son is here today with a story to tell. It holds importance far beyond the curiosity of youth. Please listen without judgment until his tale is complete."

He drew Zugo to his side and nodded for him to begin.

Zugo made eye contact with each member of the Council of Crystal Keepers. Not mixing words, he described the anger and the evil he saw in Seyes Nomed and his companions and spoke with pride of his Human friend Esán. He finished by taking responsibility for placing his people in danger.

An elderly female rose and placed her left hand on her heart, her right on the malachite marking her position at the table.

Yookotay touched his pendant. "Speak, Owae."

"Our ancient texts describe the evil intent of those lurking beyond the Dojanack caverns and their search for the Prima Crystal. The prophecies suggest that children will undo the folly of men. Evil has entered our mountain. A child befriends a child. We must pay attention and prepare for the Changing of Time. Saving the Human child is a step to saving ourselves." Owae bowed her head and sat down.

A young man stood, placing his right hand on his heart and his left on his golden topaz marker.

"Speak, Darak."

The young male's gaze traveled over the faces of those seated at the round table. "War is upon us, and this is our warning. We must fight for our right to live as we live and to protect the Prima Evolsefil. Let us gather our forces and destroy this wicked one and his companions." His hand on his marker, he sat down.

Zugo listened to each of the eleven speak. Relieved his behavior—although against the rules—was not the subject of their discourse, he learned much from the discussion. The safety of the DeoNytes and of the Prima Crystal dominated their concerns.

As the discussion drew to a close, Yookotay stood and gazed at each council member. As the DeoNyte leader, his role was to distill the feelings and beliefs of the group into an overriding truth. Using it as a guide, he then formulated a wise response to the situation.

Both hands on his heart, the ReDael of Meos bowed his head, then lowered his hands and placed them, palms down, on either side of his sapphire marker.

"I discern from heart and mind consensus regarding the threat to our existence and to our solar system as we know it. I hear the cry to battle and the cry for discreet action. DeoNytes are not warriors. The Arts of DiMensionery are beyond our experience, and Seyes Nomed is a DiMensioner. It is, however, prudent to secure our boundaries and to warn our people. Darak, I appreciate your urgent plea and honor your heart. With Fatooay, I appoint you to plan the defense of the City of Meos." Fatooay, a grizzled older male, gave Darak a brief nod.

"Now to discretion." Yookotay gazed around the table. "Protecting the Human child is vital and prudent, as is learning more of the plans of Seyes Nomed. Without knowledge, we are blind." He nodded to a young female with one blue eye and one green. "Elae, you are an initiate of the Cave of Canedari. Will you accompany my son to find his friend and carry a message to the Guardian Priestesses of Evolsefil about our concerns?"

Elae's odd eyes gleamed. "I accept the honor of this responsibility." She smiled at Zugo.

"Then accompany Zugo to find and bring the Human boy back to Meos. Please share all we have discussed with the Priestess Guardians. Sitrio and I will learn more about the DiMensioner. The rest of you warn the people and help prepare to defend the city. Are we all as one?"

The Crystal Keepers stood and took hands. Heads bowed, they remained silent for some time. In one accord, they broke the circle and dispersed in various directions.

Owae put an arm around Zugo's shoulders. "Sometimes the curiosity of youth pays off. Most often, it brings the unexpected. Be wise, young Zugo, for you have begun your walk to Doohnam." Her toothless smile beamed as she left him standing alone beside his father.

"Well, my son, you were lucky today. I honor your courage and your truth. Now, join Elae."

"Father, first please tell me about the Cave of Canedari."

Yookotay's expression grew thoughtful. "The Cave of Canedari houses the essence of our culture, the lifeblood of Myrrh and Thera, and Evolsefil, a Prima Crystal central to the integrity of the Crystal Laítise. The Chosen

Ones discover Canedari by accident or by the Council's design. I was a boy, not much older than you, when my sire introduced me to the cave as part of my initiation into the role of ReDael."

"What about Elae?"

"Elae was very young when she stumbled into the Cavern of Tennisca and discovered the Cave of Canedari. She is also a Chosen One and trains to be a Priestess Guardian. Listen with your heart, Zugo, and you will learn much from her."

"Father, what is the Crystal Laítise?"

Yookotay smiled at his eagerness. "When you return, we will discuss it. Now go. Elae awaits you, as does your friend."

Zugo returned his father's smile. "Thank you for listening and understanding."

Elae waited in the anteroom of the council chamber. Smaller than most DeoNyte females, she looked delicate—almost fragile. Zugo knew her appearance was deceiving. He liked her. More than that, he trusted her.

"So, young Zugo, we journey together."

He nodded and yawned.

"When did you sleep last?"

"It's been awhile." Zugo yawned again.

"Go rest. I'll come for you at the second chime, and we will begin our light trek."

"What about Esán?"

"Your friend is safe in the Cave of Canedari, Zugo. Get some sleep."

Zugo couldn't remember when his quarters had looked so welcoming. He downed the snack his mother had left, stretched out on his sleeping shelf, and drifted into dreaming.

Ari reached the base of the TreeOm to find her dread mirrored in her sister's eyes. Hair prickled on the back of her neck. A glance at Torgin's set jaw magnified her uneasiness. She pressed closer to Brie.

Buster bounding through the trees, tail wagging and big ears flopping, erased her growing tension. A big slobbery tongue licked her cheek. She laughed outright and tried to hug his wiggly body. "I like you, too."

Torgin responded to the big dog with a sad smile. "I wish Tam were here. I really miss her."

A high-pitched whinny preceded Tuper and Fen from the trees. The tan and cream pony, ears twitching and eyes on Torgin, followed.

Torgin threw his arms around her neck. "I knew you wouldn't leave us."

"We found her galloping through the woods, but couldn't find her saddlebags anywhere." Tuper patted the pony's flank. "They'll turn up. It's time to go." He set a brisk pace down a trail that began close to Sibine's tree.

Ari ambled beside the small stream running alongside it, where water bugs skated, polliwogs wiggled, and spotted frogs jumped from one rock to the next. *I love the morning, and I love the busy sounds of summer.* A good night's sleep, an excellent breakfast, and the beauty of the turning pushed yesterday's evil and her recent anxiety into the past. Birds sang and squirrels chattered. A rabbit with long, droopy ears peeked between the tall ferns, its nose wiggling furiously. Ari gripped Buster's collar and smiled at Torgin, who walked beside her, his arm flung over Tam's neck. Life seemed hopeful again.

Too soon, the group gazed over the grasslands. Tibin followed their gaze. "This is where we leave you. Wood Tiffs are creatures of the trees and are uncomfortable in the open. We'll tell Almiralyn where we left you and where you're headed."

Tuper pointed at the distant mountains. "See that tall, black peak directly ahead on the horizon? Keep it in your line of sight, and it will lead you to the spring in the grove of trees."

Torgin stared, his eyes shaded with a hand. "What is the mountain called?"

Tibin gazed across the grasslands. "That's NaiDisbo Peak, the mountain of black glass."

"NaiDisbo Peak." Torgin gripped the compass.

After an awkward pause, Brie hugged Tibin. "Thank you for all you've done for us. We'll never forget you."

Unable to put it off any longer, Ari bid farewell to Tibin and Tuper. "Thank you for everything. Take care of yourselves."

Fen, shyness coloring his cheeks, peeked up at her. "I owe you my life. I want to go with you, but my mother said I must stay here."

She smiled at him. "Your mother loves you, Fen. I'll see you when I come back."

Torgin bowed to the Wood Tiffs. "Thank you for everything and thank you for finding Tam."

Ari looked across the sea of green grass undulating in the morning breeze. "We have a long walk ahead of us. If we plan to reach the grove by nightfall, we'd better go."

Brie mounted Tam, nudged her in to the open, and allowed her to choose her own path through the tall grass.

Ari stared after her twin. Her misgivings manifested in the form of a shudder. With a shake of her head, she tried to push it away. "Come on, Torg." Her anxiety softened by the beauty of the world around her, she whistled for Buster and followed.

32

The countryside flew by as the early morning Onom Lira whizzed toward RemMus Lake. Sparrow stared out the window. Merrilea slept in the seat next to her. Before sunrise, Henrietta had reminded them of the Key and shooed them out the door. If the man in gray waited near, he was well-hidden. Sparrow hoped he was still sleeping.

They began their hike to Demrach Canyon in the crisp cool of the morning. Merrilea led the way up the steep, twisting path. At first, Sparrow kept looking over her shoulder; soon, the beauty of the landscape lulled her into forgetting the threat of the PPP.

Merrilea set a good pace. Sparrow did her best to match it. The higher they hiked, the more difficult she found it to keep up. "Is it much further?" She gulped a deep breath.

"Not much." Merrilea strode around a sharp bend, sidestepped to avoid a collision with two young men coming from the opposite direction, and stopped.

Sparrow covered her surprise by readjusting her pack. *By the Fathers...*

"Morning, ladies." The taller man did the talking. "Out awful early, aren't ya?"

"We like a morning hike." Merrilea smiled. "You spent the night in the canyon?"

The smaller man nodded. "It gets pretty chilly when you're up this high. We're heading down to warm up. Where're you headed?"

"Nowhere special." Sparrow forced a casual tone. "We thought we'd hike for a while, enjoy a picnic, and return later this afternoon."

"Then be careful, ladies. The trail ahead can be treacherous in spots. We'll be on our way." The taller man nodded, and he and his companion continued down the mountain.

Sparrow and Merrilea exchanged glances and hiked up the trail in silence. Paying close attention to their surroundings, Sparrow worked to match her companion's quickened pace. Soon, they had put a respectful distance between themselves and the men.

"I need a break." Merrilea straddled a log with a view of a long, winding canyon and sat down.

Sparrow joined her and pulled her ever-present sketchbook from her backpack. "What an incredible view." With quick, easy strokes, she began to sketch the breathtaking panorama.

Demrach Canyon's river and flat lands, surrounded on both sides by the majesty of the Central Mountain range, came to life on her paper. Evergreen trees that flowed from the mountaintop to the lushness of the spectacular canyon floor spilled from her artist's pen onto the page.

While she worked, Merrilea spread an old-fashioned gingham tablecloth on a flat area between them. Flasks of gering nut-redberry tea, a medley of fresh fruits, thick slices of goat cheese, and chunks of homemade bread followed.

Sparrow glanced up. "That looks yummy." She added a finishing touch to her picture and handed it to Merrilea. "I'd forgotten how wonderful it is in the mountains." She took a bite of a plump, red pommaletta and sat chewing contentedly.

Merrilea examined first the canyon and then Sparrow's sketch. "You are good, Sparrow. I could never draw like that."

"I love what I do." Sparrow tucked the sketchbook back in her pack.

After nourishing their bodies with the bounties of nature and their spirits with the beauty surrounding them, they brushed bits of stray grass and leaves off their pants and repacked. Down the trail, a small avalanche of stones alerted them to more company. Merrilea put a finger to her lips and slipped into the woods. Sparrow shouldered her pack and crept after her to a large tree. Secreted in a patch of leafy bushes behind it, they scanned the trail.

More falling stones and a smothered expletive preceded the two men they had encountered earlier. The shorter one stopped, removed his shoe, and shook it. A pebble rolled off the path. "Do you think they were suspicious?"

"Why should they be? They believe we hiked down the mountain, not from the lake."

"How'd they get so far ahead of us now?" He shoved his foot into the shoe and fastened it.

"We stopped for a rest, remember?"

The men trudged up the trail.

Sparrow bit her lip. "Now what?"

"We're near our destination." Merrilea pointed up the mountainside. "When we reach that ridge, we'll be close to the gateway. Come on."

Sparrow zigzagged between trees, laboring after her friend. The higher they climbed, the more her aching legs and lungs protested.

Merrilea offered a hand. "Almost there." They soon stood on the ridge, looking at the two men some distance below.

"Better get out of sight. If we can see them, they can see us." Merrilea ducked behind a large rock. "Wait here. I'll scout the last leg."

Sparrow watched her sprint up the trail and sucked in deep breaths of thin air. *Sure wish I were in better shape.*

"Up there!" The shout echoed through the canyon. She peeked around the rock. One man pointed toward the ridge.

Merrilea dodged from sight, then reappeared. "Come on!"

Sparrow sprinted after her. The trail widened into a flattened area where a rockslide had toppled gray granite formations and downed trees. Sparrow glanced back. The men scrambling up the mountainside chased them through the tumble of debris.

Merrilea reached the cover of trees and paused. "Sorry, Sparrow. I didn't intend for them to see me." She grabbed her hand. "We're almost there."

By following a small creek, they arrived beside a waterfall plummeting into a large pool. "This is it. You ready?"

Sparrow nodded. Together they recited the Key. "Eero Tye Como."

Beneath the surface, the water churned into a swirling mouth shaped opening.

"Now!" Merrilea leapt into the portal.

Sparrow hesitated only long enough to watch her disappear before she jumped into the gaping vortex.

A man rounded the corner as Sparrow vanished in a swirl of color. The second arrived to find his friend staring wide-eyed at a large pool, its surface rippling with the rhythmic fall of water from the rocks above.

"Where are they?" The second man scanned the area.

The first pointed into the pool.

"You're crazy."

"The dark one jumped in and vanished. You think *I'm* crazy. *That's* what's *crazy!*"

"What do we tell 'em down below?"

"I didn't see anyone." The tall man stared. "Did you?"

The shorter man shook his head. "Nope. Nothing."

The men walked away, muttering under their breath.

Merrilea put an arm around Sparrow as she stepped free of the gateway. "That was close!"

"Too close. I almost missed the gate. It wouldn't have opened a second time."

"We're both here and safe, and that's what counts."

Sparrow looked around in the dim light. "Where's here?"

"We're in the Terces Wood, not far from Almiralyn's cottage."

"How far is not far?" Her face gleamed with sweat.

"We should be there before nightfall." Merrilea laughed at the expression on her friend's face. "Don't worry. You'll make it."

Sparrow tipped her head to listen. No birds called out their presence. No small animals rustled through the knee-high ferns. The silence felt unnatural—eerie.

Merrilea directed her to a well-used path. "This is the way I used to come to visit before Esán became ill. I've missed getting away from Thera."

The sun dropped below the horizon right as they arrived in Mira's back garden.

Esán dragged himself from the Lake of Rorret into a space filled with white light and lay gasping for breath. His instincts told him he was safe. His exhausted body screamed for rest. On hands and knees, he sought a dry spot, curled into a tight ball, and slipped immediately into dreaming.

He lay on the ground, his cheek pressed against hot, red sand. Smoke billowed around him as a predator's high-pitched shriek sent grains of sand trembling and dancing. The heat fanning his body sent sweat rolling from his bald head down his neck. Through squinted eyes, he watched a thermal mirage shimmer into existence in the intense heat. Another shriek shrilled. The mirage vanished. Eyes squeezed shut, he blanked his mind. A soft, feminine voice called his name. He blinked. A woman knelt at his side. Her blue, blue eyes held a warning. She touched his forehead. The heat dissipated. Smoke changed to churning clouds and carried him into another dream.

He stood on the lip of a rocky cliff, wind tugging at his clothing and slapping color into his cheeks. An unfamiliar sound reverberated around him, shook his body, stole his breath away. He gulped in cool air. The clouds dispersed. Below, the ocean heaved and boiled. Waves rolled in, crashed upon rocks and sand, and sent saltwater spray high into the air. His heart overflowed with love for the sea. He licked salt from his lips and glanced at his companion. The dark-haired man nodded and shifted shape. Esán stared in wonder as a white sea bird soared skyward, caught an updraft, and vanished into moisture-laden clouds. Moments later, it reappeared, swooped over a rock covered with squawking birds, and landed. Esán listened to the song of water and wind and seabirds, stretched his arms wide, and...

"Wake up, Esán." The dream dispersed. For a moment, he lay still, hoping it would return, hoping that he might have shifted shape and flown.

"Esán."

Another gentle shake brought him to full awareness. He opened his eyes and stretched. A silk coverlet caressed his bare arms and rustled when he moved. He stared, bemused, at the beautiful woman smiling at him.

"You're awake." Her eyes gleamed even bluer. "Don't look so surprised. I'm real."

"I just saw you..." He sat up, feeling confused and disoriented.

"Tell me about your dreams, Esán."

Still caught in their aftermath, he forced himself to focus. "Who are you?"

"Does it matter?"

"Yes." He blinked. "Yes, it does matter." His voice sounded closer, more like his own.

"I am Almiralyn, Guardian of Myrrh."

"You have much of Mira in you. Are you her sister?"

"Mira is another form of Almiralyn. Tell me what you remember, Esán. It's very important."

Immersed once again in the strange splendor of his dreams, he described the heat of the desert, the predator's screech, and the man who changed to a bird and soared over the sea.

Almiralyn listened, her attention unwavering. His words faded into the pristine space. He smiled in wonder. "You were there in the desert."

The tip of her finger brushed his cheek. "Sleep, Esán."

He melted into satin and down pillows. Heavy eyelids closed, dropping him into the deep and healing sleep of youth.

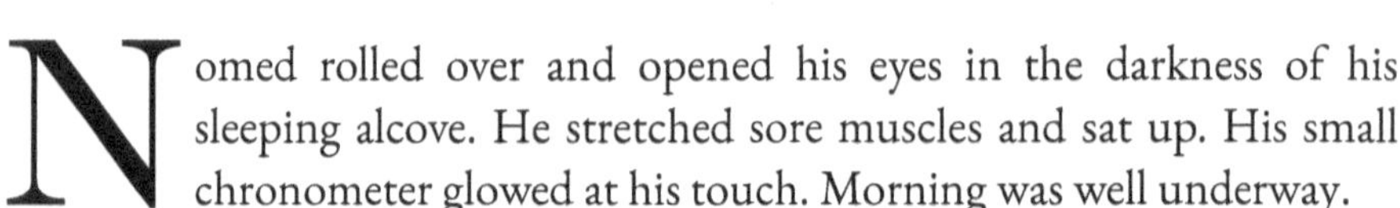

33

Nomed rolled over and opened his eyes in the darkness of his sleeping alcove. He stretched sore muscles and sat up. His small chronometer glowed at his touch. Morning was well underway.

While his agile mind reviewed the frustrating events of the past two turnings, he splashed cool water on his face, shaved, and dressed. Today *would* be fruitful—he'd see to that. Exiting his quarters, he strolled toward the fire.

In the flickering light, Dom muttered to himself. "I wish to go home to The Borderlands." He rubbed his chin and frowned. "That's not happening anytime soon."

Nomed stepped into his line of vision, a fiery warmth glowing in his eyes. Dom recognized the illusion. The DiMensioner's eyes were cold as ice and focused on him.

"Well, Dom, it's been quite a while since we spent time together. I am grateful for the news about the twins, you know. It is handy to have them nearby and related to Almiralyn. I couldn't have planned it better." He glanced around the cavern. "Where are the Pentharian?"

Dom shrugged. "I haven't seen them or Wodash. It's been so quiet this morning that I've heard too much of my mind working."

"And what, my friend, is your mind telling you today?"

"I am too old for adventure."

"You should have thought of that before you rode in this direction. And speaking of riding, your horse is a beauty. I've imprinted him, so I hope you don't care that he's now mine."

"He belongs to Almiralyn, Seyes."

Nomed sneered. "All the better."

Wodash floated into the glow of the fire. Dom shivered and wished again for the safety and quiet of his shoppe. Four Pentharian joined the group. His level of discomfort escalated.

"What are your plans for today?" Voer's lizard tail flicked.

Nomed fixed his icy gaze on the blue Pentharian leader. "You and Yuin find the twins, capture them, and bring them to me." He transferred his attention to the remaining mercenaries. "Jeet and Stee, you must destroy the gateways in the foothills and in the Terces Wood. Do you know how to accomplish this?"

Stee's emerald braids and the gold rings in his ears glistened in the firelight when he nodded. "We must spill blood and terror must penetrate the vortex. We will do this well."

"Good. Remember not to stand too close, or the portal will suck you in when it implodes."

Yuin, his expression non-committal, moved into the circle of light. "We seek also to find Yaro. He is our bloodline and younger brother." A touch of defiance gave his declaration a challenging edge.

Nomed's tone was dismissive. "Yaro can take care of himself."

Dom glanced from the ruby Pentharian to the DiMensioner. The tension between them flared, then faded. The four Pentharian turned and strode down the passageway.

Nomed's expression remained inscrutable as he watched them go. His cape swirling around his shoulders, he addressed the death shadow. "You're with me. I want an answer to Esán's disappearance. And today we will find where the Evolsefil Crystal hides."

He paused midway to the tunnel opening and looked over his shoulder. "Dom, my good friend, I suggest you get some rest. Once the twins are here, you'll be busy keeping them from doing anything silly, like the disappearing act that foolish boy pulled."

Dom listened to the DiMensioner's footsteps fade into silence and sighed. "A babysitter." He shook his head. "It could be worse. At least he doesn't expect me to wander around these caverns." A yawn stretched his mouth wide. "Sleep will help pass the time." He eased his aching body to standing and shuffled across the rough floor. Curled up on the pallet like an old alley cat, he heard the repeated cadence of his own soft snores in the empty cavern as he drifted into sleep.

From the ledge at the cliffs of ReVod, the four Pentharian gazed at the luscious landscape. Rolling hills, grassy plains, forests, rivers, lakes, and spectacular mountains surrounded them.

Voer turned to his companions. "It seems a terrible waste to destroy a land of such loveliness and wealth."

"Nomed thinks only of revenge." Stee shook his head. "His heart holds nothing but anger. I will be glad when our contract with him is complete."

"I intend to search for Yaro today." Yuin's jaw set, and his mouth tightened into a stubborn red line.

"Find the twins first. Then you can slip away. I'll cover for you. Now we have work to do." Voer shifted to a vulture and soared over the land of Myrrh. His sadness that it would soon disappear forever increased with each wing stroke.

Yaro, as a small blackbird, continued to explore the Intersect. Flying further and further from the entrance near Sibine's tree, he discovered the edge of the Terces Wood and marveled at the expansive field of slender green roots beneath the grasslands. While gliding below vast mineral deposits that gleamed in the constant light of the moon, he grew tired and landed in a small amethyst-encrusted alcove.

Above him, he knew change was in motion. *Myrrh's unraveling is about to begin, and I'm not there to see it. No matter.* He tucked his small head beneath his wing.

Brie rode on Tam, her nimble fingers removing brambles from the pony's mane. Ari and Torgin led the way through the soft green of the lowlands. Now and then, Buster sprinted after some invisible temptation and returned with his ears alert and his tongue hanging from one side of his mouth.

"Are you smiling, Buster?" Ari rubbed his shaggy head. "You're such a wonderful dog."

Torgin laughed as he dashed away once again. "Look at him go."

Brie giggled at the canine antics and then drifted back into her own thoughts. Tuper had explained that small villages and farmlands lay scattered further to the South and to the North. In this area, prairie grass grew tall and thick in the fertile, damp earth. Scattered amongst it, summer flowers blooming in rainbow colors. She smiled. *I love the way their faces tip up to soak in the sun.* Letting fear slip away, she watched bees kiss upturned blossoms and followed the journey of a butterfly until it vanished into sky and mountains.

Uncertainty, like a creeping cat, destroyed her peace of mind. *How long will it be before we reach the Sekan River?* A hand shading her eyes, she peered ahead and frowned. *We're too exposed out here. I can't wait until we reach the foothills.*

Snippets of Tuper's conversation made her tighten her grip on Tam's reins. Pentharian—shape shifters from another world—had bitten Fen. The Star of Truth throbbing warned her she would have no choice but to deal with them. *The Pentharian will find us today.* She searched her pocket. *And*

I gave my sprig of hemlock to Torgin. Even though nothing out of the ordinary caught her attention, dread played a dirge in her mind as she scanned the grassy expanse.

Up ahead, Ari and Torgin moseyed along, laughing and jostling and enjoying their trek. *I love you both so much.*

A decision to make the most of whatever peace remained eased her sense of foreboding. She slid from Tam's back and ran to catch up with her sister and best friend.

"I've never seen a prairie before. Isn't it beautiful?" Ari skimmed her outstretched arms over the tall grass. "I love how it tickles." She threw her head back and gave a hearty laugh.

Torgin grinned. "I think I'll hop on Tam. I want to see if the river is visible."

Brie caught up with Ari. Arm in arm, they watched him gallop through the tall grass.

Ari gave her a sideways glance. "You alright?"

"I'll just feel safer in the foothills."

"Me, too." Ari paused and faced her. "You're worried?"

"The Pentharian—" Buster dashed between them, saving her from an answer she didn't want to give. She scratched his shaggy head. "You're the best dog in the world." Stooping to pick up a stout stick, she threw it. A volley of delighted barks joined the song of breezes through grass as he gave chase.

Before Ari could press her further, Torgin returned, his face alive and happy. "I think I can see the river." He jumped down from Tam's back. "When we get there, I vote for a break. We haven't stopped since we left the woods."

"Sounds good, as long as it's a short one." Brie tried not to sound worried.

Buster lumbered back and plopped down in front of her. She took the stick from his mouth and lobbed it over his head.

"Dogs are so funny." Ari grinned. "The simplest things make them happy. All Buster needs is a stick to chase, and he's delighted with life." She chuckled. "Now he's trying to catch his tail."

"Buster, you crazy dog, come here." Torgin laughed.

The big dog dashed back and dropped his slobbery stick. Brie picked it up and tested its weight. "Okay, but this is the last time." Throwing her arm back, she hurled the stick with all her might.

"Wow, Brie. Good job!" Ari thumped her on the back. The big dog leapt after it and disappeared from sight. "I sure wish we could have a dog in—"

A bark of warning ripped through the late morning air. A bark of terror followed.

The twins froze. Torgin grabbed Tam's reins and tried to calm her panicked prancing.

Buster remained hidden by the tall grass, his dissonant barking the only sign of his whereabouts. Another sharp bark. A whine. And then only the sound of the breeze in the tall grass.

Brie saw her fear reflected in her sister's eyes. Tam pawed the ground and pulled against her reins.

"I don't like this." Torgin's voice shook as he fought to control the frightened pony. "What should we do?"

Before either girl could answer, triumphant growls rumbled over the grasslands. Two night-black panthers stalked into view. Their vicious teeth, encircling blood-soaked mouths, flashed in the sunlight as they lifted their heads and roared again in chorus.

Tam reared, snorted, and jerked Torgin backward.

Brie gripped Ari's arm. *At least we're together.*

Fighting to gain control of the terrified pony, Torgin watched the feline marauders move with predatory grace toward his friends. Fear flooded through him. Tam, yanking the reins, compounded his fright. Without thinking, he jumped on her back and sent her galloping away from the twins, away from the smell of death, away from his own confusion and terror.

Wind cooling his hot cheeks dispersed his fear. In the shelter of three lone trees, he pulled Tam up short. *What am I doing? I just abandoned my best friends!* A yank on the reins turned Tam around. Heart pounding, he urged her into a gallop, and raced back to where he had left the twins.

Brie stared at gleaming panther eyes and fought the urge to run. *These are the off-worlders Tuper warned us about.* One licked its blood-covered lips. A silent sob exploded in her chest.

Beside her, Ari bristled with fear and anger. "Buster! What have you done to Buster?" She started forward.

Brie grabbed her arm and pulled her around to face her. "Take out your hemlock. You might get away."

Ari pulled it from her pocket and tossed it aside. "It won't hide us both, and I'm not leaving you."

A piercing scream stood Brie's hair on end. Ari gaped and gripped her hand. The panthers reared. Front paws raking the air morphed into massive wings. Feline faces disappeared into black feathers and raptor beaks. Grass whirled and thrashed as again their screams trumpeted success. Powerful legs launched the enormous vultures into the air. They soared in a wide circle. One swooped, gripped Ari by the shoulders, and lifted her off the ground. Her panicked gaze skimmed over the grasslands.

"Hold on, Ari!" Brie choked and yelled again. "Hold on!"

Wing-whipped wind swirled the tall grass for a second time. Taloned-claws gripped her shoulders. She grasped the vulture's legs and searched the rippling grass.

Far below, growing smaller and smaller, Buster lay motionless in a flattened patch of blood-spattered grass. A sob choked her. Tears streamed down her cheeks and fell like rain to the earth below.

34

Zugo and Elae left Meos early in the morning. Elae took the lead. *"If your friend is in the Cave of Canedari, we'll have him back in Meos by mid-turning meal. What's this Human like?"*

Zugo thought for a moment. *"Esán is like light flowing through a jewel; like an old one, yet young..."* He tipped his head and smiled. *"...like the whisper of secrets. He's not afraid of the death shadow or the man with demon eyes."* Zugo gazed into the distance. *"He's a still, deep pool, clear and smooth and quiet inside."*

"How many cycles is he?"

"I think we are the same. Tell me, Elae, how often do you visit the Cave of Canedari?"

"Only during a ritual or when my training takes me there. It is sacred, and few are privileged to visit. Your father had planned to take you on your next birth celebration, but he granted me the honor. Although we go to seek your friend, today is your first step toward becoming a Crystal Keeper."

"My initiation begins today?" Zugo stared at his companion. "I didn't know."

"The Cavern of Tennisca protects the Cave of Canedari, which is off limits to the uninitiated."

"What about Esán?"

"If Canedari opens to a soul, that soul has a destiny to fulfill, involving the Prima Crystal. If your Esán is there, Evolsefil has accepted him."

Elae led the way deeper into the subterranean caverns of Meos. She understood Zugo's excitement and also his fear. Initiation meant he would be a leader. She, too, was excited, but for a very different reason. She had never met a Human, and this one sounded extraordinary. Her intuition warned her life was about to take a fresh path. This Human was part of that change.

"Zugo, we're almost there. Be watchful and be wary."

She guided him through a well-hidden door to the top of a steep stone staircase. "Here, my friend, is the test of which I have spoken."

"Please repeat after me:

> *My heart is true, my mind is clear.*
> *I swear by love and all that's dear.*
> *If it should prove that I am lying,*
> *I forfeit life and accept dying.*
>
> *If I prove true and enter in,*
> *Canedari becomes my kin,*
> *The Prima Stone holds all of me*
> *And fills my heart with what will be."*

Zugo repeated the ancient verse. When it was complete, Elae touched his forehead with the golden citrine she wore at her throat and led him down the steep staircase.

"Where are we, Elae? I see nothing but the faint gleam of the stairs."

"This is the Cavern of Tennisca, and we walk the Stairway of Retu

Erath. If you are not true of heart, the stairs melt away, and you fall forever and ever."

"What is beneath us?"

"Nothing but the distant cavern mouth and the night sky."

Zugo looked over the edge of the stairs at the distant specks of light. *I hope my heart is true.*

"Beautiful, isn't it?"

"It is. How much farther to Canedari?"

Elae paused and waited until he was on the step above her. "Do you see that glow?"

He squinted. "Yes, way out there."

"That's where we're going. Now silence. You are being asked to listen to the ancient ones speak."

His busy mind still, he continued his descent. Like a soft, exhaled breath, they began—one whispered word, then another and another.

"Zugo, son of Yookotay, listen. Listen. Listen." The whisper grew quiet and then continued. "Stay true to the stories of the ancestors but learn to accept new ways."

"Zugo, son of Yookotay, listen. Hear. Learn the patience of the elders but keep the innocence of youth."

"Zugo, son of Yookotay, hear me. Love from the center of your heart, and all things will open unto you."

"Zugo, son of Yookotay, listen and know. The young Human you seek has a gift for you. Intuition is your guide."

Whisperers flitted around him, their breath brushing his cheek and rustling through his fur. Spellbound, he paid rapt attention. In the aftermath of peaceful quiet, he contemplated the meanings behind the whispered words of wisdom.

Never taking his eyes off Elae's back, he followed her down the steep staircase. How many stairs carried him through the Cavern of Tennisca, he would never know. But he was glad to reach the bottom and stand before the double purple doors.

Elae slipped her hand into his. *"You have completed your first initiation. The Stairway of Retu Erath supported your journey."*

"There was whispering, Elae."

Her smile warmed him. *"You are a Chosen One, Zugo. Your father will be proud."*

She motioned him to place his hands on the door next to hers. A word of passage and the doors opened.

"The Prima Crystal, Evolsefil." Elae's thought filled his mind.

Evolsefil floated at the center of the room, emitting radiant energy in all directions. Brilliance flooding his eyes enhanced his sight beyond anything he had ever known. Cool, crisp, warm, and nurturing, the crystal's essence saturated him with a sense of peace and vitality. Mesmerized by its splendor, he stood bereft of words until Elae broke the silence.

"We must look for your friend, Zugo." Her soft voice helped him to drag his attention from the Prima Crystal's compelling presence.

Somewhat disoriented, he struggled to regain his sense of equilibrium. Elae's strange eyes gazing into his brought him back to himself.

Following her lead, he began a search of the cave. When he found nothing, he paused by a second set of double doors.

Elae joined him. "If Esán has been in Canedari, no sign of his presence remains."

Zugo furrowed his brow. "Now what?"

She pushed the doors open and beckoned him into a long corridor. With a finger to her lips, she stopped at a door where a pale pink crystal embedded in the smooth wood glowed with rainbow light. Zugo peered over her shoulder as she eased it open. Esán lay sleeping on a shimmering white bed.

"Your friend is an initiate."

Zugo peeked around the door frame. "What is this room?"

"Ephos is the room where initiates of the crystal heart of Myrrh recover."

Zugo tiptoed to the bed. "Esán, it's Zugo. Wake up." He reached out to touch the sleeping Human.

Jeet and Stee, in vulture form, landed before the Gateway of Kao on the north side of the grasslands at the base of the foothills. A small ravine snaked its way between two sloping hills and into a cleft between them. Under an ancient, gnarled oak, they found the swirling circular portal.

The sick lamb they had stolen from a nearby farm bleated weakly. Stee held it up and shook his head. "We will help you, wee one." He set it on the ground, and, with Jeet, transformed into panther form, and crouched low. The lamb's soft wool, where Stee's talons had gouged its tender side, ran scarlet with blood. Stee circled the trembling animal.

The song of the predator vibrated the air as both cats crept forward, maneuvering the ailing lamb closer and closer to the Gateway. Jeet flicked his claws across the lamb's unblemished side, leaving another blood-filled gash. Together, the Pentharian opened their throats and screamed. The terrified lamb turned and fled into the vortex. In a swirl of red blood and darkness, the Gateway imploded and—with a flash of lightning and a violent clap of thunder—disappeared.

Everything near the old oak withered and died. The ground beneath the cats' feet quaked in anguish. Gray clouds gathered overhead. A fissure opened, splitting the ravine down the middle. Small wildlife close to the Gateway lay dead. Birds tumbled from the sky; rabbits died in their burrows; squirrels ceased their play and fell silent and still to the ground. Jeet roared their victory.

In vulture form, he followed Stee into the air. Powerful wings created a cyclone of death below him. Their next stop—the Demrach Gateway in the Terces Wood.

Deep in the Intersect, an angry fissure cracked the crystalline space around Yaro and hurled him from the alcove where he slept. As he tumbled through space, he caught himself and glided in a wide circle. Curiosity carried him through hovering dust into the narrow, jagged crack. A sliver of light overhead ignited his hope of escape.

Below him, the fissure began to settle. The power of the closing fracture pursued him through a shower of debris. Walls collapsing snatched at his wingtips and sent adrenaline pumping through his tiny veins. With all his strength, he pressed his wings against the air and shot from the dark into dust-formed clouds.

Close to the fissure, he shifted to his natural form and savored the solid ground beneath his feet. As the chaos surrounding him registered, he felt a wave of dismay. Violent death in all its horror heralded the destruction of one of Myrrh's gateways.

Startled by his sadness and sense of futility, he marveled at how much his time in the Intersect changed him. The profound transformation brought tears to his eyes. They rolled down tattooed cheeks and dripped on the ground, where he knelt to touch the still-warm body of a brown squirrel. He stood, shoulders sagging. *I need time to come to terms with these strange new feelings.* His back to the chaos, he shifted into a soft gray mourning dove and flew toward the Terces Wood.

Esán's eyes fluttered open. "Zugo, I am so glad to see you." He sat up, and, scooting to the edge of the bed, tried to recall how he had ended up in this beautiful room. "Where am I? Who's your friend?"

The diminutive DeoNyte beside Zugo smiled. "I'm Elae, a Demi-Priestess Guardian of the Cave of Canedari. Zugo tells me the Lake of Rorret brought you here."

"The Cave of Canedari?" Esán searched his memory. "Ah, I remember. Just when I couldn't hold my breath any longer, I surfaced in a space filled with white light. But how did I get here?"

"The High Priestess brought you after Evolsefil completed your initiation."

"Evolsefil? Initiation?" His confusion doubled.

Elae smiled. "You surfaced in the Cave of Canedari, and Evolsefil, the Prima Crystal of Myrrh, initiated you into its service."

"I guess I have lots to catch up on."

Her gaze lingered on his throat. "What's that?"

He touched the cool, white cord. "The death shadow put this on me before I tumbled into the lake. If he's near and I don't do what I'm told, it freezes my lungs until I can't breathe."

"Have you tried to remove it?"

"It won't budge."

"Perhaps my father can help." Zugo moved to the door. "Let's go. We need to get to Meos as soon as possible."

Rejuvenated and ready to travel, Esán slid off the bed. Elae guided them down the corridor and pulled open the double doors. "This is the Cave of Canedari." She crossed to a glowing, quartz crystal almost twice his height. "This is Evolsefil."

Esán walked past her into the Prima's radiant light. Not daring to breathe, he circled the spectacular quartz cluster. At the center of six smaller crystals, a magnificent spire rose with the majesty of a queen. Its energy pulsed to the rhythm of his heart. Tears of wonder slipped down his cheeks.

Elae gave a soft sigh. "Isn't it beautiful!" She allowed him a moment before leading him to another set of open doors, where Evolsefil's light spilled onto a steep staircase. "This is the Stairway of Retu Erath."

When they reached the top, Zugo looked over his shoulder. "It's much shorter coming up than going—"

Lightning ripped through the night sky far below. Thunder crashed and rumbled. The stairway arched like a cat's back and snapped back into place, throwing them to their knees.

Elae was up in an instant. "Hurry!" She took off at a run.

Esán and Zugo scrambled to their feet and sprinted into the passage after her.

Almiralyn, Allynae, Sparrow, and Merrilea stared in horror at the fountain's surface, where the two Pentharian vultures lifted into the air, leaving carnage written in small, still bodies and blistered trees at what had been the Gateway of Kao.

The fissure that cracked the ravine open sliced deep into Almiralyn's heart. A released breath hissed between clenched teeth. Her legs turned to jelly. Allynae's muscular arms caught her as the room went dark.

When she opened her eyes, Merrilea sat beside her, skillful fingers resting on her pulse. Allynae and Sparrow gradually came into focus at the foot of her bed. Merrilea held a glass to her lips. Cool water slid down her throat.

Allynae moved around the bed and helped her to sitting. "Mira, you need to rest."

"There's no time." She dabbed at the tears on her cheeks. "I'm fine. I'm just so much a part of this land. When its heart breaks, mine does, too."

"At least allow yourself a quick nap." The sternness in his voice brought a smile.

"Nonsense." Her momentary weakness yielded to decisiveness. "Protecting the remaining gateways must be our priority. Each time they destroy one, Myrrh grows smaller. And my power diminishes. If they destroy Myrrh, Idronatti will fall into ruin, and Thera will begin to disintegrate."

She hurried back to Elcaro's Eye, where two reflected Pentharian vultures flew across the calm water.

Allynae came up behind her. "They're flying toward the Terces Wood."

She nodded. "Demrach Gateway is their next target. We must arrive first."

Sparrow tore her gaze from the fountain's surface. "What about the children?"

"If the Pentharian destroy the gateways, it won't matter whether we find the children. My first concern must be for the safety of Myrrh and Thera. The children will not survive the loss of either."

Allynae slid his arm around Sparrow's waist. She took a quivering breath and laid her head on his shoulder.

Almiralyn stared out the window, then turned. "Sparrow, you must begin a new painting. Your artist's instinct will help direct our course. You'll find canvases and an easel downstairs. The paints are in the supply closet next to the kitchen."

Merrilea's gray eyes gleamed. "How can I help?"

"You must lend your Myrrhinian blood to the paint, one drop in each color. This, and the ancestry you both carry, will ensure Sparrow knows what to paint."

Almiralyn paused, took a breath, and turned to her brother. "Allynae, fetch your Major Jordett. Since he is here, we'll make use of his skills. I'll join you in the kitchen."

Allynae kissed Sparrow's head and departed.

"Your paintings are more important than you realize, Sparrow. They have the potential to save us all." Almiralyn drew her into a circle with Merrilea.

In the way of women, they slipped their arms around each other's waists and stood, connected and quiet, foreheads touching before going downstairs. Major Jordett and Allynae were already in the kitchen when they arrived.

Almiralyn addressed the PPP officer. "You don't believe in Myrrh or Evolsefil, and yet here you are. I need your skills as a fighter, and I need your allegiance. If we can't defeat Seyes Nomed and the Pentharian, they will destroy Thera and Myrrh and put our solar system and the entire galaxy at risk."

The Major frowned and studied her for an intense moment. "I know Evolsefil is a crystal. Why do those from other planets seek it?"

"What do you know of the Crystal Laítise?"

Jordett shrugged. "I've heard little about it. Is it important?"

Almiralyn sank into a kitchen chair and traced an infinity symbol on the table. "A web of crystals known as the Laítise stabilize our solar system and galaxy. Evolsefil, a Prima Stone, is a crystal of great power. Its role, in combination with Corps and Demi Stones, is to hold our galaxy to its place in the universe. Because of the central position of the Clenaba Rolas System in this galaxy and Myrrh's position within it, the Guardians placed Evolsefil in the Dojanack Caverns. Seyes Nomed wants the crystal for the power it will give him. If he achieves his goals..." She noted his puzzled expression. "Time will clarify everything. Will you help us, Major?"

The Major stood in silence, hands clasped behind his back, and his eyes down. When he looked up, his demeanor composed and his gaze steady, he clicked his heels together and touched his heart. "I pledge, as an officer of the PPP and a citizen of Thera, to serve you until we win the battle, or I am no longer alive."

She held out a hand. He took it and bowed his head. She knew he would honor his pledge with his life.

"Thank you, Major Jordett. I am in your debt." She looked at her brother. "Since neither of you shape shift, saddle two horses and meet us at the gateway. Karrew, we must go." She walked into the garden. In a flash of golden light, she shifted and flew into the mist slowly gathering over Myrrh.

35

"Faster, Tam, faster!" The pony's power surged. Torgin clamped his knees tighter and searched the prairie for the last spot he had seen the twins and the Pentharian. Not far ahead, wind from an enormous vulture's powerful wings flattened the grass as it ascended. Gripped in its talons, a red-haired twin fought to hold on. The gargantuan bird flew a wide half circle and soared away toward the Dojanacks.

"Brie! Ari..." Torgin's shout died in his throat. *Whatever have I done?*

He dug his heels into the Tam's ribs. "Faster, Tamboreen!" Hooves beat the damp earth. Chunks of dirt splattered in their wake. The pony's sides heaved. Still, they arrived too late. Above them, two dark spots grew smaller and smaller until they faded from sight.

Torgin slid from Tam's sweat-lathered back and patted her side. "We have to find Buster, girl." Leading her to the spot where he had last seen the rambunctious canine, he began to search through the tall grass. At the edge of a small area trampled into flatness, he stopped. A choked sob stuck in his throat. The big, shaggy dog lay splattered with his own blood. Close to his crumpled body, Torgin found the tattered remains of a hemlock sprig. He shrugged off his backpack and squatted to touch a Buster's limp ear. "No wonder they caught you."

Unable to absorb the truth, he stared at the scarlet-streaked coat, the tail that would never wag again, the eyes that were closed forever. The deflated stillness of the body finally brought it home—*Buster is truly gone.* He stroked the blood matted fur. His sobs, released at last, quaked through him. "Oh, Buster, I am so sorry. I let you down. I'm so, so sorry."

Tears streamed down his face; devastated sobs rocked the intense quiet of the grasslands. One last hiccuped moan, and he lifted his head. A bloodied hand brushed tears from his cheeks. He stumbled to his feet, wrapped his arms around Tam's neck, and allowed the pony's warmth to seep into his cold, shaking body. "What do we do now, Tam?"

Heavy-hearted, he stared at the red stains on his hand. A frantic need to be rid of them made him pull out his handkerchief. He scrubbed his cheek, wiped each finger clean, and rubbed the smear of blood from his palm. Somehow, his actions made him feel worse. Stuffing the evidence of his failure in an outer pocket of his backpack, he looked at the mist gathering in the sky. *Where do I go from here? Maybe the map will help.*

As he pulled it out, a sprig of evergreen fell to the ground. "Oh, no. Brie's hemlock." He picked it up and inhaled its scent. "By the Fathers, I have amends to make." With a shuddering sigh, he returned it to his pocket and unfolded the map. His finger traced a path from Mira's cottage to Nemttachenn and from Nemttachenn to the grasslands.

Tam whinnied. Torgin glanced up. A tall, black man regarded him with sorrow-filled eyes. He knelt and placed his big hand on the dog's shaggy fur. "Buster, you be the first casualty of this adventure-gone-awry. We'll miss you, old friend."

"Who are *you*?" Torgin's suspicion made him sound snappish. He refolded the map and tucked it away.

"I'm Paisley James Tobinette, a friend of Almiralyn and Allynae. You're Torgin."

"How did you know?" A sense of relief eased his anxiety.

"I saw you in Alli's crystal when you first got to Nemttachenn Tower. He told me about ya."

Torgin glanced down at Buster. "Death is so quiet, isn't it? He seems so empty...so gone."

Paisley stood up and placed a gentle black hand on Torgin's shoulder. "At least he died quickly. It could have been much worse. Come, let's bury him and be on our way." He removed a shovel from his pack, extended the handle, and secured it. With a sad look at Buster, he began to dig.

"How can I help?"

The big man tossed soil to one side. "Start collectin' rocks to cover the grave."

The rhythm of the shovel hitting the dirt created background music for Torgin's hunt. Soon, he had a pile of rocks of varying sizes stacked beside the hole. Paisley lifted the limp body and placed it in the shallow grave. Torgin helped to cover it, first with dirt and then with rocks. When they finished, they stood side by side, looking at Buster's final resting place.

Paisley's gruff voice took on a soft tone. "Here lies a loyal friend who gave his life to save those he loved. May we remember him with the same joy he brought to our hearts. And may his givin' spirit inspire us to be givin', too."

Torgin knelt and placed Brie's hemlock on the grave. Tears fell unabated down his brown cheeks. "To keep you safe, Buster."

The big man brushed a tear away. "He'll always be with us in our memories."

Torgin squared his shoulders and stood. "I deserted my friends, and now I don't know what to do or where to find them."

"What makes ya think you could have saved the twins?" His new friend gazed down at him. "Without realizin' it, you made the best choice possible."

"But I panicked and ran like the PPP were after me. Will they ever forgive me?"

"You need to first work on forgivin' yourself, young one. Those twins are pretty smart. I'd be willin' to bet they're glad you got away."

Torgin hung his head.

Paisley gave him an affectionate pat on the back. "You'd best come with me. There's a man in the Dojanacks Almiralyn thinks is important. Once we find this hermit, I'll help you find your friends."

Torgin started to protest, but thought better of it. *I will be safer with a companion who knows Myrrh.* "Where's the hermit?"

"I think he's at Timreh Pass."

Torgin touched the compass resting against his chest. "Do you know how to get there?"

"In a general sorta way."

The big man's face held nothing but open interest. Torgin decided to trust him. "I have a compass Almiralyn gave me. We can ask it for directions."

"I'd appreciate the help."

Withdrawing Ostradio, Torgin held it so Paisley could see. "Show us Timreh Pass." A blur of gold glowed. The arrow stopped pointing due west. The compass face faded into a picture of a rocky trail.

Paisley gave his mustache a thoughtful yank. "I know that trail. That helps a lot. What a beautiful compass."

Torgin caressed its smooth roundness. *So much has happened since Almiralyn presented it to me.* With a heavy sigh, he tucked it away beneath his shirt and gazed toward the mountains.

A low rumbling shook the prairie. The ground heaving hurled him to his knees. Lightning flashed. Thunder crashed. Wind ripped through the tall grass and ceased. Tension-filled quiet settled over the prairie. To the north, a roiling gray mist obscured the clarity of the blue sky.

"What was that?" Torgin scrambled to his feet.

A worried expression clouded Paisley's face. "Nothin' good. Come on, boy." He helped him onto Tam's back. "We better get movin'. Myrrh's unwinding has begun." The pony's reins gathered in his big hand, Paisley led her toward the foothills.

Torgin stared at his broad shoulders and wondered if he would ever see the twins again.

As the pony and two Humans grew more distant, a soft, golden light glowed beside Buster's grave. Chealim, the Galactic Guardian of the Fourth Galaxy, stepped free and knelt, his hands hovering above the grave.

> *"Buster, hero, teacher, and friend,*
> *Your life was forfeit so others could mend*
> *The evil unfolding in Myrrh and beyond.*
> *I am here to release you from death's sudden bond."*

With each line of the chant, Buster's outline rose above the ground and became more distinct. When the last line ended, he gave a joyous bark and licked the Guardian's cheek. A soft chuckle floated over the grasslands as the big shaggy dog and his new master misted away into time.

Nomed and Wodash retraced Esán's path of the previous turning. In owl form, the DiMensioner followed his minion through the crystal tunnel, over the Lake of Rorret, and into the shaft beyond the cliff where Zugo's knotted rope hung. Swooping down to the tunnel below, they flew further into the caverns until they reached a triple fork. One passageway led to the right, one to the left, and a third continued straight ahead.

Nomed considered the left-hand passage. His instincts shouted a warning. Opting for the one leading deeper into the caverns, he flew beside Wodash's translucent body. Half expecting to find the City of Meos, it surprised him to arrive in an empty circular grotto with spoke-like tunnels exiting in eight different directions.

As he landed and shifted, a tremor quaking through the cavern pitched him down a passage ending at a low archway. Youthful voices made him retreat into the shadows and peer into a dim tunnel. Three figures raced toward him—two covered with white fur and one bald Human boy.

"Well, I'll be. At last, my luck is changing." He ducked through the arch. Two long strides brought him to the center of the tunnel in front of a fragile DeoNyte female.

With an agile sidestep, she tried to slip around him. Quick reflexes and firm grip stopped her. Esán and the second DeoNyte arrived as he passed her to Wodash, where, to her credit, she showed no fear, nor did she try to get away. With quiet dignity, she withstood the death shadow's intense cold. Serenity, the only emotion on her dark, triangular face, brought a scowl to the death shadow's thin, blue lips.

His face blank, Esán maneuvered the DeoNyte male behind him. Nothing in his mind showed his thoughts.

"We meet again, Esán Efre." Nomed kept his tone cool. "It appears destiny demands we spend time together. Please introduce your friends."

The female spoke up. "I am Elae and that is my brother, Zugo. We live in the City of Meos. This morning, we discovered Esán wandering, lost and alone. Our father sent us to show him around."

Nomed listened without taking his eyes off Esán. When she finished, he gripped Zugo by the arm and turned to Elae. "Since you are the oldest, I will ask you this question, *one time only*. If you do not tell me the truth, your brother will pay. Am I clear?"

"Quite clear."

"Where is the Evolsefil Crystal hidden?"

"Few DeoNytes know where it is."

"But you know." He glared down at her. "I see it in your eyes. Guide us there, or say goodbye to your sibling."

Esán frowned. "I don't think it's—"

"We will not—" Zugo interrupted.

"Excuse me, all of you." Elae glanced at the hand still gripping her arm. "I will lead you if—"

"Let her go, Wodash." Nomed's command met with an icy stare. His brow arched.

The death shadow released her and stepped back.

"This way." Elae walked down the tunnel, her head high, and her demeanor serene.

Nomed fell in step beside her. "Bring her brother and Esán, Wodash. We want to be certain the consequence of *any* misbehavior is swift and complete."

Esán and Zugo, held captive by the death shadow, followed.

At the entrance to the Cavern of Tennisca and the Stairway of Retu Erath, Elae faced him. "The boys cannot come any farther. The uninitiated may not enter without being harmed."

Nomed's brow shot up. "I have not been initiated."

"You are a DiMensioner and an adult. You are choosing your destiny. They are not."

He studied her placid expression and probed her mind, then turned to his henchman. "Escort our guests back to the cavern. And, Wodash, do *not* lose them. If this one is lying, then she will get to bid her brother farewell."

Elae opened the door and waited for Nomed to join her. *Neither he nor the boys realize the DiMensioner's evil will trigger a reaction in the Cavern of Tennisca. The staircase could pitch me to my death.* She suppressed a shiver, smiled calmly at Esán and Zugo, and focused on reaching the Cave of Canedari alive.

"Move." Nomed shoved her through the door.

Prepared for whatever was to come, she preceded him down the steep, stone staircase.

As Wodash stared into the inky darkness enshrouding the two descending figures. Zugo edged closer to Esán, slipped a hand around his wrist, and waited.

Nomed's startled shout echoed through the cavern. Like a magnet to steel, the death shadow shot through the door.

Spurred into action, Zugo pulled Esán back up the passageway. A quick glance assured him the silver cord around his friend's neck remained inactive. They ran as though pursued. Breathless and sweating, they arrived in the City of Meos.

"Where are we going?" Esán huffed out his question.

"To the Council Chamber. I hope my father's there."

A reddish tattooed hand shook Dom awake, yanked him upright, and shoved his spectacles into his hand. He peered up at a sneering Pentharian who marched him out to the fire.

Voer looked him up and down. "We bring your charges, old man." He nodded to Yuin. "We go now." He and his comrade strode down the tunnel.

Dom took a seat opposite Allynae's daughters. He noticed their resemblance to SparrowLyn AsTar, the woman he'd seen in the fountain. Rather than brown hair, however, long coppery curls framed lightly freckled faces. Dark eyes, so like their mother's, glowed with contempt.

"Why are *you* here?" The girl's deep voice held a distinct note of condemnation. "I thought you were loyal to Mira."

Dom let out a sigh. "I was, but I lost my mind. Now here I am, sitting in a cold, damp cavern, sharing the company of alien creatures."

"You don't sound too pleased about it." Like a melody, the second twin's voice soothed his frayed nerves.

His eyes focused on the twin that seemed less angry, he tried to explain. "I'm an old fool, but I made my choice. So please don't make my life more difficult than it is already. Nomed isn't a pleasant companion when things don't go his way, and you've caused him some frustration. I prefer not to get on his bad side, you understand."

"His friends killed Buster, Dom." Brie brushed a tear from her cheek. "How could you help someone who is prepared to destroy Myrrh?"

Dom sighed again. "I told you, I'm a stupid old man. Now, it's nap time —one of the few privileges of aging. Don't wander off or we may never find you." He scuffled away from the fire.

"Where's Esán?" The twin's deep voice hit like a knife in the back.

Dom flinched and tossed a reply over his shoulder. "From what I gather, he's somewhere in the caverns, leading everyone on a merry chase." Yawning, he slipped behind the curtained opening of the small sleeping cave.

Brie rubbed her aching shoulders and stared at the fire. "Do you think Buster died quickly?"

Ari fingered the knife hidden in her clothing. "We can only hope so. If there'd been time, I might have saved him."

"You can't blame yourself for his death. We had no opportunity to help. I wonder how Torgin's doing?"

"I'm sure glad he got away, but I miss him." Ari continued to stare at the fire. "Funny how fire has so many colors—red, orange, blue..." A sigh caught the flames and made them flicker. "Wish we had some idea what to do next."

"I think we rest. Wandering around these caverns isn't even tempting."

Brie retrieved her sleeping mat and blanket from her pack and prepared to bed down. The firelight warmed her face.

Ari curled up next to her. Soon her soft snores floated through Oche Cavern.

Brie listened to her 'older' sister's breathing settle into the peaceful rhythm of sound sleep before her own eyelids closed and she drifted into welcome slumber.

36

Nomed followed Elae—a small white beacon in an otherwise pitch-black space—deeper into the subterranean depths of Tennisca. His eagerness to find Evolsefil foremost in his mind, he failed to notice the steps changing. The movement, at first slight, broadened. The stairway swung in an arc that grew wider and steeper with each pass.

Too startled to react, he lost his footing and plunged with the heaviness of stone through space. A scream bursting from his throat brought him to his senses. Shifting to owl form, he forced his mighty wings to lift him into steadied flight. Invisible fingers snatched at his body and sent him tumbling beak over talon until, dizzy and confused, he no longer knew up from down in the bottomless cavern.

At the first sign of change, Elae sat down on a step, gripped the edges of Retu Erath, and hoped the ever-widening swing wouldn't catapult her into oblivion. She gasped as the stairway hit the bottom of its arc and swept upward. The next plunging descent pitched her stomach into her throat. The hurtling ascent dumped it back into place, rumbling and queasy. Her hands ached, her arms shook, her whole body throbbed as the staircase peaked and dropped once more. A blast of air, as cold as a late winter's night, streaked above her. She squeezed her eyes shut and whispered an ancient prayer.

The death shadow struggled against the ghostlike figures circling him. Ferocious wind dragged him deeper into the darkness. The translucent threads of his body began to unravel. The fight to weave them back together left him exhausted and numb. Forsaking his master and, even worse, forsaking himself, he gave in to the push and the pull of the whispering wind. Down he tumbled until he no longer sensed the walls of the cavern—down until he could find nothing to hold him to himself— down until he disappeared into the night sky.

With all the skill and cunning he possessed, Nomed battled against the forces that battered his owl body and sent it first in one direction and then another. Voices whispered. "Forget your humanness. Fly wild and free—without pain or sorrow. Forget the torture of loving. Forget..."

Ignoring them, he fought harder. *If I can hang onto a thread of my Human mind, I might escape these wretched ghosts.* He soared higher, the whisperers circling him like a swarm of buzzing hornets.

Gradually, the staircase ceased its pendulous swinging, and stillness returned to the Cavern of Tennisca. Beneath Elae, the stairs grew solid. Gentle hands lifted her and carried her into the depths of the cavern. A door creaked opened. More hands supported her until her feet touched the ground. Hands guided her through a darkened room into a corridor that glowed with warmth.

Elae peered at the woman beside her. "I thought I would die." The Guardian of Myrrh leaned closer to catch the soft words. "I expected to fall into the abyss of nothingness, lost forever."

"And yet you did what was necessary. Death is only an instant, Elae. And yet we fear it all our lives. What have you learned?"

Elae hugged herself. "Fear is worse than death, and I am both alive and dead in each moment." She looked up at the Guardian. "It is my choice which way I live."

"You are wise beyond your time. Come, you need to rest." Almiralyn led her into the Ephos room and helped her onto the white satin bed. "When you awaken, you will know what to do. Now, you must sleep." The Guardian brushed a wisp of white fur from her face. "You have taken your final initiation, Elae. Sleep... and dream your destiny."

Nomed found the staircase. Once assured it was solid, he shifted. Raising his arm, he sent a ball of light blazing from his fingertips. Gemstones, awakened by its touch, hurtled flashes of brilliance throughout the cavern. He dowsed his light, but not before he saw the purple doors at the bottom of the stairs. Ready to shift form if the need arose, he descended. Step by step, he drew closer to his goal—step by step, his hunger for the Evolsefil Crystal grew stronger.

The doors opened. Radiant light spilled onto the stairway, enticing him forward. Greedy arrogance ushered him into the cave. Evolsefil wrapped its radiance around him. Warmth embraced him. Power, like nectar, flooded his body. His heart, a cold and deserted place, tingled. Hands pressed to his throbbing chest, he circled the crystal, absorbing every detail of its beauty.

"Ahhhh." An exhale of understanding brought him to a standstill. *Now I understand why the leaders of DerTah want Evolsefil for their own.* Another dawning shook him to the core of his being. *I will never allow them to have it.* For the first time since he had fallen for Tianna in the village of SumnerTyme so long ago, he felt love. His heart glowed with a tenderness long forgotten. His gaze caressed the beautiful crystal. *How can I let others take you away from me?*

Certainty washed over him. *Evolsefil will be mine.* Exhilaration made him giddy. His laughter, a sound unused to being, rang out in the Cave of Canedari. Surprise cut his exuberance short. And then he threw back his head and laughed again and again, savoring the sound and the full-bodied feelings it expressed.

A rush of cold water interrupted his delighted musing. Reaching out to stabilize himself against the crystal, he floundered. The wet folds of his cape tangled around his legs. He stumbled. Churning water swept him up and carried him below the Lake of Rorret's surface, away from the Cave of Canedari and away from the Evolsefil Crystal.

Memories, like hummingbirds in search of sweet nectar, bombarded him. Diving, hovering, and darting, they ripped his emotional scars open and left them raw. Recollections came hard and fast—an abusive childhood, a father who beat him, a mother who could not come to his rescue. The Five Towers and his time there loomed large and ugly. Memories of his brother's young wife flooded his now tender heart with agony. He struggled to push them all away, but his body and mind absorbed them like a sponge.

When his emotions verged on despair, the tempestuous water tossed him onto the shore. Choking and gasping for breath, he tried to move. The world spun around him and exploded into nothingness.

Consciousness made a slow return. He opened his eyes and searched the darkness for anything familiar. Fingertips brushing across water propelled him to his feet in one scrambled motion. A light gleamed momentarily above his head. Immediate recognition of his surroundings brought with it an even more compelling realization. *I am no longer in the Cave of Canedari.*

A search of his memory brought him no sign of how he had gotten to Rorret's cavern. The cold weight of his soaked cape dragging at his body triggered water-infused memories. "Rorret!" His howl of desperation echoed off the dark granite walls.

Infuriated, he glared at the placid lake. "I don't know what you are, but you are my way to the Cave of Canedari. We have not met for the last time."

In a flash of liquid silver, he took to the air, owl wings carrying him up the crystal tunnel and back to Oche Cavern.

The Lake of Rorret reveled in the results of its labor. Images of Nomed flashed across its mirror-like surface. *Humans hide so much and this one more than most. It is an interesting time in the Dojanack Mountains.* The lake settled into fluid serenity. *But I know who you are, Seyes Nomed. And you are quite right. We have not met for the last time.*

Zugo and Esán dashed across the Meosian central square to Yookotay's council chambers, where a young female stood guard.

"Where's my father?" Zugo gulped a deep breath.

"The ReDael conferences with Sitrio. He asked not to be disturbed, Zugo."

"This is important. I have to tell him what's happening."

CleeO cast an inquisitive look in Esán's direction and knocked on the door. It opened. Yookotay looked beyond her at the two boys.

"Thank you, CleeO." He stepped aside so they could enter. Sitrio joined the DeoNyte leader, bowed, and left the council chamber, shutting the door behind him.

"I am Yookotay, ReDael of Meos." He offered his right hand, palm up. "You must be Esán."

Esán placed his right hand, palm down, on Yookotay's and his left hand on his heart. "I'm honored to meet you and to visit your city."

Yookotay smiled. "Have you been taught our way of greeting, or do you just know it?"

"I seem to know it."

Zugo waited, anxiety for Elae, making him shift from one foot to the other. *Can't my father dispense with the formalities of greeting just this once?*

"Father, Seyes Nomed and the death shadow are in the Cavern of Tennisca. Elae is with them. We must rescue her!"

"So he's here already." Yookotay did not seem surprised. "Sitrio wondered where he had gotten to when he wasn't in the upper cavern. Tell me what has occurred."

Zugo rushed through the details of how he and Esán had escaped. Yookotay listened, his focus complete. When Zugo had finished, he turned to Esán. "Do you have anything to add?"

Esán ran a hand over his baldness. "I don't believe Elae is in danger—at least not now. I don't sense fear, only peace of mind."

"And Seyes Nomed, young Esán, what are you feeling about him?"

"He's distanced from me, but still alive. And the death shadow has vanished." Esán's soft words carried strong conviction.

Zugo listened to his friend, grateful he had approached him. Esán was a gift to the DeoNytes and to Meos and Myrrh.

Yookotay ushered the boys into a smaller room attached to the Council Chamber. Carved into the stone wall was a map of the caverns of the Dojanacks. He pointed to an iridescent white sapphire. "Here is Meos." He pointed at a spot further along the wall. "Your friends are being kept prisoner here, and Zugo found you over here."

"My friends? Are they alright?"

"Sitrio says the twins are fine, but your other companion—I believe Zugo called him Torgin—is not with them."

"Did he see any Pentharian?"

"Two Pentharian left your friends in the care of an old man with gray whiskers and spectacles."

Esán frowned. "That sounds like Dom. I wonder what he's doing here?"

"Father, what about Elae?"

"She is in the hands of Evolsefil, Zugo. We dare not enter the Cavern of Tennisca when a battle rages between good and evil. Each player will meet his own fate, and we must await the outcome. I know you're worried, but have faith in the workings of Emit."

"Emit?" Esán eyes widened with questions.

"The Architect of All." Yookotay gazed at the boy. "Emit holds *All* in the palm of its hands. Emit is our protector and our mentor. We trust it to provide truth in each moment."

Esán's beautiful smile lit his face. "Oh, yes! Emit has been with me in the night when death hovered above my bed."

Transfixed by the joy in Esán's face, Zugo sighed. *He's had such a challenging journey, yet he speaks with such hope and peace.*

Yookotay returned his attention to the map. "Let's decide the best thing to do for your friends, Esán."

Zugo moved closer. "I say we rescue them. If Nomed's not there, the timing is perfect."

Immersed in his own thoughts, Esán allowed his gaze to trace the lines on the map. A strange place floating in his vision focused. Soft clouds lined a far horizon. A dilapidated cottage surrounded by rolling hills and tall, slender trees with white bark and silver leaves formed the backdrop for a DeoNyte healer who stood beside him with her fur moving in the breeze.

Zugo's hand on his arm brought his attention back to the chamber.

Esán fought to reclaim his mental clarity. "I'm so sorry."

Yookotay's serious expression intensified. "We must take you to a place of safety somewhere Seyes Nomed cannot find you. What were you envisioning?"

Esán described what he'd seen.

"Nevah Efas." Yookotay nodded. "It is a minor planet near Thera's moon. Only the true of heart may visit it. Let us move on."

Yookotay touched the white sapphire marker denoting the City of Meos on the map. It dissolved, replaced by a crystal mirror.

Zugo gaped. "I didn't know that was there."

Yookotay laughed. "You do not yet know everything, my son. Now be still. We must get permission to use a gateway."

Grasping the sapphire on the gold chain around his neck, the DeoNyte ReDael sent a shaft of blue light to illuminate the surface of the mirror. Mist rolled up and flowed onto the floor of the chamber. A tall, slender woman walked toward them, her shimmering hair mingling with the clouds in a halo of white.

Yookotay bowed his head before smiling up at Almiralyn.

"I see you've met Esán." She returned his smile. "And this must be Zugo."

Zugo stammered a shy greeting.

"What is your need, Yookotay?"

"I believe Esán should go to a safe place far from Seyes Nomed. Nevah Efas appeared to him in a vision. I request permission to use the Nervac Gateway to take him there, if you feel this is a plan of rightness."

Almiralyn's expression grew serious. "You wear the cord of the death shadow, Esán. Until it is removed, you cannot use the gateway."

Yookotay frowned. "Can you remove it?"

"No. Ari's knife is the key." She fell silent, her beautiful eyes distant. "I must go. I'm needed elsewhere. Take care of one another... and find Arienh."

The mist rolled up, obscuring Myrrh's Guardian. The mirror grew dark and smooth in the cavern wall, and the map reappeared.

"That settles it." Zugo looked triumphant. "We *have* to rescue the twins."

"You are correct." Yookotay's less-than-pleased expression conveyed his concern. "I will expect—"

A soft knock interrupted. The door opened.

"Elae!" Zugo rushed forward and pulled her into the room. "What happened? How did you get away?" He pointed at a small crystal key hanging at her waist. "Where did you get that?"

She smiled at the impetuous DeoNyte. "Patience, Zugo." Facing the DeoNyte ReDael, she bowed her head and waited.

Yookotay laid a hand on her shoulder. "Congratulations. I see you have completed your initiations."

Dignity cloaked her as she raised her gaze to his face. "I am a Light Priestess, and I am here to serve Meos."

Zugo's impatience overflowed. "Tell us what happened."

Elae described her journey into the Cavern of Tennisca with Seyes Nomed. When she finished, she appeared puzzled. "Neither the DiMensioner nor Wodash were in the cavern when I returned through it."

Yookotay pondered his options. He hesitated to leave Meos with Nomed on the loose and the Pentharian close by. Although Evolsefil could care for itself, the Guardians had charged the DeoNytes with its safety.

Resolve brought an answer. "I must remain here. Can you three rescue the twins?"

"Yes."

"Of course."

"Definitely."

Positive responses overlapped. The young trio smiled.

Yookotay placed a hand on Esán's shoulder. "Perhaps you should remain with me."

"The twins are my friends, and they are important to Myrrh's survival. I will help Zugo and Elae to rescue them." His jaw set. "We must leave now and hope Nomed doesn't arrive before us."

Elae and Zugo nodded their agreement.

Yookotay's penetrating gaze did not waver. "Take the shortest route and avoid the Lake of Rorret. Now go. Come back as quickly as you can."

Watching them depart, their youthful confidence and exuberance glowing like a corona around them, Yookotay could not dispel his fear for them. *Danger stretches its shadowed claws toward Meos, and I have no way to stop it.*

37

Relieved to be leaving the openness of the grasslands, Torgin and Paisley hiked into the foothills. Tam's ears drooped. Her beautiful head hung lower than usual. Torgin suspected she was grieving for Buster as much as he was. Without the antics of the rambunctious dog, everything seemed empty and quiet.

The big man caught his eye. "How ya doin', young one? Ya ready to ride again?"

"No." He rested his hand on Tam's neck. "She needs to walk beside us. She's missing Buster."

"They've been friends a long time." Paisley patted the pony's tawny side. "Let's stop for a break. How're ya at climbin' trees?"

"I have never climbed one. We do not have many trees in Idronatti."

"Could you climb that big oak and see if we're bein' followed?"

"I can try." He shaded his eyes, tipped his head for a better view, and considered the best way to begin. *Too bad I hate heights.*

The big man interlaced his fingers and bent forward. "Just put your foot in here, youngster. On my three, you push off the ground, and I'll give ya a boost up to that branch overhead."

Torgin, trying to ignore the anxiety beating like bat wings in his belly, put his foot in the offered hands.

Paisley inhaled and counted.

An upward thrust later, Torgin grabbed the large bough and clambered up. Avoiding even a quick peek at the ground, he braced himself against the trunk and hauled himself to standing.

"Ya alright?"

"Yes." He steadied his rubbery legs and started to climb. One sturdy branch at a time, his confidence grew stronger. He ducked and leveraged himself up to the next one. *Before today I would not have dared to climb a tree. So much has happened!*

Close to the top, he straddled a small, stout branch and wrapped his arms around the narrowing trunk. A wave of dizziness squeezed his eyes shut. He gulped a breath. *Come on, Torgin, you can do this.* Exhaling, he stared down at the vista below. "Oh, it is so beautiful."

Wind rippling through the tall grass of the prairie shifted its color from silver to green and back again. Beyond stretched the rich emerald depths of the Terces Wood. Nothing appeared to be following them. In fact, nothing seemed to move except wind and grass. He pursed his lips. *And the mist creeping across Myrrh from every direction.*

"What do you see?" Paisley sounded anxious.

"Not a thing this way." He turned to look at the Dojanacks. Two dark specks soared over the mountains. Torgin shivered. *They are flying toward us.* His fear of heights forgotten, he started the downward climb. When he reached the bottom branch, firm hands helped him to the ground.

Fear bristled into words. "Two large birds fly this way. We have to take cover. I wish I could find a grove of hemlock trees."

Paisley looked puzzled. "Why hemlock?"

"Their magic can shield us from the death shadow and the Pentharian."

"I don't know of a grove, but there's a single tree close by."

Paisley sprinted up the steep trail. Torgin dashed after him with Tam at his heels. Winded and panting, they arrived at the tree.

Torgin's quiet voice shook. "Thank you, mighty hemlock, for protecting us from evil." He tucked a small twig of evergreen into Tam's bridle, another went into his pocket, and a third into Paisley's. He patted the sturdy trunk and peered up at the sky.

Too close for comfort, the huge black vultures flew in descending circles, each one smaller than the last.

"What're they doing?" Torgin sidled closer to Tam.

"Huntin'."

As the predators circled lower, Paisley grabbed Tam's reins and pulled her into a copse of craggy fruit trees. Torgin dodged in behind them and crouched beside Paisley. The enormous birds swooped over their hiding place, banked away from the mountains, and flew off toward the Terces Wood.

"That's what killed Buster." Torgin swallowed the bile rising in his throat.

"Weren't after us." Paisley gazed after them and moved out of the trees. "There's no way they could've missed our hiding place."

"Unless they could not see us." Torgin fingered the hemlock in his pocket. "When will it be dark?"

"Soon. Let's find a place to camp for the night."

Not far up the trail, Paisley jogged onto a faint path, weaving between tall evergreens. As the sun slid behind the mountains, leaving the sky bathed in golds and oranges, they arrived at a grove of birch trees surrounding a spring-fed pool.

"This is great." Torgin slipped off his backpack. When he had spread his sleeping mat and blanket beneath a tree, he pulled out a large packet of sandwiches. "Sibine made these." He handed one to his new friend, bit into his, and grinned.

Paisley took a bite and chewed noisily. "Sibine's a great little Wood Tiff."

After they washed down their meal with a deep drink of spring water, Paisley bedded down for the night. "Better sleep while we can."

Torgin yawned, stretched out on his mat, and stared up at the darkening sky. *It's been a long, heart-wrenching turning.* A single star rose above the encroaching mist. Thoughts of Buster brought tears to his eyes.

On the opposite side of Myrrh, Allynae and Major Jordett arrived at Demrach Gateway to find Almiralyn standing in front of a translucent web of swirling color beneath a lofty Tirips tree. The two Pentharian were nowhere in sight.

"There's the gateway. Can you see it?" Allynae pointed, keeping his voice low.

The major nodded. "What is Almiralyn doing?"

"Watch."

The Guardian of Myrrh spoke in a whisper. "Eero Tye Como." At her command, the mouth-like entrance yawned wide, showing sharp points of flashing light. She clapped her hands. "Omoc Eyt Oree!" The gateway snapped shut, resumed its spinning, and shrunk to the size of a large coin.

Almiralyn's shoulders sagged. Allynae strode to her side and put his arm around her. She straightened and gave him a tired smile.

"Now what?" He held her steady.

"We wait. The Pentharian cannot destroy what they think no longer exists." She called softly to her raven protector, who perched on a limb above her. "Take this gateway to the hemlock grove and hide it. I'll maintain its smallness as long as possible."

Karrew examined her with one dark eye before clasping the spinning disc in his beak and flying off to the Northeast.

"Mira, you know you can't hold it to that size for an extended period. I hope he makes it to the grove before it resumes its full strength or—"

"It's okay, Alli. Don't worry about what *can* happen. Just keep our enemies from distracting me until I'm sure Karrew is safe."

Allynae furrowed his brow. "What do you want us to do? A Pentharian is—"

"If I am to help, you'd better tell me about these Pentharian." Major Jordett walked from the trees.

"You explain, Alli. I need to put a spell of silence and forgetting on the horses." She grabbed their reins and led them deeper into the woods.

Allynae glanced up at the sky, pulled Jordett back into the forest, and pointed at two large black shapes circling above the clearing.

The major watched their rapid descent. "Pentharian are..."

"Mercenaries, shape shifters from ReTaw au Qa." Allynae fixed a stern gaze on the Major. "They become whatever shape will help them catch their prey—any shape at all, so beware. Their venom is deadly."

Jordett pointed and spoke close to his ear. "What's wiggling in that one's talons?"

Allynae pulled him lower. "We'll know soon enough."

The enormous birds landed and materialized in their natural form at the clearing's center. Beneath an orange-scaled foot, a young Wood Tiff struggled to get free. The Pentharian jerked him to his feet with a tattooed hand and glared down at him.

The Tiffin wiped blood from a scratch on his shoulder. "You hurt me."

"Show us the gateway." The Pentharian's eyes hardened.

The terrified Wood Tiff looked around. "It's gone! It's usually right there."

"You are lying." The green off-worlder growled and loomed over the trembling figure.

"I'm not!" The young Tiff's reply was indignant. "It's *always* been right there."

The emerald alien prowled the clearing and stopped at its center. His pierced nose twitched. His lizard-gold eyes narrowed. "Someone has been here." A long finger pointed. "I see hoof prints here and footprints over there. The air smells of Humans."

Continuing to hold the Wood Tiff by the arm, the orange Pentharian joined in the search.

Allynae glanced over his shoulder. Somewhere behind him, Almiralyn remained statue-still under the trees, her concentration fixed on Karrew.

"What the..." Jordett gasped.

Allynae's attention snapped back to the clearing. The Pentharian closest to them shifted to panther, growled and crouched, blazing eyes focused in their direction.

His comrade croaked. "Come out." He held the Wood Tiff aloft by his collar. "Or I will end the life of this small one right now."

Shoving Jordett deeper into the shadows, Allynae stepped into the clearing.

"Who are you?" The orange alien examined him from head to foot.

"I'm a wood carver. My home's near here. Let the child go. He can do you no harm."

"He is our terror and our death." The Pentharian's muscles bulged under tattooed skin.

The panther sniffed the air, leapt into the trees, and herded Jordett into the open. With no sign of fear, the major moved to Allynae's side. The orange Pentharian placed the small Tiff in the branches of a Tirips tree and joined his comrade in feline form.

Allynae glimpsed Jordett's expressionless face before, back-to-back, they prepared to fight for their lives. Neither bore arms, and neither took his eyes off the circling cats.

Allynae crouched. *Timing is everything.* He tensed and leapt. His arms encircled a panther's muscular neck; his knees gripped its sleek sides. It reared. A large green anaconda hissed and slithered from his grasp. Staggering backward, he tripped and fell. The serpent's head whipped around. Its forked tongue licked the air, just missing his face. He rolled to the side and sprang to his feet. Curling its limbless body into a tight coil, the huge anaconda let out a long, high-pitched hiss. Allynae hunkered down, ready to spring out of reach. Scaled sinew shot through the air and shifted, landing with powerful muscles rippling under panther-black skin. Golden eyes locked onto his. Neither he nor the cat flinched. And neither moved.

Somewhere behind him, Jordett swore. The panther crouched. Allynae's heart constricted—blood pounded in his ears. The jungle cat leapt, claws ready to rake his flesh. A flash of silvery white caught his eye as he hurled his body sideways. Landing half sprawled, he lunged to standing and whirled around. His adversary, in Pentharian form, lay motionless on the ground.

On the opposite side of the clearing, Jordett struggled beneath the paw of his attacker. A blur of white and gold headed straight for the back of its neck, missed, and soared skyward. The panther's scream filled the woods. It crouched and shifted, vulture wings carrying it in pursuit of Almiralyn's bird form. Out of the Northeast, a streak of black shot into their flight path.

"Thanks be!" Allynae grasped the major's hand and pulled him to his feet. Above the trees, three birds circled, then banked in different directions. Karrew moved in, ready to attack. The white bird arced above them and dove, striking the vulture on the back of the neck with her sharp beak. It slowed, jerked and plummeted downward until it collapsed in Pentharian form beside its comrade. Almiralyn landed next to her brother and shifted to Human form.

"Are they dead?" Jordett stared at their adversaries, his eyes wide with astonishment.

"No, just stunned. They have a weak point at the base of the skull. I took advantage of it." She knelt by one of their fallen enemies.

"So, what do we do with them?" Jordett walked up behind her.

"Take them to the Tower of Nemttachenn and bind them there." Karrew landed on Allynae's shoulder.

Jordett stared at the blue-black raven. "Did he say that?"

Allynae winked. "Good thought, Karrew. Then at least we'll know where these two are."

"The problem will be how to transport them." The Theran major knelt to examine the closest Pentharian.

Almiralyn pulled two strands of hair from her head and tied one around each muscular neck. A snap of her fingers brought them to standing, dazed but awake. Her gaze held theirs. "Shift into small black birds."

They changed instantly.

She turned. "Alli, you and Jordett take the Wood Tiff to his family and meet me at Nemttachenn. Be quick. We have much to do." Shifting, she rose into the air. The Pentharian followed. Karrew took his place as rear guard.

"I'll get the horses." Jordett sprinted into the woods.

Allynae walked to the Tirips tree and gazed up between the leafy branches. "You can come down now."

A small face peeked through the leaves. "Who were they? Was that Almiralyn?"

Allynae lifted him down and looked him over. "Aside from a scratch on your shoulder, you seem no worse for your adventure. We'll take you home and answer your questions on the way." He handed the Tiffin to Jordett and mounted Saylo, his roan mare. "Where do you live?"

The young Tiff pointed. "My TreeOm is down that path."

The horses thundered from the clearing and through the Terces Wood.

When Nemttachenn came into sight, Almiralyn descended in an ever-decreasing spiral. With Karrew and the captured Pentharian following, she circled the parapet, dropped into the enclosed darkness of the staircase, and landed at the center of the tower's granite floor. Shifting to Myrrh's Guardian, she summoned the Sentinel.

"CheeTrann, CheeTrann,
Sentinel of Myrrh,
Keep these guests within your walls;
Do not let them stir.

In bird form, they must remain.
Harken to my plea.
Do not let them leave your care
Until I set them free."

CheeTrann's rumbling response shook the tower.

"Thank you, Sentinel." Almiralyn followed Karrew into the clearing. "That's done. CheeTrann will guard them well." Restless pacing took her around the perimeter and back.

"The Demrach Gateway is safe within the Grove of Mehloc." Karrew's ebony gaze remained fixed on her.

She paused and peered through the trees. "Where are Allynae and the major? I told Alli to hurry."

"We could fly to meet them." He landed on her shoulder.

She scratched his chest. "I'm going back to the cottage to check on Sparrow and Merrilea. You find them and tell Alli to head for the mountains. I'll join them when I can."

Karrew ruffled his feathers and lifted skyward. She followed. They circled Nemttachenn and then separated...raven to the West and white and gold bird to the East.

Nomed savored his excitement. Asleep beside the fire—fingers of flame highlighting their fair skin with its dusting of freckles and their riot of red curls—were Allynae's daughters...Almiralyn's nieces. He almost laughed aloud. *An unsatisfying situation has just become much more palatable.*

A series of rhythmic snorted snores floating from the small cave informed him Dom slept.

He yawned. *Sleep sounds good.* Certain the twins would not wander away in the dark, he stepped into his quarters and prepared for bed. Relaxed on his pallet, he laced his fingers behind his head. No matter how hard he tried to reconstruct the incident in the Cave of Canedari, the memories remained vague. A picture flashed through his mind. His heart quickened. *Evolsefil... What beauty—what power! It will be mine. And Myrrh...* He gave a harsh laugh. The jagged scar pulled at his cheek. The roar of rage came with no warning.

Memories flashed—the kitten flying across the room...Mira gathering up its lifeless body...her unwillingness to give him another chance...the march to the sunflower field...his banishment from Myrrh.

Nomed sat up. The sight of the portal mirror had infuriated him. As his savage kick sent a crack traveling upward, something inside him turned to ice. He touched the scar. *I didn't even feel pain from the cut. That turning I stopped feeling anything. My life disintegrated into shades of gray.* Painful rejection festered for a moment before he lay back on his pallet. "Memories mean less than nothing. Only destroying Myrrh and Mira matter." The sound of his voice surprised then soothed him.

Against the background of darkness, he imagined the twins slumbering by the fire and smiled. *You will be sorry, Guardian of Myrrh. The twins are mine to do with as I will.* He laughed, rolled onto his side, and slept the sleep of one whose empty life had found fulfillment.

38

Esán, unable to teleport somewhere he had not seen, hung spider-like against the cold, rough stone of a crevasse wall. Elae scaled the pitted surface above him. Zugo climbed below. Feeling his way in the dark, Esán searched for the next handhold. A loose pebble rolled away from his groping fingers and bounced several times before hitting the bottom of the chasm.

"Are you alright?" Zugo's voice drifted up from the darkness.

"Yes." He squinted, trying without success to see Elae's pale outline against the dark cliff. "I just wish we'd reach the top."

Soft words of encouragement floated down to him. "Keep climbing toward my voice, and you'll be here before you know it."

He found a solid handhold and pulled himself further upward. Elae's hand gripped his wrist and guided his ascent up the last section. A burst of energy propelled him over the lip of the chasm into a natural passageway.

Zugo arrived beside them. "What a climb!"

Elae grinned. "Let's stop for a rest so we can catch our breath."

Surprised at how quickly he recovered, Esán scanned the passage. "How close are we to Oche Cavern?"

"We're almost there. How are you feeling?"

Esán heard the concern in Zugo's casual question. "Great. I promise to tell if I'm not. Ready to go?"

Elae took the lead as they crept through the passageway in silence.

Voer, the sapphire blue leader of the Pentharian, entered Oche Cavern with Yuin. Almiralyn's nieces slept by the fire. The old man's soft snores drifted from the small cave. Seyes Nomed was nowhere to be seen. Voer crossed to his sleeping alcove. "Nomed?"

Fabric rustled. The DiMensioner's face appeared from behind the curtain. "What?"

"We cannot find our brothers; Jeet, Stee, and Yaro."

Nomed yawned. "I'll be right out."

The twins stretched and scooted closer together, their eyes filled with firelight and curiosity.

Ducking from his alcove, Nomed sneered down at them. "How nice of you young ladies to join us!" He considered the Pentharian leader. "Now, Voer, what's this about your comrades?"

"They seem to have disappeared. We have looked throughout Myrrh and have detected no sign of them."

Nomed rubbed the scar on his cheek. "Did they destroy the gateways as I commanded?"

"They destroyed Kao. The surrounding area is scorched and scattered with fallen trees and small, burned bodies. At Demrach Gateway, we found no such signs. In fact, the portal seems to have vanished. We detected the odor of Jeet and Stee and two Humans, but discovered no trace of where they had gone."

A frown stretched the scar taut. "And the other boy child?"

"I imagine he's wandering in the foothills." Yuin's defiant reply went unacknowledged.

Voer found Nomed's lack of interest in his missing comrades annoying, but he knew better than to voice his frustration. The old man stumbling from the small cave provided a welcome distraction. Mouth rounded in a yawn, Dom limped across the cavern, stopped by the fire, and cleaned gold-rimmed spectacles on the hem of his green vest.

One twin whispered to the other. "I wonder where Wodash is?"

"No talking." Nomed's order, barked in a soft voice, caused only a slight echo. "Collect your belongs, go into Dom's cave, and stay there."

The twin scowled and started to speak. Her sister elbowed her in the ribs and hauled her to her feet. As the second twin reached for her sleeping mat, a small blue pouch on a matching ribbon slipped from beneath her shirt.

Nomed grabbed her arm. "What are you wearing around your neck?"

"A pouch." The girl glared at his hand.

Eyes narrowed, he released her. "What's in it?"

"A rock." She casually tucked it away and moved to step past him.

He blocked her retreat. "What type of rock?"

"I don't know." Grabbing her pack, she dodged around him and hurried after her sister.

When he turned back to the fire, his hazel eyes gleamed with unsatisfied interest. He scrutinized the old man. "After you eat something, attend to those twins, and *don't* let them out of your sight."

Cursing under his breath, Dom perched his spectacles on his nose and rooted around in the food locker. His rebellious expression caused the blue Pentharian to glance from him to the DiMensioner.

Ignoring the old man's obvious desire to listen longer, Nomed arched a brow. "Now, Voer, you're missing three comrades?"

The disinterest in his tone made Voer's tail twitch.

The curtain whispered shut behind the twins, creating a welcome barrier between them and Seyes Nomed. They flopped down on the pallet.

"That was close." Brie's fingers closed around the Stone of Remembering. "It's a good thing I don't know what type of rock this is. If he'd asked me where I got it or what its name was, I would've had to tell the truth." She rubbed the star on the back of her neck.

"I'm just glad to be away from those awful Pentharian. And Dom—" Ari made an indignant sound in her throat. "With friends like him, do we really need enemies?"

Brie sighed. "He's not all that—"

Astonishment replaced Ari's disgusted expression. "Esán!" She smothered her screeched stage whisper with a hand over her mouth. Her eyes darted to the curtained entrance and back to Esán's bald head, where it topped a large stone on a ledge opposite them.

He put a finger to his lips and motioned them to come with him.

Ari jumped up and pulled Brie with her.

With a questioning lift of her brows, Brie pointed at the wall and shrugged.

A beautiful creature stepped onto the ledge. Another stood behind Esán.

The twins gaped.

"Friends." Esán's smile accompanied the whispered word. He pointed at one and then the other. "Zugo and Elae."

Brie shared Ari's look of astonishment when Zugo landed beside them.

A wrinkled hand gripping the edge of curtain galvanized everyone into action. Elae disappeared from view. Zugo darted to the far side of the entrance. Esán ducked behind the stone. Brie bent to tie her shoe, and Ari dropped onto the pallet, all in the instant before Dom pushed the curtain aside.

"What are *you* doing in here?" Ari's look of disgust made the old man wince.

"Babysitting." His sarcastic tone held a touch of bitterness.

Brie straightened, her gaze locked onto his. Zugo slipped behind him.

Dom's eyes narrowed behind his lenses. A flash of white knocked him to his knees. Zugo clung to his shoulders, one hand smothering his startled expletive. Esán jumped down from the ledge to help the twins press him flat on the floor. Dom quit struggling and lay still. Zugo shoved a wad of cloth in his mouth. Ari secured his hands behind his back with a short length of rope from her pack. The four lifted him and dumped him on the sleeping pallet, his back resting against the wall.

Brie grabbed her backpack. "I'm sorry, Dom. Take care of yourself."

The boys boosted her onto the ledge. Ari climbed up beside her and reached down to help Esán. He put his foot in Zugo's stirruped hands and prepared for a boost.

"Ready?" Zugo bent his knees.

The curtain whipped aside. Nomed exploded into the cave, his face contorted with anger. "Don't move, any of you."

Brie dropped to her knees behind the rock and crawled into the low tunnel.

"If you value your friends, stay right where you are." The DiMensioner's shout sent her scrambling faster, her heart pounding in her ears.

"Voer, come here. Go after that twin." His fading voice warned her the Pentharian was on the way.

When she no longer felt solid rock above her head, she stood up and listened for her sister's approach. "Ari?" Silence. "Elae?"

Pressing against the rough stone, she smothered a moan. Terror of the black emptiness doubled her over. *I can't s-stay h-here. And I c-can't go back.* She gulped in air and forced herself to move. With one hand on the wall as a guide, she ran blindly until burning lungs compelled her to stop. *I just need a moment—*

The Star of Truth shot fiery pain down her spine. Gleaming golden eyes advanced toward her. She swallowed a groan of dismay and pressed a hand against her chest. Her heart's loud hammering negated her ability to think. Fighting for calm, she crept further down the passageway.

"Time to get up." Paisley's deep voice penetrated Torgin's dreaming. "We've got lots to do today."

Torgin opened an eye. Ribboned streaks of pink and lavender stretched across the dawn sky. "Why does morning always arrive so early?" He shivered in the coolness left by the passing night.

Paisley laughed and handed him a piece of dried fruit from his pack. "Sit with me on this rock. Soon the sun'll warm ya, and you'll be grumblin' because it's too hot."

They finished their meal in companionable silence and repacked their gear. Paisley trudged up the mountain. Torgin rode on Tam, the soles of his shoes almost touching the ground, his fingers playing with the silky strands of her cream-colored mane. Although the grade grew steeper, the sure-footed pony climbed the steep trail as though it were as flat as the grasslands.

Glad to be traveling with a companion, Torgin studied the natural beauty surrounding them. He bit his lip. Hadn't Tibin said something about a black obsidian peak? Jumping down from Tam's back, he matched his long stride to Paisley's. "Do you know where NaiDisbo Peak is?"

"Yep." Paisley pointed straight ahead. "It's past those two closer mountains. Why?"

"Tibin, the Wood Tiff, told me to use it as a guide for staying on course. Is it anywhere near Timreh Pass?"

Paisley didn't lessen his steady pace. "The pass sits near the top of its neighbor, Mount GetiNar."

"What's Mount GetiNar like?" Torgin forced his tired legs to move faster.

"It's granite, coughed up from the depths of the earth. Steep cliffs on the north face got no pass-through. Lots of trees on the west side, but it's a heap easier to travel there."

"What about NaiDisbo? Is it difficult to climb?" He gritted his teeth against the pain in his cramping calf muscles.

"It's an amazin' mountain." Paisley's eyes glowed. "NaiDisbo's almost like black glass polished smooth. When you see it from a distance, you can't imagine how ya could ever climb it. But when you get there, it has steps carved in its south face."

"Who carved the steps?" He wished Paisley would slow down.

The man shrugged. "No one knows. Maybe earth dwellers sculpted them before Old Earth got blasted from the sky and scattered from there to eternity."

"Myrrh was part of Old Earth, wasn't it?" Torgin puffed in his effort to keep up. "How did it get here?"

Paisley tugged at his mustache. "Let's rest." He offered a flask of water. "Have a good, long drink."

Torgin gulped several swallows, returned it, and wiped his mouth with the back of his hand.

The big man lowered his bulk onto a fallen tree trunk, savored a drink, and stowed the flask in his backpack.

"Folks say that a couple hundred galactic sun cycles ago, a piece of Old

Earth passed close enough to Thera to be caught in its gravitational pull. To keep the two from colliding and to protect our solar system, the Guardians of the Fourth Galaxy hid the Evolsefil Crystal deep in the Dojanack Caverns and used its power to connect Myrrh's core to the core of Thera. Over time, the two became dependent on each other."

"Tell me more." Torgin sank down beside him and massaged his aching calves.

"To protect their connection from scoundrels who want to destroy the last piece of Old Earth and steal Evolsefil, the Galactic Guardians appointed five Fathers to oversee the establishment of a city on Thera, a city that would help to keep Myrrh safe. They called it Idronatti. The Guardians also trained a custodian for Myrrh."

"Is that Almiralyn?" He stretched his legs in front of him.

"Yep." Paisley rested his forearms on his knees and interlaced his fingers. "When she arrived, they hid Myrrh inside another dimension."

"Why do only children come here?"

"At first, everyone came to visit. Then the City Fathers decided they wanted total control of the people, so they commanded their research team to develop a way to erase their memories of Myrrh."

"The twins told me about the PPP and their experiments." Torgin shivered. "I like it here, but I am much more comfortable in Idronatti. I enjoy knowing what to expect. Here, I never know what's going to happen next."

"It's all about learnin' to trust your world and yourself." The big man smiled at him as he climbed to his feet. "Let's keep movin' or we won't get far today." He shouldered his pack and scratched Tam's ear.

"She's beautiful, isn't she?" Torgin mounted and stroked her neck.

"She is that, young one." Paisley caught hold of her reins and hiked up the trail.

Torgin shaded his eyes and examined the Dojanack Mountain range. He lowered his hand. "Are we almost there?"

"We should reach Timreh Pass sometime tomorrow." The big man glanced up at the sky. "Hope the weather holds."

Torgin followed his gaze. Above them, small birds circled in the late morning sun. Clouds moved in single file across the sky in a pageant of shapes and sizes.

"I love clouds." He pointed. "There's a dog with a tail like Buster's."

Paisley grinned. "Well, well, our old friend must be sayin' hello."

While they watched, the cloud morphed into another form.

"The sun's pretty high." Paisley brought Tam to a halt. "Let's stop for a bite of lunch. Then I wanna peek at that compass."

After enjoying one of Sibine's sandwiches, Torgin withdrew Ostradio from under his shirt. "What do you want to ask?"

"The best way to Mount GetiNar."

Torgin held the compass steady. "Mount GetiNar." The needle spun around and around and stopped, pointing west. The face melted away. A well-worn path leading up the side of a high mountain meadow appeared. "Show us how—"

A cascade of pebbles diverted his attention. Further up the trail, a diminutive gray creature peeked from behind a large rock.

"What's that?" Afraid to frighten it, Torgin kept his tone low.

"That be an Enots—our guide to Timreh Pass, if I can persuade him to come along."

Torgin tried not to stare at the small, boy-like creature that stepped onto the path. His slim body, about the height of Paisley's knee, appeared to be made of gray stones. Prominent round, gray eyes looked from Torgin to Paisley. Pointed ears on either side of his round face twitched. Long fingers, making the sound of rock hitting rock, flexed and straightened.

Paisley knelt. "Ya ho, young Enots. We're friends of the Lady Almiralyn. She sent us on an important mission and told us to seek the Enots if we needed help."

The gray eyes widened with curiosity. "Ya ho. What is your ending?" He spoke in a high, breathy voice.

Paisley pointed at Ostradio. "Come here and look."

Torgin extended his hand and held his breath.

More curious than timid, the Enots ambled down the trail, examined the picture on the compass face, pointed to the meadow path. "This leads to Timreh Pass. What must you know?"

Paisley stood. "How do we find that trail?"

The Enots bent, picked up a stone with his long fingers, and threw it high into the air. Catching it deftly in one hand, he studied it.

"Ya ho!" He grinned with delight. "I lead. Name called Skipt."

Paisley introduced himself and Torgin. "Would you like to ride on our pony?"

Skipt hopped from one foot to the other, and after observing her from all sides, nodded. Tam lowered her head. Giggling, he patted her nose. "Ya, me ride." A wide grin filled his tiny face.

Paisley picked him up and set him on Tam's back. Skipt curled his legs under him and entwined a piece of the mane through his long fingers. "Straight ahead until two bends in the trail, then up and up." He beamed with happiness.

Paisley led Tam up the mountain. Torgin followed, watching the Enots with interest. *What a strange creature*, he thought, *and what a strange adventure.*

39

Karrew landed at the top of a tall beech tree and looked east. His instincts nagged at him to return to the cottage. He fluffed his feathers and bobbed his head. *Allynae can take care of himself. Almiralyn will need her personal guardian sooner than she expects.*

Soaring above the trees, he contemplated the dense, gray mist obscuring the horizon. *As Myrrh's boundaries grow less distinct, so does its Guardian's.* He increased his speed until the red barn appeared in the distance. A controlled descent sent him swooping past the maple with its swing and tree house. He glided through the open kitchen window and landed on his perch.

Majeska leapt onto the sill, her amethyst eyes wide.

"How's Mira, Jeska?" He folded his blue-black wings and stared.

The cat arched her back in a luxurious stretch; gave a short, clipped meow; and jumped to the floor. He followed her down the hall to the makeshift art studio. Sparrow and Merrilea stood in front of a large painting, where Myrrh filled the canvas. Gateways swirled in the Terces Woods, the grasslands, and the mountains. Through the receding gray mist, the land emerged, clearly defined and vibrant.

Almiralyn sat in an armchair, her head resting against the padded back and her hands folded on her lap. "Well, that's more hopeful." Her fatigue-dulled gaze followed him as he landed on the top rail of a nearby chair.

He examined her with one dark eye. She, like her land, appeared faded around the edges. His wings lifted and lowered. "Mira, are you alright?"

A feeble attempt to smile ended with a sigh. "I'm fine, Karrew, just very tired."

Merrilea moved closer. "What's happening to you?"

"Each time a Pentharian destroys something in Myrrh, I lose more of myself. Even moving Demrach Gateway weakened me."

"How many gateways have they destroyed?" Merrilea helped her to stand.

"Only one. However, the magic mirror is unstable, and, as long as Demrach Gateway remains hidden in the Grove of Mehloc, it's unusable as well."

Karrew croaked his approval when Esán's aunt put a gentle hand on Almiralyn's arm and guided her from the studio and up the stairs to her room. Intrigued by Sparrow's work, he remained behind.

Immersed in her art, she removed the completed painting from the easel and leaned it against the wall. With a new canvas in place, she stared at its pristine surface. Her look of concentration changed to enlightened eagerness as she picked up her palette, dabbed her brush, and began to paint.

Not wanting to distract her and eager to check on his mistress, he flew upstairs and landed on the foot of Almiralyn's brass bed. With one eye and then the other, he noted the paleness of her skin and the dark circles highlighting the depth of her fatigue. With difficulty, he hid his distress.

Merrilea sat next to her, monitoring her pulse. "Is there anything you need, Almiralyn?"

Karrew's crackly voice rattled out an answer before Mira could speak. "The biggest danger is loosing her connection to this world. Keep her tied to Myrrh with ordinary things like eating and walking in the garden. For now, she needs to sleep." He hopped down beside his mistress and let her run cool fingers over his sleek feathers.

She closed her eyes. When she reopened them, her voice was stronger. "Go to Alli. Tell him he *must* find the children."

He gave her pale hand a gentle peck, flew out the open bedroom window, and soared over the Terces Wood.

The sun, shrouded behind the creeping, gray mist, cast its diffused glow over the land. Rain clouds gathering on the southern horizon heralded the probability of a summer storm. Allowing the wind to carry him, Karrew caught an updraft and sailed over the forest. Concern for his mistress pressed him to increase his speed. *We must stop the DiMensioner.*

His search for Almiralyn's brother took him to Nemttachenn. No sign of Allynae and Jordett sent him soaring above the woods, alert for any hint of the two men.

As he emerged into the hazy sky, a mourning dove lifted above the treetops and flew toward the Dojanack Mountains. Something about the gray-brown bird intrigued him. Before he could change course, male voices prompted him to fly in a wide circle. Through a break in the thick weave of the forest's canopy, he glimpsed two horses and their riders. With a tinge of regret, he glided between slender branches and alighted on Allynae's shoulder.

"Hey, old friend, what's up?" Allynae slowed his mount to a walk.

Karrew ruffled his neck feathers. "The small Wood Tiff?"

"We took him to his parents. The Pentharian didn't leave venom in his wound, so he'll be fine." He glanced at him. "That isn't why you are here."

"Your sister grows dimmer with the annihilation of the gateways. She's resting."

"What does she need us to do?" Jordett patted his horse's neck.

"You are to head for the mountains. If you find the children, Nomed will be somewhere close." Karrew made a gurgling sound. "If we don't stop him, Alli, his bid for revenge will wipe us all from the face of the heavens."

Allynae scratched at his feathered underbelly. "We'll do our best, Karrew." Motioning Jordett to follow, he picked up his pace.

They rode in silence until Allynae reined in his horse in the shelter of the trees at the edge of the grasslands. High in the summer sky, two dark shapes flew over the foothills. Just as they were about to disappear into the mountains, they lifted on the wind and soared over the Land of Myrrh.

Jordett halted beside him. "Do you suppose those are more Pentharian?"

"Could be." Allynae's gaze tracked the silhouetted figures. "I'd hate to encounter them without Almiralyn. Let's give them time to fly beyond the prairie."

The two men dismounted and shared water from a canteen. Karrew's restless worry drove him above the trees. The sunlight, though dimmed by the approaching storm, warmed his body. Flying north over the grasslands, he scouted the area. Nothing suggested danger lurked nearby. Only the thickening mist alluded to the evil holding Myrrh in its grip.

Pressed against the passage wall, Brie stared into Pentharian gold eyes for the second time in two turnings. Warm breath brushing her cheek froze her to the spot. A low, rapacious growl sent panic racing up and down her spine. The tumultuous beating of her heart throbbed so loud it drowned her thoughts. Rough, cold stone chafed her rigid back.

Fingers splayed, she pressed her palms against the impenetrable wall and wished she could vanish. The coolness of the panther's nose brushed the fingers of her hand and traveled up her arm. A warm, wet tongue licked a tear from her cheek. She choked back a sob and turned her head away. "Please, please let me disappear."

Behind her, the tunnel wall dissolved in a whoosh of cool air. Stumbling backward, she fought to regain her balance. Terror rolling from her throat joined with the distant wail of the thwarted hunter and faded into silence.

Forcing a calm she did not feel, she searched the pitch black space for her enemy. Her fingers touched cool, rough, and unyielding stone. She leaned her forehead against the solid barrier and swallowed a lump in her throat. Relief vanished into darksome dread as, she fought her childhood fear of the dark and the sense of isolation threatening to overwhelm her. *I need light.* She made herself focus. *I dropped my pack when the panther caught up with me. What if...*

On her knees, she searched the ground next to the wall. Shaking fingers curled around a leather strap. With a sigh of relief, she pulled it to her, withdrew a lite-stick, and thought it on. The sudden ability to see helped to disperse her fear. She tugged her pack over her shoulders and stood up. As she made a tentative investigation of her surroundings, she discovered rough stone walls, a deep cleft defined by towering cliffs, a tumbled pile of stones and debris. Half hidden to one side of the cliffs, she discovered an opening tall enough to duck through.

She gripped the lite-stick and peered beyond it into more darkness. The futility of her situation crushed her. "What do I do now?" A trembling hand tangled in her red curls as she struggled to remain calm. "Ari. Arienh, I need you." A hiccuped sob stabbed the hushed quiet. A soft voice froze her next sob halfway up her throat.

"Come. You are safe." The sweet-voiced declaration came from the opening. "Come. I'll show you the way."

Startled, Brie swallowed and held the lite-stick higher. "Who's there?" She clutched the Stone of Remembering. Comfort rippled through her. The Star of Truth tingled with warmth. The beginnings of courage escorted her to the opening.

"Come. Follow the sound of my voice."

After a calming inhale, Brie ducked through, exhaled, and held her lite-stick high. The illuminated walls of a tunnel glistened. She glanced around, trying to see who spoke the words of encouragement that continued to guide her down an endless tunnel. Fatigue tore at her calm. Fear of the dark gnawed. Tears stung her eyes. She stumbled and caught herself.

"Soon." Again, the reassuring voice whispered from the endless darkness. "Soon."

She began to listen to the rhythm of her footsteps, silently counting as they tread the tunnel floor. *One, two, three. One, two, three. It's a waltz.* She almost smiled. *A waltz carries me away from all I know. One, two, three. One, two, three. Will my friends find me, or will I be lost in this darkness forever? Ari, where are you? One, two, three.*

The sound of water brought her to a halt. The voice urged her onward. She stumbled around a corner into a modest-sized grotto. Through a jumble of glistening stones, a beautiful waterfall cascaded into a large pool. The walls glowed with green phosphorescence. Light from a hidden source sparkled across the water's surface. Air moved around her, brushing her cheek and fingering the feathers of hair that fell around her face. More exhausted than she ever remembered being, she sank down beside the pool. Using her backpack for a pillow, she dropped into dreaming.

Dom sat on the pallet in the small cave, rubbing his wrists and mumbling about old fools who should know better. Opposite him, Esán, Ari, and a young DeoNyte faced Seyes Nomed, their expressions wary. Voer had returned from his search for Brie empty-handed. Nomed's fury roiled around him like gathering clouds. Dom dreaded the coming storm.

"She's a child. How could she have gotten away?" Nomed glared at the frustrated Pentharian.

"She was right there under my nose. I had her cornered and then she vanished." His long, bluish braids tumbled over his shoulder as he expressed chagrin at his failure.

Nomed seized Esán by the arm. "Bring the others."

The fire crackled a merry song—a stark contradiction to the tension in the cavern—as Voer deposited the unwilling captives in a line facing the enraged DiMensioner.

Nomed glared from face to face. "It seems I need to place you under lock and key." He paced back and forth in front of them. His eyes blazed; his blood-red scar pulsed, as he halted in front of Zugo.

"Where—did—she go?" Nomed's clipped words carried a harsh warning.

Zugo, his pale eyes focused on the ground, remained sullen and silent.

Dom knew Nomed would probe the young DeoNyte's mind and cringed.

Zugo's hands flew to his head. "I don't know. The only way in or out of that part of the caverns is a steep stone wall. I do not believe she would climb it on her own."

Scowling, Nomed fired his next question at Ari. "Where is Yaro, the golden Pentharian?"

"How would I know?" Her eyes sparked with hatred.

Fury flared hotter as he repeated the question through bared teeth.

"I don't know." The fire in her eyes flared to match his. "And I don't care."

The sound of a slap ricocheted off the cavern walls. Ari neither winced nor cried out. She stood stone still, her head high and fists in tight balls at her sides.

Esán and Zugo, held in check by the Pentharian, stood powerless and silent beside her.

Dom cleared his throat. "Was that really necessary, Seyes?"

An unreadable expression on his scared face, Nomed glared daggers at his old friend. A snarl rattled up from his gut. He snatched it back and, nostrils flaring, glowered at the victim of his assault. Ari stared straight ahead. The print left by his slap raged red on the pale skin of her cheek. Her tear-free eyes conveyed a defiance he recognized all too well—an anger he continued to experience even today.

Imposing a tight rein on his churning emotions, he grasped Esán by the arm and prepared to march him toward his personal sleeping alcove. Hard-faced, he turned to Voer. "Take them to the small cave and make certain they cannot escape. Dom, you will guard them." He paused long enough to watch Voer and Yuin escort Zugo and Ari to the small sleeping cave.

Dom remained by the fire, soaking up its warmth and pondering Nomed's explosive behavior. *He's wound as tight as a spring. The bomb ticking inside him won't take much to ignite. I wonder what occurred in the Cave of Canedari?*

Yuin preceded Voer from the cave and stopped, his golden eyes glowing in the fire's light. "The children will not escape our knots. You watch them." His raspy voice held more than a touch of rebellion. "We go in search of our missing comrades."

Dom nodded and, relieved to see the strange aliens vanish down the tunnel, adjusted his spectacles and frowned. *Better see to it the children don't disappear again.* He left the comfort of the fire and crossed to the cave. Inside, Ari and Zugo sat trussed together, back-to-back, their hands and ankles tied with stout rope. Neither spoke when he knelt to test the knots.

He grimaced as he hoisted his body to standing. The accusation in their eyes followed him from the cave.

When the curtain swished into place, leaving them in silence, Zugo twisted to speak over his shoulder. "Are you okay?"

"Name's Ari, and I'm fine. Just furious. What... Who are you?"

"I'm a DeoNyte. My people live in Meos, deep in the mountain caverns."

He explained how he met Esán and what had happened since then. Ari described her adventures with Brie and Torgin.

After they finished, Ari squirmed to look at him better. "We have to escape. I'm worried about my sister. She's terrified of the dark."

Zugo strained to glimpse her face. "We must rescue Esán before we go after your sister. The death shadow put a cord around his neck that Almiralyn says only your knife will cut."

"You've seen Almiralyn?"

"Yes, she sent us here."

"Let's see if we can untie these ropes." Ari squirmed into position and began working with the knots at their wrists.

Esán faced Seyes Nomed and hid his defiance behind quiet words. "You didn't have to hit her. She's just scared and worried about her sister."

Nomed scowled. "You've been in the Cave of Canedari. What happened to you there?"

"I slept."

"Did you see the Evolsefil Crystal?"

Esán remained quiet.

"Don't play games, boy. Answer my question. Did you see the Prima Crystal?"

"Yes."

His response brought an inscrutable look to the DiMensioner's face. He tossed his cape on the sleeping pallet. "There's a candle by the woodpile. Bring it here."

Esán turned to leave the cave. Nomed put a hand on his shoulder. "Use your power to teleport it to you."

"I don't think I can without seeing it. Besides, it would have to travel through the wall."

"Do it." The tone demanded immediate obedience.

Strong fingers bit into Esán's fragile shoulder. He flinched and glanced up at the scarred face.

Nomed's scowl softened. "I'm sorry. I didn't mean to hurt you."

Esán looked away, narrowed his eyes, and focused. A picture of the candle formed in his mind, wobbled, then steadied. He envisioned it in front of him. It materialized, hovered for a moment, and landed at his feet. He could only stare.

Nomed gasped. "You did it! I *knew* you could."

Esán remained quiet, his thoughts masked. He had just become a tool for the destruction of Myrrh.

40

Allynae raced across the grasslands, headed for three cottonwoods standing tall and alone in the vast sea of grass. The storm gathering overhead sprinkled intermittent rain as he rode. Beside him, Jordett hunched lower on his horse. Allynae followed his example and nudged Saylo, his mount, faster. They arrived in the shelter of the trees as the clouds loosed their burden, pelting the prairie with the fury of anger long held in check. After securing the horses, Allynae produced a mottled green cape from his pack and, with Jordett, huddled beneath it. Above them, Karrew perched on a leafy branch, feathers ruffled to keep some of the wetness at bay.

Allynae glanced at his stalwart companion. "So what do you think of Myrrh, Major Jordett?"

"Please call me Jordy. I have no rank here." For a time, he seemed mesmerized by the wind-tossed grasses. When at last he turned, his face mirrored a touch of wonder. "I realize the longer I'm in Myrrh I must have come here as a child. Mira's cottage is so familiar. Why do we not recall the gentleness of this land? What makes us forget it even exists?"

Allynae rubbed his top lip, missing the mustache he had cultivated with such care before his trip to the city. "The PPP does a *mind wipe* on every citizen of Idronatti at fourteen sun cycles to ensure they won't remember."

Jordett's eyes narrowed. Ignoring the answer to his question, he gazed once again at the prairie. "Why do you suppose Seyes Nomed wants to destroy this place? Has he thought about the consequences? Thera and even our solar system could disappear."

"I don't believe he's thinking beyond his goal to obliterate Myrrh, along with my sister."

The two men fell silent, each immersed in his own thoughts.

Karrew peered from one eye and then the other. *Something is not right.* Unfurling his wings, he lifted into flight. Lightning flashed around him. The repeating boom of thunder reverberated off the tall mountain peaks. Urged upward by some unknown need, he flew higher.

Two vultures streaked from the clouds and gave chase. Karrew swooped toward the foothills, fighting the power of the wind and almost blinded by rain. The vultures closed in. He dropped lower and then soared skyward, using his superior agility to dodge clear of his adversaries. Higher and higher he flew until the lightning seemed to hold him in its current, higher and higher until thunder catapulted him closer to NaiDisbo Peak and the black obsidian Steps of Darsec. With a deep and exhilarating caw, he opened his wings and glided on powerful waves of wind. He landed at last on the barren branch of a dead Tirips tree, his pursuers left behind in the mist that rested its heaviness on the lofty peaks of the Dojanack Mountains.

Allynae scanned the sky for Karrew and swore under his breath. High overhead, two vultures descended in lazy circles toward the three cottonwoods where he and Jordett sheltered. The panicked prancing of their horses increased his sense of urgency. He stuffed the cape in his pack. "Trouble's headed our way."

"By the Fathers, I was hoping to avoid another confrontation." Jordett endeavored to quiet his horse.

Allynae grabbed Saylo's reins. "Ride for the hills. I doubt we can outrun them, but at least we can give 'em a good race." He mounted and urged Saylo into a gallop. Not far ahead, the Sekan River raged. *Once we cross the river, we'll be that much closer to the foothills.* Behind him, Jordett's mount whinnied in fright. Hooves pounding the earth brought him alongside. Neck and neck, manes flying and ears flattened against their heads, the horses raced through the wet grass. Rain and wind drove them onward. Above them, the Pentharian flew in tandem, talons extended, ready to grip their prey.

Allynae dodged the descending talons by guiding Saylo in an erratic zigzag. Jordett forced his horse to a sudden stop and then back into immediate motion, missing the talons of his enemy by only a breath. The enormous birds soared upward, preparing for a second strike. Jordett and his mount raced at a full-out gallop for the river. Allynae urged Saylo to follow. She balked, reared, and tossed him onto the mud laden ground. Screaming in terror, she bolted, galloping toward the Terces Wood.

Shaken but unhurt, Allynae lunged to his feet. A quick glance over his shoulder revealed Jordett riding in his direction. Above him, he could see only the belly of a vulture. He dove to one side. Bobbing and weaving, he fought to stay beyond the vulture's reach. It screeched, lifted higher and fanned its massive wings. Jordett rode straight for him, gripped his hand, and pulled him onto the horse's rump as a talon grazed his cheek. Impressed by Jordett's horsemanship, he wiped blood on his sleeve and held on tight.

Shared instincts sent the horse and riders dodging left, then right, then left again. Forward. Back. Around. The vultures soared upward, circled, and shot back toward their prey. Out of the cloud-covered sky, a lone raven dove and slammed into a vulture head, his sharp beak finding its mark in tender flesh. Enraged, the vulture screeched. Wings beat the grass into a frenzy as both Pentharian pursued Karrew over the grasslands and into the thick canopy of the Terces Wood.

Jordett twisted in the saddle and shouted above the roar of the river. "You alright, Alli?"

"Yes, thanks to you and Karrew. We need to go before they return."

After fording the Sekan River, they raced for the foothills. With its mane and tail whipping in the wind, their mount did not break stride until rolling hills surrounded them and his sweat-streaked body could go no further. The men slid to the ground and led the shaking animal into a ravine, where a small stream trickled between rock-strewn banks and an overhang provided shelter from the rain.

Voer and Yuin searched for Karrew until their frustration drove them to land as Pentharian. Hunger pressed them deeper into the woods and into panther form. A deer stopped, its ears twitching, its nose sniffing. It caught their scent and leapt between trees, panic turning it this way and that. Voer crouched low, his tail curled above his feline head, every muscle tensed for the kill. Yuin circled, driving the frightened deer back in his direction. Voer sprang. The deer went down. Panther teeth slashed its slender throat. Together, he and Yuin fed their hunger and eased their frustration. Rarely had either Pentharian lost its prey. The raven would die before they left Myrrh.

Karrew heard the last cry of the deer and, knowing the Pentharian would feed and then sleep, he flew up through the canopy into the water-laden sky. Occasional raindrops still fell through the mist that marched in a phantom-like parade below him. *Ominous and getting thicker. Time grows short.* He streaked toward the foothills. With luck, he would find Allynae and Jordett before night settled over the land.

Rain tap-dancing on the roof of Mira's cottage interrupted Sparrow's artist's trance. She put her palette down, cleaned her brush on a color-soaked rag, and studied her latest creation. Merrilea joined her. Both women gazed at the beautiful, white-furred creature standing beside Esán in a light so bright it obscured its source. The twins knelt side by side while a boy with a wooden flute, a mourning dove perched on his shoulder, waited in the shadows.

Merrilea bent closer. "Is this the past or the future?"

"I don't know. It just flowed from my brush. In Idronatti I sometimes paint with this kind of immersion, but here in Myrrh, I'm driven. A creative force obliterates everything else and speaks directly through my brushes. It's exhilarating." She brushed a dark curl off her forehead and yawned. "And exhausting."

The women contemplated the painting again in silence.

Sparrow put her brush in a jar and glanced at Merrilea. "How's Almiralyn?" She sighed. "How can we help when we're here and the children are out there somewhere?"

"You are helping by painting what comes from the future." Almiralyn's soft voice came from behind them, where she leaned on the door frame. Her pale face and silver blonde hair gave her a ghost-like appearance that chilled Sparrow's heart.

"What are you doing out of bed?" Merrilea walked over and reached for her wrist. Her fingers paused at Almiralyn's pulse before gliding down to clasp her hands.

"I'm gathering the strength I'll need to fly west. Your painting intrigues me, Sparrow. You realize our choices each moment weave the patterns of the future?"

The women nodded.

"Where are the children?" Sparrow studied at her finished canvas.

"In your painting, they are in the caverns of the Dojanack Mountains. In actuality, they're scattered. Circumstance have separated the twins. Torgin has found Paisley, and Esán is with Seyes Nomed."

"You used the fountain?" Merrilea leaned on the doorframe opposite her.

"I did. It shared the information I requested."

"Where's Allynae, Mira?" Eagerness infused Sparrow's question.

"Alli's fine. Not yet in the mountains, but close." Almiralyn smiled. "I think we could all use some tea."

. . .

Surrounded by faded blue walls, the women sat at the kitchen table, cradling warm mugs and listening to the rain dancing a jig on the windowsills. Majeska yawned and observed them with gleaming amethyst eyes.

Almiralyn sipped her tea and gazed at each woman. "You realize the situation demands that I leave soon."

Merrilea's peaceful expression changed to worry. "But you're so weak, Mira. What can you do?"

The Guardian set her mug on the table. "Only time can answer that question." She joined her cat by the window and ran a pale hand down the smokey-gray back. Majeska arched against her and purred as Almiralyn gave her one last pat. "I'll rest a little longer. When I'm needed, I'll know. Keep painting, Sparrow. In your heart rests our solution and our victory." Taking Merrilea's arm, she glided from the room.

Sparrow frowned and attempted to untangle her jumbled thoughts. An urgent need to return to her studio and paint brought her to her feet. The noise of her chair crashing to the kitchen floor reverberated throughout the quiet cottage and then settled back into the patter of raindrops and the soft breathing of the cat on the windowsill.

Setting the chair upright, she hurried to her studio, sat down in front of the easel, closed her eyes, and waited. Images formed and faded and formed again. She picked up a slender piece of charcoal and began. Line by line, her new sketch took shape; line by line, the story of the Unfolding continued.

41

The sound of falling water woke Brie from a deep sleep. Her brow wrinkled as her eyes flew open. *Where am I?* She peered up at the stalagmite formations on the ceiling, remembering the Pentharian panther licking her cheek, passing through a stone wall, the whispering voice, her long journey in the dark. Pushing up to sitting, she hugged herself. *I'm so alone.* Panic fluttered in her the pit of her stomach. She stared at her clenched fists, let the fingers relax, and visualized her fear dissolving.

Curiosity directed her search of the shimmering green beauty of the empty grotto. The Star of Truth's reassuring quiet calmed her and the Stone of Remembering's solid warmth in her hand kept her fear from returning.

Hunger gnawed at her stomach. Thirst from a long sleep had left her mouth tasting of yesterday. She scooted closer to the pool and touched the surface. A sad young face peered up at her.

"Don't drink the water." The girl's visage faded.

Brie came to her knees and leaned further over the pool. The face did not reappear. She sat back on her heels. For a second time, her hand clasped the velvet encased stone. She leaned forward. Sad eyes gazed up at her.

"Don't drink the water." Sorrow filled the whispered words.

"Why?" Brie gripped the rocky edge of the pool.

"Forgetting." Hopelessness and fear flickered. "Forgetting." The face faded, leaving the surface free of all but waterfall-formed ripples that caught the green light and tossed it onto the grotto walls.

Brie sat back. *Forgetting what?* She removed the ribbon from around her neck, opened the velvet pouch, and tipped the gold-veined, blue stone onto her palm. She gazed at the pool. "Forgetting." She held up the stone. "Remembering."

The Star of Truth tingled. She peered around the grotto, blinked, and looked again. Translucent figures glimmered in the soft green light. One, then two, then more appeared until they stood all around her. Men, women, and children huddled together, huge, haunted eyes fastened on her and the sacred blue stone.

"Who are you?" She eased herself to standing. "Where did you come from?"

The ghost-like figures pressed forward.

Her fingers closed around the Remembering Stone. "What do you want?"

A young girl stepped free of the circle of faces. "We, the unremembered, are answering the call of the stone. We know not who we are or where we belong."

Brie opened her hand. The center of the stone glowed. Soft blue light tinged with gold grew brighter and brighter until it overflowed her palm. The unremembered clustered closer. The radiance expanded until it cocooned everyone in the cavern within its glowing circumference. Tears slipped from haunted eyes.

The young girl's faced filled with wonder. "My name is Bonnee."

A woman pointed to herself. "I am Loeen."

"I am Reda." The short, roundish girl smiled through her tears.

"My name is Tome." The tall, thin man beamed at the woman next to him. "You are my wife, Jeen."

Each figure remembered. And as they reclaimed their names and identities, the brilliance shining from the stone grew dimmer until only a dot remained.

Behind her, Brie heard a faint whisper. "Me. Please don't forget me." She turned and held the Remembering Stone toward the young girl in the water.

"I'm Teeay." She smiled through her tears. "Thank you."

The light faded, leaving only a dark blue stone in the palm of Brie's hand.

Happy figures gathered around her. Bonnee spoke for the group. "We thank you for the gift of remembering. Some of us have been lost for many sun cycles. We honor you and wish to serve you in any way we can."

Brie returned the stone to the pouch. "How did you come to be the unremembered?"

The tall man pointed. "We drank the water from the pool. When you first drink, you forget where you are, then who you are. Little by little, you fade until you become one of the myriad of ghosts wandering the Dojanacks."

An older woman spoke up. "When you came into the caverns, we felt the pull of the Remembering Stone. We sent Bonnee to find who had brought it. She has been guiding you since you escaped from the cave where the DiMensioner imprisons your friends."

"How did I walk through a rocky barrier? Was that because of you?"

"We do not have that power." Bonnee regarded her with reverent respect. "You spoke to the wall from your heart, and it welcomed you."

Teeay floated forward.

"Thank you, Teeay." Brie shivered. "I would have taken a drink if not for you."

"The stone freed me to warn you."

"What will you all do?" Brie gazed at the Now Remembered.

"When we have paid our debt to you, we will pass on to the next world. Our loved ones are calling. Since we know who we are, we can answer their—"

Teeay squealed. The water in the pool pitched and rolled up into the shape of a rotund woman.

"It's Neuros, the Water Witch! Run, Brie!" Bonnee's terror echoed through the caverns. "Run!"

Grabbing her pack, Brie backed away from the advancing figure.

"How dare you free the unremembered!" The rotund female raged. "How dare you enter my grotto and steal my souls!"

The Now Remembered fled. Brie sprinted after them down the dark tunnel. Whispering voices surrounded her, guiding her away from the wrath of the grotto's crazed inhabitant and deeper into the caverns of the Dojanacks.

In the Grotto of Forgetting, Neuros pitched water after the Human girl. Outrage beat against the walls until, exhausted, she plunged her bulk under the pool's surface. Bosom heaving, she resurfaced, howled her despair, and broke into heart-wrenching sobs. Emerald tears spilled from her eyes like a volley of raindrops. Each rang with its own musical note as it hit the grotto floor and came to rest, its inner fire glowing.

A translucent child walked to the edge of the pool. "I'll stay with you."

Neuros regarded the figure who had once been a Human girl. A large hiccup shook her sizable breasts. She moved her watery body closer. "You would remain here?"

"If you'll let me remember, I will stay."

"What is your name?"

"Teeay."

"Then, Teeay, I will let you remember as long as *I* don't forget." She opened her arms wide.

Teeay floated into the waiting embrace and, with Neuros, withdrew into the rippling water, leaving small emerald tears glistening in the phosphorescent light.

In the subterranean cavern, Elae clung halfway down the wall of the deep crevasse. She felt certain a twin had followed her away from the DiMensioner's wrath. Unable to find the girl, she had hidden. The dismayed shriek of an unknown creature made her squeeze her eyes shut. Silence settled around her. *I believe the Human got away.* With a sigh of relief, she climbed into the passageway.

After a thorough search revealed nothing, she crept down the small tunnel and peeked around the large rock on the ledge above the sleeping cave. Zugo sat with his back to her. The twin facing her concentrated on the knots at his wrists. Elae transmitted a thought into Zugo's mind.

"Zugo, I am on the ledge."

Twisting to peer over his shoulder, Zugo jerked his hand away from Ari.

"Hold still, would you?" A touch of irritation clipped the whispered words short.

Zugo mouthed, "On the ledge."

Ari's eyes widened.

Elae jumped down, hurried to the curtain, and listened. A quick peek showed her the old man dozing by the fire. She knelt beside Zugo and the twin, her clever fingers working on the knots at their wrists.

Zugo twisted to whisper over his shoulder. "Elae, this is Ari."

The red-haired twin lifted her right elbow. "There's a knife hidden under my clothes. It will help with the ropes."

Elae disentangled the knife and pulled it from the scabbard. "Efillaeh." Emotion rose in her throat. "Where did you get this?"

"Almiralyn gave it to me. I'm sure glad you're here. Did you see my sister? Is she with you?"

"No, she isn't. I searched the passageway, but I couldn't detect any sign of her."

Ari frowned. "She has to be out there. The Pentharian returned through the tunnel alone."

Elae loosened a piece of rope, stretched it taut, and cut it. "She seems to have vanished. But we *will* find her."

Zugo squirmed. "Is that the sacred knife?"

"This *is* Efillaeh." She held it out for him to see, then sliced another rope. "The knife was formed at the heart of the Evolsefil Crystal. Only warriors with a brave heart may carry it, and only those with truth as their courage can wield its power. Almiralyn must trust you with her life, Ari."

"I-I'm just an ordinary child from Idronatti." A blush tinted her fair cheeks.

Zugo threw the severed pieces of rope aside. "None of you are ordinary. Let's go before the DiMensioner captures us again."

"Wait." Ari scrambled to her feet. "What about Esán?"

"Nomed will not let him out of his sight." Zugo marched to the wall. "If we return to Meos, my father will know how to help rescue Esán and find your sister."

Elae noted the stubbornness on the twin's face. "He's right, Ari. The ReDael is our best option." She handed her the knife. "I am honored to serve a warrior of Myrrh."

"Thanks." The girl's expression relaxed as she returned Efillaeh to its scabbard. "Let's hurry. Brie is all alone."

Elae sprang up, grabbed the rim of the ledge, and pulled herself onto it. Ari tossed up her pack. Zugo cupped his hands to give her a boost. On his count, she pushed, he lifted, and the next instant Elae gripped her arm. Zugo joined them. Quiet as the rock walls surrounding them, they crawled along the small tunnel.

In Nomed's alcove, Esán had teleported several more objects. "I'm too tired." His thin shoulders sagged.

The DiMensioner studied his pale, drawn face. "Rest. You've done well."

Esán shuffled toward the curtained doorway. Nomed intercepted him and guided him to the sleeping pallet.

"You may rest here in my sleeping alcove. I do not intend to lose you again."

Esán sank down and curled onto his side as Nomed covered him with a lightweight blanket.

"Sleep. I'll be back to check on you."

Esán felt more vulnerable than weary. *What role does Nomed expect me to play in his plans for destroying Myrrh?* Quieting his mind, he gathered his courage around him and secured it with the resolve to be true to his own heart. With this decision made, he slipped into a deep and exhausted sleep.

By the campfire in Oche Cavern, Dom sat watching Nomed rearrange the wood with a half-burned stick. A flip of the DiMensioner's wrist sent it into the fire's center, where it burst into flame.

He brushed off his hands and looked across the fire pit. "So here we are, Dom, just you and me. Where are the Pentharian?"

"They've gone in search of their lost comrades."

"How about the children?"

"The Pentharian trussed 'em up pretty good. I doubt anyone could untie those knots."

"I suggest you make sure. If they go missing again, I'll hold you responsible."

Dom pushed his spectacles up on his nose and groaned as he stood and shuffled across the cavern. He pulled the curtain aside. His mind blanked and fought for understanding. Reeling as though struck by a bolt of lightning, he crossed the cave, dropped to his knees, and scooped up the pile of severed rope. *Nomed will be livid.*

"Whatever made me leave my safe little shoppe?" The mumbled question accompanied his painful climb to standing. He winced as the curtain whooshed open behind him.

"Where are they, Dom?" The shouted words echoed through the cavern like repeated body punches.

Slowly, he faced the man with the demon eyes, his face blank and his hands spilling clean cut pieces of rope onto the ground.

As his echoed disappointment silenced, the bitter taste of anger rose in Nomed's throat. He snatched the last piece of rope still in Dom's hands and waved it in his face. "Who cut them loose? Where are they? I imagine they're headed back to Meos. Why on DerTah can we not keep our hands on them?"

Caught in a churning storm of frustration, he strode toward the fire. His first inclination—to go after them himself—meant he would have to wake up Esán. *I will keep the boy close until Myrrh is a memory.* He glared at the flickering flames. *Where is Wodash? Have the ancients in the Cavern of Tennisca destroyed him?* He doubted it, but he wasn't sure of anything.

Attempting to rein in his tumultuous emotions, he sat down and nursed a mug of spiced wine. Experience taught him that important decisions made while his anger raged never paid off.

Dom shuffled from the small cave and waited beyond the light of the fire.

Nomed savored a sip of wine and glanced at his old friend. "See if Esán is still sleeping, then join me."

The older man peeked behind the alcove curtain and took a seat. "The boy's sound asleep." He continued in a subdued voice. "He's fragile, Seyes. Be careful or you'll burn him out."

Nomed's temper flared. "I didn't ask you, did I?" The words bouncing off the cavern walls forced him to grit his teeth. He swirled the liquid in the mug and stifled his anger. "These children are driving me crazy, Dom. This should have been simple work. Come to Myrrh. Destroy the gateways. Steal the crystal. And get the SeDah away from here. But no. I run into a pack of youngsters, and the whole thing becomes a carnival. And you, my friend, have not made it any easier."

Dom sank onto a log, pressed his lips into a thin line, and massaged his arthritic hand.

"You *can* speak up, you know. I'm angry, but this cavern and its echoes will keep me under control." He downed the last of his wine and set the mug on the ground. A long stare at the fire calmed his desire to shout at his old friend. He looked up. "You have something to say?"

Dom ran his tongue over his lips and blew out a breath. "What are you planning, Seyes? Do you know or are you floundering? I've never seen you so scattered. What happened to you in that Cave of Canedari?"

Nomed pressed his palms together and scowled. "It wasn't the Cave, Dom. That abysmal Lake of Rorret dragged me under and cracked me open like an egg. I feel exposed to the world—raw. My emotions are out of control, and I can't seem to shut them down."

"Do you need all this turmoil, Seyes? Let the anger and hurt go. You've been carrying them around for a long time, my friend."

Nomed lowered hands and gripped his knees. "I came here to destroy Mira and Myrrh. I plan to finish the job, Dominee."

"You realize you'll destroy Thera as well."

"I *don't* care about the planet of Thera."

"You have a brother out there, right?"

"Why should I care about him?"

Dom stood up. "I guess the important question is, when are you going to start caring about yourself?"

Nomed glowered. "It's none of your—"

"You're right." Dom interrupted. "It's none of my business. I'm going to the cliff entrance for a breath of fresh air." Without further comment, he turned and limped away.

Nomed picked up another stick and poked the fire. Sparks jumped, formed cascades of glittering color, and rained down into the heat of the flames. *Dom's right. It's time to complete the job I came here to do.* He stood up and peeked into his sleeping alcove. The boy slept. He returned to the fire. *Let him rest. He will need all his strength for tomorrow.*

42

Torgin sat on a large rock, watching the sun slip behind the Dojanacks and the rain fade into a fine mist. Skipt had vanished, and Paisley had gone to check on Tam. The air, though still warm, carried an edge of dampness that made him shiver. The need to remain unnoticed meant no fire. Torgin sighed and hugged himself. *I miss my family and my anopi and even my nanny.*

He withdrew Brie's map from his pocket, smoothed it out on his knees, and traced his journey from the grasslands to the mountains. *Idronatti, with all its order and discipline, seems almost like a dream. And the boy who entered Myrrh through a keyhole in a magic mirror?* He shook his head. *I hardly recognize myself. Something is happening to me—something I can't quite understand.*

An unexpected deluge of memories triggered a tumult of fear. The Pentharian loomed bigger than life. Buster, lying motionless and empty, made his heart ache. And Wodash? He glanced down at the map and tapped the Tower of Nemttachenn. A chill tickled the nape of his neck. Stifling a desire to run, to leave Myrrh, and never return, he refolded Brie's sketch and stuffed it in his pocket. *Where is Paisley, anyway?*

A deep breath of rain-freshened air helped to dilute his fear. Like a sponge, the calmness of evening absorbed his uncertainties. He gave himself up to the quiet.

Above the eastern horizon, the clouds parted to show the waning moon. A distant refrain of yips and howls chorused through the night.

He jumped from his stone perch. *What animals make that noise?* He bit his bottom lip. *Are they close? Paisley said these mountains are not without danger.* Another yipped chorus increased his uneasiness. *Why did I let the twins talk me into staying in Myrrh?*

He laughed at himself. *My fear is abolishing my sense of wellbeing. Are the howling creatures threatening me? No. Right now, I am safe.*

A shower of pebbles hit the ground. Triggered apprehension swung him around as Paisley jumped down beside him, white teeth gleaming in his dark, smiling face. "Your eyes are bigger than yonder moon. Did I frighten ya?"

Torgin gave a shaky laugh. "I guess you did. What was howling?"

"Wolves."

"Wolves in these mountains?" He shot a nervous glance over his shoulder.

"Lots of things, dangerous and otherwise, live in the Dojanacks, Torgin, but they aren't here. Besides, we have shelter." He smiled. "It's time to eat and settle for the night."

Torgin followed him into the rocky enclosure. "Where's Skipt?"

"Home with his family, I hope. Strange things are happenin' in Myrrh. I'd certainly wanna be with my family."

Paisley's lite-stick glowed where he wedged it in a crevice.

Torgin settled on the ground opposite him. "Tell me about your family?"

"Ma died several sun cycles ago, and my pa..." Paisley bit his lip. "I never knew him. He liked to travel. Left when I was small and never came back."

"Brie and Ari and Esán don't know their fathers either. I can't imagine what that's like. I've always known mine, and my mother, too."

Paisley handed him the last of Sibine's sandwiches. They sat, eating and talking, while the night deepened and the mist thickened. No stars lit the sky. Only clouds, drawn like a curtain over the moon, marched warrior-like across the heavens.

To assuage his restlessness, One Man, the Hermit of Timreh Pass, strode from his cabin; inhaled the sweet aroma of eventide; and gazed at the cloud-smothered sky. *Events in Myrrh are coming to a head. Tension builds daily, and my time to meet it draws near.*

He pulled his long, wheat-blond hair over a shoulder and wove it into a braid. Dreams haunted him, dreams of DeoNytes and children and strange creatures not of Myrrh. Like the conductor of a malevolent symphony, a man in a black and silver cape summoned forth evil and destruction. This man attracted him like a magnet.

Tomorrow, I will start down the mountain. Perhaps a visit to Meos will provide some answers. Or perhaps I'll head for Almiralyn's. He flicked the braid behind his shoulder. *Her cottage is too far.* Restless pacing carried him into his hut and out again. His gaze sought the heavens. *Many cycles have passed since I spoke to another Human.*

He sat down on a hand-hewn bench and picked up a slender piece of wood. Sorrow held him still, his attention roaming from the mountains to a herd of goats to the sweeping slope of evergreens defining his small acreage. The solitude nurtured his talents and his wounded heart. The wood's silvery length, silky smooth between his hands, brought a cavalcade of memories from the recesses of his mind.

Tianna, his Tao Spirian life-mate, faced him, her eyes filled with sorrow. "My illness can only be cured on our home planet. I must leave immediately. Your destiny, and that of our child, dictates that you remain here. Take our son to Merrilea, then go to Myrrh. Your Seed of Carsilem requires solitude to mature. Almiralyn will know where you should go."

His soulmate and best friend departed that night. The next turning, he left their child with her blood-bounded sister and sought Myrrh's Guardian. A short time later, he began his solo journey into the mountains. When he reached the foothills, he whittled a walking staff from the branch of a Tirips Tree. Not long after he arrived in Timreh Pass, unable to move beyond his broken heart, he cracked the staff against a rock. He kept the two pieces as a reminder that his choices shaped his life.

He sighed. Recently, he'd picked up the straightest piece of the Tirips Tree branch and begun to whittle. A flute emerged and was ready to be completed. Taking out his knife, he admired the silvery smoothness of the wood grain and set to work with such intense focus he failed to notice the soft gray-brown mourning dove that landed on his windowsill, its bright eyes following every motion of his hand.

Morning dawned too soon for Torgin. Sleep had been elusive. Paisley's snores bouncing around the rocky enclosure hadn't helped. Nightmares sent him to strange, dark places where wolves howled and the death shadow roamed. He groaned and peered out at the new turning. Clouds continued to enshroud the morning sky with a dampness that made him long for his warm bed.

A large crow's repeated caws reverberating against the mountain nudged him to rise and shine. He yawned and sat up, his gaze darting around the small enclosure. *Where are you, Paisley?* Shivering, he stepped into the open, surveyed the thick fog, and frowned.

"Mornin', young one." Paisley appeared from the mist and held out a handful of dark red berries. "Thought you might like to add these to your breakfast."

Torgin nibbled a berry. It tasted bittersweet on the tip of the tongue, then burst into a honey-rich flavor before it slid down his throat.

"What is this?" He reached for another. "I have not eaten anything like it."

"A Dojanberry. They ripen this time of the sun cycle and stay until the winter snows fall. Have some more."

Torgin broke the last of Sibine's muffins in two and handed half to Paisley before helping himself to more Dojanberries. "How can we go anywhere when fog hides everything?"

"The mist'll lift, or at least thin out, once the sun's higher in the sky. We'll wait a bit. Hope Skipt joins us soon."

On cue, the young Enots landed on a rock above Torgin's head. "Ya ho, life is good. Mist is thinning." He jumped down beside them and removed a large pack from his back. Grinning from ear to ear, he handed them warm bread and dried apples. "Mummy sent these to fill our tummies. She says a nutritious breakfast means a good turning."

"Did you see our pony on your way here?" Torgin munched a nutty bite of bread. "This is great."

Tam ambled from the mist, nickered, and sniffed Torgin's ear.

Skipt bounced from one foot to the other, his wide grin beaming. "Ya ho, Tam."

Torgin scratched under her chin. "Glad you are here, Tamboreen." Paisley's amused smile made him laugh. "I always feel so much better after I eat."

"Me good, too." The Enots danced around, rubbing his tummy and humming a cheerful tune.

Paisley chuckled at his antics. Torgin joined in and noted that laughter added warmth and camaraderie to the moment.

When the landscape emerged from the mist, Paisley lifted Skipt to his shoulder and hiked up the steep trail. Torgin grabbed Tam's reins and followed. *I wonder what this turning will bring. Surprises for sure. Good ones, I hope. In Myrrh, I never know what is around the next bend.*

Allynae and Jordett had spent an uncomfortable night in a shallow indentation where the side of a hill had caved in. Huddled against the rough dirt wall, Allynae had slept fitfully. Wolves howled; the horse pranced and snorted; and the cool, damp mist caused his joints to stiffen. It was a relief when the dim light of early morning made pretending to sleep unnecessary.

He scrambled from beneath the overhang, knelt by the stream, and splashed cold water on his face and neck. Cupping his hands, he gulped the fresh water and glanced up as his yawning companion knelt beside him.

After washing his face, Jordett dried off with the corner of his shirt and refilled his canteen. "Where are we headed?"

Allynae rose and studied the misty side of the mountain. "There are several ways into the caverns. Who knows which one the DiMensioner is using?"

Karrew swooped from the mist and glided to a landing near the overhang. He cocked his head. "You will reach the entryway Nomed uses by dusk."

"How did you find it?" Jordett hooked his canteen to his belt.

"Dom appeared from a hidden entrance when I was flying by."

"The little traitor." Allynae scowled in disgust.

"What should we do with the horse?" Jordett ran a hand down the chestnut's neck. "We certainly can't take her into the caverns. Would it be better to release her?"

"Let's leave her here in case we need her later." Allynae pushed the saddle further under the overhang. There's plenty of water and grass. She'll be fine."

The major finished repacking his gear and glanced up at the sky. "Hope the Pentharian aren't abroad today. But I suppose if they are, we'll know soon enough."

Allynae shouldered his pack, and they began their trek higher into the Dojanack Mountains.

Karrew flew above them into the white-gray haze, wishing they could shape shift. *It would certainly speed up events. Ah, well.*

Banking left, he pressed his wings against the moisture-laden air. *Unless we stop Nomed, it seems this mist is here to stay.* He shot higher. With no end to the grayness in sight, he flew back to join his companions and landed on Allynae's pack.

"Well, what's up there, Karrew? Any sign of blue sky?"

He ruffled his damp feathers. "None, Alli. Just endless gray."

Jordett chuckled and shook his head when the raven gave him a steady, one-eyed stare.

Allynae scrubbed his prickly upper lip. "I wonder where Paisley is? He should be close to Timreh Pass."

"Who's this hermit, anyway?" Jordett adjusted his pack. "What is his role in this?"

Allynae shrugged. "Only my sister knows the answer, and she hasn't shared it with me. I wonder how *she's* doing."

Tired of listening and impatient to be off, Karrew fanned his wings. "I'll find Paisley, and then I must go to Almiralyn. Stay on this trail and keep to the left." With a sharp caw, he flew up and away, quickly absorbed in the filmy cloud cover.

Tiny fingers of sunshine poked through the gray mist to tickle the face of the dozing hermit. He'd worked late into the night. The finished flute lay on the table by the hut's only window. He had polished it to a soft luster that highlighted the silvery grain of the wood. Astonished at the clarity of its sound, he looked forward to exploring the instrument's potential.

As he sat up to stretch, the mourning dove landed on the windowsill and seemed to inspect the single room enclosed in rough timber walls. One Man smiled a welcome and savored the comfort of his home where goatskin rugs splattering a white and brown pattern across the wood floor provided a feeling of warmth. Dried plants hanging from the low ceiling filled the room with a musky, flowerlike scent and the handmade furnishings allowed him to relax after long turnings on the mountain.

The desire to stay and ignore the outer world flooded through him as he straightened the bed of sheepskins and pine boughs where he slept. He sank into the rickety rocker next to the stone fireplace. Creak, creak. Across from him, rough shelves held food and other necessities. The table and one stool finished the room's décor. It was sparse, yet welcoming. Creak. He left the rocking chair, crossed to the door, and surveyed the hazy morning. *Myrrh's in trouble and the Seed of Carsilem has completed its cycle of maturing. It's time.*

Gathering goat cheese, dried biscuits, and Dojanberries for his breakfast, he sat down at the table and eyed the gray-brown bird on the windowsill.

"Good morning, wee one. Have you adopted me, or are you only here for a visit?"

The dove hopped onto the table and pecked at crumbs and bits of cheese. "Coo, Coo."

One Man pushed a berry toward his visitor. The dove pecked at it in the one ray of sunshine escaping the cloud cover.

"Today, my friend, I'm headed down the mountain. It's been many cycles since I've ventured into the world of Humans."

He paused and gazed out the window. Sighing, he finished his breakfast, cleared the remains, and tidied the hut. After shoving a few things in a goatskin pack, he filled a water bag from the spring and slipped the flute into a soft sheepskin case. Slinging it over his shoulder, he took one last look around and pulled the door shut behind him.

He couldn't help but wonder what was to come as he traipsed through the scattered trees of the high mountain meadow. Above him the mourning dove circled and then swooped down to land on his pack. Glad for the company, he trudged down the trail into the swirling mist.

43

Grateful her lite-stick's glow made the darkness less intimidating, Brie fixed her gaze on Bonnee's fleeing form and scurried after her. Behind them, the Water Witch's angry lament faded.

Brie stopped, gripped her knees, and gulped in air. "What're we running for? Neuros can't leave the pool, can she?"

Bonnee floated to her side. "No, she can't. She's just mean, and I'm so happy to be free. Her loneliness doesn't justify stealing someone's life."

Brie straightened. "Bonnee, I have a twin sister who's probably pretty lonely right now. I need to find her."

"A twin?" Bonnee stared. "You're a twin?"

"We're identical. I'm Brie and my sister's Ari."

"I'm a twin, too." Bonnee's luminescent features brightened with remembering, then grew sad. "My sister's name is Bettee. The turning I came with my father to explore the caverns, Bettee stayed home. She hated being underground. Somehow, I got separated from Dad and found my way to the grotto. You know the rest of the story."

"Oh, Bonnee, I'm so sorry. How long have you been here?"

"I'm not sure, but seems like forever. Bettee's calling from the other side. When you're safe, I'll join her."

"If your sister's calling, go to her. I'll be fine."

"She'll wait for me, Brie. I won't leave you in this part of the caverns. Your friends would never find you. Once you're safe, I'll go, but *not* until then."

Brie brushed a tear from her cheek and held her lite-stick higher. "Thank you so much for staying. Where are you taking me?"

Bonnee floated at her side as they walked down the tunnel. "To Meos, where the DeoNytes live. Yookotay, the ReDael, should be able to help you find your sister."

"Are DeoNytes beautiful black-skinned creatures covered with white fur?"

"Yes, they're the keepers of the Evolsefil Crystal."

"What's the Evosa—" Brie stumbled over the strange word.

"It is pronounced Evolsefil." While they walked deeper into the caverns, Bonnee related the story of why the Guardians placed the Prima Crystal in the Cave of Canedari.

When she finished, Brie squinted through the darkness. "Mother's told us little bits of Myrrh's history, but she's never mentioned the crystal. I can't wait to tell her about it." She glanced at her new friend. "How far are we from Meos?"

"Quite a distance, unless you can walk through another wall."

Brie trailed a finger over the tunnel's rough surface. "I wonder if the mountains would let me do it again?"

Bonnie paused. "We're near a spot where this passage parallels one leading to Meos. If you can go through the wall, it will cut our journey in half. It's not far."

Although her lite-stick grew dimmer, Brie did not experience her usual panic as she followed her friend. *What's happening to me? I'm not afraid of the dark anymore. I wonder if my connection to Myrrh is giving me courage.*

Bonnee interrupted her musing. "We're almost there. Do you know how you passed through the wall before?"

"The panther was licking my face." Brie recoiled from the memory. "I was pretty scared and wished more than anything I would disappear. The next thing I knew, the wall was behind me."

"Here we are." Bonnee floated in front of her.

"Will you go through with me?"

"I'll be right beside you."

Brie tucked the lite-stick in her waistband, smoothed her hair back from her face, and placed both hands on the coarse, rough stone. "Dojanack Mountains, thank you for saving me from the Pentharian."

A deep, rolling voice rumbled. "Daughter of KcernFensia, the mountains welcome you. Your coming blesses us."

Who is the Daughter of KcernFensia? Awed once more by the wonders of Myrrh, she held her hands steady.

"You carry the imprint of KcernFensia." The speaker paused, then continued. "Promise you will go to the Cave of Canedari, and you may pass through the wall."

"How do I find the cave?"

"The Now Remembered know the way. Mahyinaeh blesses your journey."

The deep voice faded, and the stone melted away beneath her hands. With Bonnee by her side, she walked through, her thoughts racing. *I wish Ari were here. Where is Torgin? What's happening to Esán? And how on Myrrh do I pass through stone walls?*

After Dom's departure, Nomed stared into the flickery flames, recalling how hard he, then Davin Farlow, had worked to master the shift from Human to great horned owl. More than anything in life, he loved this magnificent bird.

He tossed a twig on the fire and watched it burn down to glowing embers. "Like that twig, I almost lost my life the first time I attempted the shift." A rush of emotions raced through him. "I remember the terror and the triumph when I succeeded as though it were yesterday."

The sun hung white and heavy above the Desert of Fera Finnero on DerTah, where Wolloh Espyro, his mentor and teacher, stood gazing at him from his one good eye. In the next instant, his crippled body transformed. A beautiful osprey soared upward in a slow, graceful spiral.

Burning with the desire to join him, Davin Farlow abandoned moon cycles of preparation and attempted to shift. His scream of terror and pain ripped over the desert. An arm, a wing, a nose, a beak—each fought for supremacy. A hand touched his sweating brow. The erratic shifting ceased. Wolloh's stern features came into focus.

"What did I tell you, Davin?" Wolloh's question probed into his psyche. "Do you recall, or have you already forgotten, the lessons of form?"

A struggle to collect his wits made him lower his eyes. "I lost my concentration in the joy of watching you fly." He peeked at his mentor. "In your Osprey's body, you become whole and I—"

Wolloh's distorted frown froze his explanation into silence. "My Human form serves a purpose, Davin. It is a constant reminder of what happens when one shifts and loses oneself in the heart of the beast. You have the talent to shape the owl. Not even I achieved this. Make the shift with focused intention, or you will end up, like me, crippled and bound to DerTah."

Davin's shoulders drooped. "I have failed you."

"I matter not. Never give up on yourself." Wolloh's knife-sharp gaze demanded his complete attention. "See the great horned owl and, on my command, become it."

Davin tensed and returned his teacher's penetrating gaze.

"Now!" Wolloh's clipped command ripped through the desert air.

The great horned owl enclosed Davin's mind and then his body. He lifted skyward, his owl's heartbeat, breath, and senses keen and piercing. Every detail of the ground below sharpened. He heard every sound. His back muscles rippled with the power of his wings. Exhilaration filled him. He flew a high, wide arch above his teacher; the blood red of the desert pulsing in his eyes until Wolloh signaled to him to land and shift.

As his owl talons touched the hot sand, he regained his Human form and bowed his head before his mentor.

The thrill of that first fight sang an aria in his heart. The great horned owl was his true nature. He embraced it with reverence and respect. He tossed another twig into the flames. Soon after that, the Dreelum of DerTah christened him Seyes Nomed.

Rustling fabric alerted him to his prisoner's presence. Esán stood bleary-eyed with sleep, the entrance curtain still in his hand, his face pale and disoriented.

"I was dreaming about you." Confusion made him mumble.

"What was the dream, Esán?"

The boy dropped the curtain and swiped a hand across his eyes. "A younger you stood beneath a fire orange sky opposite a crippled man in a black robe. When he shifted into a large white and gray bird, you attempted to shift. Your arm changed to a wing; your nose to a beak; you screamed, and I woke up."

Nomed arched his eyebrows. "You were in my memories, Esán. The bird was an osprey. The man was Wolloh, my teacher. Do you know how you strayed into my thoughts?"

A shaking hand rubbed his bald head. "I was asleep." He stared at the hand. "The next thing I knew, I was in the dream." Confusion highlighted his paleness. "It was so real I can still hear your scream in my head."

"No matter, Esán. I'm fine. When did you eat last?"

"I don't remember." He stifled a yawn.

Nomed handed him a small towel. "Go to the lake and wash up. I'll find you some food."

Esán knelt at the edge of Remmihs Lake and luxuriated in the water caressing his skin. It seemed forever since he'd bathed. When he returned to the fire, Nomed handed him a tin plate. With a good appetite, he ate dried pommaletta and cheese and a strange biscuit tasting of salt and cinnamon. Awake and strong with no pain anywhere in his body, he was excited to be alive.

Nomed finished his meal. "Today, we move forward with my plans for Myrrh. I'm impatient to be gone from this land."

Esán set his plate on the ground and fixed his gaze on Seyes Nomed. He kept his voice steady and respectful. "I do not wish to be a part of Myrrh's destruction. I love it here. Please don't ask me to harm it."

The variety of emotions flitting across the DiMensioner's face confirmed Esán's suspicion that few people dared to confront the man opposite him, let alone tell him they would prefer not to be involved in his plans. *What do I have to lose? He will do as he chooses.*

A mysterious smile warmed the cool countenance of the DiMensioner. "Well, my young friend, we shall see what we shall see." He leaned forward. "How would you like to learn to shape shift?"

"Shape shifting!" Blood rushed to Esán's cheeks.

Nomed laughed. "You have the gift."

"How do you know?"

"The same way my teacher knew I possessed the talent and instinct. To accomplish this, you must obey a few rules without question."

"What are they?"

Esán's eager response brought another smile to his mentor's face. "Concentration is key. The shift must occur in the blink of an eye. The overriding danger of shifting is that you can lose yourself in the wildness of the shifted form. If you allow yourself to stay in it too long, you will lose sight of your humanness. You must remain conscious that you are foremost a Human. Do you understand?"

"I understand." Anticipation made him feel lightheaded.

"What shape appeals to you? Think of something small at first. You can always shift to a bigger form when you become more confident."

Esán remembered the moment on the way to the Dojanacks when Nomed had shared his owl's sight and flight. The thought of it caused his heartbeat to quicken. "I would love to fly. What bird would you suggest?"

"One you sense a kinship with. Do you have a favorite?"

"I love the ruby-throated hummingbird. Also, the falcon known as the kestrel." He swallowed and reined in his excitement. "Which would be better?"

Nomed, an owl-like tip to his head, studied him. "Try the hummingbird first. Sit, collect your thoughts, picture the bird in as much detail as you can. I will guide you. If you make the shift, I will call you back into Human form, so don't worry. Just pay attention and listen to my voice."

Esán rested his hands on his knees and stared into the wavering flames.

Mira's cottage began to take shape—the tall pink hollyhocks in her back garden, the sweet smells of summer. Mindful of important details, he closed his eyes and recalled each darting movement of the hummingbird and how it sucked nectar from one flower after another. The sharp point of its beak, the ruby red of its throat, the blur of its teeny wings in motion, all formed a detailed picture.

In the distance, he felt Nomed monitoring his progress. "Embrace its mind as your mind." The command was soft and unobtrusive.

Deep in his brain, Esán perceived a stirring—a pinprick of thought, a tiny light shining.

"Good, Esán. Concentrate on its heartbeat."

His attention switched to his own heart. It pumped faster and faster until it fluttered so fast he could hardly breathe.

"*Now*, Esán. Be the hummingbird."

The change was instantaneous. One moment he sat on the log, the fire warming his face; the next, the smallest body he could imagine encased him. Tiny wings beating in a blurred motion sent him darting like quicksilver around the cavern.

A gentle mental touch brought him to hover beside Seyes Nomed. Without consciously trying, he stood with both feet planted on the cavern's floor, looking into his mentor's hazel eyes. Short gasps shook his Human body. His heartbeat slowed and steadied in his chest. Nomed remained silent and composed, with a hand on his shoulder. The wildness fell from his mind.

"You did well." Nomed's quiet, resonant voice embraced him. "How do you feel?"

Words jostled one another, trying to find expression. He laughed. "I can't describe what just happened. I yearned to make the shift, but doubted I could do it." His joy overflowed. "It was the most amazing thing ever!"

Seyes Nomed smiled a warm, encouraging smile. "I remember my first shift to a small Theran sparrow. With you, I have recaptured that memory."

"Thank you for sharing with me and for giving me this gift." He couldn't keep from smiling back.

"We're not done. Unless you're too tired, of course." The DiMensioner sat down on his upturned log.

Energy flowing like a fast-moving river through Esán's body kept him upright. "I am so full of life I'm bursting!"

"Then let's take you to the next stage. The hummingbird was a good first step. Tell me about the kestrel you mentioned. What does it look like?"

Esán's calmed heartbeat escalated. He took a deep breath. "White, blue, and reddish feathers cover its wings and upper body. Its white breast has dark ermine markings, and on each cheek, a black vertical line absorbs bright sunlight. I love it because it's a clever hunter. For extra lift under its wings, it flies into the wind and separates the feathers at its wingtips. This allows it to hover above the ground while it searches for food."

"What does it like to eat?" Nomed leaned forward, resting his forearms on his knees.

"Kestrels have excellent vision. In fact, they can see ultraviolet light." Esán pursed his lips. "They eat grasshoppers, mice, voles, and other small creatures."

Nomed rubbed the scar on his cheek. "You know a lot about it. Have you ever seen a real one?"

"Yes, they live in the fields and forests near my home. Before I got sick, I took long walks, and I would often see one. They're so beautiful and intelligent."

"Can you picture it as clearly as you could the hummingbird?" Nomed sat up, his back straight, his expression serious.

"Even more precisely."

"Then quiet your thoughts, slow your breathing, and envision it."

Once again, Esán sat on his log and closed his eyes. The image of the kestrel formed—first its proud head, then its tapestry-painted body. Its agile mind pulsed in his brain. The kestrel's quick, penetrating intelligence was a stunning contrast to the gentleness of the smaller bird. He experienced its wildness in the beating of his heart and the abrupt shift in his breathing.

Nomed's voice cut into his consciousness. "Esán, on three. One. Two. Three. Go!"

The transformation rippled through his body. Powerful kestrel wings lifted him into the air. He soared into the vastness above the underground lake. Piercing eyesight absorbed every detail of the cavern. The falcon's mind became his—they were one. A feral freedom he had never known and an exquisite pleasure in flying made him want to remain a kestrel forever.

A sharp command snapped him back into Human form. Mind screaming and body shaking from the shock of the unexpected transition, he stood panting and confused before his mentor.

"*Never* give in to the desire to remain in your shifted form, Esán. If you are so unwise, you will lose your hold on this life forever. More than that, you will lose your humanity. Do you understand?"

Esán struggled to regain his equilibrium—to force his mind to accept his humanness. The man in front of him blurred, then focused. What was he saying?

The DiMensioner gripped his shoulders, stared into his eyes, and restated his warning; then paused. "Do you understand?"

The firm hands tightened and let go. Esán's mind cleared. "I understand and will take great care." A trembling hand scrubbed his bald head. "It's just that I have experienced nothing like that in my life. The kestrel is smarter, more intense, more powerful than the hummingbird." A shrug lifted his shoulders. "I can't explain it."

"You don't have to, Esán. I *know*!" Nomed's penetrating gaze demanded his complete attention. "Listen closely. Unless I say you may do so, you mustn't shift shape on your own until you learn to return to your human body without my help. If you are unwise enough to try it, I cannot be responsible for the outcome. Is that clear?"

"Yes, sir. I won't take a chance. You have my word. Thank you for this gift. I can't wait to fly in the open air."

The DiMensioner's eyes held a secretive smile. "Soon, young Esán, you will fly through the mists of Myrrh to watch the unfolding of time."

44

Yuin, the ruby Pentharian, ate his fill of white-tailed deer and slept. He awoke with cool tendrils of fog tiptoeing over his feline body. Lethargy and an unwillingness to face the turning kept him prone. Through half-closed eyes, he watched Voer stretch, muscles undulating beneath his blue-black fur. He understood how much his leader loved the panther's fluid way of moving; the power in every muscle; its silent, predatory mind.

Embracing his Pentharian form, Yuin switched his red-scaled lizard tail as he sniffed the morning air. "It's time to find our brothers." He paused as his leader arched his feline back and shifted.

Voer rotated, his golden eyes searching. "There is a tower nearby that holds strange power." Not waiting for a reply, he changed into a vulture and rose through the trees on powerful wings.

Yuin joined him. They flew east while the rising sun pressed white light through the silvery clouds of early morning.

Nemttachenn lay half-hidden in the gathering mist. Within its granite walls, CheeTrann, the protector of the tower and the Sentinel of Myrrh, kept watch. The strange creatures Almiralyn had placed in his care—black birds that were not birds, but aliens of another world—magnified his fears for his home. The approach of two alien vultures increased his misgivings.

Small pebbles tumbling down granite steps startled the small birds into waking. Nemttachenn's Sentinel wrapped his enchantment tighter around them and waited.

Inside their stone prison, Stee clung to his Pentharian mind with tenacious focus, while Jeet picked at mites on the underside of his belly and drew closer to succumbing to his shifted form. Stee pecked at his friend's neck. Jeet pecked back. Wings flapping, Stee squawked a warning. Jeet cocked his head as though trying to understand.

Voer landed with Yuin on the ramparts of the tower and shifted. The eerie silence of the mist-filled clearing made his nostrils flare.

Yuin materialized, growled low in his throat, and sniffed the air. "Peculiar place. Let's get this over with."

Voer led the way down the stone steps, darkness absorbing his Pentharian strangeness like a sponge. A magic presence within the tower sent a rhythmic throbbing through his alien body. His home planet called to his heart. Myrrh, beautiful in its way, did not compare to the swamps of ReTaw au Qa. Another throb inspired a desire for water, for the sweet, moist air and smell of the marshlands. His mind yearned for the fluid sounds and primordial beauty of his birthplace. Longing overflowed. *Soon we will leave this land. Soon.*

When his feet touched the granite floor, the throbbing ceased. Clarity returned, but his longing remained. He turned to greet Yuin, saw the yearning in his eyes and waited.

The ruby-red Pentharian shook himself and stared up the stairs as light from the ramparts dimmed, and magic tingled overhead. "What is this tower?"

Voer responded with narrowed eyes. "It is a place of magic, which we cannot understand. Let us find our comrades and leave it behind."

A search of the tower's circular perimeter brought them to an arched doorway that proved to be a barrier rather than an exit.

"Now what?" Yuin shot a nervous glance over his shoulder.

Voer sniffed the air. "They're here, Yuin. Og dio myn oct." His guttural sounds were soft and enticing.

Wings brushed his cheek. Beside him, Yuin ducked and muttered under his breath. "What the—"

"Og dio myn oct." Voer's repeated words fell like stones into a well.

More fluttering and a squawked response turned him to the dim light of the doorway, where two small, black birds became visible. With a flurry of wings, they landed, one on the shoulder of each Pentharian.

Voer offered a palm. The bird hopped into his upraised hand, its body trembling. "We must find what holds our brothers to this shape. Already they have been in this form too long."

Yuin's lizard-gold eyes blinked. "If it is an enchantment, then we have no power to undo it."

Moving nearer to the entrance, Voer examined the shivering bird from the tip of its tail to the point of its beak. Nothing caught his eye until it turned its small head to observe him. "Yuin, I think there's something around its neck."

Voer transferred the bird to his comrade's wrist and looked closer. A single strand of pale hair gleamed against its black feathers. With the strand between his fingers, he gave a quick pull. It fell to the floor as Stee appeared, gasping for breath.

"Hurry! Jeet is succumbing to his shifted shape." The emerald Pentharian gulped in cleansing breaths of fresh air.

Yuin moved the second black bird into the dim light; Voer snapped the strand of hair; and Jeet materialized, his carnelian orange form glistening with sweat.

"T-t-too c-close." He licked his lips. "The bird almost owned me."

"How did you find us?" Stee slapped his sides to increase his circulation.

"We sensed the tower this morning when we woke up." Yuin's relief softened his features. "It is powerful. We did not know whether you were here, but it seemed worth a try."

Voer examined the entrance, then pressed a hand against the impregnability of the invisible barrier. "The tower's spell remains unbroken. We are still trapped." He shook long braids back from his face and turned to his comrades. "Suggestions?"

Stee pointed at the center of the tower. "There's a gateway here. I've felt it continuously since Almiralyn left us in this place. Perhaps we could use it to leave Myrrh."

Serious and thoughtful, Voer studied his companions. "Leaving unannounced would denote failure, something none of us want. Although I have lost any respect I might have had for Seyes Nomed, he is not paying our fee. His desire to destroy Myrrh and Thera, which he kept hidden until we arrived, goes against everything we have been taught to honor. Since the Dreelum chose not to share the DiMensioner's personal goals, we must consider where our allegiance lies."

The floor quaked. A deep voice rumbled from the darkness. "Join the Guardian Almiralyn in her fight to save Myrrh." The quaking ceased. The tower seemed to listen.

Yuin's startled gaze, darted around the space, and then fastened on his companions. "I dislike the DiMensioner Seyes Nomed. Vengeance drives him to destroy this beautiful land. He lied to us about his plans. I feel no allegiance to him, Voer, only to those who pay our fee."

Jeet's long, orange tail switched back and forth. "What of the Dreelum? If we betray Nomed, do we betray them?"

A growl from Stee drew attention in his direction. "The Dreelum lied to us about the true power of the Evolsefil Crystal. It is a Prima Crystal and vital to the continued existence of this Solar System. They would allow the DiMensioner to destroy this land and the planet of Thera to increase their power. Is that a course we wish to pursue? Our training teaches respect for other planets and cultures. Pentharian battle to free the oppressed, not to obliterate worlds." His nostrils flared. "Or *our* solar system."

Voer, his golden eyes glowing, regarded his comrades. "How do you feel about joining the Guardian of Myrrh's battle to save Myrrh?"

Yuin paced to the entrance, pressed a hand against the shield making it impassable, and returned. "If we choose to fight her fight, we place ourselves at risk of angering the Dreelum." He tossed his braids behind his shoulder and touched his heart. "I would much prefer to join the side of life and beauty than to continue on this path to destruction and mayhem."

Stee nodded his agreement. "Nomed has no understanding of what his desire for vengeance holds in store for the entire Clenaba Rolas System. If she will have us, I think we should join the Guardian's fight."

"And what of our fee?" Jeet fixed his gaze on his leader.

Fingering a bluish braid, Voer frowned. "We forfeit either it or our desire to save lives, ours and those of our Solar System."

Jeet stared into space for a long moment, then pressed a hand to his heart. "Our home means more to me than a fee. I believe the fight to save Myrrh is a fight to save ReTaw au Qa."

Voer bowed his head. "I am proud to call you my brothers. I, too, find destroying Myrrh and Thera at odds with Pentharian values. Let us make the commitment to the Guardian."

The tower quaked as he strode to the center and touched his heart. "I, Voer, swear, by the Warriors' Oath of ReTaw au Qa, to serve the Guardian Almiralyn and the well-being of Myrrh."

His comrades followed his lead. When Stee, the last of the four, completed his oath, a vortex opened at the tower's center and a cyclone of brilliant color engulfed them. Just as Voer thought the brightness would fill his senses for eternity, the vortex swirled shut. He blinked to clear his vision and faced the entrance. His hand met no resistance. The barrier had vanished.

Jeet, Stee, and Yuin filed from the tower and huddled together under the gathering gloom. Voer crossed the threshold and extended his arms to the sky in a gesture of thanksgiving.

"Was that the gateway that opened?" Jeet flicked his tail.

"I think it was the enchantment of this tower, ensuring we will keep our promise." Voer gazed at the forest and back at Nemttachenn. "The magic of the tower ties us to the future of this land. If Nomed destroys it, we die, too. If Myrrh survives, we will be free to go home."

They looked at Nemttachenn, standing tall and still in the mist. Jeet put his hand on Yuin's shoulder. "Thank you, my brother, for not giving up on us."

Stee echoed his gratitude and then turned to their leader. "Is there any word from Yaro? Do you think he will join the Guardian's fight?"

Voer stared into the distance. "I have not seen him since we began the search for the children. With luck, we will find him on our journey, and yes, I believe he will join our new cause."

"Where do we go now?" Jeet pinched the gold ring piercing his earlobe.

"After you have replenished your bodies, we go in search of the Guardian of Myrrh. Come, let us find your breakfast."

Four Pentharian melted into predatory cats and skulked into the Terces Wood.

Torgin hiked ahead of Paisley and Skipt up the mountain trail. The thick, clammy mist crept over the Dojanacks and foothills with the stealth of a Pentharian panther. He shivered and closed his damp jacket tighter around him, wishing the sun would peek through and bring some warmth back to his body.

Not far up the trail, he found Tam waiting. Her welcoming whinny made him grin.

Skipt joined them. "Ya ho, Tam. Good to find you."

Paisley hiked from the mist, stopped beside the pony, and rubbed her soft nose. "You gotta go down the mountain, girl. We'll be goin' into caverns, and we'll need to leave ya behind."

Tam whinnied and moved closer to Torgin. "She wants to stay. I'll take care of her." The tan pony nuzzled his hand. "I am more confident when she is near."

Skipt tossed a small pebble in the air, caught it, and grinned. "Boy and pony have oneness. They help each other. It is good."

Paisley tugged his mustache. "We'll have to see what happens when we get to the cavern entrance."

Torgin combed his fingers thru Tam's tangled mane. "It will be fine, Paisley." He climbed onto her back and once again took the lead.

The moisture-laden haze soon separated them from their companions. The occasional thinning of the mist allowed Torgin a glimpse farther up the trail. As he rode, he pondered his friends' whereabouts; how Seyes Nomed had brought the Pentharian into Myrrh; and where the death shadow was. He doubted the memory of the glacial cold he experienced in Nemttachenn would ever fade.

Pushing distasteful thoughts away, he let himself drift with the pleasant rhythm of Tam's gait. A delicious drowsiness settled over him. Heavy eyelids closed, and his mind grew quiet. In that peaceful place between sleep and wakefulness, he heard the soft muffled tones of a flute. His eyes flew open. Sitting taller on the pony's back, he brought Tam to a halt and listened, perplexed—only silence. And then, drifting with delicate grace, the melody began again.

He dismounted and moved to Tam's head. "Who is playing the flute in the mountains? Shall we try to find out?"

His ingrained fear nudged. *Why am I always afraid? I hate it! Whenever something new happens, my first reaction is to panic.* His spine lengthened. *Not this time.* He grabbed the reins and, with a sense of purpose, climbed toward the enticing sound.

The higher he went, the more clearly he heard the music. A thrill at the beauty and the sweetness of the sound washed over him. His composer's heart opened. He hummed an alto line that flowed in and around the beautiful melody as it continued to drift toward him through the morning mist.

Down the mountain, a wrong step sent Paisley tumbling. With a groan, he crawled to a boulder and sat massaging his bare foot and swelling ankle. "Just what I need."

Skipt peered up at him. "Ya ho, does it hurt?"

"It smarts like blazes. Besides, I feel pretty dumb." A grimace sharpened his broad features.

"You not dumb, Paisley." Placing tentative fingers on the ankle, the Enots frowned. "I go to my mother for poultice. You not move."

"First, find Torgin. I don't want him gettin' too far ahead. It would never do to lose him."

Skipt jogged up the trail, sad for Paisley, but glad the big man and tall boy had come into his life. This adventure made his tiny heart beat faster. He loved it and planned to play his part to the end.

The lilting melody enticed Torgin farther up the mountain. Flushed-face and heartbeat quickening, he followed the pull of the ethereal sound. The mist thinned and resettled. He squinted. *Did I see something?*

The music stopped, leaving only a memory to stir his heart. He hesitated. Tam whinnied. Again, the mist thinned. The hazy figure of a man faced him a short distance up the trail. Gray dampness swirled up between them, creating a curtain of curiosity.

"Did you see him, Tam?" Torgin gulped in damp air. "There is someone in the mist."

The pony nickered.

Torgin hiked up the trail, his thoughts racing. *I sense no danger, but what would I know? Things in Myrrh are never what they seem.*

Through the thinning haziness, the mourning dove observed the pony and the boy from its perch on the hermit's shoulder. It dropped its small, elegant head to capture a fly in its sharp beak. It liked the feel of this man. Gentleness, warmth, a sadness rooted deep in his heart, loneliness, too —the dove sensed them all. Above everything, he cherished the man's goodness.

The wind gusting between the mountains and the foothills ruffled his feathers and stirred the mist. Rocky cliffs and steep canyons lay shrouded in a gray cloak. A flash of intuition filled his consciousness. The people of Myrrh were fearful of the mist creeping closer to their homes and their hearts. Soon the Terces Wood would vanish in the grayness, slipping through big-leafed ferns and creeping on cotton-soft paws to press its dampness into the rough bark of oak and maple, Tirips tree and pine. The dove envisioned the Pentharian in the forest below, lifting blood-soaked noses to sniff the air.

A gust swirled up the mountain trail, dispersing the haziness. The tall boy and the man with the flute stood facing each other.

45

Fear prickled the back of Torgin's neck. He wanted to run. Tam, skittish beside him, flared her nostrils. Something was making her nervous, yet she stayed. So did he.

Nothing about the man on the trail appeared threatening. His tanned face, unwrinkled but not young, might go unnoticed but for the clarity of his sky-blue eyes. Thick hair the color of summer wheat streaked with silver hung in a loose braid midway down his back. His slender, muscular body bristled with vitality. Something about him stirred a memory Torgin could not place.

A slow smile curved the man's mouth. "Welcome to the Dojanacks." His voice—hesitant and breathy—sounded unused to forming words.

Torgin's uncertainty evaporated. "Were you playing the flute?"

"I was." The man held up the silvery instrument.

"It was wonderful. I play the flute, too, but not as well as you do. What is it made of?"

"The wood of the Tirips tree." He strolled down the trail. "Today is the first time I've played it."

Tam backed away. The man stopped. "I seem to frighten your pony. What's her name?"

"Tamboreen, Tam for short."

The mourning dove on the man's pack flew to the top of a scrawny pine. Tam ceased her restless prancing and allowed the man to stroke her neck. She nickered.

Torgin rubbed her nose. "I wonder what changed her mind about you?"

"Perhaps a smell on the wind made her nervous." He placed the flute in its sheepskin case. "I am the Hermit of Timreh Pass. Some call me One Man. What brings you to the Dojanack Mountains in these strange times?"

"You're the hermit! We've been looking for you."

"We?" The hermit peered beyond him.

"Paisley, Skipt and I, and Tam, of course. My name is Torgin. I'm from Idronatti."

"It is good to meet you, Torgin. Where are your friends?"

Skipt jogged into the sun's dimmed light. Delight replaced the worry in his gray eyes and spread into a welcoming grin. "Ya ho, One Man, we glad to see you! What brings you from home?"

"Ya ho, Skipt, there is a strangeness in Myrrh. It called me to come. Can you explain?"

The stone boy performed a quick jig, his enormous eyes looking as though they might pop from his face. "Off-worlders hunt in Myrrh. Bad magic fills the land."

Torgin couldn't contain a shiver. "Where's Paisley?"

"Big man fall. Ankle swells. He down mountain."

"Show us where he is." The hermit moved along the trail. "Perhaps I can help."

One Man and Skipt took the lead. Torgin followed with Tam. They found Paisley sitting on a large rock, his ankle elevated and pain dulling his eyes.

"Ya ho!" Skipt pointed to One Man. "This the Hermit of Timreh Pass. Lucky you not have to climb all that way."

The hermit offered a hand. "I am called One Man."

Paisley shook it and acknowledged him with a nod.

"May I look at your ankle?"

"Just be careful." Paisley grimaced.

One Man knelt and ran gentle hands over the injured joint.

Paisley clenched his teeth around the pain.

"I'm sorry." The hermit shrugged off his pack and pulled out a small pouch of herbs, a goatskin water bag, and a tin cup. "I'm going to put a compress on that ankle. You have a bad sprain. It'll be some time before you'll be able to do much walking, my friend." While he spoke, he stirred herbs and water in the cup and smoothed the mixture over the swollen joint. "After it dries, we'll wrap your ankle."

The gray-brown mourning dove landed on the rock above Paisley's head. One Man looked up and smiled. "This little fellow has adopted me." It fluttered to his shoulder.

Tam pranced nervously. Torgin tried to soothe her with a gentle pat. "What's wrong? Is it the bird, Tam? It can't hurt you."

The dove took flight and circled above them. Tam's ears twitched. Her nostrils flared, but she stood still. The bird landed up the trail, cocked its head, and shifted to a golden Pentharian.

An almost Human shriek burst from Tam's throat. Skipt disintegrated into a pile of rocks. Torgin grabbed Tam's reins and wrapped his arms around her neck. Paisley lunged to standing and immediately fell to his knees, his face contorted in pain. Only the hermit remained immobile.

"I am Pentharian, and I am your friend." The gravelly voice of the half Human, half Reptilian added to its strangeness.

"Pentharian kidnapped Brie and Ari and killed Buster." Torgin's emotions alternated between anger and fear. "You are *not* our friend."

"I am friend." The creature's response remained calm.

After helping Paisley return to his seat on the boulder, One Man addressed the alien. "You are Pentharian, and yet you say you are our friend. Please explain so we may find truth in your words."

"I am Yaro. I came to Myrrh from the planet of DerTah, where my comrades and I are what you would call mercenaries. The Pentharian are noble warriors. We fight for hire, but we pick our battles with care. We try not to harm the innocent."

Torgin clenched his hands and controlled the urge to yell.

"Why did you come to Myrrh?" One Man applied more herbs to Paisley's ankle.

"We came at the bidding of the Dreelum, leaders of DerTah, to assist Seyes Nomed in the theft of the Prima—"

"I hate you!" Torgin threw himself at the startled Pentharian. "I hate you! I hate you!" Hiccuped sobs shook his body. Blinded by anger and tears, he pummeled the hard, tattooed chest with his fists. "You killed Buster and bit Fen! I—"

"Torgin, stop it!" Paisley's groggy words faded into a moan of pain.

Torgin stumbled backward, his chest heaving and his fisted hands raised. Yaro's alien face showed only compassion. His muscular arms remained relaxed at his sides.

Tam's cool nose and warm breath on his arm brought Torgin to his senses. Choking, he lowered the fists. Tears rolled down his cheeks. He buried his face in Tam's neck and sobbed.

Skipt touched his leg. "Ya ho, you good?"

Torgin dried his tears with the back of his hand, picked the Enots up, and sat him on Tam's back. "I am good, Skipt."

One Man left Paisley's side to rest his hand on the pony's tan flank. "Tam must believe you, Yaro."

Torgin felt everyone's eyes on him. He took a jerky step back. Tam's soft, dark eyes rested on the Pentharian. Torgin glared at the tattooed face. "Did you kill Buster?"

Brown-gold braids glistened as Yaro shook his head. "I do not know this Buster."

"Buster was a dog and our friend. Two vultures killed him in the grasslands." Accusation stabbed the air between them.

"Then I did not harm your Buster. I have not been with comrades for some time." Sadness clouded his gold eyes. "I bit a small being in the strange place beneath Myrrh. I am so sad to have killed your friend."

"You didn't." Torgin's chin jerked up. "Ari saved him."

The alien's brow wrinkled. "How could that be? My venom is deadly and quick."

Torgin forced an answer between clenched teeth. "Almiralyn gave Ari a knife. It healed the wound and saved his life."

"Efillaeh." One Man pronounced the word with reverence and

something else less tangible. "I thought the sacred blade was just a legend. These *are* strange times."

Paisley eyed the Pentharian warrior with interest. "What is it you want?"

"I have found love for this Myrrh. I can no longer be a part of its destruction. If you will allow me, I will help."

"How can *you* help?" Torgin still seethed with rage and pain.

The Pentharian knelt in front of him, his Reptilian tail twitching. He bowed his head to the ground. When he lifted his head, he looked steadily at Torgin. "I will fight by your side and serve the intent of your heart."

Torgin studied the tattooed face, the golden earrings, the obsidian loop that pierced Yaro's nose, the long braided hair. In the lizard-like eyes, he saw warmth and understanding. His mind screamed, "No!" His heart sensed only truth in the magnificent alien creature. "I am honored to have you fight by my side." His solemn response surprised him.

"Well done, Torgin." Paisley smiled through his pain. "Well done. Spoken like a true warrior of Myrrh."

The Pentharian remained kneeling, his eyes level with Torgin's. "On ReTaw au Qa, my home planet, a warrior may claim a heart-brother, whom he cherishes as family. I ask you, Torgin, to be my heart-brother. If you accept, I will fight by your side, protect you with my life, and defend your home and family as my own."

Torgin's mind blanked. He bowed his head and took a ragged breath. The anger holding his body ridged melted away. His fisted hands relaxed. He squared his shoulders and met the Pentharian's gaze. "It would honor me to be your heart-brother, Yaro of ReTaw au Qa."

The Pentharian rose. "Place your palm here." He tapped a spot on his tattooed chest.

Torgin's eyes widened. He inhaled a deep breath and placed his hand.

Yaro held his gaze. "May I touch your heart as you touch mine?"

Eyes rounded, Torgin nodded.

The Pentharian's golden hand touched his chest. "Repeat after me... Comrades of Heart."

"Comrades of Heart." Torgin kept his voice steady.

"Share life and death."

"Share life and death."

"Arg doo me teekay. Dio ordek od pier." The Pentharian touched his forehead to Torgin's before stepping back. "We are now pledged to be brothers."

Torgin squirmed. "I'm sorry I hit you."

"You grieve for your friends. Let it be."

One Man joined them and offered his hand.

Yaro took it with dignity and a smile of gratitude. "Let us look to the needs of your friend." He moved to Paisley's side. "If you will trust me, I can help your pain."

Paisley nodded.

Yaro raised One Man's tin cup to his mouth and pressed one of his big eyeteeth hard against the rim. A clear fluid ran down the side of the cup.

Uncertainty sparked in Paisley's dark eyes.

"Do not be afraid. I carry both venom to kill and serum to numb my opponent. This will only ease your pain, not harm you."

Torgin moved to his friend's side. "I'll try it first if you're unsure."

"Young one, you amaze me." Paisley's voice broke, shattered by pain. "Dern blast, that hurts. Please, Yaro. I trust you."

The Pentharian spread the viscous fluid over the swollen joint.

The big man's face flooded with relief. "Thank you." His black mustache drooped around a grin. "It feels better already. Now, let's decide what's next."

While the hermit wrapped the ankle with clean rags from his pack, a lively discussion ended with decisions made. Paisley would ride Tam back to Mira's cottage with One Man as his companion. Almiralyn had been adamant—she wanted to see the hermit as soon as possible. Skipt, Yaro, and Torgin would continue the search for the twins and Esán.

After repacking his backpack, One Man held up his flute. "Before we go, Torgin, will you play for us?"

"Yes, please!" He accepted the silvery instrument, tested its weight and balance, and experimented with the fingering. After familiarizing himself with its sound, he took a breath and played.

The melody floating from the flute into the Myrrhinian sky sang of love for the mountains, the plains, and the forest. Its gentle beginning evolved into a brisk and windy passage that made Skipt's tiny feet fly over the ground. The melody transitioned to a fluid adagio, ending with a single sustained high note which Torgin held until it melted into the very fabric of Myrrh.

At first, no one spoke. He lowered the flute, staring at it with surprised wonder.

Skipt broke the silence. "Torgin, you do great music!"

One Man smiled. "You play beautifully. Where did you learn that piece?"

"I composed it as I played." Humbled and filled with awe, he gazed at the silvery instrument. "I love to compose music, but I have not played like that before."

Tears streamed down Paisley's cheeks. "I've never heard anythin' so beautiful, young one. Myrrh seemed to flow through each note."

"It sang from your heart, my brother, stirring in mine an even deeper love for this land." Yaro bowed his head.

Torgin ran a finger along the wooden grain, memorized the smoothness of the wood, the weight, the perfect balance before forcing himself to hand it to One Man. "Thank you so much. It is a remarkable instrument."

A secretive smile lit the hermit's eyes. He placed it in its sheepskin case and held it out. "This flute belongs to you. Take it and use it on this important journey."

Torgin's hands trembled as he accepted the beautiful gift and hung it over his shoulder. "I promise to guard it with my life, One Man. When this adventure is over, I will return it to you."

The hermit smiled and helped Paisley onto Tam's back.

Torgin stood beside her. "I'll miss you, Paisley."

"And I you. Today you've done excellent work, young Torgin."

He smiled as a flush tinted his cheeks. Paisley's compliment made him proud and happy. *I bet Almiralyn would be pleased, too.* The notion warmed him.

One Man gathered Tam's reins and prepared to lead her down the mountain. "I'll take good care of your pony."

"Thank you." Torgin put his arms around her neck. "Bye, Tam, I'll see you soon."

The pony whinnied and followed the Hermit of Timreh Pass down the trail.

Torgin turned to look at Skipt and Yaro. *Where are we headed?* Trepidation squeezed his stomach. *Will I ever find my friends?*

Sparrow's instincts tingled with anticipation. Her painting's subject took shape in front of her eyes as magic guided her brush over the canvas. A soft blue and red Kestrel emerged from the cloud-covered sky, followed by a raven and four creatures of shadow. Myrrh stretched, gray and somber, beneath them. To one side of the picture, a slender white hand held a mourning dove.

Sparrow put her brush down and sighed. She had painted nonstop since arriving in Myrrh. The canvases lining the walls depicted the children, DeoNytes, panthers, and birds tumbling from one painting into the next. The man with the silver-lined cape appeared, disappeared, and appeared again. She picked up a cloth and wiped her brush clean, attention fixed on her latest canvas. *I'm watching my work take on an energy of its own. Merrilea's Myrrhinian blood has brought the images to life.*

The smell of summer roses alerted her to Almiralyn's presence in the doorway. A touch of color tinted the Guardian's high cheekbones, accentuating the deep blue of her eyes.

"You look much better. Did you sleep?"

"I have slept. Something you have done little of since you arrived. Take a break, Sparrow. Your paintings have helped to restore some balance. Merrilea has prepared breakfast. Let's join her."

Sparrow followed Almiralyn into the muted lavender kitchen to find Merrilea covered in flour and giggling like a girl as she licked one batter-covered finger after the other. Washing them clean, she popped a cookie sheet into the oven and smiled with satisfaction. "A treat for the children when they return."

A wave of weariness dropped Sparrow into a chair. Merrilea placed a bowl of warm oats in front of her. "Eat, and then off to bed."

Almiralyn stirred syrup into her porridge and took a bite. "This is delicious. Thank you, Merrilea."

Sparrow smiled. "Each bite is a surprise...raisins and cherries and nuts.

Yum! What a good idea for breakfast today." She lifted her spoon, steaming from the bowl. "It even chases away the chilliness of the mist."

Almiralyn finished her meal and crossed to the windowsill where Majeska slept. The smoky-gray cat opened her eyes and purred a welcome. Outside, a fog-like haze drifted across the garden, hiding the pond and changing trees and barn into an impressionist painting. Almiralyn felt a lull in the events that had brought Myrrh to this point. The fountain had shown her only mist and mountains. Something was altering the balance of things. She wondered what and for how long.

Karrew, my dear friend, come home. She sighed and returned to the table. "To bed, Sparrow. Myrrh and the children will need your gift again soon. We'll call you when it's time to resume your work."

Sparrow responded with a slight smile. "I'm glad to rest. Which room should I use?"

"The one at the top of the stairs is ready for you."

Smothering a yawn, Sparrow left.

After they tidied the kitchen, Almiralyn and Merrilea crossed the hall to Sparrow's studio and studied the canvases lined up along the wall. As they watched, the paintings shifted and changed, their stories merging one into the other.

Esán's aunt gasped. "Are you seeing what I'm seeing? It's as though they're alive."

"Your Myrrhinian blood has given them life, Merrilea. As long as Myrrh remains at risk, these paintings will tell its story."

Merrilea moved from one animated canvas to the next and paused before one of Esán on the back of the DiMensioner's owl. "I miss my nephew. I hope he's safe."

Almiralyn put an arm around her. "So do I."

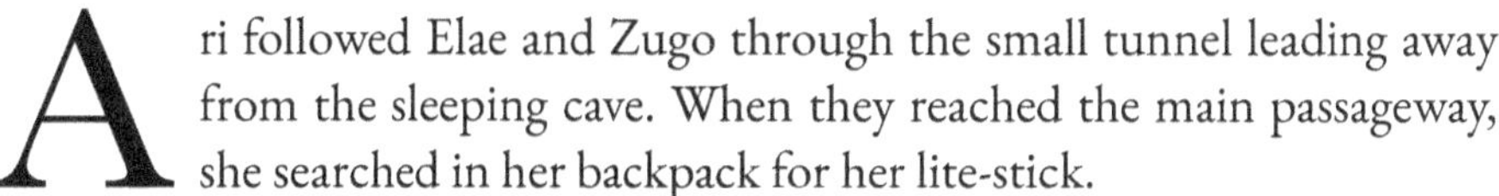

46

ri followed Elae and Zugo through the small tunnel leading away from the sleeping cave. When they reached the main passageway, she searched in her backpack for her lite-stick.

Zugo touched her arm. "Your eyes will adjust, and you're going to need both hands to climb down a deep crevasse wall. Just keep Elae in sight. Her fur will begin to give off a soft glow."

Ari re-shouldered her pack and followed the slender DeoNyte priestess. For whatever reason, she trusted these strange creatures. Elae's gentle strength impressed her, and Zugo... She smiled. *He's such a boy.*

She glanced at him as he joined her. "How long until we get to Meos?"

"It's a good way, but we'll take a shortcut. Watch your step. We're getting close to the crevasse."

Elae stopped at last, her pale eyes peering into the darkness. "This is a tough climb, and I've made it several times." Her gaze fastened on Ari. "I'll take your backpack. It will be much easier for you without it."

Ari shrugged it off and handed it over.

"I'll lead." Elae adjusted the pack. "There are hand and foot holds all the way down. I can guide your feet, but you will have to find handholds. Are you ready?"

Glad the darkness shrouded the crevasse's depth, Ari moved to the edge. *Good thing Brie isn't here. This would terrify her.* "I'm ready." With only a hint of nervousness, she watched Elae kneel and maneuver over the rocky rim.

Ari knelt and slid a foot down the wall. Elae's hand guided it to a secure hold. Lowering herself further, Ari discovered hollows and small ledges that offered safe places for her hands and feet. She could see Zugo's white shape descending above her. With apparent sensitivity for her inexperience, he maintained a slow pace, staying close enough to help, but far enough away she didn't feel pressured.

When she stepped down onto solid ground, she exhaled a sigh of relief and rubbed her chaffed palms against her pants. Zugo arrived beside her, his black face invisible but his pale eyes gleaming.

Elae returned her backpack and urged them forward. "Something has happened. The curtain of oppression in the caverns has lifted." She gasped. "The unremembered have found themselves! We must hurry to Meos. Change is afoot. The High Priestess will need me in the Cave of Canedari."

Ari hurried beside her. "What about Brie? We have to find her." Alarm made her voice more curt than she intended.

"As soon as we're back in Meos, we will ask Yookotay to send out searchers." As Elae hustled down the tunnel, a blast of orange light zoomed around a bend. The priestess pushed Ari to one side and dodged to the other. "Zugo, down! It's a Giest."

Zugo ducked, his arms covering his head.

The Giest shot further down the passageway, spun around, and, with an angry screech, zipped straight for Ari. The breeze of its passing brushed her cheek. As she turned to stare, a blaze of orange slammed into her forehead. Pain ripping through her turned the world black.

E lae placed herself between the fallen Human and the cackling ball of plasma. "Giest, be gone! Your antics are not welcome here." A Light Priestess's authority rang in her voice.

The Giest hovered in the air, sniveling. "Send me home, Priestess. Send me home."

"Make your journey to the Cave of Canedari. Evolsefil will set you free."

The blob of orange whimpered and whined. "Crystal light hurts and makes me cry. Hate you!" Sniffling loudly, it bounced out of sight.

She turned to find Zugo kneeling beside the fallen twin. "She won't wake up."

Elae knelt. "She's unconscious. Help me get her pack off. We need her lite-stick."

Working together, they maneuvered Ari until her head rested in Elae's lap. In the backpack, Zugo found the lite-stick and a small cloth, which he handed to Elae.

She dabbed droplets of blood from the damaged skin. "The Giest hit her pretty hard, Zugo. Go quickly. Bring Owae here. She'll know what to do."

Zugo sprinted down the passageway.

"And bring someone to carry Ari back to Meos." Elae's mind raced. Giests, disembodied Humans who had died horrific deaths in the Dojanacks, remained hidden in the furthest reaches of the caverns. What had brought this one so close to her home? She brushed a curl from the twin's forehead. "Ari? Arienh, can you hear me?"

A distance voice calling her name roused Ari. She moaned and murmured. "Eyelids heavy. Can't see."

"Ari, it's Elae. Can you hear me?"

An attempt to turn her head triggered blinding pain. She gasped. More darkness enveloped her. The strange voice called again and again.

Ari? Who's Ari. And who's Elae? She forced herself to concentrate and peeked from beneath one lid. *Why am I lying on the ground?* Her stomach heaved. The eye squeezed shut.

"Lie still, Ari. Help is on the way."

Help? Another stabbing pain shot through her head. She opened both eyes and stared up at a strange fur-covered creature who studied her from one pale green eye and one pale blue.

"How do you feel?"

"Real sick." A supreme effort brought her halfway to sitting.

"Here, let me help." Furry arms slipped around her and lifted her upright.

Percussive pain pounded in her head. The sour taste of bile made her gag. "Think I'm going to—"

Her companion held her while she vomited, then eased her back against the wall. Ari touched the bump on her forehead. Her fingers came away sticky and red. Her eyes hurt, her head hurt, and her stomach heaved like hummingbird wings churned inside it. With great care, she turned her head to the white creature. *Who is this? Who am I? Why can't I remember?* Exhaustion fogged her mind. *All I want is sleep.* She rested her aching head on the furry shoulder next to her.

"Stay awake, Ari. Look at me."

The effort it took to raise her head left her drained. "Who's Ari? And who are you?" Even whispering took almost more energy than she could muster.

The creature placed its hand on her arm. "You are Ari. I am Elae. Tell me what I said."

"Your name is Ari." Her throat scraped across the words.

"No, your name is Ari." The strange, calm eyes regarded her. "Say... My name is Ari."

"My name is Ari? Brie? No. I'm so confused." A tear dripped off the end of her nose.

"Brie is your twin sister." A black hand stroked her arm. "It's okay, Ari. Help will be here soon. Just don't go to sleep."

"Keep talking to me." Ari swallowed. "Who are you again?"

"Elae."

"Elae. I'm Ari. You're Elae." She repeated the words like a nonsense poem. Her stomach churned. She was about to be sick again.

Zugo arrived in Meos to find the town square crowded with frustrated DeoNytes.

"It knocked me down and screamed in my ears." An angry female rubbed her arm.

"It stole my carry pack and emptied its contents into the fountain." A young girl knelt, trying to retrieve her belongings from the water.

An older male raised his voice above the chaos. "What's going on in the caverns?"

Zugo made his way to his father's side. Yookotay looked relieved to see him.

"Was it a Giest, Father? One just knocked Ari down. It seemed half crazy with fear."

Yookotay raised his hand. The grumbling subsided. "Please settle down. The intruder was a Giest. Yes, they are nasty, but it hurt no one here. Meos has not suffered damage. Please return to your caves. Those of you on watch, please return to your posts. I must confer with my son."

Muttering about the craziness, the crowd dispersed, leave the square quiet.

Zugo followed the ReDael into the council chamber and described what had transpired since he, Elae, and Esán had left Meos in search of Brie. He paused, his thoughts troubled. "The twin was still unconscious when I left them, Father. Elae says Owae must come and also someone to carry Ari."

Yookotay summoned the DeoNyte, standing guard at the door. "Fetch Owae. Tell her to bring her herb bag."

The young female darted away.

A short time later, Owae shuffled into the chamber, her ancient face creased with worry. "Cheeca told me a Giest hurt a Human child. These are most disturbing times."

"They are indeed." Yookotay offered his arm. "Lead the way, Zugo."

"Who will carry Ari back?"

A smile twitched the corner of his father's mouth. "I believe I might have the strength to carry your friend. Besides, I want nothing to happen to you or this Human. Let's be off."

Zugo jogged down the tunnel, his thoughts chasing one another around his mind. *What is a Giest doing so close to Meos? And what made it leave the bowels of the caverns?*

Ari gradually realized she could remember very little about anything. Losing her memory terrified her as much as her head pained her. Grateful for Elae's serenity and gentle ministrations, she battled both fatigue and confusion. A wave of pain made her ill. Her stomach lurched, then settled. *Thank the Fathers. I hate throwing up.*

Elae smoothed her hair with a light touch. "I am so sorry this happened. Do you remember how you were hurt?"

"No. I remember opening my eyes and seeing you. That's all. I'm so scared."

"Stay calm. Owae is a powerful healer. She'll be here soon."

Ari fought to stay awake, but her eyelids, heavy with fatigue, started to close. Her head dropped forward.

Elae touched her hand. "They're here, Ari."

Three white-furred creatures hurried toward them—one about her size, a tall male, and an older female with an understanding smile.

The boy knelt beside her. "This is my father, Yookotay. And this is Owae, our healer."

Ari tried to commit the names to memory, but they slipped through her mind like water through a sieve.

Ancient fingers tipped her chin up. Pale, penetrating eyes searched her face. "You got hit pretty hard, didn't you? How do you feel?" The healer's voice was as gentle as her touch.

"Like someone's having a kicking match inside my head." Tears began to flow. "I can't remember anything. I'm *so* scared."

Owae reached into her bag and withdrew a small pottery bottle, which she uncorked and held under Ari's nose. "Inhale. This will help with the nausea."

Ari took a deep breath. The aroma of cool air and sunlight wafted up her nostrils. Her stomach settled.

Owae tipped three small white tablets from a second bottle onto her palm. "Open your mouth, please."

Ari obeyed.

The healer placed the tablets in her mouth. "Let these dissolve under your tongue. They should help with the pain. Now rest."

Owae's fur brushed her arm as Yookotay helped the healer to stand. "She has a concussion. We need to take her to Meos."

Ari frowned. *Concussion?*

Owae smiled at her. "Your color is better already. Let's see if we can help you stand."

With Zugo on one side and Elae on the other, Ari knelt. Dizziness hit like a whirlwind. Her stomach churned. Yookotay scooped her up in his arms. His strength stabilized her world. The spinning stopped. For the first time since she woke up without a name or memories, she felt safe.

47

Esán watched the large stone roll into place, hiding the entrance to the Dojanack Caverns. Tears slipped down his cheeks as eyes accustomed to darkness adjusted to the hazy light. The dampness felt good against his skin, and the air filling his lungs smelled of morning. *It feels like I've been in the caverns forever.*

Beside him on the high mountain ledge, Nomed stared at the gray mist, roiling in the intermittent light. An occasional thinning allowed Esán a peek of the rolling foothills nestled against the tall mountain peaks.

"Where are the Pentharian and Wodash?" His desire to know more about the DiMensioner's plans for Myrrh remained unspoken.

Nomed shrugged. "Shift to the kestrel and follow me. It is time to show you the land of my teacher."

Esán focused on the bird he had chosen for his own and inhaled. With a suddenness that caught him by surprise, his kestrel form embraced him. None of his imaginings about flying outside in the open came close to the exhilaration he felt soaring above the mist-drenched mountains. The power of his wings against the air awed him. His keen eyesight penetrating the haze to pick out minute details in the landscape below left him breathless. With Nomed's admonishment to keep his humanness ever-present in his mind, he reveled in the magic of flight.

The DiMensioner's owl soared beside him—a silhouette against the gray sky. They flew further and further into the Dojanacks until they came to an obsidian canyon. Too soon, Nomed landed between the steep walls, resumed his Human form, and called the kestrel to him.

Regaining his equilibrium after the abrupt shift took Esán only moments. "Where are we?"

"We're in NaiDisbo Canyon. Let's see if the spell I put on the gateway remains intact." The DiMensioner, his cape churning like a dark cloud, strode up the ravine.

Esán shaded his eyes and gazed at the beauty of the shimmering black cliffs shooting skyward on either side of him. At the top of the cathedral-like walls, the arch of the sky formed a cloud-covered skylight. Fragile fingers of radiance from the Myrrhinian sun caressed the glistening stone. The desire to take flight, to rise through NaiDisbo Canyon into the vastness above, almost overwhelmed him.

Nomed urged him forward. "Hurry, Esán. We have important things to do."

Not far ahead, the muted edges of a mouth-shaped opening encircled a luminescent swirl of colors. Esán stopped and stared. "What's that?"

"It is the gateway to another planet. We must go separately, so listen closely. You will go first. When I give you the word, run and jump into the middle of the light. You will land in the Desert of Fera Finnero on the planet of DerTah. Remain motionless until I am beside you. Do you understand?"

Since escape appeared impossible, Esán nodded and hoped he would have the strength to resist Nomed if necessary.

The DiMensioner's hands gripped his shoulders. He whispered a series of strange words. "Run and jump!" Nomed pushed him toward the portal.

Esán ran and leapt into the vortex. Brilliant flashes of color streaked past him. Silence embraced him until, as though shot from a cannon, he catapulted through space and dimension. Time snatched at the fabric of his being. The instant he knew it would rip him to pieces, heat hit him like the blast from a furnace and sucked him from the portal.

Sand sprayed around him as he crashed on the blood-red desert on DerTah. Stunned by the impact, he fought to accommodate the scorching dryness of the air and the heavy heat of mid-turning. With a surreptitious glance, he inspected his surroundings. Nothing but sand and the oppressive orange sky stretched in all directions. He shrugged off Nomed's warning. Midway to his knees, he froze.

At the top of a neighboring dune, air shimmered and pulsed. Flames blazed up from the desert sand, licking at the rising waves of heat. Sparks snapped and crackled around an emerging form. Smoldering wings unfurled and fanned the seared air. A creature of fire lifted with a deafening screech into flight.

Praying his minuscule movements would not attract attention, Esán lowered his body. Air trapped in his lungs burned. His vision blurred. Cheek to sand, he lay motionless.

Above him, the fire creature shrieked. Flames licked the sand on either side of his heat-soaked body. He did not move, nor breathe, nor think. His mind filled with the searing red eyes and razor-sharp teeth of the Fire ConDra. He saw its thoughts—experienced its hunger. The intensity of the creature's lust for burning Human flesh saturated him. As clearly as he knew his own name, he understood—*I must burst into flames and join the beast's fiery essence forever.* Unconsciousness overcame him; he knew no more.

I n NaiDisbo canyon, Seyes Nomed glared at the portal. It had closed behind Esán, and nothing he tried would open it. "What have I done? How will I be able to reach Esán?" His brow curved into an arc. "And how in the name of DerTah will I bring him back to Myrrh?"

Panicked, he raised his arms to the heavens. "Come to my aid. Open the portal gate." Total silence brought a wail of frustration. Rage burned in his chest. Not since childhood had he felt so desolate. A tear slid down his right cheek; traced the redness of his scar; and slipped, salty and wet, into the corner of his mouth.

Shock ricocheted through him. He spit the salt from his mouth and rubbed the cheek dry. The last time he'd shed a tear, the Guardian had banned him from Myrrh. Wrath roared up from his belly. "I hate you, Mira. How dare you send me away from the only safe place I'd ever known? All of this is your fault!" Unable to control the flood of emotions, he threw back his head and howled. Echoes bounced off obsidian walls and reverberated around him until he could hear nothing but his own anger and despair.

Brie stepped through the passage wall with Bonnee and the small band of Now Remembered. Elation at her success ebbed into an overwhelming sense something vital had changed in Myrrh. She looked around. "Something's wrong, Bonnee. Rest while I figure out what happened."

Allowing her expanded senses to encompass the caverns, she soon discovered someone or something was missing. Her connection to Old Earth deepened. She focused on her loved ones. Ari felt closer. Torgin and his companions drew nearer. *Where is Esán?* No matter how hard she tried, she could find no trace of him. Terror for his safety left her gasping. *What now?*

The Prima Crystal Evolsefil answered her call. The energy holding Myrrh to its place in the universe vibrated in every cell of her body. Relief made her giddy. The heart of Myrrh would provide the answers she needed.

She rejoined the Now Remembered. "I must go to the Evolsefil Crystal. How far is the Cave of Canedari?"

Bonnee pointed to a narrow passageway. "The cave is located down that tunnel."

Brie followed the soft glow of Bonnee's ghost-like form along the passageway to a well-concealed door.

Hovering beside it, Bonnee faced her. "We've reached the Cavern of Tennisca. The Now Remembered can go no further. If we enter the cavern, it will disperse us to the world beyond. We pledge to remain here until you are safe, but this part of the journey you must make alone."

A circle of translucent figures gathered around her. One by one, they expressed their gratitude for the gift of remembering. Jeen spoke last. "We wish you knowledge of your destiny and the return of your sister and your friends."

"Please always remember me, Brie." Bonnee's voice quivered with sadness.

Brie swallowed a lump in her throat. "You will live in my memories forever, Bonnee. That's a promise."

The Now Remembered girl sighed. "Thank you. We'll wait here until you're safe. Only then will we enter to join our loved ones."

Brie smiled through her tears and stepped into the Cavern of Tennisca. Intense darkness closed around her. Instinct urged her to turn back, but she stood her ground.

Keeping a tight rein on her fear, she squared her shoulders and began her descent down the Stairway of Retu Erath.

Ari woke up in a small, unfamiliar room where oil lamps cast shadows on rough salmon walls. Relieved her head no longer ached and her eyes kept their focus, she swung her legs over the side of the bed and sat up. Her stomach felt calm and hungry. She touched her bruised forehead. *No bump and no pain. Hmm...*

A knife in a scabbard lay beside her pillow. She picked it up and ran her fingers over the leathery roughness of the sheath. "I believe this is mine."

Withdrawing the knife, she held it closer to the oil lamp and tried to decipher the finely wrought etchings on the blade. Her mind perceived a change—one her eyes could not quite grasp—as the room melted into muted shadows. Instinct guiding her, she pressed the blade to her forehead.

Vivid images poured into her mind—a beautiful woman with brown eyes and dark chestnut hair smiled at her; a face identical to her own called her name, her voice ringing out like a melody; a brown-skinned boy, a shaggy dog, and a tan and cream pony formed and faded.

Then, the most beautiful woman she had ever seen materialized in a glowing, white-gold light. Her gentle voice filled Ari's mind. "The orange Giest stole your memories, Arienh AsTar. To retrieve them, you must find the Giest. Efillaeh will help you. Zugo and Fen must go with you." The woman kissed the top of her head and vanished.

Ari lowered the knife to her lap. "How can I exist if I cannot find the rest of my memories?" Looking up, she met the faded eyes of the DeoNyte she knew as Owae.

The healer smiled. "I have already sent Sitrio to fetch Fen. He will travel through the Intersect, so it won't take long. After you've eaten, I'll send for Zugo so you can plan your journey."

Ari studied the ancient face. "How did you know?"

"I held Efillaeh to the wound on your forehead. You and I now share a connection which no one can break. It is much like the one you share with Fen. Since you left the Terces Wood, he has ached to be with you. Now he comes to fulfill his obligation to you."

"Fen?" She touched the knife to her forehead and repeated his name. A small boy in a brown coat danced at the edge of her memory. A tree with a pretty flowered door and a black and gold snake... She sighed and lowered the knife. "The Giest didn't steal everything. I remember Fen, but what is he?"

"He's a Wood Tiff, a guardian of the trees in the Terces Wood. Come, let us fill your belly, or have you not noticed how hungry you are?"

Returning the knife to its scabbard, Ari buckled it around her waist and trailed after Owae down a softly lit hall. In the main living space, a fire burned and a pot of soup simmered, filling the air with scrumptious smells. Ari's stomach rumbled.

"I'm starving!" Ari laughed. "At least I haven't forgotten how to be hungry."

"Be at home." Owae smiled and bent to taste the soup.

Ari looked around the welcoming space, where forest green rugs complimented coral walls. Cushions in colorful piles invited her to sprawl. Oil lamps bathed the area in soft light, and a stone fountain sang of water falling through mountain canyons.

"Please sit and have some soup." Owae set a steaming bowl on a stone table.

Ari perched on a cushion-topped rock and inhaled the rich aroma as Yookotay entered the cave.

"So, Ari, you are up." He smiled. "How are you feeling?"

"I'm fine. I just remember very little." She returned his smile before turning to Owae. "Do you know the beautiful woman in my vision?"

Yookotay sat down across from the healer, his expression curious.

"It was Almiralyn, the Guardian of Myrrh. She gave you the knife."

"Oh..."

With Ari's permission, the healer shared what had occurred with the ReDael. When she had finished, he looked solemn. "I'm not sure I want to let either Zugo or you out of my sight, Ari."

"Almiralyn told me to find the Giest that stole my memories. And I have to find it, ReDael Yookotay. I don't think I can stand not remembering. Besides, I might find Brie."

Yookotay accepted a bowl of soup, took a spoonful, and nodded his approval. "We'll consider the best way to proceed once Fen arrives. Until then, I suggest we enjoy Owae's good cooking."

Ari ate a spoonful of soup, savoring it and the sense of safety she knew would not last.

48

In the cottage at the edge of the Terces Wood, Almiralyn listened to Karrew give Merrilea and Sparrow an account of Allynae's battle with the Pentharian. Sparrow paled when he described the close call with the vulture. Merrilea applauded Jordett's rush to the rescue. Both women cheered when the men made it across the Sekan River and into the foothills. Karrew, a seasoned storyteller, kept them on the edge of their seats.

When he finished, Majeska leapt into Almiralyn's lap. "What is it?" The Guardian gave her ears a gentle scratch. Majeska blinked. A low growl rumbled in her throat.

Sparrow gasped, pushed her chair back from the table, and hurried across the hall. Karrew cawed and swooped after her. Majeska landed on silent paws as Almiralyn stood up to follow. Merrilea waited for the Guardian to lead the way.

In her studio, Sparrow sat in front of a fresh canvas, blending paint on her palette. Quick flicks of the brush brought Esán's face into focus. She twirled the brush in a jar of cleaner, wiped it on a rag, and dipped it in a new color. As though driven by the creature emerging on the canvas behind Merrilea's nephew, she added red eyes in a demonic face; a body of billowing flames; a long tail lashing the air; and massive, fiery wings.

"A Fire ConDra." Almiralyn replied to the unasked question filling Merrilea's mind. "It lives on the planet of DerTah." She spoke over her shoulder, already headed for her sanctuary. Karrew soared over her head as she sprinted up the stairs. She reached Elcaro's Eye just ahead of Merrilea and Sparrow. With Karrew watching from his perch by the window, she snapped her fingers. "Show me NaiDisbo Gateway."

The water swirled. Seyes Nomed focused, kneeling, head in hands, in front of the closed portal in the canyon. The DiMensioner's spell, the one whose lingering effects she could still feel, only supported one round trip. The Pentharian mercenaries had already come one way. Seyes Nomed had sent Esán to DerTah with no way to return.

Summoning her power, she projected her image through the spinning vortex and onto DerTah's red sands. The Fire ConDra's shriek blistered the desert air. With her fragile strength waning, she placed a telepathic command in the mind of its intended victim, withdrew to Myrrh, and sagged against the side of the fountain. On the surface, a kestrel shot from the gateway and fell motionless to the ground.

Merrilea's frightened eyes searched her face. "Is that Esán?"

"Yes." She gripped Sparrow's offered arm.

"Is he alive?" Merrilea's gray eyes rounded with fear.

"Barely." Almiralyn leaned against her sister-in-law. Karrew landed on her shoulder.

Merrilea's face turned as white as Elcaro's smooth alabaster bowl. Her tears fell, scattering Esán's image one drop at a time.

A sound near the portal snapped Nomed's attention back to NaiDisbo Canyon. The small, still body of a kestrel lay at his feet. "Esán!" He knelt, slipped gentle fingers around the bird, and held it to his ear. Was there a heartbeat?

"Esán, wake up. Esán!"

The inert form did not respond.

On the verge of panic, Nomed's mind raced. *Esán needs water, and NaiDisbo Canyon is bone dry. Oche Cavern is our best option.* He placed the kestrel on the ground. The great horned owl materialized, wrapped its talons around the smaller bird, and transported it to the entrance at the Cliffs of ReVod.

Beside the fire in the cavern, with the small falcon cupped in his hand, Nomed urged water down its throat one drop at a time. "Wake up, Esán. You can't return to Human form until you're fully conscious. Listen to my voice. Open your eyes." The kestrel remained immobile. Nomed swallowed his rising dread. The impulse to yell or throw something the way he had when he was a boy boiled below the surface of his adult calm. He glanced at Dom and back at the inert body.

Dom sat opposite as his friend worked. Never had he seen Seyes Nomed so desperate or as patient. Should the boy fail to survive, he dreaded the DiMensioner's reaction.

Nomed stood up and held out the bird. "Hold him for me, Dom. I need to stretch."

Dom peered through his spectacles at the wild splendor of the kestrel—the ermine speckled breast and the blue wings, the black markings at the corner of its eyes, the curve of its beak. He looked closer. *Did its eyelid move?* He held his breath. *The slightest flutter caught his eye.* Shifting it into one palm, he ran a finger along its breast. "Come home, Esán. Come home." He stroked the ermine breast again. Totally engrossed in the kestrel, he did not notice Seyes Nomed return to sit by the fire.

A subtle movement graduated to the slow relaxation of the bird's curled toes. Its eyelids fluttered again. The breast filled with air. Dom sat the kestrel on his wrist, allowing its talons to cling to his wrinkled jacket. As he kept it steady with his hand, the bird's strength returned, one drop at a time. How long he held it upright or what he crooned to it, he would never know. His full attention focused on helping the kestrel—Esán—to survive. Only when it opened its blue wings to fly the short distance to its mentor's arm did his tears overflow.

Nomed's relief knew no bounds. With effort, he maintained his calm. When the falcon's grip steadied and its demeanor appeared alert, Nomed placed it on the cavern floor. He fixed his gaze on the small bird. "Esán."

The kestrel cocked his head as the echo repeated his name in a recurrent rhythm.

Nomed leaned forward. "If you can understand me, fly to my shoulder."

Unaware of anything but the flickering flames, the kestrel stared at the fire with first one eye and then the other, while it edged backward until firelight no longer touched its feathers.

Urgency furrowed Nomed's brow. "Esán, drop your bird form. Your time is running out."

A flutter of blue and white lifted the kestrel into the air. Its wing tip brushed his scarred cheek. Its talons gripped his shoulder.

Nomed turned his head. "Esán, you must return to Human form. Feel your own heartbeat. Let *your* mind take control. When I command you to shift, release the kestrel form."

The bird fluttered to the ground. Before he could speak again, Esán shed the kestrel, his blue eyes staring straight ahead at the orange and red flames. He staggered backward and fell into Dom's waiting arms. The old man teetered. Nomed scooped the boy up, carried him into his sleeping alcove, and settled him on the pallet. He placed a hand on his hot, clammy forehead and frowned. Dipping a cloth in cool water, he wrung it out and draped it over the pallid brow, hoping the fever would soon break.

He remained beside the pallet as the boy tossed and turned. When the restlessness eased and Esán lay quiet, his dark eyelashes resting against pale, damp cheeks, he took the boy's hand between his own and bowed his head. He couldn't remember the last time he had experienced remorse. Never had he admitted he was wrong about anything. Here, beside Esán, his regret left him shaking. *What if the boy dies?*

Without warning, Esán sat up and looked at Nomed. "The Guardian is coming." He sank back onto the pallet and fell into a deep sleep.

The curtain over Nomed's entryway rustled open. Dom peered at him from spectacle-enlarged eyes. "How is he?"

"He's just fallen asleep. Is that a good sign?"

The old man smoothed his vest and shrugged. "His fever must've broken, Seyes. You need a break. I'll stay."

Nomed stretched and came to standing. "Call me if you see any change." He crossed to the alcove entrance, paused, and looked at the old man. "I almost killed him, Dom. What was I thinking?" Without waiting for an answer, he stepped into the cavern, leaving only the swish of the curtain to fill the silence behind him.

Almiralyn gazed from her sanctuary window. She had sent Karrew to do a quick patrol of her acreage. Now, she watched his fast return with a touch of foreboding.

He swooped through the window and landed on Elcaro's rim. "Trouble comes." He puffed up his neck feathers. "Pentharian fly this way."

Merrilea and Sparrow left the bench where they were discussing the kestrel's potential fate at Nomed's hand and joined her by the fountain. On the surface, the muted silhouettes of four Pentharian vultures flew through the ever-thickening mist.

Almiralyn tugged at a tendril of blonde hair. "I wonder how the two we imprisoned escaped from Nemttachenn? How soon will they be here, Karrew?"

"Too soon." He flew into the hall and down the stairwell.

She, Merrilea, and Sparrow hurried after him through the kitchen and onto the porch.

Merrilea placed a hand on her arm. "You can't go out there, Almiralyn."

"Hiding will serve no purpose. If their goal is to kill us, they must move through me to get to you. Stay on the porch." She continued down the steps and into the garden.

Majeska joined her, eyes gleaming and tail slapping the ground. Karrew perched on her shoulder. The vultures cleared the forest and swooped over the barn. They landed in a line, shifted to Pentharian, and knelt, heads bowed. Their magnificent braids, the jewel-colored scales on their powerful lizard legs and Reptilian tails, and the exotic tattoos on their humanoid upper bodies made an astonishing and strangely beautiful picture in the back garden.

Almiralyn bowed her head in response. "Please rise."

In unison, the Pentharian came to their feet. Their leader, sapphire blue and taller than his companions, stepped forward. "I am Voer of the Clan Aves." Unwavering Pentharian eyes gazed into hers. "We come to serve you, Guardian of Myrrh. This land has filled our hearts, and we can no longer condone its destruction. We offer our loyalty and our fighting prowess to aid you."

She looked from Voer to his comrades before stepping apart to confer with Karrew. The aliens had felt the sharpness of his beak and honored his power. Two would not soon forget how one strand of her hair had kept them prisoner in small blackbird bodies. "I believe them, Karrew. What are your thoughts?"

He cocked his head. "My instincts tell they will be true to their word."

Almiralyn returned to the waiting Pentharian and acknowledged their offer. "I accept your help and your fealty."

The Pentharian leader's facial features took on the vulturian attributes of his birth clan as he placed a fisted hand on his chest and repeated the pledge made in Nemttachenn Tower. "I, Voer, promise by the oath I took as a warrior of ReTaw Au Qa to serve the Lady Almiralyn and the well-being of Myrrh." Stee, Jeet, and Yuin followed his example.

When they finished, and their features had returned to their more human appearance, she smiled. "I am honored to welcome you into my service and into my home. Will you join us in the cottage? I would know what you know and what you believe will bring this situation to a positive conclusion." She crossed to the back porch where Merrilea and Sparrow waited, wonder in their eyes.

Merrilea led the way to the kitchen. Sparrow put the kettle on and then turned to the Pentharian, who now flooded Mira's gray-blue kitchen with their rich colors. "I don't suppose you drink tea, do you?"

"We will try this tea." Voer bowed with courtly grace.

Almiralyn smiled as she looked around the room at four Pentharian, one raven, one gray cat, and two Human women. *Times are wondrous. Times are very wondrous indeed.*

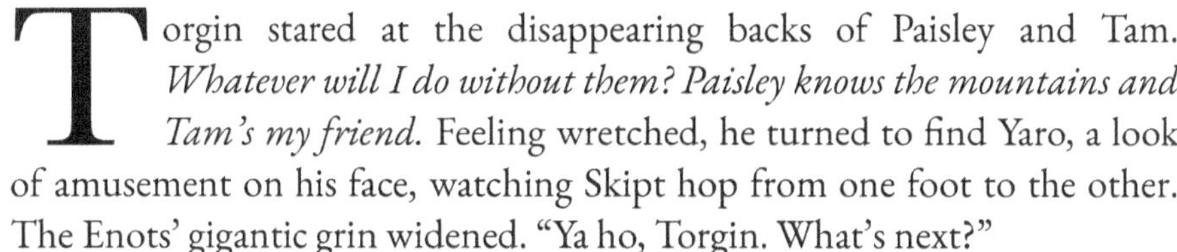

49

Torgin stared at the disappearing backs of Paisley and Tam. *Whatever will I do without them? Paisley knows the mountains and Tam's my friend.* Feeling wretched, he turned to find Yaro, a look of amusement on his face, watching Skipt hop from one foot to the other. The Enots' gigantic grin widened. "Ya ho, Torgin. What's next?"

He shrugged and nibbled his bottom lip. "I want to find my friends, but I'm not sure how." The Pentharian's understanding expression bolstered his courage. "What do you think, Yaro?"

"I suggest we journey to the City of Meos to seek the help of those who know the Dojanack Caverns."

A rush of relief erased Torgin's despondency. "That makes good sense."

Skipt bowed. "I lead the way. I lead the way. We close to the entrance that takes us there." He bounced up a narrow, steep trail that wound into scattered trees and rocky cliffs.

Yaro hiked after him, his golden scales glinting in the sunlight and his lizard tail twitching. Torgin trudged along behind, his wary gaze tracking the Enots. Skipt's love for this adventure made it easier for him to manage his own mixed emotions. *Yaro's presence helps, too.* He heaved a sigh and frowned. *I want to find the twins and Esán but...* An exposed root sent him tripping up the trail. *I miss my life in Idronatti.* He stumbled again, set his jaw, and kept climbing. *I hate never knowing what will happen next.*

He glanced ahead as Yaro disappeared after Skipt around a sharp bend. Forcing his tired legs to move faster, he pushed to catch up, jumped over a slight break in the trail, and dodged a low-hanging branch. An abrupt halt left him balanced on the edge of a cliff. The sheer drop to the foothills below turned his world into a spinning top. Vertigo squeezed his throat shut around a sudden wave of nausea. His knees went weak.

Yaro's hand on his shoulder steadied him enough to step away from the edge. He swallowed and gave the tall Pentharian a shaky smile. "Th-Thanks."

"Perhaps you should pay closer attention, young Torgin. I would not want to lose my new brother." The Pentharian's strange eyes held his for a moment before he resumed his climb.

Torgin gripped the drooping branch of a tree, fought to settle his stomach, and to slow the hammering of his heart.

Skipt's animated face peered at him. "Ya ho, you fine?"

An affirming nod sent the Enots jogging up the trail after Yaro.

Torgin inhaled a steadying breath, released the branch, and scrambled to follow. *By the Fathers, whatever made me disobey PPP rules and come to Myrrh with the twins?* A disconcerting image of the cliff edge left his stomach flip-flopping. *If Yaro had not been there—*

As the trail made a sharp bend beneath a granite overhang, Yaro paused and scanned the mountainside. "Let's take a brief rest."

Torgin leaned against the hard stone and snuck a peek at the exotic creature beside him. *How bizarre is this adventure? No one will ever believe I have met a creature from another planet. I cannot believe it myself, and Yaro is standing right here.* He forced his thoughts to focus on their goal. "Skipt, how much further until we enter the caverns?"

Skipt pointed a stony finger. "See big rock with the hollowed side?"

High above them on the switchback trail, a huge rock balanced on the trail's edge. Torgin gasped and stared.

The Pentharian appeared to assess the distance. "It will be swifter if I shift and you ride on my back." He melted into a sleek black panther.

Torgin shuddered. The memory of Buster lying in blood-soaked grass almost choked him. *I know Yaro is a shape shifter but...* He swallowed. *I did not expect a panther.*

Skipt, as usual, expressed his delight with a quick jig before darting to the panther's side. His long fingers grasping handfuls of the sleek fur, he clambered onto its muscular back and grinned.

Torgin fought a momentary inclination to walk back down the mountain in search of Tam and Paisley. Then panther eyes locked onto his. Yaro's wisdom and strength gleamed in their golden depths. His courage returning, Torgin climbed on behind Skipt, squeezed his knees into the panther's sides, and slid his fingers into its thick fur. With the smoothness of the RiaTrain in Idronatti, the huge cat sprung forward. Powerful muscles flexed in its back as it leapt with uncanny ease from one rock formation to the next, carrying them up the mountainside. A sense of freedom allowed Torgin to forget his fear and to relish the ride until, with one last leap, they stopped beside the hollowed section of the massive stone.

The Enots hopped down onto a large boulder. "Ya ho! What a great ride!"

Torgin slid to the ground and watched Yaro materialize.

Skipt scanned the Pentharian's impressive height. "Yaro too big for cavern entrance." He giggled.

Yaro's expression grew serious. "I cannot communicate with you in animal form, but I will change if the need arises." One moment he was there in front of them and the next a small brown ferret sat at their feet.

Torgin shook his head.

Skipt clapped his hands. "Perfect. Now follow."

The Enots slid behind the rock and disappeared through a narrow crevice about Torgin's height. Inside, dim light outlined rocks heaped next to a tunnel, slanting steeply downward. Skipt grinned. "This way to Meos."

Torgin trudged after him, his newfound courage leaking away one step at a time. A small paw scratched at his pant leg. He glanced down at the ferret, grateful for its presence. His fear lessened as he picked it up and placed it on his shoulder. The creature's soft warmth against his neck abolished what remained. With a sigh of relief, he felt his courage creeping back.

Skipt paused at the top of an incline. "We rest soon. I know cave. We be there in little time."

Torgin trudged after the energetic Enots, fatigue nudging him to stop and rest. With stubborn determination, he continued to put one foot in front of the other.

Skipt dodged from sight. His hollow cry wafted up the tunnel. "You come, Torgin?"

The next instant, cool air ushered him into an open area where a shaft of dim light from high overhead cast a glow across the sandy floor. Gurgling water drew him to the side of a pool where a spring bubbled up through a pile of stones. Thirst tickled his dry throat. He knelt, cupped his hands and drank deeply. Wiping his mouth with the back of his hand, he looked for the Enots. "Skipt, where are you?"

Torgin's brow furrowed, then smoothed as the ferret arched its back in a catlike stretch, jumped down beside the pool, and drank. Nose twitching, it sat back on its haunches and cleaned its face with a tiny paw. The next instant, Yaro materialized.

Torgin's hand flew to his mouth.

The Pentharian tilted his head. "I surprised you?"

"I-I just..." He shrugged.

Skipt danced out of the darkness. "Ya ho. The night will soon take the light. Let us eat and prepare to rest."

Torgin set One Man's flute to one side and rummaged in his pack. He found a handful of nuts and one last chunk of bread. Skipt added a sandwich to the scanty supply of food. Dividing everything into three piles, Torgin offered Skipt and Yaro their share.

After a quiet meal and another deep drink from the spring, he spread his sleeping mat on the sandy floor. With his backpack tucked under his head, he curled up on his side. Yaro shifted to panther and stretched his warm body around the curve of Torgin's back. Skipt snuggled up next to his belly.

Torgin listened to Yaro's deep, even breathing and Skipt's tiny snores. *I'm sleeping with a panther and a boy made of stones.* He yawned. *Maybe this is all a dream.*

Above him, the shaft of light faded, leaving the cave in darkness. The last thing he remembered before sleep wrapped him in its comfortable silence was the sound of water trickling through small stones in the spring.

Allynae and Jordett plodded through the foothills into the mountains proper. The sound of a muffled voice up the trail sent them creeping into a dense cluster of trees.

"Da Blast! That hurts! Wish I had some of that creature's venom. Whoa, Tam. I gotta rest."

Recognition of the gruff voice edged with pain nudged Allynae from the trees. Signaling Jordett to follow, he resumed the trek up the narrow trail, rounded a corner, and halted. Not far ahead, Paisley, a distressed scowl on his shiny black face, sat astride Tam. At the pony's head, a man Allynae did not recognize stood ready to help his companion dismount.

"Well, I'll be." Paisley welcomed him crooked grin. "Just the man I wanted to find." He rested a hand on the stranger's shoulder. "Allynae, this is the Hermit of Timreh Pass. One Man, this is Allynae, Almiralyn's brother."

Allynae stepped closer and offered a hand. "It's a pleasure to make your acquaintance. Mira is eager to see you, One Man."

The hermit smiled. "I desire to speak with her as well." His questioning gaze flicked to Jordett.

Allynae motioned him forward. "This is Jordett." He waited for the two men to shake hands before smiling up at his friend. "Jordy, this is Paisley."

"Howdy." Paisley's grin turned to a grimace of pain.

Allynae scrutinized his friend's face. "You've hurt your foot. What happened?"

"Help me off this pony so I can rest a bit, and I'll tell ya." Paisley clenched his teeth, inhaled, and blew out a hissed breath.

Soon, the big man sat on a stump with his injured ankle resting on a fallen tree.

Allynae settled near him. "Tell us what happened to you and where Torgin is."

"I was just darn clumsy." Paisley gave him a wry smile.

One Man listened to Paisley and Allynae exchange stories, glad that he had left his mountain home. Mira needed him, and he needed her to help him understand the unusual happenings in this land he had adopted as his home. A lull in the conversation gave him an opening to speak. "Why are the Pentharian in Myrrh? And who is this Seyes Nomed?"

Allynae told him the little he had learned about the DiMensioner. "He's made it clear his goal is to destroy Myrrh. If he succeeds, he'll also destroy Idronatti and Thera. The ripple effect could be unending."

While the men sat in silence, pursuing their own thoughts, One Man unobtrusively studied his new companions. He liked them all, but felt a particular kinship to Almiralyn's brother.

Allynae interrupted his ramblings. "Do you have any ideas about what we need to do next, One Man?"

The hermit pulled his braid over his shoulder and let his fingers travel its woven length. "I need to find Mira. Although my role is unclear, it is important for me to be in your company. The young people are beyond our reach in the caverns of the Dojanacks. Looking for them feels like a waste of precious time. Perhaps rallying our forces to stop Nomed before it is too late would be the most prudent. So, do we use this as our staging ground and put our heads together here, or join forces with Mira at the cottage?"

"We are almost three turnings from her as the crow flies." Allynae frowned.

One Man patted the ground. "Isn't there an Intersect transport system beneath this planet?"

Paisley nodded. "Ya, but few know it exists, and fewer can locate the entrances." He moved his swollen ankle and cringed. "I'm not goin' to be any help with this foot."

One Man unwrapped the injured ankle, uncorked a small brown bottle, and applied a clear, somewhat sticky liquid to the swelling.

"What's that?" The pain dropped from Paisley's face. "Looks like Yaro's venom."

"Yaro predicted you would need more. So he filled this before we started down the mountain." He tucked the bottle back in his pack.

Paisley rubbed his chin and twirled his mustache around one finger.

"Strange things are happenin' all around us." He stood up, put weight on his foot, and shook his head. "Less painful, but…"

Jordett stood up. "I suggest we return to where Alli and I camped last night. It's not far. We can make a meal, let Paisley rest a bit, and then decide about our next move."

"Sounds like a good plan." One Man moved to assist Paisley onto Tam's back.

Trees cast dark shadows over the trail as they made their way down the mountain. By the time they reached their destination, the sun had set and the coolness of evening chilled the air. Jordett gathered wood and built a small fire. One Man helped Allynae settle Paisley against the overhang and then disappeared into the woods. Within a short time, he returned, bearing gifts. Soon, the smell of roasting red marrow roots filled the air; the mist seemed less dense and the air less damp. The men relaxed, letting conversation and good food ease their weariness, anxiety, and pain.

50

Esán's nightmares—huge blazing eyes boring into his mind and fiery wings wrapping his body in a cocoon of heat and smoke—ceased while his body healed during sleep. When he awoke, he felt stronger and hungrier than he had in turnings. Dom sat at the foot of the pallet, his whiskery cheek resting on his bent knees. Occasional small snores whispered around the cave.

Esán slipped off the pallet and tiptoed to the alcove entrance. Peeking around the curtain, he found no sign of Seyes Nomed and stepped into the main cavern. A morbid fascination with the fire held him captive. Eyes glued to tiny flames dancing along the ember-encrusted edges of half-burnt wood, he remembered. The fiery desert creature rose as though it were rising from Nomed's fire and pitched him back to the desert on the planet of DerTah.

Fiery breath scorched his prone body. Blistering heat seared the air in his lungs. He knew he was about to die.

"Esán!" An urgent voice flooded his mind. "Shift!"

The sudden change to kestrel left him momentarily stunned.

"Fly, Esán! Fly!"

Lifting into the parched air, he flew over the red desert to the gaping mouth of the spinning vortex, and shot down the long, swirling tunnel, his kestrel body almost too frail to survive.

The fire hissed and crackled. He blinked. The spell broke. He stood in Oche Cavern, remembering Dom's voice. *The old man saved me.* The flames in the pit flared brighter. *Fire almost killed me.*

Hunger rumbled a welcome distraction. He rifled through a box of food, ate berries and dried biscuits, and washed them down with icy mountain water.

No longer distracted by hunger, he considered his options. Leaving Oche Cavern before Nomed returned topped the list. The Evolsefil Crystal's safety came next. He paced to the shore of the cavern lake. *What's the fastest way to reach the Cave of Canedari?* He stared at the water and laughed. *Of course...*

His kestrel form embraced him. He retraced the path he and Zugo had traveled. The crystal tunnel tingled with the recent passage of the DiMensioner. Esán glided between quartz walls until he came to rest in a small hollow in Rorret Cavern. Keen kestrel eyesight picked Nomed from the darkness.

Nomed paced back and forth along the water's edge several times before he paused and addressed the lake. "I must return to the Evolsefil Crystal. If I can accomplish the task without Esán, I will—but if I cannot, I will force him to help. Don't make me use his skills. Take me to the Cave of Canedari."

No matter what Nomed said or did, the mirror-black surface of the lake remained unruffled. Esán watched as anger drove his mentor into his shifted form. On silent owl wings, he flew a wide arc, then hovered. When nothing suggested the lake was more than water entrapped within a mountain cavern, he circled one last time and shot up the crystal tunnel.

Esán let out a breath and shifted to his Human form. If nothing else positive had come of his visit to DerTah, at least he had discovered how to return to his own body. He knelt at the edge of the lake and placed his hand on its surface. "Mighty Rorret, Evolsefil has accepted me into its service. I must return to the Cave of Canedari. Please come to my aid."

He waited, knowing he could not rush the lake. Time passed. If it did not respond, he would find Evolsefil on his own. *Time.* He shivered. *Time is such a non-thing and yet so important.*

The Lake of Rorret observed the boy, recognized his destiny, and knew he carried the life of the land. Cool tentacles surrounded him, eased him below the water's surface and pulled him deeper and deeper until he began to fight against his need to take a breath. With one last push, Rorret released him into the Cave of Canedari.

Fen could not keep from staring at Sitrio, the DeoNyte sent to escort him to Ari in the Dojanack Caverns. Almiralyn had convinced his mother to let him go. Now standing with his guide on the Intersect platform, he realized no Wood Tiff had been where he was going. Together, he and the strange furry creature repeated the words that sent them flying across the star-sprinkled night beneath Myrrh.

Three connects later, they arrived at the bottom of a stone stairway. His insides quaked at the thought of what awaited him, but he followed his heart. When Ari had disappeared into the grasslands, he knew he should go with her. Sitrio's arrival at his TreeOm scared and excited him. After learning the DeoNyte had never left the mountain caverns, Fen set fear aside and followed him to the first connection point.

Now he moved up the long, steep stairway in Sitrio's wake. By the time they reached the top, his short legs ached. The DeoNyte pulled a small lever. An opening appeared. Fen hesitated, grasped Sitrio's offered hand, and walked beside him down the long, stone passageway.

Total lack of light terrified him. The heavy burden of stone and earth over his head weighted his small body. His lungs forgot how to fill with air.

Sitrio knelt next to him. "I won't leave you, Fen. You're safe. Before long, your eyes will adjust. Come. Ari is waiting."

At the sound of Ari's name, Fen found he could breathe again. He squeezed the DeoNyte's hand. "Thank you, Sitrio."

They turned into a tunnel where soft light evaporated the darkness, and with it Fen's apprehension. Next to him, Sitrio seemed to control a need to hurry and matched his pace to Fen's shorter legs. Soon, the tunnel opened into the Meosian central square. DeoNytes of every size stared at him from huge, pale eyes. He smiled and stared back, hurrying to keep up with his guide.

Sitrio paused by a draped opening and rang a small bell. Ari pulled the curtain aside, her face wrinkled with concentrated effort. "Hello, I..."

Fen removed his hat and introduced himself. "I'm Fen, Ari, and I am so glad to be here."

She broke into a relieved smile. "Of course. Owae told me you were coming. I am so happy to see you. Come in."

In the living space, Ari sank down on a brightly colored cushion. "Join me, Fen. Are you hungry? This is Owae. She makes great soup. And this is the DeoNyte ReDael, Yookotay."

Fen made a shy bow to Yookotay and accepted a steaming bowl from the elderly Owae. Seated beside Ari, he sipped soup and listened, aware his adventure had only just begun.

Zugo observed the Wood Tiff from the archway. He had learned of them in Myrrhinian Folklore, but never expected to meet one. Fen's brown eyes reflecting the firelight and his small belly jiggling when he laughed at Sitrio's teasing.

"I fear not the dark, but only the earth piled on top of me. I am of the treetops, Sitrio. My only experience below ground is in the Intersect, where the vastness stretches below me. I'm not *buried*." He handed Owae his empty bowl.

Ari caught Zugo's eye and smiled. "Zugo, this is Fen. Now I have two friends I can remember."

Fen stood up and bowed. "It is my honor to meet you, Zugo."

Zugo bowed his head. "Welcome to Meos. Your visit to our halls honors us."

Yookotay pointed at the large cushion on the floor next to him and waited until he had settled. "Now that we're all here, let's begin to plan for your journey. I would like to go with you, but I must remain in Meos. More visitors have entered the caverns. I must await their arrival here."

Zugo turned to his father. "Where do you suggest we look for Ari's memories?"

"Two Crystal Keepers spotted Giests in the Cavern of Tennisca. I believe that is a good place to begin."

"Giests in the Cavern of Ancients? Strange times, indeed." Owae's eyes showed her alarm.

"I can lead Ari and Fen to the cavern." Zugo frowned. "But how will we know which Giest stole her memories?"

"Time will tell all." The healer's voice rang with the tenor of prophecy. "We cannot know what we do not know. You must trust the Ancient Ones within Tennisca to guide you."

Yookotay nodded. "Fen and Ari, you must walk the Stairway of Retu Erath. It will lead you to your destinies. We hope the return of Ari's memories will be part of hers."

The redheaded twin touched the knife at her side. Fen's eyes followed her movement and returned to her face. "We'll find your memories and your sister."

"And Esán." Zugo stood. *And Esán.*

Darkness more mysterious than a moonless night engulfed Brie. Each cautious step down the Stairway of Retu Erath carried her deeper into the abyss of her own fear. Terror clawed at her fast-fading calm. Panic unraveled her connection to Myrrh, destroying the sense of oneness she depended upon. Like the chaos of boiling water, her dread of the dark erased her ability to think and brought her to a standstill. A powerful storm of emotion squeezed her chest tighter. The air in her lungs, exiting in short, hissing spurts, forced her to sit. Tears streamed down her cheeks. Clutching the Remembering Stone in trembling hands, she followed her fear back to *that fateful* turning when she was barely three sun cycles.

Ari covered her eyes. Brie scrambled to find a hiding place, one her twin would not guess. The hall closet provided the perfect spot. She closed the door, dropped to her knees, and crawled to the back. Long garments brushed her hair over her eyes. Swish. Plop. Heavy folds smothered her. More clothing buried her beneath its weight. Fighting to free herself, she kicked and twisted until fright's fatigue left her motionless. Oppressive silence suffocated her, imprisoning her in nightmarish horror.

Her mother and Ari had found her, huddled under uniforms and heavy coats, tearless and mute. Brie had refused to speak about the incident. Now her tears flowed like a river, dripped from the curve of her chin, and fell into the vastness beneath her.

Sobs shook her body. Her heart ached for the touch of her sister's hand, for the sound of her voice, for her strength. She yearned to see her mother's loving smile and to hear Torgin's laughter. "And what of Esán? Where are you? Have I failed you?" A gulped breath ended in a whimper.

In the cavern-dark stillness, she regained her calm, tucked the blue pouch away, and brushed the tears from her cheeks. Fear, her shadow for so long, had faded. Filled with a sense of gratitude, she continued down the Stairway of Retu Erath.

At first, she failed to notice the subtle change traversing the Cavern of Tennisca. A warning tremor raised the hair on her neck. Uneasiness nudged her from gratitude to alarm as an immense shadowed creature emerged from the depths of the ever-night sky in a whirlpool of bloodthirsty anger. Giests formed a cyclone of color around it, their putrid stench permeating the air. Hideous laughter ricocheted off the cavern walls as the Stairway of Retu Erath quaked into motion.

Brie pitched forward, caught herself, and stumbled to sitting. White-knuckled hands gripped the step. Frigid breath formed a cloud around her. Clammy, unyielding, and evil, the cloak of the death shadow enshrouded her.

Wodash's triumphant shriek filled the cavern as coppery curls turned to gray, rosy skin blanched, and bright eyes dulled into a listless, blank stare. The girl's teardrops crystallized and fell into unending space like snowflakes falling to their death. He threw back his head and snorted a childish laugh, a sound so unaccustomed he stopped, listened, and then howled with delight. Fueled by the fierceness of hatred, he carried her across the cavern and dumped her on the ground in a cramped cave in the opposite wall.

Triumph welled up into a delight-filled chortle. "I have returned." Newfound power rolled through him. "I snatched my body from the hungry immensity of space. Piece by piece, I reassembled it and reclaimed my scattered psyche. I am whole and more powerful than ever before."

A Giest shooting by brought an evil gleam to his eyes. "And I command an army, Seyes Nomed." He gazed at the frost-coated twin. "When you arrive, I, Wodash od DerTah, will have *my* revenge."

Brie leaned against the rough stone of the cave, her frozen fingers gripping the blue pouch. A small spark of remembering ignited in her numbed mind. *I am Brie. I am Brie. My spirit belongs to me.* The death shadow's hold tightened, but in her heart a small golden flame remained, warm and alive.

51

At the Guardian's cottage, Sparrow and Merrilea watched Almiralyn and Karrew prepare to take flight with four Pentharian vultures, their goal to rescue the twins and Esán. Wind generated by the flurry of departing birds of prey whipped Sparrow's chestnut hair around her head and flattened the flowers in the back garden. Beside her, Merrilea clutched her blonde hair in one hand and shaded her eyes with the other. Karrew and Almiralyn's white and gold bird took the lead, as the formidable group soared over the Terces Wood.

Sparrow smoothed her hair. "I understand your desire to go with them." She slid an arm around her friend's waist. "I'm sorry you had to stay behind."

"It's okay. I know I would have been in the way." Merrilea tucked wisps of wing-blown hair away from her face. "At least I can help you."

SparrowLyn glanced at Majeska, sitting primly beside her. "You wanted to go, too, didn't you? We all did. Since they've abandoned us, let's make the best of it. I have a new painting flooding my mind. Come on."

In the studio, the painting of Esán surrounded by flames still sat on the easel, its message both confounding and frightening.

Merrilea winced. "I hope he's alright." She lifted it down and leaned it against the wall.

"Esán will be fine. My heart tells me it is so." Sparrow placed a clean canvas on the easel. "I need to paint. Make yourself comfortable."

Creative energy enticed her attention away from her friend and carried her to that place where nothing mattered but painting. The blank surface inspired her artistic passion. She prepared her palette of colors, selected a brush, and waited, poised to begin. Unaware of Merrilea, Majeska, or the studio, she applied a gray wash to the background, erasing white as she went. Vague pictures poured into her mind. Her brush flashed from the palette to the canvas, transforming the images into colors and shapes, highlights and shadows.

High above the Terces Woods, Almiralyn and her warriors pressed forward through the damp, clinging fog. Their first mission—to find Allynae and his companions.

In her bird form, she rode on Voer's vulture back, conserving her fragile strength. Her land shrinking away in the gray mist sent a stab of pain through her chest. The slow ebbing of her power urged her to conserve her remaining energy for the battle to come. Aware of the strength in the creature that carried her, she was grateful—grateful the beauty of Old Earth had changed the Pentharian from enemy to friend and for their support and their speed. Already they were at the grasslands, a trip which by land would have taken much longer.

Karrew flew in the company of Pentharian vultures for the first time. As he matched wing stroke to wing stroke, he reminded himself these creatures of death were kin. Occasionally, he took the lead, but more often he flew by the side of his mistress, where she clung to Voer, her white and gold feathers gleaming against the black of his broad back.

Memories of his first turning at her side warmed him. Only four chron-circles old, she had lain wrapped in a soft cream blanket, the KcernFensian sun kissing her pink cheeks. His love for her had been instantaneous. His heartbeat quickened. *I, Karrew, Raven of KcernFensia, will serve my mistress until I breathe my last breath.*

Voer hardly noticed the weight of the white bird. Honored to bear Myrrh's Guardian into battle and to fight by her side, he marveled at the clarity of her thoughts and the thoroughness of her strategy. To his surprise, he liked and respected her. He wondered, as they flew to reunite her with her brother and friends, how they would receive him and his fellow Pentharian. His broad wings pushed against the gray mist. *Almiralyn will pave the way.*

Chilled to his core, Voer realized his passenger must be even colder. Banking left, he dropped through the vapor-burdened sky, his comrades following in tight formation. Karrew confirmed the Terces Woods ended a short distance ahead and the vastness of the grassy prairie would soon open before them. Everyone required warmth and rest. Voer increased his speed and, soon, set his passenger down amongst the tall trees bordering the Grasslands.

Almiralyn shifted, stretched her long limbs, and shivered. She needed to warm up, and quickly. The Pentharian gathered wood. Soon, a fire spit orange and gold sparks into the air. She moved closer, grateful for the heat seeping into her body and the sensation returning to her chilled extremities. Across the pit, Karrew flapped his wings and fanned the fire to send more heat her way.

"I'm much better." She rubbed her hands up and down her arms. "It feels like winter instead of late summer. I can even sense snow in the air."

Stee snorted. "Snow? What is this snow?"

"Frozen water that falls in soft flakes and covers everything with white." She shivered. "You would never find snow on ReTaw Au Qa."

Yuin muttered under his breath and shifted to panther, his golden eyes made brighter by the fire's light.

Jeet laughed. "He needs a fur coat to keep the cold at bay. How long do we rest?"

Almiralyn moved closer to the flickering flames. "When we are well-warmed, we'll leave. I want to make the foothills by dusk." She stared at the glowing embers and thought of the Fire ConDra on DerTah and Esán. *Thank goodness the boy had learned to shape shift; otherwise, I could not have saved him.* She scanned the mountain-lined horizon. *Where are you, Esán; and where are your friends?*

Karrew landed next to her. "We must go. With every chron-click, the mist thickens and Myrrh shrinks within it."

Almiralyn rose and stood beside the fire. Her hair, woven into a single braid, gleamed with the luster of polished moonstone. She wore lightweight armor, which fit her form like a silver glove. Orange and yellow flames brought a glow to her skin and a light to her eyes. The Guardian of Myrrh was beautiful and stern and compelling. He watched the Pentharian stand, hands pressed to their hearts, and bow their heads.

All made ready for flight. Jeet snuffed out the fire and covered its remains with dirt. Yuin and Stee shifted.

"Will you ride on my back, Almiralyn?" Voer's respect rang clear in his throaty voice.

Myrrh's Guardian smiled but shook her head. "This time I must lead."

In a flash of golden light, she shaped the white bird and took to the air, vultures in a V formation behind her.

Karrew joined his mistress. At her side, he was complete. Together, they led the way over the grasslands.

"Dom, where on DerTah is Esán? I can't believe he's disappeared yet again." The DiMensioner paced in front of him. "Where were you?" He stopped, his scowl deepening.

Dom stood, hands behind his back, staring at the fire while the Seyes Nomed thrust his anger, like a well-honed sword, into the echoing cavern. When at last the rage dissipated and the scar on his cheek faded to a thin white line, Dom gathered his courage to speak.

"Anger clouds your thinking, Seyes. He's a boy. Where would you go if you were Esán?"

Nomed appeared to ignore the question and launched into a soliloquy. "How have I become so alone in this battle? Where are Wodash and the Pentharian? Where are the children? And if I were Esán—" He shot his old friend a fierce look. "*Evolsefil!* That is where I would go."

The great horned owl swooped from the cavern. With a sigh of relief, Dom lowered his aching body onto a log by the fire. One of these turnings, Nomed's temper would get the best of him. Dom hoped he would not be present when it did.

Nomed flew through the crystal tunnel and over the Lake of Rorret, found the knotted rope, and followed it to the tunnel leading to the Cavern of Tennisca. His battle with the Ancient Ones remained fresh in his mind. He preferred not to return to that hideous place. His dual goals— acquire the crystal and find Wodash—gave him no choice. The cavern was his only way of accomplishing both tasks.

At the concealed door to Tennisca, he shifted. *I cannot lose my temper. I will stay calm and keep my sights focused on the crystal.* Determination squaring his shoulders, he opened the door and stepped onto the landing.

Indecisión held him motionless. A walk down the Stairway of Retu Erath would be folly. But in his owl form, he could not access his magic. He would be powerless. Shoving his ambivalence aside, he prepared to shift. *I can land on a ledge if it becomes necessary.*

An intense hush accompanied his flight to the Cave of Canedari. No Ancient Ones appeared to challenge him. Nothing moved—not the stairway—not the air he breathed. Only the owl's rhythmic heartbeat told him he lived.

As he approached the double purple doors, something nagged. He attuned his owl ears to the stillness that was not as it seemed. Grateful for the silent flight of his shifted form and for its keen night vision, he flew a wide circle.

On one side of the cavern, clustered balls of light—orange, purple, yellow, and green—emitted a soft glow and the aroma of rotting flesh. Silent wings carried him toward them.

High-pitched squeals blistered his sensitive ears and sent him swooping lower. A spectre-like cloud exploded from their midst. Nomed dropped, changed course, and shot toward the far side of the cavern. The cloud pursued him hard—much too close for comfort.

A ledge jutting from the cavern wall caught his attention. With two strong downward thrusts of his wings, he landed in Human form. Lightning shot from his fingertips. The darkness ripping in two left jagged edges aglow, and the death shadow illuminated.

Casting a lasso of silver light around his henchman's neck, Nomed pulled it taut. A mental probe told him everything he required about the death shadow's plans for revenge and his army of Giests.

Nomed smiled a crooked smile at the confused and frightened spheres of protoplasm gathering near their trapped leader. His voice, sharp with authority, rang out. "Disperse or I will end his existence and yours!"

Like popcorn dancing in a hot pan, the Giests scattered, leaving trails of blurred color behind them.

His continued dissection of the death shadow's mind showed him a secret Wodash fought to keep hidden. He gave the lasso a sharp tug. The death shadow yelped and went as limp as a wet sheet. A final quick probe brought a smile of success to Nomed's face.

"So, Wodash od DerTah, you have one of Allynae's daughters."

He reeled in his prey until he floated in front of him. A dark eyebrow ascended into an exaggerated arch. Wodash cowered and lowered his eyes.

Nomed fixed a withering gaze on his captive. "Until I decide otherwise, you are mine and you will do my bidding. Do you understand?"

Wodash gave a diminutive nod.

Nomed pulled him onto the ledge. "I will end your existence

immediately, Wodash od DerTah, or we can come to an agreement beneficial to both of us. Which is it to be?"

The death shadow grimaced and knelt, head bowed. "I am yours to command, DiMensioner. There will be no more treachery."

A quick probe assured Nomed his minion was under control. He waved a hand. The lasso vanished. "Take me to Allynae's daughter. And be quick about it."

They flew unchallenged across the vast space to a small cave where a band of Giests hovered around a pale, motionless figure.

Nomed shifted to his Human shape and addressed the cowering creatures. "Your commander tells me you are excellent warriors. I will not harm you if you do my bidding."

The Giests' whined chorus echoed through the cavern. "What's in it for us?"

Nomed's eyes narrowed. "Your existence will continue uninterrupted."

"We want revenge." They countered in singsong voices. "Give us revenge."

"You will have your revenge." He hid his lie with a smile. "Stand guard at the top of the stairs. I'll summon you when you're needed."

Delighted to be rid of them, he focused his attention on Almiralyn's niece. A glowing blue orb sprang to life on his palm. "So we meet again. Which one are you?"

She lowered her eyes and sat, small and vulnerable, the blue light making her skin appear deathly cold.

"It doesn't matter, does it? You're here, and here you'll stay." He turned to the death shadow. "Guard her well, Wodash, and you may even earn your freedom. Now, I have much to accomplish." Shifting, he swooped on silent owl wings toward the double purple doors and the Cave of Canedari.

52

Ari excused herself from the fireside discussion in Owae's living space. She needed time to think. Her mind, half empty of memories, made her uneasy.

Who am I? She sat on her sleeping ledge. *A twin? Somewhere out there I have a sister who looks like me, but she remembers her life.* With a sigh, she stretched out and stared at the ceiling. *I have a mother. And I can vaguely recall who came with me to Myrrh.* One hand moved to the Efillaeh's hilt. Almiralyn's memory made her feel safe.

She sat up and covered her face with her hands. Despair welled up in her throat. Self-pity brought tears to her eyes. Something inside her snapped. She wiped her nose and dried her tears. "This will not get the best of me."

A growing sense of conviction propelled her across the cave to a small mirror. Her reflection stared back at her. "Whether I have memories or not doesn't change who I am. I'm still Ari. I'm still a twin. I have a mother and friends." Her brow wrinkled in concentration. "Maybe the past doesn't matter. It is, after all, the *past*."

She kissed her fingertips and pressed them to the mirror. Feeling less alone, she turned to find Owae watching her from the doorway. The DeoNyte's compassionate smile drew her into her arms. Owae's silky white fur pressing against her cheek smelled of cinnamon and sage. She savored the closeness and returned the gentle embrace.

Owae held her at arm's length. "You have all the courage you need, Arienh. Almiralyn entrusted you with Efillaeh. You are a warrior of Myrrh. I trust you with my life. Now, dear one, it's time to pursue your destiny."

Ari gave her a hug. "Thank you, Owae. You are one of my best new memories."

In the main living space, they found Zugo and Fen talking with Yookotay. The warmth and comfort of the healer's cave made her long to stay where she felt safe. But it was time to leave. She joined friends in a circle, with Owae on one side and Yookotay on the other.

The ReDael regarded them, his expression serious. "We send you to meet your destiny. Take care of yourselves and keep one another safe."

Owae offered an ancient warrior's blessing, one unuttered in recent times.

> *"For warriors of Evolsefil, the legacy is strong.*
> *Their duty is to solemnly right what has gone wrong.*
> *Wisdom is their credo. Insight is their gift.*
> *It rests upon their shoulders to mend the widening rift.*
>
> *Fight for right with valor. Hold the standard high.*
> *Fight for right with bravery. Sound the winning cry.*
> *Warriors of Evolsefil, we pledge our hearts to thee.*
> *Return to us victorious, so we may all be free."*

Ari gave Owae a parting hug, bade Yookotay goodbye, and, with Fen at her side, followed Zugo away from the City of Meos through the tunnel that would take them to the Cavern of Tennisca.

Esán rested at the foot of the Evolsefil Crystal for some time before he stood and placed wet, shaking hands on the crystal's gleaming surface. Energy pulsed through him, revitalizing his mind and invigorating his frail body. As his strength returned, an understanding of Evolsefil's importance to Myrrh and to the Inner Universe brought with it horrifying knowledge. If Seyes Nomed were to gain control of the crystal, he would obliterate Myrrh, its host planet, and the Clenaba Rolas System.

Esán stepped back and stared, unseeing. *I have to find a solution.* Sagging under the weight of such enormous responsibility, he shuddered and leaned his forehead against the Prima's faceted quartz face.

A whispered sound and Elae's reflection on Evolsefil's gleaming facet made him turn. Relief filled his smile. Her mismatched eyes smiled back. "Elae, I need your help. We must hide Evolsefil from Seyes Nomed without breaking its connection to Myrrh and Thera. He'll be here soon. Unless we can do something, he will destroy all of us."

Elae looked thoughtful. "Come with me. I know where we might find the information we need."

He walked beside her down the Hall of Priestesses to a silvery door. The immense room, where books lined the walls from floor to ceiling and plush carpets in muted colors covered creamy stone floors, took his breath away. Scattered throughout in cozy alcoves, small tables with comfortable chairs enticed one to sit and enjoy time and words and wonder. A fire in the palatial fireplace at the far end of the room sent its welcoming warmth to greet them.

Elae smiled at his obvious amazement. "It's called the Reading Room, and it contains works from throughout the Inner Universe."

"I've never seen so many manuscripts in one place in my life." He followed her across the luxurious chamber, down a flight of steps to a lower level, and between row after row of glass-encased bookshelves. She stopped at last in front of a case containing a single item. Her small crystal key clicked in the lock. She slid the glass door open and picked up a weathered leather-bound book.

Finding it difficult to control his excitement, Esán followed her to an alcove, where she placed the book on a small table.

"This is *EmitEnil*. It will tell you everything you need to know about the Prima Crystal Evolsefil and how to save it and Myrrh."

His hands shook as he rested them on the book's cover. "Oh my. This is —" Energy playing up and down his spine like a musician's fingers on an air keyboard throbbed through his body. His eyes widened. Blood rushing to his face made his cheeks tingle.

Elae smiled. "It's archaic, Esán, more ancient even than Old Earth. Almiralyn and Yookotay have read only small portions of it. The magic is powerful, but I know you have the talent to unlock its secrets. I'll leave you to concentrate on its content. But remember, you have very little time."

The mystery beneath his hands claimed his attention. Everything around him faded. Nothing mattered except the book. To open it, he must become it. Molecule by molecule, he grew to understand the book's makeup. Cell by cell, he wove its battered cover and many pages into the fabric of his own being.

Strong, soundless owl wings carried Nomed toward his goal. Evolsefil would soon be his. Not only that, he had Almiralyn's niece. With triumph within reach, he swooped down to land in Human form before the double purple doors.

Whispered words and a snap of his fingers swung them open. Light from the majestic crystal flared. Mesmerized, he walked around it, absorbing every aspect of its grandeur. The central spire rose over the height of a Pentharian from an opaque base to absolute crystal clarity at the top of its faceted face. Like sentries protecting their queen, six smaller crystals the size of a small child encircled it, each jutting at an upward angle from the central crystal. The overall effect was one of elegance, majesty, and immeasurable power.

Once again, he coveted it. Although he yearned to stay with the crystal, he pulled his gaze away to look around the cave. *I must find Esán.* In two long strides, he reached the doors into the Hall of Priestesses and threw them open. The energetic essence of Esán's presence still hung in the air. Liquid silver and black swirling around him, he strode down the hall, sending DeoNyte priestesses scurrying away like autumn leaves before the wind.

In the lower level of the library, Elae watched Esán immersed in the Book. Instinct nudged. She left him to continue his task, returned to the Reading Room, and crossed to the door. Easing it ajar, she saw priestesses scattering before a man in a silver-lined cape. Her heartbeat quickened. *Esán's time is running out. The DiMensioner has found his way into Canedari's inner halls.*

She locked the door and hastened to where Esán sat reading the pages of *EmitEnil*. "Seyes Nomed is here."

Esán nodded.

"Esán, he's down the hall. He'll be here shortly."

Again, the boy nodded. He continued to read.

A crash and the sound of splintering wood made her jump. Esán glanced up, frowned, and returned his attention to the open book.

Realizing she must run interference, she scurried down the corridor between the glass cases to a second set of stairs. Head high, she calmly entered the Reading Room from the far side.

At the opposite end, Nomed stood with his back to her. Unbridled power sparked as he pivoted. His scarred face hid anger—age old and violent. Hazel eyes sliced through the distance between them.

"Where is he? Don't lie." He probed her mind.

Startled, she stepped backward. "That is unnecessary." Serenity cloaked her. "He's reading a book."

"Where?" The reply was a snarl cut short.

She pointed to the stairway behind her.

Nomed teleported to her side. His hand gripping her arm made her flinch. "Show me and don't play games, Priestess, or I'll rip your mind to pieces until I discover what I need to know."

With a soft touch, she removed his hand. "This way." Her bearing dignified, she glided past him down the steps and through the lower library. A meditative state encompassed her. Nomed would find nothing in her mind but stillness and serenity.

Captivated by *EmitEnil*, Esán plunged into its contents like a diver into the sea. His goal—information about Evolsefil—forced him to skip sections dealing with the history of Myrrh, the magic of the land, and the special significance of the Dojanack Caverns. An almost imperceptible difference on the edge of a page caught his eye. He rotated the book toward the light. *Nothing.* He moved it back. *There! There it is again. If I can just...* He slid his thumbnail between two pages and applied gentle leverage. "Oh!" Golden pages covered with strange symbols lay open in front of him.

"There's so little time." He squinted. The symbols, like dancers whose choreography had unexpectedly changed, flitted around the page. "Stay calm, Esán. Just focus. Ahhh. There." Everything he needed to know about Evolsefil materialized on the page.

The sound of footsteps warned him of Nomed's approach. *I want nothing more than to devour the information word by word, but...* He shut *EmitEnil* and held it to his chest. *Nomed must never learn of this book. If he does...* His heart constricted. *I have to hide it where he will never find it.*

Nomed pushed Elae aside and rounded the corner opposite the alcove where Esán stood, a battered book clasped against his chest. For one brief moment, he locked eyes with his apprentice. In a flash of light, the boy and the book disappeared.

"No-o-o-o!" His howled denial and fists pounding on the desk rocketed between glass cases.

Blind fury whipped him around to face Elae. Grabbing her arm, he yanked her after him back through the Reading Room to the hall; and launched himself, Elae still in tow, toward the doors into the Cave of Canedari. He shoved her in front of him. "Unlock them."

Elae slid her key into the brass key plate and turned it. Before she could step aside, he yanked the doors from her grasp, exploded through, and pitched her across the room. She landed at Esán's feet, her arms encircling one of Evolsefil's sentinel crystals.

Nomed rushed forward as light exploded, imprisoning him in a tunnel that spun at a dizzying rate. Stretched like taffy in every direction, his body fought not to implode. Ahead of him, Evolsefil flashed from blinding white to pink to purple to cobalt blue, bathing Esán and Elae in rich kaleidoscope colors. Just when he thought the spinning would tear him to shreds, the young people and the Prima Crystal vanished. The tunnel flared brighter and disappeared. He crashed into a wall of black and, as limp as a rag doll, slid onto the stone floor, unconscious.

A shock wave rolled across Myrrh, spilling water from Elcaro's alabaster bowl and sending images in rapid succession over its quivering surface.

Wodash pitched out of the shallow cave in the Cavern of Tennisca with shrieking Giests scattering around him. Brie slid to the edge of the precipice. The icy fingers of the death shadow snatched her back to safety.

Ari, Zugo, and Fen rolled, like ball bearings in a wheel, down the tunnel leading to Retu Erath. In the cave by the small bubbling pool, Torgin came to his feet with Skipt clinging to his leg. Yaro shifted to his true form, golden eyes searching for the cause of his unease. The heaving foothills threw Allynae and his companions to the ground. Tam and Jordett's horse whinnied and pranced—ears back and eyes wild. At Almiralyn's cottage, the floor rolled, sending Merrilea and Sparrow to their knees and an unfinished canvas sailing across the room.

On the planet of Thera, the Central Mountains rose to meet the sky. Henrietta clung to her friend in the small village of SumnerTyme. Quakes shook Idronatti, sending the citizens of its well-ordered society scrambling from tall buildings onto the pristine streets. Their confusion multiplied as they gazed upward, where Myrrh—visible for the first time in Idronatti's history—hung partially shrouded in gray, rolling clouds. Idronattians huddled together, cowering in the shadow of the mythical land the PPP swore did not exist.

High above the grasslands, Almiralyn plummeted from the sky, white wings powerless. Karrew raced after her. Voer swooped low, caught her in free fall, steadied himself, and remained airborne, all his senses alert to the massive change occurring below them.

The fountain's water cleared. Only scattered images remained in the splashed pools on the sanctuary floor.

In Tennisca, Brie crouched in the small cave. Grateful to be alive, she watched Wodash swoop into the vastness of the cavern with his army of Giests in his wake. As the distance between them increased, life energy seeped back into Brie's numbed body and mind.

Swaddled in darkness, she registered a change. Her breathing slowed. She projected her senses across the cavern to the Cave of Canedari. Shock rolled through her. *Evolsefil has vanished.* The distant warmth of its power tingling eased her dismay. Had Seyes Nomed removed the crystal? Her heart said no.

The Star of Truth's tingling brought her attention back to the cave.

One after another, voices whispered in her ear.

"Listen."

"Listen and know."

"Listen, know, and learn."

The three voices whispered, a chorus-like song in her mind. "You are the Daughter of KcernFensia and a gift to this land of Myrrh."

Brie held the Remembering Stone close to her heart while the voices continued their repeated mantra. "Listen. Know. Learn. Listen. Know. Learn. Daughter of KcernFensia..."

The coldness of the stone floor chilling his scarred cheek jerked Nomed back to consciousness. He groaned, maneuvered his aching body to a sitting position, and strained to see through the blackness. Where his hand rested on the floor, cold water trickling over his fingers snapped his mind from its lethargy.

A faint blue light flared above the palm of his hand. Fluid iridescence caught its reflection and tossed it back. Deep rumbling laughter sent wavelets to soak his boots and to lick at his pant legs like lapping dogs.

He forced his fatigued body to standing. "I hate you, Rorret!" Anger blazing, he slogged through the water, searching in vain for the Crystal Heart of Myrrh.

Realization hit him like a fisted hand. "No! Evolsefil can't be gone!"

Fury far greater than that of a young boy banished from Myrrh coursed through his veins. Laboring through water climbing to his calves, he reached the smooth wooden doors to the Hall of Priestesses. They would not budge. Wrath burned in his gut. He whipped around, his wet cape tangling between his legs. Gathering it up, he half walked, half swam to the cavern's purple doors. They refused to grant him exit.

His back pressed against them, he fought for control. A heroic effort gradually calmed his rage. Rorret stopped rising. Little by little, Nomed reined in his temper. Drop by drop, the Lake of Rorret withdrew. The instant he felt the water recede below his ankles, Nomed loosed his sodden cape, faced the purple doors, and snapped his fingers. The doors flew wide. He leapt into the Cavern of Tennisca and shifted midair. The fire of his intent to destroy Myrrh, no matter the consequences, blazed in the owl's hazel eyes and in its heart.

Invigorated by a good contest, the Lake of Rorret churned itself into a frothing, foaming whirlpool. Once again, rumbling laughter sent a tremor over its surface. Satiated with its own delight, it settled back into its placid existence below the Cave of Canedari.

53

Karrew soared through the gathering darkness in search of Allynae and Jordett. A small campfire not far ahead caught his eye. Swooping in its direction, he discovered Almiralyn's brother and his comrades trying to soothe the pony Tam and a chestnut mare. With a cawed warning, he landed on Allynae's shoulder, shared what had happened to his sister, and explained who had rescued her and now carried her bird form.

Allynae paled. "The Pentharian leader carries Almiralyn? Go! Bring them here. I'll tell the others what's happening."

Karrew soared into the mist, rejoined the four vultures at the edge of the foothills, and within moments, reappeared above the clearing. The Pentharian followed in close formation, Voer in the lead with the white and gold bird clasped in his talons. Karrew landed on Allynae's shoulder. Voer hovered and released Almiralyn into her brother's waiting arms.

Karrew ruffled his feathers. "Get her warm, Alli. She's cold as ice." He flew to the branch of a tree and surveyed the small clearing. Paisley and Jordett stared in astonishment at four vultures who shifted to half Human, half Reptilian creatures from another world. By the fire, One Man and Allynae worked to warm Almiralyn. Karrew fluttered to the ground and waddled closer into the glowing light. "How is she?"

"She's breathing." Allynae wrapped her in his lightweight jacket and cradled her in his arms.

The hermit studied Almiralyn's motionless bird form. "Time and the settling of Myrrh will bring her back."

A blue Pentharian towered over them. "I am Voer. How is our Lady Almiralyn?"

"We'll know soon." The hermit stood and touched his hand to his chest. "I am called One Man. Will you introduce me to your comrades?"

Voer bowed his head. "It would be my honor." They walked side by side to where Jordett, Paisley, and the three Pentharian conversed.

Karrew, satisfied all was well, fluttered to Allynae's shoulder and observed the chills shivering through his mistress' body gradually lessen. A blue eye opened.

Allynae loosened the jacket and slid his hand over her feathers. "Her warmth is returning." He stroked her back. "Patience, Mira. Let me hold you a little longer."

The eye closed. Karrew tipped his head. Her labored breathing settled into a steady rhythm. When the eye opened again, he fluttered to ground. Allynae removed the jacket, set the white bird beside him, and held her steady. Karrew flapped his wings, took several steps, and paused. Hesitant attempts to mimic his movements left the white bird panting. Again and again, she rested, took a few tentative steps, and rested until at last she walked, unwavering, beside him. Only then did she stretch her gold-tipped wings and soar skyward.

Matching her wing stroke for wing stroke, Karrew flew by her side until he sensed the full return of her strength. Delighted by her resilience, he followed her circling descent through the ever-thickening gloom and landed next to her by the fire.

Almiralyn appeared in a flash of light, looking pale but beautiful. She hugged her brother. "I'm sorry I frightened you, Alli."

He returned her hug and held her at arm's length. Steady blue eyes gazed into hers. "I'm just glad you're here and safe." His lopsided smile spoke volumes.

After kissing his cheek, she turned to her gathered supporters, smiled up at Voer, and offered her palm. "Thank you for saving my life. The sudden change in Myrrh knocked me from the sky. I'll be forever grateful to you."

Voer placed his palm on hers and bowed, his braids falling in a cascade of rich color over his shoulder. "It was my pleasure, My Lady, and my duty."

She smiled at One Man. "Thank you for leaving the mountain to join us."

He responded in his soft, hesitant voice. "To assist you is my only desire. I am your servant, Almiralyn."

"Thank you, One Man. I am honored."

"What happened?" Paisley joined them.

"I believe someone has removed the Evolsefil Crystal from Myrrh. That's the only thing that would affect me in that way."

"Then we should all be dead." Allynae was matter-of-fact. "If the crystal's gone, Myrrh and Thera should've crashed into each other."

Although she maintained eye contact with her brother, she spoke to everyone. "The connection is unbroken, although it's tenuous. We must go to the Cave of Canedari to see what we can learn."

Yuin's red-scaled tail twitched. "How long will this connection hold? Can we make it there in time?"

"We must use the Intersect, and we must fly." Fatigue threatened to overwhelm her.

Paisley let out a groan. "I can't fly. Alli can't fly or One Man or..."

Voer cleared his throat and bowed his head. "My comrades and I will carry you. We will go to the Cave of Canedari together."

"What's the Intersect?" Jordett had remained quiet and watchful throughout the conversation.

Almiralyn pushed her fatigue to the back of her mind. "The Intersect is a secret transport system on the underside of Myrrh. There's an entrance quite close to here. Let's make haste."

A flurry of activity erupted as men and off-worlders prepared to depart. Only Paisley remained still.

"Come on, Pais." Allynae offered a hand. "Don't just sit there."

Paisley ignored it. "I'm no good to you with a weak ankle."

Yuin joined them. "I will carry you on my back and serve you in battle as my brother."

Paisley gulped. "I-I am a-afraid t-to f-fly."

Almiralyn laid a hand on his head. "This is the time for all of us to face our fears, Paisley. You will fly with us, and you will be unafraid."

She offered her hand. Paisley allowed her to help him to standing. Yuin shifted to a vulture. Jordett and Allynae helped Paisley climb on. One Man joined Jeet; Jordett mounted Stee; and Allynae mounted Voer's broad back.

Almiralyn shifted and soared upward with Karrew at her side. The short flight finished in Z-trauq Revir Canyon, where two tall quartz crystals guarded the gate to the Intersect. Almiralyn landed in Human form and strode between them to the shimmering cliff beyond. A whispered incantation and the clap of her hands caused its quartz face to fade away, leaving an opening into the mountainside.

Moving with cautious speed, she descended the steep crystal stairs. When she arrived on the Intersect platform, she gasped in surprise. Instead of the night sky, the City of Idronatti and the planet of Thera were visible far below.

Allynae joined her. "By the Fathers! Myrrh's no longer hidden."

Paisley gaped. "Now what?"

Almiralyn's voice rang with authority. "We continue to the Cavern of Tennisca and Cave of Canedari; we discover what has happened; and we do our best to fix it." She shared the sacred Key that would carry them to their first connect platform.

"Allynae, Voer, and Stee, please lead the way." They recited the Key and disappeared beneath Myrrh's crystal-studded underbelly.

"Paisley and Yuin, we will go next. One Man and Jeet, you will follow." She clasped Yuin and Paisley by the hands, and with Karrew on her shoulder, repeated the Key to their destination point. Before Paisley had time to protest, a flash catapulted them to their first destination.

One Man gazed in rapt delight at Intersect space as he and Jeet made two more jumps to different swirling spirals of iridescent turquoise light. Above him, crystal turned to amethyst, turned to azurite, turned to topaz. The underside of Myrrh's Dojanack range, like a geode split in half, spilled its contents into a geological wonderland of shimmering geometric designs.

Leaving frenzied concern to others, he drank in the beauty. As if in a trance, he stared, profoundly affected by the splendor stretching above him.

"One Man?" Jeet waited beside him on the last Intersect platform. "It is time. Are you ready to fly?"

"Yes." He savored one last longing glance. "I'm ready."

The Pentharian shifted to a vulture. One Man mounted and felt the powerful muscles engage beneath him. They soared toward the gaping entrance to the Cavern of Tennisca, Idronatti fully visible below them.

After the quake awakened them, Torgin and his companions did not remain for long by the bubbling spring. Skipt led them at a quick pace down one tunnel after the next, until Torgin feared they might wander forever in the black world of the Dojanack Caverns.

When he thought he couldn't take another step, Yaro paused and gazed down at him. "Rest, young Torgin. Then I will change to a panther and give you a ride."

"Thanks. I could use it." Torgin marveled at how natural it now seemed to watch his heart-brother shift shapes.

"I not ride. We close." Skipt's gray eyes glowed in the dark. "I lead the way."

Yaro shifted, Torgin climbed on his back, and the Enots led them through a multitude of passageways. When they turned into a tunnel where oil lanterns melted the darkness into soft, gold-edged shadows, Skipt stopped and looked up at the panther. "Ya ho, my friend, you must not be a ferocious cat when we enter Meos. Be ferret until we explain you."

Torgin slid to the ground and waited for Yaro to change shape. With the ferret settled on his shoulders, he and Skipt walked down the tunnel to the City of Meos.

Although the Enots provided a detailed description of the DeoNytes, Torgin was unprepared for their strange and beautiful appearance. Shyness made him glance away from the curious faces peering at him from curtained doorways. His gaze fixed on Skipt's back, he traversed the central plaza. A male DeoNyte with white fur that glistened in the lamplight greeted them by a columned entry.

The Enots boy pranced forward. "Ya ho. I Skipt, and this my friend, Torgin. We seek the counsel of Yookotay, ReDael of the DeoNytes and Keeper of the Secrets of Myrrh."

The creature nodded. "I am Sitrio, please come. Yookotay awaits you."

Sitrio steered them between the two tall coral pillars to an antechamber. At a second door, he knocked. A deep voice bade them enter.

The ReDael of the DeoNytes stood beside a round table, his palm resting on an inlaid sapphire. He knelt on one knee and offered his hand as the Enots hurried forward. "Ya ho, Skipt, welcome to Meos. We are privileged to have an Enots visit our home."

Skipt placed his hand on the ReDael's. "Ya ho, Yookotay. I bring Torgin, Human child of Idronatti. He seeks his friends and hopes you may help us find them."

Yookotay rose and smiled at Torgin. "I have met two of your friends. Now I am honored to meet you. Tell me about the creature who rides on your shoulders."

Torgin swallowed his shyness. "I carry Yaro, a Pentharian from the planet of ReTaw au Qa. He has pledged his support to those who fight to save Myrrh. With your permission, he will shift to his true form and introduce himself."

Yookotay's voice, infused with the dignity of his station, rang out in the council chamber. "Pentharian, show your true self. I will honor you as I honor Enots and Human."

The ferret jumped from Torgin's shoulder, stood up on its hind legs, and shifted. Behind them, Sitrio gasped. The golden Pentharian remained motionless, his lizard-like eyes steady and unblinking.

Yookotay's expression did not change. He, too, maintained a respectful stance.

Skipt, for once, was quiet. Torgin watched the two creatures from different worlds assess each other. Yookotay, the first to break the silence, offered his right hand palm up, his left hand on his heart. Yaro placed his left hand palm down on Yookotay's and placed his right hand on his heart. They bowed their heads in mutual respect.

A sense of wonder filled Torgin. *How beautiful they are and so different!* He realized once again how sheltered his life had been in Idronatti. *Will I ever be able to share this adventure with my parents? Will they believe I have met other races...Enots, Pentharian, DeoNytes?* His awe backslid into feeling insignificant.

Yaro's lizard-like eyes gleamed as he placed a hand on his shoulder. "What is it, young Torgin? You seem to grow smaller?"

Blood rushed to Torgin's cheeks. He shuffled his feet and met Yaro's questioning gaze. "They teach us in Idronatti that Humans are the only intelligent species in the universe." He lowered his gaze before looking at the ReDael. "I never imagined other life forms with thoughts and feelings similar to my own. Now, my life seems unimportant."

Yookotay smiled. "Meeting those different from ourselves who come from other places broadens our horizons, Torgin. But I understand how you feel. We have had many visitors who have never walked through our tunnels before. We, too, are learning new things."

Skipt's broad smile lit up his face. He bounced from one foot to the other. "I friend to Human, DeoNyte, and Pentharian. So, I grow bigger and bigger!"

Torgin, Yookotay, Sitrio, and Yaro laughed out loud.

"Skipt, you are tall among Enots, my friend." The DeoNyte ReDael looked thoughtful. "Before we leave to find Torgin's friends, we must consult the map of Myrrh."

The companions accompanied the ReDael into a room off the council chamber, where they gathered around a map carved on the wall. Only the snow-capped peaks of the Dojanack Mountains showed above the gray mist sequestering the land.

"When those peaks sink below the clouds..." Yookotay grew even more serious. "...Myrrh will disappear forever. Unless we can stop Seyes Nomed, all of us and the planet of Thera are doomed. Today the caverns quaked, the sign of a radical change." Yookotay pointed at a black void on the map.

"This is the Cave of Canedari; it is in the Cavern of Tennisca. Even on this map, it has always remained illuminated. We fear the Prima Evolsefil Crystal may no longer reside there. If this is true, it may already be too late to save our homelands."

Yaro studied the map, his expression unreadable. "Do you know for certain the crystal is gone?"

Yookotay shook his head. "We know only a strangeness exists there. My son, Zugo, the twin, Ari, and a Wood Tiff named Fen have already gone that way. I think—"

"Ari is *here*? And Fen?" Torgin could hardly believe it. "I must find them right away."

"Ya ho! A Wood Tiff in the caverns. Times grow even stranger." Skipt looked serious.

While Yaro, Yookotay, and Sitrio discussed their options, Torgin listened, feeling left out and annoyed.

At last, Yaro turned to him. "What do you think, my brother? Our best option is to look for your friends in the Cavern of Tennisca. Do you agree?"

His frustration melted into relief as he turned to Yookotay. "Will you come with us?"

"Although I'm very concerned about Zugo's well-being, Giests are abroad throughout the caverns. Some have found their way into Meos. It is my duty to protect my people, so I must stay here. Sitrio will accompany you."

He placed a firm hand on Torgin's shoulder. "You must be brave, young Torgin, for the Cavern of Tennisca will read your heart to learn your fears. Are you prepared to face those things you least like in yourself? For if not, say so now."

Torgin swallowed a lump in his throat. *Why do I feel like a coward?* He studied the rough floor of the chamber. *Can I face all the fears I keep hidden inside? Can I walk away and abandon my friends again?*

He looked up to find Yookotay and Sitrio watching him. Skipt opened his mouth to speak, but the ReDael shook his head. Torgin realized Yaro sensed his uncertainty but resisted the temptation to choose for him.

Determination replaced his doubt. "I will face whatever I must face if I can save my friends and Myrrh."

Skipt let out a whoop. "Ya, ho, Torgin, you brave Human."

Yaro nodded his approval; Yookotay squeezed his shoulder. It was time. With Sitrio leading, they set off down a long tunnel.

Excitement stirred in Torgin's belly, where butterfly wings fluttered in anticipation. Whatever was to come would come. The most important thing —soon he would find his friends.

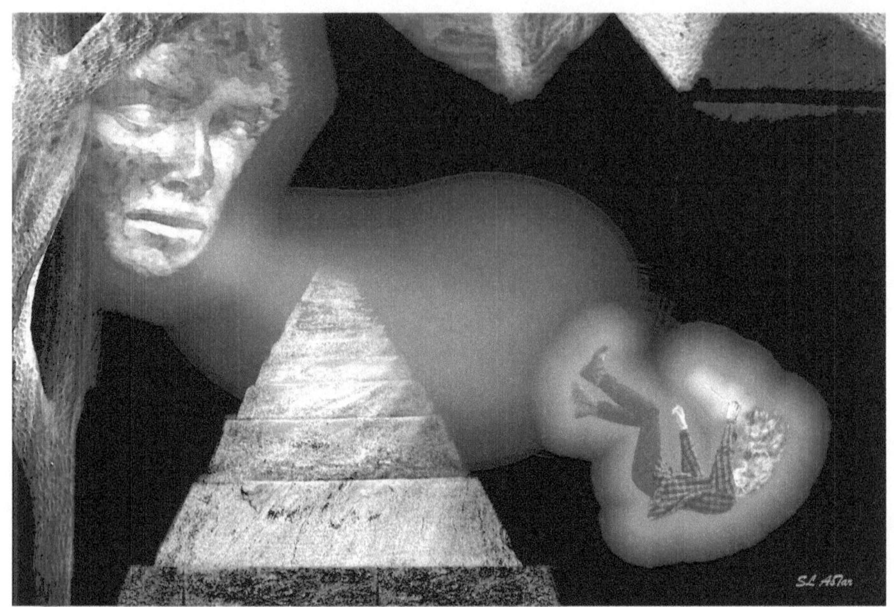

54

Bonnee and the Now Remembered huddled outside the Cavern of Tennisca, discussing the aftershocks quaking through Myrrh. She wanted to find Brie, but she dared not enter the cavern.

Three figures stumbling down the tunnel from Meos distracted her from thoughts of her friend. *A Wood Tiff in the caverns? A DeoNyte and...* She stared at the girl with curly red hair and freckles. *This has to be Brie's twin. They really are identical.*

"What just happened?" The disheveled twin steadied herself against the wall.

The DeoNyte helped the Tiff to his feet. "Whatever it was, it came from the Cavern of Tennisca."

The Wood Tiff grabbed his fallen hat and dusted it off. "You sure we should enter the cavern?"

"My memories are in there, Fen." The twin moved toward the door. "I have to find them."

Bonnee floated closer. "Ari?"

Brie's twin shot a puzzled looked at her companions. "Did you hear that?"

"What?" The Wood Tiff's voice trembled.

"Someone whispered my name."

"Ari." Bonnee pitched her voice louder. "I'm here beside you. Look closely."

Brie's sister squinted, and then her eyes rounded in surprise. "Who are you? And how do you know my name?" Her brow wrinkled. "Have I met you before?"

"We have not met, but Brie is my friend. She freed my people, the unremembered, and we brought her here."

Ari frowned. "You mean she's already in the Cavern of Tennisca?"

"She entered before the quaking began. We fear for her life."

The DeoNyte interrupted. "I'm Zugo, and this is Fen. What made Myrrh quake like that?"

Bonnee shook her head. "All I know is something is terribly wrong in the cavern, and Brie is in there."

Ari yanked the door open. "Come—"

Before Ari, Fen, and Zugo could react, screaming balls of fluorescent light streaked into the tunnel and trapped them in a circle of color, wreaking of rotting flesh.

Bonnee melted into the darkness, aware she could not help.

Ari remained motionless, her eyes darting from one Giest to the other. A sticky glob of green plasma hit Zugo. He grabbed the foul-smelling slime and, with a grimace of disgust, shook it from his fingers. Fen ducked a yellow Giest, but not soon enough. His hat flew from his head.

Amid the chaos of Giests, Ari found what she sought—an orange sphere. Her gaze locked on her target. She crept forward.

Zugo caught her eye, nudged the Wood Tiff, and pointed. "Over there, Fen."

Fen jumped up and down and waved his arms in the air.

A high-pitched scream propelled the orange Giest in Ari's direction. She froze, attention fixed on her quarry. At the last moment, it dodged into the cavern, its comrades following, shrieking as they shot past.

Ari stared into the darkness. "I'm sure the orange one is the Giest that knocked me down. How will I ever catch it?"

Zugo gave her a sympathetic look. "Since we can't fly…" He shook his head.

Fen plopped his crumpled hat on his brown curls. "What do we do now?"

Zugo nudged Fen onto the landing. "The Cave of Canedari is our best bet. At least we'll be safe there." He offered Ari his hand. "Let's go."

"Ari, wait."

The Now Remembered girl floated near the door, her eyes wide with fear. "I have promised to remain in the caverns until Brie is safe, but I cannot enter the Cavern of Tennisca. It's a long story. Please understand. I would come if I could."

Ari studied the translucent girl. "What's your name?"

"Bonnee."

"Ari, hurry." Zugo's stage whisper became more urgent. "Let's go before the Giests come back."

"Hold on, Zugo." She smiled at the Now Remembered girl. "Goodbye, Bonnee. Stay safe. I hope we meet again." Determined to find her memories and her twin, she stepped onto the landing.

Fen yanked her hand. "Over there!"

Cutting a multicolored path through the darkness, Giests in single file shot straight for them.

"Run!" Zugo shouted and dashed down the stairs.

As Ari descended, Giests swarmed around her, forming a barrier of putrid color and high-pitched screams. She covered her ears. "Get away from me! I can't hear myself think. And your putrid stink is suffocating me."

The Giests squealed louder and pressed closer. Her anger exploded. "I said get away from me. I'm warning you."

A purple blob spit in her hair.

"That's it!" She grabbed Efillaeh's jeweled handle, pulled the knife free of its scabbard, and stabbed into the closely packed circle.

Howls of pain careened around the cavern as Giests scattered in every direction—all but an orange one that hovered in the air beside her.

"Stay where you are." Her command hissed between clenched teeth. "I want my memories back!"

Frigid wind whipped around her, painting the tips of her hair and eyelashes with frost, and sending the Giest tumbling through space. Her bereft memory supplied a momentary recollection. "The death shadow... Yuck." A cloud of icy breath sent a shiver up her spine. She brandished Efillaeh. "Don't come any nearer, Wodash od DerTah. I am not afraid of you."

The creature's wicked laugh rattled around her. His horrifying face, too close to hers, sent her dodging backward. Her foot hit the edge of the step, fought for purchase, and found nothing. She plunged off the Stairway of Retu Erath with Efillaeh glowing like a torch in the vast black space.

"Ari!" Zugo's terrified shout echoed through the cavern. Fen's frantic scream chased after her. Time snatched reality away. She plummeted faster, yet everything slowed—her breathing, the blood in her veins, the beat of her heart.

"No-o-o!" The death shadow gave chase, his cold snatching at her heels. A light flickered to one side. She turned her head. The orange Giest slammed into her forehead. Memories roared through her with the force of a tsunami. *Arienh Lynae AsTar. Mother. Torgin and Almiralyn and Tam... Brie, how could I have forgotten you?* The gaping mouth of the cavern opened wider. "Brielle AsTar, I love you!" Her shouted declaration melted into the fabric of Intersect night.

His rage cooled by the Lake of Rorret, Seyes Nomed exited the cave of Canedari with the force of a fired projectile. Streaking through the darkness, he let the owl's wildness take him. A terrified scream jerked him back to Human awareness. Curiosity prompted him to investigate. Owl sharp eyes picked out a DeoNyte and a Wood Tiff huddled together on the stairs. Far below them, a falling figure pursued by Wodash and an orange Giest galvanized him into action. He shot after them.

The twin's red curls gleaming in the light cast by a molten silver knife sparked both anger and frustration. Furious his primary bargaining chip was about to tumble into the nothingness of space, he swooped past the death shadow in pursuit of the falling girl.

As he reached her, she plunged, arms and legs flung wide, through the vast crystal-encrusted mouth of the cavern. What he saw far below hit him like a shock wave. Beneath the underside of Myrrh, the buildings of Idronatti gleamed. The silhouettes swirling above the city sent another tremor through him. With all the speed he could muster, Nomed changed course and soared back to the Cavern of Tennisca, the falling twin forgotten.

From the stairway, Zugo's night vision picked out the great horned owl pursuing Ari. With both Wodash and the DiMensioner loose in the cavern, he and Fen were in grave danger. He grasped the Wood Tiff's trembling hand. "We need to go to the Cave of Canedari."

As fast as Fen's short legs would allow, they fled down the stairs. Zugo's foot hit the last step, and his hand met a solid surface. With Fen at his side, he felt his way along the wall until he found the double doors to the cave.

"Fen, I don't know the Key to open them."

"Maybe we can push them open." Fen shivered beside him. "Is it always this cold in here?" The Wood Tiff's exhaled breath hung like a small cloud in the darkness.

Zugo swung around, a fist of fear clutching at his mind. Staring him in the face, white eyes with red, odd-shaped pupils opened and closed in a hypnotic rhythm that rendered him immobile. The death shadow opened its gaping mouth. Fingers of ice slithered around Zugo's throat. Darkness flooded his mind.

Spurred into action by the cold, Fen had placed his palms on the wooden doors. "Eero, Tye, Como." They opened, and he slipped through. Turning to make sure Zugo followed, he discovered his friend frozen solid and the ugliest face he had ever encountered in his life, hovering right in front of him. A panicked scream clawed at his throat. Only a small squeak sounded. Terror left him so numb he did not notice the liquid coolness slip around his waist until it snatched him away from the doors—away from the long-fingered hands of death.

The creature's shriek shook the cave. "I curse you, Rorret. From the flames of SeDah, I curse you." With Zugo wrapped within the wintry blanket of his body, he flew away from the Cave of Canedari.

In the silence that followed, Fen sat on the damp floor, stunned, shivering, and alone.

Brie knew Ari was in trouble. She knew it with a certainty that left her breathless. A muffled cry and a scream of terror brought her to a state of alert listening. Questions, like frightened hummingbirds, darted around her mind. She forced herself to focus and extended her senses throughout the cavern. The death shadow's frozen presence and Nomed's anger snapped into focus. A DeoNyte moved in her direction. In the Cave of Canedari, a Wood Tiff huddled by himself. And at the peripheral of her expanded senses, she found Ari.

"Brie? Brielle AsTar, I love you." The words engraved themselves on her heart forever. The voice faded.

"Ari, I love you, too!" She listened intently. "Arienh?"

55

Elae opened her eyes to find Esán, pale-faced and teary, bending over her. "Elae, please don't die. Please wake up. Elae, please."

Halfway to sitting, her stomach heaved. She swallowed the bitter taste of bile and lowered herself back to the ground.

Esán gripped her hand. "Elae, I'm so sorry. I didn't know you were clinging to the crystal. When Nomed arrived, I had no choice but to teleport. Please forgive me."

Elae tried to speak. A moan and a tear were all she could manage. Her head throbbed. Every muscle and bone in her body protested when she tried to stretch her limbs. She licked her lips and forced them to shape one word. "What?"

"I moved Evolsefil." Esán leaned closer. "Can I get you anything?"

She raised her eyes and concentrated. "Water."

"What?" Oh, water." He released her hand. "Don't move. I'll find some."

She closed her eyes and lay still.

I *need something to hold water.* Across the room, Esán's gaze came to rest on a broken pottery jug lay on its side on a rickety table. He made his way through jumble piles of wood and dirt and set the jug upright.

With it cupped between his hands, he closed his eyes, studied its molecular makeup, and visualized it in one piece. A slight tremor shook it. He opened his eyes and removed his hands. The jug sat on the table, its broken pieces woven into wholeness.

After checking on Elae, he grabbed it and hurried to the door. Transfixed by the strange beauty of Nevah Efas and uncertain where to find water, he paused. To one side of the cottage, a meadow of golden grass stretched to the horizon; to the other, a forest of silver-leafed trees whispered songs of late summer. Down the hill in front of the cottage, a pale chartreuse stream meandered through a field of sweetly scented wildflowers.

Urgency nudged him into motion. At the base of the hill, he filled the jug from the stream, held it high, and blew out a relieved breath. "No leaks."

Eyes shut, he pictured Elae's still body, arrived beside it, and knelt. "Elae? Elae, it's Esán. Can you hear me?" He held his breath.

A breeze rustled her soft fur. Her chest moved with a shallow breath. *She lives.* His exhale trembled. Sitting back on his heels, he tipped some water into his cupped hand. Drop by drop, it trickled down his fingers onto Elae's parched lips. A small pink tongue captured the liquid—one drop, then another, and another—until she moaned and turned her head away.

"Elae, I wish you could tell me what to do. I don't know how to help you."

Her eyelids fluttered. A slender hand lifted and fell. Next to her, the Book of Emit lay in a patch of warm sunlight, its leather cover looking even more timeworn in the bright light.

"Thank you, Elae." He tiptoed around her, picked it up, and flipped through *blank* pages. Panic gripped him. "I need help. I need..." Words flowed across the page. As fast as his mind formulated a question, its answer appeared. *EmitEnil* seemed to know his every thought.

Elae would die, the book informed him, unless he could bring someone to her.

"Help? From whom? From where?"

The answer appeared. *Efillaeh. You must bring Efillaeh.*

He frowned. "Who is Efillaeh?"

The sacred knife honed from the heart of Evolsefil... Almiralyn will know.

He hugged the book, then placing it next to Elae, he touched her dulled fur. Her breath, shallow and hesitant, came in soft spurts. A shiver traveled her length. Again, urgency nudged.

In a pile of discarded bedding, he found a tattered blanket and covered her. "I hate to leave you, but I must go for help. I'll be back, Elae. I promise."

At the center of the golden meadow, the Evolsefil Crystal gleamed in the summer sun. Rainbows of light danced in the surrounding air. The ground vibrated with the power of its presence.

Esán placed a hand on the gleaming crystal surface. "Help me find Efillaeh." His eyelids lowered, he prayed it would give him the answer.

At the Guardian's cottage, Majeska's rumbling purr filled Sparrow's makeshift studio. Merrilea smiled at the cat curled up in her lap before returning her attention to the image emerging on her friend's canvas. A sudden desire to see more detail launched her to standing. Majeska landed on four paws and padded after her as she hurried closer to the easel. A shudder-producing chill encased her like a glove.

Concentration complete, Sparrow's brush moved from paint to canvas to paint and back in an unbroken rhythm. Dipping her brush into a dollop of burnt sienna on her palette, she added red curls to the falling figure in a cave blacker than night. Each brush stroke brought the twin into clearer focus. In her outstretched hand, a knife gleamed silver against the lightless surroundings. Sparrow narrowed her eyes, cleaned her brush, and swirled it in white-gray paint. A menacing spectre, its red pupils fully dilated, hovered above her falling daughter.

Never taking her eyes off the painting, Merrilea scooped up Majeska. Together, they watched. *If only...*

One by one, Ari embraced her returned memories until the urgency of the present hurled her from the darkness of Tennisca into cloud-muted sunlight. Wind-whipped curls slapped her face. Through tendrils of red, she beheld, far below, the City of Idronatti. *By the Fathers*! Her unhindered descent brought it closer and closer. Mind racing, she assessed her situation. The clarity of her conclusion stunned her. *I'm going to die.* She squeezed her eyes shut. *I'll never see Brielle again.* The knife in her hand pulsed. Her eyes flew open.

"Look!" Almiralyn pointed at the figure of a young girl, face down and arms and legs flung wide, rocketing in an uncontrolled fall toward them.

Allynae gaped. "By the Light of Mahyinaeh!" He felt his heart go tight with fear. "Voer! Above you!"

A rumbling response burst from the vulture as it swooped toward the distant buildings. Then, with the immense power of its great wings, it shot upward, directly beneath the falling child. Efillaeh flashed. Red hair caught the light.

Allynae's eyes locked onto his daughter's. *What if I miss? I can't miss... I won't! What if the knife...*

Ari pulled her arms and legs together and flipped. Voer tensed, timing his wing stroke for the impact. Allynae opened his arms. His daughter's back slammed into his chest. His arms closed around her. Muscles screaming in protest, he struggled to seat her in front of him. Gulping air into his deflated lungs, he leaned forward, his body a protective shield. Together they plunged on the great vulture's back—down toward the reaching spires of Idronatti.

Voer fought the impact of the added weight, accelerating their rapid descent with all his formidable strength and skill. Vulture eyes glued to the city below, he began to wonder whether he was about to die, not in Myrrh, but skewered by one of Idronatti's tall buildings.

Determined to deliver his passengers to safety, he extended his wings to their full breadth, pressed against the air, relaxed, and pressed again. Down. Up. Down. Up. The rate of descent decreased. He lifted his great vulture head. One last stroke with his mighty wings sent him soaring away from pointed spires. Only then did he realize Almiralyn and Karrew had flown by his side the entire time.

Above, Jordett, Paisley, and One Man cheered. Yuin, Stee, and Jeet soared in a wide circle, calling out in exhilarated throaty squawks.

Voer flew after Almiralyn and Karrew, the thrill of victory pulsing in his veins. The crystal mouth of the Cavern of Tennisca gaped wide. His comrades and their riders escorted him and his precious passengers into the vacuous space... the space where ancient ones whispered and evil bided its time.

Torgin gritted his teeth and struggled to match Yaro's long stride. Their quick pace, as they trouped after Sitrio, left him sweaty and panting. Tunnel after tunnel, he grew more certain they would never arrive at Tennisca. When they halted in front of the recessed door, Torgin wiped the sweat from his face. *That was too quick.* His brow creased. *I want to find my friends, right?* His stomach flip-flopped. *Are they truly here? Or is this a wild chase?*

Anticipation of the adventures to come set Skipt prancing and twitching with excitement. If he kept moving, he forgot he couldn't feel the wind or hear the birds or see mid-turning passing into evening and the sun rising in the morning. He glanced at his companions. Tension exuding from Yaro, Torgin, and Sitrio sent him reeling in a jerky, disconnected jig.

Yaro spoke in hushed tones, his exotic face serious as he and Sitrio discussed their next move. Every nerve in his warrior's body perceived danger. He knew the smell of death, and it permeated the air. His nostrils flared. *Whatever happens, I am well trained and seasoned in battle. I will forfeit my life to save Myrrh and to protect Torgin.*

Sitrio sensed the rising apprehension in the group assembled outside the Cavern of Tennisca. Although Giests were close and many, something far stronger and more powerful made Sitrio's white fur bristle. He eyed the brown-skinned boy who waited beside him, fear bright in his green eyes. The Enots pranced his anxiety in disjointed choreography. *And Yaro? Does he feel afraid?* He glanced at the strange mix of man and reptile. Only palpable alertness radiated from him.

The Pentharian had volunteered to be their scout. He would shape shift and slip under the door into the Cavern. The whole scenario left Sitrio ill at ease. He needed to do something besides wait with Torgin and Skipt. But until he knew what they faced, he would remain at their side.

Yaro placed a hand on the boy's shoulder. "I go to seek what we have lost. I will return, Torgin, my brother. Until then, rest. My heart to your heart."

"My heart to your heart. Good hunting." The concern in Torgin's sober expression mirrored Sitrio's.

The Pentharian shifted and disappeared. Only Sitrio, with his night-trained eyes, saw the tiny brown spider scurry from sight.

Torgin leaned One Man's flute against the wall. Shrugging his backpack off, he set it on the ground and sank down beside it. Sitrio joined him. Silky fur brushing his bare arm reminded Torgin of Buster and Tam. *It is so strange to have animals as friends. Even stranger are the Enots, the DeoNytes, and the Pentharian—especially the Pentharian.*

Skipt interrupted his musings. "You play?" He pointed at One Man's flute.

Torgin nodded and pulled it from the case. Wary of attracting unwanted attention, he let his brown fingers glide along its silvery wood-grained length, moving in a soundless, rhythmic pattern. In his mind, a melody took shape. Dark and filled with demons, it gave voice to his growing fear. Then, out of nowhere, a thin thread of hope evolved into a lyrical refrain so beautiful he held his breath, fearful it would go away.

Next to him, fatigue gathered Skipt in its arms. His eyelids drooped and sleep overcame him.

Torgin returned the flute to its case and let his eyes close.

Yaro arrived in the cavern amid a group of rancid balls of color. Their single-mindedness and the intensity with which they focused on revenge throbbed against his tiny body. Yookotay had explained that Giests were the disenchanted souls of men who had died searching for a legendary treasure in the fathomless depths of the Dojanack Caverns, men whose bodies the search teams had never found. Disfigured and smelling of decay, they now clustered by the door, murmuring profanities and cursing the one they called Leader.

Eight tiny legs carried Yaro away from the Giests and down the Stairway of Retu Erath. A strangeness in the rough stone made him pause. He felt the breath in it, the coursing of energy like blood through thin-walled vessels. Enlivened by it, he yearned for the time to explore and absorb its beauty.

Above him, a yellow Giest brought new orders. After much squabbling, all but two followed it across the cavern.

Yaro shifted to a small brown bat and pursued the discontented muttering into the darkness.

Fen huddled at the center of the Cave of Canedari, talking to himself. "I am so alone. Where did that horrid creature take Zugo? I miss my family and the trees and..." He pulled his hat from his head and worked it with nervous fingers. A tear leaked down his cheek. "Ari. Oh, Ari—"

A soft noise at the cave's entrance stopped his chatter. The song of wings in the air made him scramble to his feet, listening. Wha, wha, wha— so quiet he strained to follow its circular course. Wha, wha, wha. Myrrh's Guardian materialized in a glowing pool of light. Karrew alighted on her shoulder.

Fen clutched his hat to his chest and knelt. "Almiralyn?" He sucked in a breath. "Are you a dream?"

She smiled. "I'm real, Fen. Please stand."

He stood and plopped his hat on his head. *I'm no longer alone.* Strange shadows swooped into the cave and landed. His relief receded like water swirling down a drain. Sidling closer to the Guardian, he stared as the dark shapes of men dismounted, and their steeds changed into forms he did not recognize.

A smaller figure darted between them. "Fen!"

"Ari!" Sadness replaced with delight made him dizzy. "You're alive!"

She gave him a quick hug. "I'm very much alive, thanks to Allynae and Voer. I feel a bit shaky, though."

Allynae scooped her up in his arms. "Where can she rest, Mira?"

Ari squirmed to peer over his shoulder. "Wait. I don't see Zugo."

Fen scurried after her. "A horrid creature with an ugly white face froze him and carried him away."

Almiralyn caught him by the hand. "Let's find a place to recover and eat. I'll introduce you to my friends, and you can tell us what happened."

As the strange procession advanced into the Hall of Priestesses, a harried DeoNyte rushed toward them, stopped, and stood trembling, her face a picture of abject fear. "Almiralyn?"

Fen glanced over his shoulder at the four tall, imposing Pentharian. Ruby red, emerald green, sapphire blue, and carnelian orange filled the hall. Lizard-like eyes gleamed. Long braids and tattoos, not to mention scales and tails. He shook his head. *No wonder she's scared.*

Almiralyn released his hand and hurried to her side. "Don't be frightened. These are our friends and warriors of Myrrh."

"They scared us." She lowered her pale eyes and swallowed. "The D-

DiMensioner came." Her voice trembled." Evolsefil disappeared, Almiralyn, and the Lake of Rorret went berserk."

Priestesses gathered in the hallway. A regal DeoNyte came forward. "The DiMensioner took Elae and the boy with him when the crystal vanished. Why are we still alive, Almiralyn?"

"That is what we're here to discover, High Priestess Traeh." The Guardian nodded toward her companions. "We need rest and food. Then we must all confer."

Traeh gave quick instructions, and the priestesses dispersed. She accompanied Almiralyn to the end of the hall and then hurried away to resume her duties.

Almiralyn led her supporters beyond the splintered door. At the far end of the room, a fire crackled merrily in a carved stone fireplace. The Pentharian helped to arrange chairs and pillows before the warm blaze. Fen held back, while Allynae helped Ari to settle on large silk cushions.

Ari smiled at him. "You saved my life, Allynae. Thank you."

"You're welcome, but in truth, Voer saved us both, Ari." He beckoned the blue Pentharian to join him.

She offered her hand. "Thank you, Voer. I am honored to know you."

He knelt and held the hand between his. "It is my pleasure to serve you, Daughter of KcernFensia."

Ari's brow furrowed. "Isn't KcernFensia a planet? I don't understand."

Voer released her hand and rose. "You will need to discuss that with the Guardian."

Allynae gave her a mysterious smile. "We'll answer all your questions, Arienh, but now you must rest. Take care of her, Fen. Don't let her out of your sight."

Fen scrambled to his feet. "Yes, sir." He bowed so low his hat fell to the floor.

Allynae picked it up and handed it back. "Relax, my young friend. Keep Ari company while I confer with Almiralyn."

Ari watched him join his sister. "He seems so familiar." She patted the sacred knife. "I like him." She smiled. "I like him a lot."

Fen touched her arm. "I thought I would never see you alive again, Ari. Tell me what happened."

"I fell down and down and down." Her eyes flooded with the memory.

56

Brie felt the DiMensioner's rage before he landed on the ledge at the front of her prison. "Wodash! Where in SeDah are you?" His anger escalating, he flipped his cape over his shoulders and turned to glare into Tennisca's vastness.

Masking her thoughts, Brie pressed as far back into the cave as the stone wall would allow. Wodash's triumphant face emerging from the darkness sent goosebumps racing up and down her arms. When he landed and pushed Zugo toward the DiMensioner, she almost cried out.

Ignoring the DeoNyte, Nomed raised a hand. The death shadow crumpled to his knees. "You have failed me yet again, Wodash od DerTah. How could you let the twin escape? My trump card has fallen to her death."

The blood drained from Brie's head. The world tipped and spun. She made herself focus on the silver cord winding around the death shadow's neck and endeavored to make sense of what she'd just heard.

Wodash clutched at the cord with long, white fingers and forced out a strangled denial. "The twin lives."

Nomed yanked the cord tighter. "Don't lie to me. I saw her plunge through the mouth of the cavern."

Fiery tears blurred Brie's vision. Denial blazed in her heart.

"The—other—one." The death shadow's eyes bulged.

Nomed loosened the cord.

Wodash's fingers tore at it. "That was the other twin, Nomed. The one here can't escape."

A hand pressed to her mouth, her mind screamed in anguish. *The other twin. Arienh.* Brie choked back a sob.

A barked command brought a yellow Giest to Nomed's side. Its light illuminated her foot, her arm, and then her red curls. She kept her eyes pinned to the floor, fighting to control her despair.

Nomed laughed. "So you are here, after all. We are so delighted to have you as our guest." He sobered. "I am sorry about the death of your sister."

As he turned to Wodash, numbness worse than the death shadow's cold spread through her. Her dulled gaze found Zugo. She blinked, gave herself a mental shake, and forced back her tears. *I can't help, Ari, but I can help Zugo.*

A flick of the DiMensioner's wrist removed the cord from Wodash's neck. He glowered, massaging his throat with trembling fingers. Nomed ignored his discomfort and studied the DeoNyte. "Is this Esán's friend?"

"Yes." Wodash knew he sounded sulky.

The DiMensioner's eyes narrowed. "And what will he do for us?"

"He's the son of the ReDael of Meos. He wears the Sapphire of Descendant."

Nomed grabbed the deep blue sapphire and yanked. The chain snapped. A smile tugged at his scarred cheek. "What a pretty bobble." He slipped it in his pocket and spoke to the hovering Giest. "Gather your comrades. Leave two to guard the cave entrance. Bring the rest to me. We have trouble at our heels. It's time to take a stand."

Giving a high-pitched squeal, the Giest fled.

Beneath white lids, Wodash observed his master. *Can you truly expect me to follow your lead when there is no trust between us?*

The DiMensioner's piercing hazel eyes locked onto his. Chills prickled up his neck. He wondered if this was how his victims felt. Nomed's anger-saturated voice snapped him to attention.

"Hatred, my indentured friend, is as good a reason to follow as love. Hate me, Wodash od DerTah, but do not forget you are mine until I release you from my service."

He narrowed his demon eyes. "Right now, we have trouble headed this way. Our friends, the Pentharian, appear to have switched allegiance. They are flying toward the mouth of this cavern with Humans on their backs and Almiralyn and her raven in the lead." Nomed glanced at their captives and drew him to one side. "We must make plans."

The longer Wodash's focus remained on the DiMensioner, the more life seeped back into Zugo's frozen body. As the death shadow moved away, his numbed mind began to thaw.

A soft voice whispered next to his ear. "Just relax. Do nothing to attract their attention, or Wodash will freeze us all over again."

Warmth, transferred from the speaker's body to his, left him tingling. The more relaxed he stayed, the quicker the cold evaporated. When his legs could move, his companion helped him to slide further into the cave. Savoring stone cutting into his spine, he glanced at the Human beside him. "Ari? Is that you?"

The reply came in a sad whisper. "I'm Brie. Are you Zugo? Have you seen Ari?"

Distress heavy in his heart, he sought a way to communicate and not attract attention. He swallowed and tried telepathy. *"Can you understand me?"*

She nodded.

"Can you send me your thoughts?"

"I don't know."

"Try. Just think straight into my mind."

Brie grasped the blue pouch at her neck and closed her eyes.

Her mind touch, at first tentative and uncertain, grew more confidant. *"I'm Brie."*

Zugo grinned and nodded.

As though she had used telepathy all her life, Brie shared her story. Zugo told her what had happened since she crawled away down the tunnel. When he came to Ari's fall from the Stairway of Retu Erath, he hesitated.

"Tell me." She slipped her hand into his. *"Is Ari dead?"*

"She stepped off the Stairway of Retu Erath and fell through the mouth of the cavern. Brie, I am so sorry."

Brie's hand flew to her mouth, trapping a heartbroken sob. Her mind tried to understand the words it couldn't accept. *If Ari were dead, I would know.* She struggled for a semblance of calm. *I've always known when something happened to her. But with everything going on...*

The stone in her hand pulsed, calling out to her to remember. *What's the good of remembering if Ari is dead?* The Star of Truth burned as hot as a coal. *O-o-o-oh...*

"Zugo, she can't be dead. I don't know how she could survive, but if she were gone, I—would—know."

Camouflaged within the chaos of swarming Giests, a bat attached itself to the wall above Brie's prison, shifted to a spider, and scuttled into the cave. Yaro disliked the death shadow—not because he feared death, for to him death was a time-earned passing, but because Wodash lacked scruples, integrity in battle, and understanding of the value of life. He respected Nomed's power as a DiMensioner, but not his inability to move beyond hatred. Yaro held his mind quiet and crept across the ceiling.

He found the two children huddled together as far from their captors as possible. The DeoNyte, he felt certain, was Yookotay's young son. The girl child must be one of Torgin's best friends. He wanted to help them escape, but this wasn't the time. For now, they were safe enough. The DiMensioner would not harm what could buy him his life and perhaps even his heart's desire—Evolsefil. He crawled closer to Nomed.

The DiMensioner held up a hand for silence, his eyes searching the cave. Yaro did not think or move. When Nomed returned his attention to his plans for war, eight tiny legs carried the small spider away from him, the death shadow, and the children.

In bat form, he flew across the cavern. Whispered secrets tickled his ears. He landed on the Stairway of Retu Erath. The voices surrounded him, moved into his mind, and sang to him. Songs of Myrrh saturated him until he thought he would drown.

Yaro, warrior of ReTaw au Qa, listened—entranced. When the ancient ones withdrew, leaving him alone, he could not move. Rich memories nurtured his soul. His homeland pulsed with a life of its own, but not with the fullness he felt within Myrrh. Embracing his growing love for the land, he pledged, again, to fight for it and for those who loved it.

He flew up the stairs, past Nomed's guards, and shifted. Eight spider legs carried him under the door. Multifaceted arachnid eyes picked out Torgin and Skipt, sitting opposite him in the tunnel. Sitrio was nowhere to be seen. As he prepared to shift to his Pentharian form, two Giests shot from the cavern into the passageway. Scuttling across the floor, he darted into One Man's flute case. Rather than attempt a rescue and fail, he would wait for the right opportunity.

When a howl from the Giests summoned reinforcements, Torgin jumped to standing and shoved Skipt behind him. Before he could devise a plan, the stench of rotting flesh and the dissonance of high-pitched shrieks surrounded them. With his hands pressed to his ears, he tried to block out the piercing sound. Next to him, the Enots disintegrated into a pile of small gray stones that rolled away in the darkness.

Fighting the tide of Giests maneuvering him toward the door, he made a grab for One Man's flute. As his fingers closed around it, a mass of smelling, gelatinous bodies lifted him. A wave of color deposited him on a steep stairway.

With panic threatening to undermine his attempts to keep fear at bay, he shoved a Giest aside and slung the flute case over his shoulder. "I refuse to be afraid."

A ball of green flew straight at his face and spit. Another smacked the side of his head. His resolve disintegrated; fear washed over him. *I just want to go home.*

Something brushed his calf and settled on the step. Again and again—brush, plink, brush, clink, brush, plink. Small arms wrapped around his leg. Relief flooded through him. He was no longer alone.

Once the council of war was complete and plans to deal with Myrrh's Guardian and her band were ready to put into action, Wodash watched his nemesis depart for another visit to the Cave of Canedari. He gave little credence to his master's hope that Esán would return before Almiralyn and her troops arrived.

A group of squealing Giests hovering above the Stairway of Retu Erath aroused his curiosity. He soared above them. *Well, well! The boy from Nemttachenn!* His malicious laugh rattled through the cavern. "You are mine again!" He swooped down and blew a frigid cloud over his prey. Icicles formed, hung in the mist-filled air, and fell like raindrops, freezing Torgin midway between steps.

On Nevah Efas, Esán prepared to teleport. He felt the cool smoothness of the Evolsefil Crystal vibrating beneath his hand; then nothing. Blinded by sudden darkness, he walked with arms outstretched until his fingers touched the hardness of wood. He pressed his ear against a door. Silence. He opened it a crack. *The Hall of Priestesses. I'm in the Cave of Canedari.*

Almost certain neither Ari nor the Guardian of Myrrh would be there, he tiptoed to the end of the corridor, where the splintered silvery door still hung at an odd angle on one polished brass hinge. He crept closer, dropped to his knee, and peered through a jagged break in the wood. A thrill of dismay coursed through him.

Pentharian in the Reading Room! He sat back on his haunches, a multitude of questions racing through his mind. Spying again, he watched a blue Pentharian lean down to listen to someone ask a question.

I know who that is. He pressed closer to the splintered door.

"Well now, what have we here?" A harsh voice hissed in his ear.

His head jerked around. A hand clamped over his mouth. An arm picked him up and carried him down the hall. No matter how hard he struggled, he could not break free. Once through the double doors and inside the Cave of Canedari, Nomed dumped him on the smooth stone floor.

"Where is it?" The DiMensioner's eyes glinted like steel.

Esán, his mind blank as a clean sheet of paper, remained silent.

"I have Zugo and Brie. Unless you tell me where Evolsefil is, you may never see them again."

"And if you harm them..." He kept his reply calm. "You'll never know what happened to the crystal."

"I'll have Wodash deal with you."

"He'll freeze the life out of me, and I'll take the secret with me into death."

Nomed glared, his scar pulsing red with fury.

Yuin's brown bat hung upside down in the Cave of Canedari. Hypersensitive ears picked up every word of the conversation below. His dislike of the DiMensioner escalated to hatred when ropes flashed into existence and bound Esán, hand and foot.

From the swirl of Nomed's cape, the black and silver owl appeared and flew in a wide circle, its talons reaching for the bald boy.

Yuin dove from the wall and changed from bat to vulture in mid-flight. His war cry echoed through the cave and launched him in pursuit of the shifted form of the man who would destroy Myrrh. Nothing would give him more pleasure than to snatch it from the air and end its vengeful existence.

Esán stared after the disappearing adversaries, struggling without success to loosen the cords keeping him prisoner. He felt trapped and helpless.

A blue Pentharian erupted from the Hall of Priestesses with Allynae and Jordett at his heels.

"It's Nomed!" Esán struggled to sit. "He's in owl form in the cavern."

Voer shifted. Allynae leapt on his back. The next instant, they were in the air, soaring after the DiMensioner od DerTah.

Jordett knelt and tried, without success, to untie the cords. He stood up, frowning. "I'm sorry, Esán, Nomed must have done something to these knots."

Almiralyn arrived, followed by an unknown man, two more Pentharian, and Karrew. "The time has come." Myrrh's Guardian turned to the stranger. "One Man, please help Esán."

A flash of gold light left Esán momentarily blind. When his vision cleared, Almiralyn and her raven had vanished. Jeet shifted. Vulture wings carried him into the cavern. Stee, with Jordett on his feathered back, soared after him. Esán and One Man remained alone in the silent, empty cave.

57

Wodash hovered above the Stairway of Retu Erath, his hungry gaze on the boy from Nemttachenn Tower. The desire to drink his vital essence made the death shadow salivate. A war cry from the Cave of Canedari erased it. He grimaced. *My master's needs come first.*

The great horned owl swooped over his head, and Nomed materialized on the stairs. "Grab Esán!" He leapt into the darkness, plummeting like an anchor to the depths of the sea. Mid-fall, he shifted. Silent owl wings carried him upward. A Pentharian vulture soared after him, its golden eyes alight with malice.

Wodash eyed the sniveling Giests. "Guard the boy well, or you will regret it." With a final hungry look at his prey, he shot after the vulture. Like an icy cannonball, he slammed into Yuin's feathered side, hurling him away from his quarry. Hovering beyond the stairway, he watched his enemy's battle to slow his somersaulting body. A powerful downward thrust of his wings sent him soaring upward to join comrades who streaked from Canedari in pursuit of Nomed. Torn between helping his master or obeying his orders, Wodash floundered. *Obey, fool. The bald youngster comes first. You might even win your freedom.*

K arrew flew beside his mistress as they led the charge into the Cavern of Tennisca. A jagged flash cleaving the space exposed vultures and Humans to one side and Giests appearing from every direction on the other. The crash of molecules reassembling rocked the cavern. Momentary blindness held adversaries still. Then putrid balls of color exploded into action. Shrieking plasma drove vultures in a defensive pattern, dodging and weaving through their enemy's ranks. Voer and Allynae flanked Almiralyn on the right. Karrew did his best to shield her on the left as she intercepted and disabled Giest after Giest. An unexpected change in course carried her above the chaos, her escort left behind.

From his perch above the battle, Nomed drew back his arm. Like the ancient god Thor, he sent a second bolt of lightning zigzagging across the cavern. Its target—the Guardian's brother. Allynae yelled. Voer dropped, the air above him hissing with blue fire that singed his wing tips. Almiralyn streaked along the glowing pathway. Karrew raced after her.

The black and silver owl launched into flight, his trajectory carrying him straight for the Guardian of Myrrh.

O ne Man studied the boy next to him. The shaft of brightness from the hall illuminated his profile, the well-shaped bald head, the fine lines of his cheek and nose. Something stirred in One Man's heart, something long hidden. He ran a finger over a strand of cord encircling his wrists. "I see the DiMensioner has worked his nefarious magic."

"Can you do anything to help?" The boy's soft voice strummed his memory like a harp.

One Man tipped his head, then touched a knot with his fingertip. "I believe I can help." He recited a phrase, tapped the knots securing the cord to Esán's ankles and wrists, and snapped his fingers. Cords fell into a scattered heap.

Esán exhaled a relieved breath and stepped free. "Thank you. I'm Esán Efre. How did you—" A shock of recognition flashed through eyes that shifted from blue to gray; from curiosity to hope, then softened into an unspoken question.

One Man, stunned—exhilarated—fearful, swallowed. "Where are you from?" Longing rang in each word.

"The Central Mountains on the planet of Thera." The boy seemed to hold his breath.

Working his braid through shaking fingers, One Man forced words around the tightness in his throat. "Your Aunt Merrilea raised you after your mother departed and your father left."

"How did you know?" Esán's quiet question quivered with emotion.

One Man realized he had chosen not to probe his mind—knew he could read the sadness in his eyes and see the pain like iron bands around his heart. He dropped his gaze and cleared his throat. "My true name is Somay." He raised his gray-blue eyes to meet the boy's. "I'm your father, Esán."

Blood rushed to Esán's face and roared in his ears. *My father—my father—my father.* The words pounded with the rhythm of his heartbeat. He realized he hadn't spoken. With a suddenness that surprised him, his mind cleared, and he could breathe again. All the pain he had hidden for fifteen sun cycles came unbidden. "Why did you leave us when we needed you so much?"

In the Reading Room, Ari replaced Efillaeh in its scabbard and watched Paisley walk the length of the room. Fen smiled as the big man stomped his foot.

"T-thanks for the h-healing."

Paisley's stuttered apology made Ari grin. "I'm glad it helped. Let's find out what's happening in the Cave of Canedari." Halfway down the Hall of Priestesses, she came to a standstill, a finger pressed to her lips.

Paisley exhaled a soft breath. "Oh."

Fen's small hand squeezed hers.

In the light spilling from the open double doors, One Man embraced a slender boy. Esán raised his head from the man's shoulder and smiled through his tears.

"Esán." Ari sprinted down the hall. "It's really you!"

His eyes twinkled. "You're Ari. I can tell by your voice."

One Man, she noticed, kept a protective arm around his shoulders.

Esán's eyes sparkled with wonder. "This is my father."

She grinned at One Man. "I knew you seemed familiar, and now I know why." A touch of longing crept into her deep voice. "I'm so pleased you found each other."

Esán beamed. "Me, too!"

She introduced Paisley and Fen.

"Happy to meet you." Esán grew serious. "Ari, I'm glad you're here." He quickly explained Elae's situation. "Will you come to Nevah Efas with me?"

"Of—" A blast of frigid air sent her darting to the side. "The death shadow! Look out!"

Wodash od DerTah hovered, framed by open purple doors, his gaze riveted on Esán. In one swift movement, One Man stepped in front of his son.

The death shadow loomed over them. "Step aside or I'll kill the boy."

"F-father." Esán fought for breath.

One Man whipped around. Esán clawed at a white cord encircling his neck, fought for breath, and collapsed to the floor.

Ari grasped Efillaeh's handle and crept forward. Paisley and Fen moved in behind her.

One Man knelt next to his son. "Please don't hurt him."

Ari drew the sacred knife. A war whoop rang through Canedari. The death shadow whirled, inhaled, and blew. A cloud of frosty air missed her as she dropped to a crouch. Paisley staggered beside her, shook himself like an enormous dog, and kept pace as she maneuvered Wodash away from his quarry. One Man left his son in Fen's care and hurried to assist her.

Wodash hovered. Hatred glistened as cold as ice in his eyes. Unflinching,

Ari advanced, One Man and Paisley at her back. The death shadow lunged and grabbed for the knife. Faster than the snap of a whip, Ari slashed his palm with the gleaming silver blade.

The death shadow's howl shook the cave. His body, twisting and thrashing in pain, faded to a pallid, whitish gray. Pale blue fluid dripped from the long gash. As each drop splattered on Canedari's floor, he writhed, screaming like a wounded animal. "You will all pay for this." His hand cradled next to his chest, he fled.

Paisley and Fen closed the doors. As the knife crackled and sparked, cleansing itself of blue bodily fluids, Esán moaned and pushed himself to sitting. Ari hurried to his side and slid Efillaeh's tip beneath the white cord. Writhing like a snake, it fell to the floor, sizzled, and evaporated in a puff of amber smoke.

He massaged his throat and swallowed. "Thank you, Arienh."

One Man helped him to stand. "Are you alright?"

"I'm fine, Father." He turned to Ari. "We have to help Elae. She doesn't have much time."

Fen peered up at him. "How will you get there?"

"We'll teleport."

Ari's brow wrinkled in concern. "If Elae is that bad, Owae must come, too."

"Who's Owae?"

"She's a DeoNyte healer and Elae's grandmother. Yookotay will find her for us."

"Good idea, but we'll need to be quick." Longing replaced the urgency in his expression. "I have a lot I want to share, Father, and so much I want to learn, but Elae is in grave danger."

"I understand, Esán. Paisley, Fen, and I will stay here and guard these doors."

"We'll be back as soon as we can." Esán extended a hand.

Ari gripped it, her expression alive with excitement. "What do I need to do?"

Wodash flew from the cave of Canedari into the chaos of combat. The need to lick his wounds and to allow his body to recover sent him retreating beneath the stairway. His anger boiled white hot. *By the Fire ConDra of DerTah! I despise that twin, that knife, and...* Hatred-filled eyes scanned the cavern and fastened on its prey. *In the Tower of Nemttachenn, I promised you death, raven. Your end is near.*

His hollowed eye sockets narrowed in the sudden flash of Nomed's second bolt of lightning. Almiralyn and Karrew raced along its jagged path, unprotected by their Pentharian allies. The great horned owl swooped with talons outstretched, reaching for the white and gold bird.

Almiralyn shot away, taking refuge under the stairs. Looping upward, she appeared again, wing tips gleaming in the eerie light cast by the Giests. Nomed closed the gap between them. The white bird banked and streaked across the cavern. The owl arced above her, dropped, and missed. She disappeared once more beneath the Stairway of Retu Erath. Nomed hovered, waiting for her to reappear.

Wodash held his breath.

Karrew soared high above the battle as his mistress circled near the top of the stairs. She looped upward and streaked toward the hovering great horned owl. It swooped beneath the stairway, then arced above it. The white bird had no choice but to meet the owl head on.

Karrew, aiming straight for the back of the owl's black and silver neck, primed his sharp beak to tear the tender flesh.

The moment had arrived. Wodash hurtled toward his target. The impact, soundless amidst the screeching of Giests, sent Karrew tumbling head over tail into the vast darkness below. A malicious laugh rolled after him. "Roast in the flames of SeDah, raven!"

As the death shadow returned his attention to the battle, the white and gold bird dodged Nomed's talons and streaked after her falling protector.

With a howl of delight, Wodash shot forward, snatched her from the air, and pressed her warm body to his icy chest.

"Almiralyn is mine!" His shout of triumph echoed in the sudden hush that filled the cavern. Elated, he soared above Allynae and his band of Pentharian. Giests zipped around him like hornets in a frenzy. And above it all, the black and silver owl hovered, his hazel eyes glued to his henchman and the prize he carried.

Victory is mine! Wodash swooped toward the small prison cave where the DeoNyte and the twin shook in terror as Myrrh shuddered to the depths of the Dojanacks and then grew deathly quiet.

Allynae sent Jordett and Stee in pursuit of Karrew's falling body before turning his attention to Almiralyn's captor. "Get Nomed." He pressed his knees into Voer's feathered sides.

The immense vulture sailed on outstretched wings against a tide of fluorescent color. Giests drove them down toward the mouth of Tennisca. Yuin and Jeet joined in a fight to press the balls of protoplasm up into the vast cavern. Through the deafening noise and blinding light, and with the persistence and tenacity of their breed, the Pentharian caught one Giest after another in their sharp beaks and flung them away. Allynae pushed his mount faster. Voer needed no urging.

Yookotay stood at the council table, his hand resting on his malachite marker and his attention fixed on Esán as he described what had happened to Elae. Behind him, the red-haired twin, Arienh, waited, holding her impatience in check.

Esán finished with an earnest request. "We came to Meos in the hopes you would allow Owae to come with us."

In response, Yookotay summoned the young DeoNyte standing guard at the Council Chamber doors. "Go. Tell Owae what has occurred and bring her here."

A short time later, the ancient healer arrived, laden with all she would require to help her granddaughter.

Ari relieved her of her bags. "Thank you, Owae, for coming so quickly. Elae needs you." She drew her forward. "This is Esán. He will teleport us to her."

The elderly healer regarded him with interest. "I sense the power in you. Please take me to Elae."

Yookotay touched her shoulder. "She is on Nevah Efas. You may need to remain with her there."

"I have brought all I required to do what I must do."

Ari took her hand. "It's time."

Esán joined them in a circle.

"Stay safe and bring—" Yookotay's admonition went unfinished. The room was empty.

O wae gasped in surprise as Yookotay and his chamber vanished, replaced by a meadow and tall, golden grass. "Oh, my." She felt sure her astonishment matched the expression on Ari's face.

The astounded twin stared. "We're not in Myrrh anymore."

Esán laughed. "This is Nevah Efas." His gaze traveled from the chartreuse sun slipping below the horizon to where Evolsefil glowed a shimmering white against the pale mauve sky.

"How did we arrive so fast?" Owae's ancient face wrinkled in wonder.

"I thought us here." Esán gave her a lopsided smile and pointed at a dilapidated cottage. "Elae is over there."

Owae wove her way across the meadow and into the cottage. She knelt at Elae's side and placed arthritic fingers on her wrist. "Her pulse is weak. We have little time." She gazed up at Ari. "You must use Efillaeh."

Ari withdrew the sacred knife from its scabbard and held it out. "Elae is your granddaughter. Your love for her will enhance its power. You must use it to heal her."

Owae clasped the knife's handle. Whispering a quiet prayer, she touched its tip to the soles of her grandchild's feet and then to the crown of her head. Finally, she laid it over Elae's heart and sat back.

Lavender light from the amethysts in Efillaeh's handle mingled with the emerald light flowing from the etchings on its silver blade to form a cocoon of healing mist around Elae's battered body. She inhaled one shallow breath and then another. Color returned to her grayed cheeks and washed the blue tinge from her lips. Her feverish skin cooled. A tiny smile played for a moment at the corners of her mouth. With a soft sigh, she slipped into a deep and peaceful sleep.

Owae picked up the knife and pressed it to her heart. Relief and gratitude filled her. "She needs lots of rest, but she'll regain her strength." She held out the knife. "Thank you, Ari, for allowing me the gift of healing. I will never forget your kindness."

Ari smiled and returned Efillaeh to its place at her side. "It worked, Owae, because you are a Chosen One."

Esán knelt and touched Elae's soft white fur. "I thought I'd killed her."

"You found Ari and Efillaeh and brought them here. Thanks to you, she'll recover." She noted the dark circles hanging like crescent moons beneath his eyes and the translucent pallor of his skin. "When did you rest last?" She rummaged around in her pack.

"I don't remember."

She handed him a small packet of green tablets. "These herbs should ease the strain of teleporting, but you need to—"

A shudder shook Nevah Efas. Owae, Esán, and Ari hastened to the door. Although the meadow appeared unchanged, Evolsefil's vibrant energy had dimmed.

"Listen." Ari gripped the doorframe.

Nothing moved. Not a sound broke the eerie silence.

Owae urged the children from the cottage. "Something is wrong on Myrrh. Go to Yookotay. He will help you discover what's amiss."

Esán swallowed a green tablet and stuffed the packet in his pocket. "I'll return for you as soon as I can."

Ari held out her hands.

Owae watched the young people shimmer and disappear, leaving her to care for Elae and to wonder what had occurred in her homeland.

As the heart of its mistress grew cold and silent, Elcaro's Eye churned out images like newspapers on an ancient printing press.

Stillness enveloped the Land of Myrrh. Wood Tiff, Human, animal, and bird fought for breath. Trees ceased their growing. Grass withered. Water stagnated in streams, rivers, and lakes.

In Mira's cottage, Merrilea froze mid-sentence. Sparrow's brush fell from her hand and splattered paint on the studio floor. On the canvas, an ugly white face leered, its eyes brimming with evil triumph. The white and gold bird clutched to its chest appeared lifeless. Majeska's howl shattered their horrified silence. Tail thrashing the air, she ran from the room.

High in her TreeOm, Sibine gasped and placed her hands over her rounded belly. Tibin held her close, his face contorted with fear. The spirit of Nemttachenn stirred, listening intently within the walls of its tower. And in the Dojanack Caverns, white-capped waves raced across the Lake of Rorret and crashed against the shore in search of the cause of their unrest.

The Winds of Myrrh began to stir. From all directions, they gathered, whispering through the leaves of the Terces Wood, skimming over the stagnant water, and stealing through the mountain canyons. Unchecked, they sped across the grasslands, collided, and coalesced. Chaos whipped the thick, gray mist into funnels of whirlwind energy that spawned hundreds of cyclones. The heavens rocked. The winds roared. Myrrh and Thera trembled from surface to core.

Elcaro's Eye grew dark and still.

58

The great horned owl landed in the small cave, preened its black and silver feathers, and shifted form. Nomed, fingers caressing the collar of the cape that marked him as a DiMensioner, awaited the death shadow's arrival. *What a coup! Almiralyn will soon be mine and then...*

His minion touched down and knelt, head bowed, the white and gold bird clutched in his glacial grip. "I bring you the grand prize, Master."

"You have redeemed yourself and more, my friend." The DiMensioner smirked. "Rise and prepare to witness our next triumph."

Standing at the mouth of the cave, he called his army to him. A raised arm parted the wall of disfigured creatures to form a Giest-lit corridor. Through its center he threw a bolt of light that exploded above the heads of the Pentharian and their Human leader. "Come forward if you dare, Allynae Nadrugia."

Almiralyn's brother urged his mount forward until they hovered opposite him.

Nomed fixed his grim gaze on Allynae. "As you can see, the death shadow holds Almiralyn in a heart lock. I possess one of your twins and the son of the ReDael of the DeoNytes. They will die if you do not find and return Evolsefil to me. You have one turning." A gesture of his upraised hand left the cavern in total darkness and his army hidden beneath a cloak of invisibility.

Horror churned Torgin's stomach into knots as Karrew plunged to his death and Wodash, the white bird pressed to his icy chest, flew into the dark of Tennisca. He shuddered. *Almiralyn is now the prisoner of Seyes Nomed. What on Thera do I do?*

Tiny gray hands tugged at his pant leg. Bending down, he lifted the Enots to his shoulder. As he straightened, the cavern went dark—no Giests, no lightning, no DiMensioner.

Skipt tugged again. "Ya ho, Torgin, we go to the Cave of Canedari before they remember us."

Torgin's inner coward screamed, 'run', yet something held him motionless. The darkness thinned; memories flicked into focus. His strange adventure replayed, a reminder of the frightened boy who came to Myrrh and of who he was becoming.

He squared his shoulders. With new confidence, he descended the Stairway of Retu Erath. "It's time to find our friends, Skipt, and see how we can help."

Paisley paced the Cave of Canedari, his thoughts galloping round and round and always ending up where they began. *What's happenin' in Tennisca?* Only ominous silence greeted him when he peeked between the purple doors. He halted his restless back and forth to watch Fen twisting his beat-up hat in the soft light spilling into the shadowy interior from the hall.

At the center of the cave, One Man waited, a wistful expression on his face. The hermit had found his son. Paisley tugged at his mustache. *I can't imagine having a son*. Thoughts of Torgin made him smile. *Perhaps I have a small idea*. He rubbed his dark head, feeling awkward at the sudden insight.

A noise at the entrance to the cavern interrupted. Paisley peeked through a narrow crack, then admitted three vultures and Allynae. "Are the others comin'?"

Allynae dismounted. The Pentharian shifted to their true form and spoke quietly in their guttural language. Fen closed the doors.

Allynae ran a hand through his hair. "Nomed has Almiralyn, Brie, and Zugo. He's given us one turning to find and return Evolsefil to him. The Priestesses seemed positive the DiMensioner stole the Prima Crystal, but that's not the case. I'm not sure where to begin."

"Nomed didn't remove the crystal." One Man joined them. "Esán did."

Allynae looked stunned. "How could *he* move it? He's a mere boy."

Everyone began talking at once.

"Where is Esán?"

"How do we find him?"

"Do you think he can bring Evolsefil back?"

"Shhh!" Allynae knelt beside Fen. The Wood Tiff pointed at the closed doors. Yuin and Jeet shifted to panther and crouched, ready to spring. Paisley pulled Fen behind him and, with Allynae, One Man, and Voer, moved into the dimness behind them.

One door opened a crack. Tiny fingers appeared mid-way to the handle, followed by a small gray face. "Ya ho, may we please come in?"

Allynae stepped into view. "We?"

Skipt pushed the doors open further, and Torgin sidled through.

Paisley dodged between the two panthers, gathered him in his arms and grinned. "Torgin, I am so glad to see you."

Before Torgin could speak, Skipt pranced forward and pulled on Paisley's pant leg. "Paisley, we glad to see you, too."

Still grinning, Paisley introduced them to the group.

Allynae smiled and glanced at the doors. "I'm happy to meet you, Torgin. Paisley told me you were in the company of an Enots and a Pentharian."

"I don't know where Yaro is." Worry filled the summer green eyes. "He went to spy on Nomed, and we haven't seen him since."

As he spoke, a small brown arachnid crawled from the sheepskin case slung over his shoulder. A thin silver thread shimmered in the soft light. The spider dropped to the ground and Yaro appeared, a broad grin on his tattooed face.

Skipt jumped up and down. Panthers shifted and welcomed their long-lost comrade. Torgin and Fen moved away from the twitching tails, and, together, they watched the strange creatures from ReTaw au Qa greet each other in their native tongue and the ritualistic ways of their species.

"Pentharian are so beautiful, aren't they?" Torgin beamed at his friends. "Yaro is my heart-brother, you know."

The golden Pentharian beckoned him over. "This is Torgin, Human of Idronatti on the planet of Thera and the brother of my heart." Each Pentharian stepped forward with a hand on his heart, bowed his braid-covered head, and said with great respect, "Ook oadem edai. Welcome, brother."

Paisley felt a surge of pride. *The boy's done some growin' up since I found him in the grasslands.*

Fear for his sister and impatient to begin the search for Evolsefil, Allynae contained his desire to interrupt as the Pentharian reunited and welcomed Torgin as their brother. Containing his restlessness, he joined One Man and Paisley near the purple doors. "I have so many questions, ones we can't answer." He looked at the hermit. "Any idea where Esán and Ari are?"

One Man shared what had occurred in Canedari after everyone had left in pursuit of Nomed.

"I had a feeling about you and Esán." Allynae smiled. "I'm so glad you found each other."

Voer broke away from the group of Pentharian surrounding Torgin and Yaro to join them. "We are reunited." He bowed his head. "Thank you for your patience, Brother of Almiralyn."

Allynae heaved a weary sigh. "We have plans to make. Let's adjourn to the Reading Room." He glanced around the group. "We'll need someone to stay here."

Paisley and Yuin volunteered. Allynae led the strange companions along the Hall of Priestesses, his fear for Almiralyn a fierce throbbing in his chest.

Stee, with Jordett flattened against his back, plunged through the Cavern of Tennisca after Karrew. Gauging the speed of his target, the Pentharian swooped. Missed. Accelerated. Slowed. Again he dove, chasing Almiralyn's protector beyond the crystal mouth into the sky above Idronatti.

Grateful no fear emanated from the Theran major, he folded his wings close to his sides and plummeted, beak down, to the side of the falling raven. With buildings rising around them, he dropped below Karrew and unfurled his vulture wings. On his back, Jordett fought a gust of wind, steadied himself, and snatched the injured bird from its free-fall to death. Stee swooped along an empty city street, then soared straight upward to land on the roof of a tall gray building.

Jordett dismounted, cradling Karrew. "That was way too close." He gulped a breath as Stee shifted. "I almost missed."

"But you didn't." Stee's voice was steadier than he felt. "Let us see how badly he's wounded."

A gash over Karrew's heart oozed droplets of blood. Shallow, hesitant breaths barely moved his chest up and down. His black toes curled into tight little balls and remained immobile; his eyes closed.

Stee frowned. "What do you think, Major?"

Jordett's astute gaze moved to the injured bird to his face. "We must take him to the Cave of Canedari and hope Ari returns soon with Efillaeh."

The door to the stairwell edging open sent Stee into the shape of a small black fly. Darting upward, it flew a wide circle and landed on the major's back.

Two young PPP patrollers marched onto the rooftop, weapons drawn.

The shorter of the two gasped. "Major Jordett! How did you get here? We've been looking for you everywhere."

The Major regarded them with a commander's sternness. "Put your weapons away."

The tall patroller ignored the order and kept his weapon trained on

Jordett. "Maybe he isn't really the major." He glared at Karrew cradled against his chest. "What if he's a spy from..." A nervous glance at the underbelly of Myrrh produced a shudder of dread.

The shorter patrolman shot his partner a dubious look. "You'd better come with us, Major. We can't take the chance you're not who you say you are. A huge black shape flew over this building. And now, we find you here."

Jordett glared from one to the other. "Take me to your superior officer. I don't have time to stand arguing with you."

"Through there, Major." The shorter man holstered his weapon and moved toward the door. Wind whipping around a corner banged it closed. With both hands gripping the door handle, patroller held it wide enough for Jordett to step through. A gust ripped it from his grasp and slammed it shut with a resounding crash.

Stee buzzed past the major and zipped down the stairs.

Jordett flipped the lock and sprinted after him. At the landing, he pulled the exit door ajar. Stee whizzed through into an empty room across the hall. Jordett checked for patrollers, saw none, and followed.

Stee shifted. "We have to go somewhere safe so I can fly us away from here. Any ideas?"

Jordett adjusted his hold on Karrew. "Can you shape a Human?"

"Neither is it allowed, nor do I think it wise."

Jordett studied his face. "Perhaps you're right, my friend. Let's find a fire escape. We'll use the stairs."

Stee shifted to a fly and buzzed next to Jordett.

The major hurried to a door marked EGRESS and listened intently. "All clear."

Once inside, his soundless descent took them down three floors. Ducking a surveillance cam, he opened the door a small crack, noted a group of patrollers by the drop car, and eased it shut. Stee buzzed ahead of him down two more floors to an empty corridor. The numbers above the drop chute blinked, tracking the car's upward progress. It stopped at the twenty-first floor.

"They know we're here. It's only a matter of time before they find us." Jordett ducked into a nearby room. Stee materialized beside the window.

The major pointed at the fire escape. "Can you take off from there?"

Footsteps pounding down the hall spurred them into action. Stee threw open the window, climbed onto the metal platform, and shifted. Jordett followed and scrambled onto his back, with Karrew held close to his chest.

"Stop!" The shouted command ripped through the room. "Stop in the name of the PPP!"

Stee launched his vulture form from the railing. Huge wings pressed against the air and lifted him and his precious cargo skyward.

A volley of shots accompanied by yells chased them. Pain tore through Stee's body. He faltered, caught himself, and swooped along a vacant side street.

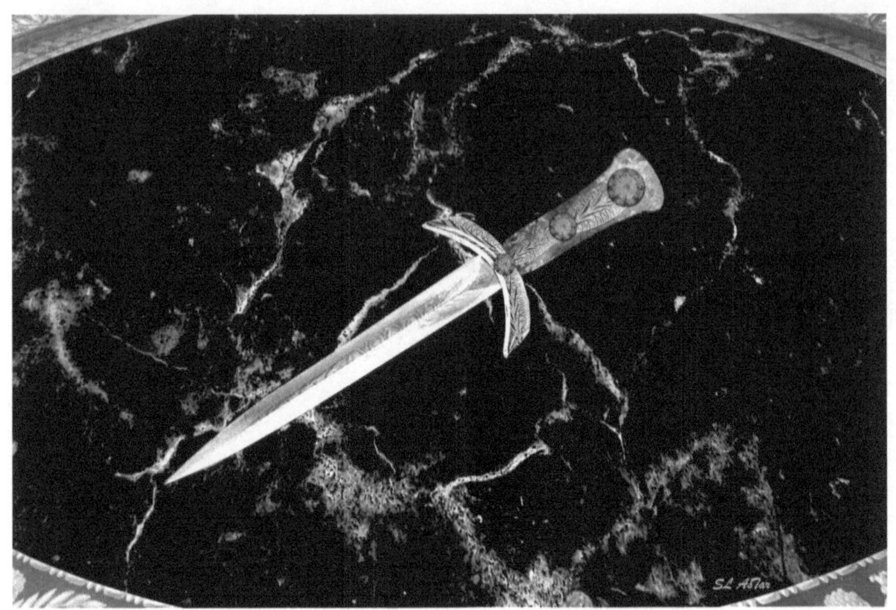

59

rie huddled next to Zugo, sharing her warmth and drawing his body's heat around her. Although the death shadow had withdrawn his attention, his chilling hatred lingered. She perceived it in Zugo, and she sensed it in herself. Across the cave, Wodash continued to press Almiralyn's bird form to his frigid chest. *Perhaps that's why the cave is so cold.*

Nomed's demon eyes locked onto hers. The bite of his thoughts pierced her brain. In his mind, triumph vibrated like a song. She tore her gaze from his face and focused on the ground.

Zugo scooted closer. *"How can we help Almiralyn?"*

She squeezed his hand and shook her head. *"Careful."*

Nomed loomed over them. "Both of you, stand up." When they didn't respond, he yanked them to their feet. "The Guardian of Myrrh and all she loves will soon cease to exist." His scar-twisted expression oozed elation mixed with hatred. "Already the land is disintegrating. Soon, I will have everything I have ever wanted!"

A mental probe knifing through Brie's mind left her gritting her teeth. She stared at the ground, her expression bland; her mind blank. He jerked her chin up and probed again. She didn't blink. Nothing registered—except her extreme dislike of the man in front of her. Nomed's scar blazed red. Rage burned in his eyes. He brought his hand back. "You little—"

A ball of white fur slamming into his stomach sent him stumbling backward. With a growl, he regained his balance and took a menacing step toward Zugo. The DeoNyte's unwavering blue eyes reflected the DiMensioner's fury with the clarity of Mira's fountain.

A look of disgust twisted the death shadow's ugly features. "Leave them, Seyes. We have more important things to do than fight with *children*."

Nomed loomed larger and more threatening. "Soon both of you will be fodder for the death shadow." He sneered at Brie. "Too bad your father will never have the chance to know you. And yours, young DeoNyte, will soon mourn your demise." His sardonic laugher echoed through the cavern. Pivoting, he glared at his minion. "Wodash od DerTah, bring the Guardian of Myrrh in *all* her *glory*!" With his cape fanning out behind him, he dove from the rim of the cave and became the black and silver owl.

Brie's hands tightened into fists. Wodash gave her a final malicious grin, bowed formally, and flew after his master, the white bird in his arms. Surrounded by a colorful entourage, they flew across the cavern and exited through the door at the top of Retu Erath.

Brie uncurled her fingers and stared at her palms. *What did Nomed mean when he said I'll never get to know my father? Does he even know who my father is?* Her frustration mounted. *I've failed everyone—Almiralyn and Ari and Zugo and even Myrrh itself.*

Sitrio's unexpected arrival in Meos minus Zugo and his companions placed Yookotay in a quandary. The details of what had occurred only heightened his concerns. He attempted to listen as his most trusted DeoNyte-at-Arms described the battle in the Cavern of Tennisca to the assembled council of Crystal Keepers. He worried about Zugo and the young Humans; but more than that, he feared for the life of Myrrh's Guardian.

Sitrio's voice, filled with the emotions of his tale, took on an ominous flavor. "Nomed and the death shadow have captured a white and gold bird and taken it to Oche—"

Esán and Ari flashed into view. A startled yelp added fuel to the fire of foreboding already burning hot in the members of the council. Frightened cries filled the chamber. Yookotay raised a hand. The voices grew quiet.

"There is no reason for panic." His calm presence soaked up the council's escalating fear. "Most of you have met Ari and Esán, and understand they are vital to the safety of Myrrh. I must confer with them. We will reconvene shortly."

Casting apprehensive looks at their leader and the two young Humans, the council members filed from the chamber.

Yookotay stopped Sitrio with a nod. "Please stay." He turned to his visitors. "What has occurred on Nevah Efas? How is Elae?"

Esán ended his update with a frown of concern. "The white bird Sitrio described is Almiralyn in shifted form. Her capture is the reason Myrrh changed so drastically."

"I know." He fingered his sapphire pendant. "With her in the hands of the death shadow and Evolsefil hidden on Nevah Efas, our homeland is in grave danger. We must bring the crystal home."

Ari tucked a stray curl behind her ear. "Is there any place on Myrrh we can safely hide it from Nomed and the Giests?"

"It must be somewhere I know, or I won't be able to teleport it there." Esán sagged against the council table.

Yookotay studied him with concern, then crossed to the map of Myrrh.

Ari hurried to his side. "What if we hide the crystal in the Tower of Nemttachenn?"

"That will work." Esán joined them. "I have been there and know it."

Yookotay nodded and smiled. "Nemttachenn might be just the place."

Sitrio cleared his throat. "I've read there's an ancient spirit guarding the tower. Will it help us, or give us away to Nomed?"

"There is one way to find out." Yookotay turned to Esán." Can you take me there?"

"I can, but teleporting demands lots of energy, so I don't know how many trips I can make. Owae gave me these green pellets to take, but I have only three left."

The ReDael pursed his lips. "Ari, have you used Efillaeh on Esán?"

"Only to cut the death shadow's cord." She rested her hand on the scabbard.

"Perhaps it will help him regain enough strength to make teleporting less fatiguing." Yookotay led the way to the council table.

Sitrio helped Esán lie down on it. Ari placed Efillaeh on his chest.

At first, the knife remained unchanged. Then a soft green and purple haze floated around his prone body. Tears welled up at the corners of his eyes. He sighed and gripped the jeweled hilt. When the glow receded, he sat up, and, after a long moment, handed it to Ari.

She replaced it in the scabbard. "What happened, Esán?"

"My illness is not of this land. Efillaeh cannot heal it. The knife has, however, given me a reprieve. I should be able to teleport Yookotay and even Evolsefil to Nemttachenn. The bigger concern is whether I'll be able to return the crystal to the Cave of Canedari." He jumped down from the table.

"We'll cross that chasm when we get there." Yookotay turned to Sitrio. "Take Ari and Efillaeh to Nomed's cavern. If Almiralyn is still alive, she will require help and healing. Select several Meosian Protectors to go with you. And Sitrio, do *not fail*. Bring the Guardian of Myrrh to the Cave of Canedari as soon as possible."

Sitrio bid his farewells, told Ari to meet him by the fountain, and hurried from the council chamber.

Ari gave Esán a quick hug. "Take care of yourself, Esán Efre."

He squeezed her hand. "You take care of yourself and bring Almiralyn back to us."

"I'll do my best." She nodded to Yookotay and departed.

In the dim light provided by their glowing guards, Zugo examined the girl beside him. The aura of magic around her reminded him of Esán. The wall of silence existing between them made him focus on his own frustrations and worries. *Where is Esán? Is he safe? What about Father and our people?*

Brie sighed and covered her face with her hands.

"Are you alright?" Zugo wiggled closer.

She lowered her hands, but kept her focus on the lines of her palm. "I miss Ari. I don't know what's happening to Myrrh. I feel so *trapped*. And what did Nomed mean about my father?"

"Shhh." Zugo cocked his head and put a finger to his lips. *"Listen."*

"Brie? Brie?" Her whispered name came from somewhere to her right.

Her eyes widened. *"You hear that?"*

He nodded toward the far side of the cave. *"I think it's coming from over there."*

Careful not to attract their guards, he mimicked Brie's slow move to her knees and then to standing. Straining to track the voice amidst the Giest's bickering, they edged along the rough stone surface.

"Maybe we imagined it." Brie's telepathic thought sounded forlorn.

He clasped her hand. *"Someone is whispering your name, and it came from over here."*

"Brie? Are you there?"

"I told you so." He kept his eyes on the Giests and nudged her ahead of him.

"Brie?"

With a quick glance over her shoulder, Brie placed her hands on the wall. Zugo choked back a gasp of disbelief. His companion had vanished. Mystified, he tapped the stone barrier.

Brie reappeared, her face a picture of surprised excitement. "There's a passageway behind this wall. Bonnee's there. She can help us find Almiralyn."

Two Giests zipped around them and hovered close to their faces. Zugo watched Brie's expression blank. He turned sullen. A purple blob flicked spittle in his fur, giggled, and, with his partner, rejoined their comrades at the lip of the cave.

Zugo scrubbed at the slime and shot a scowl of disgust at the Giest. *"I can't pass through solid rock, Brie. You go. I'll wait here."*

"Stranger things have occurred during this adventure, Zugo." She offered her hand. *"Hold on to me. We'll see what happens."*

He tried to suspend his disbelief and failed. "I'm telling you, I can't walk through solid rock."

Brie grabbed his wrist and melted through the wall. His hand hit the barrier and stopped. She reappeared. *"Zugo, please believe you can do this."*

"Go on, Brie. I'll be fine. Just hurry and bring help."

Brie glanced over his shoulder. Her eyes grew enormous. *"Look out!"* Her shout echoed in his mind. Terrified, he looked behind him, felt an unexpected jerk, and stood in complete darkness with no Giests in sight.

"Fooled you, didn't I?" She laughed with delight. "A minor distraction and you stepped through solid stone. It may not work when you're alone, but sure does when you're holding onto me."

He stared straight into her eyes. "Who are you?"

"I'm a girl from Idronatti who came to Myrrh to celebrate a friend's sun cycle. Since I arrived, many strange things have happened and walking through walls is only one of them."

A rush of respect made him smile. "I guess you'd better lead on if we're to help Almiralyn."

She pointed into the darkness. "If you stare straight ahead, you can pick out the shimmering outline of a girl about our age. Can you see her?"

His night eyes picked out the translucent form. "You are one of the Now Remembered. We sensed the change when you found yourselves."

Bonnee smiled shyly. "Brie saved us. Without her and the Remembering Stone, we would still be lost. We need to go. Nomed took Almiralyn to Oche Cavern, and it's some distance from here."

Brie followed the Now Remembered girl.

Zugo pushed on the wall, looked at his hand, and trudged after them. *I never, ever expected to walk through a stone wall. Wonder what's next?*

60

Jordett cringed as the bullet slammed into Stee's vulture side and the alien creature re-established his equilibrium and streaked skyward. The major shuddered, stared at Myrrh high overhead, and wondered if the Pentharian had the strength to fly that far.

Black wings strained against the whirling winds, ripping at rider and vulture alike. To protect the small burden he cradled next to his chest, Jordett bent lower. The raven, icy cold and motionless beneath his jacket, made Jordett wonder if he would survive.

Stee did not calculate the distance he must fly. Relieved the bleeding had gone from a gush to a dribble, he ignored the white-hot pain in his side and concentrated on staying aloft. A powerful gust of wind flung him sideward. He swore. *If I could just ride with the wind instead of fight it...*

Giving in to the currents steering him away from the Cavern of Tennisca, he caught an updraft and allowed it to send him soaring. Had he not been burdened with the ever-increasing pain, he would have relished the amazing freedom that came with being one with the elements.

A wild rush of wind hit him broadside and sent him plunging away from his goal. With agony accompanying each wing stroke, he fought to regain altitude and stability and concentrated on reaching Myrrh.

Beneath him, Jordett felt the great vulture tremble in the ferocious wind. The warmth seeping from its body left its back cold against his legs, and its struggle to breathe sent periodic shudders along its spine. He wished he could help.

A stinging blow to his cheek startled him. He gasped and looked upward. Long, dark tendrils hung from the underside of Myrrh. *The Terces Wood.* Pushing a slender root aside, he stared into the distance. *Is that an Intersect platform?* Hope stirred. He sat upright and closed his uniform jacket more securely around Karrew.

"Stee, there's an Intersect up ahead." The words ripped from his mouth, scattered in the wind. He took a breath, leaned closer to the vulture's feather-covered ear holes, and yelled again. "Intersect ahead!"

Stee dodged a large tuber and slowed his ascent. In a zigzagged pattern, he made his way through roots that became more numerous the nearer he got to Myrrh's underbelly. At last, he landed on the platform at the foot of a steep set of stairs.

Jordett dismounted at once, clutching Almiralyn's raven protector to his chest.

The emerald Pentharian materialized and collapsed on the bottom step, his side scarlet with blood. His strange face looked deathly pale beneath its exotic tattoos. "I can't go much further." A rasping gasp shuddered through him.

Jordett laid Karrew on the platform and, kneeling beside Stee, examined the hole where the bullet had entered. It had not exited the body. Not a good sign.

Taking off his jacket, he tore it into strips. Some he tied together, and some he fashioned into a thick pad he placed over the wound. "Hold this in place." He took Stee's hand and pressed it on top while he wrapped the longest strips around the Pentharian's body and knotted the makeshift bandage in place. "Stay here and don't move. Can you watch Karrew while I find out where we are?"

Stee lifted his Human-like head. Golden eyes, drenched with pain, searched his face. "I may not remain conscious for long, my friend."

Jordett placed the raven in the crook of his good arm. "I'll hurry. Hold on."

The knowledge he could lose Karrew and Stee sent him sprinting up the steep stairs. He located the lever secreted in the rough bark. The door opened, and he crawled through into the hollowed trunk of a tree. A dim opening let him into the forest.

Only subdued light penetrated the thick gloom in the Terces Wood. Wind whipped mist and leaves with such force, the ancient trees swayed and dipped in a dance of violent despair.

A branch snapped. The major scanned the area. A small face peered up from behind the fallen limb.

"You helped to save me from the monsters." A Wood Tiff boy, his brown eyes huge, stepped into the open.

Jordett knelt. "Are you Sibee?"

The Tiffin nodded.

"I'm Jordy, and I need your help."

"Sibee!" The wind dissected the single word into fragmented syllables. "Sibee, where are you?"

The youthful Tiffin dodged behind Jordett as two adult Wood Tiffs scurried from the trees and stopped, their expressions startled and suspicious.

The tallest one took the lead. "I am Tibin, and my friend is Tuper. Have you seen a Tiff? He's been missing for most of the turning, and his parents are frantic."

Jordett drew a defiant, squirming Sibee into view. "Is this your absentee?"

Tibin's stern gaze rested on the rebellious Tiffin. "Sibee, your mother's terrified monsters have eaten you."

The youngster stopped wiggling. "Didn't mean to scare her. I just—"

Jordett interrupted. "I'm a friend of Almiralyn's, and I need your help."

Tibin's brown eyes opened even wider. "What can we do for you?"

As the major explained what had happened to Karrew and Stee, the Wood Tiffs listened, their faces serious. Tibin conferred with Tuper and then looked up at Jordett. "We can't return you to the Dojanacks fast enough. The Guardian's cottage is the best place to take you."

Jordett nodded, hoping with all his heart Merrilea was still there.

The elder Tiff addressed Sibee. "Since I can't send you home in this wind by yourself, you'll have to come with us. I trust you to behave."

Excitement gleamed in the young Tiff's eyes. "I'll do what I am told. I promise."

"Just make sure you do." Tibin led the way down the stairs to the platform, where the wounded Pentharian sat cradling Karrew.

The Wood Tiffs assessed the situation—the strange creature, the bloodied side, and the pain and fatigue holding him rigidly upright.

Tuper frowned. "We must travel through the Intersect. Can you stand?"

"I'll help you." Jordett handed Karrew to the adult Tiffs. He pulled the Pentharian's arm around his shoulders, slid his own around Stee's scaled back, and hoisted him to his feet.

Stee moaned and gripped the wooden handrail.

Jordett realized the journey would take the last of his friend's energy. "Let's move out."

"We'll all travel together. Sibee, you hold tight to Major Jordett's pant leg and don't let go." Tibin helped Tuper adjust Karrew more securely against their sturdy bodies. Next, he gave quick instructions. "We have three jumps to make. Between each, we will only stop long enough to recite the Key and state our destination. When I nod, repeat after me." His funny little hat bobbed up and down and they all repeated the Key.

Jordett focused his attention on keeping Stee upright. Vaguely aware of their momentary arrival on two platforms, he heaved a sigh of relief when he felt the final one supporting them. A subdued Sibee scuttled up the steep staircase. Tuper and Tibin followed with Karrew. Jordett shifted Stee's weight and began a laborious climb, one that elicited muffled moans from the Pentharian. At the top of the stairs, a Human-sized doorway allayed his concerns about how to maneuver through a door sized for a Wood Tiff. He looked around in surprise.

"Almiralyn's barn. Thank the Fathers we're here."

"I'll get help." Tuper dashed across the hay-strewn floor and out the door. After what seemed like forever, he reappeared with SparrowLyn and Merrilea.

Cradling Karrew, Sparrow, head bent against the blustery weather, struggled to reach the cottage. Merrilea slid an arm around the Pentharian's back opposite Jordett, and they half supported, half carried the injured warrior through the howling wind into Mira's ghost-gray kitchen. By the time they crossed the threshold, the raven lay on a soft, clean towel on a table by the stove; a kettle already simmered on its way to boiling. Sparrow had gathered bandages and antiseptic from one of Almiralyn's well-stocked cupboards.

Stee groaned and sagged.

Jordett tensed. The full weight of the Pentharian tore at the muscles in his arms and chest. "He's passed out. Hurry."

The women prepared the kitchen table to receive its strange burden. The Wood Tiffs joined them, each taking a Reptilian leg. On Jordett's command, they lifted the alien body onto the wooden table.

Once they had settled the Pentharian, Tibin bowed to Jordett. "Unless you need us, we must return to our families."

Jordett shook hands with both adult Wood Tiffs. "Thank you for your help." He knelt in front of Sibee. "You know what you experienced today is a secret, one you may only share if Tibin and Tuper grant you permission."

He nodded. "I'll never tell, Jordy. I *promise.*"

With Sibee between them, Tibin and Tuper scurried across the garden, and disappeared in the wind and the mist.

Not allowing himself to give in to the exhaustion threatening to knock his feet out from under him, Jordett walked to the sink, splashed cold water on his face, washed his bloodied hands, and swallowed a long, cool drink.

Merrilea handed him a towel. "I realize you are beat, Jordy, but I need your help. If I can't remove the bullet from Stee, we'll lose him. I checked Karrew. His ribs are bruised. We won't know for a while if the impact punctured his lung. He's alive, but..." She shook her head. "Sparrow will concentrate on him while you and I work on Stee."

He tossed the towel on the counter. "Have you ever removed a bullet from anyone before?"

"Only from a farmer's dog, but I don't have a choice."

He saw the determination in her face. "Tell me what you need." He rounded the table to stand by her side.

Esán sat on the wooden bench in the council chamber in Meos, nibbling hard-crusted bread and berries provided at Yookotay's request. He listened to the DeoNyte ReDael give instructions to two guards and realized how much Zugo's father loved his people and took to heart his responsibilities as their leader. With danger lurking in every shadow, Yookotay was doing his utmost to ensure the safety of his community prior to leaving for Nemttachenn.

When the guards had departed, he ate a crust of bread. "Do you require anything before we go, Esán?"

"I am much better. I didn't realize how hungry I was. Thank you." He stood up and brushed the crumbs from his hands. "Are you ready to leave?"

Yookotay smiled and clasped the offered hands. "Take me to Nemttachenn."

The walls of the council chamber morphed into the clearing where the Tower of Nemttachenn's ramparts disappeared in the swirling gray mist.

Esán observed with interest while Yookotay's candid gaze absorbed his surroundings—the trees whipping in the wind, the clouds churning as though a giant cook were stirring them with a ladle. "Have you ever been outside the Dojanacks Caverns?"

"I have not. Come." Yookotay walked to the arched door leading into the tower. "Let us summon the Sentinel of Myrrh."

CheeTrann's imposing presence filled Nemttachenn. Raging winds had inspired dreams of collapsed mountains tumbling across the landscape and forests burning with such fierceness the tower melted. The gradual ebbing away of the essence of the land, Evolsefil's disappearance from the Cave of Canedari, and the death shadow's capture of Almiralyn brought it to full wakefulness within a cocoon of anticipation.

The boy walked to the tower's center. "The spirit is here. Can you feel it, Yookotay?"

The Sentinel's booming voice filled the circular space. "I am CheeTrann, Sentinel of Nemttachenn, and you, young one, are Spirit Boy, rider of the Great Horned Owl. The Crystal Keeper of Evolsefil, the chosen ReDael of the DeoNytes, accompanies you. What is it you seek within my tower?"

Yookotay walked to the tower's center. "We come to ask your help to save Myrrh and its Guardian."

The tower quaked. "For one centuria, I have waited in the depths of Nemttachenn to rise and protect my mistress and her domain. You have my word that I am sincere in my desire. The off-worlders can confirm my allegiance."

Surprise lit the boy's stormy blue eyes. "The Pentharian were here?"

"Almiralyn placed two of them in my care. A single strand of her hair around their necks imprisoned them as small black birds. Their comrades rescued them. The four Pentharian pledged their hearts to Myrrh and her Guardian."

The ReDael started to speak.

"Let the boy talk, Yookotay." The disembodied voice boomed. "He is a Chosen One and must live his destiny."

Esán summarized the story of Seyes Nomed, Evolsefil's disappearance, and the capture of Almiralyn. Before continuing, he took a long, cleansing breath. "CheeTrann, I will teleport Evolsefil to you if you promise to protect it from the DiMensioner. The Prima Crystal's return to Myrrh will help us save the land and Almiralyn."

"Bring it hither, Spirit Boy. I pledge to hide it so no one will know it is here, and to protect it with all the power I possess."

The ReDael examined Esán's face. "Can you transport it without returning to Nevah Efas, or must we travel there first?"

"We have to travel there, Yookotay. I can't teleport Evolsefil unless I see it. Owae and Elae must return with us. I know I can't go back for them later."

Yookotay scrutinized the dimness of the tower. "CheeTrann, an injured priestess of the Cave of Canedari and a DeoNyte wise woman must return with us. Are they welcome within the walls of Nemttachenn?"

"I am honored to receive them. You have my word as CheeTrann, Protector of Myrrh. They will be safe in my tower."

Esán knelt with head bowed and his right hand on his heart. "Thank you, CheeTrann. I am pledged to your service and in your debt."

"Rise, Spirit Boy. Stand with pride. You and I have no debt. We are of one accord. Go. Bring the Prima Crystal Evolsefil back to the Land of Myrrh."

Esán stood up. "Why do you call me Spirit Boy?"

"Your spirit is far stronger than your body, young one. It fills the surrounding space with a radiance that obscures your physical shape. Soon, you will no longer need the body to carry your soul. Fly, young one, for Myrrh trembles on the verge of death."

With Yookotay's hands clasping his, Esán let his mind fill with the colors and smells of Nevah Efas; the feel of the soft breeze rippling the golden grass in the meadow and the tinkling sound of silver leaves rustling. Nemttachenn blurred; Evolsefil, its beauty muted by the absence of inner light, came into focus.

Yookotay's sorrow-filled gaze examined the crystal. "We may be too late."

Esán touched the dulled surface. "It still carries a seed of light, but we must hurry."

He led the way through the field of flowers to the cottage where Owae sat with Elae's head in her lap.

The healer lifted tired eyes to the ReDael. "Yookotay, why are you here?"

"To transport you and the crystal home to Myrrh."

"My granddaughter is too weak to travel." She stoked Elae's white fur. "I will remain with her here."

"Esán cannot make this trip again, Owae. You must come now." Yookotay picked up the sleeping priestess.

The wise woman gathered her things and followed him through the tall golden grass to where Evolsefil sat in the morning's first light. Forming a semi-circle around the crystal, they prepared to leave the haven of Nevah Efas.

Yookotay signaled Esán. The boy bowed his head and touched the dulled quartz surface.

61

Ari and eight sturdy DeoNytes had made good time reaching the tunnel leading to Oche Cavern's small sleeping cave. Now they huddled, waiting for the order to begin their daring campaign to rescue Almiralyn.

Sitrio shrugged off his backpack and pulled out a crystalline-coated net. "Owae and the High Priestess of Light created this to help us send Giests into the Beyond."

"Does it work?" The younger DeoNyte sounded skeptical.

"If it doesn't, we distract them and lead them away from Nomed's cavern." Sitrio beckoned Ari forward. "Please describe the tunnel."

"It's low and rocky and ends on a ledge above the cave. Let me be your scout. I'm smaller and quicker than Daehe." She nodded at a stocky male.

Sitrio looked doubtful. "We can't afford to lose you or the sacred knife."

"I'll give you Efillaeh." She unbuckled the scabbard, handed it to Sitrio, and dropped to all fours in front of the opening.

When she reached the end of the tunnel, she discovered four Giests guarding the cave. She picked up a pebble and pitched it into the midst of the quarreling circle of colored plasma. The targeted Giest squealed and smacked its yellow neighbor. A second pebble hit the turquoise blue one beside it, and a third pelted a green, glowing mass. Laughing out loud, Ari clambered back up the passage. If the pebbles didn't tempt them to pursue her, she knew her laughter would.

As soon as she reached the mouth of the tunnel, a DeoNyte helped her to stand and slapped the scabbard into her hand. The first Giest slammed into the crystal net, now stretched taut across the opening, shrieked, struggled, and faded from sight. A turquoise one followed, and then the green one. The fourth Giest whipped around and shot back down the tunnel.

The younger DeoNyte's skeptical gaze examined the net. "What's it made of?"

"Crystalline dust from Evolsefil." Sitrio ran a black finger over a shimmering strand.

"Now what?" Daehe peered down the narrow shaft.

Sitrio looked beyond him. "Giests aren't too bright, so let's hope our last one went for reinforcements—more putrid balls of slime—not the DiMensioner."

"Or the death shadow." Ari fastened the scabbard around her waist and gave it a pat.

Bedlam erupting in Oche Cavern brought Wodash storming from Nomed's sleeping alcove. "*What* is all the ruckus about?"

A Giest circled the cavern. "They all gone. Gone. Gone."

Its incoherent explanation annoyed him even further. "Go find them and bring them back." He paused just long enough to make certain they obeyed.

Several Giests flew into the small cave and hovered by the tunnel entrance, muttering to themselves.

A blue one floated near the ledge, moaning and hissing under its breath.

"No Noise." Others joined in a warbling chorus. "No Noise. No Noise. No Noise."

Wodash stuck his head into the cave. "Be still, all of you. Find out what happened to your comrades, or you'll never make noise again."

In a flurry of color, the Giests formed a single line and flew up the tunnel.

Wodash rejoined his master and Dom.

Nomed glared. "What was all the racket about?"

"A couple of Giests took off down a tunnel and disappeared, and you'd think something swallowed them." Shaking his head, he returned to his post by Almiralyn.

Suspended in a frigid world, the Guardian of Myrrh fought to hold on to her humanness. *I must remain conscious.* She repeated this thought with the rhythm of a poet's rhyme and snuggled deeper into the nubby blanket.

Whenever Wodash left her side, a subtle warmth crept through her feathers and soaked into her numbed mind. Awareness of Nomed's presence nearby kept her motionless. She did nothing to disturb her appearance of suspended animation or to alert her captors of her returning sense of self.

While the DiMensioner's hard-edged voice described the battle in the Cavern of Tennisca, Dom studied the wall above Nomed's shoulder. Appalled that the Guardian of Myrrh lay frozen on the pallet beside Wodash, he wondered again what held him to Seyes Nomed. His restless fingers pulled at his green vest, twisted each of its gold buttons, yanked at his gray mustache, and pushed his spectacles higher on the bridge of his nose.

"You are loyal to me, my friend, because I saved your life." Amusement filled Seyes Nomed's voice, but not his eyes. "You know I will dispose of you without a second thought if you give me cause."

"Stay out of my mind, Nomed. You are well aware I hate that Almiralyn is your prisoner. You also know I won't betray you. I may be a coward, but I'm not a stupid one."

Nomed's acerbic laugh chilled Dom to his core and made Wodash stare hard at his master. They were all expendable, every one of them. Almiralyn's capture had given the death shadow a new status with the DiMensioner, but Dom realized even he wasn't foolish enough to think the act assured his existence.

"Where are those Giests?" Nomed glared at the alcove curtain. "Find out what's keeping them, Wodash."

"Why me?" He scowled. "Send the old man. He's been sitting there being worthless."

"*You* are the only one not affected by their wretched smell, and they trust you. Go. We have things to discuss, don't we, Dominee?"

At the end of the narrow shaft, the DeoNytes waited, soundless and ready. Giests crowded the mouth of the tunnel, searching the darkness. When nothing appeared to block the entrance, they shot into the passageway. With savage cries, Sitrio and his DeoNyte jerked the net into place and, corralling the shrieking balls of plasm, vanquished them one by one.

When the last one hit and crystalline dust thrummed a final dirge, Ari grinned. "It worked."

Sitrio nodded. "Let's disappear before Wodash or Nomed comes to find them."

Brie followed Bonnee's shimmering figure along a narrow passageway that twisted and curved through subterranean gloom. She glanced at Zugo. *We actually escaped.* A triumphant grin flickered and faded. *Wish I could see Nomed's face when he discovers we're gone.*

Bonnee rounded a sharp corner and motioned the small procession to a halt in front of a steep wall of tumbled rocks.

Brie studied it and then looked at their Now Remembered guide.

Zugo narrowed his eyes. "Does the slide block the passage?"

Bonnee's soft glow dimmed and brightened. "Halfway up is an opening large enough for us to slip through." She floated upward, focused on their path.

Brie calmed her mounting trepidation and scrambled up the haphazard pile, one rock after the other, until she hauled herself onto a large boulder. The Star of Truth tingling a message down her spine brought her to a standstill. She rubbed her neck and squinted into the darkness.

Zugo climbed onto the boulder and almost knocked her over. "Hey. Warn me next time you plan to stop, Brie." He clutched her arm to steady himself.

"Sorry." She stared beyond him, her thoughts racing.

Bonnee floated beside them. "Is something wrong?"

"What's over there?" Brie pointed where her intuition instructed.

"I don't know, but the tunnel to Oche Cavern is in the opposite direction."

The Star tingled again, stronger and more insistent. Brie responded. "My instincts are telling me to go that way. I realize it sounds crazy, but I believe it's important."

Zugo squirmed. "Take the lead or tell Bonnee where to go." His tone held a note of impatience.

"To the left, then straight ahead, Bonnee. Would you mind going first? I see better when you're in front."

Bonnee floated up the incline. Brie followed, a sense of premonition building. "Is there a way down the rockslide?"

The Now Remembered girl paused. "Stay here. I'll see what I can discover."

Anticipating her usual frightened response to the dark, Brie slid her hand into Zugo's and chanted her mental mantra. *I am not afraid of the dark. Darkness doesn't scare—*She gasped. *No palpitations. No chills. I don't like it, but I'm not afraid.*

Bonnee appeared above them. "This way. Watch for patches of loose gravel as you begin your descent. Once you pass them, the climb down is easy."

Brie allowed the DeoNyte to guide her from one rock to the next. A misstep sent a cascade of smaller stones down the steep side. As Zugo released her to sidestep the miniature avalanche, Brie lost her footing and skated over the gravel. His hand gripped her arm. He pulled her against his chest and held her until the cascading stones hit the bottom and settled into the silence. She trembled. "I c-can't go any f-further."

"You're fine, Brielle." Zugo hugged her.

Bonnee floated next to her, a luminous glow in her eyes. "The rest of the climb is much easier, and there's plenty of light."

"Tell us what you found, Bonnee." Brie didn't hide her eagerness to know.

The Now Remembered's ghost-like form quivered. "You'll find out soon enough. We're almost there."

Zugo tested the next rock. Scrambling onto it, he offered his hand.

Within a short time, they stood on a smooth surface where soft light spilled onto rough stone walls.

Brie's sense of expectancy increased. "Look, Zugo, a flight of steps carved right out of the mountain." Unable to resist the insistent pulsing of the Star, she descended.

At the bottom, she discovered a large door made from black oak and lit by simple lamps, one on either side. Embedded in the center of an intricate design carved in the polished wood, a golden topaz gleamed like the sun. Crescents of luminescent moonstone encircled the central stone. Around them, twelve deep blue stars of gold-veined lapis lazuli caught the light and glistened.

Zugo gaped at Bonnee. "It can't be!" His voice held a tremor of awed excitement.

"Would someone please tell me where we are?" Brie looked from one radiant face to the other.

Zugo's eyes gleamed. "If we're where I think we are, we're about to see something few have seen."

Bonnee smiled. "You're an initiate of the Cave of Canedari, Zugo, so you have the power to open this door."

"My initiation was only a short time ago, and I haven't studied its secrets yet."

Her companion's voices melted away as Brie, enchanted by the beauty of the intricate mandala, let everything else fade from her awareness. Mesmerized by the richness of the gemstone design and the grain of the dark, satiny wood, she pressed her palms against the door, closed her eyes, and opened her heart to its beauty.

A soft breeze sent curls tumbling around her face. Her mind cleared; the beat of her heart quickened. She laughed softly. *I know how to open the door.*

She stepped back to re-examine the jeweled pattern. Below the central topaz crystal, a lapis star the size of her palm gleamed in the warm light. Eager yet calm, she explored its edge until she discovered a series of raised bumps. With her fingers placed between them, she pulled. The star moved. She rotated it one point to the right, released it, and pushed the door open. Excitement ushered her into a space that left her breathless.

Zugo crowded behind her. His gasp died away into a silence saturate with wonder.

From a hidden overhead source, light illuminated the dome-shaped cavern. In the manner of a geode cut in two, the faceted amethysts covering the curved ceiling and walls sparked with radiant light. Clear quartz crystal pillars sent rainbows, like miniature ballerinas, pirouetting throughout the space. At the cavern's center, a huge circular pool reflected the prismatic light. Equally spaced around it, twelve moonstones shone with a luster that shifted from white to pale blue. At the pool's center, on a platform of polished amethyst, a throne, carved from pink tourmaline and inlaid with emerald, sapphire, and ruby, commanded the space like royalty. Overcome by its power and beauty, Brie pressed a hand to her heart and let her tears fall.

"ReNin RepPosu—the Throne of Netydis." Zugo's exhaled breath rustled her hair. "I never imagined I'd be standing here."

The Star of Truth's throbbing urged Brie to cross to the pool. She knelt at an opening in the moonstone circle, and, guided by an inner knowing she could not ignore, searched beneath the pool's surface. In a hidden niche, she discovered a small lever, pulled it, and smiled. Through a gush of gurgling water, four large white stones emerged to form a path connecting the pool's edge and the platform. She stood and placed a foot on the first stone.

"Brie, wait for me." Zugo started to follow.

Bonnee floated beside him. "Stay with me. This is her destiny. We are her witnesses."

As though in a trance, she stepped from one moonstone to the next until she stood on polished purple. Unaware of anything but the pull of the tourmaline throne, she sank onto the cool seat and rested her hands on the smooth inlaid arms. The Star of Truth's tingling warmth mingled with that of the gemstones surrounding her. The world blurred into mist and sky. Images formed in fast succession.

Esán, Almiralyn, and Ari, mountains, forests, and plains flashed before her. Villages and well-kept farms came and went. Pentharian and Wood Tiffs, the noble spirit of Nemttachenn and the slow ebbing away of Myrrh, appeared and faded. Places she had yet to see and people she had yet to meet paraded like clouds across the heavens. Evolsefil filled her heart and then shattered. An explosion shook the galaxy, tearing the fabric of Space and Time into a jagged black hole of nothingness.

Zugo gazed transfixed at the Human girl, now a dim outline on the glowing pink throne. Superimposed around her, the form of an adult woman gradually took shape. Long red hair hung to her waist and framed a face of such loveliness he was certain his heart would break. Dark auburn lashes outlined chestnut eyes that seemed to see far beyond the domed grotto. She rose and cried out with such devastating sorrow that tears streamed down his cheeks. Beside him, Bonnee's translucent figure trembled. When silence settled over the cavern, young Brie, her brown eyes huge and luminous, stood observing him.

"I know the destiny of Myrrh. We must hurry." She ran across the stone path toward a small door at the opposite end of the amethyst cavern.

Zugo cast a last glance at the throne and raced after her. Not far ahead, she waited impatiently at the bottom of a winding staircase.

"Please hurry! We have so much to lose if we don't make it." She didn't wait to explain, but jogged up the steps, circling higher and higher above him.

Wishing he understood what she had learned and where they were going, he mounted the steps in her wake.

Motivated by the knowledge she had gained on the throne, Brie sprinted up the stone stairs with Zugo and Bonnee close behind and entered a chamber shrouded on three walls by deep purple drapes. The fourth wall, a massive stained-glass window, angled away from the room's center and paralleled the night sky below. Framed by the plush curtains, the window's fading pattern appeared lifeless.

Brie's heart tightened. *Myrrh is dying*. Running her hand along lush velvet folds, she followed them until she found a hidden door.

"I can't go in there." Bonnee drifted backward. "What if it leads to the Cave of Canedari?" She shook her head. "I'm not ready to leave you."

Zugo gave the Now Remembered girl an impatient frown. "Bonnee, as long as Evolsefil is not there, you'll be safe. Besides, it might not be Canedari."

"You may be right, Zugo, but I don't wish to take the chance."

"I'm positive you won't be sent anywhere, Bonnee." Brie looked at her friend. "Stay with us. We need you, and we want you. You have important things to accomplish on Myrrh before you join your sister."

Bonnee released a sigh that trembled through her translucent form. "If you're sure I won't be called into the Beyond, I'll come with you."

Brie smiled and pressed her ear to the door. The muffled voices on the other side were barely audible. Pushing it open, she stepped into an enormous room, where books lined shelves from floor to ceiling.

Zugo peered over her shoulder. "The Reading Room. And look who's here."

At the end, a group of Pentharian and Humans gathered before an ornate fireplace. Brie walked toward them, Bonnee and Zugo flanking her.

A Wood Tiff darted forward. "Ari, you're back already!"

Her lilting voice rang out. "I'm Brie, Fen, and I wish to meet my father."

All conversation in the room ceased; all heads turned her direction. A tall man with salt and pepper hair separated himself from the group. His startled blue eyes fastened on hers. Silence, broken only by the occasional hiss and crackle of the fire, filled her with a sense of suspended time. She took a step, her eyes never leaving his. Another step and another, and then he stood in front of her, his arms open and waiting. Her tears overflowed as she wrapped her arms around his neck. For the first time, her father's arms embraced her; his heart beat next to her heart; his tears melted into those on her cheek.

"How did you know, Brielle?"

"ReNin RepPosu showed me."

Allynae broke their embrace gently and held her at arm's length. "You sat on the Throne of Netydis?"

"Yes, Father. We have so much to discuss."

She saw the pride in his eyes and knew he saw Myrrh's future in her.

62

With Jordett's help, Merrilea removed the bullet and stitched Stee's side. Respecting the strange tattoos covering his torso, she matched the jagged edges of his wound, careful to preserve each exotic design. Now the emerald green Pentharian slept on the kitchen table, his every breath audible to those who awaited his awakening.

Exhausted, she picked up a mug, stepped onto the back porch and, sinking into a chair next to Jordett, savored sweet, fragrant sips of Mira's favorite tea.

Karrew rested by the stove, slowly filling with life. Sparrow had cleaned the wound in his chest, waited for Majeska to curl up beside him, and tiptoed away to her art studio. Merrilea did not doubt that images filled her mind and called her to paint.

A sudden restlessness prompted her to finish her tea and follow her friend. From the art studio doorway, she followed the brisk movement of

Sparrow's hand as it flicked from palette to canvas. Burnt sienna, blue, flesh, and brown, swirled to form the faces of children. Each one—Esán, Torgin, the twins, and the DeoNyte—seemed to have grown beyond her earlier works. A translucent child joined them, where they gathered around a figure she could not see.

"You're amazing." Merrilea moved closer to inspect the emerging painting. "They could almost walk off the canvas."

Jordett came up behind her. "It's exquisite, Sparrow."

Absorbed in her work, she nodded, dipped her brush, and continued.

Merrilea guided the major around the room, showing him each finished canvas and answering his questions. He paused in front of a picture of Esán suspended halfway between kestrel and Human. "Can he really do that?"

"We believe the paintings depict actual events." Merrilea slipped her hand into his and drew him back from the lineup of pictures. "If you stand here, you can see them merging from one into the next."

Sparrow cleaned her brush. "I've never painted like this in my life. The images come unbidden. If I try to take control, I can't make it work." She studied her canvas, wrinkled her bow in thought, and added a shadow.

Merrilea sensed Jordett's energy flagging and glanced at his strained features. Fatigue saturated his eyes and set his mouth in a thin line. "You'd better sleep while you can, Jordy. More changes are coming—I can feel them. When they do, you'll need all your strength and your wits."

"Wish we knew more about what's happening out there." Frustration flattened his tone. "Almiralyn may need me, but I do not know how to find her."

"We could ask Elcaro's Eye, but all it shows is the mist." Merrilea realized she still held his hand and, with a self-conscious smile, withdrew it. "Let's check on Karrew, and then I'll show you where you can rest." On the way to the door, she paused to see how Sparrow was progressing.

Jordett joined her. "You're an extraordinary artist, Sparrow. I've seen nothing like these on Thera."

"Thank you, Jordy." Distracted for only a moment, Sparrow considered her painting and added a series of details to the background.

Merrilea led the way to the kitchen, where she bent over the raven, Karrew.

"How is he?" Jordett stifled a yawn.

"No change since I checked him last. It's almost as though he's suspended in time. There seems to be nothing we can do but watch and wait."

Majeska's amethyst eyes rounded as she arched her back in a luxurious stretch and sat grooming herself with her pink tongue. Stretching once more, she circled around herself and lay down with her spine pressed against Karrew's.

Merrilea ran a hand along her sleek, gray side. "It seems odd for a cat to care for a raven. But right now, *everything* happening is strange." She preceded Jordett upstairs to a small guest room and pushed open the door. "You can rest here, Jordy."

"You get some sleep, too, Merri."

The tenderness in his expression made her heart flutter and blood rush to her cheeks. "I'll wake you when you're needed." Her voice, she was glad to note, was steadier than she felt.

After Merrilea left, Jordett stretched out on the bed. *She's quite a woman.* He yawned and adjusted the pillows. *I wonder if she... Get over it, Jordy.* Another yawn, and with a soldier's ability to catch a nap at will, he fell asleep, dreaming of dark tunnels, where a huge hazel-eyed owl and the white face of death pursued him.

Torgin leaned on the back of a chair, listening to his best friend explain what she had learned from ReNin RepPosu. He pursed his lips and studied her changing expressions, the way she stood, and the sound of her voice. *She seems so different.* He looked closer.

Her red curls framed her sparsely freckled face; her chestnut brown eyes sparked with flecks of light. *What's changed?* He squinted and tapped his chin. *The dignity in her demeanor as she speaks to her father is more assured than I have noticed before.*

He regarded the others in the room. *Do they see the difference?* The adults paid close attention, listened, and then responded with nods of approval to the answers she provided. Voer even complimented her for her insight.

Torgin looked from one to the other, his ego doing a disjointed jig. He blushed. *I think I'm jealous of my best friend.* The realization caused him to squirm.

Yaro walked up beside him. "Are all of Idronatti's young people as remarkable as you and your friends?"

Grateful the Pentharian couldn't see his festering jealousy, he responded with a touch of sadness. "Prior to this adventure, we were just ordinary. Something about Myrrh has changed us all."

"What makes you feel sorrow, my heart-brother? Does your friend seem so different?"

He peeked up at Yaro from beneath his lashes and realized the Pentharian *could* see his jealousy and understood. "Have you ever been jealous of your friends?"

"I have, Torgin, and it was not a comfortable feeling. Like you, Brie has been through much. She also struggles with the changes occurring in herself and those she loves. Give her and yourself time to absorb everything."

Brie caught Torgin's eye and smiled. He flinched and looked away. "I'll try, Yaro. Thank you for understanding."

Emotions churning, he walked over to stand by the fireplace. *The twins are Allynae's daughters and the Guardian of Myrrh's nieces. I am an ordinary boy from Idronatti.* His heart sank. *I am not good enough.*

Behind him, Brie's father's voice took over the conversation. Everyone listened with intense interest as Allynae assigned each member a task. Torgin kicked a small twig into the fire. He yearned to be included, but his fluctuating feelings acted like an insurmountable barrier. By the time Allynae called his name, Torgin was so engrossed in self-pity he hardly heard it.

Skipt pulled on his pant leg. "You here or not?"

His face burned. Avoiding Brie's eyes, he joined the circle of Almiralyn's allies.

"I speak to you last, Torgin Whalend, because your job is so important. You are the keeper of the secrets of Myrrh." He pointed at the compass hanging around his neck. "With the help of Yaro, Paisley, and Skipt, you must rid the Cavern of Tennisca of the remaining Giests and prepare the Cave of Canedari to receive the Evolsefil Crystal when it returns."

He paused. "Do you have questions?"

Torgin bit his bottom lip. "What do we do when we've accomplished our task?"

Allynae smiled. "Once you have secured the cave and a DeoNyte guard is in place, you and your companions must decide your next move. You'll know what it is when the time comes."

Torgin touched the smooth, round edge of the Compass of Ostradio. Embarrassment burned his cheeks when Brie's questioning gaze came to rest on his face. Forcing a steadfastness he did not feel, he attempted a smile. "I am honored to be given this assignment, Brie, but even more important is that you stay safe."

"And you, Torgin, take care of yourself. When we come together again, the future of Myrrh will be decided. You are, and always will be, my best friend." She rose on tiptoe and kissed his cheek, then walked over to join One Man, Jeet, and Fen where Bonnee floated near the fire.

Allynae rested a hand on his shoulder. "The only constant in life is change, young Torgin. Can you not sense it in yourself?"

He saw only understanding in Allynae's rugged features and nodded. "Thank you for—" His discomfort made him look away.

Brie's father gave his shoulder a reassuring squeeze. "Go. Your companions await you."

Torgin studied the strange group and reviewed what each would do to save Almiralyn and Myrrh. Jeet, One Man, Fen, Bonnee, and Brie headed for Nemttachenn. The Wood Tiff's job was to escort them through the Intersect, the fastest and safest way to travel. Allynae, Zugo, Voer, and Yuin prepared to join Ari and her DeoNytes at Nomed's cave. Yaro, Paisley, and Skipt talked by the splintered door, waiting for him. Torgin's gaze sought Brielle. His heart ached at his inability to let go of his jealousy.

From a crack in the double purple doors, Torgin and his team watched Giests searching the huge cavern.

"Ya ho." Skipt smothered his mischievous laughter behind small gray hands. "No Brie and Zugo. Big Mystery."

Torgin grinned at the stone boy, then turned to his heart-brother and Paisley. "What will the Giests do now?"

Paisley rubbed his stubble-covered chin. "It depends on how afraid they are of Wodash and Nomed. They'll either go tell 'em their prisoners are gone or they'll hide."

Yaro made a quick decision. "I'll find Ari." He touched his pale gold palm to Torgin's. "Guard the entrance to Canedari with your life, my brother. I'll be back soon." A brown bat materialized.

Torgin peeked between the purple doors and eased one open. "It's clear."

Yaro's small mammal shot through, and, dodging frustrated Giests, flew to the top of the staircase. A quick shift sent him scuttling under the exit door on eight spider legs.

In the passageway, he shifted again to the brown bat and followed the scent of Human and DeoNyte along a smaller passage and into a round cave. At the sound of whispered voices, he changed to Pentharian and waited.

A group of shadowy forms approached with Ari in the lead. She gripped the hilt of her knife when he stepped away from the tunnel wall. DeoNytes surrounded her, crouched and ready to fight if necessary.

Yaro introduced himself. "I am heart-brother of Torgin, Human boy of Idronatti and friend of Almiralyn. Brielle told me of your coming."

"Brie!" Ari's delight shone in her eyes. "Where is she?"

"She's on her way to Nemttachenn, where she will meet Esán. My comrade Jeet, One Man, Fen, and Bonnee go with her."

Ari sighed. "Sometimes I wonder if I'll ever see her again."

Sitrio offered his hand. "It is good to see you, Yaro. What brings you this way?"

He described the happenings in the Reading Room, including Allynae's assignments. "I am scouting the surrounding area for Torgin and our friends. We must secure the Cave of Canedari for the return of Evolsefil and then help to free Almiralyn."

Sitrio frowned. "Do Giests still guard the Cavern of Tennisca?"

"Many remain there. We have not yet discovered the means to be rid of them."

Ari glanced at Sitrio, who nodded. "We have a way." She explained how the crystal net worked.

Sitrio then proposed a plan.

Yaro listened with a slight smile. "It is good. Come. We have much to do."

They arrived at the cavern entrance and reviewed their plans. His shift to the spider ushered him into the darkness of Tennisca, where he changed to a bat and flew to the Canedari to rejoin Torgin and his companions. After a quick update, he explained the plan he and Sitrio had devised.

Torgin grinned. "Do you mean I am to fly with you?" Excitement glowed in his summer-green eyes.

"Me fly, too!" Skipt jumped up and down.

Yaro shared a smile with Torgin. "Of course you will fly, too."

Paisley gave the boy from Idronatti and the Enots a lopsided grin and nodded at Yaro. "I'll stay right here to make sure no unwanted guests enter Canedari."

The golden Pentharian shifted. With Paisley's help, Torgin mounted onto his powerful, feathered back and helped the Enots to settle in front of him.

"Ya ho!" Skipt chortled his delight. "This big adventure. Ya ho, hey!"

Paisley opened the double doors and stepped away. Vulture wings unfurled and Yaro swooped into the midst of the squabbling Giests, with his passengers screaming and laughing on his back. Panicked, the odorous balls of protoplasm scattered in all directions, their vivid colors forming blurred tails in their wake. One by one, Yaro herded them toward the exit into the passageway where Ari and her DeoNyte escort waited.

At the top of the stairs, Torgin and Skipt dismounted, let Yaro's bat form attach to Torgin's shoulder, and darted through the door, slamming it shut behind them. Joining Ari and the DeoNytes, they corralled shrieking Giests and drove them into the waiting crystalline net. Yaro shifted once more to the vulture and added his terrifying squawk to the cacophony of chorused of sounds.

Above the chaos, an orange Giest lingered, watching his comrades hit the shimmering net and vanish. It circled, hovered, and circled again before howling in terror and disappearing down a side tunnel.

"Ya ho!" Skipt pointed. "One got away."

Yaro shifted to Pentharian beside Torgin and the Enots, his lizard-like eyes glinting. "Go on to Nomed's cave. I'll join you there."

Changing to bat, he followed the scent of his quarry, hoping it would lead him to Nomed and the Guardian of Myrrh.

63

The Intersect sped by, taking Brie and her companions from one swirl of turquoise to the next. Five jumps carried them through the star-studded sky to a platform near the Tower of Nemttachenn. The exit from the stairs ushered them into a hollow tree at the edge of the clearing. Jeet ducked through the opening, shifted to a small black bird, and circled upward. One Man made a stealthful search of the area. At his signal, Fen slipped into the woods, gulped a great breath of fresh forest air, and grinned. Brie ducked into the open, happy to see the turning's light. Bonnee hesitated.

"I promise you'll be fine." Brie reassured her with a smile. "I wouldn't have brought you here if I thought the Beyond would claim you before you're ready."

Her eyes brimming with tears, Bonnie floated from the hollow trunk, her translucent form soaking up the mist-muted browns and greens of the Terces Wood.

Brie gave her an encouraging nod. "You'll be at my side until this quest ends."

One Man waved them over to the tower, urgency etched in the lines of his face.

Bonnee's bottom lip quivered. "What about Nemttachenn?"

"Until you are ready, you're safe with us. Stay here with Fen, Bonnee, while I awaken CheeTrann, Myrrh's Sentinel."

Hurrying to One Man, she glanced skyward. "What do you think is keeping Jeet?"

"He'll be here soon." The hermit's questioning gaze rested on her. "Sure you want to go in alone?"

"I'm certain." She inhaled a steadying breath, entered, and walked to Nemttachenn's center. "Protector of the Land of Myrrh, come forth."

An ancient voice shook the tower. "Twin Child of KcernFensia, I have awaited your coming."

"CheeTrann, Sentinel of Myrrh, I have looked forward to our meeting. Have you seen my friend Esán?"

"Spirit Boy returns from Nevah Efas with Evolsefil. Accompanying him are an injured Priestess of Light and a DeoNyte Wise Woman." The Sentinel paused. "You travel in strange company, young one. Never have I witnessed Wood Tiff, Human, and off-worlders together. Is the translucent child one of the unremembered?"

"Yes, she is. Her people have regained their memories and join the battle to save our land."

"Myrrh is in peril." CheeTrann's deep rumble rolled through the tower. "And the peoples of the solar system have come together. It is a strange time. It is a hard time. It is the time of The Unfolding."

Brie bowed her head. "CheeTrann, I thank you for your help."

"Spirit Boy approaches, Daughter of KcernFensia. Shelter with your companions in the woods until he and Evolsefil are safe within my walls."

Brie strode from the tower, noted Jeet had returned, and hurried to join the adults. "Quick. Take cover in the forest. Esán and the heart of Myrrh will be here soon."

Within the safety of the Terces Wood, One Man helped to protect Bonnee from the raging wind. Jeet held Fen's small hand to keep him steady. A faint roar shook the clearing. Mist roiled around the granite tower, obscuring it from sight. A howling gale whipped through the trees. The entirety of Myrrh quaked and grew quiet.

The mist churned and thinned as Esán stepped into the clearing, dark circles under his eyes but triumph on his face. "Evolsefil has returned to Myrrh." His elated shout broke the intense silence. "It is in danger of losing its life spark, but it's back."

One Man, his expression overflowing with relief, hurried from the trees and embraced him.

Brie smiled at them. "I've met my father, too, Esán."

His eyes widened, and his beautiful smile erased the fatigue from his face. He moved from his father's embrace to give her a hug. "I'm so glad, Brielle. Come on, let's check on Elae and Owae."

The companions entered Nemttachenn to find Yookotay with the DeoNyte priestess in his arms and Owae, looking harried and concerned, by his side. "She needs rest and quiet, and it's much too damp for her here in the tower."

Jeet gazed at her from his impressive height, his carnelian orange tail twitching and gold piercings gleaming. "I will take her to Almiralyn's cottage. I go there to check on my blood brother, Stee, and the raven, Karrew."

Owae's pale eyes studied the alien creature as she placed a protective hand on Elae's arm. "Can you carry us both? I don't want to leave my granddaughter even for an instant."

"It would be my honor, Wise One." Orange braids cascading over his shoulder, he bowed to Yookotay. "Do I have your permission, ReDael of Meos?"

"Thank you, friend. I am delighted to entrust my people to your care."

When Jeet, with his DeoNyte riders, had lifted into flight and soared over the Terces Wood, Brie, along with her companions, trooped back into the tower and gathered around the crystal's dimmed presence. Resting her hands against its smooth termination, she closed her eyes and envisioned the spark of life growing brighter. "Send your roots into your land, Evolsefil."

The granite walls trembled; the floor quaked. CheeTrann's deep voice filled Nemttachenn. "The heart of Myrrh strives to regenerate. We must guard it well, for the DiMensioner will soon know it is back. Let the mist remain to protect and hide us until Evolsefil rests once more within the Cave of Canedari."

Brie pressed her hand to the velvet pouch containing the Remembering Stone. "Thank you, CheeTrann."

"Together we will defend it and rescue the Land of Myrrh from the hatred of Seyes Nomed." The rumbling proclamation faded, and the Sentinel withdrew.

Esán stood beside her, fatigue settling around him like the mists enshrouding the land. A weary smile told her he understood how tired she felt.

He held out a battered book. "This is *EmitEnil*, Brie. It contains the history and legacy of Myrrh and the story of the Prima Crystal Evolsefil. It will help you save the land."

She touched the worn cover. Energy tingling up her arm brought with it the knowledge the tome did not belong to her. "You must keep it, Esán. It speaks to you in ways I do not yet understand. Please share what you've learned."

He slid his thumbnail along the edge of the ancient parchment. The pages flipped open. Words danced across the golden surface. Esán let out a reverent sigh. Brie bent over the *Book of Emit*, absorbing its magnificence and its gifts.

In the Guardian's upstairs sanctuary, Elcaro's Eye roiled and grew still. New images rose from its depths. Myrrh sighed with relief as Evolsefil's unfurling fingers of light penetrated the darkness in the ground below Nemttachenn. The trees of the Terces Wood ceased their high-pitched whining, and the power of the winds lessened. Villagers and farmers felt the painful bands of impending doom fall from their hearts. DeoNyte and Wood Tiff, Giest and Pentharian, all sensed the change. In his cavern in the Dojanacks, Seyes Nomed stopped mid-sentence. His left eyebrow ascended to an exaggerated arch and the scar on his cheek stretched taut by a sudden realization... *Evolsefil has returned to Myrrh, but not to the Cave of Canedari where it belongs. So where is it?* His eyes narrowed. *Very soon I will know.*

A vulture's high-pitched shriek announced the arrival of a Pentharian warrior. Merrilea, hoping for news of her nephew, hurried across the porch to the door and stared. Two DeoNytes, creatures she had never expected to see, rode on its back. The oldest one struggled to keep her companion upright. Merrilea hastened down the steps and ran to the vulture's side. "How may I help?"

The wrinkled, black face flooded with relief. "I am Owae. This is my granddaughter. She's been ill. Can you help her down?"

Merrilea reached for the fur-covered body and maneuvered it to the ground, then assisted Owae.

The elderly female drew in a breath. "Thank you. Is there somewhere she can rest?"

Jeet materialized, bowed his head to the women, and scooped up the younger DeoNyte.

"This way." Merrilea led them upstairs to a small bedroom at the end of the hall. After turning back the bedcovers, she helped the Pentharian settle the beautiful white furry creature between the cool sheets.

"Thank you, Jeet." Merrilea kept her voice low. "We moved Stee into a room across from the kitchen. He's resting well. Jordy is with him."

He nodded. "I'll see you downstairs."

The older DeoNyte squeezed her pale eyes shut. When they opened, some of her exhaustion had faded. After checking on her granddaughter, she explained the events that had brought them to Almiralyn's cottage.

"You've seen Esán." Merrilea wanted to cry with relief. "How is he? Where is he?"

"He's exhausted from teleporting the crystal to the tower." Owae lowered into a chair by the bed. "But I believe he's better than when you last saw him. Your nephew is with his father at Nemttachenn."

"Somay is here?"

The DeoNyte's expression softened. "He has lived in Myrrh for many sun cycles. The peoples of the land know him as One Man, the Hermit of Timreh Pass."

Merrilea sank into the armchair at the foot of Elae's bed. Confusion, relief, elation, and concern ebbed and flowed like the ocean tides. *Perhaps Somay will be the right donor for Esán.*

Elae stirred. Her strange eyes, one the pale green of a spring leaf and the other soft blue of the morning sky, opened and rested on Merrilea. She blew out a breath and struggled to form a question.

Owae leaned closer. "I'm right beside you, Elae."

"Grandmother, I am so glad you're here."

The healer rose, smoothed the tasseled fur away from her forehead and kissed her. "Sleep, dear one. I'll be close by."

The beautiful eyes closed, and she slipped into a deep and restful slumber.

The DeoNyte elder smiled. "She's stabilizing. What she needs most is rest and quiet. Would it be possible to make a cup of tea?"

"Yes, of course. Let's go downstairs." Out of habit, Merrilea took Elae's thin wrist between her well-trained fingers. The pulse beat soft but strong. She placed the small black hand on the coverlet and led her guest from the room.

They found Sparrow in the kitchen, pouring hot water into Mira's flowered teapot. She smiled at Owae. "You are even more beautiful than my painting of you."

Over a cup of fragrant tea, the women exchanged stories like old friends catching up on the latest events in one another's lives. Grateful for the respite, Merrilea felt her stress and fatigue lessen and noted a spark of vitality brighten Sparrow's tired face.

When Owae had drained the last drop of the sweet Dojanberry brew from her cup, she joined Esán's aunt by Karrew. Shallow breaths lifted his injured chest. Although his taloned feet had uncurled, they remained limp and lifeless.

The DeoNyte healer examined his wound and the ribs underneath. "You're a lucky raven, Karrew. Your injury only bruised your ribs." She rubbed her low back and sighed. "I have a salve in my pack that will help to heal his wounds and lessen the pain. I'll check on Elae and bring it down with me." With a slight limp in her gait, she left the room.

Merrilea sat at the table, happy for a moment of silence. Sparrow emptied her china teacup, washed it, and put it in the rack to dry. Paint-splattered fingers caressed Majeska under her chin until a rumbling purr filled the kitchen.

Owae returned with a small pottery jar of white cream and applied it to Karrew's battered chest. His eye fluttered open. "You must remain quiet, my friend." She crooned a series of soft notes and stroked his feline companion's back. "Let yourself rest in the stove's warmth and Majeska's protective presence."

Merrilea held out her hand. "May I see your cream?"

"Of course." Owae smiled and slid the jar across the table.

Merrilea pulled out the stopper, inhaled the scent, and smiled in surprise. "It smells lovely, and I feel so relaxed and invigorated. What's in it?"

"Myrrhnica, jolendula, and other medicinal herbs. I make it myself." Owae rested a gentle hand on Karrew's feathered side. "The bruised ribs will take longer, but the wound itself is healing."

Jeet preceded Jordett into the kitchen in time to hear her explanation. "Would your cream work on a Pentharian?"

"I'm sure it would." Owae retrieved the jar. "Where is your comrade?"

Stee rested on a double bed, his emerald body glistening with sweat. Merrilea supported his head while Owae gave him a sip of water. After adjusting his pillow, the healer examined the Pentharian's wounded side. "Your work is exceptional. He's lucky you were here." She applied the white cream to the bruised, tattooed skin. "The wound will heal, but the internal damage requires time or Efillaeh. Rest is the best medicine for him now."

Jordett and Sparrow were deep in discussion when they returned to the kitchen. The major looked at the orange Pentharian. "We must go to Nemttachenn. If Sparrow's paintings are any sign of coming events, Nomed will be on his way there soon."

"Sparrow's paintings?" Jeet's lizard eyes blinked.

Jordett smiled at Sparrow. "May I show him?"

"Of course." She pushed her chair back and escorted them to the studio.

Merrilea watched from the doorway while Jeet and Owae studied the canvases and marveled at how they reflected the ongoing events in Myrrh.

Jordett paused next to her. "A lot is happening. How are you holding up?"

"I'm fine, Jordy. Just tired. I never seem to get enough sleep and I worry about Esán constantly."

He put an arm around her shoulders. "He's with his father. That has to help."

She resisted the temptation to rest her head on his shoulder. "It does, but I want to know for myself he's alright. Let's see what Sparrow is working on."

He removed his arm but clasped her hand. She let her blonde hair cover the warmth rising to her cheeks and joined the group by the easel.

SparrowLyn put the finishing touches on a kestrel, owl, and vulture soaring over a mist-covered terrain above a majestic granite tower. Wiping her brush, she tipped her head and studied her work.

Jeet took one last look at the series of prophetic paintings. "You are a woman of much magic." Again, the lizard-like eyes blinked. He turned to Jordett. "You are correct, my friend. We must go to Nemttachenn."

In the kitchen, Jordett accepted a pack of supplies. "When I come back, Merrilea—"

A tremor shook the cottage and pitched her into Jordett's arms. His exhaled breath brushed her cheek, and then he was gone.

Sparrow ran into the room, her dark eyes rounded with fear. "What was that?"

Unable to think, Merrilea grabbed her hand and, with Owae following more slowly, dashed into the garden.

The wind's incessant screaming ceased as the whispered name Evolsefil repeated over and over.

Owae raised her arms to the sky. "It's time!"

Merrilea's gaze found Jordett. His steady gaze met hers.

Jeet took Sparrow's hands in his. "You do not understand your power; but like your namesake, you have gifts not obvious to the casual observer. My heart is honored to have seen your work." His reptilian eyes glanced from her to Merrilea. "I promise to protect your children with my life." With a bow of his head, he shifted to his vulture form.

Jordett echoed the Pentharian's pledge, then climbed onto the vulture's broad back and focused his attention on Merrilea.

She blushed and handed him the pack of supplies. Their fingers touched; her heartbeat quickened. His expression left her breathless.

The enormous bird of prey ascended into the clouds and flew toward Nemttachenn.

Sparrow studied her with a smile, lightening the weariness on her face. "Have I missed something?"

Merrilea shot her a dimpled grin. Linking arms with both Owae and Sparrow, she strolled with them across the garden to the cottage.

A spark of life deep in Karrew's consciousness flared. Pain shooting through his side left him on the verge of wakefulness. Warmth creeping over his body comforted him. Rhythmic, reoccurring breath pulsed against his spine, reminding him to breathe. Each painful inhalation forced him closer to full awareness.

Gentle fingers massaging his aching chest with a sweet-scented cream reduced his pain and warmed him further. He opened an eye. An ancient face framed by white fur peered down at him. A voice crooned a lullaby, easing him to sleep. Sometime later, more muffled voices penetrated his slow return to consciousness.

A tremor shook him. The warm presence against his spine moved. A damp nose nudged his body until he began to respond and then helped him to roll upright. A wave of dizziness hit and passed. He tipped his head and found Majeska observing him, her amethyst eyes steady and knowing. She licked her right paw and rubbed her ear until she seemed satisfied both were clean. He watched her speak the language of cats, grateful for her friendship.

Merrilea, Owae, and Sparrow entered the kitchen. Karrew gazed at them from his place by the stove and realized that women of Thera and Myrrh had saved him. He lived and so did his mistress; but for how long, he could not tell.

While Paisley stood guard in Canedari, Allynae, Voer, Yuin, and Zugo gathered around the fireplace in the Reading Room, discussing the best means of reaching the DiMensioner and Almiralyn.

Allynae glanced up after a thoughtful silence. "Zugo, what's the quickest way to Oche Cavern?"

"We must swim the Lake of Rorret to the crystal tunnel. From there, it's only a short distance to Nomed's cave."

Allynae shuddered. "Isn't there another way?"

The young DeoNyte shook his head. "The lake is the fastest… if Rorret will welcome us. What are you worried about?"

"I hate to admit it, but I don't know how to swim."

Voer, who had been standing by the fireplace, sat down next to him. "I will become a dolphin. You can hold on to my dorsal fin and swim beside me."

"I don't swim either." Zugo's steady gaze held his. "But if Rorret helps, it won't let us drown."

Allynae thanked Voer with a warm smile. "How do we attract Rorret's attention?"

"We see if it'll answer my call." Zugo led the companions down the Hall of Priestess.

Paisley met them at the doors to the Cave of Canedari, his dark face solemn and expectant. "Yaro found Ari and her band of DeoNytes. Torgin and Skipt are with him now helping to herd the Giests into a crystal net Owae made. What're your plans?"

"Zugo suggests we ask Rorret for help." Allynae worked to keep his surging doubt under control.

"I'm not sure if it will respond, but here goes." Yookotay's son and heir squared his shoulders and called out in a steady voice. "Lake of Rorret, Keeper of the Underground Waterways, I, son of the ReDael of the DeoNytes, call upon you to serve Myrrh and the Lady Almiralyn. Please come to our aid."

A section of the white marble floor slid away, revealing clear, dark water. A languid tone flowed into the cave. "I am Rorret, appointed by the Guardian of the Land to protect against terror. Why do you summon me from the depths of my watch?"

"We need your help to rescue Almiralyn from the DiMensioner and Wodash, the death shadow."

"What has kept you so long, young Zugo? It has been some time since Nomed and his band of Giests returned to Oche Cavern with the white and gold bird that is our Lady."

Allynae stepped to Zugo's side. "How did you see this?"

"Ah, brother of Almiralyn, I flow in all the waterways of the Dojanack Caverns and learned this from the reflections of my sister lake. The white bird remains hidden in the alcove where Nomed sleeps."

Voer knelt at the water's edge and pressed a long-fingered hand to his tattooed chest. "We must go to Oche Cavern."

The lake roiled. "Pentharian warrior, we meet again, but I do not know of your brother."

The ruby red Pentharian came forward. "I am Yuin, blood relative and comrade of Voer. He tells me of your grandness."

"The Lake of Rorret is at your service." The water beneath the floor rippled into stillness.

Allynae forced a calmness he did not feel. "If we are to rescue Almiralyn—"

"Patience, Allynae." Rorret's watery voice held a touch of annoyance. "Introductions are important. I must know who joins with me."

Aware the lake could be cantankerous, Allynae swallowed a caustic retort. "Rorret, I understand the need to learn of those who swim in your depths."

"Don't humor me, Brother of Almiralyn. Your sister is my mistress. I will carry you to Oche Cavern as soon as introductions are complete."

"Can you take us all the way?" Zugo knelt next to the opening.

"Son of Yookotay, where water flows, I have access. Your challenge is to hold your breath long enough to make the crossing." Irritation laced Rorret's words with sarcasm. "Who cowers in the shadows?"

Allynae beckoned Paisley forward. "This is my friend, Paisley. He's standing guard here until Evolsefil returns."

"The crystal has already returned to Myrrh." Water splashed over the edges of the square opening. "Why is it not here? Do you think I cannot protect it?"

Voer touched his heart. "We honor your power and your ability to defend Evolsefil. When Almiralyn is safe and Nomed defeated, Evolsefil will return to your excellent care. Time is of the essence. I know you feel the life of Myrrh ebbing."

The surface of the lake swirled over the marble floor, lapped at everyone's ankles, and receded. Rorret's voice filled the cave. "Join me. I agree to carry you to Nomed's cavern."

Voer edged Allynae away from the opening. "Show no fear or Rorret will amplify it with everything it can find in your mind to feed it."

Allynae nodded and returned to the side of the opening as Yuin and Voer lowered themselves into the lake and shifted to freshwater dolphins.

Zugo slipped in, his hand grasping Yuin's dorsal fin. "Come on, Allynae."

Shoving his fear aside, Allynae slid into the cold water. Voer steadied him. He took a deep breath and, with the dolphin, dove beneath the surface. His grip tightening on Voer's fin, he willed himself not to put temptation in Rorret's way.

Paisley watched them disappear and the marble floor slide into place. *Sure glad I'm stayin' here.*

With his back pressed to the stone wall, he sighed. *Turmoil continues. How are Torgin and Skipt? Is Tam safe?* He tugged at his mustache. *And what of Karrew? Does he live?* His mouth opened in an exhausted yawn; sleep threatened. Stoically, he began a patterned pacing before the double doors into the Cavern of Tennisca.

64

Torgin couldn't squelch his dismay when his heart-brother disappeared in pursuit of the orange Giest. Beside him, Skipt jumped up and down, pointing after the Pentharian. A girl's deep voice intermingling with those of the DeoNytes created a delightful diversion. Taking the Enots by the arm, he strode down the passage. "I have someone special to introduce you to. Yaro can take care of himself."

Not far along the passageway, Ari conferred in a serious tone with Sitrio. Skipt pranced to her side and made a comical bow. "Ya ho. You, the other twin. I Skipt, Enots and warrior of Myrrh."

Ari's eyes sparkled as she returned the bow and offered her hand. "I'm Arienh AsTar, twin of Brielle and warrior of Myrrh. Nice to meet you."

"Me pleased, too." He gave her hand a vigorous shake.

"Hey, Arienh." Torgin grinned down at her.

With a chortle of delight, she threw her arms around him, stepped back, and studied him with open curiosity. "*Where* have you been, Torgin Wilith

Whalend? Have you seen Brie? How is she? Where is she? Which Pentharian flew after the Giest?"

He started to laugh. "One question at a time, but first... I'm so happy to see you. Will you ever forgive me for deserting you in the Grasslands?"

Ari hugged him again. "You saved yourself, Torgin. I never even thought to be angry."

Sitrio welcomed them with a nod and smile and then returned to the serious business at hand. "I've assigned two DeoNytes to guard the entrance to the Cavern of Tennisca and two to help Paisley in the Cave of Canedari. Our next step is to decide the best way to reach the DiMensioner's hideaway."

Ari tugged a red curl and pursed her lips. "I think the sleeping cave is our best bet. They won't expect us to go back there, and even if Giests are guarding it, we have the net."

His friend's confidence nudged Torgin's ever present jealousy. The temptation to walk away stalled when Sitrio turned to him.

"What do you think is the best plan, Torgin? The small cave or cross the Lake of Rorret?"

"If the cave is the quickest—Wait! Let's ask Ostradio."

Skipt danced a happy jig. "That good idea."

Torgin removed the leather thong from around his neck. Sitrio, Ari, Skipt, and the remaining DeoNytes gathered around him, their attention focused on the blue compass.

"Show us the safest and shortest way to—" He glanced at Sitrio.

"Oche Cavern." The DeoNyte nodded as the needle spun in a blur of gold and ended pointing NW. The image of the tunnel rose above the compass face and shimmered into nothing.

"Thank you, Torgin." Sitrio patted him on the back. "The small cave it is."

Ari squeezed his hand. "You're the best, Torg. Come on, let's go."

Torgin glanced sideways at the twin. Like Brie, she seemed so different. *But then, this unbelievable adventure has changed me, too.* The realization produced a slight smile. Shrugging off jealous thoughts, he trotted along beside her, glad to be her friend and happy to be at her side.

K eeping Almiralyn's rescue in the forefront of its thoughts, Rorret refrained from playing with her brother's mind, and carried its passengers through the winding underwater channels leading to Oche Cavern. When they could no longer hold their breath, it brought them up under the channel's low ceiling.

Gasping for air, Zugo and Allynae brushed water from their eyes and worked to equalize the pressure in their ears. The two Pentharian dolphins blew water from their air holes and waited to continue.

"The next time I bring you up, you will be on the far side of the lake in Oche Cavern, near Nomed's command post. Surface in silence or you will give yourselves away. Remmihs Lake will help you cross without alerting Nomed. Rescue Almiralyn, and you will save Myrrh."

Allynae began to speak, but Rorret interrupted. "I've just said more than I have in many cycles. Let it be, brother of Almiralyn. Let's finish this journey."

Zugo and Allynae filled their lungs with air and held fast to the dolphins' fins as they dove beneath the surface. Rorret pulled them even faster through the underground waterway. This leg was the longest. It would be difficult for the DeoNyte and the Human to hold their breath as long as necessary. With luck, it would pass them off to Remmihs before they lost consciousness.

V oer felt Allynae's grip on his dorsal fin tighten and fear threaten to overtake him. He knew Zugo battled with his instinct to breathe. *We'd better come up soon.*

As though in answer to his thought, the water pressed them upward. A deep feminine voice sounded in their bursting ears. "Be silent... silent... ever so silent..."

When Zugo and Allynae broke the surface, fighting the need to gulp in loud, wrenching mouthfuls of air, Voer left them with Yuin to recover. Unlike the Lake of Rorret, this lake made him uneasy. His thoughts hidden, he dove beneath the water.

Shifting to frog, he explored the water's edge; in bat form, he flew up to the high ceiling and crisscrossed the cavern's breadth and width. Below him,

Giests gathered near the cavern entrance. Dom sat by the fire, cleaning his spectacles and muttering to himself. Neither Seyes Nomed nor his henchman, the death shadow, were visible.

Voer returned to Remmihs Lake to search for a place to rest and recuperate. Allynae and Zugo would need to warm up before undertaking a rescue attempt. A rocky ledge jutting over the water a suitable distance from Nomed's camp caught his attention. He swooped down to investigate. On its far side, he discovered a small, dry cave, where warm air rose from a pool at the back. *A hot spring. This will do.*

Although preferring not to reenter the lake, he shifted to a dolphin and swam to where Allynae and Zugo floated, shivering, beside Yuin. Preparing to dive, he waited for Allynae to take several deep breaths and dove.

With his mind masked, he guided his charges to the cave. Grateful to arrive and to move away from the Remmihs, he shifted to his natural form and helped Allynae and Zugo onto the shore. Soon, the four companions huddled together close to the hot springs.

Zugo shivered all the way to the center of his bones. His beautiful white fur, plastered against his body, made him feel naked and vulnerable. Allynae had stripped to his undergarments and spread his clothing on the rocks to dry. The Pentharian seemed unaffected by their time in the water.

In soft whispers, Voer, Yuin, and Allynae discussed their options. Zugo tried to listen, but his mind wandered back and forth from their voices to a strange vision he'd experienced on the way to the cave.

Glowing gemstones and shimmering crystal stalagmites provided a backdrop for a DeoNyte female pirouetting ahead of him, tempting him to let go of Yuin; enticing him to follow.

Zugo frowned. *Why did Remmihs Lake play with my mind when Rorret took care not to?* Suddenly alert, he moved closer to his companions.

"Listen!" He put the urgent thought in their minds. *"Listen! Quit talking."* Could he make himself understood using telepathy? He tried again. *"Stop talking. This is Zugo. Look at me if you can hear me in your mind."*

Voer tilted his head from one side to the other and placed a finger on his thin, red lips. Yuin and Allynae looked perplexed and grew quiet. The sapphire blue Pentharian drew Zugo into the circle of adults, his eyes filled with questions.

Zugo put a hand on the Pentharian's scaly knee, concentrated his intention, and touched his earhole. *"Voer, can you hear me?"*

Voer's mouth rounded in surprise. He nodded and turned to their companions.

Allynae and Yuin exchanged confused glances but remained silent.

Voer pointed at Zugo, then tapped his temple, and mouthed a slow explanation. "He speaks in my mind."

Allynae moved closer to Zugo, a look of concentration on his craggy face.

Voer whispered in Yuin's ear in the language of ReTaw au Qa. Yuin acknowledged his understanding. Both Pentharian focused their serious gazes on Zugo.

"Nomed has control of Remmihs Lake." Zugo described his vision.

A strange sound from Allynae made them all focus in his direction. Pointing at himself, he mouthed the word 'vision' and pointed at the lake.

Yuin frowned, then nodded.

Voer smiled. *"Good job, Zugo."*

Zugo grinned. *"Thanks. Now what?"*

"Rest and think." The Pentharian mouthed the same message to Yuin and Allynae.

As he curled up next to the warm pool, Zugo could sense the lake straining to hear.

S kipt crept down the tunnel to the sleeping cave. When he saw no one, he slipped on to the ledge. His small nose wrinkled. *Giests.* He scrambled down the wall and crossed to a dark curtain at the cave's entrance. The reek of Giest forced him to step back. Muffled squabbling in the cavern confirmed their proximity.

I promised Sitrio I'd return at once. He shot a glance over his shoulder. Curiosity overruled his promise—and his good sense. His eyes mere slits, he squatted and lifted the corner of the curtain.

Giests of every color converged on the minuscule opening. Skipt disintegrated into a pile of gray stones as they flew helter-skelter around the cave. Forcing down his desire to reassemble and run, he remained still.

Wodash appeared at the entrance, a sneer magnifying his ugliness. "What are you doing?"

A green Giest hovered. "Curtain moved."

"Just a little." A yellow one squawked from its side.

"Nothing here." Their squeaky song shrilled through the cave.

"Stop!" The word rocketed through the cavern, cracked against the wall, and bounced back, again and again.

A red-faced Seyes Nomed charged from his sleeping alcove. "What in DerTah is all the ruckus? Can't you keep *anything* under control?"

"Everything is under control." Wodash sent two Giests to investigate the tunnel while he walked the circumference of the small cave. "All that ruckus for nothing." Kicking the fallen curtain aside, he smirked with delight and knelt to examine a pile of small gray stones. "What have we *here*?"

Skipt's heart pebble skipped a beat. He gawked at the terrifying form leering down at him.

When the two Giests crashed headlong into the crystal net, Torgin, fear for Skipt screaming in his mind, dropped to all fours and scuttled down the tunnel. When he reached the end, he paused. *What if—?* He pushed the thought away and dared to peek around the large rock.

Wodash knelt over Skipt, his jowl quivering with glee.

Dismay squeezed Torgin's fragile courage dry. *I can't...* Memory flared and faded. *I will not leave my friend.* Not giving himself time to change his mind, he stepped onto the ledge. Wodash od DerTah raised gleaming red eyes to his face.

Torgin concentrated on his hatred of the death shadow. Not even his relief registered when the pile of gray stones reassembled into an Enots and darted under a rumpled blanket in the corner. Trapped in Wodash's frigid cold and more courageous than he ever remembered being, he kept his mind blank.

The confusion in the cavern brought Voer in bat form from the hot springs on another scouting mission. He arrived in time to see Wodash capture Torgin and Skipt dart for cover. Attached to the cave wall, he delayed until Wodash departed, then flew down the tunnel. At the end, six DeoNytes and Ari waited with the crystal net stretched over the opening. He shifted to a fly, zipped beyond the net, and landed in Pentharian form. "Ari."

The twin pivoted and stared. "Voer."

"Where did you come from?" Sitrio joined them.

Voer related the recent events in Oche Cavern and explained that Allynae, Yuin, and Zugo waited for him on the other side of the lake.

"You mean Wodash has Torgin?" Ari clutched the sacred knife and started toward the tunnel. A tattooed hand caught her gently by the arm.

"Wait, Ari, we must work together. If we succeed the first time we attack, they won't capture anyone else. We may even rescue Almiralyn."

"Torgin's fear of the death shadow might undermine his ability to control his thinking." Dread filled her voice.

"All the more reason for us to make careful plans." Voer drew her into the circle of DeoNytes.

Torgin, numbed but conscious, felt the death shadow lift him from the ledge. Too soon, he stared up at the scarred face of the DiMensioner.

"We have a spy." Wodash gripped his shoulders with glacial hands.

Chills coursing through him left Torgin shaking, whether from cold or fear he could not tell.

"Release him." Nomed scowled at his henchman. "I need him conscious to search his mind."

The death shadow hesitated, then obeyed.

Torgin collapsed to his knees and wrapped his arms around himself.

"Stand up." Nomed's snarled command hit like a slap.

Torgin's legs refused to move. He moaned and huddled lower, his heart pounding in his ears.

Nomed stepped closer. "Stand up *now*, or I will make sure you never get up again."

The fury in his tone threatening to undermine Torgin's newfound valor, he forced the fear away. Still, his physical body would not respond.

Wodash jerked him to his feet. "Do not forget, Seyes, this boy is mine when you're done."

Nomed and death shadow locked gazes for an instant before Torgin felt the DiMensioner's attention refocus on him.

"Tell me where Evolsefil is, and I will let you go." Nomed's voice had become honey sweet.

Torgin didn't blink or think. He shoved his hands in his pockets and focused on the cold that turned his breath white when it met the warm air in the cavern. In a game of hide and seek, the DiMensioner pursued his memories—one after the other until Torgin knew his brain would explode. No matter how hard he tried to keep his thoughts away from Evolsefil and the Tower of Nemttachenn, they stubbornly returned to first one and then the other.

Paper crinkled in his pocket. *Brie's gift.* He forced his mind to remember every detail, every line—and to forget everything else. Almiralyn's cottage loomed in his memory. *A haven.*

"Empty your pockets." Nomed barked the command like an angry dog.

The ebb and flow of the tall grass between the Terces Wood and the Sekan River... climbing through the foot—

The DiMensioner grabbed his arm and yanked his hand free of his pocket. "What have we here?"

Torgin snatched his hand away and crumpled Brie's map into a tight ball.

Nomed caught his wrist in an iron grip. "Drop it or I will break your hand. You will never play music again, I promise you."

Excruciating pain shot through his palm. His fingers uncurled. The crumpled paper fell to the ground.

Tears filled his eyes when the DiMensioner unfolded it and laughed. "A map of Myrrh." His tone mocked Torgin and everything he loved and valued.

Nomed pulled his knife, grabbed Torgin's throbbing hand, and stabbed his middle finger. Holding it over the drawing, he whispered a chant in a strange language. A droplet of blood dripped on the Grasslands. The DiMensioner squeezed out a second drop that splattered across the Terces Wood. A third crimson bead formed on the tip of his finger. It fell, hovered above Brie's gift, and with a suddenness that took Torgin's breath away landed on Nemttachenn Tower.

Nomed's mind probe shot from his head through his entire body. Gasping, he crumpled to the ground.

Laughter echoed through the cavern. "I should have guessed. Where else but Nemttachenn." His amusement turned ugly. "Almiralyn's Myrrh is about to meet the same fate as your map, young Torgin." Ripping it to shreds, he flung it into the fire.

All but a single fragment flared and disappeared in tiny plumes of smoke. One solitary piece floated on a wave of heat and landed by Torgin's bleeding hand. His fingers closed around the blood-soaked tower.

Dom watched Nomed from his place near the cave where Almiralyn remained imprisoned in an icy web of Wodash's making.

When Wodash appeared with Torgin, Dom used this distraction to slip unseen into Nomed's alcove. Kneeling by the white and gold bird, he wrapped her carefully in Nomed's cape. "Mira!" His urgent whisper trembled. "There's little time. Wake up."

The bird convulsed in his arms. *What's causing her so much pain?* Her white-feathered body wrapped in shimmering liquid silver convulsed again. He slipped his arm around her and yanked the DiMensioner's cape away. A blue eye opened and looked up at him. He held her close to his chest, tears streaming down his wrinkled cheeks.

65

V oer landed beside the hot springs and explained the simple plan he and Sitrio had developed to Yuin, Zugo, and Allynae. "The timing is critical." He paused and squinted over the lake.

"Listen! Listen!" The echoed words repeated over and over throughout the large grotto. Voer shifted to bat once more and flew to investigate. Near the alcove entrance, an orange Giest hovered in front of Nomed. Its stringent demands mingled with the babbling chaos created by its comrades. Torgin lay in a heap at the DiMensioner's feet. A small brown ferret skulked from shadow to shadow until he reached the fallen boy.

Voer hastened back to the hot springs. After a quick explanation, he and Yuin, with Allynae and Zugo secure on their vulture backs, soared over the lake.

Torgin raised his head in time to see Ari and her DeoNytes stretch and anchor the crystal net across the entrance to the smaller cave. *I'm not alone.* A spark of courage reignited. After a moment of satisfaction as three Giests hit the crystalline net, he eased himself to sitting and watched the two vultures and their passengers circle, herding more Giests into the trap.

Close by, Nomed and the death shadow struggled to gain control of their army. A silver lasso materialized above the DiMensioner's head, whirled, and rocketed through space, missing Zugo by a breath. It snapped back to Nomed's hand again and again, its hiss and crackle cutting through the air in an echo-repeated rhythm.

Insistent pressure against Torgin's knee wrenched his attention away from the battle. Ferret gold eyes sought his, their message clear. He blanked his mind and glanced over his shoulder at the chaos in the cavern. Picking up the ferret, he placed it around his neck and made a slow ascent to standing. *Nomed might know where Evolsefil is, but he won't have Almiralyn to bargain with.* Again, he masked his thoughts.

His attention glued to the DiMensioner's back, he dodged beyond the alcove curtain and halted in surprise. Dom huddled on the pallet, rocking a white bird and sobbing.

The ferret leapt to the ground and shifted to the gold Pentharian. Dom's eyes widened in fear. Torgin cleared his throat to explain. Yaro shook his head and took the bird from the elderly man.

"The DiMensioner probed my mind and discovered where Esán hid Evolsefil." Torgin lowered his gaze; shame warmed his cheeks.

Yaro pursed his red lips in a soundless shhh and handed him the white bird. He assisted the old man to his feet. "You will do what I ask?"

Dom nodded, staring up at the tattooed face.

Nomed pivoted at the center of the frenzied activity in the cavern. His lasso sailed out, hovered above Allynae's head, and missed. A flip of his wrist sent it into oblivion. He rounded on Wodash. "Get those creatures under control."

Scanning the craziness overhead, he assessed the possibilities for success.

The Pentharian traitors and their riders circled, herding his undisciplined army toward the occupants in the sleeping cave. Although the Giests continued to outnumber his adversaries, their numbers decreased at an alarming rate. His eyes narrowed. *My only chance is to escape with Almiralyn.*

Waves crashing against the shore of Remmihs Lake sounded an alarm. Nomed whipped around, looking for the twins' friend. Signaling Wodash to join him, he ripped the alcove curtain from its adhesive fasteners and found himself face to face with his quarry, the white and gold bird cradled in his arms. Beside Torgin, Dom regarded him from behind his spectacles. A golden Pentharian flashed from sight.

Nomed's hand shot out and snatched a brown bat from the air. Sharp teeth pierced his finger. A paralyzing cold careened up his arm. Reality blurred. His ears rang. Fear mixing with rage, he flung the bat against the wall and pulled a vial from his pocket. A shaking hand uncorked it. He drank the contents as his legs gave way and he stumbled to his knees.

The sluggishness spreading through his body changed to searing heat and normalized. He grabbed his cape from the pallet. *I almost died.* Through clenched teeth, he hissed and an angry command. "Wodash, bring the boy and the Guardian."

Without a backward glance, he shifted to the great horned owl, shot across the cavern, and streaked along the tunnel to the cliff entrance. His henchman landed by his side, Torgin and the white bird frozen within the wasteland of his bulk. Giests formed a silent guard around them.

S kipt gave chase. "Ya Ho! The DiMensioner got Torgin! The DiMensioner got Almiralyn!"

Ari ran after him, grabbed his arm, and knelt to speak to him. "Skipt, you can't save them by getting caught." Fear for Torgin and Almiralyn overflowed his gray eyes. "I'm frightened for them, too, Skipt. We'll discover where he took them. We have to. Let's find out what the others are planning."

"I couldn't penetrate the wall of screaming Giests to intercept them." Allynae's dismay rang clear as he shared his frustration with Voer and Yuin. "There were just too many packed together."

Sitrio joined them, carrying the crystal net. He scanned the cavern and almost smiled. It appears the horrible things are gone for now.

Yaro ducked from the sleeping alcove and joined them, rubbing his bruised temple. "I bit Nomed." He shook his long braids back from his face. "He had the antidote."

Allynae patted him on the back. "You did your best, my friend." Worry replaced his obvious frustration. "We must follow at once. They'll head for Nemttachenn, and we can't afford to let them arrive before we do. Sitrio, will you come with us or remain here?"

"I'll stay here to place guards at the entrance to this grotto and secure all the ways into the Dojanack Caverns. The Cave of Canedari will be ready to receive Evolsefil when it's time." He handed him the crystal net. "You might find this useful."

Allynae accepted the Giest-catcher. "Thank you, Sitrio. Be safe. Yuin, you take Zugo and Skipt. Ari and I will ride with Voer."

"I'll fly ahead to warn the others and find my heart-brother." Yaro shifted to a golden falcon and shot down the passageway.

"What about Dom?" Ari didn't hide her disgust.

The old man waited by the fire pit, fumbling with his spectacles. Perching them on his nose, he met Allynae's stern gaze. "I am Almiralyn's servant, Alli."

"For how long, Dom?"

"Until I no longer walk this land." The shame on his face and earnestness in his voice suggested he told the truth.

Ari cut her eyes at him. "Don't believe him, Allynae. He's a traitor."

Voer spoke up. "He was trying to save Almiralyn, Ari."

"I don't care. He—"

Allynae's hand on her shoulder stopped her tirade. "We must hurry. Dom, please fetch Tam and the chestnut mare, from the bottom of the mountain trail and then get Gemlucky. Nomed enchanted the stallion. Beware of the fire in his eyes."

Looking grateful not to be chastised for his misdeeds, Dom straightened his hunched shoulders. "I'll find them, Alli, and bring them back to the cottage."

Ari walked down the tunnel with Zugo. When they reached the entrance and emerged into the sun's brightness, she squinted and inhaled a deep, invigorating breath. Beside her, Zugo, long accustomed to the dimness of Meos, absorbed the view of mist-shrouded mountains and the huge white ball of light burning through the grayness. *What would it be like to stand in the open air for the first time?*

Before she could ask, Allynae lifted Zugo onto the back of the ruby Pentharian's vulture and placed the Enots in front of him. Yuin peered over his shoulder, spread his massive wings, and carried his passengers skyward. Zugo's dark face registered astonished delight. Skipt bristled with excitement and clapped his hands.

Allynae helped her mount Voer's feathered back and climbed up behind her. She remembered her first flight in his arms and felt grateful for his reassuring presence and the Pentharian's. She glanced back and smiled. Allynae responded with a gentle squeeze. With a sigh, Ari prepared to enjoy the blissful feeling of soaring over the beauty of the misty Myrrhinian landscape.

Dom's gaze followed the Pentharian silhouettes. His heart throbbed with shame. The reasons he'd sided with Seyes no longer seemed valid or important. He couldn't help but hope he would never see the DiMensioner again. Muttering under his breath about old men who make bad choices, he began his trek down the mountain. His aged bones already ached with the effort of staying upright on the steep, rocky trail.

In the cottage kitchen, the strength returning to Karrew's body left him invigorated and his instincts sizzling. He cocked his head. *Almiralyn is in trouble. It is time to fly to her assistance.* Stretching his good wing brought no discomfort. A tentative attempt on his injured side sent a stinging ache through his chest. Craning his neck, he examined the wound. The edges, where Owae's healing herbs had penetrated the skin, had knit together to form a jagged line. An acute spasm knifed through his pectoral muscle. He exhaled to ease the throbbing. Cawing softly, he flew to Almiralyn's kitchen chair and then to the end of the table. Taking a moment to catch his breath, he assessed his body's response to flight. *The pain is not unbearable. I think I will manage. I have to.*

Majeska watched him, preparing to leave while she licked a paw and rubbed it with fastidious care over her ear. Jumping to the floor, she padded to the back door, which stood ajar. Karrew's eyes, bright as sun-soaked obsidian, followed her. She gave the door a push with her nose. Cool air filled the room and wafted down the hall.

Owae watched from the back porch as the cat and the raven disappeared into the Terces Wood. She shook her head. *It's too soon, Karrew, but I understand.* She returned to Almiralyn's cozy kitchen, where the walls showed faint signs of another color change. The desire for companionship carried her across the hall to the art studio.

Sparrow and Merrilea huddled together, their attention focused on the stark, cold painting on the easel. Enclosed in a cage of ice, Torgin, his green eyes huge, his black eyelashes crystallized, cradled a beautiful bird with gold-tipped wings. A formless field of white with a nightmarish face hovered in triumph over them.

Owae moved to their side and gasped. "Watch Almiralyn."

The bird's sapphire blue eye looked directly at them, blinked, and closed.

Merrilea started for the door. "Let's check the fountain. Perhaps it will tell us something." She jogged up the stairs two at a time, with Sparrow at her heels.

Owae took one last peek at the painting and hurried after them. By the time she entered the sanctuary, a series of quick images flashed across the surface of Elcaro's Eye. As though the fountain understood what the women needed to know, an image emerged from the water's depths.

Beneath the branches of a Tirips tree, Nomed and Wodash plotted their next move. Above their heads, hidden in its silver leaves, a golden falcon listened to every word.

"I bet that's a Pentharian." Sparrow leaned closer.

"Look at the Giests." Owae's pale eyes narrowed as the scene shifted, showing blobs of color huddled together in small, silent groups. "Until today, none of them have been outside the caverns since before their deaths. I almost feel sorry for them."

The image blurred, changed, and cleared.

"It's Jordy." Merrilea clutched the rounded rim of Elcaro's bowl.

In the clearing surrounding Nemttachenn on three sides, Jeet introduced Jordett to Yookotay and a man hidden from view. They spoke in hushed voices, dispersed in different directions, and vanished into the mist. The carnelian Pentharian flew to the top of the tower, his eyes straining to penetrate the grayness enshrouding them all in a silent prison.

Ripples erased the image and replaced it with another.

Inside the tower, Fen and Bonnee watched Esán and Brie study a battered book. "I feel as though I am being filled while I read." Brie bit her bottom lip. "It's like I've been thirsty all my life and *EmitEnil* is quenching it, word by word. And look what's happening to the Stone of Remembering." She held out her hand. On the palm, the stone glowed bright cobalt blue.

Merrilea's eyes remained fixed on her nephew. "Esán looks so different."

"*EmitEnil* is filling him, too." Owae put an arm around her. "Myrrh is being absorbed into his very essence and he into hers."

Sparrow moved closer to the DeoNyte healer. "Look at the way he's watching Brie. He seems intrigued, or curious, but then so am I. She is so..."

"Grown up?" The DeoNyte smiled.

A new image fluttered into view. Evolsefil glowed, illuminated by the Sentinel of the tower's misty blue essence.

"CheeTrann knows the opposing sides are moving nearer." Owae pressed her aged hands to her heart. "It waits to see what its role will be in the final battle."

The reflection faded and refocused.

High above Myrrh, Pentharian raptors soared through the mist, carrying Ari, Allynae, Zugo, and Skipt closer to the tower and to their enemies. Like the oarsmen in a longboat, they maintained a strong, unbroken rhythm. The powerful wings carried them toward the confrontation that awaited them in the Terces Wood.

A haze swirled up around the clearing and onto the fountain's surface, obscuring the water and leaving unanswered questions in the minds of the anxious women who watched.

66

Calm and cold as the iciness imprisoning Myrrh's Guardian, Nomed folded his arms over his chest and stared at the tower. His scar pulsed, a reminder of the young boy's promise of revenge. He felt the sting of the glass shard cutting his cheek and warm blood running down his stoic boyish face. Anger raged as deep and fiery now as it had that fateful turning. *I will be avenged, and Esán will become my apprentice to train and to conquer.* His jaw tightened; his chin lifted. *And... the Prima Crystal will be mine, alone.*

Jordett waited in the woods surrounding Nemttachenn Tower, his patience dwindling. The clammy cold of the billowing mist penetrated to the marrow of his bones. He shivered and turned up the collar of his uniform jacket. *I wish I could do something besides hide.*

A golden Pentharian flashed into sight.

"By the Fathers, Yaro, couldn't you warn a man when you're about to materialize from nothing?"

Yaro's eyes showed momentary confusion. "I bring news from Dojanacks." He provided details, then waited.

Jordett frowned. "Have you seen Nomed?"

"He is near. Our time is short."

Glancing skyward, Jordett knit his brow in frustration. "Intercept Allynae and tell him to make haste, Yaro. We are too few to take a stand against the DiMensioner."

The soft swish of the Pentharian's shift rippled through the mist as a golden falcon soared upward.

Jordett glared into the gloominess. *Where are you, Seyes Nomed? And where is your henchman, Wodash od DerTah?*

A group of Giests slipped between trees, spotted a uniformed Human and hovered. Their green leader hit Jordett's forehead and knocked him to the ground—senseless, silent, and empty as an unfilled cup. The Giest hung above the body, sniffed it from head to foot, and, with a crooked smile on its distorted features, rejoined its comrades.

They continued their aimless meandering until the Meosian ReDael emerged from the mist. A large wad of purple spittle coated the DeoNyte's face. Fighting for breath, he crumpled to the ground, a misshapen pile of white fur.

A strange man stepped from the trees and waved a hand in their direction. A wall of tingling energy chased them into the woods and held them at bay. Squabbling in confusion, they watched him drag the DeoNyte deeper into the forest, wipe the purple slime off his face, and conceal him beneath the branches of a broad-leafed bush. The stranger whispered a phrase that caused the air surrounding the ReDael to shimmer and the Giests to fly free before he faded from sight.

Muttering amongst themselves, the plasmic creatures drifted on, listening for the call of their master.

At Nomed's behest, Wodash circled high above the tower where Jeet stood guard. Hidden by the mist, he eyeballed his target before dropping from the grayness, his ugly mouth a gaping, icy pool. The Pentharian gasped and started to change shape. A blast of frigid air froze him halfway through the shift. A strange conglomerate of bird and Pentharian—one arm, one wing, a feathered back and vulture's tail, a humanoid head and torso—balanced precariously on the parapet's rim. The Pentharian's humanesque features flashed surprise and then went as blank as a cleaned slate.

The great horned owl swooped from the mist. Nomed, his hazel eyes gleaming, appeared beside the fallen Pentharian. "A work of art, Wodash...a genuine work of art." His caustic laughter rang out in the oppressive atmosphere at the top of the tower.

Wodash winced at the sound, then gasped. Existence-threatening warmth washed over him. Weak-kneed and shaking, he gagged. "Evolsefil, the S-s-sentinel—" Energy waning, he launched his failing body from the parapet.

The black and silver owl shot past him. Landing in the woods opposite the tower's east-facing entrance, he materialized and flipped his cape behind his shoulders. The silver lining flashed like mercury in the dim light.

Hatred for his master welled up in Wodash's chest. He descended to stand beside him. *Do you even care I almost expired? Are you aware of the power that fills Nemttachenn?*

Nomed angled his head to look at the mass of glacial coldness next to him. "Will you never learn to hide your thoughts, idiot? No wonder the boy could read every one." Scorn laced his tone. "And you didn't expire. You and your traitorous imaginings are right here." He sneered at his henchman. "If you want to make it beyond this turning, Wodash od DerTah, at least attempt to mask your feeble mind."

Pulling his shoulder-length hair back from his face, Nomed secured it at the nape of his neck and scrutinized Nemttachenn. The tower sent a rhythmic pulsation throughout the Terces Wood. Whatever resided within knew where he and Wodash were hiding. Instinctively, he moved further into the trees, motioning the death shadow after him.

Yuin deposited his passengers behind Nemttachenn and slipped into the trees. From his hiding place, he saw Skipt dodge under a bush and disintegrate into a pile of pebbles. Zugo crouched in the shadows. As Nomed and Wodash withdrew and the Giests continued their marauding patrol of the clearing's perimeter, two gray eyes, and the gray stones reassembled into a running Enots who darted through the tower's entrance. Zugo, a blur of white, dashed after him.

Yuin scanned the clearing. Satisfied his charges were safe, he peered through the mist at the top of the tower, squinted, and frowned. A vulture's wing hung at an odd angle over the granite parapet. Yuin shifted to a Terces blackbird, shot upward, and circled. Jeet, caught midway between Pentharian and vulture, lay half on and half off the rampart. Voer, Allynae, and Ari strained to move him to safety. Alighting, Yuin shifted and helped to lower him to the roof.

He addressed Voer. "What happened?"

The Pentharian leader touched Jeet's orange-brown braid. "I don't know. Arienh, will the knife help?"

Ari withdrew Efillaeh from its scabbard. "I bet Wodash did this." She touched the blade to Jeet's forehead and then to his heart.

Yuin knelt and clasped his comrade's icy hand.

Cold crept over Jeet's body, numbed his mind, and suspended him in a place without time. CheeTrann's blue light wafting upward through the tower roof kept him from toppling to the clearing below.

Faint voices drifted around him. Someone lowered him to safety. Something touched his brow. The cold melted away. It rested on his heart. He inhaled, completed his shift to the vulture, and then materialized in his true form.

Yuin helped him to sit with his back against the granite parapet. "How are you, my brother?"

Jeet pushed long, carnelian braids back from his face and looked at his comrade. His gaze traveled to Voer and Allynae and came to rest on Ari and the sacred knife. "I am alive. Please help me stand."

His Pentharian comrades on either side of him assisted him to his feet. His nostrils flared as he inhaled the damp air. He stuck out his tongue, absorbed the flavors of the Terces Wood, and licked his lips. In the way of his kind, he touched his forehead to Voer's and then to Yuin's and celebrated their friendship in the language of ReTaw au Qa. He offered Allynae his palm. "I am in your debt, brother of Almiralyn."

Allynae placed his palm on the Pentharian's. "I'm glad I was here."

Jeet knelt in front of Ari, gold eyes glinting with reverence. "You gave me back my life. I honor you as my comrade and fellow warrior."

"I am privileged to fight at your side, Jeet." Ari replaced Efillaeh in the scabbard and smiled. "And you are most welcome."

Allynae handed Yuin the crystalline net. "Go with Jeet and do your best to decrease the number of the Giests roaming the woods."

Yuin studied his boyhood friend and fellow warrior. "Are you well enough to join in our battle?"

"Together we will rid the forest of those plasmic vermin." Jeet shifted and perched on the parapet, surveying the mist-soaked landscape.

Yuin embodied his vulture form and alighted beside him. With the Giest-catcher firmly in their beaks, they began a search of the perimeter.

Something nagged at Ari to pay attention. She curled a strand of red around her finger, tugged, and turned towards the man behind her.

"Brie is here in the tower, Allynae. I have to find—"

A golden falcon swooped past her and materialized as Yaro. Compelling need bristled around him as he acknowledged Voer with a nod and hurried to her side. "You must come with me, Daughter of KcernFensia. Nomed imprisoned Torgin and Almiralyn in a cage of ice. Unless we can free them, they will perish." He addressed Allynae. "Yookotay, One Man, and Jordett hide in the mist. They await your instructions."

Ari chewed her bottom lip. "What about Brie? She's here, Allynae. I need to see her so much."

Sympathy, understanding, acceptance flitted one after the other over the craggy features. "I know you wish to join your sister, Arienh, but you are the bearer of Efillaeh. Your allegiance must be to Almiralyn and Myrrh."

She peered at the spiral staircase leading to Brie, swallowed her desire like a bitter pill, and shook herself. Pivoting, she looked from Allynae to Yaro. "I'll go. If you see Brielle, please tell her I miss her."

Allynae squeezed her shoulder. "I promise."

Yaro flashed to his vulture form. She mounted and pressed her knees against his muscled sides. As he lifted into flight, she glanced back at the tower, the longing to be with Brie, a knot in her chest.

Mixed feelings racing, Allynae climbed onto Voer's shifted form, gasped when they launched into the air, and shelved his desire to accompany Ari. *I know I'm needed here.*

The massive vulture landed in the trees at the edge of the clearing as several Giests drifted by, muttering and squabbling amongst themselves, their fear making them more dangerous than ever. Voer folded his wings and vanished. Allynae glanced around and gulped down a startled gasp. Alert panther eyes blinked a warning. A cool black nose nudged him deeper into the forest.

CheeTrann felt the malevolent presence of the DiMensioner od DerTah and the death shadow growing stronger. Rising from its resting place, it cast a spell of invisibility around the Heart of Myrrh. "Evil approaches, Spirit Boy and Daughter of KcernFensia. Prepare to do battle."

Esán and Brie hid *EmitEnil* within Evolsefil's clustered crystals. Hand in hand, with Fen, Bonnee, Skipt, and Zugo by their side, they formed a barrier in front of it.

CheeTrann returned its attention to the evil surrounding the tower.

Tam pranced uneasily beside Jordett's chestnut mare. Patience, never her strong suit, ebbed. Her instincts shouted a warning—her Human boy and her mistress needed her. A toss of the head sent her creamy mane floating around her like a halo. Restlessness prodded her to take action. She forced her thoughts to grow quiet. *Where are they?* Mind chatter intruded —*Up the mountain. Up the mountain. Up the mountain.* Ignoring the unbidden mantra, she searched further afield. The Terces Wood filled her senses. She dropped her nose, chomped a mouthful of grass, and concentrated. Within the patterning of Myrrh, faint, ghostly imprints of Torgin and Almiralyn whispered a call for help. Quenching her thirst in the small spring, she swished her tail in farewell and left the mare to wonder at the mystifying behavior of ponies.

Too little time. Too little time. The thought played a repeated tune in her head as Tam wound her way through the foothills, wishing she had wings to fly to her loved ones.

As she approached the final slope into the grasslands, a screech of rage— high, shrill, and whipped by the wind—brought her to a standstill. Nostrils flaring, she strained to pick up a scent. Her ears swiveled and twitched. The scream, in the language of horses, shrilled again—nearer, more dangerous.

Tam's heart raced. Every fiber in her body tingled with anticipation. Hoofbeats pounded toward her, slowed, and fell silent. An uneasy hush settled over the grasslands. Time ceased. Nothing disturbed the misty quiet.

Taut muscles easing, she resumed her trek down the trail. But her nostrils, her ears, every nerve ending remained alert—ready to warn of approaching peril.

Hesitant to walk into the open, she paused at the base of the foothills. Through the encroaching gray haze, she watched the grasses ebb and flow in the wind. Only their soft swish, swish, filled her ears—no animal sounds, no birds, no hoofbeats. If danger were near, she could neither hear nor smell it.

One step, two, and then a third carried her into the exposed vastness of Myrrh's grassland prairie. The distant sound of the river beating against its banks matched her urgent need to gallop unrestricted. Resisting, she ambled forward. The mist wafted, swirled, and opened a momentary path. A trio of trees thrashing in the wind brought her to stillness. Her instincts screamed.

Muscles, knotted in expectation, twitched. She stretched her neck to its fullest and sniffed the air. The mist billowed and thinned. In a single ray of sunlight, power rippling through every muscle, a black stallion regarded her from hatred-burdened eyes.

"Gemlucky?" Her soft nicker drifted between them.

The stallion neighed and tossed his head. "TroeEen." He pawed the ground.

Tam saw her friend; her instincts saw an enemy poised to kill. The startling realization she was the intended victim rocketed through her.

The misty curtain dropped like a guillotine. Ears flattened, she raced for the river. TroeEen's thundering hooves forced her faster. Fiery breath burned her flank. She jogged right. Like a wicked shadow, he galloped past her. She dodged left and back again. He blocked her path, her demise blazing in his coal-black eyes. She crow-hopped backward and squealed. Mane and tail flying, he reared. A descending hoof raked her shoulder. Sharp teeth closed on her neck. Shying away, she broke his grip, and stood blood-covered and trembling.

Anger boiled in her belly. Fury at Gemlucky's transformation changed her fear to determination. She whinnied again, reminding him of friendship and good times.

He pranced forward, then back, snorted, and shook his head.

"Almiralyn." She countered his aggression.

His sides heaved as a final terrifying scream vibrated the air. Wheeling about, he galloped into the mist, his hoofbeats fading in the distance.

Relief buckled her knees; sheer willpower kept her upright. She breathed in the scent of blood, blew out through her nostrils, and twisted her ears to listen. The only sounds in the prairie—wind in the tall grass and the low roar of water caught against its will—urged her to move. A stab of pain left her panting. She limped the remaining distance to the river.

Weariness threatened to claim her as she sought the far riverbank. Her pain-ridden mind balked. She forced herself to think—to remember her Human and her mistress. A tentative step into the fast-flowing current chilled her. She ignored the piercing cold and her rising fear and slogged deeper. Fast moving water knocked her legs from under her. Clambering against the powerful undertow, she regained her footing and forged ahead. The opposite shore seemed inaccessible. Fatigue, as fearsome as TroeEen, robbed her of courage and dissolved her determination in the icy currents of the rushing river.

A distant volley of urgent barks tugged at her fast fading awareness. With a supreme effort to stay afloat, she searched for its source. A big, shaggy dog, his tail wagging and his ears flopping, ran back and forth along the sandy bank.

Buster! Water surged over her head. Legs pumping and lungs bursting, she fought her way to the surface. Another volley of barks ordered her forward. Her hooves found the bottom. One exhausted step at a time, she reached the shallows. Fatigue quivering in every muscle, she waded ashore.

The big dog plopped down on the riverbank, his pink tongue hanging from the side of his mouth, his eyes alert and happy. Touching her nose to his, she nickered. Like a wisp of the advancing mist, he faded away.

Buster. Tam whinnied her joy. Her old friend had saved her.

She sniffed the air. Change rode on the wind. The time to find her mistress and her Human boy had arrived. Shaking herself free of water, she trotted toward the Terces Wood.

Hidden in the tall grass on the far side of the river, the black stallion watched.

67

*S*o *cold. So, so cold.* A shiver frozen at the base of Torgin's spine released and careened upward. His body's shuddered response reminded him of his first encounter with Wodash in the Tower of Nemttachenn. Gritting his teeth, he peered between the icy bars. Sudden realization stunned him—*I can still see.* Amazement flared. *I can think. Why?* His fear thawed into a deepening sense of awareness. *I am different. That has to be it.*

The Guardian's white bird form cradled in his arms stared up at him from one shimmering eye. *What does she expect me to do? Even if I can think, I can't move.* He barely noticed the air fighting its way in and out of his lungs. His slow, steady heartbeat pumped sluggish fluid through narrowed arteries and veins. *It's so strange to sense my blood flowing. Am I conscious of it normally?* He couldn't remember. The white bird's sapphire eye closed.

Beyond the frigid cage, he saw nothing but trees and mist. If only the grayness would go away and let the sun warm them. He scanned the narrow bit of forest he glimpsed between the bars. A silhouetted shape detached itself from the leafy background and crept in his direction. Amethyst-colored eyes in a sleek gray face stared up at him. Torgin tried to move. Pain left him gasping. *How can I hurt so much when I am so numb?*

The white bird opened her eye and followed the movements of the prowling cat. Above the cage, a raven's soft caw floated down to them. *Do something, Karrew. Do something soon before HE comes back.*

Bushes close by rustled and settled. Torgin strained to hide his thoughts. Silence returned to the forest. Only the top of the trees whispered in the Myrrhinian wind. Again the leaves moved, then parted to show red curls glowing in the dim light. A twin held a low branch aside for a black panther to step into the narrow space around the cage. *Yaro?* Crystal tears formed and fell, each plinking its sadness on the frozen floor of his prison.

Yaro shifted and knelt. The twin peered over his shoulder. "We're here, Torg." Her whispered words were just discernible. "We'll get you out."

Ari. Torgin blinked his eyes. Another tear bounced and rolled between the bars, where Yaro picked it up and pressed it to his heart.

Only his rigid state prevented Torgin from sinking to the ground in relief. *I am not alone.*

A ri walked the perimeter of the icy prison, her acute gaze absorbing every detail. A rounded top arched above Torgin's head. Solid ice bars, about two fingers' width apart, enclosed the diameter of the circular space. Anchored in the ground and secured to the tree above it with chains of solid ice, it emanated a strange and noxious power.

"Do you think Efillaeh will cut through the ice, Yaro?" She kept her gaze fixed on Torgin. "Shall I try?"

He blinked in response.

Yaro straightened, his Pentharian body half-hidden in the surrounding grayness. "I'll do some scouting before you do anything."

Raven wings flapped a clear warning of danger. Majeska faded into the gloominess of the forest. Torgin whimpered his dismay and squeezed his eyes shut.

"Hide, Arienh." Yaro tensed and scanned the trees surrounding them. "And mask your thoughts."

Ari ducked behind a thick, leafy bush as Wodash's grotesque bulk floated from the trees and enveloped the prison. She suppressed a horrified shuddered but could not stop the goose bumps racing over her body.

The hideous creature of death exhaled a cloud of arctic cold that hovered and then, crackling like ice breaking on the river, enshrouded the prisoners.

Ari crouched, knife in hand. Only Yaro's firm grip on her shoulder kept her from giving herself away.

Torgin's tears welled up and froze, blurring the small slice of forest within his line of sight. The white bird convulsed in his arms and grew still. Holding her closer, he felt her lungs rise and fall in a constant rhythm against his chest. Gratitude melted the tears and cleared his vision.

The death shadow's ghost-pale face hovered opposite him, red pupils fully dilated, and blue lips sneering. A scarred hand reached through the cage bars. One long finger traced the curve of Torgin's cheek, leaving a burning trail in its wake. "You are mine, boy. You are mine. Soon, I will devour your desire to live. How do you feel about that?"

Torgin didn't blink, think, or move one muscle.

Wodash's hand lingered above Almiralyn. "Dare I touch the esteemed Guardian of Myrrh?" His hideous mouth twisted into a frown. "Would Nomed even know?" He withdrew his hand and curled his fingers into a boney fist. His nostrils flared. "Soon, boy. Soon." Unwrapping his body from around the cage, he floated away toward Nemttachenn.

Torgin stared into the mist. *Are my friends still close?*

The reason One Man left Timreh Pass awaited him here at Nemttachenn Tower, and yet he felt helpless. *What keeps me a silent watcher in this eerie haze?* As he crept closer to the clearing, a silvery glimmer arrested his attention. Fading into the fog-soaked forest, he crept toward it.

After sending Wodash into the trees, a mute spectre with a mission, Seyes Nomed flipped his cape silver side out. Knowing Allynae and Voer would seek the cause of the sudden burst of shimmering light, he strode from the woods to stand opposite the arched entrance to the tower.

His voice exploded across the clearing, across the forest, the plains, and the mountains of Myrrh. "I, Seyes Nomed, DiMensioner od DerTah, claim Evolsefil and the boy, Esán, for my own. I will banish anyone who tries to thwart my plans to LlEh to burn forever in the flames of their own fear."

A slight movement attracted his attention. He almost laughed out loud at a man and a panther creeping through the trees, unaware the death shadow stalked them. Catching his henchman's eye, he gave a nod.

Wodash closed in and froze his prey mid-stride as they dodged back toward cover.

Nomed flashed to their side. "What a surprise...the brother of Almiralyn and his pet Pentharian." He leaned in close to Allynae's face. "You will die like everyone else in the land, Allynae Nadrugia, but first you will see your sister's bones stripped clean by the NoiRrac Beetle od DerTah." He opened his hand. A reddish-brown bug ran around his palm. "I brought this one just for your sister."

Allynae's hate-filled eyes glared back at him.

In a diabolical drawl, Nomed continued. "They multiply within chron-clicks, you know. This is the female. You can see that by her dried blood color and the egg sac she carries. Alone, she's quite harmless. The NoiRrac male is much more striking, the rich red of fresh let blood." The wind lifted his silver cape. "Put them together—" He paused for effect, never taking his eyes off his adversary's face. "And they are deadly." He held the beetle closer. "Don't worry, Allynae. I have a male, and when the time comes, I will reunite them." He sneered. "Hundreds of hungry red beetles will devour Almiralyn in no time at all."

A wave of his hand and the insect vanished, replaced by a stout silver rope. On command, it secured both man and the panther. Nomed smiled. "That should keep you where I want you until you're needed." A sneer twisted his mouth. "By the way, brother of Almiralyn, how's your head? When I saw you a few turnings ago, it was a bloody mess."

Realization flooded Allynae's eyes. He pressed his lips into a thin line and stared straight ahead.

Nomed observed his reaction with a cold stare. "Take them, Wodash, bind them to a tree, then return to me. We have much to do." His malicious laugh vibrated the air surrounding him. He flipped his cape, whirled it around his head, and vanished in a cloud of black doom.

Inside the tower, Brie paled. "Nomed has my father. I have to help him." She started for the entrance.

"Wait, Brie." Esán put a hand on her shoulder. "You can't go out there. That's exactly what Nomed wants. We need you here to assist with Evolsefil. I can't move the Prima Crystal alone."

"I just found him." She stifled a sob and pressed a fist to her heart. "I don't want to lose him before I've had time to know him."

Bonnee floated to her side. "Remember ReNin RepPosu, Brie. You must have courage. We need you, and so does Myrrh."

Esán withdrew *EmitEnil* from Evolsefil's crystals and handed it to her. "Let's keep reading, so when Nomed makes his move, we're ready."

Brie pressed the book to her chest and then allowed it to fall open in her hands. Esán joined her, and they began to study the sacred text while Skipt, Fen, and Zugo stood guard and the Sentinel of Myrrh kept watch.

The Now Remembered child's restlessness carried her to the wall opposite Nemttachenn's entrance. With an uneasy glance at her companions, she melted through the thick granite and emerged in the mist. Careful to avoid the DiMensioner, she explored the trees bordering the clearing. Trussed to a large tree, she discovered the Guardian's brother and the blue Pentharian, Voer.

Allynae stared at the silver ropes that bound him and looked back at her.

She nodded her understanding. "I'll bring help as soon as I can."

She found Yookotay under the broad-leafed bush and Jordett, conscious but lost in his emptied mind, further along the clearing's perimeter. As she made her way to the side opposite the arched entrance, One Man emerged from the mist.

Bonnee floated toward him. "Where is Ari? I am eager to find her and the sacred knife."

"She's with Yaro, looking for Torgin and Almiralyn. Have you seen the Guardian's brother?"

"Wodash tied Allynae and Voer to a tree." She gave him directions and faded into the fog.

Alert for Giests, she floated within the trees, her mind seeking answers. Surmising that Nomed and Wodash would hide their prisoners close by, she expanded her search. Not far beyond the limits of the area patrolled by Nomed's strange army, she discovered Torgin and Almiralyn trapped in a cage made of ice. A sleek gray cat, a raven, one gold Pentharian, and the mirror image of Brie, a silver knife gleaming in her hand, surrounded them.

She floated through the mist to join the circle.

"Bonnee." Ari peered beyond her. "Is Brielle with you?"

"No, she's in Nemttachenn with Esán. We need you to free Allynae and Voer. They're bound by a magic cord."

"As soon as we've freed Torgin and Almiralyn, I'll come with you."

Returning her attention to the cage, Bonnee shivered. "They look so cold."

Eyes narrowed in concentration, Ari studied the ice prison from every angle. With each attempt to slice through the bars, Efillaeh grew colder and heavier in her hand. She wielded the blade again. Her fingers turned numb; her head spun. The knife slipped from her grip. "I can't move." She choked on her fear. "I'm fr-e-e-zing."

Karrew flapped his wings and croaked. "Get her away from the cage. The Spell will attach her to it."

Yaro picked her up and carried her into the forest, where he helped her to sit against a tree. Tingling energy enlivened her. Blood rushed to her cheeks, tinting them with a healthy pink glow. The coldness vanished. She glanced up. Tree branches reached down to fill her with their magic. "Thank you, WeHem." She smiled at Yaro. "Thank you both."

The Pentharian stared at her. "What happened?"

"She rests against a hemlock tree." Karrew landed on Yaro's shoulder. "Hemlocks are Stewards of Myrrh's magic. This one countered Nomed's spell."

"Can we use hemlock to undo the spell on the cage?" Bonnee floated up to the group.

Raven feathers ruffled and settled. "We would need a whole grove to accomplish the task."

Ari hurried to retrieve Efillaeh. "Can Aunt Mira access the power of the sacred knife in her bird form?"

Karrew cocked his head. "All it needs to do is touch one feather, but how do we get it to her?"

Bonnee floated closer to the Pentharian. "What if you shift and take the knife to her?"

Yaro gazed at the raven. "Even if I changed to something small enough to pass between the bars, I doubt I would survive."

"You wouldn't." The feathers around Karrew's neck puffed up twice their normal size.

The discussion continued, one plan after the other rejected.

A movement near the cage focused Bonnee's wandering attention. Majeska, unaffected by the spell or the cold, was digging a hole. Dirt sprayed out behind her. Bonnee's eyes widened. "I'll go into the cage."

Ari frowned. "Won't it hurt you?"

"I might be dispatched to the land beyond." She shrugged. "Brie says that won't happen until I enter the Cavern of Tennisca at a time of my choosing."

Yaro fingered the gem in his earlobe. "Can you pick up the knife?"

She held up her translucent hand. "No, but you could."

The golden Pentharian's intense gaze studied her. "What are you suggesting?"

"You cannot pass between the bars, right? But you could go *under* them."

"Yes, but in a smaller form." He frowned. "The cold and magic would destroy me."

Ari touched his arm. "Please, let her explain what she's thinking."

"Look, Majeska is already burrowing under the cage. If you became a mole and completed the tunnel while I slip between the bars, you could shift into me as you emerged. You can do that, right? I mean, use my patterning so you are not at risk?"

"I have never shaped a Human, nor do I wish to do so. Our laws forbid it."

"Please, Yaro." Ari's entire demeanor pleaded. "It may be the only way to break the spell."

"It is *forbidden*." Stern and unapproachable, he bowed his head.

Bonnee floated closer. "You have my permission, Yaro. You would not be taking my form against my will."

Karrew flapped his wings. Pain registered as a full-bodied shudder.

Ari withdrew the knife from its scabbard. "Yaro, lift him down so I can help him?"

"No." The raven's rasping caw ended with a choking sound. "Save Efillaeh's magic for Almiralyn."

"But, Karrew—"

"No, Ari." His gaze held hers for one long moment, and then he looked at Yaro. "Tell them why you cannot assume a Human shape."

Yaro knelt in front of Ari and Bonnee. "Torgin is my heart-brother, and I have sworn allegiance to Almiralyn. I take neither of these things lightly, but I cannot take the form of a Human. If I were to do so, the leaders of ReTaw au Qa would ban me forever, along with my children and my children's children. They would strip the ability to shift shape from all of us." He bowed his head. Golden tears slid down his cheek. "We must find another way."

68

Camouflaged by churning gray fog, the death shadow hovered above the trees of the Terces Wood. Below him, lack of visibility and too many obstacles made it impossible for the Pentharian vultures to use their crystal Giest-catcher. Wodash smirked with satisfaction, and, giving a high-pitched whistle, shot upward.

Giests of every color swooped from the clouds to intercept their enemies. The Pentharian released the net, flashed into two dragonflies, and zipped out of range. In the emptiness they left behind, spheres of protoplasm dodged and zigzagged to keep from colliding.

A yellow Giest floated beyond the chaos, its bulgy eyes never leaving its quarry. Intent on capturing a dragonfly, it shot after them.

The death shadow's scowling face brought it up short. "Is this what you are looking for?" He held up a frozen insect.

"Two." The Giest squealed and pointed. "Two fly away."

"Then find the other one and bring it to me." Landing at Nomed's side,

Wodash held out his hand and uncurled his long fingers. "We have a Pentharian in the guise of a dragonfly."

The DiMensioner's narrowed eyes failed to hide a spark of glee as he picked up the insect and broke one fragile, iridescent wing. "Too bad it's frozen *and* injured." His snigger turned to a pernicious sneer. "Perhaps we should break more than a wing."

A blur of black fur exploded from the woods, slammed into Wodash's deathly cold, and crashed to the ground.

Nomed looked at the frozen panther and shot his henchman a complacent smile. "Good work, my friend." His sardonic laughter surged through the clearing. A glance at his palm squelched it. "Where on DerTah did the dragonfly go?"

The death shadow shrugged. "I doubt an insect with a broken wing can do us much harm."

"Never underestimate your enemy, Wodash, or your friends." The DiMensioner tossed him a silver rope. "Secure that bothersome feline to a sturdy tree and come back here."

Swearing under his breath, he tethered the Pentharian to a stout oak. *Someday I'll get my revenge, Seyes Nomed.*

Karrew observed the flecks of panic glinting in Torgin's eyes as his heart-brother's repeated attempts to hack through the enchanted bars failed. Jumping from his perch, he landed on the Pentharian's shoulder. "Efillaeh can't help with this."

Yaro stared at the knife, handed it to Ari, and knelt by the cage. "I promise we will free you, my brother."

"Listen." Karrew fluttered to a low branch and cocked his head.

Dried leaves crackling and twigs snapping, almost indiscernible at first, grew louder and louder.

Majeska's ears twitched. Her amethyst eyes rounded; her tail flicked.

His pain forgotten, Karrew circled upward and swooped back to his perch. "Tamboreen heads this way."

The bloodied pony hesitated in the trees at the edge of the small clearing, whinnied softly, and limped forward. A large gash on her neck and a tear on her flank oozed droplets of crimson.

"Tam, you're hurt." Ari hurried forward and offered her a palm. The pony snorted and sniffed it before nickering her approval.

Yaro, following her example and waited for Tam's soft neigh, before examining her injuries. "You've been in a battle, my friend."

Karrew hopped to a branch near the pony. "How is she?"

The Pentharian stroked her neck. "Her wounds are clean, but she's lost much blood."

Ari shot a stubborn glance at the raven. "I need to help her." Without waiting for a reply, she withdrew Efillaeh. "Hold still, sweet Tam. This won't hurt."

As the twin placed Efillaeh on each wound, soft green light shimmered around it and tendrils of purple from the amethyst-studded hilt cauterized the lacerated edges. The pony's pain-dulled eyes grew brighter. Her hide glowed with healing. When the knife's radiance faded and the tendrils withdrew, Ari returned it to the scabbard and patted the tan neck. "I've missed you, Tamboreen."

Tam snorted and pranced closer to the cage, where her Human boy, his eyes bright with fear, cradled her mistress in his arms. As she walked their prison's perimeter, her hide prickled and her nostrils stung from the aroma of dark magic. She stopped, her ears twitching to hear the crackling chorus of enchanted ice pressing against the moist summer air.

A sapphire eye followed her as she made a second circuit. *My mistress lives!* Tam pawed the ground. Torgin's eyes gleamed with love and trust. She swung her head from side to side, switched her tail, and trotted the circumference. Her hooves striking the ground created a steady rhythm. Round and round she went, picking up speed with each circular orbit. Round and round until the ground quaked, and the cage quivered.

"Look!" Bonnee floated closer. "It is vibrating."

Tam circled again. The frozen bars thinned; color flooded Torgin's cheeks. She neighed and reared. Her hooves crashed down on the side of the cage. The chains of ice anchoring it to the ground snapped. She reared again.

A pungent yellow haze hissed from the damaged prison and hung in the air, obscuring its occupants from view.

No one moved in the smothering silence that followed.

And then—starting small—a tiny breeze fluttered leaf tips, lifted single strands of Tam's mane, and grew steadily stronger. North, south, east and west, the winds of the land came to the aid of the Guardian of Myrrh. Trees swayed a celebratory dance. Yaro nudged Ari away from the cage and under cover of the hemlock's branches. Tam pranced backward, with Bonnee sheltering beside her. Wind whipped and swirled, whisked the virulent haze into an opaque froth, funneled it high in the sky, and flung it into oblivion.

The clearing grew quiet. Tempest-tossed but smiling, Torgin stepped beyond the shattered remains of the ice cage and walked to Tam's side. Karrew landed on his shoulder. "Never underestimate the love of a pony."

Tam nickered her agreement, nudged her mistress, and nibbled at Torgin's check.

S eyes Nomed pondered his next move. He could not account for one twin, two Pentharian, and an adult Human. *Do I wait forever or take the crystal and leave this land that I hate?* Eyes narrowed, he flipped his cape once more to silver. After confirming his minions were in place, he strode into the clearing and shouted one clipped, commanding word.

"Esán!"

The boy appeared inside the entrance to Nemttachenn.

"Come out here and bring the twin with you."

"This is as far as I'm willing to come."

"Are you so afraid of me? I taught you to shape shift and showed you the way to your other gifts. Do you not trust me?"

"I fear your plans for Myrrh, DiMensioner."

"If you give me Evolsefil, Esán, I will free Almiralyn and your friend. Tell the girl I will even consider releasing her father."

The red-haired twin appeared by Esán's side. Her mind opened to his touch, but gave him only what she wanted him to see.

Curious to know what had changed her, he studied her more closely.

"Return to DerTah, Seyes Nomed." The confidence in her voice caught him off guard.

"Not without Evolsefil."

"Then remain here in this land you hate, for the Prima Crystal does not belong to you." She took Esán's hand, and they withdrew into the tower.

Nomed stared at the empty entrance, furious, bemused, and surprised at the sense of disquiet the young people engendered. "Bring her father, Wodash, and be quick about it."

The death shadow vanished and reappeared with Allynae in tow. Nomed checked the silver cords that kept him weak and controllable.

"Twin, show yourself. I have your father."

Brie appeared, her demeanor as confident as Nomed's. Neither flinching nor dropping her gaze, she matched his determination.

"It would be terrible to lose him now that you have found him." Nomed kept his voice soft, but his hazel eyes glinted steel hard.

"If you take Evolsefil, we will all die." Her melodic voice was unyielding. "My father would not expect me to betray Myrrh to save his life."

Nomed kicked Allynae, bringing him to his knees. "Tell your daughter to obey me, or you die right here in front of her."

Allynae, pride shining in his eyes, smiled. "She has known me only a short time, yet she understands me well. It appears we are much alike, DiMensioner. She knows I could not ask her to cause the demise of Myrrh and Thera by attempting to save me."

Nomed's anger, an inferno of hatred, blazed. He raised his hand and spoke a single word. A fiery sword snapped into view, its sharp blade glinting in the dim light.

The twin's gaze did not waver. "Free Almiralyn and Torgin, and release all our comrades, including my father, and we will give you and Wodash safe passage off Myrrh." Her eyes glazed over. Her voice filled the clearing like a song. "I saw you from the Throne of ReNin RepPosu. This is a fork in your journey, Seyes Nomed. Your destiny is yet undecided. Do not tempt fate, or she may abandon you."

He gripped the hilt of the sword with two hands. Fury powered the rise of the blade above Allynae's head.

A flash of blue streaking from Nemttachenn's entrance knocked the sword from his grasp. Esán's kestrel arced skyward. A howl of frustration filled the clearing as the DiMensioner shaped the great horned owl and soared upward, powerful wings thrusting him after his prey.

Wodash fired a foul look in Brie's direction, yanked her father to standing, and pushed him toward the trees. "Today has been lucky for you, brother of Almiralyn. Let's rejoin your friend." He gave him another shove, then gaped. Where Voer's panther had been, the silver cord, still tied in magic knots, hung limp and empty. The Pentharian had disappeared. Growling under his breath, he secured Allynae to the tree and flew after his master and the blue kestrel.

Karrew felt nothing but dread when the bars of the cage melted away and the prisoners stepped free. Below him, the friends expressed their relief and excitement in different ways. Yaro took the white bird from Torgin and patted the boy on the back. Majeska meowed and rubbed her silky body in and out between his ankles. Bonnee smiled.

Ari hugged her friend. "Torgin, you're so brave. Are you alright?"

"I think so." He seemed dazed but unhurt as he leaned his forehead against Tam's. "I never expected to see you again." She nibbled his neck. He laughed and scratched her ears. "You're the best pony in the galaxy."

Karrew flew to Yaro's shoulder and peered at his mistress, trembling in the Pentharian's arms.

"She has been too long in bird form." Yaro spoke with the quiet knowledge of a shapeshifter. "I can feel her wildness, her desire to be free. If I let her go, she will fly away, and we may lose her forever."

Ari gazed up at the Pentharian. "Is something wrong?"

"Almiralyn is too much bird. She cannot shift back to Human."

Pulling Efillaeh from its scabbard, Ari held it up in the dim light. "Maybe this will help."

The bird squirmed away, her gold-tipped wings beating against Yaro's chest; her beak tearing at the flesh on his arms.

"It's Efillaeh, Almiralyn. You gave it to me, remember?" She stepped closer but, at the bird's obvious terror, hesitated and looked at Karrew.

He tilted his head. "Release her, Yaro. Only Evolsefil can help her now."

"If I let her go, she may not come back to us." Sympathy filled Yaro's golden lizard eyes.

"And if you don't let her go, she will die." Karrew's words dripped with sadness. "When the time is right, she'll return. Release her."

Yaro loosened his hold. The white bird shuddered, flew to an oak branch, and swooped away through the trees.

Majeska gave a sharp meow and vanished after her.

Karrew bobbed his head. "Save Evolsefil and you will save Almiralyn." With a final caw, he followed her into the Terces Wood.

Yaro herded his charges away from the shattered ice cage and down a narrow trail. "You heard Karrew. We can save the Guardian of Myrrh, but first we have to save the Prima Crystal. We can't do either if Wodash or his Giests find us."

The sound of pounding hooves exploded through the woodlands. Tam snorted and moved closer to Torgin, wild fear in her eyes.

Yaro sniffed the air. The hair on the back of his neck prickled. "Into the cover of the forest and—"

A black stallion zigzagged between trees, erupted onto the trail, and came to a halt, his eyes blazing.

Ari dodged behind a large oak. "That's Nomed's enchanted horse."

Yaro vanished into a panther and prepared to protect his charges.

With his heart pounding against his ribs, Torgin strained to see the shadowy forms on the trail.

Eyes the color of sun-soaked amber shone in the dim light as the Pentharian panther crouched. TroeEen pranced a restless dance, every muscle in his body twitching, his flanks lathered with sweat. The panther flattened his ears and growled. Backing along the narrow track, the stallion jerked his head up, then down, and charged. Yaro's feline form leapt into the trees and reappeared behind the enchanted horse. TroeEen rounded, smoke pouring from flared nostrils, and reared. Its hooves hit the ground, just missing the panther's head.

Tam nudged Torgin's side. The message in the piercing softness of her eyes spurred him into action. Adjusting his flute across his shoulders, he leapt up onto her back. She snorted and tossed her head.

His shout sliced the air. "I'll find Almiralyn and bring her to Nemttachenn." His knees digging into the pony's sides, he sent her in a mad gallop through the trees.

TroeEen shrieked with rage. Mane and tail flying, the enchanted horse charged after the pony and the boy.

Yaro materialized in his natural form. "That was too close. The outcome might not have been in my favor had I fought that stallion."

Ari walked from behind the oak. "What about Torgin?"

"My brother must follow his heart. Our goal must be to reach Nemttachenn without getting caught."

"Look." Bonnee pointed. The crystalline net shimmered at the side of the path. "You can use it to protect yourselves."

Yaro handed the Giest-catcher to Ari. "Ride on my back and wrap it around you. Bonnee, lead the way and warn us of trouble."

He shifted to a panther. Ari mounted and hugged his sides with her knees. Following the Now Remembered girl's translucent form, Yaro carried his passenger toward Nemttachenn and what he sensed would be the final battle.

69

Huddled together inside the Nemttachenn's entrance, Brie, Skipt, Fen, and Zugo watched the soaring kestrel and the owl vanish into the clouds roiling above Myrrh. From the corner of her eye, Brie saw Wodash drag Allynae into the trees. *If only I dared to follow...*

"I feel trapped." Zugo glared at the clearing. "Your father needs our help. My father is out there somewhere. What if he's hurt, and we're stuck in here?"

"And I need to find Ari." Fen pulled his hat off, crumpled it, and squashed it back on his head.

Brie mustered a slight smile for the Wood Tiff. "I do, too, Fen. But none of us want to be caught by Wodash or his Giests."

Skipt pointed a gray finger at the sky over the tower. "DiMensioner chase Esán."

Crowded closer to the entrance, the companions watched the kestrel circled one more time. The great horned owl swooped lower, decreasing the distance between them. Wodash closed in fast. Giests tightened their formation around the tower. The kestrel banked and streaked from sight into the churning sky.

Above the trees on the far side of the clearing, two vultures appeared, a glittering Giest-catcher stretched taunt between them. Making a broad sweep of the outer perimeter, a third vulture sent screeching blobs of color careening into the net.

As each one disappeared, Skipt jumped up and down, cheering. "Ya ho, Pentharian!"

"Here comes Esán." Fen waved his hat.

The small falcon swooped from the roiling gloom, blue wings flashing in the light, and hovered over the clearing. Black and silver bursting from the cloud cover sent him dodging through the trees. The great horned owl shot after him. Soaring up again just beyond the owl's reach, the ermine-breasted kestrel, looped high above Nemttachenn, descended in a spiral that ended in a long swooping glide, and landed at the clearing's center. It ruffled its feathers and vanished into the form of Esán as Wodash landed by the tower entrance.

Nomed materialized from a flurry of black plumage and wings, flipped his cape over his shoulders, and faced his apprentice. "What an exhilarating flight. Now I believe it's time to claim my prize." He moved to close the gap between them.

"I'm not your prize, DiMensioner." Esán took a step back. "Nor is Evolsefil. Leave Myrrh and never return. You have done more than enough damage."

Seyes Nomed threw back his head and laughed. "And you think you can just send me away?" He glared at the slender, bald boy.

Esán remained silent and unafraid.

Quick as a thought, the DiMensioner flashed to his side and gripped his arm. "You are *mine*, Esán, whether you like it or not."

"I will *never* be yours." The boy spoke with cool confidence.

Nomed yanked him around and glared down at him.

Zugo started forward.

Brie grabbed his shoulder. "No. We can't help Esán if we get caught by Wodash."

The DiMensioner's eyes narrowed to hazel slits. Esán met his gaze, his own unwavering. "Enough." Nomed placed two fingers on his lips. A long shrill whistle cut through the mist and echoed across the land.

The sound sent Giests scattering in every direction. Three vultures swooped in to take advantage of their confusion.

Nomed yanked Esán opposite the tower's arched entrance. "Esán is mine, and he will do my bidding. Without him, you cannot move the crystal. I have Almiralyn and Torgin, Yookotay and the Theran major. They are of no help to you. Allynae is tied to a tree and quite helpless. Come out of the tower, and I will let them live."

Brie herded her companions into the interior shadows of Nemttachenn.

Fen shivered. "What do we do now?"

"Wait." She kept her attention focused on Esán. "We wait."

"Twin, if you do not come out here now—"

"Don't do it, Brie." Esán called out, his voice as calm as his stoic expression.

"Did I ask you to speak?" Nomed snarled. A slap rang out across the clearing. A red welt blazed on Esán's pale face.

"Leave the boy alone, Davin."

Nomed's spine snapped straighter. Maintaining his hold on his apprentice, he faced the man who advanced toward him.

"Who are you?" His grip tightened on Esán's arm.

"Look at me, Davin Farlow. Do you not recognize your own brother?"

Esán shot a startled look, first at the DiMensioner and then at his father. The red handprint on his face burned brighter.

"Somay?" Incredulity rang out across the clearing.

One Man stopped a short distance from his brother. "My mind is not yours to probe, Davin. I'm not one of your minions. And please keep the death shadow under control. I do not fear him or you."

"What is it you want?" Nomed tightened his grip on Esán's arm.

"I want you to release my son, Davin."

Nomed tore his gaze from his brother's face to stare at the boy beside him.

"You are my nephew. No wonder..." He left the sentence unfinished and looked back at One Man.

"I won't let him go, Somay. He's mine, even more so now. We are of the same blood. I will train him to be more powerful than you can imagine."

An almost imperceptible nod sent Wodash creeping toward One Man.

Brie stifled a shout when Ari stepped into the clearing behind the death shadow.

Her twin brandished the silver knife. "If you move one more step, Wodash od DerTah, Efillaeh will slice you to ribbons."

Wodash turned his foul-looking head to peer over his shoulder. The sacred blade flashed in her steady hand. Intense brown eyes stared back at him. Allynae stood at her side. The death shadow did not move.

Brie peered across the clearing, her eyes never leaving her sister's face.

Merrilea couldn't stop worrying about Esán. Feeling trapped and fidgety, she stood at Almiralyn's kitchen window and watched Stee pace in the garden, as though walking would miraculously heal his side and let him fly. Upstairs, Owae sat with Elae. In the studio, Sparrow's brush flicked nonstop across her canvas, her concentration so complete she seemed unaware of the present or her companions.

Merrilea's fingers drummed an agitated rhythm on the windowsill. Shaking herself free of the dread threatening to consume her, she climbed the stairs to Mira's sanctuary. For the umpteenth time, she stood beside the fountain. Overwhelmed by fatigue and worry, she gripped the alabaster bowl, leaned forward, and stared into its fluid depths. Her tears splashed and disappeared, absorbed, one with the water and the magic.

"Please show me Esán." Another teardrop and another...

The water's rippling rhythm ceased. Mist swirled up to caress her cheeks and dissipated. A picture steadied on the clear, smooth surface.

Silence hung like a shroud over the Land of Myrrh. Not even the wind murmured. Trees and creatures listened, alert and afraid. In every hamlet, village, and farm, the citizens of Myrrh looked to the enchanted tower in the Terces Wood.

Nemttachenn shimmered into view. Elcaro's Eye zoomed in on the clearing, where Nomed held Esán by the arm, his gaze locked on Somay. Wodash hovered motionless, hate-filled eyes on Ari and Allynae.

Pounding hooves ruptured the strained silence. TroeEen exploded from the woods, his fiery eyes flashing like black flames in the dim light. Torgin and Tam zigzagged through the trees and burst into the clearing a short distance behind him. The stallion came to a halt in front of his master.

"At last." Nomed threw Esán onto the stallion's back and sprang up behind him. With a handful of black mane in one hand, he steadied Esán with the other, and, wheeling TroeEen around, rode straight for the tower.

CheeTrann pitched Brie, Fen, Skipt, and Zugo into the clearing just before horse and riders bolted through the tower's entrance, the death shadow in their wake.

Brie jumped up, ran after the crazed animal, and disappeared. Thunder shook Nemttachenn. The ground rolled in a series of wavelike swells. Blue light flashed from every crack and fissure in the tower walls. Blocks of granite catapulted skyward.

Zugo grabbed Fen and pulled him into the shelter of the trees. Skipt dodged a falling chunk of granite and scurried after them. Ari ran toward the arched entrance, only to be thrown to the ground. One Man helped her to her feet, and, ignoring her protests, drug her into the forest. Tam reared, unseating Torgin. Allynae sprinted to the boy's side, hauled him to standing, and corraled him and the terrified pony away from the quaking clearing.

The water in the fountain grew foggy. Merrilea's grip on the edge of the bowl tensed. "Esán." Her throat tightened. "Nomed has my nephew." A tear fell. Ripples chased each other across the surface and then calmed.

Sweaty and frothing at the mouth, TroeEen charged over the granite floor from one collapsed side of the tower to the other. He bucked, snorted, and lunged toward Evolsefil where Brie waited, the Stone of Remembering glowing in her hand. Slamming to a stop, he threw Esán and Nomed from his back into a pile of arms and legs on the ground.

TroeEen's panicked scream echoed throughout the Terces Wood. More crazed than ever, the black stallion pawed the air above Brie's head. Calmly, she stepped aside as Gemlucky's memories chased him from the chaos in the quaking tower, across the clearing, and into the Terces Wood, his pounding hoofbeats joining the rumbling roar issuing from the Nemtachenn.

One Man and Allynae ran across the clearing toward the demolished tower with Torgin and Ari. The ground heaved, dumping all four to their knees. Ari scrambled up and vanished into CheeTrann's blue haze.

The fountain's water swirled, spraying droplets into the air.
"No!" Merrilea gripped the rim. "Please, don't stop now. Please—"
The surface stilled.

Nomed sprang to his feet, yanking Esán with him, and whipped around to face Evolsefil. He froze, his face a picture of conflicted emotions. Ari and Brie stood between him and the crystal heart of Myrrh. Efillaeh glowed in the hand of one twin; a blue stone shimmered on the palm of the other.

Nomed's expression turned to iron-cold hatred. "Out of my..." Angry words snapped with the sharp crack of a whip and then slurred. The wildness in the scene decelerated. Time warped. Evolsefil, dimly visible in the blue haze, attracted him like a magnet. One deliberate step at a time, he dragged his nephew forward.

Brie and Ari did not flinch or move. No sign of fear attracted the death shadow. Power, invisible yet tangible, enveloped them.

In a voice stretched by time, Nomed drawled, **"E v o l s e f i l   i s   m i n e ,   t w i n s .   S t e p   a s i d e ."**

They remained an obstacle, still as stone and unaffected by his commands. Esán struggled to break free. The DiMensioner seized his shoulder.

CheeTrann rumbled. Time sped up. "Release Spirit Boy, and you may leave unharmed."

Nomed's eyes blazed. His scar burned red. He passed Esán to Wodash and raised his arms. A bolt of lightning flashed across the tower, cut through CheeTrann's blue light, and opened a path to Evolsefil.

The DiMensioner yanked the boy from his henchman's grasp and shot along the path. Light blasting from an opening in the floor caught them mid-stride. Nomed jerked Esán into the circle of his arms while dizzying spirals of orange, red, and gold spun around them.

Wodash struggled to move away, only to be hauled, howling in frustration, into the churning vortex.

CheeTrann's booming roar shook the clearing. Light blazing brighter and swirling faster, blurred colors one into the other. The rolling motion of the floor hurled Brie and Ari to the ground, coppery curls tumbling over their faces as they buried their heads in their arms.

A loud slurping noise erupted from the tower's center. And then they were gone—Esán, Nomed, and Wodash—sucked down into the gaping void like a sinking ship in a whirlpool.

"Esán!" The twins scrambled to their feet.

One final quake sent them into each other's arms. The hole closed. Silence as shattering as CheeTrann's roar gripped the clearing. Nothing moved.

Breaking free of their stunned lethargy, Ari and Brie ran forward. "CheeTrann, what have you done?"

The Sentinel of Myrrh rumbled one last time and withdrew into the hidden depths of the tower's scattered remains.

Merrilea held her breath as disjointed pictures flickered across Elcaro's reflective surface.

In the clearing, the mist began to fade. Confused and frightened, Giests flitted back and forth, then bolted toward the Dojanacks.

Near the edge of the Terces Wood, TroeEen stopped face to face with Dom and the chestnut mare. While the old man murmured softly and stroked her lathered neck, the filly spoke in the language of horses. Gemlucky began to remember. Gradually, the wildness faded from his eyes.

Zugo and Torgin, the first to leave the safety of the trees, dashed a zigzagged path across the clearing. Skipt and Fen dodged around granite blocks and followed.

Allynae strode purposefully forward.

One Man remained still, his expression reflecting the loss of the son he had so recently found.

Beside Elcaro's Eye, Merrilea, released at last from the paralysis that held her upright, sank to the floor, sobbing.

N omed's arms, strong as prison bars, pressed Esán against his chest. Cringing at the thought of being possessed by his uncle forever, he wondered if he would he see his father again...the twins...his Aunt Merrilea? Endless space, even darker than the Cave of the Ancients, swallowed him. He felt himself shrinking into its vastness.

A s they plunged through pitch-black nothingness, Nomed's mind raced. Consumed by unimaginable fury, he tensed his jaw and gnashed his teeth. *I underestimated CheeTrann and those twins.* His nostrils flared; his grip tightened around his nephew. *All I worked for—gone— beyond my reach. How will I ever destroy Myrrh?*

Unexpected heat blasting the breath from his body increased his raging anger. He hit a mound of red sand, lost his hold on Esán, and, with fins of fine granules shooting skyward, slid to a stop in a wide trough between desert dunes. Wodash skidded to a halt on one side of him and his nephew on the other.

"Don't move." Nomed jumped up, untied his cape, and threw it into the air, where it remained, its silver lining up, hovering above his head. "Get under here now!"

E sán shoved thoughts of escape away. Beneath the DiMensioner's cape was the only place he would survive the Fire ConDra od DerTah.

B rie and Ari exited what remained of the tower, their faces so alike and yet so different. Allynae gathered them in his arms and hugged them close to his heart. When he finally held them at arm's length to make sure they were unharmed, Ari smiled through her tears. "Hello, Father." She wiped a tear from his cheek.

One Man peered through the shattered entrance of Nemttachenn, shuddered, and turned to the twins. His questioning eyes asked what Brie knew he could not verbalize. She shook her head. He fell to his knees and buried his face in his hands. She could see in Ari's expression the sorrow they all shared.

Allynae helped his friend stand. "We'll find him, One Man, even if we have to search the entire galaxy."

"At least Evolsefil is still in Myrrh." The hermit's face reflected his struggle between anger and sadness. "Now we must discover a way to return it to the Cave of Canedari."

Torgin and Zugo hurried toward them from the trees. Suddenly, everyone began talking at once. "Where is Yookotay? What about the Pentharian? And Major Jordett?"

The Now Remembered girl floated into their midst. After telling Allynae where to find the Theran major, she turned to Zugo. "I can lead you to Yookotay." The young DeoNyte blew out a relieved exhale and followed her into the woods.

Allynae returned with a lost-looking Jordett leaning on his arm and brought him to the twins.

Ari's eyes widened. "He has no memories." She turned to her sister. "You can help him, right?"

Brie nodded and removed the velvet pouch from beneath her shirt while her father helped Jordett to sit on a large granite block. Tipping the Remembering Stone onto her palm, she pressed it against his forehead.

The stone's blue glow surrounded Jordett. His eyes brightened as images flooded his mind and recollections stabilized. When the blue glow faded, Brie returned the lapis stone to its velvet home.

Gratitude and wonder filled the major's expression. "Thank you, Brie. I remembered nothing at all." His eyes narrowed. "I have much to think about." With a shiver, he surveyed the rubble. "What happened here?"

Yookotay and Zugo joined them. Three Pentharian vultures landed and shifted. Yaro, Voer, and Jeet strode across the clearing.

While Allynae shared recent events with the new arrivals, Brie clasped Ari's hand and drew her aside. "I missed you, sis!"

Her twin hugged her. "I wondered myself if we'd ever be together again. I have so much to share."

The Star of Truth tingled on the back of Brie's neck. "When this adventure is done..."

70

Merrilea sat in the art studio, her face buried in Owae's soft fur. As though she were a child, the healer rocked her gently and crooned a DeoNyte healing song. From the doorway an emerald Pentharian, his strange eyes filled with compassion, looked down at her and then let his gaze travel to Sparrow's almost completed canvas.

Sparrow worked steadily. Quick strokes added a highlight to a swirl of saturated colors encasing Nomed and Esán. Another intensified the dismayed faces of the twins. She wiped her brush clean, swished it through a puddle of color on her palette, and applied a final splash of gray to the chunks of granite hurtling around the Tower of Nemttachenn.

"I saw it all." Merrilea snuffled and blew her nose. "Nomed has Esán, and they are not in Myrrh. How will we ever find him?"

Sparrow faced her friend. "Allynae and Jordy will do everything possible. Let's go where we can all sit and decide what to do next."

In the pale lavender kitchen, Stee observed the woman who had saved his life struggling to regain her composure. He fingered the line of stitches in his side, pleased by how quickly his wound had healed. Somehow, he would repay her and the DeoNyte healer.

A shimmering dragonfly fluttered with drunken grace through the open window and landed on his hand. "It is a brother." Stee showed the wounded insect to women. "Its wing is broken."

Owae produced her jar of salve and smoothed a drop on the fragile appendage. The dragonfly lifted into the air. Once it cleared the table, Yuin materialized, holding his injured arm against his side. A grimace of pain twisted his alien features. He nodded to the elderly DeoNyte. "Thank you." He turned to Stee. "My comrade, I am grateful. I was unsure whether anyone would recognize me."

Merrilea walked around the table. "May I look?"

The weary Pentharian nodded.

Her sensitive fingers examined his tattooed forearm. "A bone near your wrist is broken, Yuin. I'll splint it and put your arm in a sling."

Stee pulled out a chair and helped him to sit. "How did this happen, my brother?"

"Seyes Nomed." Yuin recounted the events at the tower.

"That's it." Merrilea stood up and slapped the table with her hand. "I *must* find a way to Nemttachenn. I can't stay here doing nothing when Esán is in trouble."

Stee rose. "I will take you. My side is much better."

Owae, her pale eyes filled with sympathy, touched her shoulder. "Merrilea, prepare yourself in the event you do not to find him."

Sparrow hugged her friend. "You go, but I'll remain here. I have at least one more painting to do."

"And I will stay to care for Elae and Yuin." The DeoNyte healer smiled a toothless smile.

Yuin cradled his arm and frowned his frustration. "I wish to go, too."

Stee put a hand on his comrade's back. "My brother, I understand your need, but we do not know for certain Nomed is truly gone from Myrrh. The ladies would appreciate your protection."

Yuin's expression grew hard. "I have never liked that DiMensioner." He bowed to Owae and Sparrow. "I will protect you."

Stee, his emerald green scales glinting, preceded the women into the garden and shifted.

Merrilea climbed the vulture's massive wing and settled on his back. When he lifted into the air, she gasped and then giggled. The trees passing beneath her perfumed the land with their freshness. Wind tugged at her hair and kissed her cheeks, easing the pain in her heart. Like a child caught in a dream of flying, she reveled in each moment.

More quickly than she expected, she saw a group of adults gathered in a rubble-strewn clearing. Her relief when Jordett waved was instantaneous. The vulture landed, and the major helped her dismount. "We'll find him, Merrilea. I promise you, we'll find him."

Stee materialized, and together they joined Allynae, where he finished telling Yookotay what had occurred. One Man opened his arms. Merrilea burst into tears and threw hers around his neck. He let her cry, stroking her hair and consoling her in his soft, throaty voice.

The twins made their way through the fallen granite blocks to the tower's entrance. Brie turned to her sister. "I have to call forth Myrrh's Sentinel and fetch *EmitEnil*. You stay here."

Ari rested a hand on Efillaeh's hilt and shook her tangle of curls back from her face. "I'm going with you."

Brie smiled. "You're sure? I have no way of knowing how CheeTrann will react."

"I don't intend to lose you again." Her sister nudged her into the lead. "Let's get this done."

Brie led the way through the blue haze obscuring the crystal to the tower's center. "CheeTrann, Sentinel and Protector of Myrrh, come to our aid."

As the request melted into silence, a deep rumble shook the ground.

Gradually, the opaque form of a man took shape. Tall and majestic, he gazed down at them, his eyes glowing, his shoulder-length white hair and neatly trimmed beard framing his ancient face. "Daughters of KcernFensia, I answer your call. To protect the land and to bring its Guardian back to herself, you must rekindle Evolsefil's inner *light*." He waved a hand. The blue haze faded, leaving the dulled Prima Crystal exposed with the *Book of Time* nestled within the crystal cluster at her base. With a regal bow, the ghostly Sentinel vanished.

Ari swallowed. "Did you see what I saw?"

"If you saw the figure of a man, yes." Brie smiled. "We have just seen the venerable Protector of Myrrh in his true form."

B rie and Ari gathered their companions near the crumbled entrance to Nemttachenn. "We must return Evolsefil to the Cave of Canedari." Brie nodded as Allynae and Yookotay joined them. "If we can rekindle its light, the crystal might help us understand how to send it home."

"How do we regenerate it?" Allynae studied his daughter.

Brie held up *EmitEnil*. "Esán and I found this passage: The children of many will return the crystal to *light*."

Ari looked around. "We are the children of many races."

Brie nodded, then frowned. "The only thing we're missing is music. Without it, Evolsefil cannot return."

One Man walked over and put a hand on Torgin's shoulder. "You have music."

Torgin blushed, withdrew the silver-wood flute from its sheepskin case, and held it up. "One Man made this and gave it to me." He beamed. "It has a beautiful sound."

"Ya ho, I can dance and sing." Skipt's boundless energy sent him galloping around the clearing.

Brie smiled at the Enots' eagerness. "We will need to circle Evolsefil. But first we must memorize the verse Esán and I learned from *EmitEnil*, so we can repeat it over and over until the crystal's *light* returns." With the battered open book in her hands, she recited the lyrics in her clear musical voice.

"Music fills the hearts of all, the hearts of all who know.
Children bring their innocence, their joy, that all may grow.
Here we stand, each gathered 'round, touching hand to hand,
Calling back the light and love you bring to this great land.

Hear us call, Evolsefil! Ignite your sacred spark!
Let it shine in clustered quartz, a beacon in the dark.
We, the children of the land, pledge our love to thee,
Open up the light within that we may all be free."

After they had repeated the lyrics several times, Brie organized Zugo, Skipt, Fen, Bonnee, Ari, and Torgin in a circle around the crystal cluster. A survey of the group made her frown. "We need a Pentharian. Who is the youngest?"

Yaro grinned. "I am the youngest and the heart-brother of Torgin. However, I am not a Penthary."

"But as you say, you are Torgin's heart-brother." She smiled. "Tam, please stand in for all living creatures in Myrrh."

The tan pony tossed her head and nickered.

Ari held up a sprig of the dark green conifer. "And I have hemlock to represent all things that grow."

Brie removed the Stone of Remembering from its blue pouch and, along with *EmitEnil*, placed it within the ring of sentinel crystals at Evolsefil's base. Then she took her place between Torgin and Ari and nodded to her father, who motioned the adults to form a protective circle around them.

Torgin lifted the flute and began to play. The melody, ancient and sad, related the history of Myrrh. Youthful voices blended with the fluid current of notes, repeating the verses from *EmitEnil* over and over again. Torgin's music changed. Adagio to allegro and back to andante, it flowed. Rich and brilliantly hued, it picked up the words of the children and gave them life. Brie's beautiful voice rose and fell. Beside her, Ari's tenor tones rang out deep and clear. Skipt, his small face rapt with joy, joined in. Together the children of many sang, their voices floating across Myrrh.

The luminescent core of the crystal glowed brighter and brighter until it fully illuminated the central Prima spire. Fine threads of pure gold shot up from its base in a radial pattern, creating a golden halo around it. The six sentinel crystals throbbed with light that expanded to every man, woman, and child and every Wood Tiff and creature that crept from the woods.

From the throne of ReNin RepPosu, Brie had seen a preview of the future. Now, as Torgin's music and the children's voices spread through Myrrh, the events unfolded before her. Awed, she looked up as Evolsefil's returning brilliance penetrated the grayness and called forth the sun.

Sibine and Tibin and their new babe entered the clearing. Tuper followed with Sibee and his wide-eyed mother. Around them, Nyti flitted on gossamer wings, eyes shining as the mists rolled away and the crystal glowed.

Brie knew her mother's brush captured those gathered at Nemttachenn. With each stroke, as with each note Torgin played, a filmy image appeared inside Evolsefil's majestic central spire. Keeping her voice steady, Brie continued to lead the children through the verses, never letting them falter. Tears spilled down her cheeks as the faint figure took on form and substance.

Within the crystal heart of the land, the Guardian of Myrrh appeared tall and strong, her face gentle and her sapphire-blue eyes gleaming with life. Pale blonde hair floated around her, catching the light and enclosing her in a rainbow corona. Karrew perched on her shoulder, his black feathers lustrous and full. At her feet, Majeska sat with amethyst eyes shining. The Land of Myrrh seemed to hold its breath. Only the music of children rippled across time.

Torgin's melody changed. The smoky-gray cat, her ears alert and her tail waving like a conductor's baton, stepped free of the crystal. Almiralyn's majesty encompassed the clearing as she followed.

Brie bowed her head. The Guardian of Myrrh had returned. Evolsefil, the heart of this last remnant of Old Earth and the Prima Crystal of the galaxy, glistened in the sunlight, its spark rekindled.

Karrew flew to a tree near his mistress to listen as, one by one, the children ceased singing. Finally, only Torgin's melody filled the clearing. With the radiant elegance of Almiralyn flowing around him, he took a final breath and played one last sustained note that seemed not to fade, but simply to infuse Myrrh with its beauty.

A hush fell over those gathered, and then everyone began to speak at once. The Guardian raised her hand. "One at a time, please."

Brie spoke up first. "Almiralyn, we were so afraid for you and so glad you're back."

"Nomed has Esán." Torgin informed her. "CheeTrann opened a portal, and they disappeared."

"We have to find him." The twins nodded at each other.

Skipt danced forward, excitement sparking around him. "Wodash gone, too."

Almiralyn's gaze came to rest on One Man, where he waited with Merrilea and Jordett. "We will find your son, Somay, but there is much to do here before we embark on any such venture."

Zugo began to protest. "We can't just leave him…"

Yookotay silenced him with a stern look.

Almiralyn gazed at the young DeoNyte. "I want to locate him, too, Zugo. We cannot return Evolsefil to the Cave of Canedari without Esán, but Myrrh hangs visible above Idronatti. The sooner we hide it, the better, or we will have bigger problems than Nomed to deal with."

She turned to survey the demolished tower. "First, we must shield Evolsefil from prying eyes." Arms raised in supplication, she spoke for all to hear. "Sentinel of Nemttachenn, come forth."

A low rumbling shook the clearing. Blue light spun up through the rubble. "Mistress, I celebrate your return." CheeTrann's faint masculine figure trembled. "How may I serve you?"

"Rebuild Nemttachenn around Evolsefil. Guard the Prima Crystal until we can transport it to the Cave of Canedari."

"As you will, My Lady. Everyone, take cover in the woods before I begin."

Hurrying to comply, the twins led Bonnie, Skipt, and Fen into the forest. Allynae urged Merrilea and Almiralyn after them. Torgin guided Tam into the trees where Yaro and the Pentharian sheltered near One Man and Jordett. Yookotay and Zugo crept deeper into the woods.

Karrew flew to a better vantage point, one closer to his mistress, cocked his head, and studied her face. *She is beautiful. And stern.*

Blue light enveloped the clearing. A rumbling quake catapulted pieces of granite high above the trees. Like reversed action, they reassembled themselves into a tower. From big to small, they found their place until Nemttachenn stood whole, and CheeTrann's protective blue haze shimmered around it. The ground ceased its quaking tremors; birds began to sing, and the companions surged from the woods.

Almiralyn's voice rang out. "CheeTrann, your continued guardianship of Evolsefil will insure the existence of Myrrh and Thera."

"I will not fail you, My Lady." The ancient Sentinel's ghost-like form wavered.

Ari called from her place by her father. "Where did you send Nomed?"

Allynae put a gentle hand on her shoulder. "Patience, daughter."

"Sentinel of Nemttachenn, where did the DiMensioner, Seyes Nomed, go with Wodash and Spirit Boy?" Almiralyn reframed the twin's question with gracious diplomacy.

"Where his heart took him." The blue haze faded, leaving the tower strong and forbidding in the returning rays of the sun.

Almiralyn faced her allies. "We are not yet safe from Seyes Nomed or from others far more powerful. Our enemies are many. Some wish to destroy this last stronghold of Old Earth. All crave the power of the Prima Crystal Evolsefil.

"A good plan is vital before we begin a search for Esán. The DiMensioner will not harm him, and Esán has the resources to take care of himself until we rescue him."

Standing apart from the group, Brie listened to Myrrh's Guardian. Karrew landed on her shoulder. "Thank you, Daughter of KcernFensia."

"For what?" She offered her arm and lowered him to eye level.

The raven cocked his head. "For saving Evolsefil and bringing Almiralyn home."

"I only did what was necessary. It was your love that saved her, Karrew."

"Everyone did their part, Brielle AsTar." He flew to join his mistress, his blue-black wings glistening in the sun.

Brie crossed the clearing to where a smiling Sibine stood, cradling Adin, her wee Tiffin in her arms. Tibin stood protectively beside her.

"He's so beautiful." Brie touched the Tiffin's soft, brown curls.

Tibin smiled the proud smile of a new father. "This babe blesses our lives." He bowed his head before leaving his mate's side to join the group around Almiralyn.

Sibine smiled up at her. "You are always welcome in our TreeOm, Brie. As Adin's name giver, you are his wise one and mentor. Please come often."

"I will." Brie gave her a quick hug, kissed Adin's forehead, and followed Tibin.

"We'll all return to the cottage and make plans from there." The Guardian gazed at her assembled allies. "But first, I must take care of an important matter." She smiled at Bonnee. "If you are ready to join your twin sister in the Beyond, Evolsefil will send you."

Bonnee floated closer to Brie. "I am ready to go as long as you no longer need me, Brielle."

"You've waited long enough, Bonnee." She smiled at her twin. "Ari is here with me. And I've found my father. It's time for you to join Bettee."

With a radiant smile, Bonnee followed Myrrh's Guardian into Nemttachenn. Brie and Ari joined them. Like a curtain drawn, CheeTrann's blue haze parted, forming a path to the beautiful quartz crystal.

Almiralyn gazed at the translucent girl. "It is time. Please enter the Heart of Evolsefil."

Her eyes bright with tears, Bonnee floated into the gleaming spire and faced her friends. Brie clasped Ari's hand. Almiralyn whispered an ancient blessing, and the Now Remembered girl shimmered away, leaving Evolsefil's center clear.

The Guardian smiled at her nieces. "It is done."

As their aunt exited the tower, the blue haze filled the pathway, and the crystal vanished.

Brie sighed. Ari hugged her. "Come on. We have lots of planning to do."

Outside, Karrew and Allynae dispatched Tam to meet them at the red barn and asked Tibin to escort the adults to the cottage via the Intersect. Four Pentharian vultures waited to transport Brie, Ari, Torgin, Zugo and Skipt.

"Ya, ho! We fly!" The Enots clapped happily, his smile almost bigger than his face could hold.

Allynae and Almiralyn watched the vultures of ReTaw au Qa and their passengers lift into the air. Karrew landed on his mistress' shoulder. "What a strange adventure."

"And it's not over yet." Allynae looked at his sister. "I'm sure glad you're back and safe."

She smiled. "I am happy, too." Her smile hardened as she glanced at the tower. "Our time of peace will be short lived, Alli. Evolsefil's power has increased one hundredfold. Nomed and others will feel its pull."

Allynae's brow furrowed. "You mean the golden threads have magnified its intensity?"

"Its base is solid gold, Alli. Evolsefil is now the Prima Crystal for the Inner Universe."

Allynae rubbed his stubbly upper lip and shook his head. "Oh, my. How will we ever keep it hidden?"

She scratched Karrew's breast feathers. "We find Esán, rescue him, and bring him home to help move her back to Canedari." She glanced up at the patches of blue sky appearing through holes in the dispersing cloud cover. Her gaze returned to his face. "Your daughters are at the heart of it, Alli. And Esán is the key to more than we know."

He nodded. "I figured that out. And Torgin?"

"He will continue to surprise himself and everyone else. Even Paisley will play his part." Her eyes narrowed. "The most important thing now—we must return Myrrh to its hidden dimension and regroup. See you at the cottage." She raised her arms. Shimmering golden light surrounded her as she soared upward in the shape of the white bird.

Allynae departed for the entrance to the Intersect in the woods behind Nemttachenn.

Karrew circled the clearing. His mistress, the gold tips of her wings gleaming in the Myrrhinian sun, joined him. Together they flew over the trees of the Terces Wood.

In the upstairs room, the statue of Myrrh's Guardian gazed into the alabaster bowl. Droplets ceased their endless cascade. The water stilled. Musical notes rose to the surface and floated into the air, forming four lines. As each line glowed a bright azure blue, a song rang out across the land.

> *The children of many bring truth to light,*
> *Their courage challenges the DiMensioner's might,*
> *The Unfolding sets the stage to reveal*
> *Their futures and then their destinies seal.*

As the last sung note faded, three words formed on the water's surface, melted into a mist, and floated out the window and over the Land of Myrrh...

GLOSSARY

Glossary - In this book

Many (but not all) names of characters, places, and things in the VarTerels' Universe™ are anagrams. A printed glossary for this book starts on the next page.

Glossary - View Online

A searchable glossary of the VarTerels' Universe™ is available to you online at:
www.skrandolph.com/glossary

Adin - Wood Tiff baby; parents Sibine and Tibin

Allynae Nadrugia - Alli, Almiralyn's brother, born on the planet of KcernFensia, joined to (married to) SparrowLyn AsTar

Almiralyn Nadrugia - Mira, the appointed Guardian of Myrrh, born and trained on the planet of KcernFensia

Anopi (piano) - air keyboard made of crystal and obsidian and played by Torgin

Ari - Arienh Lynae AsTar, daughter of Allynae and SparrowLyn, twin sister of Brie

Benisuss - (business) business district in the City of Idronatti

Bettee - sister of the Now Remembered girl named Bonnee

Birchberry - golden berry used in jams and jellies

Bonnee - one of the unremembered/Now Remembered freed by Brie and the Stone of Remembering

Brie - Brielle Ralyn AsTar, daughter of Allynae and SparrowLyn, twin sister of Ari

Buster - Almiralyn's dog

Cave of Canedari (radiance) - cave within the Cavern of Tennisca where the Evolsefil Crystal resides

Cavern of Tennisca (ancients) - cavern in the Dojanack Mountains, the home of the Cave of Canedari and the Stairway of Retu Erath

CheeTrann (enchanter) - Sentinel of Nemttachenn/Protector of Myrrh who resides in an enchanted tower in the center of the Terces Wood

CleeO - DeoNyte female

Clenaba Rolas (balance solar) – one of four solar systems in the Fourth Galaxy from the Great Central Sun

Cliffs of ReVod (Dover) - cliffs outside the entrance into the Dojanack caverns used by Seyes Nomed

Daehe - DeoNyte male

Dalan - doorman in Torgin Wilith Whalend's apartment building in Idronatti

Darak - young DeoNyte male

Davin Farlow - Seyes Nomed's birth name

Demi-Priestess - initiate level of the Priestesses of Canedari

Demrach Canyon (charmed) - canyon in the Central Mountains of Thera
Demrach Gateway - portal connecting the Central Mountains to Myrrh
DeoNyte - furry white creature found in the depths of the Dojanack Mountains in Myrrh
Deora - Henrietta's friend in SumnerTyme in the Central Mountains of Thera
DerTah (hatred) - small planet in the Clenaba Rolas solar system
Desert of DerTah - informal name for the Desert of Fera Finnero
Desert of Fera Finnero (fear inferno) - largest desert on the Planet of DerTah
DiMensioner - first of three rankings in the Order of Esprow
DiMensionery - metaphysical arts including shape shifting, telepathy, teleporting, etc.
Dojanack Mountains - diverse and beautiful mountain range on Myrrh
Dojanberry - small blue berries found in the Dojanack Mountains
Dom - old man who runs Antiques by Q in The Borderlands; trusted subject of Almiralyn; friend of Seyes Nomed, full name Dominee
Domlenah (homeland) - apartment districts in Idronatti
Doohnam (manhood) - the coming of age for DeoNyte males
Dreela - male leaders on the planet of DerTah
Dreelas - female leaders on the planet of DerTah
Dreelum - plural of Dreela and Dreelas
Drotti - slang for Idronattian
Efillaeh (life heal) - sacred knife formed in the heart of the Evolsefil Crystal
Elae - DeoNyte Priestess of Light and friend to Zugo
Elcaro's Eye (oracle) - fountain protected by Almiralyn; coveted throughout the Inner Universe for its ability to show past, present, and future events
Emit (time) - creator/architect of all things
EmitEnil (timeline) - ancient book of knowledge, The Book of Emit
Enots (stone) - small creatures made of stones who live in the Dojanack Mountains
Ephos (hopes) - healing room in the Hall of Priestesses
Esán Efre (Sean Free) - son of Somay, nephew of Davin, nephew of Merrilea
Esor Trazuq Canyon (rose quartz) - canyon in the Dojanack Mountains

Evolsefil (loves life) - crystal heart of Myrrh; the power that keeps Thera and Myrrh from colliding, the central crystal in the Crystal Web

Fadin - vendor in The Borderlands

Fatooay - older DeoNyte male

Fen - a teenage Wood Tiff

Fire ConDra - creatures of fire found on the planet of DerTah

Gateway of Kao (oak) - portal in the foothills of Myrrh

Gemlucky - coal black stallion belonging to Almiralyn

Gerolyn - SparrowLyn's mother; the twin's grandmother

Giest (from poltergeist) - mass of colored plasma, the remains of evil Humans who haunt the deepest caverns in the Dojanack Mountains

Grotto of Forgetting - grotto in the caverns of the Dojanacks overseen by the Water Witch Neuros

Grove of Mehloc (from hemlock) - grove of ancient and mystical hemlock trees in the Terces Wood

Henrietta - the elderly woman who lives across the hall from the twins

High DiMensioner - second highest ranking in the Order of Esprow

Holistic Healer Zarron - Esán's physician in Idronatti

Homelanders - citizens of Myrrh

Humanesque - Human-like

Idronatti (tradition) - the only city on the Planet of Thera; the city in which Myrrh is hidden in another dimension

Idronattian - citizen of Idronatti

Jeen - unremembered/Now Remembered woman

Jeet - carnelian orange Pentharian from the Planet of ReTaw au Qa

Jolendula - Myrrhinian herb similar to calendula

Jonn Menalow - Allynae's alias as provided by Dom

Karrew - Almiralyn's raven, protector from the planet of KcernFensia

KcernFensia (frankincense) - planet in the Clenaba Rolas solar system, Almiralyn's birthplace

Lake of Rorret (terror) - lake in the caverns of the Dojanack Mountains

Lite-stick - "stick" that gives off light

LlEh (hell) - DerTahan version of hell

Loeen - unremembered/Now Remembered woman

Mahyinaeh - goddess of the planet of KcernFensia

Majeska - Jeska, Almiralyn's smoky-gray cat

Major Jordett - Jordy, a military officer in the Peoples Plan Protectors

Meos - center of the DeoNyte realm in the caverns of the Dojanacks

Meosian - citizen of Meos; the ways of Meos

Merrilea - Merri, Esán's aunt

Moon Cycle - one month, forty-two Myrrhinian turnings (days)

Mount GetiNar (granite) - granite mountain in the Dojanack range

Mountain of Niar (rain) - crystal mountain in the Dojanack range

Myrrh - last remaining piece of Old Earth; secreted in a hidden dimension paralleling the planet of Thera

Myrrhinian - citizen of Myrrh; the ways of Myrrh

Myrrhnica - Myrrhinian healing herb similar to arnica

NaiDisbo Canyon (obsidian) - black canyon in the Dojanack Mountains

NaiDisbo Peak - obsidian mountain in the Dojanack range

Nans - vendor in The Borderlands open market; wife of Saaul

Nervac Gateway (cavern) - portal in the Dojanack Caverns

Neuros - Water Witch of the Grotto of Forgetting in the Dojanack Caverns

Nevah Efas (safe haven) - tiny planet near one of Thera's moons where only the true of heart may go

NoiRrac (carrion) - carnivorous beetle from the planet of DerTah

Oche Cavern (echo) - Nomed's command post in the Dojanack Caverns

Order of Esprow (powers) - organization whose members are trained in the Arts of DiMensionery

Owae - DeoNyte healer; Elae's grandmother

Paisley James Tobinette - Pais, a Myrrhinian comrade of Allynae

Pendant of ReDaelship (leadership) - sapphire pendant worn by the leader of the DeoNytes

Pentharian - half Reptilian, half Human shape shifters from the planet the ReTaw au Qa, mercenaries

Penthary - Pentharian youngsters

Pommaletta - red, apple-like fruit grown on Myrrh

Quwee - type of fruit used in Idronatti for juices and teas

ReDael (leader) - leader of the DeoNytes

Reda - unremembered/Now Remembered woman

ReDaelum - sapphire of leadership

Redart Sector (trader) - district for blue-collar workers in Idronatti

Remmihs (shimmer) - lake in Oche Cavern in the Dojanack Mountains
RemMus Lake (summer) - lake in the Central Mountains of Thera
ReNin RepPosu (inner purpose) - the throne of destiny in the sacred amethyst cavern in the Dojanacks
Repoc/repocs (from copper) - coins used in Myrrh and in The Borderlands
ReTaw au Qa (water/aqua) - small planet in the Clenaba Rolas solar system composed primarily of water; the home of the Pentharian
Retu Erath (true heart) - stairway in the Cavern of Tennisca
RiaTrain (air train) - subway train in Idronatti that floats on air
Ria Transport (air) - taxi or limo that moves over the streets on a cushion of air
Saaul - vendor who lives in The Borderlands; husband of Nans
Saylo - chestnut mare belonging to Almiralyn
SeDah (hades) - expletive used by Seyes Nomed and Wodash
Sekan River (snake) - river that runs through the grasslands of Myrrh
Seyes Nomed - Davin Farlow, the DiMensioner od DerTah, Somay's brother
Singtil - small village in the Central Mountains on the planet of Thera, Sparrow's family home
Sibee - Wood Tiff youngster
Sibine - Tiffet, female Wood Tiff; Tibin's mate
Sitrio - male DeoNyte; assistant to the ReDael of Meos
Skipt - Enots youngster
Somay - Nomed's brother; also know as One Man and the Hermit of Timreh Pass; Esán's father
SparrowLyn AsTar - mother of Ari and Brie, joined to (married to) Allynae
Standin - stepfather of SparrowLyn AsTar
Stee - emerald green Pentharian from the Planet of ReTaw au Qa
Steps of Darsec (sacred) - stairway carved in the side of NaiDisbo Peak
SumnerTyme - small town in the Central Mountains of Thera; home of Esán Efre and his Aunt Merrilea
Sun Cycle - one year, thirteen Myrrhinian months, 546 turnings
Sun Cycle Celebration - birthday
SunRise Mountain - mountain in the Central Mountain range of Thera
Sun Turning - one day, thirty six earth hours

Tamboreen - Tam, Almiralyn's tan and cream pony

Tansy - young girl from The Borderlands; daughter of Nans and

Teeay - unremembered/Now Remembered girl who saves Brie

Terces Wood (secret) - enchanted woods of Myrrh

The Borderlands - buffer zone between the city of Idronatti and Myrrh

Thera (earth) - small, earth-like planet in the Clenaba Rolas solar system

Theran - citizens of Thera; ways of Thera

Throne of Netydis (destiny) - Throne of Destiny; ReNin RepPosu

Tianna - Esán's mother

Tibin - leader of the Wood Tiffs; Sibine's mate

Tiffet - female Wood Tiff

Tima - boy from The Borderlands; son of Nans and Saaul

Timreh Pass (hermit) - pass at the top of Mount GetiNar in the Dojanack range on Myrrh

Tirips Tree (spirit) - most ancient trees growing in Myrrh

Torgin Wilith Whalend - Torg, the twins' best friend, Idronattian

Tower of Nemttachenn (enchantment) - tower in the Terces Wood

Traeh - DeoNyte Priestess of Light

TreeOm - tree home of the Wood Tiffs

TroeEen - name given to Gemlucky, Almiralyn's horse, by Nomed, Mighty One in the language of DerTah

Tuper - male Wood Tiff

V-Chip - small computer chip on which data is stored

VarTerel - highest ranking achievable in the Order of Esprow

Voer - sapphire blue leader of the Pentharian

WeHem - unified spirit of the hemlock trees

Wodash od DerTah (Shadow of Hatred) - creature who feeds on the fear of death; a death shadow

Wolloh (hollow) - High DiMensioner from the planet of DerTah, Nomed's teacher

Wood Tiff - small guardians of the trees of the Terces Wood

Worldness Way - street in The Borderlands

Yaro - youngest Pentharian; golden in color, Torgin's heart brother

Ylenol Springs (lonely) - spring near One Man's hut on Timreh Pass

Yookotay - ReDael of the DeoNytes, Zugo's father

Yuin - ruby red Pentharian from the planet of ReTaw au Qa

Z-trauq Revir Canyon (quartz River) - canyon in the Dojanack Mountains
Zugo - young DeoNyte male who befriends Esán Efre

SYMBOLISM

Amethyst - perfect peace, balances emotions, mind, and body
Carnelian - protects against envy, fear, and rage
Emerald - the bringer of harmony
Golden Topaz - conscious attunement, lightness of spirit
Gold - enhances inner beauty and brings understanding
Lapis Lazuli - emotional, mental, and physical purity and clarity
Malachite - equalizing, balancing, and healing
Moonstone - understanding one's destiny
Myrrh - rejuvenation
Obsidian - stone of protection and grounding
Quartz Crystal -harmonize, heal, transform
Rose quartz - gentle love, calming
Ruby - stimulates nurturing, wisdom, health, knowledge
Sapphire - communication, intuition
Tourmaline - creativity, love, and spirituality

ACKNOWLEDGMENTS

Over the course of the past several years (now in 2026, approaching two decades),, many have offered their insights into *DiMensioner's Revenge*, its characters, and their adventures.

To editor and author Linda Lane, who opened my mind to the technical needs of good prose and my heart to the passion of writing, I express my gratitude and heartfelt thanks. Under her mentorship, *DiMensioner's Revenge* and VarTerels' Universe™ have come into their own.

To Tom Krantz, for his help, his support, and his ability to make me laugh at myself. Without him, publishing the VarTerels' Universe™ would still be a dream.

To Ann McIntire, for her willingness to read, reread, and critique each volume of the VarTerels' Universe™.

A special thank you to that unidentified administrative assistant who scribbled on one of my many rejection letters *do not think self publishing will get you anywhere* which opened my eyes to a new opportunity!

And to Aaron Shepard for holding my hand through his practical self publishing guide books *Aiming at Amazon* (2007) and *POD for Profit* (2010) as I started down this wonderful indie path.

And to the following steadfast supporters, I express my deepest appreciation for their time, their honesty, and their patience:

Leslie Randolph, critique partner, for keeping me focused on the tasks at hand

Debbie Stilson, copy editor, for her patient work on the revised version of *DiMensioner's Revenge* and her stalwart support throughout the writing of VarTerels' Universe™

Suzanne Nordstrom, copy editor, for searching for and finding every error in the original manuscript for Book 1, no matter how small

JoAnna Pepe, for encouraging me to write

Emma Randolph, for painting the Terces Wood and for reading and rereading without complaint

Meredith Bird, for creating the map of Myrrh

Arminda Crane Horton, for being the first to read the manuscript and for loving it from the beginning

Brenda Crane and Cameron Russell, my great nephews, for loving what I write

Sally York, for always believing in me and encouraging me to keep writing

My beta readers from Kitt II and Kitt III, for their support and thoughtful suggestions

Stephanie Sheppard, photographer, for her photographic contribution of the great horned owl

Hamlet Fort, Tyra Clemmenson, and Chi Davis for allowing me to use their images to create chapters heading in the book

TheLea Brooks, Amy Horton, Marcia Matthews, Beverly Moller, Judy Seaton, Barbara Talcott, and Priscilla Wagner, for encouraging me to keep going and finally to publish

ABOUT THE AUTHOR

FROM DANCE STAGE TO WRITTEN PAGE

STORYTELLER

Dance, humanity's most ancient narrative art, captivated S.K. Randolph as a child living and dancing in the British Crown Colony of Bermuda. After graduating from the University of Utah with a BFA in Ballet, her dance career spanned four decades of performing, mentoring, teaching, choreographing, and directing. Over sixty of her original choreographic works were brought to life for theatre audiences around the globe, establishing her deep foundation in pacing, movement, and narrative structure. She was the Ballet Mistress of the Colorado Ballet and the Alberta Ballet as well as cofounder of the Bermuda Dance Theatre. For the last two decades of her dance career, she educated the next generation of creatives, as Director of Dance at Interlochen Center for the Arts, named the "#1 Best High School for the Arts in America", and at St. Paul's School.

S.K. at the helm of her forty-foot boat leaving Seattle, Washington on a transformative seventy-five day voyage up the Inside Passage to Sitka, Alaska. Then a decade writing while living afloat swinging on the anchor rode in one remote Alaskan cove or another.
2010

DIGITAL ARTIST

S.K., a pioneer in the digital art sphere, has been creating original digital art since 1997. Utilizing a unique, self-taught technique, she transforms photographs into vibrant, otherworldly masterpieces using Adobe Photoshop. Today, her VarTerels' Universe™ series features nearly 500 of these hand-crafted digital illustrations.

VOYAGE TO WRITING

In 2010, S.K. retired from the dance world to live with her partner on their boat in the world's largest temperate rainforest along the remote and rugged coast of Alaska. Isolated in nature, she spent a "gap decade" afloat honing her writing, refining her digital art style, and mastering shipboard skills (including catching dinner). It was during this creative voyage that she transitioned her storytelling from the dance stage to the written and illustrated page, self-publishing her first novel, *DiMensioner's Revenge*, in 2011.

TODAY

Now, in 2026, S.K. is currently writing the twenty-first installment of her saga. She and her partner reside in the lower-48 states, living on the side of the largest flat-top mountain in the world. From her mountain studio, she continues to cultivate her "Illustrated by the Author" Science Fantasy series, VarTerels' Universe™, dedicating her life to the timeless journey of a true storyteller.

S.K.'s website
www.skrandolph.com

Facebook
facebook.com/skrandolph11

Substack
skrandolph.substack.com

An epic science fantasy saga told through art and words
in companion shorts and illustrated novels,
available as paperbacks and eBooks.

Illustrated by the author, color in eBooks
and black and white in paperbacks.

Presented in suggested reading order.

DiMensioner's Revenge

Illustrated by the Author
VarTerels' Universe™ Book 1
Part I - UnFolding
Novel
642 pages, 73 illustrations

Four young people from a regimented city discover their destiny when they journey to Myrrh—the hidden remnant of Old Earth—only to find themselves hunted by a vengeful DiMensioner, his death shadow, and alien mercenaries determined to destroy everything they've come to cherish.

Available as a paperback with black & white illustrations and eBook with color illustrations.

Gifts

VarTerels' Universe™ Book 2
Part I - UnFolding
Novella
34 pages

A pregnant art student must deceive a ruthless surveillance state about her twin daughters' true father, the brother of a powerful Guardian, or become the perfect hostage in a deadly political game.

Available in the paperback *Agothany 1* and as an individual eBook.

Discovery

VarTerels' Universe™ Book 3
Part I - UnFolding
Novelette
32 pages

Fourteen-year-old Torgin must choose between protecting his passion for music and spying on the only friends who understand him in a dystopian city where the government controls every aspect of life.

Available in the paperback *Agothany 1* and as an individual eBook.

Rescue

VarTerels' Universe™ Book 4
Part I - UnFolding
Novella
31 pages

In a dystopian city where surveillance is constant and conformity is mandatory, twin sisters Ari and Brie must navigate secret portals and evade ruthless patrollers to rescue a lost boy and return him home before their forbidden act lands them all in the dreaded Five Towers.

Available in the paperback *Agothany 1* and as an individual eBook.

ConDra's Fire

Illustrated by the Author
VarTerels' Universe™ Book 5
Part I - UnFolding
Novel
504 pages, 59 illustrations

Kidnapped to a hostile desert planet, Esán must survive while his friends race to rescue him, unaware that their rescue mission will unleash ancient powers and reveal family secrets that could destroy three worlds.

Available as a paperback with black & white illustrations and eBook with color illustrations.

Encounters

VarTerels' Universe™ Book 6
Part I - UnFolding
Novella
29 pages

When a vengeful DiMensioner forms an unholy alliance with a death shadow to steal a legendary crystal and destroy the Guardian who banished him, he discovers that the children he saves along the way may hold the key to his own redemption—or his ultimate damnation.

Available in the paperback *Agothany 1* and as an individual eBook.

Metamorphosis

VarTerels' Universe™ Book 7
Part I - UnFolding
Novella
31 pages

Wrongfully banished from his home planet and left disfigured by a catastrophic magical accident, Laurent must shed his arrogance and accept his broken reflection before he can master the ancient art of dimensional magic and discover his true purpose.

Available in the paperback *Agothany 1* and as an individual eBook.

MasTer's Reach

Illustrated by the Author
VarTerels' Universe™ Book 8
Part I - UnFolding
Novel
686 pages, 60 illustrations

As the UnFolding reaches its climax, teenagers wielding legendary artifacts must evade deadly hunters across multiple worlds while uncovering shocking truths about The MasTer's identity and a centuries-old conflict that threatens to destroy the Eleo Preda people forever.

Available as a paperback with black & white illustrations and eBook with color illustrations.

Wanted

VarTerels' Universe™ Book 9
Part I - UnFolding
Novella
33 pages

A fugitive with a dark past escapes prison only to discover he's being hunted by a powerful mystical league that wants to control his untapped ability to bend reality itself.

Available in the paperback *Agothany 1* and as an individual eBook.

Jaradee's Legacy

Illustrated by the Author
VarTerels' Universe™ Book 10
Part I - UnFolding
Novel
336 pages, 51 illustrations

Separated as children during a brutal genocide, birth-mate twins Rayn and Rethdun must survive across galaxies while carrying the genetic legacy that could save their dying civilization or destroy them both.

Available as a paperback with black & white illustrations and eBook with color illustrations.

Agothany 1

An anthology of
the Companion Shorts
Gifts, Discovery, Rescue Encounters,
Metamorphosis, and *Collision*
in VarTerels' Universe™
Part I - UnFolding
256 pages

Available as a paperback.
Each Companion Short also
available as an individual eBook.

Incirrata Secret

Illustrated by the Author
VarTerels' Universe™ Book 11
Part II- CoaleScence
Novel
428 pages, 45 illustrations

Racing against ruthless enemies across mystical dimensions, the Universe's youngest VarTerel and a prophesied leader with legendary eyes must rescue kidnapped mentors from a cloud-shrouded island where a phantom octopus guards secrets that could reshape their world—or destroy it.

Available as a paperback with black & white illustrations and eBook with color illustrations.

Lessons

VarTerels' Universe™ Book 12
Part II- CoaleScence
Novella
26 pages

On the desert planet of DerTah, blind oracle WoNadahem Mardree must overcome devastating loss and her deepest fears when a mysterious shape-shifting DiMensioner arrives seeking knowledge, challenging everything she believes about fate, power, and love.

Available in the paperback *Agothany 2* and as an individual eBook.

Corps Stones

Illustrated by the Author
VarTerels' Universe™ Book 13
Part II- CoaleScence
Novel
438 pages, 52 illustrations

A young VarTerel and her friends journey to 1969 New York City to recover three stolen Corps Stones before their entire solar system collapses into chaos.

Available as a paperback with black & white illustrations and eBook with color illustrations.

Fishing

VarTerels' Universe™ Book 14
Part II- CoaleScence
Novella
30 pages

A twelve-year-old boy with extraordinary powers must survive slavery, betrayal, and the relentless pursuit of a deadly league that murdered his parents and will stop at nothing to control him.

Available in the paperback *Agothany 2* and as an individual eBook.

Duplicity

VarTerels' Universe™ Book 15
Part II- CoaleScence
Novella
30 pages

A sworn protector with shapeshifting abilities and a future Guardian destined to unite worlds must outwit a ruthless League of sorcerers determined to claim her before she can fulfill her destiny.

Available in the paperback *Agothany 2* and as an individual eBook.

Mocendi's Gambit

Illustrated by the Author
VarTerels' Universe™ Book 16
Part II- CoaleScence
Novel
328 page, 35 illustrations

Stripped of her protective Star of Truth and held captive aboard an enemy ship young VarTerel Brielle AsTar must trust an unlikely ally—a former enemy seeking redemption—and escape through folded time before The MasTer's followers destroy everything she loves.

Available as a paperback with black & white illustrations and eBook with color illustrations.

Destiny

VarTerels' Universe™ Book 17
Part II- CoaleScence
Novella
32 pages

Brielle AsTar, the youngest VarTerel in the Inner Universe, must hide her genetically engineered babies and their surrogate mother from ruthless spies while battling a dangerous gene threatening to resurrect an ancient evil.

Available in the paperback *Agothany 2* and as an individual eBook.

Cimondeli

VarTerels' Universe™ Book 18
Part II- CoaleScence
Short Story
12 pages

Sixteen-year-old Desty has never seen the sky, but when she ventures beyond her underground refuge for the first time, she discovers her telepathic gifts, befriends a majestic flying lizard, and learns that healing a poisoned world may begin with bridging the divide between enemy tribes.

Available in the paperback *Agothany 2* and as an individual eBook.

Queen's Quest

Illustrated by the Author
VarTerels' Universe™ Book 19
Part II- CoaleScence
Novel
420 pages, 44 illustrations

A young VarTerel, a bearer of cosmic seeds, a musical genius, and a street-smart boy with magical spectacles must unite their extraordinary powers to shatter an impenetrable dome, defeat a rogue demi-god, and complete a universal cycle before time runs out.

Available as a paperback with black & white illustrations and eBook with color illustrations.

Collision

Prequel to VarTerels' Universe™
VarTerels' Universe™ Book 20
Part II- CoaleScence
Novella
64 pages, 14 illustrations

A genius physicist barely out of university must lead a team of Galactic Guardians wielding ancient instruments of power to rescue Earth from total annihilation, even as enemies from his past conspire to ensure the planet's destruction.

Available in the paperback *Agothany 2* with black & white illustrations and as an individual eBook with color illustrations.

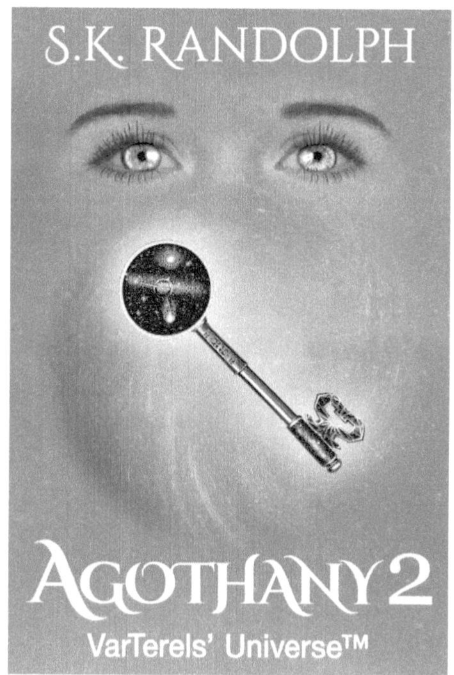

Agothany 2

An anthology of
the Companion Shorts
Lessons, Fishing, Duplicity
Destiny, Cimondeli, and *Collision*
in VarTerels' Universe™
Part II - CoaleScence
284 pages

Available as a paperback.
Each Companion Short also
available as an individual eBook.

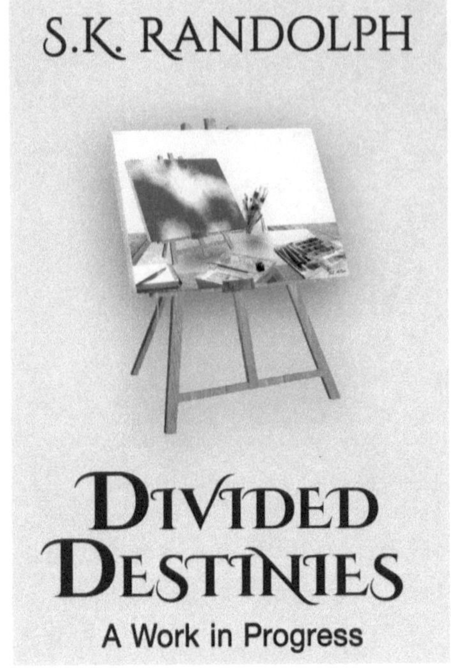

Divided Destinies

Illustrated by the Author
VarTerels' Universe™ Book 21
Part III- QuicKening
Novel
a Work In Progress

Divided Destinies is a work in progress with a targeted release date of late 2026. An illustrated novel, it starts QuicKening, Part III of the VarTerels' Universe™.

See www.SKRandolph.com for current status and subscribe to S.K.'s newsletter to receive progress updates.